UNFINISHED SYMPHONY

MUSIC IN THE NIGHT

Also by
Virginia Andrews

VIRGINIA ANDREWS®

THE NEW

UNFINISHED SYMPHONY

MUSIC IN THE NIGHT

BCA

LONDON   NEW YORK   SYDNEY   TORONTO

CONTENTS

UNFINISHED SYMPHONY

Prologue

&

The New York City skyline took my breath away. As Holly and I approached the sparkling city, I reflected on the rush of events that had brought me all this way. Too excited to rest yet too tired to talk with Holly, I decided to write Alice Morgan and thank her for sending the picture that had catapulted me into this odyssey, this journey to find my past.

Dear Alice,

Thank you, thank you, thank you for sending me that clothing catalogue with the picture of the model who looked just like my mother. Kenneth and I agreed with you, and Kenneth contacted the catalogue company and they gave him the name of the model, Gina Simon, and her address. And you'll never guess where I'm headed right this very minute as I write this letter. Los Angeles! Hollywood! Well, actually, I'm in New York City now (or driving through it at least—we just passed the Empire State Building!). Kenneth's friend Holly offered to drive

1

me to New York, and then Holly's sister Dorothy and her husband, Peter, have volunteered to let me stay with them in Beverly Hills. Can you believe it?

I'm a little scared to be traveling so far on a dream, though. What if this Gina Simon just turns out to be a woman who looks a lot like Mommy? Or maybe even worse, what if she is my mother? What does that mean? Then who is buried in her grave in Provincetown? And why hasn't she let me know that she's okay, that she really didn't die in that car crash? Maybe she got sick and lost her memory. If Mommy has amnesia she might need me now more than ever. I just have to go. I have to have the answers to all these questions.

You would think that with all the excitement of finding a clue about my mother I would be happier. But leaving Provincetown almost broke my heart. I know when I last wrote you I told you that I was lonely, and that Grandma Olivia was giving me a hard time, and that certainly hasn't changed, but Cary and I have grown so close that it was painful to leave him. And to watch little May cry as she waved good-bye was just awful. They really have become like family to me. And Cary, of course, has become much more. I'll have to tell you all about it when we talk.

Well, Alice, I hope to have news for you soon, and I hope you are enjoying life back in Sewell. I really do miss West Virginia. And you of course! Say hi to everyone at school and keep your fingers crossed!

Love,
Melody

2

1

A Glimpse into the Future

Holly's crystal shop looked small inside because every available space was utilized. The air reeked of incense and there was some kind of Far Eastern music playing. Large crystals, all shiny and jagged, stood on antique tables at the center of the shop and tall oak bookshelves lined the side walls. I turned my gaze to the books alongside me and noticed that the shelves were filled with titles describing meditation practices, astrology, faith healing, the afterlife and paraphysical wonders, whatever they were.

Along the back wall was a long glass case crowded with birth stones, as well as amethyst, blue topaz, citrine, garnet and other minerals set in earrings. On the shelves behind the glass case were boxes of incense, teas, Tarot cards and herbal medicines. The ceiling was covered with charts of the constellations, along with posters explaining the powers of various stones. Above the cash register, framed in flowers, was a photograph of a man Holly said was the Buddhist guru who had taught her about meditation. A curtain of multicolored beads hung in the doorway that led to the rooms in back of the shop.

We'd only been in the shop a few moments when a young man in a wheelchair, whom I knew had to be Billy Maxwell, parted the curtain and appeared. He had silky ebony hair that reached his shoulders and framed his face, a face that had an angelic glow because of his rich, almost alabaster complexion. As soon as he saw us, his light green eyes brightened and a gentle smile appeared on his face. Perhaps because of his disability and dependence upon his arms and shoulders, his upper body was firm, muscular, obvious even in his loose, light blue shirt. He wore a pair of dark jeans, white socks and sneakers. There was a large, round gem in a gold casing dangling on a gold chain around his neck and his right ear was pierced and filled with a turquoise stone earring.

"Hi, Billy," Holly said as he wheeled himself closer, his eyes fixed on me.

"Hi. You got here earlier than I expected. How was your trip?" he asked her, while still concentrating on me.

"Good. This is Melody."

"Pleased to meet you," Billy said, extending his hand. He had long, soft fingers and a palm that was warm against mine.

"Hi," I said. There seemed to be such peacefulness in his face, a calmness that helped me feel at home.

"So you're on a big journey," he said, sitting back.

"Yes," I answered, unable to hide my nervousness.

"The Chinese say a journey of a thousand miles begins with a single step and you've taken that single step. That's usually the hardest," he added. "Now the momentum will take over and carry you to where you have to go."

I nodded and then glanced at Holly, not sure what I should say or do. She laughed.

"You'll get some good advice here, Melody. Billy's the best tour guide in our galaxy."

4

Billy smiled but kept his eyes on me. It was strange, having him look at me so intently, but I didn't feel intimidated or self-conscious. I felt his sincerity, his concern and it was as if he and I had known each other for years instead of minutes.

"What's been happening here?" Holly asked before we started across the shop.

"Well, Mrs. Hadron's daughter gave birth prematurely early this morning, but the baby is doing well. She stopped by to thank us for the smoky quartz—it really helped her daughter get through the crisis. And Mr. Brul was here this morning to tell you that the variscite helped him recall a past life. He had vivid details to share."

"Past life?" I asked.

"Yes. He saw himself in England, mid-nineteenth century. He said he was a bookkeeper, which made sense to him. He's an accountant now."

"You mean you believe we all have former lives?" I asked, looking from him to Holly and then back to him.

"Yes," Billy said smiling. "I have no doubt."

"Well, for now we'll have to concentrate on her present life," Holly said. "This way, honey."

"I'm sorry I can't help with your bags," Billy apologized.

"We'll be fine," Holly replied. "See you in a few minutes."

"Welcome again, Melody, and don't worry. There is good energy surrounding you." His eyes grew small. "Things will work out for you," he said with confidence. It was as if he really could look into the future.

"Thank you," I said.

The door chimes rang as two elderly women entered the shop. While Billy attended to them, Holly led me through the curtain of beads to the living quarters at the rear of the shop.

"Our rooms are right back here," she explained. I followed her through the doorway to a short hallway.

5

There was a small living room on the right with a sofa, a smaller settee, two easy chairs, a glass table and two standing lamps.

"This is Billy's bedroom," she said nodding at the first door on the left. "It makes it easier for him to be closest to the shop. I have the next room and you can take this room across the hall," she said opening the door.

It was a very small room with one window that opened on the rear of the building. There wasn't much to look at: just a driveway that provided access to garbage trucks and a small, fenced in area for someone's dog. The dog was in its doghouse at the moment, with just its large black paws visible. The window had light brown cotton curtains and a window shade with a quarter moon and a star painted on it. There was a large ball-shaped mauve candle on the nightstand. The dark pine bed had a light brown comforter and matching pillows. It looked comfortable. Actually, the room was cozy with its tan carpet, its dark pink walls, lamp, rocking chair, table and matching dark pine dresser. A set of chimes dangled in the corner above the chair, barely moving at the moment.

"This room gets a lot of use," Holly explained. "Many people who belong to our network of friends pass through New York going one way or another and stop over for a short visit. I know it's small but . . ."

"It's fine, Holly. Thank you."

"Why don't you just settle in. The bathroom's at the end of the hallway. Freshen up. I'll do the same and call my sister. Then we'll have some dinner. Billy does all the cooking, you know."

"Really?"

"And he's quite the gourmet."

"I forgot what you told me about why he's in a wheelchair. Did you say he was shot?"

"Mugged, about five years ago not that far from here. He ran and the mugger shot at him and shattered Billy's spinal cord."

6

"How horrible, but I'm glad you told me. I didn't want to say anything wrong."

"Don't worry about that. Billy is quite at peace with himself and his condition. Because of his spirituality, he pities more people than pity him. I can't think of a moment when he was depressed these past few years. Anyone who comes in here feeling the least bit sorry for himself usually leaves feeling ashamed of his own self-pity after they talk to Billy. And he's a wonderful poet, published in many literary magazines. We'll get him to read you something later."

Holly put her arm around my shoulders and squeezed.

"Just like Billy said, everything's going to turn out fine, Melody."

I nodded. The discoveries, the quick decision to make the journey and the ride to New York, as well as how overwhelming the city was, suddenly filled me with a deep fatigue. I felt my body sink, my legs soften, my eyelids turn to lead.

"Take a rest," Holly wisely advised. As soon as she left me I lay down and dropped my head to the pillow.

A tinkle, like the sound of glasses being jiggled in a dishwasher tray, woke me. For a few seconds, I didn't know where I was. The sun had gone down and the room was filled with shadows. Someone had come in while I was asleep and turned on the small lamp by the rocking chair. I sat up to grind the sleep out of my eyes. The window was slightly open and the breeze that passed through made the chimes hanging from the ceiling tap, which solved the mystery of the sound.

I heard a gentle knock at the door.

"Yes?"

Holly, dressed in one of her bright yellow dresses with a yellow and green headband, her silver crystal earrings dangling down to her shoulders, poked her head through the open door.

"You've been sleeping quite a while. Getting hungry?"

7

"Yes," I said.

"Good. I spoke to my sister Dorothy and everything is set. As soon as we know when your flight arrives, I'll call her and she and her driver will meet you at the airport. My friend is working on the ticket now and promises to call within the hour. Billy's been preparing a feast. Freshen up and come out when you're ready," she said.

"Thank you, Holly."

"You're welcome sweetheart. Oh," she said before closing the door again, "I spoke to Kenneth. He sends his regards and his best wishes," she added, but I picked up a change in her tone.

"Was something wrong?"

"He just sounded a little down. Maybe he misses us. Misses you, especially," she offered.

"He's probably working twenty hours a day."

"Twenty? More like twenty-two," she said with a small laugh. Then she closed the door and I got up and opened my suitcase to pick out something to wear. After I had washed up, fixed my hair, and changed, I went out to the kitchen. The aroma of the food was tantalizing and made my stomach churn. Billy, bent over a table obviously built lower to accommodate him in his wheelchair, turned as I entered. Holly was in the shop with a customer.

"Hi. How are you doing?" Billy asked.

"I feel better after my nap. Looks like I slept longer than I thought I would. Can I help?"

"Everything's done," he said nodding at the table he had set. "Holly will close the shop in about ten minutes and we'll have dinner. Oh, let me light the candles," he said. "I like to dim the room when we eat. It heightens the sense of taste when you diminish the power of the other senses. Did you know that?"

"No."

"It's true," he said, laughing at my skepticism. "Didn't you ever notice that food tastes better in the dark? Assuming it's good food, that is." He lit each candle and then returned to his work table.

"How long have you been cooking?"

"Since I became a vegetarian. It's just a lot easier to cook for yourself and besides, preparing good food is an art and very self-satisfying. Most people today think it's an ordeal, but that's because they don't take pride in what they do. They don't look for the essence, the inner rewards. Life for them is full of burdens. They're never at ease and they rarely enjoy their own accomplishments. Their days are full of stress and negative energy."

He turned back to me.

"I don't mean to bore you with a lecture. Holly says once I get started, I'm like a clock that won't wind down."

"No, really, I don't mind," I said. "Why are you a vegetarian?"

Billy paused in his food preparation and turned his chair so he could face me.

"I follow many Buddhist traditions and consider all animal life sacred, but other religious groups practice vegetarianism as well. In the Roman Catholic Church, for example, it has been practiced monastically by Trappists since 1666 and among Protestants by Seventh-Day Adventists. I believe that the killing of animals is unnecessary and cruel and can conceivably lead to disregard for human life. It's also a healthier way to live, as long as you don't neglect your protein."

He smiled.

"Now you think I'm some sort of kook, right?"

"No," I said, "but I know a lot of people in Cape Cod who would be unhappy if people stopped eating fish."

"Oh, well, for that I make an exception," he said with a wink. "I'll eat net-caught fish on occasion, as long as I know there are no chemicals added."

"Something smells very good," I admitted.

"Tonight's menu," Billy announced, sitting up straighter in his chair. "We shall begin with chilled okra-yogurt soup, then an orange, walnut and romaine salad, followed by rice, carrot, mushroom and pecan burgers

9

on toasted seven-grain bread. For dessert, I have prepared a carob cake with carob ricotta icing. Something special in celebration of your arrival," he added.

My silence brought laughter to his lips.

"Don't know what you're in for, huh?" he said.

"It sounds . . . interesting," I said, and he laughed harder.

"What's going on in here?" Holly asked as she entered the room.

"I just described the menu to Melody and she was speechless. Then she said it was interesting. How's that for diplomacy?"

"Oh. Don't worry, Melody. You're in for a delightful surprise," Holly promised.

"Did you close up?" Billy asked. She nodded.

"Then let the feast begin," he declared, slapping his hands together.

Once again I asked to help, but Billy insisted I was the guest of honor. It amazed me how quickly he could move about the kitchen, spinning himself on the wheels of his chair. Holly turned the lights down and took her seat.

The soup was delicious and refreshing. The salad was very good, but I was most surprised by the vegetable burgers because they did resemble meat in their texture and even their flavor.

"How do you do this?" I asked, munching away.

"He has magic hands," Holly said.

Billy asked questions about Cape Cod, my life there and my life before in Sewell, West Virginia. He was a good listener, absorbing every detail. Occasionally, he and Holly exchanged a look that told me they had discussed me and my situation at length.

"You have to realize," he said when I completed my explanation as to why I was on this trip, "that places change people. We react to our environment, to the other people around us, to the climate and especially to the sort of energy force that is there. Even if this woman is your mother, she might be more of a stranger to you now than you would expect."

10

"I hope not," I said mournfully.

"Just be prepared," Billy advised.

"I don't know how to prepare for something like that."

"Maybe I can help you," he said, his eyes intense.

The telephone rang and Holly spoke to her travel agent friend. When she hung up, she told me my flight was set for the day after tomorrow.

"It will bring you into Los Angeles about eleven A.M. Pacific time. I'll call Dorothy and give her the flight number and time," she added, returning to the phone. My heart began to pound now that my plans were becoming a reality. When I looked at Billy, I saw he was smiling softly at me, his eyes full of comfort. It helped me relax again.

This time when Holly hung up, she shook her head.

"Dorothy will take you to some Beverly Hills restaurant for lunch, where you will eat a piece of celery and a cupful of pasta for a hundred dollars, I'm sure," she said. "Think of my sister as someone who has to be humored. La La Land is just Disneyland for the rich and famous."

"Oh, now let her make her own conclusions, Holly," Billy said charitably. "Who knows? She may enjoy that world."

"Not this down-to-earth girl. You listen to me, Melody. Get in and get out. Find out what you have to find out and if it isn't what you expected or what you want, put yourself on the next plane out and come back here if you like before you return to Cape Cod," Holly said. "Also, ignore ninety percent of what my sister tells you and be skeptical about the other ten percent."

The phone rang again. Holly spoke to someone for a few moments and then, when she hung up, she announced she had to leave for a while.

"I have to do an astrological reading for someone. It's way past due. I hate to leave you your first night here, but . . ."

"She'll be fine," Billy said.

"Will you read her one of your poems?"

"If she would like," he replied, turning to me.

"Oh yes, please," I said. "But I insist that you let me help clean up."

"No problem. I'm a gourmet cook and all gourmet cooks let people help clean up."

He and Holly laughed and I smiled widely. I had been in New York only a few hours, but I felt more at home here than I had at the homes of my so-called relatives and family. Maybe Billy was right; maybe there was such a thing as positive energy and maybe he would give me enough to help me get through the dark valleys and tunnels that loomed ahead. The question was, would I find any light at the end?

After I straightened up the kitchen and put dishes and cooking implements away, I stopped by the living room where Billy sat gazing at a notebook in his lap.

"Come on in," he said. "I was sitting here thinking about what I had written that would be most appropriate for your circumstances and it's taken me all the way back to my rebirth."

"Rebirth?"

He nodded and flicked some strands of hair from his eyes. He had that soft, angelic smile on his lips again. I had never met anyone who seemed so at peace with himself. It reminded me of the deep calm before a storm, when the whole world seemed to be holding its breath. Cary called it Mother Nature's deception, claiming she tricked us into believing all was well just before she sent the furies down around us.

"Yes, rebirth, for I was dead to so much before my . . . my death," he said. "I was like most people, blind and deaf, confused by the clatter and noise, chasing material things, living on the lowest level and never hearing the song."

"The song?"

"The spiritual song, the voice deep within us all, the voice that links us to each other, to every living and even

12

non-living thing. Even the man who shot me is part of this overall spiritual essence, and in that sense, we're part of each other, forever."

"Did they catch him?"

"No, but that doesn't matter. He shot himself when he shot me. We're eternally tied together by that act."

"You mean you could forgive him for it?" I asked, astounded.

"Of course. There's nothing to forgive. The negative energy that was in him is what must be driven away. He was captured, a prisoner of that, just as I was captured and for a while made prisoner by the bullet that shattered my spine."

"How can you be so positive?" I asked with curious astonishment.

"I was lying on my hospital bed, feeling terribly sorry for myself, cataloguing all the things I would no longer be able to do, regretting how much I was dependent on other people, in truth, wishing I would die," he explained, "when suddenly Holly stopped at my bed accompanied by her guru, an elderly man from India who had eyes like crystals themselves. It was part of their charity work to visit the infirm and give sick people hope. Right from the start, I felt something about him, some inner strength that he was able to share with me, instill in me. He taught me how to meditate and opened the doors to my new self. I dedicated my first poem to him. He has since gone back to India. That's a picture of him in the shop.

"After that Holly came to me and offered me a job in her shop and I agreed. I've been here ever since.

"Let's see," he said, flipping the pages. "Ah, yes. This was when I first began to write poems. I wasn't working here long. I had read some poetry in this Village newspaper and thought I would like to try putting my thoughts down, too. Want to hear it?"

"Very much, please."

He stared at the pages for a long, silent moment and then in a very soft, low voice, read.

"I had come to the end of daylight
and faced the doorway of darkness.
But when I touched my face,
I realized my eyes were closed and my skin was
  cold.
All that I thought I loved and needed was gone
and I was naked, shivering in misery.
They were measuring me for a coffin.
Suddenly, I heard a voice calling from within
  myself.
I turned my eyes around to look back,
to look down, to look deep
and I saw a single candle.
It drew me closer until I could reach out
and put my fingers in the flame.
Slowly, meticulously, I burned away my dead
  body
and when it was gone, I was no longer naked."

He looked up slowly.

"It's beautiful," I said, "but I'm not sure I understand."

"I had to crawl out of my old, now crippled body, burn it away because it literally imprisoned me. Once I found the inner light, true spirituality, I was able to go beyond the physical body and reach a higher place. Someday, you will too. Everything you love and think you need looks lost. You're on a search because you feel naked, without meaning or hope; but you'll see that you have everything you need inside yourself and you didn't have to take a single step in any direction."

I said nothing. We gazed at each other in the silence and then he smiled.

"You've got that look in your eyes again. You think I'm a kook again."

"No," I said, laughing. "Actually, I hope what you say is true."

"It is, but these are discoveries everyone has to make for himself or herself. I can only show you the way, point you in a direction."

14

"Is that why Holly called you the best guide in the galaxy?"

"Yes," he said with a laugh. "All right, enough lessons for one evening. Want to go for a walk?"

"A walk?"

He laughed at my surprise.

"Well, you'll walk and push me along," he said.

"Oh. Sure," I said, hoping I hadn't insulted him with my astonishment.

"It's pretty warm out. You don't need a jacket." Without any hesitation, he turned his chair around and wheeled himself out of the living room, through the kitchen and out into the shop. I almost had to run to keep up. We paused outside the door for him to lock it and then he asked me to push him up the street. At the corner, we crossed and went down another street, past the shops, a few restaurants and a small theater. The sidewalks were crowded with well-dressed people, and I enjoyed seeing their glamorous hustle-and-bustle lifestyle.

When we reached the N.Y.U. campus, Billy had me pause to listen to some speakers. Some were making political speeches, others were ranting about the coming of the end of the world. At one corner a man played a guitar and sang folk songs to a small group that had gathered around him. He had his hat before him and people were putting in change and dollars.

Farther down, a group of young men sang spiritual songs a cappella. They were very good and they, too, had a basket out for contributions.

"What do you think?" Billy asked me as we moved down the sidewalk, past homeless people asking for handouts, a man arguing with a tree, and a black boy who looked like he couldn't be more than twelve playing the bongo drums.

"Now I understand why Holly calls New York a carnival of life."

Billy laughed and asked me to wheel him toward a bench where there were no people and little noise. I sat and we watched the traffic, the groups of tourists and city

15

dwellers making their way to and from their destinations.

"It was on this corner," he suddenly said.

"What was?"

"Where it happened. I was running in that direction," he nodded to the left. "It was about two in the morning. I was a student here, you know."

"Oh. Doesn't it bother you to come here?"

"No. It intrigues me. I can give you this advice, Melody Logan," he said in a deeper, darker voice that made my spine tingle. "Seize the moment, confront the face of that which frightens you and search until you find a way out. Don't let anything shut you up inside yourself. Wherever you go, whatever you see, when you are most afraid, think of this corner, of those shadows, of me sitting here and staring back through time at myself, at the gunman, at the sound of the pistol, at myself folding on that sidewalk and then, suddenly rising up out of myself and standing taller than before."

He reached out and took my hand and I felt as if his courage and spiritual strength moved into me. I smiled.

"Thank you, Billy."

"Thank yourself, cherish yourself and don't let anyone make you feel small."

He sat back and suddenly looked exhausted, as if he had spent all his energy on me.

"Maybe we should go back now," I suggested. He nodded.

Holly still hadn't returned by the time we arrived.

"Can I help you with anything?" I asked.

"I'll be fine," he said, smiling. "Thank you."

Billy wheeled himself down the corridor, first to the bathroom and then to his room. I prepared for bed myself. As he went by to go to his room, he paused at my door.

"Good night, Melody."

"Good night, Billy," I called. He wheeled into his room and I marveled at how cheerful he was and how

16

well he had driven the shadows of loneliness from his door.

I wasn't in my room five minutes before those shadows began closing in on me. Here I was in a strange place, away from anyone I loved or who loved me, feeling like a wanderer who had lost all sense of direction and no longer knew her way home.

From what well of faith did Billy Maxwell draw so much strength?

I lay there in the dark thinking about Cary, hearing his laughter, recalling flashes of his smile, his beguiling eyes, even his smirk. Thinking about him made me feel better. I closed my eyes and concentrated on the memory of the sound of the ocean, visualized the sight of the tide rushing in to wash the shore.

And soon, the shadows of loneliness sunk back. Sleep, like the tide, washed over me.

I was drifting out.

When I woke the next morning, I was embarrassed by how late I had slept. I practically jumped out of the bed, washed and dressed. Holly and Billy had already opened the shop and were dealing with customers.

"I'm sorry I slept so late," I declared when the customers left.

"That's all right, honey," Holly said. "You must have been exhausted. Billy told me you two went for a walk," she added.

"I guess all the excitement of being in New York tired me out."

"I'll get her some breakfast," Billy called out as he headed for the kitchen.

"I hate being so much trouble."

"You're no trouble. After you have some breakfast, we'll go get your airline tickets," Holly said. "Then, I'd like to show you some of New York. What would you like to see the most?"

"I don't know." My mind reeled with the possibilities, the things and places I had only read about and Alice and I had spoken about back in Sewell when the two of us planned a future trip together. What had once been a childhood fantasy was now a reality for me.

"I guess I'd like to see the Empire State Building and Broadway and the Statue of Liberty and the Museum of Natural History and . . ."

"There's only one day," Holly said, laughing.

"I'll show her most of that," Billy called from the kitchen. "Got some fruit, a bowl of multi-grain cereal, juice and coffee in here waiting on you, Melody."

"You'll show me?" I asked, not hiding my astonishment well. He and Holly looked at each other and then laughed.

"Billy gets around as well as anyone," Holly said. "He has a van with a lift and a specially engineered steering wheel."

"Gift from my parents," he said, and I thought, how strange that he had never mentioned them before.

"I can't take you away from the shop. I . . ."

"What do you mean? I'm due a vacation anyway, aren't I, Holly?"

"More than one," Holly replied. "Better eat breakfast so you can get started," Holly said. "Go on," she urged. "Stop being a worrywart."

I laughed and went in to have my breakfast. Afterward, Holly and I drove over to the travel agency where her friend worked and I picked up my airline tickets. Having them in my hand with the itinerary spelled out before me made me suddenly frightened. Would I really get on that plane tomorrow and fly across the country to stay with people I didn't know and search one of the country's biggest cities for a mother who might not want to see me?

Billy had his van in front of the shop when we returned. He showed me how the lift worked and then took his place in the driver's seat. Holly waved good-bye as we drove off for my tour of New York, Billy looking as excited about it as I was.

"It's always fun to see familiar things through virgin eyes," he explained. "It helps one appreciate what one has more."

Seeing the Empire State Building in the distance was one thing, but to ride right up to it and look up was another.

"You want to go up?" Billy asked.

"Can we?"

"Of course. I'll pull into that parking garage there and we'll take the elevator. It's a beautiful day for it. We'll probably see into Canada."

"We will?"

"No," he said laughing.

"You probably think I'm a country bumpkin," I said, grimacing.

"Absolutely not, and what if you were? It would be refreshing and honest," he replied. Billy could turn anything negative into a positive, I thought. How could anyone be so perfect?

Billy moved about the city as if it were just a small town no bigger than Sewell. The hordes of people, a veritable sea of bodies and faces moving up and down the sidewalks, the legions of cars, the noise and commotion seemed not to exist. He wheeled himself along barely noticing any of it, while my eyes raced back and forth, up and down, taking in everything.

The elevator ride to the observation deck of the Empire State Building was the most exciting I had ever taken, and when we stepped out and over to the railing, I thought we were literally on top of the world. I squealed with amazement. Billy laughed and gave me some change for the telescope through which I could see the Hudson River and clear across to New Jersey.

Afterward, we drove up to Broadway and past all the theater marquees, the great electric signs and through Times Square, a place I had seen only on television and read about in books. My heart pounded with excitement. I couldn't wait to write to Alice. Billy decided we should

19

have lunch in the world famous Chinatown, where he could get his favorite—vegetable lo mein. While we were there, he bought me a beautiful hand-painted fan.

After lunch, we went out to the Statue of Liberty. The sky was still mostly blue and there was a warm breeze from New York Harbor. When we returned to shore, I realized Billy was more tired than he pretended and I told him it was time to go back to the shop, claiming I was tired myself. I wasn't. New York had a way of injecting its energy into me. The panorama of people, things to see and do was mesmerizing and helped me forget all my worries and troubles.

Back at the shop, the three of us sat and had some tea while I ranted on and on about the things we had done and seen. Afterward, Billy went into his room to meditate and Holly and I took care of the customers. I was fascinated with how much people were intrigued by her crystals and gems, how much they wanted to believe in the powers. All sorts of people came in to buy and inquire about the items: old as well as young, men and women alike. Some were frequent customers and many testified to the claims Holly made about her stones.

When Billy emerged from his room, he looked revived. Once again I offered to help him with dinner, but again he told me I was the guest and he enjoyed the preparations. After she closed the shop, Holly and I sat in the living room and relaxed while Billy made dinner. I told her about the poem he had read and the things he had said.

"He's a wonderful person. I'm happy he became my partner."

"He said his parents gave him the van, but he didn't mention any more about his family to me. Where are they?"

Holly grimaced.

"They live upstate and they are quite happy he's not there, too. They don't accept his way of life now. His father calls him a hippie."

"Oh, how sad."

"Billy isn't happy about it, but he's resigned and he accepts it."

"Does he have any brothers and sisters?"

"An older brother, an attorney. He sees him whenever he comes to New York; or, I should say, once in a while when he comes to New York. I don't think he calls every time. He wanted Billy to go home and live with their parents, but Billy won't be treated like some handicapped person, as you've probably already noticed."

"He's amazing," I said. "Inspirational."

Holly nodded. Then she turned a bit serious.

"I've been working on your charts, Melody," she said. "Now that I know more about you and the events, and I can pinpoint things, I can get a clearer picture."

"And?"

"I don't think you're going to find what you want," she said gently. "Maybe you should turn around and return to the life you have, the people you know you can count on."

It was like a clap of thunder above my head. I sucked in my breath and smiled.

"You know I can't," I said softly and she nodded. "But after being with Billy and learning from him, I'm not as afraid as I was."

"That's good."

"I'm very grateful to you for what you've done for me. I don't know if I would have had the courage to do this if it weren't for you, Holly. Thank you."

She didn't smile.

"I hope I've done the right thing," she said.

I could only wonder what it was she saw in the stars that made her even doubt it.

It's better, I thought, not to ask.

2
&

Innocence Lost

Billy wheeled himself out to watch Holly and I get into her car the next morning. After I loaded in my luggage, I paused to say good-bye and he took my hand into his and looked deeply into my eyes.

"Often, most of the time, I should say, we feel like ships passing each other in the night," he said. "We spend so little quality time with each other, barely getting to know each other, but I don't feel that way about you, Melody. You have been kind and trusting enough to open your heart to me. Thank you for sharing."

"Sharing? Sharing what?" I asked with a smile. "My problems?"

"Your problems are part of who you really are, but you didn't just share your problems. I got to see your excitement. I was able to feel your energy and it's strengthened me."

I looked at him with astonishment. How could I strengthen anyone at the moment: me, trembling on the sidewalk, terrified of the journey ahead of me.

22

He leaned forward and removed the gold chain and unique locket he wore around his neck. Then he handed it to me.

"I'd like you to have this," he said. "This is a lapis lazuli. It helps release tension and anxiety, but more important, it will enhance your ability to communicate with your higher self. It has helped me a great deal."

"Then I shouldn't take it," I said.

"No, it's all right. I want you to have it. Please," he insisted.

I saw he wouldn't be satisfied until I accepted his gift, so I took it and put it on. He smiled.

"Thank you, Billy." I leaned down to kiss him on the cheek, which automatically turned crimson. Then I hurried to the car.

"Mind the galaxy while I'm away," Holly called back to him. He laughed and waved as we drove away. I looked back and waved again until we rounded a corner and he disappeared from sight.

"It's funny. I haven't been here two full days, but I feel like I've known Billy for years and years," I said.

Holly nodded.

"That's the effect Billy has on everyone. I'm glad you had a chance to spend some time with him before you left for California," she added.

California! Just the way she said it and the way I thought about it made it seem like another planet. I sat with my knees together, my hands nervously twisting on my lap as we wove our way out of the city and toward the airport. Think of something pleasant, something calming, I told myself.

On the way to the airport, Holly described her sister in more detail, but admitted they hadn't seen each other for nearly a year.

"I won't go out there, and even when she comes here, I feel like I'm embarrassing her. She's seven years older, so there's nearly a generation between us, but deep down she's really very kindhearted."

"It's very nice of her to do all this for me, a complete

stranger," I said, wondering just how deep was deep down.

"Dorothy loves being magnanimous. It makes her feel even more like a queen," Holly said, laughing. "I have something for you to give her." She reached into her pocketbook to produce a small jewelry box wrapped in paper decorated with the ram, the sign for Aries, Dorothy's sign. "It's a bracelet filled with amethyst. The gems for the Aries are amethyst and diamond, but she has enough diamonds. You'll see."

"I'll make sure she gets it right away," I promised, tucking the tiny box away in my purse.

"Thanks. Well," she said as the airplane hangars came into view, "we're almost there."

My heart thumped like a parade drum at the sight of all the cars, the limousines and buses, people scurrying everywhere and skycaps loading luggage. Horns blasted, policemen shouted at drivers and waved at pedestrians to make them walk faster. Airplanes thundered overhead. How would I ever find my way through this maze of activity? Everyone else looked like he knew where he was going and was going there fast. I felt like I was floating through a dream and could be bumped toward one direction or another.

"Now don't worry," Holly said, seeing the expression on my face. "As soon as we pull up, the skycap will take your bags and give you your baggage receipts. Then he'll tell you what gate to go to for boarding. The directions are posted clearly inside the airport," she assured me. "And if you have any questions, there will be someone from the airlines nearby."

I took a deep breath. I was here; I was actually going. She pulled to the curb and we stepped out. The skycap took my bags and stapled the receipts to my ticket.

"Gate forty-one," he mumbled.

"Gate forty-one?"

I tried to get him to repeat it, but he was already helping someone else. I turned to Holly.

"I can't stay parked here any longer. They just give you

enough time to drop someone off. You'll see a television monitor inside with your flight number and gate number, along with the time your plane takes off."

"Thanks for everything, Holly."

"You call and I'll call you," she said. She held my hands and stood looking at me. Then she shook her head. "Your mother must have been some blind woman to leave a daughter like you behind," she said. She hugged me and I held on to her, held her as if she were a buoy keeping me afloat in this ocean of people and noise and activity.

She turned and got back into her car, flashing a final smile my way. I watched her drive off, waving and looking after her until she was gone. Now I was really all alone, without a friend in the world. Two elderly people brushed past me roughly, neither realizing they had almost knocked me over with their suitcases. I was standing in the wrong place. I clutched my purse and headed inside before someone else trampled me.

It wasn't much different inside. People were rushing by, pulling luggage on wheels, calling to each other. At the desk, a man was arguing vehemently with the attendant while the people behind him all wore looks of annoyance and frustration. How they could all use Billy Maxwell's calming words and meditation, I thought, shaking my head.

"What's so funny?" a young man in a dark gray suit asked. He had curly blonde hair and impish-looking hazel eyes with a dimple in his right cheek that appeared when he pressed his lips together. He carried a black briefcase and an umbrella.

"What? Oh. I was just watching those people and seeing the steam coming out of their ears."

"Steam?" He turned and looked at the line. "Oh." He smiled pleasantly. "You're a seasoned traveler, huh?"

"Who? Me? No sir. This is my first trip on an airplane, ever!" I exclaimed.

"Really? Well, you don't look it. Where are you going? Wouldn't be Los Angeles by any chance, would it?"

"Yes," I replied. "I've got to go to gate forty-one."

"That's easy. I'm heading that way, too." He nodded to his left. He took a few steps and paused when I didn't follow. "I don't bite," he quipped.

"I didn't think you did." I said nervously, and started after him.

"I'm Jerome Fonsworth," he said. "Unfortunately, I have to travel a lot so I *am* a seasoned traveler." He grimaced. "Hotel rooms, taxis and airports, that's my life. What a life," he concluded with a smirk.

"Why do you travel so much?" Like everyone else, he walked at a quick pace. I nearly had to jog to keep up.

"I'm in banking and I have to go from Boston to New York or to Chicago or Denver often. Sometimes I go to Atlanta and sometimes I go to Los Angeles. Today, it's Los Angeles. Ever hear of that movie, *If It's Tuesday, This Must Be Belgium?*"

I shook my head.

"Well, anyway, that's me. Busy, busy, busy. Sometimes, I feel like a bee," he muttered, swinging his briefcase as he walked. He stopped suddenly and turned to me.

"Look at me," he said. "Do I look like a man in his late twenties or a man in his late thirties, early forties? Don't lie."

"I don't lie," I said, "especially to strangers."

He laughed.

"I like that." He paused and tilted his head to consider. "You know, that makes sense. You have to know someone to care enough to lie to him. I don't lie much to strangers either." He thought and nodded. "Well?"

"You don't look like a man in his forties," I said.

"But I look like a man in his thirties?" He waited, his eyes tightening.

"Early or mid-thirties," I admitted.

"That's because my hair's starting to thin out at the top of my forehead and that comes from stress. I'm really only twenty-eight." He started to turn and stopped. "What did you say your name was?"

26

"I didn't tell you my name, but it's Melody, Melody Logan."

"Melody? Don't tell me you sing and you're on your way to Los Angeles to become a star," he said disdainfully as he continued walking.

"No, I'm not going there to become a star," I replied, but I didn't think he really heard me.

"Right up here," he said, indicating an escalator. "You've got to check your purse, so if you have a gun in it, you'd better take it out now."

"A gun!"

"Just kidding," he said.

When we reached the entryway, I watched him put his briefcase on the table and realized they were looking at an X-ray screen. I put my purse on the moving table and walked through the metal door. A ringing sound started and the attendant stepped up to me.

"Have any change or keys in your pockets?"

"No, ma'am," I said.

"It's probably that necklace. Put it in the basket," she ordered.

Jerome Fonsworth stood watching and smiled at me. Slowly, I took off the necklace Billy had given me and put it in the basket. Then I walked through the gate again, this time without the ringing sound.

"Okay," she said, offering me the basket to take out my necklace. I did so quickly and put it on. Then I grabbed my purse and joined Jerome.

"I should have told you that would happen. I always have to take off this watch." He checked it as he slipped a shiny gold watch back on his wrist. "You're going on American, flight one-oh-two also?"

"Yes."

"We have almost an hour. Want a cup of coffee or something?" he said, nodding toward the cafeteria.

"I might have a cup of tea."

"Stomach's woozy?" he kidded.

"As a matter of fact, it is," I said. I didn't see why I should be ashamed of being nervous. I bet he had been nervous the first time he had traveled like this, I thought. He heard the defensive tone in my voice.

"It's all right. The reason mine isn't woozy is because it's turned into a tin can from all the fast food I eat on the road and all the plane food I eat. Come on," he said and led me into the cafeteria. He ordered a coffee and a doughnut and a cup of tea for me.

"Thank you," I said when he insisted on paying for it.

"It's no big deal. I'm a bank executive in my father's bank. Money grows on trees," he said and indicated a table near the front of the cafeteria. We sat and he handed me my tea.

"Do you really hate your job as much as you claim?" I asked.

"Hate it? No, I've gotten so I don't feel anything about it. I go through the paces, do what I have to do, and then go home," he said. He didn't look at me when he spoke. His eyes continually wandered. Like everyone else around me, he seemed to be a bundle of wild energy. I thought he might just go poof and rise to the ceiling in a small cloud.

"Where is home?"

"Boston. I told you that," he said. "You weren't listening, Melody Logan." He waved his long right forefinger at me. "See, I remembered your full name. Pay attention to everything and everyone when you travel," he advised. He bit into his doughnut and then offered it to me.

"No thank you."

"You'll calm down once you're in the air," he assured me. "Actually, flying's the best way to travel. You put on earphones, sit back and fall asleep. Most of the time, I've got to work on the plane because I'm behind in my paperwork. I hate paperwork."

"What exactly do you do?"

"I work on commercial loans," he said. "It's not as glamorous as what people do in Hollywood. So why are you going there? Vacation?" He continued to look

28

around after he asked me questions, as if he didn't care what I would answer or he was looking for someone else.

"No, I'm going to meet my mother."

"Oh." He turned back. "Your parents divorced and you live with your father?"

"Not exactly," I said.

"You don't have to tell me your private business. I'm just being nosy to pass the time. Your name's Melody, but you don't sing?" he asked. He looked to his right, chewing his doughnut quickly, actually gobbling it.

"I play the fiddle."

"Fiddle?" He turned back to me and laughed. "Not the violin?"

"It's different. I was brought up in West Virginia where playing the fiddle is very popular."

"Oh. I thought there was something unusual about your accent. Fiddle huh? Well, I suppose that's nice." He swallowed the last morsel of his doughnut and licked his fingers. "I'm hungrier than I thought. I think I'll get another doughnut."

"Oh, let me get it this time. You bought my tea," I offered.

He laughed.

"A woman of independent means. I like that. Sure. Get me a plain . . . no, make it a chocolate doughnut this time," he said. I reached into my purse, opened my wallet and took out two dollars.

"Is this enough?"

"Yes," he said, shaking his head. "It's more than your tea cost so it's not exactly a fair exchange," he warned.

"That's something a banker would say," I replied and he laughed harder.

"Thanks."

I went to the counter and picked out the doughnut. His eyes were still full of laughter when I returned.

"I'm not used to women buying things for me. The girls I know belong to the leech society," he said, taking the doughnut. "Come on, share this one with me, okay?"

29

"All right," I said and took the half he broke off. We ate in silence.

"I was in Los Angeles two months ago for a convention," he said when he'd finished his half.

"Did you like it?"

"Los Angeles? I stayed at the Beverly Hilton. That's the way to see Los Angeles . . . chauffeurs, the best restaurants. Matter of fact, that's the way to see any place. Where's your mother live?"

I rattled off the address because I had committed it to memory soon after Kenneth Childs had given it to me in Provincetown.

"West Hollywood. Could be nice," he said. "How come you've never been there before?"

"She hasn't been there that long," I replied. He saw from my face that there was much more to the story, but he didn't look like he wanted to pry anymore. He nodded and then looked around again.

"I just remembered I gotta make a phone call. Would you watch my briefcase? I'll be right back," he said and jumped up before I could reply. He hurried down the terminal. The way he was burning up energy, he probably would look like forty or fifty soon, I thought.

I sat back and watched the crowds of people moving along, the children clinging to their parents' hands and the couples who also held hands or walked side by side. Where were all these people going? I wondered. Were any of them first time airplane travelers like me?

Suddenly, Jerome appeared again, looking all out of breath.

"I got a new crisis," he said, "here in New York."

"Oh, I'm sorry."

"I've got to return to the city." He picked up his briefcase and then he paused. "The trouble is I had to get these papers to Los Angeles today. Listen, could you do me a great favor? I would be willing to pay you."

"What is it?" I asked.

"There will be a man at the airport waiting at the gate when you arrive. He'll be holding a sign that reads

30

'Fonsworth.' Just give him this briefcase. I'll be calling and telling him to expect you. Okay?"

"Just give him the briefcase?"

"That's it," he said. "Okay? Here," he added taking a fifty-dollar bill out of his wallet.

"Oh, you don't have to give me any money for something so simple," I said.

"I insist."

"I won't do it if you insist on giving me money. If we can't do little favors for each other . . ."

He smiled.

"You know, I had a feeling it was my lucky day when I saw you standing there and smiling like that. Thanks. And if we ever run into each other again, I'll be sure to buy you another cup of tea."

He pushed the briefcase toward me.

"A man will be standing with a sign . . . 'Fonsworth.' He won't be hard to find," he declared and then he walked off, disappearing in the crowds of people who had just come off airplanes.

I finished my tea and got up. The briefcase was a little heavier than I had anticipated, but it wasn't too heavy. I walked down the terminal until I reached gate forty-one. There were many people there already. I asked the attendant what I had to do next.

"You'll get your boarding pass at the desk," she instructed and I got into line. Ten minutes later, I reached the desk and handed the attendant my ticket. She gave me my boarding pass and I sat and waited with everyone until the flight attendant announced our plane would begin boarding.

My heart began to beat madly again. When I heard my seat number, I joined the line and made my way to the airplane. The attendant at the door smiled warmly at me and directed me to the right.

"You have the aisle seat," she said. I found it quickly. There was an elderly man in a light brown suit sitting by the window already, his eyes closed. He opened them when I sat beside him.

31

"Hello there," he said.

"Hello." I put the briefcase under the seat in front of me and buckled my seat belt, just as I had been instructed. Then I smiled at him again.

"Going home?"

"No. I'm going to Los Angeles for the first time," I said. "How about you?"

"Going home. I visited my brother in Brooklyn. He's too old to travel anymore so I come to him. Used to be, we took turns. It's not easy to get old, but you know what they say, it beats the alternative," he added and laughed, his thick-lensed glasses bouncing on the bridge of his nose.

"How old is your brother?"

"Ninety-four, two years older than me," he replied.

"You're ninety-two years old?" I asked, astonished.

"Years young. If you think of yourself as being old, you're old," he said plainly. He did have remarkable young-looking light gray eyes, more hair than I thought a man of that age would have and a face that, although crossed with deep wrinkles in his forehead and temples, was not that weathered. He was slim, but he certainly didn't look fragile and weak.

"I'll have to ask you to tell me your secret," I said, smiling.

"You mean the secret to keep bouncing?" He leaned toward me. "Do what you have to do, but let someone else do the worrying," he replied and then he laughed again. "It's all up here." He pointed to his temple. "Mind over matter. So, are you in college?"

"Not yet," I said and told him a little about myself. He had a hearing aid, which I thought had to work very well. He seemed to hear everything I said.

I didn't realize how long I had been talking until the pilot announced we were the next plane to be approved for takeoff. I sat back, holding my breath.

"Is this your first time in an airplane?"

"Yes sir, it is," I said.

"Remember what I told you," my elderly friend said

with that twinkle in his eyes. "Let someone else do the worrying."

He closed his eyes and sat back, looking very relaxed. I was lucky to be sitting next to him because he had a calming effect on me. How could I be nervous when a man in his nineties was so brave?

Once we were airborne, he told me all about his life. He could remember the Spanish-American War, as well as the First and Second World Wars, of course. It was mind-boggling thinking about all the changes he had seen. He and his brother had worked with their father in the garment industry when they were only ten and twelve years old. He had had many different jobs in his life and finally had become an insurance salesman, married and moved to California where, he said, he made some money in real estate. His wife had died nearly fourteen years ago. I heard about his children and his grandchildren. He talked so much I didn't realize how much time had passed. We had our lunch and then he took a nap and I read a magazine. I fell asleep for a while myself and when I woke up, I heard the pilot say we were close to Los Angeles.

"Remember," my elderly friend said, his hand over mine, "stress and worry, that's what puts age in you. Now, time, time's just a reminder that we ain't here forever."

"Thank you," I said.

After that, it all happened so fast, the plane landing, getting my things together, saying good-bye to my new friend and leaving the airplane. My heart was thumping so hard and quickly, I was afraid I'd faint before I set eyes on Holly's sister. I didn't have to look long. She was right there at the gate doorway, unmistakable, an elegant beauty in a wide-brim white hat, a lace coat over her milk-white silk dress. She wore matching silk gloves and large diamond earrings. Her hair was a sleek cap of pale shining gold, pulled back from her face to show a sculptured profile and unlined face.

Holly had warned me that her sister Dorothy was

supporting a number of plastic surgeons in Beverly Hills. Holly called it Dorothy's Wrinkle Panic. The mere sight of a line would send her into a frenzy and put her on the phone with her cosmetic surgeon. Her nose had been trimmed, her eyelids and skin tightened so often, her face resembled a mask, but she did have Holly's youthful hazel eyes. Her lips were fuller. Later, I would learn that, too, was because of something else her plastic surgeon had done.

Beside her stood her uniformed chauffeur, a handsome young man with turquoise eyes and hair the color of fresh straw, trimmed close at the sides with a sweeping wave over the top. He had a cleft chin, and a sharp, strong-looking jawbone and high cheekbones. At the moment, his firm mouth was curled up slightly in the right corner, a laugh in his eyes as he contemplated me, wide-eyed and terrified walking into the terminal.

Dorothy was a tall woman, at least four or five inches taller than Holly. Her chauffeur was easily six feet two or three, I thought. He was trim, movie star sleek with that perfect Hollywood tan I saw on the faces of stars in fan magazines. The caramel tint emphasized his aqua eyes.

Dorothy waved. Beside them stood two uniformed policemen studying everyone who came from the plane. I waved back and hurried along.

"Melody?"

"Yes," I said.

"I just knew it was you. Didn't I, Spike?" she said as I approached.

"You had a good description," he said, widening his handsome smile.

"Oh dear me, look at you. You're so sweet," she said. "Isn't she just the freshest little thing you've ever seen, Spike?"

"Yes, ma'am," he said gawking at me, a silent laugh on his lips.

"Welcome to Los Angeles," Dorothy declared. "My sister has told me all about you, but of course, I want to get to know you for myself. I'm sure half the things she

34

told me are either exaggerations or figments of that wild imagination of hers. Spike, take her briefcase. Briefcase?" she asked herself, raising her eyebrows as soon as she said it. "Why would you be carrying something so . . . ugly? Couldn't my sister provide you with a suitable bag? Something more feminine?"

"It's not mine. I'm doing someone a favor," I said and gazed past them, looking for the man with the sign.

"Favor?" Dorothy looked at Spike. He shrugged.

"I met someone at the airport in New York, a banker. He was on his way here when he had an emergency and had to go back to the city. He asked me to take this to Los Angeles and give it to a man who held up a sign with his name, Fonsworth," I said still looking past them. "But I don't see him."

"What nerve," Dorothy said. "Especially to burden a young girl coming here for the first time." She looked at Spike again, whose smile had evaporated and been replaced with a frown that put furrows in his forehead. His eyes went to the policemen behind me and then he reached quickly for the briefcase, practically pulling it out of my hands. I thought he was being rather rude and I was about to protest. After all, it was my responsibility. He stepped away quickly.

"Did you have a nice flight, dear? Sometimes it's bumpy and they always manage to serve you your food just when it's bumpy. I don't fly unless I can fly first class anymore, not that it's less bumpy, but at least you know you'll be a little more comfortable. So, you must tell me all about yourself and your adventure and of course, tell me all about my sister. I hope you don't believe half the things she claims to be able to do. We'll have lunch," she added before I could utter a syllable. "After Spike gets your luggage."

She took a deep breath. Spike remained a few steps in front of us.

"I really want to get that briefcase to the man," I said. "I promised and I feel responsible."

"Of course, dear. Spike?"

35

He turned as we reached the long corridor.

"The gentleman she's looking for must be down at the baggage carousel, don't you think?" Dorothy said.

He paused, looked past us, and then started to open the briefcase, but it was locked.

"I don't think you should do that," I protested.

"I'll be right back," he told Dorothy as he headed into the men's room.

"Why doesn't he let me take care of the briefcase?" I asked.

"I swear, I have no idea," she said. "He's an actor, of course, and like all of them, he's moody and unpredictable. Everyone in L.A. these days is either trying to get into the entertainment industry or selling real estate. Enough about Spike. Please tell me about you. Where did you meet my sister?"

I told her about Provincetown and Kenneth, Holly's arrival at the beach and how we became friends.

"She still drives that ridiculous circus car?"

"Yes," I said, laughing and thinking about the bright psychedelic colors.

"She had her ears pierced when she was only eight, you know. She had a friend do it and she had to be taken to the doctor before infection set in. My father was furious."

Before Dorothy could continue, Spike reappeared, but without the briefcase.

"Where's Mr. Fonsworth's briefcase?" I demanded instantly.

"In the garbage bin. Let's get moving," he said to Dorothy.

"What? Why did he do that?" I cried.

"Quiet," he said gruffly.

"Now just a minute," I began, determined to make him explain. He surprised me by seizing my arm at the elbow and pulling me forward. Before I could protest, he turned to Dorothy.

"Drugs," he said.

"Oh dear."

"What?"

"That briefcase was lined with something called cocaine. Ever hear of it?" he said sarcastically. "That's probably why the police were waiting at the gate. They got a tipoff; he found out and planted the case with her," he told Dorothy and then looked at me. "If they would have stopped you, you would have been in great trouble. Maybe we all would have," he added.

"But . . ." I looked at Dorothy, whose eyes were almost as wide as mine. "He was a nice young man, a banker. Surely, this is a mistake," I cried.

Spike shook his head.

"He must have spotted her a mile away," he told Dorothy.

I pulled my arm out of his grip and swallowed over the huge, aching lump in my throat.

"That's not true. He had an emergency, and how would he know I would do such a thing anyway?" I asked.

"If you refused, he would have looked for someone else or given up for today. You just transported a lot of cocaine across the country and you might even have brought it to Mrs. Livingston's home," he added firmly.

I felt myself wilt, the tears burning as I looked at Dorothy. She wagged her head at Spike, flashing him a cool, chastising look.

"Oh don't be so harsh on her, Spike. She didn't know." She patted me on the shoulder. "It's nothing, dear. These things happen in today's mad world, but we won't worry about it now. Let's just get her luggage and go, Spike. I'm absolutely famished. We'll go directly to The Vine on Beverly Drive. Wait until you taste their baked goat cheese salad, Melody, and their grilled eggplant sandwich."

Thinking about the trouble I might have gotten myself into just as I had started out on this journey made my throat close. I took a deep breath of relief and shot a glance at Spike, feeling ashamed that I had gotten so angry at him when he was just doing what he thought he had to do to protect all of us. He was silent as we continued down the terminal toward the baggage area, where I spotted a man in a light blue jacket and dungarees holding a small sign with the word "Fonsworth" written on it.

"Don't look at him," Spike ordered.

We hurried by him to the baggage carousel. However, I couldn't help but glance back at him once in a while. As the crowd thinned, he turned and rapidly left the terminal.

"I'm sorry," I told Dorothy. "I had no idea what that man had given me."

"It's all right, dear. Please, I hate unpleasant things. When something nasty happens, I just buy myself something new to wear and make myself feel good again." Her eyes drank me in from head to toe. "That's what we'll do for you later, buy you something nice to wear. I'm sure you don't have the right things. You need something more fashionable if you're going to traipse around Beverly Hills."

"Oh, I can't ask you to do anything like that."

"Of course you can't, but I still can do it," she said with a laugh.

I spotted one of my bags and Spike scooped it up.

"I almost forgot," I said, digging into my purse. "Holly sent you this."

I handed her the small package wrapped with the sign of Aries. Dorothy rolled her eyes.

"Oh no, what magic charm did she deliver this time?"

Without opening it, she dropped it into her own purse. I thought how much Holly would be disappointed, but before I could say anything, my second bag appeared and I pointed it out to Spike. We showed my receipts to the attendant at the door and Spike carried my bags out to the limousine. It was a long, sleek black Mercedes with plush leather seats, a bar and a small television set in the rear. Spike opened the door for us and we got in. The leather smelled brand new.

"I'm really sorry about what happened in there," I

said again. The more I thought about it, the more ashamed I felt for endangering people who were being so kind to me.

"I don't hear you," Dorothy sang. "I don't hear unpleasant things. I've trained myself to be deaf when I have to be, so you might as well stop talking about it. Let's talk about you again. Tell me about this place . . . this coal mining town and how you came to live in Provincetown," she said. "I'm actually fond of the Cape, but we only stay in Hyannis. That's where the Kennedy's live, you know. Spike, please take the fastest route to The Vine," she told him when he got behind the wheel. "I'm absolutely starving to death back here."

"Yes, ma'am," he said and winked at me as he pulled out of the parking lot and onto the road.

With all that had happened, I hadn't even looked up at the magnificent blue sky. We shot into traffic and we were soon on one of California's famous freeways. I was really here, and somewhere, not far away, my mother might be, too. If I ever needed her, I thought, I need her now.

3

&

Hopes Dashed

*T*raveling through Los Angeles was very different from traveling through New York City. Everything seemed so much farther apart and there weren't nearly as many tall buildings, even though there seemed to be many more streets. However, Spike obviously knew his way around because as soon as we ran into a line of heavy traffic on the freeway, he took an exit and began to wind the limousine through the city streets. Dorothy said it wasn't the nicest area of Los Angeles, but even the poorer areas looked bright and dazzling to me. Sidewalks glittered and giant billboards advertised new movies. However, I did notice there weren't as many people walking the sidewalks as there were in New York. Here, everyone seemed to be in cars. Minutes later, Dorothy eagerly pointed out the sign that read CITY OF BEVERLY HILLS.

"Home," she declared with a deep, grateful sigh. The way she spoke about it made it seem as if Beverly Hills were an island on which she felt safe and secure from the rest of the world.

Spike drove up to the front of The Vine, a restaurant

with a hunter green railing smothered in vines and bright pink and red bougainvillea. There was an outdoor patio that looked nearly filled with patrons. Waiters and busboys in starched white shirts and black pants with black suspenders scurried about gracefully, moving like invisible people past the obviously well-to-do clientele, all of whom were thick in conversation.

The restaurant's valet hurried to help us out once Spike came around to open the door.

"Merci," Dorothy said with a wave of her glove.

When Spike got back into the car, I wondered where he would go to eat, but I didn't have time to ask. Dorothy swept us down the cobblestone path to the gate of the patio, where a very attractive young woman waited at the hostess station.

"Mrs. Livingston," she said, flashing a smile made for toothpaste commercials, "how are you?"

"Starving, Lana. Meet my sister's young friend, Melody. She's just flown in from New York. This is her first time in Los Angeles and I thought I would introduce her first to The Vine. So get us a good table," Dorothy insisted.

Lana turned and studied the patio.

"I have number twelve open," she declared as if it were an amazing accomplishment.

Why was it so important where we sat? I wondered. All of the chairs looked the same and the patio with its fountain and bright flowers looked beautiful no matter where you were sitting.

"Bellissimo," Dorothy approved. Lana started down the cobblestone patio and we followed until she stopped at a table nearly perfectly centered. Dorothy beamed with satisfaction and after we sat Lana handed us the menus encased in leather folders the same hunter green shade as the railings.

"We have an angel hair pasta special with red peppers and portobello mushrooms today, Mrs. Livingston."

"Oh, that's good. *Merci.*"

As soon as Lana left us, Dorothy leaned toward me.

41

"This is usually a table reserved for movie stars," she said. "It's where everyone can see you."

"Oh." Why did she want everyone to see us? I wondered. It made me feel more self-conscious about my hair, my clothes, everything I did.

I looked at the menu. The prices were shocking. Everything was à la carte and the salads were almost as expensive as the entrées. Simple things were described so elaborately, I wasn't sure I recognized them. What was a heart of celery?

"Don't you think a second about the prices," Dorothy said, anticipating my reaction. "My husband Philip writes off everything I spend one way or another." She laughed. "He says since I do so much to help the American economy, the least the government can do is subsidize me."

"What does your husband do?" I asked. "I don't remember Holly telling me."

"He's an accountant and a financial manager with some very impressive clients," she replied, lifting her eyebrows. Then her face filled with the excitement of a starstruck little girl. "Oh, I think that's somebody sitting in the corner over there," she said, nodding right. I turned.

"Somebody?"

"A television star, right?"

"I don't know," I said.

"I'm sure it is. Well, let's see," she said, turning back to the menu. "Why don't we have the angel hair special after the goat cheese salad, okay? Do you like iced tea? They make it with a touch of mint."

"Yes, ma'am."

"Please don't call me ma'am, Melody." She gazed around nervously to see if anyone nearby had heard. "That makes me sound so old. Call me Dorothy."

"Yes, ma' . . . Dorothy," I said and she smiled and nodded with approval, holding the brim of her hat as she did so. The waiter came. He spoke with a thick Spanish accent. I had trouble understanding what he said, but

42

Dorothy had no problem. She gave him our order and added, *"Por favor,"* the Spanish for "please." I already had noticed how she liked to throw French, Italian and Spanish expressions into her conversation, flicking her wrist as she did so.

"I don't imagine you ate very well on the plane, did you, you poor thing?"

"I was too nervous," I admitted.

"That's okay. I'm always too nervous to eat when I travel. Philip's never too nervous to lose his appetite over anything. Now, let's get right down to your problem," she said, pausing only when the busboy brought us our iced tea. "As I understand it, you want to find out if this woman is your mother, a woman who came out here to be a movie star. You were told she was killed in a car fire and they even shipped her body back to Province-town?"

"Yes."

"It sounds very, very complicated. I discussed it with Philip and he agrees we should simply hire a private detective. After all, why should a young girl go investigating such a thing?"

"Oh no," I moaned. "This is something I have to do myself. Thank you, but I do," I insisted.

"Really?" She stared at me a moment and then rolled her eyes. "Well, I suppose you can start yourself. I'll have Spike take you around. He's very good when it comes to weird things, as you saw, but you must listen to him," she admonished. "I wouldn't want anything to happen to you while you're my guest," she said. Then she thought about what she had said and added, "I wouldn't want anything to happen to you under any circumstances."

"Thank you, Dorothy. I do appreciate your concern for me and what you're doing," I said.

"Now, now, let's not think about it. I'll become deaf," she threatened again. I started to laugh. "So," she continued without catching her breath, "tell me more about my dear little sister. Does that crippled man still live with her in the rear of that hole-in-the-wall shop?"

43

"I don't think of Billy as being crippled," I began and described my trip to New York and what Billy and I had done together in so short a time. She listened, a small smile on her face. I had the feeling she was studying me rather than paying attention to the things I said.

"It's so wonderful to be young and impressionable," she declared with a sigh. "It's almost a shame to introduce you to the hard realities of the real world. Holly always refused to face them. But you saw how my sister lives, like some hippie, some gypsy. And she's so pretty and bright when she wants to be. I could find her an adequate husband in a heartbeat, if she would let me, but *que sera, sera.*"

I was about to protest and explain that I thought Holly was happy as she was and lived a good life, but our salads arrived. They looked delicious. However, the portions made me smile and shake my head. A half dozen forkfuls would clean the plate. I felt guilty having her pay for it.

"It seems like a lot of money for this small amount of food, Dorothy."

"Nonsense. It's more than enough. You've got to watch your diet, especially here, my dear. Just look around at these women. Look," she ordered and I realized she really wanted me to do it now.

I looked around the restaurant as subtly as I could. There were many attractive women, all with beautiful hairdos and expensive-looking clothes. It was obviously a place for the rich and beautiful.

"Everyone watches her figure. Competition, competition, competition, my dear. Every woman is competing with every other woman here."

"For what?" I asked.

She laughed.

"For what? For the eyes of a man, what else? Many of these women want to be in pictures or with powerful men. But don't worry, I'll explain it all to you later. Just from the little you have told me about your background, I know you have so much to learn, and I do enjoy helping a young woman become . . . sophisticated," she de-

44

clared. "Now don't eat too quickly. You don't want to seem like some naive young girl from the Midwest. Besides, this is the best table. We should enjoy our moment in the spotlight. See, people are wondering who we are already," she said, nodding at people at other tables. She was right—they were looking our way. Dorothy adjusted her hat and smiled at someone.

"You can be friendly," she said, still nodding and smiling at people, "but don't speak to anyone first. Let them come to you. Always wait for them, and never tell anyone too much," she warned. "The more mysterious you are, the more your stock goes up. That's the way Philip would put it." She nodded at someone to our right. "Don't worry, you'll learn. After a while," she assured me.

"I'm really not here for any of that, Dorothy," I said softly. "I'm just here to see about my mother."

"Of course, but like everyone else who comes here, you'll soon fall in love."

"Fall in love? With what, with whom?" I asked.

"Why, with yourself, dear. Who else?" she said and laughed. "I'm sure," she added when I just stared at her, "that that is exactly what happened to your mother."

After what proved to be one of the longest lunches of my life, our meal followed by cups of cappuccino and fruit tarts that cost as much as the meal itself, we finally left. Spike was right there with the limousine, waiting. He held open the doors and I did feel like someone very special because of the way pedestrians paused to look at us and the way the hostess and other staff members fawned over Dorothy. She was like a sponge, soaking up their artificial smiles and growing fatter on that than the miserly portions we had been served. I did get a glimpse of the bill and Holly wasn't far off when she had told me what it would cost. Dorothy had paid over seventy-five dollars for lunch!

We rode past other expensive-looking restaurants, up

Santa Monica Boulevard to what Dorothy announced was the world famous Rodeo Drive.

"I'll take you there tomorrow, my dear, to find you something adequate to wear."

Spike made a right turn and drove us past beautiful large homes, one more elaborate than the other with their Grecian columns and tall hedges. As we drove, Dorothy rattled off the names of movie stars, singers and dancers I had seen in films. She also knew the names of film directors and producers who lived in various houses because her husband Philip had some of them for clients.

Finally, we slowed before a two-story English Tudor bigger than any house I had ever seen. It had a steeply pitched roof, side-gabled, with tall, narrow windows with multi-pane glazing. There was a massive chimney on the left crowned by three decorative chimney pots. The walls were brick contrasted with wooden claddings. It was the sort of house I had seen only on the covers of romance novels.

"Home sweet home," Dorothy declared as Spike turned into the pink tile driveway lined with Tiffany glass lamps. The lawn looked like an emerald carpet, with every blade cut perfectly. There was an enormous weeping willow on the left, its tearful branches nearly reaching the ground, and on the right was a thick oak that looked proud and majestic as it towered over the flowers, rock garden and yellow, white and pink bougainvillea that clung to the tall wooden boarder fence beneath it.

"Your house is so big!" I exclaimed. "I didn't think houses could be so big in a city. It's a mansion!"

"I suppose it is a mansion. We do have twenty rooms," she said, "if you count the help's quarters, Philip's office, Philip's gymnasium . . ."

"Gymnasium. Twenty rooms!"

Dorothy laughed.

"Philip complains that it's never big enough, especially when I host my women's club meetings."

Alongside the house was a three-car garage, but because the entrance was on the side, it made the house appear even longer. I saw windows above the garage, too.

Spike parked in front of the arched doorway and quickly came around and opened Dorothy's door. As soon as she stepped out, he rushed around the limousine to open mine and reached in to take my elbow and help me out. I felt silly having someone do the simplest things for me, but I was afraid to make a social error.

"Take her bags to the pink room, please Spike," Dorothy commanded. "We have many guest rooms, but I think you'll enjoy this one the most. It suits young people," she said. Spike glanced at me with a small smile on his lips and then opened the trunk.

"Let me acquaint you with our house before you settle in for what I'm sure is a much needed rest," Dorothy told me. I followed her to the front door, which seemed to open magically as we approached.

A short, stout, bald-headed man with bushy gray eyebrows and a pug nose greeted us. He wore a dark blue suit and tie and had a light complexion with rust-tinted spots along the crests of his cheeks and the base of his forehead. His skull was peppered with what looked like freckles dropped randomly along the middle and down his temples. His thick lips were almost the same shade of orange.

"Hello, Alec. This is Melody. She will be staying with us for a while."

He nodded.

"Very good, madam," he said in sharp, clipped tones with just the slightest nod. His light gray eyes swept over me, making me feel as if I had to pass inspection before entering the house. After a moment, he stepped aside and we entered.

The entryway had dark, rich-looking brown tile that complemented the walls paneled with dark cypress. Above us a teardrop glass chandelier glowed. The stairway, winding up with a mahogany balustrade and detailed spindle work, was polished to a pristine glow.

Spike started up with my bags, Alec right behind him, but I followed Dorothy deeper into the house.

On the right was a very large living room with a dark pine grandfather's clock that bonged the hour of three. All of the pieces of furniture were oversized to fill the great space. Light blue satin curtains draped the windows and the marble floor was covered here and there with large Persian oval area rugs in a matching blue. There was so much to visually gobble, I could only shake my head: great oil paintings depicting scenes in cities like Paris and London, as well as grand gardens, all in elaborate gilt frames, glass sculptures that looked like they cost hundreds of dollars, porcelain figurines so dainty and perfect they were surely hand-painted, silver and gold candelabra, antique swords . . . how could anyone be so rich?

"Cozy, isn't it?" Dorothy asked proudly.

Cozy? It was a room in which one could run tours, not relax, I mused, but only nodded.

She showed me the den, with its rich, plush leather sofas and chairs, Philip's office, the dining room with a table that could seat twenty at a time and the kitchen that looked more like a kitchen for a restaurant. She was especially proud of her ovens, although she was quick to say she never even boiled water for tea.

"That's Selena's job," she declared and introduced me to her cook, a very short and very plump Peruvian woman with eyes as dark as peat moss. "Selena lives in the rear of the house," Dorothy explained. "Spike has an apartment over the garage, but my maid, Christina, lives in West L.A. She arrives here at seven in the morning and leaves after dinner, usually about eight. Philip pays them all off the books," she added in a whisper.

"Off the books?"

"Things accountants do to stave off the greedy government. Let's go settle you in. I'm sure you want to shower and freshen up after your trip."

"Yes, I do. Then I'd like to visit the address."

"The address?"

"Where my mother might be," I said.

"Right away?" She grimaced. "Surely, you want to wait until tomorrow."

"I'd rather do it as soon as possible. It's why I'm here," I emphasized. She raised her eyebrows.

"I keep forgetting how much energy young people have," she said. "Very well, if you insist. We'll have Spike ready for you in an hour."

"Thank you, Dorothy, and thanks for showing me your house. It's wonderful."

She beamed.

"I've done most of the decorating myself. With the help of professionals, of course. Holly's been here only once. Can you believe that? I think she's afraid to return, afraid to face the fact that she might like it here," she added with a wink.

I doubt that, I thought. Holly was impressed with spiritual, not material things, I wanted to tell her, but I kept my lips sealed tight.

We climbed the stairs. Alec had already unpacked my things, hanging up what had to be hung and putting my other things in the dresser drawers. It embarrassed me to realize he had done all this and especially handled my underthings.

I was so shocked by the bedroom though, that I didn't even have time to feel embarrassed. This wasn't a room, but a chamber fit for a princess. I couldn't believe the posh splendor, the opulence! The walls were covered in silk damask, colored a delicious strawberry pink, richer than the pale mauve of what I thought had to be at least a two-inch-thick carpet. There was a king-size white pine bed, the wood somehow treated so it had strands of blush pink through it. There was a canopy and over the bed itself was a soft, furry coverlet. Even the walk-in closet was bigger than any room I had slept in. It had shelves for shoes and a mirror and a small dressing table at the rear. But there was also a vanity table and matching dressers in the room itself.

All of the fixtures in the bathroom were brass. The

floor was a whitewashed tile. There was a whirlpool tub, a glass stall shower that looked like it would fit a whole family and double sinks. Mirrors everywhere caught my look of amazement. This was the guest room! What could Dorothy and Philip's master bedroom be like?

"I can't believe how wonderful your house is, Dorothy," I said again.

"I'm glad you'll be comfortable," she replied.

"Comfortable! This is a palace. How could anyone not be comfortable?"

She laughed.

"Are you sure you want to go dragging yourself into West Hollywood so quickly? Why not pamper yourself a bit, dear? Take a whirlpool bath, rest, watch some television on your own set. We'll have some hors d'oeuvres before Philip gets home and then we'll have a nice dinner—"

"It sounds wonderful, Dorothy, but I'd feel guilty. I'm not here to enjoy myself. I'm here to find my mother," I reminded her.

She sighed and shrugged.

"Everyone is in such a rush these days. Well, I'll tell Spike to be ready."

"Thank you. For everything," I said.

She flashed a smile and left me to take a shower and change my clothes. I was tired, nearly exhausted, but my excitement over being here and being so close to finding Mommy was stronger. I got into the shower and let the warm water wash over me until I tingled and then I got out, put on a pair of jeans and my best blouse, brushed out my hair, took a few deep breaths, closed my eyes and thought about Billy Maxwell and Holly sitting beside me, advising me on how to calm my nerves and gather my energy, energy I needed now more than ever.

Then I rose and set out to find my mother.

Thinking about the time that had passed since Mommy had left me with my stepfather's relatives in

Provincetown, I was suddenly plagued by a new, albeit foolish fear. Had time and events changed me so that she might not recognize me, especially if she was suffering from some form of amnesia? It hadn't been all that long, but I felt so different. When I confronted her, how would I begin? It seemed ridiculous to walk up to someone and say, "Hello, remember me? I'm your daughter. You're my mother." If there were other people standing around, they would surely think I was mad.

As I stepped down the carpeted winding stairway and through the entryway to the front door, I felt myself shrink. It was an illusion, of course, stimulated by the size of everything around me, but more important, by the size of the task I was about to begin. I took a deep breath and stepped outside.

Spike was leaning against the limousine reading a copy of *Variety*. He looked up at me and smiled. Then he folded his paper and opened the rear door, stepping back in one graceful motion with a very affected and deliberate theatrical bow.

"Madam," he said.

"Thank you," I said in a voice barely above a whisper. I started to get in and paused. "Oh, here's the address," I said, handing him the slip of paper that might have held the key to my future. "Is it far away?"

"Nothing's far away in this town except a good part," he commented.

I got in and he closed the door and went around quickly to the driver's seat.

"Would you like to look at this?" he said, offering me the copy of *Variety*.

"No thank you," I replied.

He shrugged.

"I just thought you'd like to see what a Hollywood paper looked like. It's filled with all sorts of news about actors and actresses. You've never read one before, I bet," he muttered.

"No. I haven't had a reason to," I explained.

51

He laughed as he started the engine.

"I'm not trying to be an actress or anything," I added when the smirk remained on his lips.

"Every woman is an actress and therefore would love to be in movies," he quipped.

"Not me. And every woman is not an actress," I snapped back at him.

He laughed again. The patronizing smile that remained on his face was infuriating.

"I want to go to college and do other things," I continued, wondering why it was so important to me to explain myself.

"Your mother came out here to be an actress, didn't she?" he asked as we proceeded down the long driveway. My shoulders stiffened.

"If you're trying to be an actor, why are you a chauffeur?" I asked in reply.

He turned and looked at me to see if I were being serious.

"It takes a lot of time, intense studying, knocking on doors, hundreds of auditions until you get that one big break," he whined. "In the meantime, unless you were born with a silver spoon in your mouth or unless you have some rich friends who are willing to stake you, you take any job you can that pays for groceries and rent. This isn't a bad job for me. Mrs. Livingston gives me a lot of leeway. Whenever I have an important audition, she gives me the time off, even if it means she has to use a taxi service."

"How long have you been here trying to be a successful actor?" I asked him.

"Three years, seriously at it," he replied.

"Have you been in any movies?"

"I had a few bit parts. I have my Screen Actors Guild card. That's more than a lot can say. I was in a play six months ago. It ran nearly a month, too."

"Then you must be good," I said. He turned to flash me one of his handsome smiles.

"I am. I just have to get everyone else, the important

people, to see it," he said. "After a while it's all just your lucky stars anyway," he added. "Being in the right place at the right time."

"Do you believe in astrology?" I asked.

"Hey, I'll believe in anything they want me to believe in as long as it means I get the part," he said.

"It's that important to you?"

"Are you kidding?" He turned back and gazed at me as if I had just arrived from another planet. Then he smiled. "After you're here for a while, you'll understand," he said. "It's in the air."

"I hope I'm not here that long," I muttered and gazed out the window. Spike continued to watch me in the rearview mirror. I allowed my eyes to meet his briefly before I turned to stare almost blindly at the passing scenery. I couldn't help but be nervous about what was only minutes away. My stomach was doing somersaults. Spike finally noticed my anxiety and took some pity on me.

"It's been some time since you've seen your mother, huh?" he asked softly.

"Yes."

"And you're not even sure it is your mother?"

"No," I said, "although everything points to her being my mother."

He shook his head.

"What a gig. This address, it's an inexpensive condo development. Most of the owners sublet to people tying to break into the business."

"The business?"

"That's what we call Hollywood, the biz," he said. "We have our own lingo." He laughed.

"It's like another country," I muttered, but loud enough for him to hear, which made him laugh even harder.

"You really wouldn't want to be famous, in show business? I bet you have some sort of talent."

I continued to stare out the window.

"I play the fiddle and some people say I'm very good."

"There, you see. A number of country music stars have become famous actors," he said.

"I'm far from a country music star," I said, shaking my head. How easy it was for someone to fall into the trap and start believing in his or her own fantasies, I thought. Was that what had happened to Mommy?

"You gotta think positive about yourself. Look at me. I must go to ten, twenty auditions a week and most of the time, I don't even get a call back, but do I let that discourage me? No. I just keep coming back at them. Sooner or later . . . sooner or later," he chanted.

I gazed at him, wondering if he, not me, was the one who should be pitied.

"It's just down this street," he finally said, after making a right turn. My heart seemed to stop and then pound, pound, pound like someone beating on a locked door. I held my breath as he slowed the limousine.

"That's it," he said, "The Egyptian Gardens. I just love the names they give these places."

I peered out the window. Tall hedges walled in the pink stucco complex that wound around the pool in an ell shape. The buildings were only five stories high, each unit with its own small balcony. Some had flower boxes with plants overflowing the sides. All had a small table and chairs. Although the pink shade was bright, the buildings looked worn, tired, chipped and battered in places. The lawn was spotty, some of the bushes looking sickly with many branches without blossoms.

There was a directory of the residents just to the right of the main gate above which was the name of the complex scrolled in dark pewter. Spike was right. I saw nothing Egyptian or even vaguely Arabic about the place and like him, wondered why it was called The Egyptian Gardens. The main gate opened and two young men in shorts and polo shirts, wearing sneakers without socks, walked out laughing. They were both slim and good looking, both with wavy dark hair. They were so identical, in fact, they looked like they could be twins.

"Pretty boys," Spike mumbled. He got out and opened

54

my door. For a moment I thought my legs wouldn't work, but I pushed myself up and stepped out. "I'll wait right here for you," Spike said.

"Thank you," I said, or at least I thought I had. I wasn't sure I actually made the sounds. He tilted his head.

"You okay?"

I nodded and crossed to the main gate. I looked up at the directory and read the names until I found Gina Simon. My fingers trembled as I reached up to press the button next to the name.

"No point in doing that," I heard a female voice say and turned as a young woman with bleached blond hair came up beside me. She was in a pink tank top and white spandex shorts and had her hair tied in a ponytail. She jogged in place as she spoke, her pretty face flushed, small beads of sweat across her brow. "It doesn't work. They were supposed to fix it last week and the week before and the week before, but nothing gets done fast around here." She took deep breaths and continued to lift her feet in rhythm. "Who you looking for?"

"Gina Simon?"

"Oh, Gina. Sure. She's right across from me. Four-C. Come on," she said and jogged through the main gate. She paused, holding the gate open, and continued to lift and drop her feet as she did so. "It's not locked. So much for security here."

I followed her in and she continued to jog down the walkway. I walked quickly, just about jogging myself to keep up. She paused when we reached the pool. Three young women in bikini bathing suits were sunning themselves on lounges. I gazed about quickly to see if Mommy was at the pool as well. I was relieved she wasn't. I didn't want to meet her in front of all these people.

A tall, very thin young man with short light brown hair sat dangling his legs over the diving board.

"Hey Sandy, how was your workout?" he asked the young woman who had let me into the complex.

55

"I nearly got hit by an idiot on a motor bike near Melrose," she said.

One of the women on the lounges sat up and braced herself on her elbow. She had long, reddish brown hair. Except for her nose, which was very pointed, she had nice features, too.

"Did you lose the five pounds?" she asked, rolling her eyes and smiling like a cat.

"I'm getting there," Sandy said. She spun on her heels and looked at me. "C'mon, before they eat you alive," she said and the three young women laughed. I hurried after her. She took me around the pool, down a walkway to the steps of the second building. Once inside, she stopped jogging.

"I'm trying to lose weight for an audition. It's a photo shoot and you know how the camera puts the pounds on you. The elevator's right down here," she said, indicating the corridor on her left. "I'm Sandra Glucker, but my show business name is Sandy Glee."

"My name's Melody," I said.

"Perfect," she said, shaking her head. "I love it. Actress, dancer, singer?"

"No," I said.

"No?" She stopped walking and turned back to me. "Are you a writer?"

"No," I said, smiling. "I'm not in the business."

"Oh. Oh," she repeated as if just realizing there were other kinds of people in California. She looked at me again. "You're pretty enough to be."

"Thank you."

"Gina Simon. How do you know, Gina? Oh, don't mind me. You don't have to tell me. I'm just someone addicted to gossip, but it's not as bad as some of the other addictions around here."

We stepped into the elevator and she pushed the button for the fourth floor.

"We know each other from someplace else," I said and hoped that would be enough for her.

"Someplace else? Is there someplace else?" She

56

laughed at her own remark. I smiled and the elevator door opened. "You're from Ohio?"

"Ohio?"

"That's where Gina's from, some small town near Columbus, I think. So, what, did you meet in school or something?"

"School? No." How old did she think I was? Even more important, how old did she think Gina Simon was?

"What, is it top secret? There's Four-C," she pointed to the door down the hallway. Instead of going into her own apartment she watched curiously as I walked toward apartment 4C.

I gazed back at her and flashed a nervous smile. Then I took a deep breath and knocked on the door.

"The door buzzer works," she said. "At least, it should."

"Oh. Thanks." I pushed it and waited. So did she. No one came to the door. I pushed the buzzer again. The seconds seemed more like minutes.

"She's probably not there. Maybe she went to an audition. Didn't you call first?"

"No," I said sadly.

"Too bad. In L.A., you should always call first. I'll probably see her later. You want me to tell her you were here?"

"No," I said and realized I said it too quickly. I smiled. "I was hoping to surprise her."

"Oh. Oh! I love surprises. So does Gina, I'm sure." She snapped her fingers. "You're not her sister, are you? She told me she has a younger sister. You are, aren't you?" she followed before I could speak. "That's terrific. She'll be so happy. She misses her family so much."

"She does?"

"Of course. Deep down inside, no matter how beautiful she looks and sophisticated she seems, Gina is a simple girl. That's why everyone loves her. You want to wait in my place?"

"Er, no. I'll just come back later. Thanks," I said.

"You sure. Because—"

"No, thanks," I said, my heart thumping fast. I hurried into the elevator and hit the button for the first floor. As the doors closed, Sandy Glee stepped out to look at me one more time, her face full of confusion.

The minute the doors opened, I rushed out. Then I did jog down the walkway, past the pool, where everyone looked at me, and to the gate. I hurried out and to the car.

"What happened?" Spike asked, stepping out to open my door.

I shook my head.

"She wasn't there, and . . ."

"And what?"

"I don't think it's my mother!" I cried.

4

A Different World

"Do you want to go right back to the house?" Spike asked me.

"I don't care," I wailed and curled up in the corner of the seat. I've come all this way for nothing, I thought, for a dream, a child's dream. I should have done what Dorothy suggested: had a private detective do the footwork first. But even that idea was silly. Where would I get the money to pay him? Grandma Olivia wouldn't have given it to me for that. She couldn't care less whether or not my mother was really alive unless it meant I was out of her hair, out of Provincetown and away from her precious family.

"I'm sorry you were disappointed," Spike continued, "but in L.A. you've got to learn how to live with disappointment."

"I don't want to be in L.A.!" I cried.

"Sure you do. You haven't seen the best of it yet," he replied. "Look at those houses up there. They call that the Hollywood Hills. The views are terrific. See how some of them are built on the edge of the hill? I bet they get a thrill when the earth shakes, huh?"

Despite myself, I peeked through my hands to look at the houses.

"And you're so close to the ocean here. If you want to go and relax or get some sun, hey, all you do is drive a few miles. I'll show you," he said and made another turn, sped up and headed west. "Say you're at work, see, and you've had a bad day, so before you go home to the old lady, you take a little detour," he rambled. "Back in the boondocks, you'd stop in some grungy tavern and moan over your suds. But here . . . hey, look over there. See that building. That was used as the front shot in *Gone with the Wind.* That's Tara!"

I glanced out the window.

"This is a movie studio," he continued. I sat up and gazed at the long white buildings and the trucks. Minutes later, Spike told me to look straight ahead, and there it was . . . the Pacific Ocean. Just the sight of the waves and the vast silvery blue water pulled at my heart. I thought about Cary and May and walking on the beach with Kenneth's dog Ulysses at my heels. I remembered the wind in my hair, the smell of the salt air, the sound of the terns above me, the wonderful feeling of being alive and part of nature.

Spike was right. We started out in a city and moments later, here we were, parking on a bluff overlooking a long stretch of beach.

"Let's walk over to the fence and look down over the Pacific Coast Highway." He got out and opened my door. I took a deep breath, felt myself relax, and then stepped out. "C'mon, follow me," he urged.

We walked over the grassy area where there were benches and where some older people were sitting around their portable folding tables and playing cards.

"This is Santa Monica," Spike explained. "It's a great little beach community, full of European tourists as well as locals. There's the Santa Monica Pier," he said pointing down the beach. "See the Ferris wheel. There's a merry-go-round there, too. It's fun! People are just coming off the beach," he added, nodding toward the shoreline below us. Cars rushed by on the Pacific Coast Highway and in the distance, the sun hovered between two clouds and just over the horizon. "That's Malibu," Spike said, continuing his explanation. "Pretty, isn't it? Sometimes, when I don't get anywhere in an audition, I stop by and just gaze out at the sea. It gives me a fresh outlook, boosts my morale, know what I mean?"

"Yes," I said. "I've been living in Cape Cod. I know the power of the sea."

"Oh yeah, right. I forgot. For some reason, I keep thinking of you as small town, West Virginia. You can't get away from that accent," he kidded. "Actually, it's cute and I bet some casting directors would love it."

I nodded and bit down on my lower lip, trying hard not to show my emotions.

"My parents were a lot older than most when they had me," Spike volunteered. "My mother was nearly forty and my father was in his fifties."

"When you were born?" I asked, thankful for the change of subject.

"Yeah. I guess they woke up one morning and looked at each other and said, 'You know what? We forgot to have children.'" He laughed. "Dad passed away last year. He made it to seventy-nine."

"Where are you from?"

"Phoenix. My mother still lives there with her sister in one of those golden age communities. She's a golfer, addicted. Whenever I do call her, all she talks about is her handicap and the great putt she made. I told her when she dies, I'll have people ride in golf carts behind the hearse." He laughed again and then shook his head. "She didn't think it was funny."

We both stood there, staring out at the sea. There were sailboats that looked like they were pasted against the darkening blue horizon, and farther out was what looked like a cruise ship heading southwest.

"If you want to go to the beach one day, I'd be glad to take you," Spike offered.

"Thank you, but I don't know if I'll be here all that much longer."

"I bet the Livingstons wouldn't mind how long you stayed. You should take advantage."

"I don't want to take advantage of their hospitality," I said, "and besides, I have people waiting for me back in Provincetown."

"People? You mean, a boyfriend?" he asked with an impish glint in his eyes.

"Yes," I admitted.

"What's he do?"

"He takes care of his father's lobster fishing boat right now and in the fall, he'll be harvesting cranberries."

"Sounds . . . nice," Spike offered, but his head was turned in a way that kept me from reading his eyes. Did he mean it? Did he really have a longing for something more substantial than acting or trying to be an actor, or was he just humoring me?

"It *is* nice," I said defensively. He glanced at me with a small smile on his lips.

"You're too young to cash in your chips and settle down, Melody. Look out there. It's a big, wide world to explore. There's so much to do and see."

Our eyes met. If he wasn't being sincere, he was a good actor after all, I thought.

"So what convinced you the woman wasn't your mother?" he asked finally.

"She comes from the Midwest, Ohio, and she's apparently a lot younger than my mother," I said.

"But she looks like your mother in that catalogue?"

"A lot like her. Different hair color, but that's nothing," I said.

"Well, people lie about their age here. It comes with the territory. Hollywood is a young person's world, especially for women, and triple especially for a woman who wants to be a model or in films."

"Really?"

62

"Absolutely," he said.

"This woman claimed to have a younger sister though, and my mother has no brothers or sisters," I said.

"So? People manufacture their pasts here. It's as if they stepped out of a movie of their own making," he continued. "Before you give up, I'd try again. Why don't you try calling her later?"

"I didn't get a phone number," I said.

"She'll be listed, especially if she wants to be an actress or model. She wants to be easily contacted."

I nodded.

"I guess we should get back," I said. "Dorothy wasn't too happy about my shooting off right away as it was."

"Sure," he said. He flashed me one of his warm smiles, took my hand and led me back to the limousine. When he opened the door for me, the people who were playing cards looked up to see who I was and drivers slowed their cars to glance our way. Everyone here was so eager to spot a celebrity, I thought. For the first time since we had arrived, I actually wished I was one. Was I starting to catch the disease?

When I returned to the Livingston's mansion, Dorothy came rushing down the hallway to greet me.

"What happened? I've been sitting on pins and needles waiting. I should have had Spike call me from the limousine. Well?" she asked.

"I still don't know anything for sure," I said and explained what had happened and why I was filled with new doubts.

"You poor thing. To come all this way and be so disappointed. Why couldn't that dreadful woman have been there?" she said, bunching her lips together.

"Spike says I should try to call her now."

"He does? Well, I suppose you can do that, too. But we're going to have dinner in about a half hour. Philip's already home and getting dressed."

"Dressed?"

"We always dress for dinner. Don't worry. Just put on the nicest thing you have to wear," she said. "Tomorrow,

I'm taking you to Adroni's on Rodeo to get you something fashionable."

"Oh, I really don't think—"

"Remember," she sang, "I get deaf."

I smiled.

"Thank you, Dorothy."

"My sister, the psychic, you should excuse the expression, called before to see if you arrived all right. I asked her if she was such a psychic, how come she doesn't know the answers to her questions before she asks them." Dorothy laughed at her own joke. I smiled, imagining Holly's reaction. "I forgot all about the little gift you handed me at the airport, so I had to pretend I had looked at it. I did a few minutes ago. Where does she expect me to wear these things?" she added shaking her head. "Anyway, I told her you would call her tomorrow. She was off to do some sort of hoodoo, voodoo thing."

"Thank you," I said, heading for the stairway. "I'll be right down."

"Don't worry yourself about the woman, dear. If she's not your mother, you're still welcome to stay here and enjoy Los Angeles for as long as you like."

"Thank you," I called back and hurried up the stairs to my plush room.

It wasn't until I plopped myself down on the bed that I realized just how tired I was. Young or not, I finally realized the time difference. After all, for me it was three hours later than it was for everyone here. I'll just rest for a few minutes, I thought and lay back, closing my eyes. A sharp rap on my door woke me immediately. I sprang into a sitting position.

"What? Yes?"

The door opened and Alec gazed in at me.

"Mr. and Mrs. Livingston are waiting for you in the dining room," he announced.

"Oh. Oh, I fell asleep! I'll be right there," I cried and hopped off the bed. He grimaced and closed the door.

I splashed cold water on my face, practically tore off my blouse and jeans, and pulled on my dress. I ran my brush through my hair once and then hurried out of the room and down the stairs.

The Livingstons were at the far end of the long table. Mr. Livingston sat at the end. He was dressed in a dark sport coat and navy blue tie. His thinning dark brown hair was parted on the right side and cut neatly around his ears. He glanced up at me, his hazel eyes sweeping over me quickly before turning downward again to look over the bridge of his narrow, bony nose, under which he wore a well-trimmed mustache. He had thin lips and a soft, almost round chin.

"Hello dear. I'd like you to meet Philip. Philip, this is Holly's little friend, Melody."

"Hello," he said quickly and flashed a smile that swept across his lips so fast, it was as if someone had turned a light on and off.

"Just sit right there, dear," Dorothy said, nodding at the seat across from her. She wore a black evening dress with puffy sleeves and a frilly, square collar, a pair of teardrop diamond earrings with a matching necklace and bracelet, and at least two more rings than she had on when I had first met her.

I took my seat and Philip looked up instantly at Alec. He moved quickly to begin serving us.

"I told Philip all about your little episode today," Dorothy continued, "and he made a wonderful suggestion. Tell her, Philip," she said.

"You're doing fine," he replied, glancing at me and then at his plate as he drummed his fingers on the table. Alec began serving us bowls of what looked like clear chicken broth with some rice and carrots.

"Philip says this woman has to have a social security number. Everyone has a social security number. He will call the business manager at the catalogue company and check the number to see if it's under her name or your mother's name. Isn't that a wonderful suggestion?"

I nodded and looked at Philip. He began eating his soup.

"Just common sense," he muttered between slurps.

Then he paused, his spoon perfectly still before him, not a tremble in his hand. "Of course, people have been known to produce phoney identification and get a new social security number. We'll see," he added.

"So you see, dear, you don't have to spend any more time chasing down this woman. Just relax and enjoy your visit," Dorothy said.

Philip twisted the right corner of his mouth so deeply it looked like his lips were made of pale pink clay.

"It won't be something I can do overnight," he muttered.

"That's all right. I'll still want to meet this woman," I said.

"Philip thinks that might be dangerous."

"I didn't say dangerous. I said unpleasant."

"Well, that's practically the same thing," Dorothy insisted.

He put his spoon down and sat back. Alec moved instantly to remove his soup bowl. I had barely eaten half of my small portion and took two quick spoonfuls when I felt Alec hovering over my shoulder. Dorothy didn't dip her spoon into the cup more than twice, but that seemed to be enough.

A small dinner salad followed, accompanied by the thinnest slices of bread, paper-thin slices that crumbled in your fingers.

Our main course was veal medallions in a lemon sauce, accompanied by string beans and mashed potatoes with a flavor I couldn't recognize. Everything was delicious, but as I ate, I noticed Dorothy watching me and recalled her warning about eating too much. I could have eaten more, but I stopped.

Philip made little conversation but he was interested in my description of the lobster fishing business and the Cape Cod tourist business. He said he had some clients interested in investing in a hotel chain that serviced the Cape and he was not keen about it.

Dinner was followed by coffee in a silver service and a

custard dessert. It had been a wonderful meal and I said so as I thanked them.

"Maybe we should ask Selena to prepare lobster for us tomorrow night, Philip, in Melody's honor," Dorothy said as the meal came to an end.

"Lobster's overpriced these days," he grumbled.

How could anyone with this much money worry about the price of lobster? I wondered.

"Oh nonsense," Dorothy said.

"I don't enjoy eating things that I know are over-priced," he insisted.

"I really don't need to have lobster, Dorothy."

"Of course she doesn't," Philip said, nodding. "She gets it dirt cheap back on the Cape and it won't be as good here. Think of something else," he said. "I've got some work to finish in my office," he explained as he rose. I realized he was not quite as tall as Dorothy. "It was nice meeting you," he added, nodding as he walked away.

"Philip's the most efficient man I've ever known," Dorothy said shaking her head. "He reviews the house-hold accounts once a month and makes brilliant sugges-tions to save money. He says he does it for his clients, why can't he do it for himself? I suppose that's true. Well, do you want to find something to read? You can look in our library. I try to keep up with everything. I belong to three book clubs."

"First, I'd like to try to call Gina Simon," I explained.

"Oh. Well then, why don't you use the phone in the parlor. You'll have some privacy there," she suggested.

"Thank you," I said, trying to remember where the parlor was in this big house. She must have read that in my face.

"Just go down the corridor to the third doorway on the left, dear. There's a phone book on the shelf of the small table."

"Thank you."

"You're welcome. I'll be in after a while and then we

can go to the den and watch some television if you like. *Desperate Lives* is on tonight. Do you watch it? Philip calls it nothing more than a soap opera, but it's so much more than that, it's . . . just more," she said.

"No, I haven't heard of it," I said.

"Haven't heard of it? Oh dear. Well, maybe you'll like it," she said and I went to the parlor. I found the phone book and discovered three Gina Simons, but the address pointed out the right one. With my fingers trembling again, I lifted the receiver. It was an antique brass and ivory dial phone and I misdialed the first time and got a phone number that was disconnected.

I dialed correctly the next time, but after only three rings, an answering machine came on.

"This is Gina Simon. I'm sorry I'm not able to take this call. Please leave your name, the time of your call and a brief message at the sound of the beep," the voice directed. I listened closely. It did sound like Mommy, but there was an affectation, an attention to diction I didn't recognize. I waited and called again just to hear the voice. It sounds like her, I told myself. It must be Mommy.

Dorothy entered the parlor, a small white angora cat in her arms.

"This is Fluffy," she said. "Isn't she beautiful?"

"Yes, she is."

"Philip won't let me keep her in the house proper. She stays with Selena. He says whenever she's permitted to run through the house, she leaves hairs everywhere. He's so finicky about the house. If a piece of dust is out of place, Philip knows it."

She sighed and sat in the soft cushioned chair across from me, the cat purring in her lap.

"So, did you try calling that woman?"

"I got an answering machine," I said. "It sounds like my mother."

"Did you leave a message?"

"No. I wasn't sure what to say."

"She might have been there, listening," Dorothy said,

nodding. "People often do that here. They wait to see if it's someone important and then they answer. If it's not someone important enough, they let the machine take the call. It's a power thing, Philip says."

"Power thing?"

"Yes, you just don't speak to anyone. It diminishes your importance."

"I can't imagine my mother thinking that way."

"Well, if this woman wants to be someone in the industry, she behaves that way, believe me. I've met enough of them."

I thought about it. What was it Billy Maxwell had told me just before I had left New York . . . be prepared to find a very different woman, even if she was my mother. Perhaps that was very true.

"I wish the world we lived in wasn't so conscious of every little thing," Dorothy said, dreamy-eyed as she petted the purring cat in her lap. "Philip wants me to be perfect, to remain perfect. If I have a hair out of place, he asks why I didn't go to the beauty salon this week," she said a bit more mournfully than I would have expected.

"He doesn't seem like that," I told her. She snapped out of her reverie and raised her eyebrows.

"He's a man, isn't he? They're all the same, waving a magnifying glass over you, checking for wrinkles, for age spots, measuring your bosom, your waist, your hips, looking for an ounce of ugly fat.

"I have a personal trainer," she continued, "who comes to the house three times a week. It's such a bore, but I bear it for Philip's sake. And my own, I suppose," she said with a sigh. "Well, a woman has to do all she can, doesn't she?" she added.

"I'm not sure. I've never really thought about it I guess," I said.

"Of course you haven't. You're still young and beautiful. You have a way to go, but believe me, one day you'll wake up and look in the mirror and notice a little wrinkle here, a little more puffiness there and you'll realize it's going to take some work to look beautiful.

"Of course," she continued, "if you're bright enough, you won't settle for just anyone and you'll marry someone substantial as I did, so he can provide you with the best there is when it comes to cosmetic surgery."

"Surgery?"

"Now don't sit there and flatter me and tell me you didn't notice how firm my buttocks are for a woman of my age without thinking I had something done," she said smiling.

"I didn't really notice, but . . ." An operation on her rear end?

"It's nothing more involved than a tummy tuck. I can't tell you how many times I've had that done. Oh, and my eyes of course. Some people are so lucky. They're born with genes that help them to remain young-looking longer. Philip's mother, for example, hardly had a wrinkle in her late seventies and look at Philip. Well, it's always different for men anyway. They can have wrinkles. It makes them distinguished-looking, but we girls . . .

"Well," she said with a little more animation in her face, "do you think our sexual relationship would be as strong as it is if I didn't keep myself attractive? There's an article about it in my latest issue of *Venus*. According to scientific studies, a successful relationship means a husband and wife make love on the average of five times a month, even at our ages. I told Philip about it and he said his own research indicated between four and six times. We mark the calendar. You probably noticed it on the wall by our bed. Philip appreciates order in his life.

"Oh, I know what men do when they have ugly wives," she continued, ignoring my gaping mouth, "especially in this town," she said, nodding. "A woman has to work on her relationship. That's her job. And I don't mind telling you I'm very successful at it.

"You saw how the young male waiters were gazing at me at The Vine," she said, batting her eyelashes and smiling. "They have no idea how old I am, and they'll never know," she said firmly. "You guard your age like you guard your life. Never tell a man your true age. Always subtract five to seven years at the least," she advised.

"Oh no," she said suddenly, rising to her feet. *"Desperate Lives* has started. Quickly," she ordered and marched out of the parlor.

I sat there for a moment, trying to digest the things she had told me the way you would try to digest food that was far too spicy. The words kept repeating themselves.

"Come along, dear!" she shouted.

I rose and joined her in the hallway. She turned in to the den and flipped on the television set. Then she plopped herself into her overstuffed chair, curling her legs under her lap, and gazed at the television screen like a teenager about to see her teen idol. I sat on the sofa beside her and listened to her little moans and sighs as one handsome young man after another paraded before us on the large television screen.

But fatigue began to rise in my body like mercury in a thermometer. I felt my eyelids getting heavier and heavier and drifted off a few times, only to be wakened by her shouts at the television set, complaining about something a character said or did, as if she thought they could actually hear her.

"Doesn't that just get you infuriated," she railed, turning my way. I nodded, even though I had no idea why she was so upset. "And I hate it when they leave you hanging like that. But," she said, smiling suddenly, her mood swinging radically in the opposite direction, "as Philip says, that's how they get you to tune in night after night and how they get to sell all those products. You look tired, dear. Perhaps you should go to bed. I know it's late for you."

"Yes, I guess it's all finally caught up with me," I said, rising. "Thank you so much for everything."

"Nonsense. Tomorrow, right after breakfast, we'll go to Rodeo Drive and get you something proper to wear. Don't," she said, raising her hand to stop any protest, "say anything that will make me deaf. Philip and I have

71

no children. I was never fond of the idea of being pregnant and Philip really can't tolerate little people very well anyway. But we both enjoy doing things for young people now and then. When they're deserving, as you are, of course." She smiled. "Have a good night's rest."

"Thank you," I said again, too tired to argue anyway, and went upstairs, taking the steps as if I were already walking in my sleep.

Despite my exhaustion, before I turned out the lights and crawled under the cover, I lifted the phone receiver and dialed Gina Simon's number. It rang and rang until the answering machine came on again, and again, I listened closely to her voice, feeling more and more confident that it sounded like Mommy's voice. Or was I just wishing it did?

And why wasn't she picking up? Had she gone away? Maybe it would be days, weeks, before I stood face to face with her.

I lay my head back on the pillow and closed my eyes, grateful I was too tired to continue thinking, but still apprehensive as to what tomorrow would bring.

5

A Bitter Pill

Once again it was a gentle knock on my door that woke me, but this time a pleasant-looking woman with strands of gray running through her dark brown hair entered. The breakfast tray she carried was laden with a silver coffee pot, cup and saucer, a plate, silverware, eggs in a dish, a croissant, jelly and butter and a tall glass of freshly squeezed orange juice. Alongside everything was a small vase with a single fresh red rose.

"Good morning," the woman said. She had a pretty smile brightened with the warmest blue eyes I had ever seen. She was about five feet two with a small bosom and hips definitely too wide for Dorothy's taste. Her forearms were strong, but she had small hands. "I'm Christina, Mrs. Livingston's maid. She asked me to bring up your breakfast this morning."

"Oh, you didn't have to do that," I said, sitting up and struggling to get my eyelids to stay open. "What time is it?" I gazed at the clock in the belly of a light blue ceramic seagull. "I've never slept this late."

"It's all right, dear. Mrs. Livingston insisted," Christina said, placing the tray on a bed table she'd retrieved from the closet.

"You have two, two-minute soft-boiled eggs," she said, lifting the cover to show me. "Did you want anything else? Hot cereal, different juice? I have freshly squeezed grapefruit or prune."

"No, this is fine, but I could have come downstairs," I said, uncomfortable with all her fussing.

"Only Mr. Livingston comes down for breakfast as a rule," Christina replied with a smile. "He reads the morning papers and doesn't mind eating alone. Mrs. Livingston always takes her breakfast in bed. Do you have everything you need?" she asked, walking into the bathroom. "More towels, anything?"

"I'm fine at the moment," I said, drinking my juice. "Thank you."

She nodded at me and watched me take a few bites of the croissant.

"I hear you're from the East and this is your first trip to California," she said.

"Yes."

"I've never been to New York, but I hope to go one of these days. I have a daughter who can't be much younger than you," she added. "Her name's Stacy. She's starting community college this year, working at a department store and taking some courses. She wants to be a grade school teacher."

"That's great," I said. "I guess she likes working with children."

"Yes, she's a great help with my others. I wish we could afford to send her full-time, but . . . we just can't at the moment."

"How many children do you have?"

"I'm raising four," she added.

"Four?"

How did she manage raising four children while working as someone's maid, and have such a pleasant personality? I wondered.

"The youngest is six, a boy." She paused at the

doorway. "Just leave everything beside the bed. I'll be up later," she told me. "Let me know if you need anything," she added as she left.

I couldn't help feeling quilty about being pampered so much while I had yet to make contact with Mommy, so I ate the delicious breakfast quickly, then showered and dressed, taking more time than usual with my hair. Dorothy had made me so self-conscious about my looks I was afraid she would rush me off to the beauty parlor if I didn't look pretty enough to greet the California morning.

Mr. Livingston was just leaving the house when I came down the stairs. He wore a pin-striped suit and maroon and white tie. He stopped at the front door to look up at me as I descended.

"Good morning," he said.

"Good morning."

"I hope you had a good night's rest," he said without a smile.

"Yes, thank you."

"Well, enjoy your day," he added. He looked uncomfortable speaking to me alone. He fumbled with his briefcase and then hurried out the door.

I thought about dialing Gina Simon's number again, but imagined I would only get the answering machine. It was better to go over there in person. I had to wonder if Sandy Glee had told her she had a visitor and then described me to her.

"Excuse me, miss," Alec said, seemingly appearing out of nowhere. "You have a phone call."

"A phone call? I do?"

"Your name is Melody, is it not?" he asked sharply, as if he thought I was being critical.

"Yes."

"Then, you have a phone call. You can take it in the parlor," he said nodding in that direction.

"Thank you."

I hurried in and lifted the receiver.

"Hello."

"Hi," Holly said. "Sorry I missed you yesterday, but I had a reading to do and by the time it was over, I thought it might be too late."

"That's all right."

"How are you doing? Did you meet the woman in the catalogue yet? Kenneth called me early this morning to see if I had heard from you."

I told her about my visit to the apartment complex and the things Sandy Glee had told me about Gina Simon.

"I'm not getting good vibes, Melody. Remember what I told you. Pack up and come back if things aren't what you hoped they would be," she said.

"I will," I promised.

"Good. How's my sister treating you?"

"Like royalty," I said. I told her about my room and my breakfast in bed.

Holly laughed.

"I hear you. She's a character, huh? And Philip, did he say more than two words?"

"About seven or eight," I said, laughing. It was so good hearing Holly's voice, hearing the sincerity and the warmth. "It's nice of you to call, Holly. It's nice of you to care."

"Would you be any different if roles were reversed?" she asked. "Billy sends his regards, too."

"Tell him hi and I'll call you guys as soon as I know . . . anything," I said.

"Okay. Take care and don't let Dorothy talk you into a face lift while you're there," she warned before hanging up.

Before I had even set the phone down, Dorothy appeared.

"Good, you're up," she said as she entered the room. "The stores are just opening."

"I'm sorry I overslept. I'm usually up a lot earlier than this."

"Overslept? Nonsense. A woman needs her sleep.

76

That old fashioned idea about beauty rest happens to be true. If you don't rest your skin, it gets old faster. I never get up much earlier than this unless I have a very important reason. Anyway, I've called for the car. I just have to tell Selena what Philip wants her to make for dinner tonight and then we'll be off to the shops."

"Dorothy, really, I just want to go back to the apartment complex, see Gina Simon and—"

"You need something decent to wear first. Then you'll go," she insisted.

"Really, I—"

"Deaf," she said, shaking her head with her hands over her ears. "Meet me outside. Spike's bringing the car around."

She left for the kitchen. There was nothing to do but let her be generous, I thought, and then pay another visit to The Egyptian Gardens.

Anyway, I couldn't help but be impressed with the stores on Rodeo Drive. Papa George and Mama Arlene, who had lived next to to us in Sewell, West Virginia, used to say their grandparents came to America thinking the streets were paved with gold. This was the closest anything came to that, I thought. The designer clothing stores with their richly draped mannequins in the windows, the grand art and antique galleries, the beautiful restaurants and expensive jewelry stores all made it look like shopping for the rich and privileged. Everywhere I looked, I saw Rolls Royces, Mercedes, and other expensive automobiles, as well as limousines like ours with chauffeurs in uniforms opening doors for people who looked like they were all in a contest to outdress each other.

"Right here, Spike," Dorothy ordered and turned to me to say, "I know this boutique well. They have the sort of clothing young girls like these days. You'll see," she promised.

When we entered the store, I thought it was going out of business. There were so few things on display, each item was treated like a special work of art. Toward the rear of the store was a bar where a bartender prepared cappuccinos, lattes and espresso for the customers. The saleslady recognized Dorothy immediately and hurried over, her high heels clicking on the Spanish tile.

"Enchanted, Mrs. Livingston. How have you been?" she asked, her hand out limply. A gold bracelet filled with diamonds dangled from her small wrist. She looked like she had spent a half a day preparing her makeup and hair. Not a hair was out of place and she had the most even pancake complexion I had ever seen, which made her look tan down to the base of her neck, after which there was a milk-white line. Dorothy just squeezed her fingers quickly.

"Very well, thank you, Farma. This is my sister's friend from the East Coast. She had to rush here and wasn't able to pack her better things. So I thought we would just pick up something nice for her to wear during the day and something for the evening."

"Oh, how nice," Farma replied and gleamed at me with dollar signs in her eyes. "We just received this Italian pants suit in a perfect color for . . ."

"Melody," Dorothy said. "I knew you would have something appropriate."

"Come dear," she said, drinking me in to measure my size. "What a delicious little figure you have."

"Doesn't she?" Dorothy said.

I never felt anything as soft as the material out of which the pants suit had been made. It was a creamy white color with swirls of pink through it and it did fit perfectly. When I gazed at myself in the mirror, I felt my ego swell. Then I glanced at the tag dangling from the left sleeve and I almost fainted. It was fourteen hundred dollars!

"She looks fantastic," Dorothy said. "What a wonderful choice for day wear," she said, without even checking the price. "Now, let's think about something for the evening. I plan to take her to Chasens tomorrow night, and you never know who might walk in."

"Oh, I have a darling black dress, just in from Paris."
Farma hurried off to get it and I spun on Dorothy.

"Dorothy, look at the price of this!" I exclaimed. She
gazed indifferently at the tag.

"What of it, dear? Decent things are going to be
expensive these days."

"But this—"

"Please," she said widening her eyes, "don't embarrass me. I know all the salespeople in these stores and
they know me. Oh, that does look sweet," she said when
Farma brought out the thin-strapped evening dress.
Reluctantly, I tried it on and it also fit perfectly, flatter-
ing my figure, but it was eighteen hundred dollars! I
couldn't swallow after Dorothy told her to wrap up the
evening dress.

"She'll wear the pants outfit now," she declared.

"Very good," Farma said.

"Dorothy . . ." I stood, astounded.

She stepped up to me so she could lower her voice.

"If I don't spend my money, Philip will only invest it
in one of those dreary annuity funds and tie up the
money for years. As it is, I never get to spend all of my
monthly allowance."

"You have an allowance?" I asked, amazed at the idea
of a grown woman being given an allowance.

"Of course I do. And if I don't use it, I can't get him to
raise it, can I? He's too smart. He'll simply say I don't
spend what I get now, so why raise it? All of my friends
get allowances and I happen to be at the top. I don't
intend to lose that position," she added.

"Besides," she continued, "I don't enjoy giving my
money to charity as much as I do buying something for
a pretty young girl. It makes me feel . . ." She smiled.
". . . feel younger myself. I used to have a figure like
yours . . . naturally. Now go put on that suit. We're going to go someplace special for lunch and many of my
friends will be there."

She smiled triumphantly.

"When Spike takes you back to the apartment complex, people will pay more attention to you and be more impressed with you. They'll take you more seriously. You'll see. Here everyone's impressed by clothes and cars first, and then they consider the person wearing the clothes and driving the car. You'll learn."

"I feel like they should have given me a passport when I left the East Coast," I remarked and she laughed so hard she had to tell Farma what I had said. Then they both laughed again.

While I changed into the Italian pants suit, Dorothy bought herself three blouses and two skirts. The bill at the end of our visit was enough to keep a family of four in food and shelter for months back in Sewell, I thought, but I dared not utter another complaint.

Before Dorothy had Spike take us to lunch, she insisted on buying me a pair of shoes to match the pants suit and a pair for the evening dress. Then we had lunch at a little café off Rodeo Drive where a sandwich cost as much as an entire meal anywhere else in America. Dorothy seemed to know everyone there, introducing me as her sister's close friend. I listened to them chatter about clothes and jewelry, and all the things they had bought that morning. Everyone managed to get in how much they had paid, as if the higher the cost, the more justified they were in buying it.

My head was spinning from this spending whirlwind by the time Dorothy had Spike drive her home. Alec was brought out to carry my packages up to my room, and then I was finally excused to pay another visit to the apartment complex.

"You look great," Spike said. "You belong in expensive clothes."

"Nobody belongs in things that cost this much. It's outrageous," I said. He laughed.

"It's supposed to be. This is Hollywood. Later, I'll take you up to Grauman's Chinese Theater and you can look at the footprints and handprints of the stars."

"I'd rather find the footprints of my mother," I

mumbled and sat back, hoping this time I would have more success.

Now that I knew the buzzer on the directory at the front of the complex didn't work, I simply entered through the main gate and followed the path past the pool. There were a half dozen young men and women sunning themselves on the lounges, some holding reflectors under their chins. Unlike the first time, no one paid any notice to me. I didn't see Sandy Glee anywhere. As I approached the building in which I knew Gina Simon's apartment was located, I heard a loud, familiar laugh. A woman I was sure was Mommy came out of the entrance accompanied by a short, stout man with thinning gray hair and a bulbous nose. He had thick lips and was wearing a pair of thick-lensed eyeglasses that made his eyes look like the eyes of a dead fish.

I knew it was Mommy because when she saw me, she gasped, brought her hand to the base of her throat, and paused. Her escort looked at her curiously and then at me. Mommy regained her composure with a deep breath and smiled at the man.

"Anything wrong?" he asked. I stood waiting, my heart thumping like a parade drum. "You forget something?" he followed when she didn't reply.

"No," she said quickly. "It's all right."

"Well, we had better move along. Gerry Spindler is the sort of producer who likes to be the one who's late for a meeting, not the person he's interviewing. Not that I think there's a doubt about you, sweetheart. He'd have to be made of stone to pass on you," the stout man said and laughed grotesquely, his jowls shaking and his lips curling. Mommy fixed her eyes on me as they continued toward me.

"Mommy!" I exclaimed when she was only a few feet away.

"Pardon me?" she said.

The stout man brought his head back.

"Mommy, what's going on? Alice found your picture in a catalogue and sent it to me in Provincetown and Kenneth found out who you were and where you were," I said quickly. "Grandma Olivia gave me the money to come out here. Mommy, don't you recognize me?"

"What?" she said laughing.

"Who is this?" the stout man asked.

"I have no idea," Mommy said. Her eyes turned as cold as two small stones in a West Virginia mountain brook.

"It's me, Mommy. Melody. Don't you recognize me? Really?"

"First, honey," she said in a sharp, hard voice I didn't recall, "I could never be your Mommy. I'd have to have been six when I had you."

The stout man roared with laughter.

"And second, I never saw you before in my life. I wish they would fix that damn security system here," she told the stout man. "Any riffraff can walk in off the street and you know what we have walking the streets around here these days."

"Yeah," he said nodding and gazing at me.

"Mommy . . ." Tears burned under my eyelids. I tried to swallow so I could continue, but the lump in my throat felt like a chunk of coal.

"Maybe it's someone's idea of a joke," the stout man offered. "Anyway, don't worry about the security system. You get this job and you'll be able to move into a classy place, honey. And so will Mr. Marlin."

"Please, listen," I finally uttered. Mommy glanced at me and then quickly threw her head back to brush the hair from her eyes. I was shocked by how empty she could make her eyes, as if she knew how to turn all her emotions off. She tightened her hand around the arm of her fat escort and continued down the walkway as if I didn't exist.

I stood there, gaping after them, watching her disappear around a turn. She laughed at something the man said and then threw me one final disdainful look before she disappeared. I sank to the stone bench at the side of the walkway, stunned, feeling cold, actually shivering in the hot California sun. Despite her coldness, there was something in Mommy's eyes that told me she had recognized me, that she wasn't suffering from amnesia, but at the same time, there was something that said, "Be gone, don't you dare come back into my life, especially now."

How could she pretend to be a woman in her twenties? She looked it, but she knew she wasn't, and how could she leave me standing here, amazed and in shock after I had come so far? I buried my face in my hands and started to sob. I had come all this way to be ignored and rejected by my own mother, who I had hoped would be so happy to see me it would even cure amnesia. I took a deep breath and sat back. I remained there, staring, shaking my head, feeling nauseated and sick. Tears streamed down my cheeks, dripping off my chin, but I made no attempt to wipe them away.

A handsome dark-haired, young man and a very pretty blond-haired woman came hurrying down the walkway. They both glanced at me and smiled as if seeing someone bawling on a bench was just part of the scenery around here. They hurried into the building, their laughter tinkling behind them. Above me, a window was open and Latin rhythms came pouring out. This was not a place to be mournful, I thought and rose to my feet. I actually wobbled for a moment, the world around me taking a spin. I held on to the back of the bench and waited for the vertigo to pass, but it lingered like cramps that wouldn't dissolve.

"Hey, what are you doing?" I heard and turned to see Spike standing there. "You all right?"

"No," I wailed.

"What happened? I've been waiting and waiting. I thought I had better come in and see if I could find you. Hey," he said and lunged at me to prevent me from crumpling to the cement walkway.

Only minutes later I woke in his arms. He was sitting

on the bench with me in his lap, gently slapping my cheek.

"Melody . . . Melody . . ."

"What happened?"

My eyes fluttered open again and the world came back into focus.

"You fainted," he explained.

"Oh. I'm sorry," I said, feeling horribly embarrassed. Fortunately, no one else had come by to gawk. We were still alone. Spike helped me sit up.

"You all right? Take a deep breath. Go on. That's it. What happened?" he asked when the color returned to my face.

"I met her," I said. "Right here. She came out of the building with some man and I was no more than a foot away from her."

"So?"

"It was my mother, but she pretended she didn't know me. She said she couldn't be old enough to have had a daughter my age and she laughed at me." I started to sob again. "She told the man I was some sort of riffraff coming off the street. She wished they had fixed the security system so I would be kept out."

"Take it easy," Spike said and put his arm around my shoulders. "She was probably putting on an act for that guy."

"But why? Why was that more important than me? I came across the whole country to find her and she hasn't seen me for so long. Why?"

He shrugged.

"She probably had an audition or something and maybe the guy was a producer she was stringing along. I don't know. This is Hollywood."

"You keep saying that as if it justifies everything that goes on around here," I snapped back at him. "I don't care if it's Hollywood. People should still be decent to each other, especially mothers to their daughters."

He smiled at me as if I had said the silliest thing.

"You know something," he remarked, nodding as he

gazed at my disdain, "you could be quite an actress. You've got integrity. You can reach down into the emotion well and draw up the right responses."

"I don't want to be an actress! I don't want to be in Hollywood! I'm not pretending to feel bad. I *do* feel bad! I want my mother to acknowledge me and explain why she has done these terrible things," I cried.

"Maybe she will, one of these days," he said calmly. "But now's obviously not the right time. Come on. Let's get out of here. I hate complexes like this, filled with people trying to make it in the business. You can cut the desperation in the air. It's depressing," he said as he stood. "Come on." He held out his hand for me. I took it and stood up. "You okay? You think you can walk?"

"Yes," I said.

"Great." He kept his arm around me and we started down the walkway. The sight of a chauffeur walking with his arm around a young woman in an expensive Italian pants suit drew some eyes as we passed the pool again. It almost made me laugh, but my heart was too heavy for any sort of joviality. All I could think of was Mommy's cold, indifferent eyes and her voice cutting through me like a band saw.

I got into the limousine and Spike drove us away. He continued to make excuses for Mommy as we went along.

"If she is your mother, when you confront her alone, she'll be different," he assured me. "You caught her by surprise, that's all."

"She's definitely my mother," I said. "The instant I set eyes on her in person, I knew and she knew me. She just . . . made herself so different."

"That's—"

"Don't say it," I warned. He laughed.

"Hey, you've got to step back, catch your breath and try again. You'll get to the bottom of it all, I'm sure."

I didn't reply. I gazed with empty eyes at the scenery that flew by, no longer seeing the beautiful flowers and plush lawns, the glitzy stores and exciting billboards.

This was a place I'd rather not be in, I thought. I closed my eyes and wished I was walking on the beach. I concentrated as hard as I could until I could hear the waves lapping at the shore and could see the whitecaps sparkling in the New England sunshine. It put a smile on my face.

"You okay?" Spike asked, watching me in the rearview mirror.

"Yes."

"Good. Hey, did I tell you I have a chance for a really great part tomorrow?"

"No."

"It's a recurring role. Know what that means?"

"No."

"Well, if I get the part, I'll be in this episode and then the writers will write me into others, so I'll work on a regular basis and really get some exposure. From there, the sky's the limit," he said. "It's not a very big role to start, about thirty lines, but it's the impact on the show that counts. You want to see the script, maybe help me rehearse?"

"Help you rehearse? How can I do that?"

"I'll do my lines and you'll read the others. I'd like to have you hear me recite. You've got a fresh ear and would probably hear my mistakes."

"I don't know anything about acting, Spike."

"That makes you an expert around here," he said and laughed. "Come on. You don't want to just hang out with Dorothy, do you?"

"Not really," I said. It was probably unkind to say that about someone who had been so generous and hospitable to me, but I really wasn't in the mood to hear about expensive clothing or beauty tips. How I wished I could drop in on Holly and Billy. If only they weren't so far away. I longed to run up the stairway to Cary's private workroom and throw myself into his arms, too.

But I was here, among strangers, with my own mother being the biggest stranger of all.

"Will you? Please," he said.

"Okay," I replied.

"Great," Spike said. "I appreciate it."

When we arrived at the Livingston residence, Spike pulled the limousine around to the garage instead of to the front of the house. He opened my door and directed me to a side door that took us upstairs to his apartment.

"Don't mind any of the mess in here," he said, throwing some clothing into a pile behind the sofa. "Between driving for Mrs. Livingston and preparing for auditions, I don't get much time to be a housekeeper. Is it stuffy in here?" he asked, throwing open a window.

"It's all right," I said. There was a pile of scripts on the sofa. He hurriedly cleared them away to make a space for me. "How about something to drink? Beer, juice, water?"

"I'll just have some water, thank you," I said.

"Sure." He rushed into the kitchen. I gazed around the bland apartment. There was nothing on the walls and except for the scripts piled here and there and the clothing and dishes scattered about, there was no personality to the place. It reminded me of the thrifty motels Mommy, Archie Marlin and I stayed at during our trip up to Provincetown. Now that seemed ages and ages ago. It was hard to believe the woman I had just confronted was the same woman, but she was. I was positive about that and right now, it started to make me angry.

"Wow, what a look on your face!" Spike said returning with a glass of ice water. He handed it to me and I drank.

"She had no right to treat me like that. I don't care who was with her," I said.

He nodded.

"You'll tell her, I'm sure," he said. "I'll tell you something," he said, stepping back and scrutinizing me from head to toe as he nodded, "when you get angry and your face gets all flushed and your eyes look like they have candles burning behind them, it's rather exciting."

He put his hands together, thumb to thumb like a film director and gazed at me through the opening, moving about as would a camera director searching for the best perspective. I shook my head and laughed.

"You're always in a movie," I said.

"That's life, a movie. I'm trying to get good reviews, that's all," he said, laughing at his own joke. He poured himself a glass of beer and then handed me a script with the pages marked.

"*Desperate Lives?*" I said, looking at the title page. "This is Dorothy's favorite show."

"I know. I haven't told her I'm going for a part in it yet. She would make me too nervous. Okay, here's the setup. I'm Trent Windfield, who has discovered he's more in love with his girlfriend's sister than with his girlfriend. Her name's Arizona."

"Arizona? That's a state," I said, finding the name on the page.

"That's what her parents named her because they have this multimillion-dollar ranch there. In this scene, Trent decides to tell Arizona how he really feels about her. The problem is he's a graduate student and she's only a high school junior. Her father, a man with a fiery temper, would have him shot."

"How does Arizona feel about Trent?" I asked, gazing at the lines.

"She's always had a crush on Trent, but she never dreamed it would turn into anything. She's over-whelmed, but excited, titillated. It's a dream come true. Ready?" he asked, standing before me.

"Okay, I guess."

"Top of the page," he said. I watched him lower his head and then raise it slowly, his face changing, his eyes filling with emotion.

"No one knows I'm home," he said. "I drove right to your house." He fell to his knees at my feet. It took me by surprise and I gaped at him. "Read your lines," he coached out of the side of his mouth.

"Oh." I looked at the pages. "Why? Why did you come here first, Trent?"

He took my hand.

"Because the things I said to you just before I left . . . the things I told you I was feeling haunted me. I couldn't study. I couldn't talk to anyone. All I've been doing is thinking about you. Every time I look at another girl, she has your face, Arizona." He leaned on my knees and drew closer.

I gazed at the pages again.

"If you're teasing me, this is cruel," I said.

"It would be like teasing myself, like being cruel to myself," he said. "I know this is biting into forbidden fruit, but I would chance being thrown out of Paradise just for one of your kisses," he said.

I started to look at the pages again when his fingers slipped under my chin and gently lifted my face so he could lean over and kiss me softly on the lips. My eyes went wide.

"Arizona," he said. "Your name is branded on the front of my brain."

He kissed me again, this time putting his hands on my shoulders to hold me and draw me closer, making his kiss harder, his tongue moving through his lips and slipping in between mine. Surprised, I sat back.

"I knew you loved me just as much. I knew it," he said and flooded my face with kisses, running his lips down to my neck. His hands went to my waist.

"Spike," I said.

"Trent," he replied, and covered my mouth with his again, his kiss forcing me back on the sofa. His right hand moved off my waist and up over my ribs until he reached my breast.

"Wait," I cried.

"There is no time to wait," he said, still acting as if we were in his scene. But my words were my own. I wasn't reading off a page. In fact, the script had fallen from my hands. Spike pushed me down on the sofa, his lips moving to my chin, my neck and then his fingers separating the jacket of the pants suit so he could lift it and slide his hands under my silk blouse. When his fingers reached my bra, I twisted and turned to break free.

"Don't be afraid," he whispered in my ear. "This is the way grown-ups make love."

"Spike, stop!" I cried. His lifted my bra and soon the tips of his fingers were sliding over the top of my breast, strumming my nipple as his lips continued searching my neck, my face, his left hand against my head, trying to get me to return his kisses.

I brought my knees up higher and then, with all my strength, pushed into his stomach. He lost his balance and fell off the sofa. I didn't wait to give him a chance to recuperate. I shot up and turned away from the sofa, straightening my clothing quickly.

"Are you crazy?" I demanded.

He sat back, a wide, silly grin on his face.

"I'm just getting into my scene. What are you getting so excited about?"

"That's not in your scene," I accused.

"It's what we call improvisation. It helps you to build your part. You get into the character. That's all. Come on," he said, patting the sofa again. "Let's try again and when you get into it—"

"I'm not getting into anything," I said, backing away. "If this is acting, I'd rather do someone's laundry," I added.

He laughed.

"Melody, really—"

"Thanks for the introduction to dramatics," I said, heading for the door. "You should do real well. Good luck," I said and charged out of his apartment, down the stairs, bursting into the sunshine.

Maybe everyone was crazy here. Maybe like Spike said, everyone was moving in his or her own movie. Mommy certainly seemed to be.

Instead of heading back into the house, I walked down the tiled driveway and out to the street. The sky was hazy now and there was a nice cool breeze even though the sun was still strong. Traffic went by at a leisurely pace, people glancing at me curiously. Gardeners trimmed hedges and swept leaves and debris from the fronts of beautiful homes. I walked with my arms folded under my breasts, my heart still pounding from my episode with Spike.

And then I paused to watch a little girl with long golden pigtails being lifted out of a car by a woman who had to be her mother. She clung to her with loving desperation and gazed over her mother's shoulders at me. Happy, secure, she flashed me a sweet smile and then waved as if we knew each other. I waved back and for a moment I felt as if I were waving at myself, years and years ago, when I was about her age and my stepdaddy was alive. Of course, I didn't know then he was my stepdaddy. I thought he was my real daddy. He loved me just as much as any real daddy could.

The woman carried her little girl into the big, beautiful house where she would be secure and safe and where even the thought of something unpleasant was left at the doorstep. I stood there, smiling and thinking about her. I don't know how long I was standing there, but suddenly I realized there was an automobile stopped nearby and someone looking at me.

It was Mr. Livingston.

He waved.

"You all right?" he asked.

"Yes," I said. "Thank you. I was just taking a little walk."

"In Beverly Hills, that's considered strange," he remarked. "Don't go too far," he said, raised his window and drove on. I watched him turn into the driveway and then I headed back myself. Maybe it was strange to be alone here and think.

I would do what Spike had suggested. I would confront Mommy again, hopefully when she was alone, and if I had the same result, I would get myself back on the plane as quickly as I could and I would fly away, leaving Mommy and my past behind me.

6

❦

Devil's Bargain

Alec greeted me at the door when I returned from my short walk and in a very stiff and formal voice informed me that Mr. and Mrs. Livingston wanted to see me immediately in the parlor.

"Melody, dear, where have you been?" Dorothy asked the moment I appeared. She was seated on the settee and Philip was sitting across from her in the thick cushioned arm chair, his posture regal. They looked like they had been having a very serious conversation. "Philip just told me he saw you wandering aimlessly about Beverly Hills. Why didn't you come right in and report to me about your second visit to that Egyptian whatever?"

"I just wanted to be alone for a while," I said. I certainly wasn't going to say anything about Spike and the little drama in his apartment. "I wasn't wandering about aimlessly. I knew where I was going. Doesn't anyone just take a walk here? Why did they build sidewalks?"

"You poor dear. Come in here this instant and give us the details about your visit," she insisted and patted the seat beside her.

Philip sat staring at me, his fingers pressed together in cathedral fashion, his beady dark eyes looking quite disapproving. I walked in slowly and sat. Then I took a deep breath and began.

"I met her," I said in a voice that even sounded like the voice of doom to me, "and she pretended not to know me."

Philip nodded and glanced sternly at Dorothy.

"It was what I anticipated," he said, "even from the little I knew about this bizarre situation. Dorothy—"

"Now hush, Philip. We will solve the matter ourselves," she said, but he didn't look relieved.

"This is not one of your social games, Dorothy. I told you what I thought when I first heard about this. We sympathize with your situation, Melody," he said, directing himself to me, "but we're certainly not equipped to solve the problem as Dorothy implies. This sounds to me more like a police matter. Someone is surely defrauding someone here," he continued. "Perhaps an insurance company. I simply can't have myself attached to the issue in any way. I have a major responsibility to my clients, who are all high-profile, and I can't afford to have any negative publicity. You seem like an intelligent enough young woman to appreciate that."

"Yes sir. I'm sorry. I'll leave tomorrow."

"You don't have to leave so quickly," Dorothy said, but not with the same firmness she said most everything else to me.

"I don't want you to feel we're throwing you out. You're a friend of my sister-in-law and Dorothy made her sister some promises," he added, eyeing her disapprovingly. "You can stay for a while as long as you don't bring any of this mess to our doorstep, but from what it sounds like to me, my best advice to you is to return to where you call home and the people who care for you," Philip said.

"Yes sir," I replied in a small voice that started to crack.

"You can report what you know to the proper authorities and let them take the necessary action," he continued. "I'll assist you in doing that, if you wish."

"That's not why I came here. I don't care about any of that. I wanted to find out what really had happened to my mother. I wanted to see if she needed me."

There were tears in my eyes as I spoke, but they defied gravity and remained firmly under my lids.

"I see. Well, Dorothy knows that if you require some money for your return trip . . ."

"I have everything I need. Thank you," I said.

"Okay. I'm sorry for your trouble. You're a very nice young lady and I'm sure you'll regain your composure and go on to do something worthwhile with your life."

"Oh, she's going to do a lot more than that," Dorothy said. "She's an exceptional young lady."

"Yes, well, I'll just go up and get ready for dinner." He shot another, even sterner look at Dorothy. "Don't put yourself in a position where you're giving advice you shouldn't be giving, Dorothy."

"I think I know what I can and can't tell someone, Philip."

"I certainly hope so," he said with his eyes full of warning. He glanced at me and then rose and left the room.

"I'm sorry," I said. "I don't want to make any trouble for you. Maybe I should leave right away. I can stay in a motel until I make travel arrangements."

"Of course you won't do something like that. Don't you listen to him. He's just being . . . just being Philip Livingston," she said, as if that explained or justified it. "Now I want to hear all the details. Go on. Tell me everything from start to finish," she begged, leaning toward me, her eyes wide. For a moment I had the feeling she was treating me and my problem as if it were all another episode of her favorite soap opera. Nevertheless, I related the events as they occurred, leaving out my scene with Spike. When I was finished, she sighed deeply.

"Maybe Philip is right, dear. Maybe you should get on with your own life. Not that I want to chase you away, but . . ."

"My mother is part of my life," I said.

Dorothy smiled and shook her head at me as if I had said something ridiculous.

"Family can be such a burden. Look at what I have with Holly."

"Holly is a very happy person and she has a lot of friends and knows a lot of wonderful people," I shot back. "I can't think of anyone who's been nicer to me."

"Oh she has a heart of gold, especially when it comes to helping other people, but will she ever help herself? Not Holly. She was always like that, always off on a cloud. I tried to get her to be more substantial and do more with her life, but there's just so much you can do and then, then you've got to do what Philip said, go on with your own life. Philip does give the best advice. He always has. Sometimes, I feel he's more like a father to me than a husband." She smiled. "Are you all right, dear? Is there anything else you want to tell me?"

"I'm tired," I said. Dorothy was so wrapped up in herself, she would never hear anything she didn't want to hear anyway, I thought. "I'll just go up and rest for a while."

"Of course. Take a whirlpool bubble bath and suddenly the world will look much better to you. Believe me, it will. If I'm depressed, I just go to the spa and get a facial and take a mud bath and a massage. What good is money if you don't use it to make yourself happy and drive away the gloomies?" she added with a thin little laugh. What she said reminded me of our shopping spree and all she had spent on me. I was sure now that Philip would be very upset once he found out, despite what she had told me.

"I'd like you to bring that evening dress back to the store, Dorothy. I won't be needing it now and—"

"You certainly will. Won't you go to some nice affair back East? And just think how envious all the other young women will be when they see you in a designer dress."

I stared at her, too tired to argue.

95

She rang a bell and a few seconds later, Christina appeared in the doorway.

"Christina, will you please draw a bubble bath for Melody?"

"I can do that myself," I said.

"Please, just do it, Christina," Dorothy emphasized firmly.

"Yes, Mrs. Livingston," Christina said and left to do it immediately.

"Really, dear. You have to let the servants do their work otherwise . . ." She laughed. "Otherwise we won't need servants and they would be without jobs, and Christina is someone who can't afford to be without a job. She has a flock of children to feed. Enjoy your bath. Alec will call you to dinner."

She rose and stood there for a moment gazing at me.

"I wish you were able to stay for a while longer. I have so much to teach you," she said and then shook her head with a twist of pity on her lips and left.

You have so much to teach me? I thought and gazed around at this palace in which two people shared wealth beyond my imagination, but seemed to be like strangers to each other. I don't want to learn about getting the best table in a restaurant or how to keep a wrinkle off my face. No, I wanted to learn something much deeper. I wanted to learn where I truly belonged. If I stayed here ten years more, I didn't think I could get Dorothy Livingston to understand that.

My legs felt like they had turned to stone beneath me when I rose and started for the stairs. It was another bright day outside, but inside my heart the sky was overcast with long, thick clouds of despair. As I approached my room, I heard Christina singing by the whirlpool tub.

"I've put in some scented bubble bath for you," she said when she heard me enter.

"Thank you."

She looked at me closely.

"Did you have a bad day?" she asked.

I started to shake my head, but my lips trembled and my chin quivered. I had to bite down to keep from releasing a sob.

"You poor girl," she said, coming to me. I couldn't help myself. I started to cry. She wrapped her arms around me quickly and held me to her, stroking my hair. "There, there, now, nothing is as bad as all that."

"Yes it is," I wailed. "My own mother refused to recognize me today. She ran off and left me with relatives back East and then I think she pretended to die so she would be rid of me forever," I blurted.

Christina looked shocked for a moment and then she nodded slowly, her lips firm.

"Any woman who denies her own child must be in trouble," she declared. "It's not natural and it has to be painful for her."

"Do you think so?" I asked, wiping my eyes.

"Oh yes. When you become a mother, you'll understand," she said with a smile. "Your child is part of you, always your baby. It hurts to see them grow up because you know they're growing away from you, but that's a different and healthy kind of letting go.

"I'm sure your mother will contact you," she said and squeezed my hand softly.

"She doesn't know where I'm staying."

"Then she expects you'll be back," Christina assured me.

"I don't know," I said, thinking about it. I wanted to share her optimism, to make everything terrible look small and insignificant, to believe that after a storm there was always a rainbow, but I had been disappointed so many times already.

"Have more faith, dear," she said. "Relax, eat a good dinner, get a good night's rest and tomorrow, tomorrow will look a lot more promising."

Her smile was like the sunshine after the rain. I couldn't help but smile back.

"Thank you," I said. "Your children are lucky to have such a good mother."

"Oh, I tell them that all the time," she joked. She had me laughing again and for an instant I felt like my old self, full of sunshine and laughter.

I enjoyed my whirlpool bath, soaked and relaxed and practiced meditating. I thought about Billy Maxwell overcoming his personal disaster and I grew stronger. I was even hungry and looking forward to dinner.

Right after I got dressed, there was a knock on my door and Christina poked her head in.

"Everything all right?"

"Yes, thank you, Christina."

"You have a call," she said. "Just leave the bathroom as it is. I'll come back before I leave and take care of it all," she added, closing the door so I would have privacy. I imagined it was Holly calling again. Maybe Dorothy had called her and told her what Philip had said. Holly would want me to fly back to New York and stay with her for a while. I had to admit it looked like the best idea.

"Hello."

"Melody," Cary said. What a surprise it was to hear from him.

"Cary!"

"I called Holly and got her sister's number. Are you all right? How was the trip?"

I spoke quickly, in minutes summarizing everything that had happened, beginning with the near disaster at the airport. He listened silently until I was finished. I realized it was already late in the evening back East.

"Sounds like you've had a terrible time from the day you left New York," he said.

"But how are you?" I asked.

"Things are not too good here, Melody. I'm actually calling you from the hospital."

"The hospital! What happened to you?"

"It's not me. Dad's back in the cardiac care unit. He had another heart attack. I think he brought it on himself this time, complaining about being restricted, insisting on doing more than he should."

"Oh Cary, I'm so sorry. How's Aunt Sara?"

"You know Ma. She just keeps herself working so she won't think about it."

"And May?"

"Not so good. She misses you a lot," he said. "Which is about half as much as I do. But I understand why you have to be away," he added quickly.

"I do miss you very much, too, Cary."

"What are you going to do now?"

"I'm not sure yet. I'll call you as soon as I know," I promised. "If you can, tell Uncle Jacob I hope he feels better."

"I will."

"And take care of yourself, Cary. You can't do everything for everyone," I said, knowing him.

He laughed.

"Look who's talking. Guess who I saw this morning at the hospital?" he said. "Grandma Olivia. She couldn't help herself. She had to ask me if I had heard from you. I told her I was calling you tonight and she made me promise to give her the latest news."

"She's just hoping her investment pays off and I stay away forever," I said dryly.

"But you're going to fool her," he said and then laughed nervously.

"Right now I think the only person I've been fooling is myself," I moaned.

"I saw Kenneth in town this afternoon. I didn't speak to him. I saw him just as he was driving away. He looked . . . more straggly, if that's possible. I guess he's not taking very good care of himself."

"That's too bad. I was afraid something like that might happen."

"We're all just falling apart without you around here," Cary said.

"Oh, Cary."

"I don't know if I said it enough to be sure you believed me, Melody, but I love you. I really do."

"I believe you, Cary, and I do miss you."

"Take care of yourself and don't fall in love with any movie stars," he kidded.

"You don't have to worry about that," I said, laughing.

His good-bye was like a ribbon in the wind, lingering for a moment and then drifting away with the end of the phone call. I held the receiver for a few minutes after the line had gone dead, as if by doing so I could hold on to Cary's voice and my warm memories of him longer.

When I went downstairs for dinner, I found the air even thicker than usual, if that was possible. Philip uttered barely a word, eating and staring ahead as if he were alone in the room. Dorothy tried to make small talk, telling me about a new makeup she had discovered and a skin cream that made her feel as soft as a baby.

The food was a treat, a Mexican dish called a fajita. Dorothy told me Mexican food was very popular in Los Angeles.

"Because there are so many of them here and most of them are good cooks," she explained.

After dinner she wanted me to watch television with her; it seemed Philip rarely did anything with her at night. He usually had work to do in his office, or if he wasn't working, he was reading. Dorothy had said he hated television unless he was watching the financial reports, which she thought were abominably boring. I wondered what had brought these two people together at an altar to pledge undying love and devotion until death did them part. It seemed the only romance in Dorothy's life was the romance she watched with religious devotion on her soap operas.

I thought about the things Christina had said and I thought about Cary and May and Kenneth, and all the people who needed me back in Provincetown. Wasting any more time seemed sinful. I would do no more of it, I pledged.

"I'm going back to The Egyptian Gardens one more time," I declared after dinner. That brought animation into Philip's face. "And I'm not going to leave until I get some truthful answers."

"Tonight?" Dorothy asked.

"Yes, right away," I said.

"Really, Melody, do you think that's wise, especially at this time of night?" Dorothy asked. She looked to Philip for support.

"I wouldn't suggest you do that," he said. "It's not very intelligent in light of what you have already experienced."

"Sometimes, we have to do what our hearts command more than what our minds demand," I replied.

"Inevitably that leads to disaster," he retorted.

I said nothing more, but they both understood I was going.

"I'd rather not have our limousine involved," Philip said as he rose from the table.

"I'll just call a cab."

"Philip," Dorothy said.

"I'm afraid I have to be firm on this," he told me.

"I understand. You've both been very kind and I'm grateful for your hospitality."

"It's not the first time my sister-in-law has put me into a difficult situation," Philip remarked.

"Why don't you wait until morning, Melody? Maybe then things—"

"Regardless of whether it's day or night, I don't want our car involved," Philip repeated, raising his voice. Dorothy sat back as if she had been slapped.

"I'll just go catch a cab," I said rising.

"You don't catch a cab in Los Angeles. You call for one to pick you up," Philip said. "I'll see that Alec does that for you."

He marched out of the dining room.

"Please be careful, dear," Dorothy said.

"I will." My heart racing ahead of me, I hurried upstairs to get my purse. Actually, I was happy Spike wasn't going to be driving me anyway. I wasn't sure I could look him in the face after what had happened in his apartment.

The cab was just pulling in when I stepped out of the house. I hurried to it and gave the driver the address. I was off for what I had decided would be my final attempt to approach Mommy. If I failed, in the morning I would go back East.

The Egyptian Gardens looked different in the evening, even seedier, if that was possible. Some of the lights in the lanterns along the walkway didn't work and some of the lights on the buildings were dead as well. The shadows draped longer, deeper, darker. The gate squeaked when I opened it and entered. Ahead of me at the pool, two young men were talking and drinking something from tall glasses. They turned my way as I continued past them. Just as I reached the far corner and started toward Mommy's building, I saw a man step out of the doorway and pause to light a cigarette. The flame of his match danced on his face and hair for a moment and I gasped and retreated into the shadows. It was Archie Marlin. I'd recognize him anywhere.

He still had short orange-red hair and skin the shade of milkweed, with freckles on his chin and forehead. Everyone back in Sewell always said he looked ten years younger than he really was, although no one knew his exact age. No one knew very much about Archie Marlin. He never gave anyone a straight answer to questions about himself. He always joked or shrugged and said something silly. But he had filled Mommy with enough promises to sweep her off her feet and have her go off with him.

I held my breath as he walked past me, a slick, small smile on his orange lips. He strolled down the walkway and went around the corner. I let out my breath, my heart pounding. I didn't want to face him just yet, if ever; but seeing him was the last and final assurance that the woman upstairs in that building was beyond a doubt my mother.

My legs felt as thin and weak as a scarecrow's legs of straw as I entered the building and went to the elevator. When the doors opened, I stepped in quickly and pressed Mommy's floor. My heart seemed to have risen into the base of my throat. How horrible, I thought, how horrible that I should have all this trepidation about seeing my own mother. In moments I was standing in front of her doorway, hesitating, my fingers lingering over the buzzer. Finally, I stabbed at it and waited.

The door was thrust open and Mommy was standing there in a bathrobe, her hair unbrushed, no makeup on, her eyes glassy. She wobbled and spoke before she saw who it was.

"What did you forget now, Richard?" she asked and then focused on me. Her expression froze, first with a glimmer of delight and then quickly with a look of annoyance. "You again?" she said.

"Mommy . . ."

She stared, then she leaned out farther to look up and down the hallway.

"I see I won't get rid of you so easily. Get in here," she ordered as she dragged me into the apartment.

Mommy closed the door quickly behind me, gazed at me sourly and then walked into the living room. She kept her back to me.

"Why are you pretending not to know me, Mommy?" I asked and wiped one of my tears away quickly.

"Because I don't know you," she said. "I don't know anyone from that life. I can't, I just can't," she said, slamming her fists against her thighs and spinning on me. "Why did you come here? How did you find me?"

"Alice saw your picture in a catalogue and sent it to me. I brought it to Kenneth and he studied it and said he felt sure it was you. Then he called a friend in Boston who helped track you down for me."

"Kenneth?" She relaxed her lips into a tiny smile, and

then realizing what she had done, drove the angry, hard look back into her eyes. "I don't know anyone named Kenneth, except Ken Peters at ICM. You've got to go back," she said. "Tell them . . . tell them I'm not who you thought I was and—"

"But why, Mommy?"

"It's better for everyone all around," she said. She folded her arms under her breasts and stiffened her shoulders like one of Kenneth's statues, firming up her resolve, strengthening her resistance. I just started to cry more openly. "Stop it," she said. "Don't you see? You'll mess everything up, ruin my chances just when I was starting to get someplace. I might have a good part in a movie and another, better modeling job. I'm meeting important people. Just when it's finally happening, you pop out of nowhere and nearly sink my boat."

"I don't understand, Mommy." I took a deep breath. "How did you do this? You had everyone back home believing you died. There was a body. You're buried in the family plot back in Provincetown."

She laughed, went to an imitation ivory cigarette box on the yellowish brown coffee table and took out a cigarette.

"You mean Olivia Logan permitted the poor corpse to be deposited in her precious family ground even though she believed it was me?" She laughed again, found a match and lit her cigarette. Then she fell back into the worn, cotton print easy chair and stared at me as she puffed away. "You look good," she said. "You filled out nicely. Jacob didn't throw you out on the street, I guess."

"He's very sick, Mommy. He had a heart attack and nearly died. Now he's back in the hospital."

"Doesn't surprise me. He's too much like his mother to enjoy life or let anyone else enjoy it. Probably finally soured his own heart." She took a deep breath, shook her head and gazed through the sliding glass doors of the balcony. "I can't have a daughter your age," she said. "I wouldn't get a decent job in this town."

"Why not?"

"It's just the way it is. Young people get everything here, especially women. Look, you don't belong with me, honey. I'm not a good mother. I never was and I never will be. It's just not in my nature."

"Why not?" I asked.

"Because . . . because I'm too self-centered. Chester was right about that. Don't you remember? It was always Chester who did the important things for you, not me. And you spent most of your childhood next door with Arlene and George."

"Papa George died, Mommy," I said sadly.

"Did he?" She nodded. "He was pretty sick when I left. I didn't think it would be too much longer. You see," she said, snapping her head up and firing a look of fear my way, "you see how short life is, how quickly your chance to do something fades? I won't get a second chance out here, Melody. This is it for me. That's why I did what Archie suggested when the accident happened."

"I don't understand, Mommy. What happened?"

"Archie was really in an accident," she said, waving her cigarette. "He was returning from a party at a bar where there was supposed to be a gathering of producers and agents. He had one of his younger clients with him. The girl was really very young, but had everyone fooled, except Archie of course. Anyway, he had me lend her my identification for the night. On the way back, Richard, as you know he's called now, lost control of the car and as soon as it crashed, it caught fire. He was thrown, but the girl was trapped and killed.

"When the police found the body and my identification, Archie and I discussed it and decided it would be better if I took advantage of it to cut myself off from family. So I took on a new identity. I'm Gina Simon, Gina Simon, do you hear? Everyone here thinks I'm years younger than I am!" she added in defense. "I can't get anywhere unless I'm this young, so I did it. Don't look at me like that," she fired. "I knew you were doing well and you were with family. It wasn't as if I left you stranded somewhere."

"Family," I said, my face twisting with rage. "You left me with a family that you knew disliked you."

"Yes, but you're not me," Mommy said. "I figured that in time they would see that and not punish you for being my daughter. And they're all well off, even Jacob."

"Not anymore. His business is struggling and it's hard work and now that he's very sick—"

"You can't live with me. Why did you come here? How can I take you in? Go back and wait until I get established and make a lot of money and then I'll send for you," she promised. "You've got to go before anyone realizes who you are. Where are you staying?" she asked quickly, realizing there might be people who already knew.

"I'm staying with Holly Brooks's sister, Dorothy Livingston, but not after tonight," I said.

"Holly Brooks? I know that name."

"She's a friend of Kenneth's."

"Oh. Oh yeah. Is she living with him?"

"No, she lives in New York City. She's been very nice. She helped me get here."

"And this Dorothy . . . what does she know about us?"

"Just what I've told her . . . how you pretended I was someone you didn't know."

"Good. Go back and tell her you came here again and you had made a mistake. Then go back to Jacob and Sara."

"I can't go back to Jacob and Sara," I said. "If I go back, I have to live with Grandma Olivia."

"Olivia? Why?" she asked. I sat on the sofa and began to tell her the story of my discoveries, how I had visited with her mother, my grandmother Belinda, and how I had learned that my mother's father was really Judge Childs.

"I finally understood why Kenneth and his father don't get along. He blames his father for his losing you," I said.

Mommy smiled.

"Kenneth," she said softly, reminiscing. "I suppose if things had been different, he and I would have married.

106

You don't know how handsome he was and bright. All my girlfriends were crazy about him. He was always different, always exciting to be with." Her smile faded. "But when I learned the truth and brought it to him, it was as if I had hit him with a sledgehammer.

"They're all so prim and proper on the outside, the blue bloods who made me feel inferior. I was the poor, discarded little girl, the waif living off of Olivia's kindness and generosity. How she continually reminded me of it. She took me in just to reduce the embarrassment, but she hated every moment I was there and she brought her boys up to think of me as contaminated. Only I fooled her, didn't I? I won Chester away from her and for that, she hated me forever.

"Was she smiling at my funeral? I wish I had been there just to watch the hypocrites," Mommy said and puffed her cigarette violently.

"No, she wasn't smiling. She was dignified. It was a very nice funeral. Kenneth was there, too."

"Poor Kenneth. Was he very upset?"

"Yes."

She sat back, pleased.

"It's not so bad to bury yourself once, especially when you're burying the ugly past too." She stared blankly at me. "But that's all gone, six feet under, Melody. You can't dig me up. It's not fair. I've finally thrown off the chains, the weight of my past, and I have opportunities now, new friends . . ." She gazed around. "This is just temporary. After my next few jobs, I'll be living in a plush condo, maybe in Brentwood. Archie assures me," she said.

I looked down, my heart so heavy I thought it might fall out of my chest.

"Why does Olivia want you to move in with her now?"

"Because Uncle Jacob's so sick and because she wants to keep the lid on any scandal. I told her I wanted to live with Kenneth since he's really my uncle, but she says that will only stir gossip."

"Oh, she's right about that. Olivia knows her territory.

Maybe it's not a bad idea anyway. It's a beautiful house. I did enjoy living there when she wasn't breathing down my neck or screaming at me for one thing or another."

"She wants to find a proper school for me and she said I have an inheritance from Grandma Belinda's half of the Gordon fortune."

"That's great. So you see, you should go back and quickly."

"But . . . it's not money I want or a snobby girl's school, Mommy. Olivia isn't my mother. She's not even my real grandmother. I'm afraid to live with her, afraid she'll make my life as miserable as she made yours."

"She wasn't completely at fault. I brought a lot of it on myself," Mommy confessed. "I was angry at them, all of them, and I wanted them to pay for my unhappiness."

"They'll always see you when they look at me," I said. "Olivia does, no matter what she tells me, and Uncle Jacob certainly does. Even Kenneth," I added and she perked up.

"Oh?"

"He had me model for him just the way he had you model," I said.

She widened her eyes.

"Really? And you did it?"

"Yes. He's created a wonderful new piece of sculpture. He says it's his greatest work, *Neptune's Daughter*. But the face on the sculpture is more your face than it is mine," I told her. I saw she liked that.

"Stand up," she asked suddenly. I did so. "You really did fill out. You're a very attractive young girl. Kenneth doesn't miss much." She thought again for a moment. "Didn't you like it at all back there, meet anyone nice?"

"Cary's nice, very nice. I miss him and I love May, but I've missed you, Mommy. I really have. I don't like being . . . alone. It's not fair."

She nodded and crushed her cigarette.

"It did bother me to leave you, to lie to you," she said. "Maybe not as much as you would have liked it to have bothered me, but it did. I didn't like leaving you behind, but there was just no other way to do all this. You understand?"

I nodded, even thought I really didn't.

"I had to listen to Archie. He's had much more experience with all this," she said in defense. "What are we going to do?" she asked herself.

"Please, let me stay with you, Mommy."

She gazed at me and smiled.

"You were always a sobering influence on me, weren't you, Melody? When I stayed at Frankie's bar and grill too long in Sewell and came home, I would take one look at your face and feel so damn guilty I lost my buzz in an instant. I hated you for that, too," she admitted, "but later, I would love you for it, as much as I could love any child, I suppose."

She straightened up.

"I don't have very much here, yet," she said. "It's not even a drop in the bucket compared to what Olivia has and what she can offer you."

"I don't care about that, Mommy. I should be with you."

"You can't be with me," she whined. "I just can't have a daughter your age."

I thought quickly, remembering what her friend Sandy had thought.

"I could be your younger sister. You told people you had one," I suggested quickly.

"How do you know that?"

"I met some woman here the first time I came. Her name was Sandy and she thought I was your younger sister surprising you," I said.

"She would." She smiled and looked at me. "We do look like sisters. I mean, I look young enough to be your sister, don't' I?"

"Yes, Mommy, you do."

"See," she pounced jabbing her forefinger at me. "That's just the problem. You can't call me Mommy. A younger sister doesn't call her older sister Mommy, does she?"

"I won't."

"You'll forget."

"I won't," I insisted.

She relaxed as she thought about my suggestion.

"If I had a younger sister here, it would certainly make everyone believe me even more," she thought aloud.

"That's right, it would," I said nodding.

"You can only call me Sis or Gina. You can't even forget and call me Haille."

"I never did, Mommy."

"Mommy!"

"Well, there's no one here right now," I said quickly.

"Archie's not going to like this. He'll be furious with me," she said with a shake of her head.

"He has no right to be furious with you. You've done everything he wanted, haven't you?"

"Yes, yes I have," she said. She stared at me and then she smiled. "He won't be unhappy when I tell him he has another prime client anyway," she said.

"Another prime client?"

"You, silly. You're beautiful. You can become a model and an actress, too. We'll tell everyone I called you out here to develop your career. Just like me. Then we really will be sisters!" she exclaimed. "Maybe we'll even get to do something together."

I shook my head.

"I could never—"

"Sure you could. It's so easy. You smile when they want you to smile and you bat your eyelashes when you have to and before you know it, you have an assignment and they're paying you hundreds of dollars an hour just to pose."

"I don't know if I can do that," I said, recalling what I had learned from Spike already about the business.

"Believe me, you can do it," she said. "Okay, you can have the second bedroom and we'll try it. If it doesn't work out, you have to promise you'll return to the Cape and go back to school. Well? You wanted to be with me, this is how you can be with me. Make up your mind."

110

I stood there, speechless for a moment. Could I really turn down a chance to be with Mommy again? To wait for the perfect opportunity to find out who my father was? Before I had a chance to really think about her suggestion, we heard the doorbell.

"Who the hell is that so early?" she muttered and rose to go to the door. It was Sandy Glee.

"I saw you," she sang looking past Mommy at me. "I saw you from my patio coming up the walkway. So, Gina. Aren't you going to introduce me to your surprise?"

"Melody," Mommy said turning to me, "you see why you can't keep any secrets here. Everyone's a snoop. This is my kid sister," she said, eyeing me warily.

"I knew it," Sandy remarked with a clap of her slender hands.

"She's coming to stay with me for a while and try her luck in Hollywood like the rest of us nitwits."

"Richard's going to represent her, too?"

"Yep."

"Good. Welcome to the fight," Sandy said. "I'm having a few people over tomorrow night for a pot luck dinner if you want to introduce her around," Sandy said. "About seven."

"We'll be there," Mommy promised.

"See you later, Sis," Sandy said waving. She left the apartment and Mommy spun around to me with a wide smile on her face.

"It worked. I knew it. I do look young enough to be your sister. In this town everyone believes everyone else's lies. It's a perfect place for people who hate the truth.

"Welcome home, Melody," she said sincerely. "I can finally throw my arms around you."

Even as she hugged me, giving me the affection I so desperately needed, I had to wonder: What had I gotten myself into?

7
&

New Beginnings

Mommy made us some coffee and we sat and talked in her small kitchen, catching up on what had happened to both of us since the day she had left me in Provincetown.

"I really did hate leaving you behind," she said. "You remember how hard it was for me to do that, don't you? I think I cried all the way from Provincetown to New York City, but Archie, I mean Richard, was right in advising me not to take you along. It was a hard trip, struggling for work along the way, trying to get meetings with important people in the big cities, going from one cheap motel to the other, sometimes barely having enough money to feed ourselves. You would have hated every minute. Many nights you would have been left alone in some crummy motel room. Some of them didn't even have television sets in the rooms.

"How could that life compare to being in the fresh ocean air, going to a good school, eating well . . . You understand why I did it, don't you, honey? You don't blame me anymore?" she asked, her voice shaking.

I took a deep breath and shifted my eyes away so she

couldn't see how deeply I had been hurt. Kenneth had once told me I might as well have had translucent skin. It was that easy to see my thoughts and feelings. However, there was no sense being dishonest and lying to my mother now that I had found her, I thought.

"I used to hate you for it, Mommy," I admitted. "I used to sit there in Laura's room and listen hard through the walls for the phone to ring and hate you for not calling, hate you for making promises you wouldn't keep."

"I know. And that bothered me, too, but Richard kept saying, 'If you call her and can't send for her, it will be even more cruel, won't it?' He was right."

"He wasn't right. I needed to hear your voice, Mommy," I insisted.

She slammed down her coffee cup so hard it nearly shattered on the table.

"You've got to stop blaming me for things. I can't have any stress," she whined. "Stress brings on age and wrinkles and makes you look terrible and then you can't get jobs. The camera picks up every little detail, you know. They don't want you if they can't use you for close-ups. I won't get any work. Is that what you want to happen? Richard won't stand for it anyway. He won't let you stay here," she warned.

I gazed around the apartment, just realizing what she was saying.

"Does he live here, too?"

"Well what do you think? You have no idea how expensive it is to live and work in Los Angeles. Apartments like this are hard to come by. What would be the point of both of us having our own apartment and paying two rents?"

"Are you married?" I asked, holding my breath.

"No, we never got married. I don't want to get remarried for a long, long time; but Richard is . . . well, he's more than my agent; he's my financial manager. He takes care of all our money needs. He does that for all his clients."

113

"How many clients does he have?" I asked.

"A half dozen, but none earn as much as I do right now, so you see why it's so important everything remains smooth for us," she repeated. "No more talk about the terrible past," she said, waving her hands over the table. "I don't want to hear about how you suffered and I don't want to be reminded about what I did when I lived there. Don't ask me any questions about any of them, and don't even bring their names up in front of me," she ordered. "That's the rule if you want to live here, understand? I mean it, Melody." She glared at me, her eyes colder than I ever recalled them.

"Even Kenneth?" I asked.

"Yes, yes, yes, even Kenneth. Nobody. I forbid it. I didn't have a life before this. That's the way I want to think now. It's what Richard says I should do. These are changes we had to make for our own well-being. I hate being selfish, but it's a good selfishness because it helps us find success."

"Why did he have to change his name, Mommy? I never believed that story about Archie being his nickname."

"You're right. Archie was never his name. It was his older brother's name and he took it so he could be thought of as older when he first left home. That's a big difference between men and women. Men like to be thought of as older. They don't get punished for being older and turning gray with wrinkles, but we do.

"Anyway," she continued, "his brother got himself into big trouble with loan sharks and the like and as soon as Richard found out, he dropped that name like a hot coal so they wouldn't mistakenly come after him. That's why he never liked to talk about his family. He was ashamed of them. His father wasn't any better. Now, don't mention any of this in front of him. Understand? He would be furious with me. He's very sensitive about it."

"I won't say a thing," I said, not really believing the story anyway.

114

"Good. As long as you do what you're told, we'll be fine. I think," she said, still not sure.

She looked at me hard again and then tilted her head, smiling.

"I like that outfit you're wearing."

"Dorothy Livingston bought it for me."

"Did she? You and I are almost the same size. We can share things, but you've got to take good care of whatever I give you to wear, okay? Some of my things are very special and designed for auditions. Did you bring a lot of your own stuff to California?"

"Not a lot, no."

"Where are your things?"

"At the Livingstons'."

"Well, I guess you'll have to go get your stuff. Don't tell her too much when you go back." She thought a moment. "I know what you should say," she added with excitement. "Tell her you're going back to Provincetown. You probably won't see her again anyway, and that way, she'll tell everyone else who asks about you that you left."

"Why don't I just tell her the truth?" I asked. She laughed.

"You never tell anyone the truth if you don't have to, honey. That's something you keep in your back pocket as a last resort. Take it from someone who's had to make her way on the road of life the hard way. I know from where I speak. The less you tell people about yourself, the better off you'll be later. There's always a jam to get out of and the truth can reduce your options. Richard taught me that lesson real well," she said, nodding.

"Okay," she continued, "let's look at where you'll sleep." She rose to go to the doorway of the second bedroom.

I followed her and she snapped on the light. A dull glow fell from the ceiling because the fixture was full of dust.

"This is going to be your room. We have only one bathroom, as you see, so don't hog it. You can help me

115

keep the whole place clean. It's too much for a working girl to do that and stay pretty enough for an audition at a moment's notice anyway. That's why it looks a little disorganized right now," she said, but I remembered that Mommy was never a very good housekeeper. My stepfather Chester and I did most of the heavy cleaning in our trailer back in Sewell.

I studied the small bedroom. The walls were a faded pink, scratched, scuffed and chipped. Even the guest room at Holly's in New York with its one window was more comfortable and cozier-looking than this bare-walled, dusty room with a bed now covered with clothing, cartons of files, old issues of movie magazines and trade papers. The thin rug was badly worn in places, its thin threads frayed and unraveling. The curtains on the two windows were limp from dust and bleached from the sunlight. Large cobwebs dangled in the corners of the ceiling. I noticed a pile of what looked like thin briefcases in the right corner.

"You'll have to clean up a bit in here, but don't lose anything."

"What's that in the corner?" I asked.

"Oh, that you can't touch. Those are Richard's watches, antique watches. He sells them on the side. A friend of his got him into it here and he's made a nice bundle of pocket money doing it."

"He sells antique watches? I thought he was an agent with a half dozen clients."

"Everyone trying to break into the business does something else in the meanwhile, Melody. Most of the people living here work as waiters or waitresses in restaurants, some valet park cars, some even pack groceries. Anything to keep food on the table and pay the rent until you hit it big."

"I know. Dorothy's chauffeur is an actor. He told me he was in a few movies."

"What's his name?" she asked quickly.

"Spike. I don't remember his last name."

"Spike. I know ten Spikes if I know one," Mommy said with a laugh.

We both turned as the door opened and Archie Marlin entered. The moment he set eyes on me, his face became flushed with surprise and then anger.

"What the hell? How did she get here?" he demanded. He closed the door sharply and stood facing us with his hands on his hips, a cigarette dangling from the corner of his mouth. He pulled it out. "Huh?" he said pointing the cigarette at me. "Did you send for her behind my back?"

"No, Richard. A friend of hers from Sewell saw my picture in the *En Vogue* catalogue. She sent her the catalogue and Melody brought it to someone who knew advertising. He tracked me down for her and she came out to L.A. to find me."

"That's just great," he said throwing up his arms. "That's just what we need right now. Your daughter," he said with disgust.

"But no one knows she actually found me, do they, honey?" she asked me.

I shook my head.

"Big deal. What are we going to do with her now?" he asked, as if I were some puppy left on their doorstep. "And just when I had everyone believing you were young enough to play their parts."

"That's not going to be a problem. We worked it out," Mommy told him.

"Yeah? How?" he said. He dropped himself into the worn easy chair, ashes from his cigarette raining down on his pants and the chair. He didn't seem to notice or care.

"Sandy thought she was my younger sister. Remember the story you told me to tell? That I have a younger sister back home in the Midwest?" she said, nodding to get him to remember. I imagined he had trouble keeping track of all the lies they had spread from West Virginia to California.

"Yeah, I remember. So?"

117

"So don't you see?" She turned to me. "Melody came after me, following me, looking for a career herself," Mommy said. He turned from her and gazed at me with sudden interest.

"Younger sister? Looking for a career herself, huh?" He sat forward. "Come a little closer," he ordered.

"Go on, honey. Richard doesn't bite," Mommy said with a smile.

I took a few steps toward him and he raised his lusty green eyes to look at me, lingering over my body in a way that made me feel naked beneath his gaze. His lips curled.

"Yeah, she's a looker now, ain't she? How old are you again? Never mind. From now on, you're twenty-one, see?"

"Twenty-one?" I looked at Mommy, but she just smiled and nodded. I turned back to Richard. "No one will believe that," I told him.

"Of course they will. They won't care if you're lying or not anyway, which is more important. Yeah," he said nodding and smiling as his eyes burned through my clothes, "I can find her some work."

"I'd rather find my own," I said and he stiffened.

"You got any money?"

"Yes. Grandma Olivia gave me traveling money."

"Well, that's not much. The rent here's high and groceries and everything else costs a lot. If you're going to stay with us, you're going to have to pull your fair share, right Gina?" he said.

For a moment I had forgotten that was the phony name Mommy had taken for herself. I squinted with confusion and then remembered and looked at her.

"He's right, Melody. You're big enough and old enough to make your own way now. And besides, Richard might just make you a star too."

"I might," he said nodding. "I always thought she was a pretty girl, being she's your daughter," he said, smiling at Mommy. She beamed. "So," he said sitting back, "you saw your mother in the *En Vogue* catalogue. I got

118

her that job," he bragged, "and we made some money on it, didn't we, Gina?"

"Yes, we did, Richard."

"Course, we spent it all, but I got her another job yesterday too. I just wrapped up the deal, honey," he said.

Mommy squealed.

"Oh, that's wonderful. See, honey? I am making it here. What's the job?"

"You're going to demonstrate some new perfume over at the Beverly Center and then be a model for makeup demonstrations," he declared.

Mommy held her smile, but it lost most of its bright light.

"Well, what about that role in the movie, Richard?" she asked softly.

"We'll see. They're still thinking about you," he said. "You might get a call back tomorrow in fact."

Her smile warmed again.

"Good. Well, Melody has to return to where she was staying and get her clothes and things, Richard."

"Oh yeah? Where were you staying?" he asked me.

"With the sister of a friend in Beverly Hills," I replied.

"Beverly Hills? Well, well, well, ain't we coming up in the world?" He laughed. "You sure you want to lower yourself and come live here with us common folk?"

"I was leaving their house tomorrow morning anyway," I said. "Mrs. Livingston was just doing her sister a favor by helping me."

"All right. I'll take her to go fetch her things. I like driving around Beverly Hills, gives me a chance to pick out the house I'm going to buy real soon," he said with a faraway look in his eyes.

"Oh, that's so nice of you, Richard. You see, honey? We'll work it all out as long as you listen. Isn't that right, Richard?"

"That's right," he said sternly gazing at me. "As long as you know who's running things around here and do exactly what I tell you to do."

119

"He knows what's best for us, honey," Mommy said. I looked from her to him, his glaring eyes full of self-satisfaction and I nodded to myself, recalling Christina's words and thoughts. Mommy did need me now more than ever. Somehow, someway, I would free her of the hold this slimy man had over her, I pledged.

He seemed to sense the challenge I threw back at him. He pulled his shoulders up, curled his lips and nodded at the door.

"Let's go. I have important things to do."

"Thank you, Richard," Mommy told him. "It's very nice of you." He shrugged.

"As long as she does her fair share, it's no skin off my teeth," he said. "And," he added firmly, threateningly, "as long as she remembers she's your sister and not your daughter."

"She won't forget. See you soon, Sis," Mommy said with a laugh. Richard gazed at me, his head tilted, a wry smile on his lips now.

"Well, what do you say?"

I looked back at Mommy, whose face coaxed me to do what was expected.

"See you soon . . . Gina," I managed, even though the word wanted to choke my throat.

Richard Marlin roared with satisfaction and opened the door.

"Miss Simon," he said stepping back with an exaggerated bow, "shall we fetch your things at the Livingstons'?"

I walked out, my heart pounding, but my spine as straight as Grandma Olivia's could be when she was faced with a challenge. Maybe she was right, I thought. Maybe I was more like her than I wanted to admit.

"So, tell me how you've been since we left you back at the Cape," Richard said as we drove out of the parking lot. He had a different car, an older car with dozens of dents and scratches and a crack in one of the rear

120

windows. The passenger seat in front had a deep tear in it, too. He glanced at me. "You don't look the worse for it. I'd say they fed you well, didn't work you too hard."

"I managed to get along," I said and he laughed.

"I bet you did fine living with those clam diggers."

"They're not clam diggers. They're lobster fishermen and they harvest cranberries. It's hard work and you've got to know the sea and—"

"Right, right. It's great if you want to get up with the worms and break your back every day. That's not for me, not for Richard Marlin," he boasted. "I'm going to have the easy life and soon, too. I've already started doing better than most out here."

From what I saw, I thought he had been living better when he was a bartender back in Sewell.

"What happened to your other car?" I asked. "It was much nicer."

"What? Oh. It don't pay to have a nice car in the city. People are always knocking into it, and if you have a nice car, someone's bound to steal it for parts anyway. Lots of big actors and producers have old, beat-up-looking cars like this one," he assured me. "So they won't be noticed so easily, see? Once people find out you're an agent and a manager, they hound you to death hoping you'll take them on as clients."

"So you're afraid of having too many clients?" I asked, incredulous.

"I've got more than I can handle now. We're going to make it big, your mother and me. You'll see." He looked at me closely and then turned back to the road. "You sure you want to stay with us?" he asked. "We won't have time to do any baby-sitting."

"I don't need baby-sitting."

"This is a place for grown-ups, people who can deal with hard realities," he bragged.

"Really? From what I've seen, it looks like a land of make believe, a big sandbox," I replied. He turned to me, his eyebrows raised and then he laughed.

"Maybe you will get along here after all."

When he saw the Livingstons' home, he whistled through his teeth.

"Why the hell do you want to leave this?" he asked. "Why don't you just stay on until they throw you out?"

"That's about what Mr. Livingston's doing," I remarked as we pulled into the driveway.

"You better wait in the car," I suggested when he went to get out.

"What's that supposed to mean? You too haughty now? Think I'm an embarrassment? Think these people are better than me?" he asked angrily.

"No, but if Dorothy Livingston sees you, she might describe you to her sister, who will tell people back in Provincetown, who might be angry enough to tell the police about what you and Mommy have done. There's a stranger buried in the Logan family plot and Olivia Logan is not the sort of woman who would look fondly on that," I said. "She's a powerful woman, too, with friends in high places. She might even get the FBI after you," I added.

He thought a moment, looked at the house, and then nodded as he sat back.

"Yeah, right. Good thinking. You do have a head on your shoulders. That's good. I'm tired of doing all the thinking for everyone," he said. "Go on. Make it fast. I got things to do," he ordered and I got out of the car quickly and went to the front door.

Alec came to the door almost immediately after I had pressed the buzzer. He looked out at the car in the driveway and then stepped back with that habitually disapproving grimace on his face. Dorothy and Philip appeared in the hallway, both coming from the den. Alec closed the door and walked away without a word as they approached me.

"What happened?" Dorothy asked. "I've been very worried since you left and so has Philip," she said. I glanced at him, but he still looked more concerned about his own reputation than anything else.

I thought about Mommy's advice concerning the truth and decided she wasn't right. I wasn't going to get caught up in her and Richard's web of lies.

"We met and I'm going to stay with her," I said quickly. "She needs me."

"You mean she owned up to who she was?" Philip asked.

"Yes."

"Well, why did she do such a terrible thing before? Why did she deny knowing her own daughter?" Dorothy demanded.

"She had her reasons," I said, "but it's all cleared up now. I'll just go get my things."

I started for the stairs.

"But . . . will you really be all right?" Dorothy asked.

"I think she knows if she'll be all right, Dorothy," Philip said, obviously happy to be rid of me. "She's old enough."

"No she's not. She's—"

"Dorothy," he snapped.

She bit down on her lower lip and watched me climb the stairs. I hurried into the room and threw my things together quickly. I gazed at the black evening dress in its box, thinking that if I just left it there, Dorothy would have to take it back.

"I won't take it back," I heard Dorothy say as if she had been reading my mind. I turned to see her standing in the doorway. "You might as well take it with you, Melody. Otherwise, it will just collect dust."

"I don't mean to be ungrateful, Dorothy. You've been wonderful and kind and generous, but—"

"No buts, ifs, or maybes. I just want you to know I hope the best for you, Melody. You're a sweet young lady," she said, coming into the room and sitting on the bed. "Actually," she said, looking down at her hands, "I wish I could do something as significant for my own sister, but she and I . . . we never saw the world the same way. Oh, we love each other, I suppose, as much as two sisters can, but I know Holly thinks I have no purpose to

123

my life other than satisfying myself. She doesn't know who I am," she said with tears in her eyes. "I have my mountains to climb, too."

I smiled at her.

"I'm sure she knows that, Dorothy. She cares a lot about you and she thinks a lot of you. She told me you would be wonderful to me and she was right. Thank you very much." I took the box with the dress in it and she smiled.

"Good luck to you and please, please don't hesitate to call me if you need someone. Don't worry about Philip. He'll growl, but he'll do the right thing in the end."

I nodded and she hugged me.

"I do wish I had had a daughter like you," she said. "I wish I had someone else, someone who needed me. Philip's about as self-sufficient as anyone can be. It's good to be needed and wonderful to be able to help someone in need."

"I know. That's why I want to be with my mother," I said.

She nodded.

"She's very lucky. I'm sure she doesn't deserve you."

Dorothy followed me out and down the stairs. At the doorway we hugged again. Philip was nowhere in sight. He wasn't the sort who cared to say good-bye anyway, I thought. Tomorrow, he would forget my face.

I hurried out and to the car, turning once to wave. Dorothy lifted her hand and held it for a moment before she closed the door softly. Loneliness, I thought, had nothing to do with money or wealth; loneliness had to do with the heart. If it beat only for one, it was only half used.

"What did you get, a good-bye present?" Richard asked, eyeing the box when I got into the car.

"Mrs. Livingston was very generous. She bought me some clothes."

He glanced at the box and saw the name inscribed on the cover.

"That's a pretty expensive boutique in Beverly Hills," he said as he started the engine. "What is it?"

"A black evening dress."

"Oh yeah? Well, what do you need with something that expensive now?"

"She wanted me to have it," I said dryly.

He backed out of the driveway and looked at me. "I got an acquaintance who can turn a new dress like that into hard cash, which we could use. Especially since you ain't worn it yet and I bet it still has the tags on it, right?"

"Yes."

"Good."

"I don't want to sell this," I said. "It was a present. It meant a lot to her to give it to me."

"Is that so? What are you, a millionaire? You going to pay the first six months rent for us? You going to buy tomorrow's groceries, pay the electric and gas bills? Pay for my car insurance? I gotta cart you girls around town to the auditions, to the jobs. That takes gas money, upkeep. There's expenses here," he whined. "If you want to be part of this, you gotta put in your share. How much money did the old lady back in Provincetown give you for traveling?" he demanded. "Huh?"

"She bought my tickets and gave me . . . five hundred dollars," I said. She had given me two thousand, but I knew where Richard's questions were heading.

"Well, where's the money?"

"I spent nearly all of it coming out here," I said.

"What's left?"

"A hundred dollars."

"That's all? All right. Give me seventy-five and keep twenty-five for pocket money so I don't have to give you any for a while. Go on, give it to me," he said. "I'll need to have some seed money to find you a job now, too."

I opened my purse and counted out the seventy-five without his seeing how much was really there. When I handed it to him he shoved it into his pocket without another word.

"Good. That makes sense. I'll find you work," he promised.

I curled up in the corner of the seat and gazed out the window as Beverly Hills fell behind us.

"There's my house," Richard claimed, nodding at a large home with Grecian columns in the front. "It's only a matter of time," he said with a confident laugh.

Matter of time? Matter of centuries, I thought, but kept it to myself. My eyes filled with tears of determination. Somehow, somehow soon, I had to get Mommy away from him and away from all this.

As soon as we returned to the apartment, Richard told Mommy about my evening dress, but when Mommy saw it and then tried it on, she moaned and pleaded for him to let us keep it. She did look absolutely beautiful in it.

"I'll get a job where I'll need to wear something nice like this, Richard. Won't I?" she asked, spinning in front of the mirror. "And then, instead of having to rent something, I'll have it. And how about the wonderful, important parties you told me we would be attending soon? I'll need to look good for you, won't I? Oh please, let us keep it."

"People will be impressed Mommy has something so expensive," I added, "and clothing is important to people in the business, isn't it?" I offered to support her.

Richard glared at me.

"How do you know what's important to people in the business?"

"I met an actor who told me all about it," I said.

"Oh, you met an actor. Big deal."

"She's right though, isn't she, Richard? You've told me that. That's why you needed the money for your nice jackets and suits," Mommy added.

He squirmed in his seat.

"We could get a nice piece of change for that."

"Mommy's got work and you said you were sure you could get me work soon anyway," I chimed.

He reddened with fury.

"That's right, Richard," Mommy said, checking her reflection in the mirror.

"You're going to keep calling her Mommy," he snapped at me. "You're bound to make a mistake in front of strangers."

"I won't," I insisted.

"You better call me Sis or Gina even when we're alone, Melody," Mommy advised. "Get into the habit."

"All right. I will. You look beautiful in that dress, Gina," I added, enjoying the way Richard twisted in his seat as the prospect of losing the money for the dress sunk in deeper.

"Richard," she whined. "I've waited so long for something nice."

"All right, all right. Just this once, I'll change my mind, but next time when I decide something—"

"We'll listen. We promise," Mommy said.

He smirked, turned a suspicious eye at me and then went to watch television while Mommy and I got my room organized.

"The Livingstons must be so rich, Melody," Mommy said. "Such expensive gifts. But soon, I'll be able to buy myself things like this. I'll be driven in my Rolls to Beverly Hills and stroll into the most expensive stores, too," she said and pretended that my dingy room was a designer's boutique. "The salespeople will come rushing over, each eager to help me, to show me the latest fashion," Mommy continued. I sat on the bed and watched her pose as if she were gazing at a dress. "Yes, that might work. What's that? Only five thousand dollars? What, is it on sale?"

She laughed and then spun around to look at herself in my evening dress once more. I laughed, too.

"It's beautiful," she said and sighed. Then she looked at me. "But it's really yours."

"No, it isn't Mommy, it's yours. I want you to have it, keep it in your closet."

"Really? Thank you, dear. But please," she said,

whispering, "try, try to call me Sis or Gina." She gazed at the doorway. "Especially when he's here."

I nodded. She gave me a quick hug and then left to be with Richard.

It felt strange going to sleep in their apartment that first night because it reminded me of the trip from Sewell up to the Cape. I recalled the nights on the road, sleeping in motel rooms with them sleeping together nearby, just as they were tonight.

Back then I could only think of my stepdaddy and wonder how Mommy could hold and kiss someone else so quickly after my stepdaddy's death. Maybe she was afraid of being alone, so afraid she would even cling to someone like Archie Marlin. He took advantage of her vulnerability and replaced her fears with pipe dreams. Was Mommy just too grief-stricken to notice? But what about now? What was her excuse for letting him rule her life now?

I felt so small and alone myself, sleeping in this dismal little room. If Mommy hadn't realized what sort of a man Archie Richard Marlin was by now, how could I hope to open her eyes? He held up the promise of glamour and fame, riches and respect. What could I offer in its place except the truth? And for Mommy, the truth might be too painful a pill to swallow.

Like so many other people in Los Angeles, dreams, no matter how false or impossible, were something she would much rather have. At least, I thought, I had found her, and at least now, there was a chance.

I was up before either of them the next morning. I made coffee and toasted some nearly stale bread. They didn't have much more to eat for breakfast, no cereals or eggs and very little jam or butter. Nevertheless, the aroma of freshly brewed coffee brought them out of the bedroom.

"Now this is more like it," Richard said. "I usually have to go out for some coffee. Your sister can't get her eyes open fast or wide enough to boil water first thing in the morning."

"Oh, Richard."

"What, am I telling her something she didn't know about you?" he said and laughed.

"We need some groceries," I said.

He raised his eyebrows.

"So, you still got a few bucks. While we're off to the mall for your sister's job, you go buy what you want," he said.

I made up my mind that was just what I would do.

"Clean up our room, too, while we're gone," he ordered. "I'm tired of living in a pigsty and until you start working and bringing in money, you'll earn your keep that way."

"I gave you money," I reminded him. He reddened.

"What money?" Mommy asked.

"Just some of her pocket money, hardly anything, but I need it to go riding up and down the valley seeing people and trying to get her a job, don't I? Well, don't I?" he pursued.

"Yes, I suppose so," Mommy agreed. It seemed there wasn't anything he couldn't make her think or say.

They drank their coffee, nibbled on some of the toast and then went to get dressed. I waited until they left and then I called Holly and told her where I was and what had finally happened.

"So you've decided to stay?"

"Yes," I said. Although I didn't tell her how Philip wanted me to leave, I did tell her how sad I thought Dorothy really was.

"She can't buy enough things to keep the darkness from her door," I told Holly.

"I know. It's a conversation she and I have had before. Maybe I should make another trip out there soon."

"I wish you would. She does miss you," I said.

"Listen to you, giving other people advice and trying to help them while your future is still uncertain. Don't take on more than you can handle, sweetheart, and call me if you need me."

"I will. Thank you, Holly."

As soon as I hung up, I called Cary, hoping he might just be home. He wasn't, but Aunt Sara was eager to talk.

"Jacob's very sick," she told me. "It was worse this time. And now Cary's got me worried, too. He barely gets any rest between going on the boat, looking after our business and running up to the hospital. I'm on my way up there now."

"I'm sorry, Aunt Sara. I wish I were there to help you."

"Are you all right, dear? I haven't even asked you how your search is going. I'm sorry."

"That's all right. You have enough on your mind. Just give Cary my phone number, please, but tell him not to call until he really has a free moment. It's not any sort of emergency."

"I'm afraid it is here," she said in a tiny voice. "We all try to be strong for Jacob, but it gets so hard to keep our spirits up."

I heard her start to sob and then she quickly excused herself and hung up. I felt awful about being away from Aunt Sara and the family when things were going so poorly. I felt myself pulled in every direction. Mommy also needed me, but she seemed to have chosen her predicament. Cary and Aunt Sara and May had no choice.

Where did I really belong?

It seemed like I had been searching for home forever. Just when I thought I'd found it. . . .

8
ॐ

A Star Shines

After I got dressed, I went downstairs and asked a man working on the grounds where the closest grocery store was. He spoke broken English mixed with Spanish words, but I remembered enough from my high school Spanish class to communicate with him. The supermarket was a little more than three long blocks away. When I got there and saw all the delicious produce, I wanted to fill my cart, but thinking about the long walk home kept me from going wild. It was already hot and sticky, with only little puffs of clouds lazily sliding toward the horizon. A nice day for a stroll but not for lugging groceries around.

A handsome young man with dark brown hair was just turning in his apron at the next counter when I checked out, and I caught him looking my way as I was paying the cashier. As I walked from the store, struggling not to spill anything out of my two bags and hoping the bottoms wouldn't burst, I heard someone behind me say, "You look like you could use a third arm."

I turned to see the handsome young man from the

store. In the sunlight, his hair held hints of copper. His laughing eyes were hazel with long eyelashes. Although he wasn't what I would call muscular, he was well proportioned, sinewy, sleek, his face very masculine, especially around his mouth.

"I could carry one of those for you," he offered. "I won't steal your food," he added with a soft smile when I hesitated.

"How do you know where I'm going?" I asked.

"The Egyptian Gardens, right? I saw you there yesterday. I was at the pool when you went by. I live there, too," he said. "I'm walking that way anyway," he added, "going home." He shrugged when I didn't reply. "Light's changing."

"What?"

"We can cross now," he said, indicating the traffic had stopped.

"Oh."

He reached out and took one of my bags.

"Better hurry up," he said. "This is one of the shortest lights in L.A."

He grabbed my elbow and gently directed me across the street. We walked quickly and didn't speak again until we were on the sidewalk.

"I don't blame your hesitating to accept my offer. I don't trust my groceries with strangers either," he said with that silly, impish grin again. "Strange women are always approaching me and offering to carry one of my bags."

"Very funny."

"My name's Mel Jensen."

"Melody . . . Simon," I said.

"There. Now we're no longer strangers," he quipped. "I can carry your groceries all the time."

"Just because we exchanged names doesn't mean we're not still strangers," I replied and he turned very serious.

"You're right. Besides, around here, you're never sure the person is giving you his or her real name anyway," he said with a tiny turn in the corner of his mouth, and I felt myself turn a bright crimson. He was looking straight ahead, so he didn't notice. "But that's my real name and I intend to make it a household word," he bragged, now turning to see my reaction.

"What are you selling?" I asked and he laughed, the light in his eyes getting even brighter. He paused when he saw I wasn't kidding. "You're serious? You think I'm a salesman?"

"Well, you said household, so I thought . . ."

"What are you doing in L.A.?" he asked, suddenly very curious and suspicious. I looked away before replying.

"I'm visiting my sister," I said.

"Sister? Simon," he thought aloud. "Oh, you're Gina Simon's sister?"

"Yes," I said. I never thought of myself as a good liar and I had doubts that I would be able to fool people the way Mommy and Richard Marlin wanted. I was positive people would see through me or hear the hesitation in my voice and know immediately I wasn't telling the truth, but if Mel Jensen saw my deceit, he ignored it.

"Of course," he said nodding, "you two do look a lot alike. I suppose you want to be an actress and a model, too?"

"Not really, but my sister's agent thinks I can be. He says he's going to try to get me a job while I'm here," I replied.

"Stranger things have happened. The doorman at the Four Seasons got offered a small part in a television pilot. The pilot was picked up and he got a recurring role in it. Now he's an actor who drives up to the Four Seasons in his own Mercedes and has doors opened for him."

"Are you an actor, too?"

"No, I'm a dancer, jazz, interpretive, that sort of thing. However, if they made musicals the way they did when Gene Kelly and Fred Astaire were alive, I'd be in

133

the movies," he claimed. "Anyway, this job packing groceries and stocking shelves is just something to keep a roof over my head while I fight the good fight. I share an apartment with two other guys, who both happen to be actors. Aren't you and your sister from the Midwest someplace?"

"Yes," I said quickly, hoping he wouldn't press me for details. I didn't know all the lies Mommy and Richard had spread about themselves.

"I'm from Portland."

We turned into The Egyptian Gardens and I stopped to take back my second bag of groceries.

"That's all right," he said. "I'll go up to your sister's place with you. I'm not in any rush. I'm not waiting for anything. I have an audition tomorrow morning and then I'll be hovering around the phone." He laughed and we walked down the pathway to Mommy's building. "You should see the three of us when we've all gone for something and the phone rings. It's a mad dash. Lately, all three of us have been disappointed, but my luck's changing. I can feel it."

"I hope so," I said.

"Thanks. See, we can't be strangers any longer. You're already wishing me luck."

He stepped into the elevator with me and carried my bag of groceries to the door of Mommy's apartment.

"Thank you," I said as he put the bag into my arms.

"Just an added service we provide at the Bay Market," he replied with a soft, beguiling smile on his lips. "What are you doing with the rest of your day?"

"I'm . . . cleaning," I said.

"It's so hot today."

"I have to do it," I said.

"When you take a break, come on down to the pool and I'll introduce you to some of the other tenants."

"I'd like that," I said hesitantly.

"See you later then," he replied and started for the elevator.

I don't know why I said I might go to the pool, I thought. I don't even have a bathing suit. I put away the groceries and began to clean the apartment. From the gobs of dust and the cobwebs I found, I realized neither Mommy nor Richard had ever done much cleaning since they had moved into this place. The pail of water turned black from my dipping the mop in it after two or three swipes of the kitchen floor. The windows were so crusted with grime, they made the outside world look gray even on a beautiful day.

The bathroom was even dirtier. Stubborn mildew had formed in every crack and space, and when I moved a small rug near the tub, I jumped back a foot because of the size of the bugs that came crawling out.

Finally, I turned my attention to the bedrooms. The little balls of dust under the beds were like tumbleweeds. There wasn't any vacuum cleaner either, so I had to sweep under the beds and wash by hand the places the mop wouldn't reach. I didn't know whether Mommy would want me to go into her and Richard's dresser drawers, but I saw she wasn't folding her clothes any better than she used to fold them back in Sewell. I did most of our washing and ironing back then, too.

Clothes were draped over chairs and there was a pair of jeans and a blouse crumpled on the floor. While organizing one of her dresser drawers, I found a light pink two-piece bathing suit and I thought about Mel Jensen's invitation. It was still very sunny and warm outside and I was about due for a break.

When I tried on the bathing suit however, I realized it was very revealing. I was going to take it off and look for another, more modest suit, but all I found was another bikini, this one even skimpier.

I stood up and gazed at myself in the mirror again. The suit fit well. I was a little bigger in the bosom than Mommy so the top was snug. My hips were more narrow, but the suit was like new and not stretched. I turned around, gazing at myself from different angles, not unhappy with what I saw. I didn't approve of girls who flaunted themselves, but I didn't see why I should be ashamed of having a nice figure. I could use a little tan, I thought, and conjured up Mel Jensen's soft, handsome, inviting smile. Did I have the nerve to go down to the pool in this suit? Just the thought of it was titillating.

While I was considering it, the phone rang. It was Cary.

"I tried calling earlier," he said, "but when the answering machine came on, I decided not to leave a message. You wouldn't know when to call me anyway. I'm in and out so much."

"I went shopping for groceries."

"Shopping for groceries? Where are you? What did you tell Ma? She can't remember anything these days. What's happening?" He fired questions at me without taking a breath.

I told him about my confrontation with Mommy and summarized her story quickly.

"So they sent a strange woman's body to Provincetown? I can't believe it. That's against the law, isn't it?" he asked.

"I suppose so," I said.

"What about the woman who's in the grave? Isn't anyone looking for her?"

"I don't know all the details, but there are a lot of people here who have left their families behind forever. Besides, I think it was mostly Richard Marlin's doing," I added. "Mommy seems . . . under his control, but I'm going to get her out of here," I said and explained why I wanted to stay in Los Angeles and try to save her from Richard's evil grip.

"Maybe she doesn't want to be saved, Melody," Cary said.

"I've got to try."

"Why? She didn't care about you. Look at what she did. If your friend back in West Virginia hadn't found that picture in the catalogue, do you think your mother would have ever called again?" he argued. "She was just like those other people you mentioned, people who forgot their families."

I knew he just wanted me to go home to him, although what he was saying was not untrue.

"That's just it, Cary. I did see the picture and I did find her and I know she needs me. One day she's going to find herself all alone here. Once Richard decides he can't get anything more out of her, he'll leave her stranded."

"She should have thought of that herself. You don't belong there," he insisted. "They're criminals, sending a stranger's body to be buried as if it were your mother's. Grandma Olivia's going to be furious."

"Maybe you shouldn't tell her anything just yet."

"What do I do when she asks, lie? Is that what you're learning how to do out in L.A.?"

"No."

"Your mother's a good teacher," he muttered. "We both know that."

"Look Cary, no matter what she's done, she's still my mother. You'd feel the same way."

"No, I wouldn't," he said quietly and I could hear the sadness in his voice.

"How's your father doing?" I asked.

"There's been no change. He's still in the cardiac care unit in the hospital. It was raining here this morning, a small storm, so we didn't go out in the boat. I'm depending on the cranberry crop to get us through the year anyway," he added. "There's going to be a lot of work to do soon."

"Maybe I can come back to help," I suggested.

"And then what, return to L.A.?"

"I just don't know, Cary."

"You probably like it out there. Hollywood," he spat. "It's a lot more glamorous than living in an old house and harvesting cranberries. I don't blame you," he said in a tired voice. "I wish I could run away from my responsibilities, too."

"I'm not running away from my responsibilities, Cary Logan. I'm running toward them. I'm trying to help my

mother," I said firmly, determined to make him understand.

"Right. Well, you know where I'll be. Give me a call
sometime, if you *have* time," he said, not disguising his
frustration and anger.

"Oh, Cary, you know I'll call."

"I gotta get back to the hospital," he said. "I left Ma
up there with May. Bye."

"Cary."

The phone went dead. I held the receiver in my hand a
moment and then put it back on the cradle, my heart
feeling like cold stone. Cary didn't do well with sadness
and hardship. He turned inside himself and bitterly
closed up like a clam. It was the way I had found him
when I had been left there to live with Uncle Jacob and
Aunt Sara, and it had taken a while to get him to say two
friendly words to me. I felt just horrible not being there
at his side when he needed me so much.

But when I gazed around this small apartment and
thought about Mommy completely under Richard's control, I knew I had to stay. I had to try. It was times like
this I wished there were two of me. I would send my
other self back to Provincetown. I should have been the
one to have a twin, not Cary, I thought.

A rich peal of laughter came flowing up from under the
patio. I went out and listened. Two young women were
walking down the path toward the pool. They were both
in bikinis, even skimpier than the one I was wearing.

I do need a break, I thought, just a small intermission
from all these troublesome thoughts. Just for a little
while, I'll pretend to be one of them. My only fear was
that whatever madness drove them would be contagious
and what Cary suggested would come true. I'd find it was
easier to just run away into my dreams and fantasies,
and like everyone else here, not worry if they had any
reasonable relationship to the truth.

Despite that fear, I searched for and found a beach
towel at the bottom of the closet and a pair of sandals. I

scooped up Mommy's coffee-stained and cigarette-burned terry cloth robe and slipped it over myself. Then I headed down to the pool, telling myself it was just for a little while. No harm done. Right?

"This is Melody Simon," Mel Jensen told the stout, light-brown-haired man on the lounge beside him. "Melody, meet Bobby Dee," Mel said.

"Greetings," Bobby Dee muttered. He held the sun reflector under his chin and glanced at me quickly.

"Bobby's the drummer for the Gross Me Outs, a rock band who cut their first single last week."

"Oh. Congratulations," I said. Bobby Dee grunted. Mel pulled up a lounge chair so I could be beside him. Across the pool Sandy and two of her friends were sunning themselves, surrounded by two other young men. Everyone looked at me when I took off Mommy's robe and laid it neatly on the lounge. Mel's smile widened.

"You better put on some suntan lotion," he suggested. "You're a bit pale in places that have obviously not seen the sun in a while." He handed me his bottle of lotion.

"Thank you," I said and rubbed some lotion over my legs and arms.

"I can get your back for you," he volunteered.

"Watch out. That's how he starts," Bobby Dee mumbled. "First it's the back and then it's the arms and then—"

"Never mind, big mouth," Mel said. He took the lotion and stood behind me. His hands felt warm on my skin, but the lotion was cold and I jumped.

"He's the guy with the magic touch." Bobby lowered his reflector and really looked at me. "You don't sing, do you? We're looking for a new lead singer."

"I sing when I play the fiddle," I said. "But I'm not good enough to be in anyone's band."

"Fiddle. You mean as in hoedown music?"

"I guess so," I said. Mel rubbed the lotion into my

arms and then spent some time on my shoulders and neck. "Thank you," I told him. I had the feeling if I didn't speak up, he'd keep at it all afternoon.

"No problem."

"Hell's a Poppin' has a fiddle player in their band," Bobby said. "They got a gig in the valley, at Market Square off of Ventura. Ever hear of them?"

"She just got here, Bobby. She doesn't even know what you mean by the valley," Mel said.

"Oh yeah?" He studied me a moment and then went back to his sun reflector.

Sandy and one of her girlfriends dove into the pool and swam over to us. The young men jumped in after them.

"Hi again," Sandy called and raised herself up to look at me.

"Hi."

"You've met Mel, I see," she said.

"At my office," he told her.

"Watch out, he bites," she warned, laughing as she pushed herself away.

"Why is everyone warning me about you?" I asked him.

"Jealousy," he said. "Beware of the green-eyed monster. It possesses everyone around here eventually."

Bobby grunted.

"Look who's talking," he said. Mel spun on him.

"What, you're not jealous of Tommy and the Loafers?" Mel asked him.

"It was just luck that they got that contract instead of us," Bobby replied.

"You're still jealous," Mel said. "See?" he told me. I smiled, lay back and closed my eyes. Someone turned on a radio and the music drifted our way. The sunlight was warm. There was laughter around me. It was easy to forget problems. I could get used to this, I thought shamefully.

"Are you going to Sandy's party tonight?" Mel asked.

"I think so," I said.

140

"Good."

I opened one eye and glanced at him. He was on his side, turned toward me.

"Why don't you bring your fiddle to Sandy's tonight," he suggested.

"I didn't bring it to California," I said.

"You didn't? Why not?"

"I . . . didn't think anyone would want to hear a fiddle player," I said.

"Doesn't Jerry have a fiddle?" Mel asked Bobby.

"Yeah. We'll dig it out for you. I'll bring it tonight."

"No, I'd rather not. I'm really not that good," I said.

"If there is one place in the world modesty doesn't work, it's L.A.," Mel said. "Here, you're considered weird if you don't blow your own horn."

"Then I'll be considered weird," I said firmly, "because I don't."

Bobby laughed.

"She plays the fiddle, stupid," he said, "not the horn."

"I bet you're good," Mel insisted. I didn't reply. "Come on," he said poking me, "let's get wet."

He got up and dove into the water, a smooth, graceful dive that barely made a splash.

"Come on in," he said when he surfaced. "It's great."

I looked at Bobby, who shrugged and said, "I took one bath already this week."

Mel treaded water and Sandy and the other girls began to splash him. He splashed back. It looked like they were having fun so I got up and sat at the edge of the pool. Mel swam over and seized my ankles.

"Come on. You won't drown. It's only five feet deep." He tugged and I went forward, falling into his arms and into the pool. The girls came to my rescue, splashing him so much he had to dive under. I joined in, but when they turned to me, their eyes widened with shock. I paused, curious.

"What's wrong?" I asked.

Sandy swam forward.

"Your suit," she said and I looked down at the top of

my mother's bikini. In water the suit became transparent. I was as good as naked.

"Oh no," I wailed, wrapping my arms around my breasts.

"Just wait a minute," Sandy said and climbed out of the pool. She got my towel off the lounge and returned. I got out and she wrapped the towel around me. Everyone was looking at us, and some of the men who had arrived were shaking their heads gleefully. Even Bobby Dee was laughing at me.

Embarrassed to the bone, my face and even my body turned so red I looked like I had gotten a bad sunburn.

"Thanks," I told Sandy. "It's one of my . . . moth— my sister's suits. I didn't know it would do this," I explained. I looked at the others and then grabbed the apartment keys off the table by the lounge and fled.

When I got up to the apartment, I looked at myself in the mirror. This suit was obviously not meant for bathing, I thought. I got out of it quickly, dried off and put on my clothes. As I was drying my hair, I heard the buzzer. It was Mel, bringing the rest of my things.

"Now that was a dramatic exit," he said when I opened the door. "You're definitely an actress. You made a big first impression."

"Thanks a lot. I'd rather not have been noticed. I didn't realize that suit wasn't meant for swimming. I borrowed it from my sister's dresser drawer."

"No explanations necessary. I kind of liked it," he said, leaning in close to me.

"I wonder why," I said sarcastically, and then reached for my robe and sandals. "Thanks for bringing these."

"No problem. I'll see you at Sandy's," he said. "Dressed?"

"I'm not showing my face," I wailed.

"That's silly. Everyone understands. Something like that happens around here regularly."

"Not to me," I cried. He laughed as I closed the door.

When Mommy and Richard Marlin came home, I took Mommy aside and told her what had happened.

"Oh, I haven't been down at that pool ever," she said. "Those suits are for modeling jobs. You don't want to get too much sun when you're my age. It brings out wrinkles," she explained.

"It was very embarrassing," I said and she just laughed.

"I bet it made you instantly popular with the young men around here," she said, with a tinge of jealousy in her voice.

"I'd rather not be that popular."

"Of course you would. The more men looking at you, the more important you are," she told me. "Take your time giving any one of them your individual attention. You've got years and years to go before you do what I did, chain yourself to one man."

"Is that what it was like for you, Mommy? You felt trapped all the time?"

"Yes," she confessed easily. "And please, remember, don't call me Mommy," she whispered.

Richard came out of the kitchen.

"You bought quite a bit," he said. "There's actually some real food in this house for once."

"Well, we don't have to worry about it tonight. We're going to Sandy's party," Mommy reminded him.

"I can't go, Sis. Not after what happened this afternoon."

"Nonsense, Melody."

"What happened this afternoon?" Richard asked. Mommy told him and he laughed. Then he looked at me seriously.

"I think I got you a job. I described you to this producer and he wants to see you tomorrow. After I drop Gina off at the mall, I'll take you to the studio."

"Oh Melody, that's terrific, and so fast, too. Now the girls around here will really be dying with jealousy."

"The green-eyed monster," I said nodding, recalling Mel's words.

"What?"

143

"Nothing. What kind of a job is it?" I asked Richard. "What do I demonstrate?"

"Don't be so smart. It happens to be an acting job," he said, "in an independent movie."

I looked at Mommy, who beamed.

"But I've never acted," I said.

"So you'll learn," Richard said. He looked around and nodded. "She did a good job with the place, didn't she, Gina?"

"Yes. Thank you, honey."

"Maybe, maybe this will work out after all," Richard said, smiling like a Cheshire cat. It was a smile that sent chills down my spine. Suddenly, I was feeling like a cornered mouse.

My little incident at the pool made me the star at Sandy's party. The moment the three of us came through the door, there was a cheer. I was embarrassed by the attention, but thought everyone was very friendly. The party was already in full swing by the time we arrived since Mommy had taken forever to put on her makeup and decide on how she wanted to wear her hair.

"Besides," she'd told me, "in Hollywood, being on time is a sign of weakness. Always be fashionably late."

Mel had helped Sandy with the food, bringing her things that were ready-made at the supermarket. They started with recorded music, but Bobby Dee and his band began to play as more guests arrived. The apartment wasn't much bigger than ours and it seemed to me everyone who lived in the complex was there, and it wasn't long before everyone was dancing. Even people standing and talking were moving to the rhythm of the music as they spoke. If ever fun was infectious, it was infectious here, I thought, unable to keep myself from swinging and moving to the music and laughter around me.

Almost all the conversations I heard were about auditions, parts, agents and producers. What amazed me the most was how easily everyone accepted Mommy as about their age. In her micro mini and her black tank top with her hair pulled back into a ponytail, she did look more like my sister than my mother. I understood why the lie was so easily accepted.

My thoughts were interrupted when Mel asked me to dance with him. As we spun around the room I noticed Richard had moved off to talk to two pretty women while Mommy danced with someone who called himself Stingo. He had hair as long as mine and wore two silver earrings. Mommy's laughter was soon heard over the music. Every once in a while, she glanced my way and beamed a smile. She looked happy, like someone who had been rejuvenated. Was it possible to really turn back time, to be young again?

Suddenly, Bobby's band stopped playing and he announced to the crowd that there was a new talent in their midst, a fresh, innocent voice. I had no idea who he was talking about until he produced the fiddle and called out my name. Mommy looked as surprised as I was.

"No," I said shaking. "I told you I wasn't that good."

"We'll be the judge of that," Bobby declared. "Come on, we're all bitter friends here," he added with a smile.

"Go ahead," Mel urged.

"I can't. I—"

"Just do it or he'll keep bugging you. That's Bobby."

Reluctantly, I stepped forward and everyone cheered. Mommy and Richard stood beside each other watching with interest and surprise. Although Richard looked pleased, a strange look came over Mommy's face. If I didn't know better I'd have thought she was jealous.

"This is a song an old friend taught me," I began as I took the fiddle. The crowd grew still, but I tried not to think of them and instead thought of Papa George and his pleasure whenever I played for him. "It's an old mountain folks song about a woman whose lover dies in a feud. She mourns him so much that her heart turns into a bird and flies away, up to join his soul."

Someone laughed and someone else said, "Shut up, you idiot."

I lifted the bow and began, singing softly at first and then lifting my voice and closing my eyes. When I ended, there was dead silence.

"That was great," Mel said just loud enough for everyone to hear. There were murmurs of agreement and then there was loud applause and cheers.

"Looks like you got a real good new client, Richard," Bobby shouted across the room. Richard smiled and nodded.

"Do I know talent when I see it or don't I?"

"Is that a question?" Someone shouted and there was more laughter. Bobby and his band started again and the wild, happy mood returned.

"That was very sweet," Mommy said coming up to me. "You didn't waste much time getting to know everyone and letting them know you played the fiddle."

"I didn't. It just—"

"But I really don't think that kind of music is successful in Hollywood these days, Melody, so don't get your hopes up."

"Oh, I don't expect the fiddle to make me famous. I didn't even want to play it now. I didn't come here for that."

She laughed.

"Oh, maybe you did," she said with a wink. Without another word, she grabbed the arm of a tall, dark young man and went off to dance again.

As I walked through the room everyone congratulated me on my performance and Sandy gave me a big hug.

"You're great," she declared. "You're going to make it."

"Make it? Make what?"

"Success, silly," she said before rushing off to dance. Mel stepped up beside me.

"You're a hit. No one has moved into this complex and won everyone's attention so quickly," he declared.

"I'm not looking to do that."

"What are you looking for then? A job in the supermarket? I can help you get that," he teased. "Somehow, I think you want more, just like the rest of us."

"No," I insisted.

I looked around at the gathering of young hopefuls, everyone believing something wonderful would happen if only they tried hard enough. They came from all over, the East, the Midwest, northern California, each of them waiting to get their big break. It wasn't wrong to have ambition, but there was a line, a difference between ambition and false dreams, dreams that would only bring pain and disappointment. I had no idea where the line was or who was crossing it, but I wasn't going to be one to do so, I vowed. Yet I could see how easily someone could be tempted to believe in fairy tales. I couldn't deny the compliments and encouragement had me daydreaming about being a famous musician.

Cary's words came thundering through my memory. *It's more glamorous than living in an old house and harvesting cranberries. I don't blame you.*

"I'm tired," I told Mel as my thoughts came back down to earth. "I've had a big day." I flashed a smile at him and grabbed Mommy's arm as soon as she danced near me. "I'm going back to our place. I'm tired, Sis."

"Whatever," she said, barely hearing me. She was too involved in her dancing.

"Hey, it's so early," Mel said as I headed for the door.

"Jet lag, I guess," I replied shortly.

"You're going to miss a good time. Things haven't even begun yet," he coaxed, still holding onto my hand.

I pulled it away gently.

"There'll be other good times," I said. "Thanks."

His disappointment was written across his face.

"Yeah, you're welcome. Anytime," he said turning away.

I slipped out of the party quickly and went across the hall to our apartment. Once I closed the door behind me, I let out my long-held breath. My face was flushed. The breeze coming through the window was too warm to bring any relief so I went out onto the patio and sat there, looking over the tops of the buildings at the brilliantly shining constellations.

I wondered if Cary thousands of miles away was looking at the same stars. I missed seeing the way they sparkled over the ocean, making wishes on shooting stars as I walked along the beach. Was the ocean calm tonight? Were the waves gently lapping at the shore? As much as I wanted to hear Cary's voice, I knew it was too late to call him. Everyone was probably asleep anyway, I thought.

I heard a car alarm go off on the street in front of the complex. It sounded like a wounded animal, an injured stray dog, its high-pitched scream lasting a good two minutes before it stopped. Then, it was relatively quiet again. My eyelids drooped. I got up and got ready for bed. The moment my head hit the pillow, I was asleep.

But a few hours later, I was woken by the sound of Mommy and Richard's laughter. They came bursting into the apartment, both sounding drunk and not caring how much noise they made. Mommy shouted.

"Where's my talented little sister?" She laughed and came to my doorway. "The hit of the party. How'dya like that, Richard?"

"I love it," he called to her and she laughed again. I pretended to be dead asleep, but I opened my eyes and saw her wavering in the doorway. "Everyone thinks that was very cool, Melody . . . being a hit and then walking out of the party. Very cool. Looks like I taught you more than I thought," she said, "but just don't forget who's the teacher."

"Come on to bed, Gina."

"I'm coming."

She stood in the doorway glaring in at me. I didn't move.

"Sleep tight, Sis," she said. Then she laughed, wiped her forehead and stumbled away. I heard something fall on the floor with a crash and I heard her curse.

148

"Get to bed before you destroy the place and ruin all the good work your sister done," Richard teased.

Mommy cursed again and then she went into their bedroom and slammed the door. The whole apartment shook.

I heard their muffled voices through the walls, Mommy raising hers and then Richard yelling something. After that, I heard Mommy's sobs and wails. Finally, it grew quiet.

She can't be happy here, I thought. She just can't. Tomorrow, tomorrow I'll start talking to her about going back. I'll remind her about my inheritance and how we'll have money and how she could do whatever she wants if she would only stop trying to be someone she isn't.

It was like I was in the land of ghosts, everyone trying to be another person and their true selves floating around them, waiting to return to their lost bodies. Ironically, that's what Mommy had to do . . . return to her body, to her name, to the identity she had buried in a grave back in Provincetown.

Would she ever want to be Haille Logan again?

I hoped so, because Haille Logan was my mother.

9
&

Take One

I woke to the same sound of shouting and muffled cries I had heard before falling asleep. By the time I rose, got dressed and went out to put on a pot of coffee, however, it was quiet again. Richard emerged first, looking furious. He poured himself some coffee and began mumbling aloud.

"It's like pulling teeth sometimes. Why do I have to put up with this?" he muttered. "She acts like she's doing me a favor. LET'S GET IT STRAIGHT WHO'S DOING WHO A FAVOR HERE," he shouted toward the bedroom.

"What's wrong?" I asked and he spun on me.

"What's wrong? Everything's wrong. She drank too much, as usual, thanks to you, and then she went into one of her crying jags and kept me up all night. Finally she passed out and now she's miserable and hung over."

"Because of me?" I asked, confused, but he ignored my question.

"She moans and fights me. She knows she has to get up and look good. MY REPUTATION IS AT STAKE

HERE!" he added, again shouting in Mommy's direction. She finally emerged wearing sunglasses and walking with small, careful steps like someone who was walking on eggshells. She went directly to the coffee pot.

"You can't wear those sunglasses all day, Gina. I told you to stop drinking ten times last night if I told you once, didn't I? Didn't I?" he asked furiously.

"I'll be fine," she said.

"Sure. You'll be fine. You'll look and act half dead and they'll fire you and once again, they'll blame me. Another market will be lost to me and my other clients!" Richard exclaimed.

"Your other clients?" She tried to smile, but that seemed to make her head ache, because she immediately grabbed her forehead.

"Does anyone want anything to eat?" I asked. Mommy didn't reply, but Richard turned away from Mommy and looked at me.

"No. And get dressed," he snapped. "You have to go with us. I'm not coming all the way back here to pick you up. Your appointment is in West L.A."

"Dressed? I am dressed."

"Put on something . . . sexier. Don't you have a miniskirt or something?"

"No, I—"

"Go look in Gina's closet," he ordered. Mommy smiled.

"Yes, go do that, Melody. Only, don't wear my other bathing suit."

She laughed.

"Oh, you're so funny," Richard said. "I have all the responsibility here. I'm the one putting his neck out. It's about time I was appreciated. I mean it," he said sternly.

She raised her sunglasses off her nose. Her eyes were bloodshot and very tired looking.

"I appreciate you, Richard. You have no right to say I don't."

"Well, if you're not in tiptop shape when I deliver you, you put me in a bad light," he said. He turned to me.

151

"Didn't I tell you to pick something out? We're behind schedule because it took so long for me to get her out of bed."

I gazed at Mommy. She lowered her glasses again and sipped her coffee. She hadn't even said good morning to me. I went into their bedroom. It looked like war had been fought in their bed: the blanket twisted, the sheet pulled up, one of the pillows on the floor. Mommy's clothes from last night were piled over her shoes beside the bed. I found a miniskirt and matching blouse in her closet and put them on.

"That's more like it," Richard said. "You women have got to understand how to put your best foot forward when I bring you someplace," he lectured.

"It's not our feet they're interested in," Mommy quipped and then laughed.

"Very funny. Let's get moving," he ordered.

He didn't give me time to clean anything up. I barely had time to turn off the coffee pot before he marched us out of the apartment, mumbling angrily behind us that we put pressure on him by taking so long to get ready.

"He's a slave driver," Mommy said loud enough for him to hear. "But he's right. I'm lucky I have him looking after me."

"If he was looking after you, why did he let you drink so much?" I asked her.

She glanced at me and then stiffened.

"He didn't let me. You heard what he said in the kitchen. He tried to get me to stop."

"Why did you do it?" I pursued.

"Because I'm not the hit of the party like you, Melody. I'm not perfect, but there's a lot worse than me around here," she added in a louder voice, mostly for Richard's benefit.

"I'm not perfect, Mom . . . Sis, and I didn't go there to be the hit of the party. Honest."

"It doesn't matter. Who cares what these losers think around here anyway? Most of them will be gone in six months. You'll see," she said.

I got into the rear of the car and Mommy got into the front. None of us spoke as Richard made his way through the city streets, cursing at drivers, mumbling about why he should be living in a nicer neighborhood by now.

"And I would be, too, if I'd only got the sort of cooperation I need."

"I'm sorry, Richard," Mommy said when we pulled into the mall parking lot. "I know I was a bad girl."

"Just try to do a good job in there. Important people come to this plaza and someone could easily spot you. Remember what I told you . . . exposure, exposure, exposure . . . that's the name of the game."

"Right. I'm sorry," she said and leaned over to kiss him. He didn't soften much, keeping his back straight, his eyes forward.

"I'll be back to check on you later," he said. It came out as a threat. Mommy turned to me before getting out.

"Good luck, honey," she said, "and listen to whatever Richard tells you."

"I don't know what I'm doing or—"

"Will you get going, Gina," Richard ordered. "You're already a few minutes late."

"Yes. Right away," she said and left the car. Before I could get into the front seat, Richard started away.

"Where exactly are we going?" I asked.

"Live Wire Studios," he said. "A friend of mine is doing us a favor, giving you a chance."

"But I don't understand. How do I start acting without a single lesson?"

"The director teaches you everything you have to know right on the spot. It pays real well. We could make a half a year's rent on this one assignment if you do it right," he said.

"A half a year's rent?" So much money, I thought, and dependent on me.

"That's right and that's only the beginning. I've been telling your mother how good it could get, but she goes off on a bender like this and nearly ruins things from time to time," he said. "It hasn't been easy for me, no matter what you think."

"Maybe she's not really happy here then," I offered. He was silent. "Why did you say it was my fault, what happened last night?"

"You upstaged her," he said, "and Gina hates being upstaged, especially by someone who's supposed to be her younger sister."

"Upstaged? But . . . I didn't mean to do anything like that."

"Sure," he said with a smile. "None of you women mean anything."

"It happens to be the truth," I snapped.

I glared at the scenery. The buildings and the neighborhood began to look more seedy and run-down. Where were we going?

Finally, he made a turn into a driveway. I saw a building with something called an Adult Reading Store in front of it. The driveway wrapped around behind it to another building that looked like an attached garage, but above the doorway was a sign that read LIVE WIRE STUDIOS.

"Here we are," Richard said.

"This is a studio?"

"Most of the studios look like this," he explained. "People who don't know Hollywood have this fantasy, this glamorous view of it. It's just another warehouse, just another factory churning out fantasy instead of shoes or chairs. That's all. Now remember," he warned, "you're twenty-one years old. Oh, I told them you were in a small film back in West Virginia."

"What?"

"It's nothing. Everyone makes up his or her resumé here. The film was called *Cherry Blossom*. You played Cherry."

"What?"

"Stop saying 'what,'" he ordered, turning around. "Now don't tell them any more than they need to know about you. And do what the director wants quickly,

154

without questions, understand? You'll be here most of the day. I'll pick you up at five."

"You're not coming in with me?"

"I have other clients, other meetings," he said testily. "I can't be baby-sitting you. You want to be a movie star, this is how you start."

"I don't want to be a movie star," I said gazing at the worn-looking doorway to the dull brown stucco building. I noticed there were no windows.

"So? You'll grin and bear it, fame and fortune. I should be so unlucky." He opened my door. "Come on, get going. I'll be right here at five," he said and stepped back.

I got out slowly, too slowly for him. He reached in and pulled me by the arm.

"Will you get going," he said. "Everyone has to do his part to keep this operation going. You want to be with us, earn your keep or go home?" he threatened. "Now what's it going to be?"

"I'm just going to make a fool of myself," I said.

"So what? Besides," he said with a sly smile on his lips, "something tells me you won't make a fool of yourself. In fact, you might just be a bigger star than your mother will ever be. And then you'll only have me to thank."

He got into the car again and nodded at the studio door.

"The director's name is Parker, Lewis Parker."

He turned the car around and drove out of the yard, leaving me standing in front of the studio. I took a deep breath, swallowed back my confusion and fear, and went to the door. It opened to a dim, shallow hallway. There was a very tiny office on the right with paper piled on the small desk and stacks of what looked like scripts scattered on the floor. A poster of a woman clad in a see-through nightgown, hovering over a man wearing handcuffs was on the wall above the desk. The poster read SLEEP WALKER. SHE WAS HIS BEST NIGHTMARE.

I continued down the hallway to another door above

which was an unlit red light bulb with the words DO NOT ENTER WHEN LIT beneath it. I knocked on the door and waited and then knocked again. Maybe there was no one here, I thought. It looked deserted.

Suddenly, the door was opened and a curly-haired, young black man in dungarees and a loose fitting T-shirt greeted me.

"Can I help you?" he asked.

"I'm Melody Simon," I said, my voice cracking.

"Oh, yeah. Good. Parker, the other girl is here," he called over his shoulder. "I'm Harris. Follow me," he said, turning back to me.

"Get her in here," someone shouted from behind him and Harris stepped back, smiling.

"Come on," he said.

I entered slowly. There were wires everywhere and lights on poles. I saw the cameras, three of them all pointing toward what looked like a bedroom, where a cameraman was adjusting some lights. A very buxom platinum blond–haired girl who didn't look much older than I was sat on the edge of the bed, her arms behind her as she leaned back, her breasts bare. She had a tattoo of what looked like a snake coming up and out of her cleavage. She wore nothing but a pair of flimsy panties, and she chewed bubble gum, blowing a bubble and snapping it before wiping it back in with her tongue. I must have gasped aloud.

A plump bald-headed man spun around in a chair.

"Over here," he called. "I'm Lewis Parker. You the girl Marlin sent? What's your name again?" he asked.

I was still too stunned to speak. I shook my head instead.

"Hey," he said. "We haven't got time to waste. I have to do four scenes and two setups today."

When he rose from his chair, I could see he was very fat and I wondered how he'd fit in the chair. He waddled rather than walked toward me and stopped, drinking me in from head to foot, a pleased smile spreading like melted butter over his jowls and thick, fleshy lips.

156

Because he was so heavy, his eyes looked small, sunken in his large head.

"Marlin was right," he said. "A looker. Great. Delores," he cried and a woman who looked like she was in her fifties, but who also had bleached blond hair and wore lots of makeup, came out from behind a rack of costumes. "Get her dressed and on the set, will ya? Make sure she looks . . . innocent. I like that. Good."

"Yes, Lewis."

She marched toward me.

"Hello," she said. "Step over there. We don't have a dressing room."

"Dressing room? Why would we need a dressing room?" Lewis Parker said and Harris and the cameraman laughed. "We're all friends here."

"I don't understand," I said, shaking my head and stepping back. The half-naked young woman sat up and suddenly took interest in me. "What is this? What kind of a movie are you making?" I asked.

"What's she talking about?" the woman asked, looking at Lewis Parker.

"What is this? What kind of a movie are we making? This is Live Wire Studios," Lewis Parker said. "You're Melody . . . somebody, right? You were in a blue film before, something called . . . what's it called, Harris?"

"*Cherry Blossom*. She was the lead," Harris said.

"Right. So. You know what to do. We're on a tight schedule."

Lewis Parker started back toward his chair. The cameraman looked my way and stopped fiddling with the equipment. I shook my head again and took another step back.

"No, I don't do things like this," I said. "I never did."

"What?" Mr. Parker spun around as quickly as his heavy legs allowed. "What do you mean, you don't do things like this?"

"I don't know what Richard told you but . . . but I can't do this," I cried.

"Hey!"

I turned and ran out the door, down the short corridor and burst out to the parking lot. For a moment I stood there, confused, undecided as to which direction to take. Then I hurried down the driveway to the busy city street, my heart thumping. When I reached the sidewalk, I started in one direction and then another, unsure of my surroundings. I took a step off the sidewalk as cars whizzed by, and one driver blared his horn, sending me flying back, my stomach almost in my throat. Tears streaked down my cheeks. I took a deep breath and closed my eyes. Richard must not have known what kind of assignment he'd gotten me. He just couldn't have expected me to actually take the job. . . .

"Get hold of yourself," I ordered my frantic body. When I opened my eyes again, I saw a phone booth by the gas station across the street. I thought I might call Dorothy and ask her to have Spike pick me up. This time I waited until the light changed and then I hurried across to the booth and dug into my purse to find some change. It wasn't until I took off the receiver and started to put in the coins that I realized I couldn't call Holly's sister. Her husband would be furious with her, especially if she got involved in something like this. It wasn't fair for me to do this to her after all she had done for me, I thought.

But I didn't know where I was and I had no way to get back to the apartment. I thought a moment and then dialed information and asked for Mel Jensen's phone number. There were three Mel Jensens, but I knew I had the right one when I mentioned The Egyptian Gardens. I got the number and dialed. Someone picked up after only one ring.

"Hello."

"I'm looking for Mel Jensen," I said.

"Oh," the voice said, dripping with disappointment. "Just a minute. Someone for you," I heard him say and Mel got on.

"Hello."

"I'm sorry to call you, but I didn't know who else to call. My sister is working at a mall and—"

"Melody?"

"Yes," I said.

"Where are you? I hear a lot of traffic."

"I'm on a street corner. I'm lost and . . . I don't know how to get back and I thought—"

"What's the address? Where are you?"

"The address?" I looked at the street sign and then read it to him.

"Okay. I know where that is. Wait right there," he said. "It'll be a good twenty minutes."

"Thank you."

After I hung up, I looked for a place to sit and wait, but there weren't any benches around so I went into the coffee shop on the opposite corner and sat at the counter. I ordered a cup of coffee, but barely sipped it, watching the clock. When fifteen minutes had passed, I went out again and stood on the corner. While I was waiting I saw a man I thought might have been Harris come out of the studio and disappear into an alley. Almost ten minutes later, just when I was starting to get nervous, I heard a car horn and saw Mel. I was never so happy to see anyone. He pulled over and I got in quickly.

"What the hell are you doing down here?" he asked.

I started to cry, sucked in my breath, and told him.

"Marlin wanted you to be in an X-rated film? Some break," he said. "They can make good money. I'm not saying he lied about that. Does your sister know?"

"No. So you think Richard knew it was that kind of job?" I asked.

"Are you kidding? Those jobs are right up Marlin's alley. Well you did the right thing walking out like that. These things can come back to haunt you when you do get decent work and become a star."

"I'm not going to become a star, any kind of star. That's not why I came here," I protested. Wouldn't anyone believe me?

"Why did you come here?"

"Just to visit," I said. After a moment I added, "But

159

now that I'm here, I hope I can talk my sister into going back home with me."

Mel laughed.

"I don't know your sister that well, but she looks like she's been bitten, just like the rest of us. Don't get your hopes up."

Now that I was in his car and we were driving away from Live Wire Studios, I swallowed back my panic and felt my heart stop pounding.

"Thank you so much for coming to get me," I said.

"You sounded terrified. I borrowed my roommate's car. I don't have a car myself."

"Oh. It was nice of him to lend it to you."

"Yeah. So why did you leave the party so quickly last night?"

"I was feeling exhausted. You didn't see how dirty my sister's apartment was and how much work I did."

He laughed.

"I bet. She's no Suzy Homemaker, huh?"

"No. She never was."

"What, did your parents spoiled her?"

"My father did," I said. It wasn't such a lie, I thought. "He and I ended up doing most of the work, even the cooking."

"What about your mother?"

"She died when we were very young," I said.

"Oh, sorry."

"I can't believe what Richard wanted me to do," I muttered, still half in shock.

"It doesn't surprise me. To a manager or an agent, it's easy money."

"I have to find some other way to earn money while I'm here," I moaned.

"I can always get you a job at the supermarket," he said, half kidding.

"Could you?"

"You'd like that?"

"I'd do anything, anything but what Richard was trying to get me to do," I replied.

"Okay, I'll see about it. I'd take you somewhere for something to eat, but I have to get to work. I have the afternoon shift today."

"That's all right. You've done a lot for me already."

"How about paying me back by going to dinner with me later?"

"How's that paying you back?" I asked, laughing.

"I like your company," he said and smiled. "Well? I'll be out at six-thirty. We can go around seven. You like Italian? I know a great little place only two blocks south of us."

"Okay," I said. "But I should be taking you out. I wish I could afford to."

"Don't worry about. It's my treat."

I thanked him again when we arrived at The Egyptian Gardens. After he dropped me off I hurried up to the apartment and quickly changed out of Mommy's miniskirt and blouse, putting my own clothes back on. I was calm enough to make myself some lunch and settle down. I did some more cleaning to keep my mind off what had happened and spent the remainder of the afternoon reading Mommy's movie magazines on the patio. A little after five I heard her and Richard come in. I got off the lounge and entered the apartment to meet them in the living room.

Richard stood there with his hands on his hips, glaring at me furiously. Mommy looked almost as angry, her hands clenched in fists at her side.

"What did you do, Melody?" Mommy asked softly. "What did you do to Richard?"

"What did she do to me? I'll tell you what she did," Richard said, stepping toward me before I could offer any response. "She put a nail in my coffin here. She hurt my reputation and completely destroyed a lucrative market for me. I had three other girls set to get jobs with Live Wire Studios and they canceled all of them. You lost those girls a lot of money and they needed it badly," he said. "I'm not even counting my lost commissions."

"Melody, how could you do this?"

161

"Mommy, you don't understand," I cried.

"There," he screamed, his forefinger jabbed at me. "She keeps forgetting. She'll call you Mommy in front of these people here and you might as well kiss your career good-bye."

"Melody, I've pleaded with you not to call me Mommy."

"I know. I'm sorry," I said. "I'm just upset. I won't forget anymore." I took a deep breath. "I did what he told me to do. I went into the studio and there was a half-naked woman sitting on a bed and they wanted me to . . . to be in this movie."

"So?" Mommy said. "Richard told you how much money you were going to make. I bet it was twice if not three times what Kenneth paid you to model naked for him," she added.

I felt my heart stop and then start racing. The blood seemed to drain from my face. I tried, but I couldn't speak for a moment. The lump in my throat was as hard as a rock, unmovable.

"What? You get undressed only for certain men when you feel like it?" Richard quipped. "When I get you a job where you can help us, you decide to be Miss Prim and Proper? You run out of the studio, make me look like the fool of the year?"

"Sis, that was different. What Kenneth was doing was art. You know that," I finally said, unable to believe she didn't see the difference.

"A lot of people think of this as art too, Melody. You have to be understanding and you can't be a snob," she said.

"A snob? But Sis, they wanted me to get undressed and be in bed with this other woman and—"

"What of it? I've done it," she said.

"You have?" I asked, not wanting to believe her.

"Of course. How do you think we got the security and first and last month's rent for this place? You know how much money that is? And I got it with just two days' work," she said proudly.

I just shook my head in disbelief.

"You can't stay here without earning your keep," Richard insisted. "We're not running a shelter for the homeless."

"I'll earn something. Mel Jensen thinks I can get a job at the supermarket," I spat back at him.

"The supermarket? That's what you want to do?"

"Yes. I'd rather sweep floors and stack groceries forever than do what that fat man wanted me to do back in that so-called movie studio."

"Well, you raised a pretty smart girl," Richard said to Mommy. "Supermarket Wonder. Great. In the meantime you can keep this apartment spotless and see to our laundry. If you won't be a movie star, then be a servant. Maybe that's all you're capable of being."

I looked at Mommy for support, but she just nodded.

"Richard's right, honey. With the three of us now, we won't be able to afford a housekeeper or dry cleaners if you don't work where Richard wants you to work."

"I don't mind doing the cleaning and looking after the laundry," I said. Surely Mommy didn't fully understand what Richard was doing to her and what he would have done to me if I had let him. We're the ones exposing ourselves, embarrassing ourselves, lowering our self-respect and he was the one collecting the money for it. I had to make her understand and if it took my having to be someone's little slave for a while in order to do so, I thought, so be it.

"Good," Richard said, marching out of the living room to the bedroom.

"Sis, you don't know how terrible this place was. You couldn't have done something like that."

"Don't be stupid, Melody. You can't be a child anymore. You're here, make the most of it, take advantage. You have a built-in manager and agent. Do you know how hard it is for new talent to get representation?"

"Talent? What kind of talent does it take to strip off your clothes and do X-rated things in front of a leering cameraman?"

"You'd be surprised," Mommy said. "The camera doesn't lie. If you're not sincere when you perform, the camera will expose you."

"Oh, you're exposed all right, and then some. Sis, listen," I said, but Richard came marching back into the living room. His arms full of shirts and pants and a few pairs of shoes on top.

"See that these things are washed and ironed. We can't afford the laundry. And I want these shoes polished so I can see my face in them. I've got to look twice as good now that you have screwed things up," he claimed as he dumped everything at my feet.

I looked from the pile to Mommy, but she just turned and walked into the bedroom.

"Of course," Richard said softly after she was gone, "if you want to turn around and go back to Cape Cod . . ."

I glared at him with hot tears in my eyes and then I started to scoop up his clothes.

"Not yet," I said. "I haven't finished what I came to do."

He saw the firmness in my face and his smile evaporated.

"Just watch yourself," he said. "You're playing out of your league and you're playing on my turf."

"I'm not playing," I replied and began to take everything into my room.

An hour later while I was ironing Richard's shirts, Mommy poked her head into my room to tell me they were going out to dinner.

"We can't afford to take you, honey," she said. "I'm sure you'll find something for yourself here."

"Someone's taking me to dinner," I said softly, not looking up at her.

"Oh? Who?"

"Mel Jensen," I said. When I looked up at her I saw a look of surprise on her face.

"Really? Well, you be careful," she said. "Watch what

164

you say, what you tell him. Men can get you to trust them too much too fast," she warned.

"I suppose you'd know," I said. Her back straightened and a sharp look came into her eyes.

"Don't be disrespectful, Melody."

"I'm not. I'm just . . . Sis, when can you and I sit down and have a real conversation? When can we be like we used to be, just for a little while?"

"I don't know," she said, a little sadly. "I don't know if we ever can. That's why . . . that's why it might have been better if you never came looking for me, Melody. I'm sorry," she said. "I just don't know."

We stared at each other a moment and then she returned to the living room and left with Richard. My heart felt as if it had sunk like a chunk of coal into my stomach. I sat on the bed and buried my face in my hands, choking on dry sobs. Billy Maxwell was so right when he said people changed because of where they were and what they were doing. He warned me to expect Mommy might be a very different person. But was she different? Perhaps she was the same woman she had always been, but the woman I had refused to permit myself to see. I took a deep breath and sat straight, wondering what I should do. Should I just leave her, try to forget I had a mother, or should I remain and do battle with her fantasies and her phony knight in shining armor? How would I ever get her to listen to anything I had to say?

I was in such a confused and troubled state of mind I forgot all about Mel until he came knocking on the apartment door.

"Ready?" he asked when I opened the door.

"Oh Mel. I forgot. I'm sorry." I looked down at myself wearing an apron over dungarees. "I'll just be a minute," I said. "Come on in."

I rushed into the bedroom to pick out something to wear and then I hurried into the bathroom to brush my hair and put on some lipstick. Mel sat on the sofa laughing as I paraded back and forth.

"It's all right. Take your time," he called.

I took a deep breath, closed my eyes and tried to calm my nerves before appearing before him again.

"Voilà," he said, standing. "Remarkable metamorphosis. You look great."

"I don't feel great," I moaned. He opened the door and stepped back so I could pass.

"So, tell me, how did Marlin take your not going through with the assignment?" he asked as we descended in the elevator.

"He was furious. He said I hurt his reputation."

"I bet. Not to mention his pocketbook. I was offered those kinds of films, too."

"You were?"

"Sure. A lot of would be's think that's the way to get into the business, and unfortunately they get taken advantage of. This is a tough place, a city with sharp teeth that devours the pure of heart," he remarked.

"Then why do you stay?" I asked.

"It's where it's at," he replied with a shrug. "And, I'm not so pure at heart." He put his arm though mine and led me out of the complex.

The restaurant was small and cozy, just as he had described and the food was delicious. Mel talked about himself, telling me all about his home and his family. Every time he asked me questions, I had to check myself to be sure I wasn't saying anything that would give away all of Mommy and Richard's lies. I tried to say as little as I could. Finally, he sat back and narrowed his eyes.

"Getting you to talk about yourself is like pulling teeth. Why is that?"

"I don't know," I said shifting my eyes down quickly. He continued to stare.

"Are you really just visiting or did you run away from home?" he pursued. I raised my eyes and smiled.

"Run away from home? What makes you think that?"

"I've met a number of runaways and they act a lot like you, evading, giving only the bare minimum when asked a question."

166

"Well, I'm sorry to disappoint you. I'm just visiting," I said and he laughed.

"Fine."

"I am!"

Why was it every man I met could be so infuriating, thinking they knew me better than I knew myself?

"They've got great spumoni," he said and ordered some for us.

"I hate to see you spend your money on me," I told him, calming down slowly. "I know how hard it is for you."

"That's okay. Actually, I asked you out both to be with you and to have you celebrate with me. I got a part in a theatrical production that will open in two months. I had auditioned for them so long ago, I forgot all about it and wrote it off, but out of the blue, my agent received a call and called me just before I left to pick you up tonight."

"Congratulations. That's wonderful, Mel."

"I expect you to be in the front row opening night," he said. "Now," he continued, turning more serious, "what this means, I realized, was I have to give up my job at the supermarket. I spoke to the manager this afternoon and told him I had someone responsible to take my place. He thought it was fine. So, congratulations to you. You'll get your job in about three more days, if you really want it."

"Good," I said. "Now Richard won't be able to complain about me. Thank you."

"Of course, I think you should aim higher. You have talent and you look great," he said. "But you've got to want it, be hungry for it."

"But I *don't* want it," I said and he stared at me with that curious smile on his face.

"Maybe that's what intrigues me the most about you," he said.

"What?"

"Your ability to resist the temptation, your lack of ego. You're just the type who succeeds," he added.

I looked at him, at that impish grin on his face. It

amazed me how other people saw things in me I never saw in myself.

After we walked home, Mel asked me if I wanted to come up to his apartment.

"We could listen to some music. My roommates are out for the night."

"I don't know," I said. "I promised my sister I wouldn't stay out late."

"It's not late," he insisted. "I'd like to dance for you, too."

"Dance?"

"Sure. I'll show you what I did at the audition for this show. Okay?"

It sounded interesting so I agreed and we went up to his apartment.

"You'll have to excuse the mess," he warned me at the door. "Remember, three guys live here."

It didn't look anywhere near as cluttered and dusty as Mommy's apartment had been before I had started to clean it. I told Mel and he laughed.

"Want something to drink? More wine, perhaps?"

"I suppose wine's all right," I said and he poured me a glass. After he did, he went in to his bedroom to put on his dancing clothes. I heard the music first and then suddenly, he leaped into the room, wearing the tightest top and pants I had ever seen, so tight they left nothing about him to the imagination. He spun on his toes and lifted his legs so high, I lost my breath, especially when he did it right in front of me.

The music became faster, the beat harder. He mixed ballet steps with slides and turns that were dazzling. Finally, he stopped and stood before me, breathing hard, his face flushed with excitement. I felt flushed myself from the wine and his performance.

"Well?"

"You're wonderful," I said. "I can't imagine you not succeeding."

He laughed and stepped closer. The music continued, softer, slower. He reached out to take my hand.

I started to shake my head, but he pulled harder until I stood and we were dancing cheek to cheek, his hard, fast breathing on my neck. When I caught sight of us reflected in the window, it looked like I was dancing with a naked man. My own breathing quickened as his slowed and then he smiled at me and kissed me softly. I felt him push against my thighs.

"You're so sweet," he said. "I really like you." He kissed me again, but I didn't let his lips linger on mine. I stepped back, bowing my head and, when I looked down at him and saw how excited he was, I felt my heart flutter and my breath grow short.

"I've got to get home," I said.

"Melody . . ."

He stepped toward me.

"I really do, Mel. Please."

"Okay," he said. "I don't force myself on anyone, but I hope you like me."

"I do, but not that way. I'm sorry," I said. "I'm sure there are a lot of girls who would love to be up here with you," I added.

He smirked.

"Very few like you. Okay, I'll give it time," he said. "Consider this my first audition. Maybe, you'll give me a call back, okay?"

I laughed and tried to shift my eyes from his very revealed body. I found my purse and headed toward the door.

"If you wait for me to change again, I'll walk you home."

"No, that's all right. Thanks for dinner."

"I'll call you about the supermarket job," he said.

"Thanks."

I hurried out the door and when I looked back, I saw him standing there, smiling after me. I waved and descended the stairs, feeling as if I were fleeing.

But was I fleeing from him or from myself? For the first time, I thought I was really more afraid of my own weakness and desire. This was a place filled with many

169

different kinds of temptations. The Egyptian Gardens might as well be the Garden of Eden, I concluded and half expected a snake to come up and whisper in my ear as I crossed the courtyard to our building and made my way up to our apartment.

The phone was ringing as I entered. I hurried to it and after my first hello, I heard nothing.

"Hello?" I said again. I heard a deep breath and then . . .

"Where were you?" Cary asked.

"I was out to dinner, Cary. What's wrong?"

"Dad's dead," he said. "He had another heart attack in the CCU and he died." He laughed strangely. "I couldn't think of anyone else to call but you and you were out to dinner."

"Cary, I'm so sorry."

"Yeah, well, it won't be the wrong person in his grave, will it?"

"Cary—"

"I'm tired. It's very late here. I ran down to the docks when I came home and I just stood there looking out at the ocean and thinking about all the trips he and I made together. Funny," he said huskily, "now you and I are both without fathers."

"I'll be back as soon as I can, Cary. I promise."

"Okay," he said in a small voice.

And then he hung up and left me crying for both of us.

10

&

Revelations

After I hung up the phone, I sat on the sofa in the dark living room and cried softly, thinking about Cary, little May and Aunt Sara and what they all must be going through. I wondered how Grandma Olivia and Grandpa Samuel were taking the news of their son's death. Nothing could be worse than losing a child, I thought, no matter how old the child was at the time, or how aloof and cold at heart you were.

Uncle Jacob had resented my coming and living with him and his family, but most of the time I thought that was because my presence made the loss of his Laura that much harder to bear. Right from the beginning, Aunt Sara treated me as if I had been sent to replace Laura, but I knew as far as Uncle Jacob was concerned, no one could ever replace his daughter. He had been hard, sometimes downright cruel to me, but I also recalled moments when he gazed at me with softer, kinder eyes, especially after he had heard me sing and play the fiddle, and often, when he didn't think I was aware of his gaze.

He was a hardworking man who wanted to provide for

his family as best he could. His religious zeal often made him cold and unpleasant to me, but on more than one occasion, Cary hinted that his father had become more devout and sterner after Laura died, somehow blaming himself for her death. When he was in the hospital the first time, he had asked to see me at his bedside, and because he thought he was dying, he confessed to me that he and my mother had done something sinful together when they were young. At the time he made it seem that he blamed himself for my mother's wild ways later on when she was older. Afterward, he denied saying these things. Ashamed of what he had told me, he found my presence even harder to bear. I'm sure he was happy when I decided to leave to find my mother, as happy as Grandma Olivia was to see me go.

I closed my eyes and took a deep breath. Minutes later, I fell asleep and didn't waken until I heard the door open, followed by loud laughter.

"Why is it so dark in here?" I heard Richard say before snapping on a lamp. The shock of light made me blink and rub my eyes as I sat up quickly.

"Well, well, look who's waiting up for us," he said.

"Why are you still up and dressed? How was your dinner, Melody?" Mommy asked. "You didn't drink too much wine or anything, did you? Did you bring Mel up here?" she scanned the room as if to look for evidence of his having been in the apartment. She wobbled a bit but took a step closer and focused on me with some effort, finally noticing how red my eyes were and the streaks tears had made down my cheeks. "What's going on now?" she demanded.

"Uncle Jacob," I said and swallowed, taking too long for her.

"What about him? I can't imagine anything about him that would interest me," she told Richard, who laughed. "Well, what did he do?"

"He died," I said. "His heart gave out at the hospital." She stared, the news having a sobering effect on her. I saw her face move through a myriad of emotions, from shock to sadness, to anger and then indifference. She smirked first at Richard before turning back to me.

"His heart, as you call it, gave out a long time ago. I don't wish anything bad on anyone, but I can't pretend to be terribly upset about it," she said, the mirth all gone from her eyes and lips.

"But you grew up with him and Daddy. You can't be so uncaring," I replied.

"You don't know anything about what my life was like growing up with Jacob as a so-called brother, Melody," Mommy flared back at me, "and I can't forget how he treated me afterward when all the trouble began for me and Chester."

The anger in her eyes stunned me so much I was speechless.

"I don't like anyone bringing bad news to Gina," Richard said, suddenly pretending to be very protective. "Especially news about her past, and especially the night before she has an audition."

"Yes," Mommy said, smiling with a proud gleam in her eyes. "I have something exciting to try out for tomorrow, a part in a television sitcom. I've got to get right to bed. That's why we came home so early," she added.

I looked at the clock. Early? It was a little past one o'clock. What was late supposed to mean?

"You should go to sleep yourself," Richard said. "You have a lot of work ahead of you, too." He laughed and headed for the bedroom.

"I do feel sorry for Sara and the children," Mommy said, her voice somewhat softer. "Sara was always nice to me." She sighed and pulled her head back a little as if to swallow back some errant tears. Then she looked at me with a small smile on her lips. "If you think you should go back for the funeral, it's all right. I . . . can't have anything more to do with them. Whatever tears I would spill would be one more tear than his mother will anyway. Believe me," she said.

"You hate her very much, don't you?" I asked.

The corners of her mouth whitened with her rage.

"Yes. I won't deny it. I do, and she has no love for me either, Melody." Her eyes glared hotly and then her expression returned to one of self-pity. She groaned. "I hate going to sleep feeling upset," she said as she turned toward the bedroom. "I wish you hadn't told me about it."

I watched her go in and close the door and then I rose and went to bed myself. Maybe I should return to the Cape, I thought. Maybe the mother I had hoped to find did die and was buried back in Provincetown. What had happened to Mommy to make her so selfish? Or had I been too blind to realize that that was her true self?

Mommy was right about going to sleep with sadness like a rock on your chest, however. I tossed and turned, sobbed and sighed through most of the night, unable to get Cary's sad eyes out of my mind.

I finally fell asleep just before morning and slept so soundly, I didn't hear Richard and Mommy get up. I did wake when I heard him shout my way.

"Well, this is a fine thing. We don't have coffee made. What sort of a maid did you hire, Gina? Turns out she's lazier than you."

I got up quickly, throwing on one of Mommy's light cotton robes, and stepped out into the living room. Richard was already dressed and Mommy, dressed rather nicely, I thought, came out of her bedroom, too.

"I'll make some coffee," I said. "It won't take long." I started toward the kitchen.

"We can't wait," Richard said, his eyes fixed hard on me. I realized I wasn't wearing much and he seemed to be able to look right through my flimsy night clothes. "We'll get something at the studio. Clean up our bedroom while we're gone. I left some more of my things for you to iron," he added and started toward the front door.

Mommy looked at me, her face somber.

"Wish me luck," she finally said.

"Good luck."

"Thank you," she said, flashing a smile. Then she followed Richard out of the apartment. I listened to their footsteps disappearing down the hallway toward the elevator and then I went into the kitchen and put on some coffee for myself. I sat there, more or less in a daze, sipping coffee and nibbling on some toast and jam. Before long, my mind wandered back to memories of myself and Cary on the beach. I thought about Kenneth and his dog, Ulysses, and remembered first meeting Holly and the fun we had talking like sisters.

How could Mommy want this kind of a life? I thought. Despite herself and the mean things she had said to me last night after I had told her about Uncle Jacob, her eyes did soften occasionally. Deep in her heart, I told myself, she wants to go home. I've just got to get her to realize it.

Still wearing my nighty and Mommy's robe, I cleaned up their bedroom and began ironing Richard's pants and shirts. I worked without thought, moving like some kind of a robot, dazed by the tragic events. A little after noon, I finally put the work aside and went into the bathroom to take a shower. I stood there letting the warm water beat on the top of my head, my eyes closed, the stream flowing over my face. Finally, I shut off the shower and stepped out from behind the curtain.

For a moment, I was confused. I knew I had brought in a towel and my clothes, but there was just a hand towel on the rack and none of my clothes were in sight. Not trusting my own memory, I figured I had intended to do these things, but because of being in such deep thought, hadn't. Dripping wet, I ran out of the bathroom to my bedroom. As soon as I entered, the door closed behind me, only I hadn't been the one to close it.

Richard stood there, leering at me, and he was stark naked himself!

Silent screams stuck in my throat.

"What are you doing? Where's Mommy?" I finally shouted and rushed to the bed to pull the top sheet off and throw it around me. Brittle as thin glass, his laughter crackled across the room. He stepped forward, not making any attempt to hide his manliness from my sight.

"I told you to stop calling her Mommy," he said, still smiling.

"Where is she? What are you doing?"

"She's at her audition. She'll be there most of the day. There are a lot of actresses trying out for the part, so I thought, why hang around? I decided, while waiting, I might as well make myself useful. I've been wondering why you would run out on such an easy job for a lot of money yesterday, and I figured out it's simply because you're too innocent. You need to grow up, and fast, or you'll never amount to anything. Consider this an extra service. Call it my generosity," he continued, moving closer and closer until he was only inches away.

I turned and looked down rather than into his face. His breath stank from alcohol and began to upset my stomach. I felt it do flip-flops.

"Come on," he said, "I know you're looking forward to this."

"Get away from me!" I cried.

He put his right hand on my shoulder and his left on my waist, forcing me to turn to him.

"Relax and enjoy," he said bringing his lips close to mine. I swung my head and tried to pivot out of his grasp, but he tightened his hold and pressed his lips against my mouth. I gagged and kicked out, catching him between his legs with my knee. His face exploded like a balloon bursting and he crumbled, clutching his lower stomach.

I didn't wait. I pushed past him and started to run from the room, holding onto the sheet. Somehow, he managed to reach out, clutching the end of the sheet and holding on. It tugged me back until I let go and fled the room, totally naked. I returned to the bathroom and slammed the door shut, locking it after me. Then I stood there for a moment gasping, sobbing, listening. My heart was pounding so, I had to lean against the door to brace myself. The memory of the stench coming from his mouth made me dry-heave.

"You little bitch," I heard him shout. He came up to the door and tried the handle. "Open up. How dare you knee me like that? I'm letting you stay here, aren't I?"

He pounded the door with his fist and I screamed. Then he stopped and all was quiet for a long moment. I tried to hold my breath so I could listen, but my lungs were stretched to bursting and the thump, thump, thump of my heart was echoing in my eardrums.

"You'll be sorry," he finally said in a loud whisper between the door and the doorjamb. "I could have taught you something, made you grow up overnight. You would have been sophisticated enough for anything, but Richard Marlin doesn't allow himself to get turned down more than once. It's your loss," he added. "You hear?"

He punched the door again. I cried out and backed away, afraid he would break the door down. After a while I heard only silence and then, when I drew closer to the door and put my ear against it, I heard him walk away. I didn't come out. I sat on the tub and waited, my arms folded tightly under my breasts, my sobbing slowing and my breathing returning to normal. I heard the front door open and close. All was quiet. Was it a trick to get me to open the bathroom door?

I waited and waited, listening, hoping he would grow impatient if he were still out there, but I heard nothing. Suddenly the phone rang. It rang and rang and I imagined that if he were still there, he would be too concerned the call was for him and he would have answered it. More confident that he was gone, I unlocked the door as carefully and as quietly as I could. I hesitated and then in fractions of an inch at a time, opened it until I could peer out.

I didn't see him anywhere. I looked across the dining area to my bedroom. The door was wide open. Was he waiting inside the room again? I tried to swallow, to stop my heart from its racing again, but I couldn't. His attack had made my legs weak and my whole body trembled as I opened the bathroom door wider and wider until I stepped out, and then waited, terrified he would suddenly appear and lunge at me. He didn't.

My courage growing, I practically tiptoed across the floor to the doorway of my bedroom. There I paused to listen. I heard nothing. I took a deep breath and walked into my bedroom, gazing around quickly, clenching my hands into little fists with which to pummel him should he pop out at me. He wasn't anywhere in sight. I closed the door quickly and then, my heart fell. What if he were hiding in my closet?

I waited, listening again for a moment. Hearing nothing, I went to the closet door and pulled it open. The wind from my jerking open the door shook the clothes on the hangers, but thankfully, there was no Richard Marlin hiding and waiting to pounce out at me.

I got dressed as quickly as I could and then I fled the apartment, feeling trapped and in danger of a horrible repeat performance if I remained there. I didn't look at anyone when I hurried down the walkway. Like someone in a race, I shot through the main gate and charged down the sidewalk. I walked as quickly as I could, not looking back, crossing streets, fighting traffic, hurrying along as if I knew where I wanted to go. It felt good to move quickly. It stopped my body from trembling and the farther away from The Egyptian Gardens I walked, the safer I felt. Finally, tired, my body in a heavy sweat, I paused at a corner, undecided in which direction I should continue. I gazed at the street sign that read Melrose Avenue, and then I looked around at other people.

Up until this moment, I hadn't noticed anyone or anything. I had walked with blind eyes, focused only on fleeing Richard's awful grasp. Now I found myself in a very curious area of the city. Young people with blue, green and pink hair, dressed in leather jackets and jeans walked past and in front of me. Many had tattoos covering their arms and chests. Two girls even had rings in their noses! I felt like I had stepped onto another planet.

I backed up, turned and started walking in the opposite direction. Everyone in this city really did seem to be in his or her own movie, I thought, feeling as if I had wandered onto a movie set. I didn't know whether I should laugh or cry. After I walked a few minutes, the neighborhood changed again and I slowed my pace, quickly realizing that I was lost. I stopped again and gazed around, this time seeing a small store window on my left that read MADAM MARLENE, READINGS. I saw the crystals and the tarot cards and thought about Holly and Billy. It brought a smile back to my lips. Impulsively, perhaps searching for good memories at a very troubled time, I stepped into the small shop.

There was a dark cherry wood table and two chairs at the center of the little room. The crystals were in a small glass case on the right and at the rear of the shop the was a doorway like the one at Holly's shop, curtained with strings of beads. When I entered, a small buzzer had gone off. A short, dark-haired elderly lady came through the doorway of beads. She wore a shimmery white shawl over a dark blue dress and had silver earrings with crystals that glittered like diamonds in between the long strands of hair falling over her shoulders. Her dark eyes were large but she made them appear even larger with smudgy kohl eyeliner.

"Hello," she said. "I'm Madam Marlene. Would you like a reading?"

I shook my head.

"Um . . . I . . . I just . . ."

"You look upset," she said. "Please," she added pointing to the seat by the table. "Rest a moment and tell me what troubles you."

"I'm lost," I said. "I'm new here and I don't remember how to get back to my apartment complex."

"Which complex, my dear?" she asked, her smile soft and friendly. She looked to be about fifty and not much more than five feet tall.

"The Egyptian Gardens," I said.

"You're not very lost. Just go down two streets, make a left and you'll run into it after about ten minutes. I think there's more troubling you though, isn't there?"

I nodded and gazed around her shop.

"I have a friend in New York City who has a crystal shop and who does astrological readings for people. Her name's Holly."

"That's interesting," Madam Marlene said, and a knowing twinkle came into her eyes. "You really came in here because you wanted to know something, yes?" she pursued, her head tilted slightly and her eyes even more luminous as the dim overhead light caught them in its warm glow.

I thought a moment and then nodded.

"I wanted to know if someone I loved would ever return to me," I said.

She nodded as if she had always known I would show up on her doorstep.

"Sit down. Please," she said.

"I just left my apartment quickly," I said. "I don't have any money on me."

"Oh, that's all right," she said. "You can send me something later." She sat at her table, motioning for me to sit down across from her. She reached out immediately and took my right hand into her hands and held it, closing her eyes. Then she nodded to herself and looked down at my open palm.

"You have already been on quite a rugged road," she said, "with many twists and turns. Your life has more valleys than most, but I see some very high places too. I see you have lost loved ones, yes?"

"Yes."

"Yet you have strong energy. What is your name?"

"Melody."

"I see music in you, yes. This person, this loved one who is lost has been lost for a while."

"Yes," I said.

She looked at my hand again and then she reached out

180

to touch the locket Billy Maxwell had given me. She turned it in her fingers a moment.

"Lapis lazuli. Someone you like very much and someone who likes you very much gave it to you."

"That's right," I said.

"You are like a comet, something beautiful and full of energy floating through space, searching . . . searching for a home, your real home."

"I am," I said, excited that she seemed to know so much about me.

"Someone you're searching for is coming," she said, closing her eyes again. Seconds later she opened them, and this time there was no smile on her lips. "Where you are looking for love, there is no love. You will have to change direction. But don't worry. Your energy is too strong to be defeated. Do not be afraid to turn toward the darkness, for often what we think is sunlight is merely the reflection coming from our own glow. Do not look for love in the usual places," she concluded and sat back as if reading my palm, feeling my energy and predicting my life had exhausted her.

"Thank you," I said standing, uncertain if I'd be able to follow her advice.

"Oh, it's my pleasure. It's always a pleasure to read a heart as big as yours. Here," she said opening a drawer in the desk to pluck out a business card. "This has my address. I usually get twenty dollars, but you can send me fifteen."

"Thank you," I said, taking the card from her wrinkled hand.

"Your locket will bring you much luck on your journey. Keep it with you always," she called as I went to the door.

"I will. Bye."

I stepped out, feeling revived, calmer. It would take time to understand all she had said, but I would think about it. Since I had been with Holly and Billy I paid more attention to these things and I wasn't so quick to laugh at anyone or anything that seemed new and different to me. I was leaving myself open to new ideas and experiences. But there were still some things I could definitely do without.

Dreading facing Richard again, I headed back to the apartment, following the directions Madam Marlene had given me. A little over half an hour later, I turned into the main gate and with great trepidation, made my way to our building and then to the elevator. When I stepped out and walked to the apartment door, I paused. I had to tell Mommy what he had tried to do, I decided. Maybe now, maybe finally, she would see him for what he truly was.

I opened the door and entered, surprised to find them both sitting in the living room. Mommy looked like she had been crying all afternoon. Her eyes were bloodshot; her face streaked with makeup that had run. Richard sat there looking calm, his legs crossed, a drink in one hand and a cigarette in the other. He gazed up at me with a confident smirk that put a chill in my heart.

"So you decided to come back," Richard said.

"What did you do, Melody? Run away afterward?"

"Yes," I said defiantly gazing back at Richard as I spoke. "I did. I was too scared to stay here. I was afraid he would come back and try again."

"Ha!" Richard said and crushed his cigarette in the ashtray. "Listen to that."

"Melody, how could you?" Mommy asked.

"How could I what?" I looked from her to him and then back to her, realizing he had told her some lie. "It was him, Mommy. And I don't care if I called you Mommy," I added quickly for his benefit. "He attacked me in the bedroom. He came into the bathroom while I was taking a shower and he—"

"Liar. She's just like I said," Richard interrupted. "Conniving, sly. Tell the truth for once, will you."

"The truth?"

"I was sitting here, right where I am now, relaxing, planning on making some important calls, when all of a sudden, she comes out of the bathroom after taking a shower and parades naked right in front of me," he told Mommy. "She walked right up to me as if she were fully dressed and smiled. Go on, tell her," he challenged me.

"No," I said, shaking my head. "That's not what happened, Mommy. He took all my clothes out of the bathroom and when I came out and went to the bedroom, he was waiting for me and he was naked!"

"Did you ever hear such a story, Gina? Look, Melody, you've been trying to compete with Gina ever since you arrived. You made a spectacle of yourself down at the pool and then you tried to steal the limelight at the party. I get you a job, but it's not good enough for you. Oh no. You'd rather we support you, too."

"Mommy, listen . . . he was there, in the bedroom, waiting for me. He told me he was going to educate me. He—"

"Educate you? This story gets more and more stupid every time she opens her mouth. Listen, sweetheart, you're going to have to do better than that if you want to make it in Hollywood."

"I don't want to make it in Hollywood! And neither do you, Mommy. You have to come home. You have to leave this place," I cried.

"See?" Richard Marlin said jabbing his finger at me. "That's been her plan all along . . . to mess things up for you so you would leave. She's jealous of her own mother. I've seen it a hundred times, and especially out here. Now she says she doesn't care if she calls you Mommy. She'll do it deliberately in front of people and make you the laughingstock of the whole industry. She's already made us a mountain of trouble because of what she did at Live Wire."

"Mommy . . ." I said, turning to her. She shook her head at me.

"I'm very disappointed in you, Melody. I really don't know what to say."

"Say you believe me. Say you know he's lying and that he's a phony who can't do anything for you out here, that all he's doing is getting you silly little jobs or selling you to sex merchants," I begged.

Richard sat back looking very satisfied. Mommy bit down on her lower lip and looked away.

"Mommy—"

"Keep it up; keep it up. Keep calling her Mommy," Richard chanted like a cheerleader at a football game.

"Maybe Richard's right, Melody. Maybe it's better for all of us if you go back. This isn't working out."

"You believe him, Mommy?" I choked, barely able to whisper the words.

She didn't reply. I saw the grin on Richard's face and I glared back at him hatefully. He looked so confident and Mommy looked so weak and under his control. My frustration and pride overflowed.

"Maybe you deserve him then," I said and fled to my bedroom to pack my bags.

Twenty minutes later, after the phone had rung, I heard Richard yelling, blaming Mommy for not getting yet another part. Then I heard him leave the apartment. Minutes later, Mommy came to my bedroom. She wore her sunglasses again and she looked very pale and unhappy.

"I guess you heard," she said. "I didn't get a call back from today's audition. Richard says it's because I'm too distracted these days."

"Maybe it's because you're not meant to be an actress, Mommy," I said and closed my bag.

"No, I can do it. I know I can. It's just taking a little longer than we expected, that's all."

"I didn't do what he said I did, Mommy. It was the other way around. I swear it."

"It doesn't matter, Melody. Richard's right. You don't belong here. I don't know what I was thinking when I agreed to let you stay."

"You were thinking like my mother," I told her. "You were thinking about doing the right thing."

She smiled.

"You were always the dreamer."

184

"Me?" I started to laugh. "Look around you, Mommy. Look where you are. This place grows dreams like . . . like we grew weeds back in Sewell."

"I meant you were a dreamer because you saw more in me than there is. I'm sorry, honey. I'm not the mother you want me to be."

I nodded. Maybe, finally, she was speaking the truth. I sat on the bed and stared into my lap.

"What are you going to do? Do you have any money?" Mommy asked.

"Yes, I have most of my money. I didn't tell Richard the truth. He would have taken it all. I have my return ticket, too. I'll go to the airport and get myself on the first flight I can," I added.

"And go back to Provincetown?"

"Yes."

"Good. I'll be happier knowing you're safe, and you'll be safe there," she said.

"You mean then your conscience won't bother you, don't you, Mommy?" I shot back at her.

She started to get angry and then her shoulders sank and she nodded.

"Yes," she admitted. "I guess it's time for the lies between us to stop."

I stared at her, trying to blink away my disbelief.

"Chester was always a better father to you than I was a mother," she said and then she laughed. "And the funny thing was he wasn't your real father. Though that didn't bother him at all."

"Mommy," I said sucking in my breath, "when you left me in Provincetown and I discovered the truth about you and my stepdaddy, I started to think that Kenneth was my real father. I just knew you had to be lying about Grandpa Samuel. Please, please, tell me the truth."

She looked at me for a long moment and I thought she was just going to shake her head and walk away, but she came farther into the room instead.

"I hated them," she said, "as you know. When Judge Childs told me he was my real father and therefore

Kenneth and I were half-brother and half-sister, I felt as if he had reached his hand into my chest and ripped out my heart. I felt so betrayed, Melody. You can't imagine. Here were all these high and mighty people always making me feel like someone inferior because my mother had me out of wedlock and Olivia had to take me in like some wayward orphan. They never stopped reminding me how grateful I should be, how lucky I was.

"And all the while . . . the lot of them were no better, and in fact, much worse. They were deceitful, greedy people, liars and charlatans, so I decided I would get back at them. When they realized I was pregnant, Olivia was ready to pounce, to point her finger at me and shout, 'See, see, this proves how low-down and no good she is, how she's nothing more than a tramp.'

"But I fooled her, I fooled the whole lot of them when I turned the tide and accused Samuel of being the father of my unborn baby. Olivia," Mommy smiled at the memory, "almost died of embarrassment. She was sick and in her room for days. I told her I would expose the whole sinful lot of them. I would shout it in the streets.

"Chester . . . Chester always loved me. He was quick to take my side, especially when I went to him and cried on his shoulder. He promised to look after me, no matter what. I played them all against each other. Chester and Jacob fought. Olivia pulled her tail between her legs and crawled into a hole. I felt sorry for Samuel, but he was someone to pity anyway, letting her bulldoze him all the time, pretending he didn't know she was really in love with Nelson Childs, who had an affair with her sister, my mother. They were hideously cruel to her. They put her away in that institution and made me ashamed of my own mother.

"Nothing I did to them equaled what they had done to me, Melody. I regret nothing except . . . except what I had to do to you. I'm sorry, but I know you're going to be all right."

"Not until I know the whole truth, Mommy. I want to know who my real father is. You've got to tell me."

She nodded and turned her back to me as she turned her gaze to the window.

"I was wild. I wanted so much to hurt them all, to keep hurting them, embarrassing them. I drank, hung out with older friends, flirted with everyone. And then one night, after I had been out drinking, I decided to walk home. It was a warm night, full of stars. I remember getting dizzy every time I looked up at the sky.

"Suddenly, he was there in his car beside me. I turned and he rolled down his window and asked me why I was walking alone so late at night. He sounded so protective, so concerned. He said he would drive me home so I got into his car, only he didn't drive me home. He drove me to a beach road and he talked about his unhappy life, how he was married to a beautiful woman and making a lot of money, but how he was still dissatisfied. His life was missing something, some excitement, and he said whenever he saw me, no matter where I was or what I was doing, he was filled with that once-in-a-lifetime excitement."

Mommy turned to me.

"You have to understand how it was for me, Melody. No man had ever spoken to me like that. I was swept off my feet and this man . . . he was successful and well-to-do and he was telling me I was more important to him. How could I resist?

"I made love with him and it was special. We met often, secretly and then I became pregnant with you and it all went out of control. It wouldn't have done me any good to reveal his identity. He wouldn't leave his family for me, and when Olivia attacked me, I made my decision to get my revenge. I never told anyone the truth, not Chester, not Kenneth, no one."

I held my breath until I could hold it no more.

"Who was he, Mommy? Is he still in Provincetown?"

"Yes, honey, he is," she said. "His name is Teddy Jackson. They call him T.J.," she said.

I know my heart stopped beating for a moment. I know my blood drained from my face. I felt the room spin. Mommy grasped my hand. I closed my eyes and battled for a breath.

"Are you all right?"

I didn't reply. I waited until my heart started beating again, swallowed and nodded.

"His son," I said, "Adam Jackson, tried to be my boyfriend when I first arrived."

"Oh no. Did you want to be his girlfriend?"

"No, I hated him. He's arrogant."

"Good," she said. "For a moment I thought I did to you what Judge Childs had done to Kenneth and me."

"I think I had a feeling about Mr. Jackson, Mommy."

"He's spoken to you?"

"From time to time, and whenever he has, he's been very nice."

"He'll never come forward and admit it, honey. He has a family, a position in the community—"

"I don't care. I just wanted to know who he was," I said. "Thank you for that, Mommy."

I stood up. Madam Marlene had been right when she read my palm. I was looking for love in the wrong place.

"Maybe you shouldn't go yet, Melody. Maybe you should stay another day."

"No. I don't belong here, Mommy, and Cary needs me. He needs me far more than you do," I said.

My mother stared at me as if I was a stranger and then she nodded.

The lies would end between us and like two people who had finally lifted the masks from their faces, we finally saw each other for who we truly were.

And we both knew we would have to live with that forever. For better or worse.

11

Home Again, Home Again

I decided to leave without any other good-byes. I felt confident that Mommy would make up a story to tell to Mel Jensen and the others. Lying came as naturally as breathing to her now. Maybe it always had. I took a cab to the airport and arranged to fly what they called the red-eye from Los Angeles to Boston. For a while I flirted with the idea of returning to New York to visit with Holly and Billy, but the summer was drawing to a rapid end. I still had my last year of high school to complete, and I was tired of throwing myself into other people's lives.

It was time to grow up anyway I told myself, to put my childhood beliefs back into my box of fantasies and close the lid forever on my past, on my hope of having a real mother and a real father. I was truly an orphan. The only man who had wanted to be my father was dead, and the man who really was my father had kept it a secret and was happy that he had escaped responsibility.

In a real sense, my mother had died twice: first, when she and Richard Marlin had invented their deception

189

and sent a dead stranger back in my mother's coffin; and now, when I had found her and had failed to revive any real mother–daughter feelings in her. She was truly a stranger to me. I shed no tears walking away from her and I could hear her sigh of relief as she closed the door behind me. Her ordeal was over. She could go back to living the life, and the lie, she always wanted.

On the flight back to Boston, there wasn't anyone in the seat beside me on the plane, and for that I was grateful. I was in no mood to make conversation, and after my near tragic experience with that man in New York who had tricked me into taking his drug-laden briefcase, I was wary of strangers anyway. I simply closed my eyes and welcomed the drowsiness. I slept for most of the trip.

When I arrived in Boston, I made my way to the bus stop and bought a ticket to Provincetown. It was late morning by the time the bus headed out on the highway. I didn't leave enough time to get breakfast, but I had little appetite anyway. I felt numb, beaten, drained of any resistance and energy. The monsters in the shadows were too big and too powerful and there were far too many. It was better to retreat and to accept and be what fate seemed determined to have me be.

With that darkness well entrenched in my heart, I thought it was best to take a taxi to Grandma Olivia's and Grandpa Samuel's as soon as I arrived in Provincetown. Grandma Olivia was the true monarch of this family. She seemed to be the only one capable of determining destiny. She was the one who had decided how my grandmother Belinda would live and where she would live. She was the one who ruled Uncle Jacob and Aunt Sara's family. She even dominated Judge Childs. Certainly, she was the one who ruled her own house, and despite what my mother believed, Grandma Olivia was the one who had banished Mommy to a poorer, harder life in the coal mining town of West Virginia.

It was time to recognize that power and bend to it. I had no more defiance in me. I felt like a flag at half mast.

When the taxi pulled up the driveway of Grandma Olivia's house, my sense of defeat thickened. I moved lethargically, exhausted, my head down, up the walkway to the front of the house and pressed the buzzer, resembling someone who had come to offer her surrender.

Above me, the late afternoon sky had turned a deep, dark blue. The air smelled fresh, crisp, but I was much too nervous to enjoy the beautiful day. Grandma Olivia's maid, Loretta, opened the door and stood looking at me, her face wearing a mask of indifference. I imagined working for Grandma Olivia had toughened her. She moved through her day like some cog in a machine, reliable, consistent, but uncaring. She revealed no reaction to my appearance. I could have been a traveling salesman, for all she cared.

"Will you please tell my grandmother that I am here, Loretta," I said in a tired voice and stepped into the house. She lifted her eyebrows and gazed at my suitcases.

"She doesn't have to tell me," I heard and turned to see Grandma Olivia at the top of the stairway, gazing down at us with her regal posture. She wore clothes of mourning, a black blouse and a black ankle-length skirt, which somehow made her look taller than she was. Her white hair was brushed and pinned back as usual, and there wasn't the trace of any makeup on her pallid face.

"That will be all, Loretta," she continued as she took a step down. "You can return to your dinner preparations."

"Yes, ma'am," Loretta said with a slight curtsey. She hurried away.

"So you've returned, as I knew you would. Giving you that traveling money was a waste, but it's your waste, not mine," she added. "I will keep the document you signed and deduct it from your trust fund."

She continued her descent, sliding her hand along the mahogany balustrade as she walked, her head high, her shoulders and back perfectly straight.

"I don't have to ask you what happened. I can see it on your face: disappointment, disillusionment. Or should I

191

say a final awakening? At last you see her for what she is?" she asked, not hiding her pleasure.

"It's because of the man she's with—" I began.

"Oh, don't blame it on someone else," she interrupted with a wave of her hand. "It was always that way with Haille. Someone was eternally making excuses for her, finding someone or somewhere else to place the blame and the responsibility for her selfish, cruel acts." She paused and smirked. "I assume she faked her death in order to end even a semblance of responsibility for you," she said smugly. Her eyes were unflinching. She had the confidence of a predator who knew she had her prey trapped.

"Yes," I murmured, my own eyes down. Even now, even after all I had been through, I still couldn't help being ashamed of Mommy.

"Humph," Grandma Olivia said. I looked up at her, tears burning under my eyelids, but kept trapped there, the last vestige of my pride. She shifted her eyes away from me, but when her gaze returned to my face, I thought I detected a hint of sympathy. "Well," she continued, "I suppose it was something you had to do, something you had to see for yourself. You can provide the details at some later time, if you like. I certainly have no burning desire to hear them.

"But," she continued with that characteristic strength I hated, respected, and envied all at the same time, "that part of your life is over and we must go on. This family must continue to strive to maintain its position of respect in the community. It would be best, obviously, if no one hears of this scandal. As far as I'm concerned, we buried your mother. I'm not going to go and dig up some unfortunate soul. Haille's as much dead to me anyhow, and from the looks of you, you feel the same. Who have you told about all this?"

"Just Cary," I said. "Kenneth Childs will know, too."

She thought a moment.

"Kenneth will keep it to himself. I'll have a word with

192

Cary to ensure he does the same," she said with a curt little nod of her head.

"You don't have to worry. Cary doesn't gossip, especially about our family," I said and she smiled, but a cold, hard smile that turned her stone eyes into glittering glass.

"Our family, is it? That's good. That's what I want to hear." She nodded, her smile softening just a bit. "You did right coming here," she said. "You have good sense. As we discussed before you went on this futile journey, you will live here from now on." She paused, her face hardening again. "You know, I am sure, about my son's passing while you were away?"

"Yes," I said. "I'm sorry."

"So am I, but we bury the dead so the living can continue to strive. Jacob was a good man, but he was a sufferer. He took things too much to heart and his heart was so weighed down, it collapsed. There's a lesson to learn," she said widening her eyes at me. "You have to build a casing around your heart to protect it. You don't give away your affections, your sympathies, your feelings cheaply, because every time you do, it costs you.

"There are many lessons you will learn here," she said, continuing to fix her gaze on me so intently, I dared not look away.

"As I told you before you left, you have, I have noted, demonstrated some qualities of character that, although in the rawest form now, can be cultivated so that you will grow into a stronger person, a capable person. But this will happen only if you listen and obey. I don't intend to relive the painful past I endured with your mother," she warned. "You will behave while you are under this roof and you will do nothing that will bring discredit to this family."

"Maybe this isn't such a good idea," I suggested. "Maybe I should go back to live with Aunt Sara."

"And learn what? Self-pity? Ha. Besides, she has enough to do caring for her handicapped child."

193

"I can help her. I can—"

"Waste your life," she concluded. Her cold eyes softened a bit. "Everyone expects I will look after you, now that your mother is supposedly dead anyway. How do you think it will look if I permit Sara to endure another burden immediately after losing Jacob?"

"So you're worried about your own reputation," I said and she stiffened so quickly it was as if an electric shock had passed through her.

"I was hoping you would see that what I am offering you is an opportunity other girls your age would die to have. Yes, I have selfish motives, but they're not motives for myself. They're for this family. Family name, honor, reputation, these are the really important things, Melody. You will learn that and understand it after a while.

"People without family pride are weak, and their weakness and lack of control affects their entire family. Look at that woman you insist on calling Mother. Does she have any pride in herself? Well, does she?" she demanded.

"No," I admitted hesitantly.

"Do you want to be like her?" she pursued. I raised my eyes and she smiled after one glance at the fire in them. Then she nodded. "There's more of my family blood in you than you care to recognize," she said. "Very well. You'll take the room that once belonged to Haille. I've had it prepared for you, anticipating this day. Even though you have come to live here, you are to look after yourself and your own things. Loretta is my maid and will not have time to wait on you hand and foot. Besides, that's how we went wrong with Haille: we gave her too much, spoiled her. Actually, Samuel was the one who indulged her, and you know the thanks he got for that.

"I expect you to continue to do well in school. I also expect, no *demand,* that you conduct your social and personal affairs only on the highest levels. Never do I want to hear even a hint that you've been doing some of the terrible things young people your age do these days. No drinking, no drugs, no promiscuity and you are not

194

to parade around in any of those silly, risqué clothes young people today think are fashionable.

"I will arrange for your preparatory schooling after high school graduation so that there will be a smooth transition after you complete this last year," she said in a calmer tone. "However, as I said, there are things you will learn from me just by living here and observing, things you can't learn in any school. You can go up and rest now. You look tired. If you want some supper, come down in two hours."

"Where's Grandpa Samuel?" I asked.

"He's asleep on a lounge in the back. That's how he spends most of his time these days . . ." Her voice was so low it was as if she forgot I was in the room. Then suddenly she noticed me staring at her. "Well? Is something wrong?"

"I'm not sure which room was my mother's," I said quickly, gazing up the stairway.

"First door on the left," she said. "It's been cleaned and so has the bathroom. Make sure it all remains that way. You'll find some clothes in the closet and the dresser drawers to wear. I had them bought for you the day after you left, anticipating this day," she added triumphantly.

"I wish I had the same crystal ball," I replied dryly.

"You will," she said with confidence. Then she looked at me as if she was deciding whether or not to say, "Welcome home." She remained silent, nodded, and then turned to go down the hallway to her parlor.

Feeling like someone who had been given the key to a motel room and told to find her way herself, I started up the stairs. When I reached the first door on the left I paused, took a deep breath, and opened it. My new home, I thought as I gazed inside the room.

If there had been any trace of femininity in this room before, Grandma Olivia had erased it. It looked almost as Spartan as a room in a nunnery. The walls were papered dark brown with no pattern and there were plain white curtains on the windows. The bed was a simple one without a headboard and was covered with a beige blanket and pillow case. There was a small desk in the corner, and it was equipped with a few pads, pens, pencils and a sharpener. The only other furniture was a plain dark pine wood dresser with six drawers and a nightstand of matching dark pine next to the bed.

There was no vanity table and no mirror other than the mirror above the sink in the bathroom. Of course, there was no phone in the room and no television set or radio. When I opened the closet, I found a half dozen simple dresses, two ankle-length skirts and some color-coordinated blouses. In the dresser drawers I discovered underthings, socks, and a few wool sweaters, for which I would be grateful when the weather turned colder.

I opened my suitcase and took out the two expensive outfits Holly's sister had bought me and I hung them in the closet. They almost looked comical next to such simple, inexpensive and practical clothing. I put the matching shoes on the closet floor and completed my unpacking, finding a place on the nightstand for the Chinese fan Billy Maxwell had bought me. I promised myself I wouldn't let too much time go by before calling him and Holly and thanking them both again for all they had done.

My unpacking completed, I sat on the bed for a moment and stared through the opening in the curtains at the ocean in the distance. The blue sea looked inviting, peaceful, soothing. At least I had that view whenever I felt trouble, which I imagined would be often in this house.

Gazing around, I wondered what this room had been like when my mother lived here. Grandma Olivia must have gone through it with the fury of a hurricane and torn away anything that suggested my mother had lived here. It was a good-size room. I could make out where some shelves had once been hung on the far wall. On them my mother probably had her dolls and stuffed animals. From the little Cary had told me, I understood that Grandpa Samuel had spoiled her and bought her whatever her little heart desired. I wondered if it had all been consigned to the basement along with those pictures Cary had once showed me, or if it all had been given away, even burned. Grandma Olivia was not incapable of doing something like that.

I lay back on the bed. The trip had been exhausting even though I slept on the plane and on the bus. I realized what I was feeling was a deep emotional fatigue. The kind of weariness that gripped my very bones. Just dozing on a plane or bus wasn't enough to quench it. I was hungry, though. I thought I would just close my eyes and take a short rest, and then, as Grandma Olivia said, go down to dinner.

But when I opened my eyes again, it was so dark I couldn't see the door. The sky had become overcast, shutting out the stars. I blinked, sat up, and listened. The house was quiet, barely creaking. I fumbled for the light switch on the small lamp by the bed and squinted when it came on. Then I looked at the clock. It read two A.M. I had not only slept through dinner; I had slept right into the night!

A feeling of panic like a little trickle of ice water ran down my spine. I had intended to phone Cary right before or after dinner and let him know I was back. He would be upset that he wasn't the first one I had called or seen. Now it would be hours before I would be able to tell him I was back. And I wanted to get over to see Kenneth as soon as possible, too. There was so much to do and here I was sleeping the valuable time away.

After waking to such alarm, of course I couldn't fall back to sleep. That famous jet lag everyone warned me about was taking its toll. My body didn't know what time it was and my stomach, angry at being forgotten, growled and churned. I rose, went to the door and peered out. I could see a faint light in the hallway and over the stairway. The door creaked as I opened it farther. Then I practically tiptoed out and down the stairs, each step on the staircase betraying me with a groan as I descended. I didn't want to disturb anyone, but I needed to eat something, some milk, a piece of bread, anything.

On my way down the hallway toward the kitchen, I saw there was light coming from the parlor. When I reached the doorway, I paused and gazed in to see Grandpa Samuel slouched in an easy chair, his hands on his stomach, his mouth open as he slept. On the table beside him was a decanter of brandy and a partly filled goblet. I continued on to the kitchen where I made myself a turkey sandwich, which I ate quickly, feeling like a thief.

Suddenly, I heard a gasp and looked to the kitchen doorway to see Grandpa Samuel standing there looking as if all the blood had drained from his face.

"My God," he said, stumbling forward and stopping, his eyes wide. "Haille?"

"No, Grandpa. It's Melody," I said. "I'm sorry I woke you but—"

"Melody?" He scrubbed his face hard with his palms and then looked at me again, a dazed look in his eyes. "Melody?"

"Yes, Grandpa. I was hungry. I fell asleep and missed dinner and—"

"Oh. Oh, yes, Olivia told me. She had Loretta look in on you." He shook his head. "For a moment there . . . your mother used to come home late like this and go to the kitchen to gobble something. Lots of times she'd had too much to drink," he added in a whisper, "but I wouldn't tell Olivia. I'd make sure she got some food in her and then I'd send her up to bed.

"Well now," he continued, still sounding a bit confused, "well, I guess it's late. I should go up. Olivia's probably given up on me again." He looked at me askance. It was as if he still didn't trust me, trust reality. "I didn't hear you come in, Haille," he said after a long moment. He shook his head. "I'd better go to sleep. I'll lock the front door again. Olivia locked it when you didn't come home on time and said to let you sleep in the streets, but as usual, I unlocked it when she went upstairs."

"What? Grandpa . . . it's me, Melody," I said softly, puzzled by his behavior. Maybe he was sleepwalking. And talking.

He smiled.

"Let it be another one of our little secrets, okay? Now don't you oversleep tomorrow morning," he warned, waving his right forefinger at me. Then he smiled. "Good night."

He turned, and slowly made his way toward the stairs, looking more like an old man than ever, as he shuffled away. I cleaned my dishes and wiped up the table, careful to erase all traces of my midnight snack. When I got to the stairway, however, Grandpa Samuel was just pulling himself up the final steps and groaning as he made his way to his and Grandma Olivia's bedroom.

I went up to my room quickly and closed the door. Then I got undressed, put on one of the new nightgowns that were in the dresser drawer and crawled into bed. Finally my stomach was settled, but now my mind raced as I tried to figure out Grandpa Samuel's strange behavior. I didn't look that much like my mother, did I? I wondered. And after I had told him who I was and he seemed to remember, why did he forget again and talk to me as if I were Haille, as if he was living twenty years in the past?

"There, you see. It's Melody, our grandaughter. Melody, not Haille," Grandma Olivia insisted when I entered the dinning room to have breakfast the next morning. I was still lounging in bed when I heard the two of them walk by my room earlier that morning, and I scrambled to shower and dress as quickly as I could. Grandpa Samuel gazed up from his bowl of oatmeal and nodded, smiling at me as I took my seat at the table.

He was dressed in a sports jacket and wore a tie, but he had done a poor job shaving his face. There were patches of gray stubble on his chin and along his jaw.

"He was raving last night," Grandma Olivia continued, "talking stupidity again, telling me Haille was back."

"Good morning, Grandpa Samuel," I said, concerned that he'd give away my early morning wandering. His eyes looked glassy, distant, however. I gazed questioningly at Grandma Olivia.

"He's slipping away," she muttered, "into his dotage."

"What's that, Olivia?" he asked. "What about the cottage?"

"I didn't say anything about any cottage, you fool," she snapped. "I want you to see the doctor about that hearing aid today. I told Raymond to take you over there."

"Oh. Fine, fine. I've got time today," he said and she laughed.

"You hear that? He can find the time in his busy schedule today."

I gazed at him. He was so different and it had happened so quickly, I thought. I turned again to Grandma Olivia, who saw the confusion in my face.

"He's been like this ever since Jacob's death," she explained. "It hit him like a sledgehammer and aged him years in minutes."

Grandpa Samuel blew on his spoonful of oatmeal and gazed absently ahead, looking through me.

"Oh, how sad," I said.

"As is much of life," Grandma Olivia instructed. "That's why it's important to learn how to deal with unpleasantness, how to accept what you can't change and move on to what you can. Don't ever waste your time again on lost causes. Time is too precious. You're young now, so you think you'll be young forever, but one day you'll wake up and find yourself unable to count the wrinkles and the gray hairs and you'll have aches and pains where you never had them before."

She turned back to Grandpa Samuel.

"If you keep blowing on that same spoonful, Samuel, it will turn to ice. Eat it already."

"What's that? Oh, yes. I have time today. I have time," he muttered.

"I don't know why I bother," Grandma Olivia said. "He'll soon be in the room next to my sister. You'll see."

"Maybe with time—" I said.

"With time he'll grow worse. There's no sense wasting tears over it. What are your plans for today? Do you have everything you need for the start of school? I believe that's next week if I'm not mistaken."

"Yes, it is. I've got everything I need. I was hoping to go visit Cary and Aunt Sara and May," I said.

"That pathetic woman. All she does, day and night, is cry. Her eyes are so bloodshot, it's a wonder she can still see out of them."

"I'm sure it's been very hard for all of them," I said, remembering how awful I felt after my stepdaddy Chester died.

"Jacob had a good insurance policy. There's adequate money for the way they live, and I made sure they had a little more. They won't starve or go without necessities," she said tersely.

"I'm talking about more than money," I said, amazed that she showed no emotion when she talked about the death of her son.

She laughed as if I had said something hilarious.

"Yes, when you find out what that is, let me know."

"I already know. It's love, concern, friendship . . ."

"No one loves anyone more than he or she loves him or herself. You'll discover that."

"I hope not," I said.

"You already have," she replied. "What could be more intense than a mother's love for her own child? And yet, your mother loves herself more. Don't think romantic love is any different. Men and women crave each other, pledge all sorts of things to each other when they're young and in love, and then, time goes by and they begin to grow apart. Their own interests become most important again. Before you know it," she said gazing at Grandpa Samuel, who was blowing on another spoonful of oatmeal, "thirty-five years have gone by and you hardly know the man who shares your bed. And if he doesn't end up calling you by some other name, you're fortunate.

"Don't place too much faith in romantic love, Melody."

"What *do* you believe in, Grandma Olivia?"

"I told you, family, name, reputation, self-respect." She dabbed her lips with her napkin and rose. "For today and only today, I'll permit Raymond to cart you over to Sara's before he takes Samuel to the ear doctor, but I don't intend to have him do that every time you get it into your head to go there.

"Samuel," she snapped. "Do you intend to play with your food all morning?"

"What? Oh? Is it time to go?"

"It was time to go a long time ago," she said wistfully. The sadness in her voice caught my ear and I stared at her for a moment. She quickly realized I was looking at her and rose from the table. "Finish your breakfast, Melody. I'll have Raymond wait for you in the drive."

As soon as I had finished breakfast, I joined Grandpa Samuel in the car. When Raymond brought me to Aunt Sara's, I expected Cary would have already left to go on the lobster boat, but when I got out of the car and knocked on the door, it was he who opened it and gazed out at me, his eyes first full of surprise and then, full of joy.

"Melody! You're back!"

"Hello, Cary," I said smiling.

He started toward me to embrace me and then saw Grandma Olivia's car pulling away.

"What was Raymond doing here? Where are you suitcases? How long have you been back in Province-town?" he asked, rapidly firing his questions at me.

"I got in yesterday, but I was so tired from the trip that I fell asleep as soon as I put my head on the pillow and slept into the night," I said.

"Slept? Slept where? You went to Grandma Olivia's house first? Why?"

"Where are Aunt Sara and May?" I asked instead of replying.

"Inside. What's going on? Why did you go to Grandma Olivia's first? You're going to stay with her after all, aren't you?" he demanded.

"Yes, Cary. I am."

"Why?"

"You remember we had this discussion before I left, when I had learned Judge Childs was my real grandfather and Kenneth was my uncle."

"Yes, but—"

"None of that's changed, Cary, and with my mother really not dead and buried—"

"But no one knows it and with Dad gone—"

"That's just it. I . . . just think it's best for now. Your mother has enough to do and, well, now, especially with everyone believing my mother's dead and buried, Grandma Olivia thinks this is better for all concerned. But just as I promised before I left, I'll see you every day," I added quickly.

His green eyes seemed to pierce right through me as his lips curved up in a disdainful smile.

"I didn't think you'd go through with it after your trip to California, but I guess now that you've tasted wealth and glamour, you'd rather live in the mansion, right?"

"No, that's not it," I protested, shaking my head.

"There's no question she can do far more for you than we can," he continued, folding his arms across his chest and pulling his shoulders back. "I don't blame you."

"Stop talking to me like that, Cary. You don't understand."

"Oh, I understand. That's my trouble. I understand too much," he said.

This time I permitted the burning tears to course down my face.

"Visiting my mother was a disaster. First, her boyfriend Archie, or Richard Marlin, or whoever he really is, tried to get me into a pornographic movie and Mommy approved," I said. Cary's cold smirk evaporated a bit. "Then he tried to . . . tried to rape me and she believed him when he said it was my fault. She was happy to see me go. She has everyone believing she's not much older than I am. She told them I was her sister and I had to pretend to be her sister.

"I have no parents anymore. No one who truly cares about me!" I cried.

"You have me, Melody, and May and my mother. . . . You know she needs someone to fill Laura's place in her heart."

"That's just it . . . Laura's place. I appreciate that, but I've got to become myself and I'm afraid, Cary. I'm afraid that now, more than ever," I confessed, hiding my eyes as I did so, "your mother will want me to be Laura. I'm sorry," I said. I wiped away more tears. He was silent.

"I know what you mean but . . . I just . . ."

"You think I want to live with Grandma Olivia? She's cruel in ways I don't even understand, but she's strong, Cary, and if ever there was a time I needed someone strong, it's now."

"I'm strong," he proclaimed.

"You are, but you have to be strong for your mother and your sister first, especially right now," I said. "Later, when the time is right, I want you to be strong for me, too."

That brought a warm smile to his face. He thought a moment and then he nodded and stepped closer to embrace me. I loved the feel of his strong arms around my body. I wished I could sink into him and be safe and secure behind the walls of his love forever and ever.

He kissed away a lingering tear and brushed back my hair.

"I thought I had lost you forever," he said. "I thought you would fall in love with Hollywood."

"I hated it, Cary, at least the part I saw. It's not the

place for me or for my mother, but she just hasn't realized it yet. I'm afraid that when she finally understands, it will destroy her."

"Grandma Olivia is right, Melody. You need to forget about Haille. You've come home to us. You need to start thinking about the future." He looked up at me sheepishly. "I never thought I'd ever agree with her about anything."

"I know. I hate to say this, but I think we both have a lot to learn from her."

He laughed and then grew serious.

"You saw how bad Grandpa Samuel is, I suppose."

"Yes. It's as if something snapped in his head when your father died."

Cary nodded and tears glistened in his eyes, too. He swallowed quickly and then smiled again.

"Well, May will be very happy to see you, and so will Ma. Come on in," he added, stepping aside. He kissed my cheek again and we entered the house.

May was at Aunt Sara's feet reading and Aunt Sara was doing some needlework, her hands working mechanically, her mind obviously elsewhere. Aunt Sara lifted her eyes slowly and when she saw me, her face softened into the most loving and wonderful smile, the smile I had wished to find on my own mother's face but didn't.

"Melody!" She put her needlework down and the action caught May's attention. The moment May saw me, her face exploded with happiness and she jumped up to run into my arms. I held her tightly and then she pulled back and began signing with such speed, I couldn't keep up.

"Slow down," Cary signed. "She's so full of questions she will exhaust you much quicker than any cross-country trip."

I laughed and stepped forward to embrace Aunt Sara.

"I'm so sorry, Aunt Sara."

"I know, dear. He fought hard. The doctors said he fought until the end. He did not go 'gentle into that good night.'"

"Not Dad," Cary said proudly. "He was a real Logan."

For a moment I thought about Grandma Olivia's words concerning family dignity and I smiled at Cary's pride.

"Come, sit with me and tell us all about your journey. Where are you suitcases? Has Cary brought them upstairs already?" she asked looking from me to him. Cary didn't say anything.

"I'm going to stay with Grandma Olivia for now, Aunt Sara. With Grandpa Samuel the way he is and all, I think she wants my company," I explained. It wasn't such a terrible white lie, I thought. Actually, I hoped it was true.

"Oh. I see," she said fighting hard to hide her disappointment. She forced a smile. "Well, she can do so much for you. Of course you should stay with her. That's very good. So then, that woman wasn't Haille after all?"

I looked at Cary, whose eyes told me he hadn't said a word to her.

"No, Aunt Sara, the woman I found was not the mother I was hoping to find."

"Oh, how sad." She nodded with a small smile. "But at least you're back here, home with us, with your family again. You must tell us all about California. I've never been there."

I sat beside her on the sofa and told them about my trip. May sat at my feet, watching my hands, and Cary sat in what had always been his father's chair, listening, his eyes fixed on me.

We had lunch and then Cary and I took May for a walk along the beach, just as we used to do.

"While you were away, May and I came out here often. I'd pretend you were with us. It was easy because she can't hear, so I could talk aloud to you. I don't know how many times I told you I loved you."

"I heard you each time," I said. He tightened his hold on my hand.

"Can you stay for dinner?"

"I think I'd better go back for dinner, but I want to see

Kenneth this afternoon and I was hoping you'd drive me out there," I said.

He turned away quickly.

"What's wrong?"

"I was out there yesterday," he said. "Kenneth's . . . different. I think all of it, finishing his big work, your friend's discovery of Haille, your leaving . . . all brought back painful memories, memories he was able to bury in his work."

"What's wrong with him?"

"He was drinking a lot. Actually, I found him sleeping on the beach, Ulysses whining beside him. I helped him into the house. He had obviously been out there all night."

"Oh no, Cary."

"I don't know if you should go there."

"More than ever, Cary. I should go there more than ever," I said.

I said it with such determination and strength, I even surprised myself.

"With all your unhappiness and all your own problems, you think you can go and help someone else?" he challenged.

"Because of all that," I replied, thinking about some of the things Grandma Olivia had said. "It's important to learn how to deal with unpleasantness, how to accept what you can't change and move on to what you can."

"And you think you can change Kenneth's unhappiness?" he asked with skepticism and amazement.

"Yes," I said gazing out over the blue waves that rolled toward us. "Yes, I do."

12

The Downward Spiral

*T*he wind picked up considerably as we drove down the bumpy beach road to Kenneth's house. I could see the ocean spray bouncing off the rocks, and the seagulls looked like they were struggling to stay on course. The sky was still quite blue, but over the horizon long somber clouds with ominously gray faces were snaking toward us.

"Bit of a nor'easter coming," Cary said. "We'll get some heavy rain tonight."

We stopped beside Kenneth's jeep, and noticed that he had left the driver's side door wide open. Getting out of the truck slowly, I stepped up to the jeep and peered in at the empty beer bottles and the empty fast food bags on the floor, some old french fries and packets of ketchup beside them.

"I think he burned out his battery," Cary said, gazing over my shoulder. He nodded at the dashboard. "Looks like he left the headlights on all night after he returned from whatever bar he was at."

I shook my head, my heart thumping in anticipation as we turned toward the house. The door was unlocked as usual, but it, too, was partially open. The house was even a worse mess than it had been before I had begun working for Kenneth. It looked like he hadn't washed a dish in the kitchen since I had left. Food was caked on plates. Glasses, some still with wine, whiskey, beer and flat Coke in them, were scattered everywhere, even on the windowsills.

I knocked on the bedroom doorjamb before gazing in, but Kenneth wasn't there. I didn't know how he could sleep in the bedroom anyway. The blankets were half off the bed, as were the sheets. There was a pillow on the floor, along with clothing and shoes he had discarded. I waded through the mess and then stopped and stooped down to pick up the picture of Mommy and me I had once found under the bed.

"Boy, it smells in here, doesn't it?" Cary said. I saw some rotted food and what looked like a pile of vomit in the corner. "Disgusting. What's that?"

"A picture of myself and Mommy. Did you check the bathroom?"

"Yes. He's probably in the studio," Cary said. He shook his head as he gazed around the room. "I told you things were bad, but I didn't know how bad they were."

"Okay. Let's go find him," I said and we walked through the house, both grateful for the fresh air. I gazed down at the small pool where Kenneth kept Shell the turtle and some fish. Two dead fish floated on top of the water and Shell was nowhere in sight.

The door to the studio was wide open. I stood in the doorway, sweeping my eyes over the bottles, the plates, the paper and cans. A chair was overturned and the small sofa looked as if it were missing some of its stuffing.

Kenneth was sprawled at the foot of *Neptune's Daughter*. He was folded in the fetal position, one hand holding a nearly empty bottle of whiskey. His cheeks were unshaven, his beard very straggly, his hair long and untrimmed. He wore a stained pair of dungarees, no shoes and a faded brown T-shirt ripped down the right side. His eyes were shut tight and his mouth was twisted in a grimace. It looked like he was having a terrible nightmare.

Ulysses, sleeping at his side, rose with great effort, and came to greet us, his tail wagging emphatically.

"Oh, Ulysses, you poor baby," I said as he licked my hands and my face. "When was the last time you were fed?"

"He's probably been eating off plates, leftovers," Cary remarked.

We both looked at Kenneth again. He hadn't stirred.

"Maybe we shouldn't wake him," Cary said. "I told you I did that before, but I didn't tell you he wasn't so nice about it."

"We can't leave him here like this," I declared, took a deep breath and went to him. He smelled awful but I knelt down and carefully pried the bottle of whiskey out of his fingers. Cary rushed over to take it and put it on the table. Then I shook Kenneth's shoulder gently. His mouth closed and opened, but his eyes remained shut. I shook him again, harder.

"Kenneth. Kenneth, wake up. It's Melody. I'm back. Kenneth. Kenneth!" I jerked his arm and his eyes snapped opened with a start as he groaned. He shot up so quickly, I nearly fell backward to avoid being struck by his swinging left arm. Then he fixed his eyes on me and rubbed them into focus.

"What?"

"I'm back, Kenneth. It's Melody."

"You're back?" He scrubbed his face with his palms, dropped his head as if he were going to fall asleep again, and then lifted it slowly, gazing at me harder. "You're not a vision, a dream? You're really here," he said smiling.

"Yes, Kenneth. I'm really here. What's going on? What have you done to yourself?"

He smiled.

"Done to myself? Nothing. What you see here has been done to me, not by me," he replied. "So . . ." He finally noticed Cary standing to the side. "Oh, the beach rescue service has arrived, huh?"

"Hi, Kenneth. I think you drained your battery in the jeep. You must have left the lights on last night."

"Most likely," he said nodding.

"I have some jumper cables in the truck. I'll give it a boost and get it running for you."

Kenneth brought his hand to his temple, to his mouth and then bowed.

"My family thanks you."

Cary laughed and then looked at me and saw I didn't think any of this was funny.

"I'll just go charge the jeep while you two talk," he said and hurried away, Ulysses at his heels.

"Talk? We're going to talk?"

"What's happened to you, Kenneth? You weren't like this when I left."

"I don't know," he said quickly and struggled to get to his feet. I moved to help him, but he pushed me away. "I can do it myself," he said, but he wobbled when he stood and had to put his left hand against the statue. He opened his eyes and smiled. "I knew I created this for a reason."

"It has a lot more reason to be than that, Kenneth. It's spectacular," I said, glancing at *Neptune's Daughter* again. There was no question the face was my mother's face.

"Right. Art for art's sake, to bring out the beauty that is otherwise unseen, unheard, untouched around us. I am a prophet, a singer of songs, a . . ." He groaned. ". . . a man with a terrific hangover."

He staggered over to the sofa, grabbed a pillow and flopped down, nearly turning the sofa over at the same time.

"Why are you drinking like this? You're killing yourself," I said.

"No, it just looks that way. I can go on like this indefinitely. So," he said coming more to his senses, "I did hear from Holly a few times. Apparently, our Miss Cape Cod did pull a fast one, huh? She performed a death and resurrection, just as we all suspected?"

"Yes, she and her so-called agent took advantage of a situation to fake her death. The woman in the car with

Richard Marlin was borrowing my mother's identification and was first mistaken for Mommy and then deliberately made out to be her."

"Olivia's not going to appreciate less than blue blood bones in her sanctified ground."

"Why is everyone so worried about what Grandma Olivia thinks?" I moaned.

"I don't really worry about it. I'm amused by it, actually." He thought a moment. "I shouldn't be at all surprised. Haille liked to pretend she was someone else all the time, especially movie actresses. When she met strangers, she would give them a fictitious name, make up a whole history for herself and do it rather convincingly."

"Then she's in the right place," I said and began cleaning up the studio.

"Don't do that. I don't care about it being clean and organized anymore. You are looking at my last work," he said staring at *Neptune's Daughter.*

"Stop it, Kenneth. You're not going to let this be your last work. You're too young to retire."

"Retire?" He laughed. "Yes, retire is a good word for it. Kenneth Childs, renowned New England sculptor, has declared his retirement. I like the sound of that."

"I hate it because it's full of self-pity," I said. His eyes widened.

"Whoa. Et tu, Melody? Then fall Kenneth Childs."

"I understand, Kenneth, because I've been wallowing in it as well." I put another pillow back on the sofa and sat beside him. Then I told him what had happened in California and why I had left. He listened, his eyes regaining some of their spirit and light as I spoke, especially when I described my mother and how young she looked.

"Then she's still very beautiful?"

"Yes, but there are many beautiful women in Hollywood, most with more talent, and all probably with more reputable and reliable agents. Richard Marlin is just some lowlife that has her beguiled," I said.

He nodded.

"I feel sorry for her. She was just as much a victim as I was. I feel sorry for you, too," he added quickly.

"I don't want you to. I'm not going to think about it anymore and I'm not going to try to make something happen that can never happen."

He looked at me with new interest.

"I see. You're learning to grin and bear it, huh?"

"Yes, and I want you to learn as well." I paused and then added, "You were actually lucky you didn't end up with my mother. Grandma Olivia is right about people making excuses for her. She is what she is not because of what happened between you two, not because she discovered your father is her father, but because it's in her to be who she is. She was always selfish, Kenneth. You know that's true."

He laughed.

"Where did you find all this wisdom and knowledge?"

"It was a long journey," I said dryly, "through a rain forest of tears. Just because she lost you as a lover doesn't mean she had to turn me away, to deny me as her daughter, does it? When do you stop blaming your father for every mistake you make and start blaming yourself?"

His eyes widened.

"You don't understand," he said in a hoarse whisper, his head shaking.

"I understand. Don't you think I wanted to love her, too? Don't you think I wanted to have a mother? When I was growing up and I had so many questions, girl-talk questions, don't you think I longed to have her spend hours and hours with me and not talk about herself and her pimples or her new ounce of fat? Do you think if you had been able to marry her, you would have changed her?"

"I don't know," he admitted. "All I do know is I would have liked the opportunity." He sighed deeply. "Okay, Melody, okay," he said. "I'll stop wallowing in self-pity, but I don't know about my work." He looked at

Neptune's Daughter. "This project just seemed to drain me. Maybe I gave it everything I had."

"I doubt it," I said. We heard the jeep's horn and looked toward the doorway. Cary gave us the thumbs-up sign.

"He's a good kid. Hard news about his father. There's a lot falling on his shoulders now. Did you come back to live with them?"

"No, I'm going to be living with Grandma Olivia. Remember how the arrangements were already made just before I left for California?"

"Yes, I remember, and I remember thinking it was a good idea. You'll learn a lot from her."

"That's what she keeps telling me," I said dryly. He laughed and then he reached out to stroke my hair.

"It's nice to have you back, even though for your sake I was hoping it would have worked out otherwise."

"Thank you, Kenneth. Um, can I make a small suggestion at this time?"

"Why not?"

"Could you take a shower or a bath soon?"

He roared with laughter and pulled his hand away from my hair.

"Okay, I deserve that."

"In the meantime, I'll clean up some of this mess."

He shook his head and sighed.

"You're a bad influence on someone who wants to wallow in self-pity, Melody."

"Good," I said, which brought another smile to his face. I had the feeling there hadn't been too many since I had left.

"You did wonders with him," Cary said as we drove away some two and a half hours later. We left Kenneth eating some warm food and promising to rest and stay off the whiskey for a while.

"I don't know how long it will last though," I said sadly. "He's come to the point where his art isn't enough. He needs someone real to love and to love him."

"I can understand that," Cary said, reaching to squeeze my hand softly.

"Yes, me too."

As we bounced over the beach road, I gazed back at Kenneth's house. Ulysses had come to the gate, but he didn't, as usual, follow the truck most of the way down the beach road barking after us. Cary gazed in his side mirror.

"Ulysses is showing his age, huh?"

"Yes," I said sadly. "And he's the only companion Kenneth has."

During the drive back to Grandma Olivia's we watched the clouds blow in from the north, creeping over most of the sky. By the time we turned into the driveway, it had begun to rain.

"What are you doing about the lobster business?" I asked Cary as we came to a stop in front of the house.

"Roy's been running it. Theresa's been helping him, too. She asks about you often."

"She turned out to be the nicest girl at school, as far as I was concerned. I don't care what the snobs think of the Bravas."

Cary laughed. The Bravas, as the half black and half Portuguese residents of Provincetown were called, weren't easily accepted by the girls Grandma Olivia considered of respectable lineage.

"I've got the cranberry crop to worry about now anyway. Because of the warmer weather this year, they're a little ahead of schedule," Cary said. "Most of the berries are already a bright red. Usually, we don't begin harvesting until October, but I think we'll be at it by the third week in September this year."

"This will be my first cranberry harvest. What do I need to know so that I can help you?"

"Well, these cranberries will all be for juices and sauces so we do what's called a 'wet harvesting.' First, we flood the bog until the cranberries are completely covered with water. Then we bring in fat-tired trucks called 'water reels' or 'eggbeaters.' They're driven through the

215

bog and the spinning reels on the machines loosen the berries from the plants and they float to the surface. That's when the hard work begins."

"What do you mean?"

"We assemble a corral using boards and canvas hinges, and encircle the cranberries, drawing them to one end of the bog. A pipe is placed just beneath the surface of the water, and this pipe leads to a pump on shore which sucks the berries into a metal box called a hopper. The hopper separates everything and then the berries are loaded into trucks."

"You sound like you know exactly what to do," I said.

"Maybe, but I've never done this without Dad."

"You'll do fine, Cary, and I'll be there beside you."

He laughed.

"You'll be in school," he said.

"I'll take some days off," I promised.

"Play hooky? You have a chance to be class valedictorian, don't you?"

"It's not as important to me," I said, "as helping you."

He smiled and leaned over to kiss me. It was a short, sweet kiss, and when he pulled back, I looked so deeply into his green eyes that I felt I was really connecting with him, with his soul, with who he was. His eyes were like magnets. I moved my lips toward his again and we kissed, only this time longer, harder, embracing each other tightly.

"I'm glad you're back," he whispered. "I had nightmares that I would never see you again."

"Fill your head with only good dreams, Cary. I'm back and I won't ever leave you again," I promised.

He was so happy it brought tears to his eyes. We started to kiss again, when I looked out over his shoulder at the house and saw a window curtain move on the second floor. I was sure it was Grandma Olivia gazing down at us.

"I better go in, Cary, before it really starts pouring."

"Right. When should I come by tomorrow?"

"Wait for me to call you. I'd like to visit Grandma Belinda, if I could."

"Sure, I'll take you," he said.

"You should be spending all your time with your mother, Cary. She must be so sad. And lonely."

"I can't sit there all day and watch her cry, Melody. It makes me crazy to see how sad she is. The best I can do is work hard and show her that everything will be all right. I'll take care of things."

"I know you will," I said, nodding. "I'll call you tomorrow."

I gave him a quick kiss and hopped out of the truck. He watched me cross in front of it and smiled at me as I walked to the front door. He didn't start the engine until I opened the door to go in. I waved and he started away.

With the sky so overcast and the lights either off or turned low, it was dismal and dark in the house. I felt a chill run through my body and folded my arms across my chest as I hurried up the stairs. When I reached the second floor and turned toward my room, I found Grandma Olivia waiting at my door. Without a greeting, she opened the door for me and stood back.

"Let's talk," she said, grimly.

Keeping my head down and my arms still folded, I walked by her and into the room. She closed the door softly behind her.

"Where were you all day?"

"I went to Aunt Sara's and spent time with her and May, and then Cary took me to see Kenneth," I replied.

"It would probably be better if you stopped going out to that beach house so much now," she declared.

"Why?"

"There's enough suspicious gossip going on. It will only add to it."

"I can't hide from every whisper in Provincetown," I said.

She stiffened.

"You will lead an exemplary life here. No one will have any reason to utter the smallest suspicion or tale of indiscretion," she demanded as if she could order the future at will.

"I'm not going to stop seeing Kenneth. He's my uncle, my real uncle."

"Don't ever say that to anyone, do you understand?" she snapped, moving to stand over me. Her eyes looked more haunted by her own fears than rage at me. Nothing appeared to terrify her more than the community learning Judge Childs was my grandfather and had been her sister's lover.

"I have no intention of rattling any of the skeletons in our family closet, Grandma Olivia. It wouldn't serve any purpose except to hurt people who have already suffered too much because of them."

She smiled, relieved, and nodded.

"That's right. That's good thinking."

"How is my grandmother?" I asked firmly.

"Belinda is . . . Belinda. She was taken off the medication that turned her into a vegetable, if that's what you mean."

"Good. I'm going to see her tomorrow. Don't worry, you won't have to waste any gas. Cary's taking me," I said quickly.

"That's the main reason I wanted to talk to you," she said. "You've grown too close to Cary. I understand why," she continued, crossing to the window. The rain had become harder and the wind was flinging the heavy drops at the house, drumming a wild beat upon the roof. "You were alone; you were in strange surroundings but you had a contemporary to talk to and befriend you. However, now that you are here, you've got to create some distance between the two of you."

"Whatever for?" I asked and she pivoted quickly.

"Cary is a good, responsible young man, but too limited for you now. You can't make the mistakes I made," she warned. "There would be no purpose for taking you in if I didn't teach you that," she added.

"Being with someone you love can never be a mistake," I replied.

She shook her head.

"When you've grown out of these foolish romantic notions, you will be strong enough to take on the responsibilities I have in mind for you. Besides, you're not thinking of your immediate future. You will finish this school year, go to a prestigious prep school which will prepare you for the best colleges, where I am sure you will meet someone from a distinguished family and form a meaningful relationship."

"You talk like you have my whole life planned out for me."

"I will do the best I can, but you must be cooperative and obedient," she continued, obviously not at all concerned with my feelings. "I've been thinking about you all day and I've concluded that you can begin your training immediately. For that purpose, I have contracted with an excellent tutor, a Miss Louise May Burton, who happens to be a retired charm school teacher. You will begin your lessons the day after tomorrow, so don't make any silly plans to wander the beaches, or go sailing or visit anyone."

"Lessons? In what?"

"Etiquette, manners, behavior. You are going to attend schools populated by the daughters of only the best families, people of stature, good breeding, pure blood."

"There's nothing wrong with my manners," I complained.

She laughed.

"How would you know, my dear? Have you ever been with people who recognized the difference?"

I stared at her a moment, my anger simmering my blood into a rolling boil. Yes, my mother was a great disappointment, but there were many people in my life who were warm and decent. Why, Papa George and Mama Arlene would make any of Grandma Olivia's blue bloods look like savages when it came to true and good feelings and decency, I thought.

But Papa George was dead and Mama Arlene had moved away, a small voice reminded me.

219

"That's settled then," Grandma Olivia continued. "You will limit your contact with Kenneth Childs and with Cary and you will be a good student of manners."

"I won't limit my contact with Cary," I challenged.

"If you won't on your own accord, I'll have to speak with Sara. And," she said smiling, "you know what sort of influence I have with Sara. They are, despite what dribbles in from that dying lobster boat business and their silly cranberries, dependent upon my charity to an extent you don't fathom. Why even that pathetic house really belongs to me," she revealed. "My son needed to borrow the money for the mortgage."

"You wouldn't dare do anything to hurt them," I countered.

She fixed her eyes on me with a firmness that put ice into my veins.

"Not unless you force me too," she said. Then she smiled. "I suppose you could always run away and live like your dead mother. Think it all over and I'm sure you'll conclude that your best chances for a decent life are here with me and with what I will do for you."

"Why are you really doing all this for me?" I asked her, suddenly more curious than angry.

"I told you, for the family's sake," she said.

I shook my head.

"There's another reason."

"There is no other reason . . . for anything," she declared and then turned to leave my room.

The rain grew heavier, its drum beat pounding on my heart as well as on the house. I saw Cary's loving smile, his deep green eyes revealing his great need for me and great trust. How could I disappoint him? Grandma Olivia's threats scared me. I thought about the fury in her face.

Some time ago, she had trusted her heart to someone who had betrayed her and from that betrayal my mother was born, a woman she couldn't control or mold. I was her last chance for revenge.

But revenge against whom? Against what?

Was it someone or was it merely a world she had come to despise? Maybe it was both, I thought.

I was sure that in the days to follow I would find all the answers, only I was just as terrified of making the discoveries as I was of not.

I was floundering in a world of adult quicksand. Who would throw me a line to pull me out? Kenneth? Judge Childs? My Grandmother Belinda? Cary? Everyone seemed to be floundering just as much.

Only Grandma Olivia, only she seemed to walk on firm ground. I had to admire her for that, and suddenly, I was filled with a new fear.

What if she got her way and I became the woman she wanted me to become?

Would I become her?

Then surely, she would have her revenge.

Grandpa Samuel did not join us for dinner. When Loretta began serving, I inquired after him.

"Samuel's not up to coming down to dinner tonight," Grandma Olivia said and began to eat her soup.

"Isn't he hungry?"

"He doesn't remember when he ate and when he didn't," she remarked acidly.

- "Well, that's terrible, isn't it?" I pursued.

"Yes," she said and paused. "I'm debating whether to have a nurse move in to help take care of him or—"

"Or what?"

"Have him placed in the home Belinda is in. The doctor will be examining him again in a few days and we'll know what he thinks we should do."

"Surely, he'll get better. He's just overcome with grief," I said.

She dabbed her mouth daintily and signaled for Loretta to remove her bowl.

"Really Melody, I don't know if we have room on our door to hang it," she said.

"Hang it? Hang what?"

"Your medical degree. I didn't know you had one," she said humorlessly.

"I'm just saying that it's possible, isn't it? He just needs some tender love and care. It's very painful to lose someone you love," I shot back. Sarcasm dripped from those thin, smug lips of hers.

"Of course it's painful, but tragedy and sadness must be subdued if you are to be of any value to anyone, including yourself. If all you are going to do is wallow in tears, you might as well throw yourself into the grave with your loved one. I may sound insensitive to you, Melody, but I am a realist, pragmatic. All the success, all that we have, is a result of that strength.

"And the irony is," she continued, "the weaker, more sensitive members of my immediate family are totally dependent upon my strength. Where would they be without me? Where do you think Samuel would eventually end up, and Belinda and Sara? All of them. Even you," she added.

She nodded at Loretta, who began serving the entrée, but who looked terrified of doing anything that would interrupt. Grandma Olivia continued.

"I don't expect gratitude. I don't need to be continually stroked with thank-yous, but I won't be despised for my actions either. Is that clear?" she demanded.

I glanced at Loretta, who looked like she was waiting for my reply before she would serve me, too.

"Yes, ma'am," I said.

"Good." She began to eat while I poked at my food. "You may go visit Belinda tomorrow. You should, now that I think about it. Tell her about Haille. Give her all the details about her daughter. A good dose of reality might be beneficial," she said, nodding and smiling.

We stared at each other a moment and then we ate quietly, neither of us saying another word until we were finished. Loretta was there to remove the dishes in an instant and quietly announced that she'd be bringing out dessert momentarily.

"I'm tired and I've had enough to eat. You should take your time. Try the crème brûlée. It's very good," Grandma Olivia said and retreated to the parlor.

I had no more appetite and left the dining room soon after her. When I passed the parlor, I saw her sitting in her grand cushioned chair, suddenly looking very small, exhausted and alone. She had a book in her lap, but she wasn't reading anymore. She was staring out the window at the slow downpour, watching as the sky poured out the tears she'd never allow herself to shed.

I went upstairs to my room, but when I reached the second floor, I heard a door open and close and saw Grandpa Samuel coming down the hallway. He spotted me and hurried toward me. He wore a pair of pajamas and a dark blue velvet robe, but he was barefoot. His hair was disheveled. It looked like he had been running his fingers through it for hours.

"Haille," he whispered. "I'm glad you're back."

"No, Grandpa. I'm Melody," I said softly with a smile. "Melody."

He shook his head and looked back as if he was afraid of being overheard.

"She's gone and done it. I told her it wasn't right, but she forbade me to utter a word. She said it was a family disgrace and if I should so much as drop a hint in public or to Jacob and Sara, she would have me thrown out. She would tell everyone I was responsible for your pregnancy after all. Can you imagine? I think she meant it."

"Grandpa."

"I'm not saying she's not right. Maybe she is better off where she is, but Haille, you—"

"Grandpa, it's me, Melody," I said. I reached out and took his hand. He turned and looked into my face.

"What?"

"Look at me closely. I'm not my mother."

"You mustn't tell her I told you," he said. He looked very frightened.

"Tell her what? Who are you talking about? Belinda?"

He shook his head.

"I'm not responsible," he said, pulling his hand from mine and backing away. "You can't blame me."

"Grandpa."

"I'm going to bed. Things will look different in the morning. They always look different in the morning. But if you don't believe me, you go into the basement and you look. You'll find the papers. Shh," he said bringing his finger to his lips. "Don't say a word. Don't let her know I told you," he warned me. "Just pretend you found the papers yourself," he added and hurried away, looking back only once before going into his bedroom and closing the door.

What papers?

Was it all part of his madness? Like Ophelia in *Hamlet,* had he been driven insane by the death of someone he loved? If he didn't come out of his constant state of confusion he would end up in a rest home, I sadly thought.

Or were there more skeletons dangling in a closet I had yet to discover? Was it not just madness but painful memories that did this to him?

I heard footsteps below. Grandma Olivia was coming up the stairs, and for now, I thought, I would keep Grandpa Samuel's words to myself.

In my room I lay on the bed, my thoughts tumbling through my mind, making it impossible to sleep. Grandpa Samuel's words echoed in my ears and when I did finally drift off to sleep, it was of secrets and lies and whispers from beyond the grave that I dreamt. I tossed and turned for most of the night before I finally gave up on sleep.

I lay there with my eyes wide open for the longest time. The rain had stopped but the wind continued to whistle and blow over the big house, scratching at the window and whispering a name. My nightmares had stirred a voice. I could not make it out, but I knew it was a secret deeper than I had ever fathomed.

13
&

How Sweet It Is

After breakfast the next day, Cary came by to take me to see Grandma Belinda. I waited at the parlor window so I could rush out to meet him as soon as he pulled into the driveway. I didn't want him to have to see the look of disapproval on Grandma Olivia's face. He would surely ask me about it and I would have to tell him her feelings concerning us. If there was anything I wanted to avoid at the moment, it was family turmoil, especially when it could be traced back to me.

Yesterday's storm had passed and the small vanilla scoops of clouds looked like they were melting over the powder blue sky. The instant I saw Cary's truck, I ran out to greet him. As we drove away from Grandma Olivia's dreary home, Cary and I remarked on how bright the sun seemed, how clean and clear the air, how beautiful the grass and flowers. It filled me with a renewed sense of hope and reminded me of when I was younger and I believed life would be like one long and perfect summer day, a day just like this one.

I was about to see my closest relative again. I hoped

that taking her off her medication had cleared her head. I couldn't wait to hug her and talk to her about everything, especially all my dreams and plans for the future. At least Belinda had time to listen, I thought. At least I had someone neither Mommy nor Grandma Olivia could take from me.

As we drove up to the rest home, Cary talked about the times his twin sister Laura had gone to see my grandmother before Uncle Jacob had forbidden any further visits. Cary hadn't talked about Laura for quite a while. When I had first come to Provincetown, just pronouncing her name seemed to bring pain to his lips.

"Why did Laura visit her so often, Cary?" I asked. He thought for a moment, his memories brightening his sea-green eyes.

"Belinda took to Laura the first time she met her. It was as if they recognized something soft and loving in each other, some secret the two of them shared. No matter who else was present, Belinda directed herself only to Laura. No one knew about the first time Laura visited her up here. In fact, if I recall, my father didn't discover it was going on until the third or fourth time, and only then because some spy of Grandma Olivia's told her about the visits. She called Dad and he chastised Laura for going; after all, Belinda was the black sheep of the family. We weren't supposed to mention her name, much less visit her.

"But Dad always had trouble forbidding Laura to do things," Cary continued. "Whenever Laura and I did something he didn't approve of, Dad would direct himself mainly to me, barely looking at Laura, as if she hadn't been involved at all. He never thought he let his soft spot show, but it was obvious he always thought things were my fault anyway, as if I was the one who should have known better or should have been more responsible. Laura would fly to my defense, of course, taking as much blame as she could, but Dad wouldn't hear of it. He would accuse her of trying to protect me."

Cary laughed, as he continued remembering.

" 'But Dad,' she would exclaim, 'Cary wasn't even there!'

" 'No matter,' Dad would growl back. 'He should have been there to stop you or warn you.' "

"Once," he said turning to me as we drove up the side road toward the rest home, "I took quite a beating for the both of us. He whipped me with a thick leather strap and I had so many welts on my rear end I couldn't sit for days. I had to lie on my stomach. Laura came into my room and sat beside the bed, crying as if she felt the pain as much as I did. I tell you, I stopped feeling sorry for myself and didn't feel as much pain. One of my tears would draw ten of hers, so I had to stop crying or she would drown the two of us," he explained with a laugh.

"Anyway, she would bike all the way up here to visit Belinda, and Belinda really looked forward to her visits, from what I heard. I think Grandma Olivia was jealous. Laura never biked over to visit her." He smiled, turning to me. "Like you, Laura cared more about other people than she cared about herself, especially those who were less fortunate, whether it was because of lack of money or lack of love."

We pulled into a parking space and got out of the truck and made our way to the entrance of the home. A pretty nurse greeted us just inside the lobby. Her name tag read MRS. WILLIAMS. I hadn't seen her before. She didn't look much older than her late twenties.

There weren't as many residents sitting there as the last time I had visited, but once again, my appearance, and especially Cary's, too, drew all their attention, quieted their conversations, interrupted their checkers and card games.

I explained who we were and whom we had come to visit, but before Mrs. Williams could respond, Mrs. Greene stepped out of her office and drew our attention as she came toward us, her high heels clicking over the tile floor.

"Well, it's been some time since your last visit," she

said. "You led me to believe you would be here frequently," she added as if she had caught me in a lie.

"I've been away," I explained. She smirked and turned to the nurse. "I'll see to them, Mrs. Williams."

"Yes, ma'am," the nurse said and returned to the other residents.

"Your grandmother is in the garden," she said, glancing quickly at Cary. "This is a family member, I assume?"

"Yes, he is. How is she doing?"

"Quite well, actually. I should warn you that since you've been here, Miss Gordon's formed a friendship with one of our other residents, Mr. Mandel, and the two of them spend most of their time together."

Cary smiled but Mrs. Greene didn't even acknowledge him.

"It's just a companionship, of course," she continued, speaking through her tight jaw as she led us through the lobby and down a corridor to a side door that opened on the gardens and walkways, "but we encourage such things. We find it's good for their mental health to develop relationships with other residents."

"You talk about them as if they're some other species," I remarked. Cary's eyes widened, surprised at my tone of voice and confrontational demeanor, but I recalled this woman's attitude about me the other times we had met, and I was sure she was somehow on Grandma Olivia's payroll.

"The elderly practically are some other species," she replied, not skipping a beat. "However, only someone who has to work with them day in and day out would understand, I'm afraid."

She flashed as artificial a smile at us as I had ever seen and then nodded toward Grandma Belinda and a short, bald man sitting on a bench. He had a dark wood cane and leaned on it as he sat. His glasses had slipped down the bridge of his nose until they tottered at the very crest of his narrow nostrils. He wore a blue suit jacket, but pants of a lighter shade, almost gray actually. His tie was awkwardly knotted with one half far longer than the other and his socks sagged around his ankles.

As we approached I was hoping Grandma Belinda would remember me. When her face brightened, I thought she had.

"Well, look who's here, Thomas, my grandnephew and grandniece," she said and I realized that because I had come with Cary, she assumed I was Laura.

"No, Grandma," I said. "It's Melody, not Laura."

"Melody?" She looked at Cary.

"That's right, Aunt Belinda. It's your granddaughter, Melody. How are you?"

She looked from him to me and blinked rapidly. Even though she appeared to be struggling with her memory, she was far from as pale and drained as she had been the last time I had visited. She looked bright, her cheeks a little rosy. She had taken care to brush her hair neatly, and she even wore a little lipstick. I saw she was holding on to Mr. Mandel's left hand. He smiled up at us, nodding.

"Oh," Grandma Belinda said. "I want you two to meet Mr. Mandel. He used to be an accountant and can still add lots of numbers in his head, big numbers!"

"Don't exaggerate, Belinda. I'm not anything like I was," he said jovially. "Pleased to meet you. I guess I'll let you visit with your family, Belinda," he said, rising and patting her softly on the back of her hand.

"You don't have to leave, Mr. Mandel," I said, seeing the disappointment on Grandma Belinda's face.

"No, no, I have to talk to Mrs. Landeau about her tax shelter investments. I promised her. You go on. Here, take my seat," he said to me.

Grandma Belinda looked sadly after him as he wobbled away on his cane. Then her eyes shadowed, growing deep, dark, her face turning angry and resembling Grandma Olivia's face.

"I know what she's up to, asking him for advice," she muttered. "She had her eyes on him the moment he came over to sit with me in the dining room. Green with envy, that one. I bet she hasn't a cent invested in anything anymore. She's just lying to get him to pay attention to her. I know that type. They can't stand to see someone else happy."

Cary laughed. I shook my head at him so he would stop; I didn't want Grandma Belinda to think he was laughing at her. Then I sat beside her, taking her hand into mine.

"Grandma, don't you remember my coming to see you before?" I asked. "Don't you remember our talks?"

She glanced up at Cary and then smiled at me.

"Of course, I remember. How are your parents?"

Cary and I exchanged looks of disappointment. Should we confront Grandma Belinda with doses of reality or was it better to assume the roles her confused mind assigned us?

"Look at me, Grandma Belinda. I'm Melody, Haille's daughter, your granddaughter. I'm not Laura. I've come to tell you about Haille. I went to see her in California."

She stared at me, pressing her lips together. Then her face turned harder, her eyes colder.

"I don't have a daughter," she said. "Everyone has to stop saying that." She turned to look after Mr. Mandel, her voice full of rage. "Now you've gone and chased Mr. Mandel away and that Corina Landeau is going to get her claws into him. Every time I find someone, someone tries to steal him away. My sister's no exception either." She turned back to us and her face suddenly softened again with a sweet smile. "How's your mother? You tell her I enjoyed the cookies and if she wants to make me some more, I won't object."

"Grandma," I said with more desperation, "please, try to remember my other visits. I'm Melody, Melody, Haille's daughter."

She continued to look after Mr. Mandel and from the faraway look on her face, I could tell she wasn't listening to me. I sighed deeply and Cary put his hand on my shoulder.

"Grandma Olivia wanted me to come up here and give

230

her a dose of reality. I think she knew what I would find," I said bitterly.

"She was here," Grandma Belinda said, her gaze still fixed away from us. "She paid me a visit. I suppose I'm to be honored."

"Who was here, Grandma?" I asked.

"Her majesty, who else?" she said, turning back to us. "She told me Haille was dead, killed in a car accident long ago. So you see, I can't have a granddaughter. I don't have anyone. I had Mr. Mandel, but now—"

"That's not true, Grandma. She lied. You have me, Grandma," I said. "Please, look at me, remember me. I visited you before. Don't you remember?" I cried, practically pleading with her. She stared at me, her eyes empty.

I turned to Cary and so did Grandma Belinda.

"How's your mother, Cary?" she asked. "Does she still do that beautiful needlework?"

"Yes, she does, Aunt Belinda." He smiled and she nodded.

"I used to do needlework, but my fingers are too clumsy now. That's what happens. You get older and your fingers get clumsy." She shook her head sadly and then turned back toward Mr. Mandel and pressed her lips together so hard little white lines of rage formed.

"Just look at her beaming over there," she muttered under her breath. "He's talking and she's beaming. She doesn't have a penny invested. I told him, but men don't listen. Some other woman bats her eyelashes at them and they go chasing after them. You understand, don't you?" she asked turning back to me as if she just realized I was sitting beside her. She smiled. "Just look at you. Look at you. You look so grown up, Laura. So grown up. Don't fall in love too fast," she warned as she turned back to look at Mr. Mandel. "Why don't we just walk over there and I'll pretend to need him to help me with my money, too. Yes," she said, pleased that she'd come up with a solution to the problem.

"Grandma . . ."

She continued to stare after Mr. Mandel.

"It's no use, Melody," Cary said. "She's not going to remember. You're just wasting time and facing more disappointment."

"But she is all I have left, Cary. I have no other family," I moaned.

"You've got me," he said emphatically.

"I thought she'd remember," I said, gazing at her wistfully. "I thought we'd have some time together, but obviously Grandma Olivia made sure we wouldn't," I added. "She came up here and confused her. She did it deliberately."

"Let's go, Melody."

"She's jealous of everything, even the fragile relationship I was building with my grandmother. She just came bursting in here and swept it all away."

"Melody, you're getting yourself all worked up. Come on," he urged.

"Do me a favor," Grandma Belinda said when I stood up. "Just go over there and ask Mr. Mandel to come back. Tell him I need him right away."

"He'll come back to you, Grandma," I said. "You're much prettier than she is."

"I am?" She brightened again and nodded. "Yes, I am much prettier, aren't I?" she agreed, brushing the sides of her hair with her palms. "He'll see that. She's got that mole on her chin with tiny hairs. I don't even have many wrinkles, do I?" She turned to us, raising her face to the sunlight, her eyes closed, her lips pursed like a young flirt.

"No, Grandma, you don't," I said and touched her cheek. She opened her eyes and gazed up at me.

"You look like an angel now," she said. "Your mother must be very proud of you."

"She is," Cary said quickly. "Very proud."

"That's nice. That's the way it should be."

She turned back to glare in Mr. Mandel's direction. Cary tugged my hand and I stood up beside him.

"She'll be all right," he said.

"You're right," I said. I leaned over and gave her a kiss on her cheek, but she didn't notice. Her gaze was locked on Mr. Mandel. "Bye Grandma. I'll come back. I promise."

"Don't forget the cookies," she called as we started away. I looked back at her once before we left the garden. Mr. Mandel had left the other woman and was hobbling down the path toward her and she looked very contented, very happy.

"Maybe it's time you started thinking more about yourself, about us," Cary said as we left the rest home. "Maybe it's time we both looked to the future and not to the past, huh?"

"Maybe," I agreed, but I wasn't as confident as he was that the past would let us do that.

I said nothing to Grandma Olivia about her visit to the rest home. I wasn't going to give her the satisfaction of knowing that she had once again gotten her way. When she asked about my visit, I said it was fine and left it at that. If I was to survive in her world, I had to learn to play the game her way. For the time being, I would pretend to be the young woman she wanted me to be.

The next day, as Grandma Olivia had promised, Miss Burton arrived at the house to begin my education in etiquette, making me feel from the start that I wasn't much better than some hick who had just arrived on these precious Cape Cod shores. I was sure it was how Grandma Olivia had described me to her.

She called me down to the parlor and introduced me.

"Miss Burton, I'd like you to meet my granddaughter, Melody," Grandma Olivia said, and I looked at the tall, thin woman who stood so straight, I thought she had a steel rod for a spine. She had very small shoulders, the bones of which pressed up sharply against the dark blue cotton dress that hung over her body in a straight line. Its hem reached her ankles and it was buttoned at the collar.

Miss Burton said nothing but held out her hand.

"Hi," I offered, shook her hand quickly, backed away

233

and looked at Grandma Olivia, whose head bobbed slightly in approval.

"Until school begins, Miss Burton will meet with you promptly at nine A.M. each weekday morning. After school begins, you will arrange your schedules accordingly."

"For how long?" I asked.

"For as long as it takes to turn you into a lady," Grandma Olivia replied curtly.

"I think I am a lady," I returned. Grandma Olivia grinned coldly and looked at Miss Burton.

"As you see, you have a real challenge here, Louise."

"I'm sure we'll do what we can," Miss Burton said, still scrutinizing me intently.

"Then I'll leave you to begin. I know you need all the time allotted for your lesson. And then some," Grandma added and walked out of the parlor. For a moment Miss Burton and I just looked at each other, sizing each other up like two combatants. Then she cleared her throat and took a step toward me as if someone had given her a shove from behind.

"I can help you only if you want to be helped," she said grimly.

"I don't think I need to be helped," I replied honestly, since she wanted to be frank.

"Oh, my dear," she said smiling and shaking her head, "you most definitely need to be helped."

"Really?" I said dryly. "And how can you tell so quickly, or are you basing everything on what my grandmother has told you about me?"

"I make my own evaluations of people. Let's simply begin with your entrance this morning. Mrs. Logan introduced you properly to me. A young person is always introduced *to* an older person, but you don't say 'Hi.' The very least you say, is simply 'Hello.' This is acceptable in any situation except, of course, after a very formal introduction. We had a somewhat formal introduction. You should have said, 'Hello, Miss Burton, I'm glad to meet you,' or 'How do you do, Miss Burton.' Furthermore, a formal verbal greeting should be accompanied by direct eye contact, which indicates that you are actually paying attention to the person you are acknowledging. You let your eyes wander to Mrs. Logan, the room, me, Mrs. Logan, back to me again," she lectured. "Should I continue?" she asked.

"I guess," I said, feeling a tight knot form in my stomach.

"An older person extends his or her hand first to a younger one, as I just did, but you don't take someone's hand limply as if yours is boneless or as if you're grasping an empty glove. Of course, you don't squeeze too hard, but you should be firm and you should look the person directly in the eyes when you shake.

"Next," she continued without skipping a beat, "is your dreadful posture. A person who stands erect and sits erect looks best, looks confident, looks like someone of worth. Rounded shoulders, slouching, folding your arms across your body as you are now doing . . . all this shows your sloppiness and lack of refinement immediately. Your shoulders should be back, chin in and slightly up, abdomen and stomach in, back straight and knees relaxed. You may keep your arms at your sides, relaxed, as well. Now, let me see you take that seat," she said nodding toward the overstuffed chair to my left.

I eyed it like a challenge of great proportions, positive that whatever I did would be wrong. Nevertheless, I stepped up to the chair, turned, looked directly at her and sat. She laughed.

"What's so funny?"

"You don't really sit like that. You would never be so stiff, nor do you flop into a chair. Sit softly and keep your knees together," she added, nodding at my legs. "The only people who want a view of your undergarments are degenerates. You should sit a bit sideways to keep from sprawling into the chair."

"These pillows are so soft that I—"

"More reason to be aware of your posture and how you appear to others in the room."

"I don't think I look especially sloppy," I protested.

"You don't look sloppy, but you don't look like a young woman of refinement, a woman of quality, stature, a woman who would attract someone of like ilk," she insisted. "You are part of a very distinguished family now. You have a responsibility to be distinguished yourself, and sitting in a chair with your knees wide enough apart to drive a truck between them, slouching when you stand, moving in jerky motions, gawking, all of that makes you look more like someone brought up by uneducated, unsophisticated people of low quality."

"That's not true. I was brought up by good people, decent people who cared about other people and—"

"Then why don't you try to make them proud of you, proud of what you can become and proud of who you now are?" she retorted before I could continue my protest.

I swallowed back my pride and indignation.

"I will be only as good a teacher as you permit me to be and you will be only as good a student as you allow yourself to be. Shall we begin or for the next hour would you rather we debate whether you need my help or not?" she asked firmly, never relaxing her proper posture or letting any warmth into her cold brown eyes.

"I'll try," I finally said, breathing deeply, determined not to cry.

"Good. Then let's begin. Walk out and walk in again, pretending we are meeting for the first time. Keep thinking about your posture as you enter the room."

I rose and left the parlor. For a moment I was tempted to rush out the front door. Then I gazed down the corridor and saw Grandma Olivia watching me. I knew the satisfaction she would get from seeing me flee. She would just nod and say she knew I didn't have it in me to rise to her level. Furious at the thought of her ridicule, I pulled back my shoulders, held my head high, and returned to the parlor.

Miss Burton offered her hand and I shook it firmly and said, "Hello, Miss Burton. I'm pleased to meet you."

She smiled and nodded toward the chair. I sat as she had instructed and placed my hands in my lap.

"Very good," she said. "We'll make a lady of you yet."

"I think being a lady comes from more than knowing how to say hello," I told her.

"Of course it does my dear. The guiding principle of etiquette is thoughtfulness. There are ten commandments of everyday behavior. Never," she began, wagging her long, thin and bony forefinger at me, "talk only about yourself, never gossip, never ask personal questions or pry, never intentionally embarrass anyone, never stare or point at someone, never chew gum with an open mouth or snap it, or make bubbles, never display affection in public," she said, pausing for breath. "From what I understand, that's a commandment you young people today violate often."

"I don't," I protested.

She shook her head.

"You must become your own best critic and to do that, you must not lie, especially to yourself. That's what happens when you lie to others; you end up lying to yourself."

"But —"

"Didn't you kiss someone right out here in this driveway recently?" she asked.

I sat, my mouth agape. Grandma Olivia told her about my kissing Cary?

"Don't keep your mouth open like that. It's not only impolite, it's unbecoming."

"I —"

"Kissing in public is showing affection, wouldn't you agree? Let's move on," she said standing. "Today we want to concentrate on eating."

"Eating?"

"Mealtime manners, my dear. Please, follow me to the dining room."

I rose and started toward the door.

"Always permit the older person to leave first," she instructed. Embarassed, I stopped and allowed her to walk out first. "Please, come along," she said. "There is no need to wait that long behind me."

I shook my head and followed her to the dining room, feeling like a puppy being housebroken. As we passed the stairway, I noticed Loretta standing in the shadows, gazing down at me. Her face was shrouded in the gloom, and I could only wonder whether Loretta would turn out to be my only friend in this cold and heartless home. Or would she, too, prove to be another of Grandma Olivia's minions, too frightened to do anything but her bidding?

If only I knew I could trust Loretta, I would reach out to her and tell her to watch closely, I was about to beat Grandma Olivia at her own game.

My first opportunity came at dinner that night. As I headed toward the dining room, I heard voices in the parlor and paused by the doorway in time to hear Grandma Olivia say, "He's become impossible, a blithering idiot. I can't permit him to be seen in public anymore. I want you to call in some favors and put him at the head of the list, Nelson."

"But I thought the doctor said that might only exacerbate his condition," Judge Childs replied.

"What about my condition? Don't you think it's been more than exacerbating for me?"

I stepped forward and the Judge saw me.

"Oh, Melody!" he exclaimed getting up to greet me.

I held out my hand the way Miss Burton had instructed, standing erect and holding out my arm fairly stiffly to prevent him from embracing me. I was uncomfortable with him showing me any affection in front of Grandma Olivia. I knew that if she suspected the relationship I was developing with my grandfather she would destroy it as quickly as she had my fragile bond with Grandma Belinda.

"Good evening, Judge Childs," I said. "It's nice to see you again."

He paused as if struck dumb for a moment and then smiled and took my hand for a very quick greeting, glancing at Grandma Olivia as he did so. She nodded approvingly.

"I'm happy to see you've come back."

"Thank you," I said with a tight smile, hoping he would go along with my ploy.

"Er . . . we were just . . . relaxing before dinner," he explained with some awkwardness.

He looked as dapper as ever, albeit a little older, grayer, his face a bit thinner. He wore a navy sports jacket and khaki pants, a striped cravat tied loosely around his neck.

"Isn't Grandpa Samuel coming to dinner?" I asked. "I haven't seen him all day."

"No," Grandma Olivia said sharply. "His condition is worse. The doctor will be seeing him in the morning."

"Is there anything I can do to help?" I asked, wishing I could will Grandpa Samuel well again.

"There is nothing any of us can do," she replied dryly. Just then, Loretta came to the doorway, and with a small curtsey announced dinner was ready.

"Finally," Grandma said, rising. Judge Childs held out his arm to her and she took it quickly, the both of them heading for the doorway. I stepped aside to let them leave first and then quickly followed them down the corridor.

"You must tell me about your trip West," the Judge said when we were all sitting at the table. "Perhaps you can come by one day to visit," he added, after throwing a nervous glance at Grandma Olivia.

"I'd like that, Judge Childs," I said, unfolding my napkin and placing it in my lap. Grandma Olivia studied my posture as I sat straight, my spine pressed firmly against the back of my chair.

As soon as the soup was served and Grandma Olivia picked up her spoon, the Judge and I began to eat. Except for Grandma Olivia's house, I had never eaten anywhere where there were so many pieces of silverware next to the plate. Miss Burton had explained that we always start with the implement of each type that is farthest from the plate. We ate quietly for a moment, Grandma Olivia and I eyeing each other. When the level of our soup became too low for the spoon, Grandma Olivia scraped the bottom of her soup dish, loud enough to be heard.

I tipped mine, lifting the near edge and pointing the bowl away from myself.

"I believe this is the proper way to do it, Grandma," I said, delighted to see her face redden. The Judge started to laugh, but stopped the moment he saw the rage in Grandma Olivia's eyes.

"I know the way to do it. I wasn't ready yet," she replied.

"Your spoon sounded as if you were," I said. Although I was determined to see my plan through, I was beginning to think I might have to take things a bit slower.

She pressed her lips together and tilted her bowl properly, but she only took one more spoonful. When we had both finished, we left our spoons in the soup dish, moving almost simultaneously and looking like two competitors vying for a prize in mealtime etiquette. I saw the question marks in the Judge's eyes.

Trying not to grin, Loretta removed the dishes and returned with our appetizers, clams on the half shell.

"I assume you've visited with Sara and the children since your return," the Judge said. "How are they doing?"

"As best as can be expected. Cary and May really miss their Dad. And, of course, Aunt Sara is just so sad," I replied.

"Please give Sara my best when you see her again," he said. "I will have to do something to help that poor family," he added, shaking his head sadly.

When Grandma Olivia began to eat her clams, the Judge and I dug into ours. The clams were served on cracked ice arranged around containers of cocktail sauce. We speared the clams with our shellfish forks and dipped them into the sauce and ate them in one bite.

"Sweet," the Judge said, patting his belly contentedly. Our salads followed and then our entrée, which tonight was lambchops. I almost choked on my meal when the Judge took one by the bone and gnawed at the meat. I could only imagine what Miss Burton would say to that! Grandma and I cut ours daintily and ate in small bites. When I was finished, I put my knife and fork on the plate and sat back. Loretta took my dishes and silverware, and then collected Grandma Olivia's. The Judge didn't relinquish his until every morsel was gone. Then he smacked his lips and remarked about the flavor of the meat.

"This is one of the best restaurants in Provincetown," he quipped.

"And the price is right," Grandma Olivia muttered. The Judge roared with laughter and then sat forward, his elbows on the table as he clasped his hands.

"So, Melody, you're about to start your senior year, then," he said. "I bet you're excited about that."

"Yes, I am," I replied honestly.

"I'm thinking of Rosewood for her as a prep school," Grandma Olivia said, always anxious to put in her two cents' worth.

"Oh yes, a fine place. I think Congressman Dunlap's daughter is there this year, if I'm not mistaken."

"You're not," Grandma Olivia said.

Loretta brought in our coffee and a lemon cake, which the Judge eyed covetously. When Grandma Olivia lifted her cup, she spilled some of her coffee into the saucer. It was as if a solo performer at a concert had hit a sour note. She froze for a moment and then continued, sipping her coffee and then putting the cup back, her attention shifting to the lemon cake.

"Shouldn't you replace that saucer, Grandma?" I asked her. She fired a look at me and sat back.

"Loretta," she called. Loretta appeared. "I'd like a new saucer, please."

"Right away, Mrs. Logan," Loretta said and hurried back to the kitchen. The Judge's smile widened. Grandma reached forward again for the lemon cake. She cut herself a piece and passed the cake plate to the Judge.

"I was told that the plate is to be passed counterclockwise, Grandma. Wasn't that correct?" I asked, trying to sound as innocent as I could manage, considering my knees were knocking. Her face turned so purple, so fast, that I was worried she might do some actual harm to herself. She took the cake plate back so quickly, her hand trembling so much the cake slipped to the edge. In an effort to balance it again, she overcompensated and the cake fell, splattering in front of the Judge, who pulled back to avoid being hit by the icing.

"Whoops," he said with a laugh. Loretta came charging toward the table.

Grandma Olivia, as red as a sunburnt tourist, jerked her chair away from the table to permit Loretta full access to the mess.

"No harm done," the Judge said. "I'll eat that anyway it looks, Loretta."

She smiled at him but shifted her eyes toward Grandma Olivia as if she felt she would somehow be held responsible.

"Nonsense," Grandma Olivia said. "Loretta, take that back into the kitchen and make it look presentable again."

"Yes, ma'am," she said, hurrying away with the smashed cake.

"I would have eaten it off the table," the Judge said to lighten the moment, but Grandma Olivia glared daggers at him until he sat back like an obedient little boy. Then she turned slowly to me.

"If you hadn't interrupted like that—"

"I was trying to practice what I've been taught, Grandma. I'm sorry, but Miss Burton says we shouldn't save our best manners for the outside world. She says the people with whom we live deserve our best manners even more."

"Miss Burton?" the Judge asked.

"Someone I hired to teach her the finer ways," Grandma replied quickly.

Loretta returned with the cake somewhat repaired, only this time she went around the table and served us each our piece.

"Looks scrumptious, doesn't it?" the Judge said.

"Yes, it does," I said and cut my piece with my fork. Grandma Olivia only nibbled at hers and left more than half on the plate.

Just as Loretta returned to take away the dishes, we heard the doorbell. She paused for orders.

"See to that first, Loretta," Grandma said.

"Expecting someone?" the Judge asked.

"Not at all," she said, obviously annoyed to be disturbed. A moment later, Loretta returned with Cary behind her. He was carrying a covered pie dish.

"Oh, sorry I got here too late, Grandma," he said, "but Ma sent over a homemade cranberry pie. I picked some early berries and she made it just this afternoon."

"Hmm . . . I've never cared much for cranberry pie," Grandma Olivia said, sniffing haughtily.

"I love it," the Judge said, winking at me.

"Then you take it," she said with a wave of her hand.

"Thank you. And Cary, you thank your mother for me," he said as Cary stepped forward with the pie.

"Put that in a box for Judge Childs, Loretta," Grandma Olivia commanded. "You should have brought it earlier if you expected us to eat it tonight," she told Cary.

"I had some things to do at the dock and . . ."

"Oh, don't worry about it," the Judge said. "It won't go to waste, that's for sure."

Cary stood there awkwardly, waiting for an invitation to sit at the table, but Grandma Olivia wasn't offering any. He glanced at me and then smiled at the Judge.

"May I be excused?" I asked. "I'd like to go for a walk on the beach."

She glared icily at me.

"It's getting late," she said sternly.

"Late?" the Judge asked and looked at his watch as if he were the one who somehow mistook the time.

"For walks on the beach," she explained. "I thought you had problems at the dock, Cary."

"It's all been fixed, Grandma. I can stay for a short visit," he said, practically pleading. Reluctantly, she nodded.

I rose.

"Thank you, Grandma. Judge Childs, I enjoyed dining with you tonight. I hope I'll see you soon."

"Anytime you want, my dear. Just come right over," he said, smiling happily. Thankfully Grandma Olivia was too wrapped up in her own steam to think the Judge's invitation odd.

I left the table and accompanied Cary to the back door. When we stepped outside, I felt as if I had thrown off shackles. The night air never felt so refreshing.

"What's going on in there?" Cary asked. "You could cut the tension with a knife."

"Grandma and I are practicing good table manners," I said and laughed. "It appears she is not as perfect as she thinks she is. I think I'm going to have some fun with all this proper this and proper that."

Cary took my hand and we walked down to the beach. The ocean was calm, the tide lapping softly at the shore. In the distance I saw the tiny lights of a tanker. Stars glittered just above the water, some looking like strings of sparkling diamonds. There was no moonlight, but the evening was clear enough so that the heavens glowed down over us.

"You sure you want to live with her?" Cary asked. "She looked meaner than ever tonight. Where was my Grandpa? After the whole pie thing, I was afraid to ask," he explained.

"She has him shut up in his room. I overheard her talking to the Judge. I think she's getting Grandpa Samuel placed in the same home my grandmother is now in," I said.

"Is he that bad?" Cary asked, unable to keep the tremor from his voice.

"He's babbling, confusing things I don't understand and he's not looking after himself, Cary. Unfortunately, I think she might be right. He needs help."

"It's like everything's falling apart around us," Cary said sadly. "Ma won't break out of her depression. And May is so unhappy."

"I'll come by tomorrow," I promised, "and spend time with them."

"Thanks. I know they both miss you terribly."

We paused, both gazing out at the water. He slipped his arm around my waist and I leaned my head on his shoulder. I felt his lips on my hair, my forehead and then on my temples. I lifted my head toward him and we kissed, a long, soft kiss. Then he embraced me and turned me around toward him so he could kiss me again. I heard his breathing quicken.

"I love you, Melody. I don't think an hour goes by that I don't think of you, even when I'm asleep," he said.

"Cary, We have a problem," I said pulling away and taking a few steps down the beach.

"What?" he asked, following me slowly.

"Grandma Olivia doesn't want us to spend so much time together. She's practically forbidden it."

"What? Why?"

"She's planning out my life, designing it, and in her design, there is no place set aside for you," I told him, uncertain how to soften the blow.

"What? But—"

"So, I think it would be best if we don't let her know how much time we spend together. The less she knows about it, the better. She'll only make trouble for us, for you," I said.

"How can she do that?" he asked worriedly.

"Any way she wants. And every way you *don't* want." I said. "Why cause problems anyway, if we don't have to? The more I see of the adult world, the more I realize it's built around millions of white lies that get strung into chains of illusion and deception anyway. I'm tired of fighting it, Cary. If we have to steal our happiness, we'll steal it," I said firmly.

He smiled.

"As long as I'm with you, I don't care how we do it," he said.

"For the time being, I'm going to let her believe I'm doing everything she wants. It will make things easier for all of us. Your mother doesn't need any more turmoil in her life at the moment. None of us do," I said. He nodded.

"You're getting to be a pretty strong person, Melody."

"Whether I want to or not," I replied. He laughed and then embraced me again for another long kiss. This time his hands moved over my arms and my waist, climbing to my breasts. I moaned and sank against him, my legs weakening.

"Cary."

"I missed you so much," he said. "When can we be together like we were?"

"Soon," I promised. "Soon. We better get back now though."

He nodded reluctantly. As we approached the rear of the house, I gazed toward the basement stairs, recalling when Cary had first shown me pictures of my mother and revealed she had been living with Grandpa Samuel and Grandma Olivia, growing up with my stepfather and Uncle Jacob as if she were their sister.

"Grandpa Samuel mumbled about some other secrets hidden in the basement, Cary. Do you think it's true? Or just his delusions talking?"

"I'm sure that's all it was," Cary said, but as we passed the stairway, I felt the shadows drawing me, beckoning, promising revelations that would chill me to the bones.

Someday I would have the courage to see.

But for now, I needed my courage just to make it through the day.

246

14

ஜ

Sacred Moments

*E*xcept for Theresa Patterson, whose father had worked for Cary's father and now Cary, I had made few friends at the high school. After I had played my fiddle and sang in the variety show at the end of the school year, people took more notice of me, but since I was in California I hadn't spent time with any of the other girls during the summer. A few were curious about where I had been, and when I told them I had been to Hollywood visiting friends, they were more than interested. Since I couldn't really reveal the details of my trip they soon grew bored and stopped finding excuses to drop by my locker and chat.

On Tuesdays every week after school, I spent an hour or so with Miss Burton. Since our initial first meeting, I felt less defensive and even began to like her. Her husband had died five years ago, and both her children lived in Florida. In many ways she was just as lonely as I was.

"Etiquette," she explained during our second session, "is really nothing more than the Golden Rule put to work. You are simply developing ways, manners, behavior to treat people as considerately as you would like them to treat you. You show them respect and expect them to show you respect. You treat older people with veneration and hope that when you are older, that's how you will be treated. You practice etiquette at meals so you don't do anything unappetizing. You wouldn't want it done to you. And there are always the problems that come from wondering how to behave at special occasions, how to behave with royalty, with high government officials, et cetera. Etiquette gives us the guidelines that make us comfortable in these settings.

"Isn't it nice to know how to introduce someone to somebody whose name you've forgotten? Why embarrass that person or make him or her feel bad? Isn't it comforting to know how to properly thank people, invite people, console people, what to do at weddings, funerals and birthdays? All of this will certainly come in handy when you're in the business world or looking for a career," she explained.

I stopped resisting, and listened and learned. Whenever I could, I pointed out Grandma Olivia's failures and mistakes, although now I usually chose them one at a time. I especially liked to do it in front of one of her distinguished guests.

Finally, one day she paused at the dining room table when we were eating alone and said, "I know why you're criticizing my table manners or my dinner invitations, but I want you to know it no longer bothers me as much as you hope it will. Furthermore, I am happy you are learning these things and despite yourself, are becoming refined. In the end when you are finished being a brat, you will come to me and thank me," she predicted. Deep down I couldn't help but wonder if she was right and from that day forward I stopped correcting her.

I really did have to try and keep some peace since it was just the two of us in the house now. At the end of the first week of school, I had returned home to learn that

Grandpa Samuel had been taken to the rest home. I didn't realize it until Grandma Olivia and I sat at the dining room table that night. After Loretta served us our appetizer, Grandma Olivia announced Grandpa Samuel's fate without a crack in her voice or a tear in her eye.

"I had to have Samuel taken to the home," she said. "He's become impossible."

"He'll be there forever then?" I asked.

"As long as forever is, yes," she replied.

I nodded.

"I'll visit him whenever I visit Grandma Belinda," I declared.

"Don't be surprised if he forgets who you are entirely. According to the doctor, he's only going to get worse," she said.

"I'm so sorry. I wish there was something we could do to help him."

"That's old age. The weight of grief, disappointment, a lifetime of struggling take their toll sooner on some than it does on others. It will be your fate as well as mine. It's best to prepare for it rather than try to deny it. Only the weak live in illusion. I don't expect you to like me, but I'm hoping you will come to respect what I'm trying to do with and for you," she continued.

"Both my sons are gone. My daughter-in-law remains a frail, pitiful creature. I have a deaf mute for a grand-daughter and a grandson who keeps hoping his pipe dreams will come true. Yes," she said with a smile, "I do know about Cary's foolish dreams of building boats."

"They're not foolish."

"It's foolish from a business standpoint. He'll always be a plodder, not much of a student, not much of a businessman and certainly not capable of supervising the family fortune. You, on the other hand, will be. It's a great responsibility . . . family. Each great family is like a kingdom unto itself. Whether this one survives or not will rest solely on your shoulders some day. That means you, too, will have to make decisions that won't be popular, but will be best for everyone. Either you will have the strength and will to do it or you won't.

"Every decision you make now, every choice has an impact on the fate of this family. Remember that and you will do well," she advised. "It wasn't easy putting my husband into a home, but it had to be done and it was. Moaning about it won't help him or me," she said, sounding like she needed to convince herself more than me.

"I'll stop in to see him," I repeated.

"Do that, but don't come begging me to bring him home if that's what he asks you," she warned. "I will not allow it."

She looked like an alabaster statue set in the dining room chair. Her decision was unquestionable. I nodded, ate my supper in silence and eagerly retreated to my room to do my homework and leave the long, lonesome shadows she cast through the house.

The days and weeks went by. I devoted most of my time to my schoolwork, not only because that was what Grandma Olivia wanted, but because I truly enjoyed it. The dramatics teacher tried to talk me into trying out for the fall production, but I resisted. I wanted to give Cary and May all my free time. I was there when Cary began the cranberry harvest, and although I didn't play hooky, I was beside him right after school, sometimes bringing May home so he could be free to supervise the work.

Aunt Sara snapped out of her sorrow as best she could. She had spent so much of her adult life caring for Uncle Jacob, anticipating his needs and wants, it was hard for her to stop the routine, stop wondering what favorite food of his she would prepare each night. For a while she continued to wash and iron his clothes, under the guise that Cary might use them. Cary did try to wear some of his father's things, but he had trouble doing it. To take for himself Jacob's possessions, however few, was to admit, each time, that his father was truly, finally, gone.

When I came home from Aunt Sara's I occupied my time by writing letters to Alice Morgan in Sewell, telling her all about my mother. I thought Alice deserved to know since she was the one who had discovered Mommy's picture. Alice called after she had read my first letter. She consoled me and promised to come to Provincetown the first opportunity she had. I never heard from Mommy, of course, but I did call and speak to Holly and Billy a few times. Holly was very concerned about Kenneth and I promised to visit him as often as I could and give her a report.

Kenneth was much better than he had been when I had first returned from California, but he still hadn't started working on anything new. He spent more time than usual at his favorite local pub, and some days he fished or visited a friend in Boston. I felt like a spy, but a good spy since I was making my reports to Holly.

Another sore point around my new home was that Grandma Olivia refused to permit me to get my driver's license or take driver's education. She said the car was the downfall of young people today, and I, a budding debutante, should have men driving me around or use our chauffeur. She did allow me to have a bicycle and I was soon a regular sight along the sides of the Provincetown streets. Although it was quite a ride, I peddled my way out to Kenneth's occasionally on weekends.

One Saturday, I found him walking alone on the beach. He was dressed in his ragged jeans and a T-shirt and was barefoot. I caught up with him, but he didn't acknowledge my presence for quite a while. Instead, he just stared at the water, and when he finally did turn, I saw his eyes were bloodshot, as if had been crying. Or on another drinking binge.

"What's wrong, Kenneth?" I asked, holding my breath.

"Haven't you noticed anything different?" he asked, spreading his arms wide and gesturing across the beach, back toward his house.

"Different?" I gazed around and then it hit me. "Ulysses," I said.

"I buried him this morning."

"Oh Kenneth, no,"

"I woke up this morning, but he didn't. It was like him to die quietly. That dog was never a problem, even as a puppy. He was patient, undemanding, sensitive to my moods." He smiled. "Better than any woman I've known. No wonder they call them man's best friend. We were a team," he said, his voice catching. "I'll miss him."

"I'm sorry, Kenneth. I'll miss him, too."

"I know you will. He took right to you, as I recall," he said trying valiantly to smile. He took a deep breath and we walked along the beach together, the deep silence of sadness linking us during our somber thoughts. Finally, he paused and turned to me with a genuine smile.

"So, you're burning up the academic playing fields, I hear, and look like a shoe-in for class valedictorian."

"Who told you that?"

"Cary," he replied slyly.

"He's been here?"

"Often, lately. I've decided to hire him to build me that sailboat," he said.

"Really, Kenneth?"

"Really."

"That's wonderful. He must be so excited!"

"He's got some good ideas. In his own way, he's a very creative young man, and, he's crazy about you."

"I know," I said blushing.

"What's Her Highness think of it?"

"Forbids the thought," I said.

"Hmm. What are you going to do? She rules with an iron hand," he warned. "And when she brings it down, she usually smothers the victim like an ant."

"She's hard, but we've come to a bit of a truce these days. She hasn't had much to complain about. I'm doing well in school. I'm Miss Burton's favorite pupil, and I listen attentively to Grandma Olivia's nightly lectures about people, responsibility, the importance of family, family, family," I added in a pretend deep voice. Kenneth laughed.

"You little devil. You're humoring her to death, aren't you?" he asked.

"I'm being . . . diplomatic," I said and he laughed harder. We heard a horn and turned to see Cary bouncing down the beach road in his truck.

"Here comes my sailboat engineer," Kenneth said. "I wonder if he's come to see me about it or if there's been some diplomatic maneuvering here for a rendezvous," he teased. My cheeks turned crimson. He laughed and we started toward the house.

"Cary Logan," I cried as we approached him, "why didn't you tell me about the sailboat you're building for Kenneth?" I stood with my hands on my hips. Cary looked at Kenneth, who wore a wide grin.

"I wanted it to be a surprise," he said, shifting the rolled up papers he carried under his arm. "I've got the plans completed, Kenneth," he said.

"All right. Let's spread them out on the table in the studio and study them. I bought some Portuguese bread this morning and your favorite cheese, Melody," he told me.

"Is that a hint to make everyone a sandwich?" I asked suspiciously.

"Now I see," Kenneth said to Cary, "that she is just as quick as you said she was."

Cary roared as the two of them went in to the studio. I joined them fifteen minutes later with our sandwiches and some lemonade. Cary's sailboat plans were on the table and I thought they looked very impressive and professional.

"It looks huge," I remarked.

"Six thousand eight hundred thirty-four pounds with a twenty-nine-and-a-half-foot deck. The cabin will hold up to six people comfortably," Cary said. "You see it has a relatively long waterline, which gives us optimal volume and at the same time favors speed. This double-chine hull with a flat-bottom plate gets us quick immersion of the upper—"

"Cary, you're losing her," Kenneth gently pointed out.

"What? Oh. Sorry," he said.

"I think you might safely say he's got a passion for this," Kenneth remarked.

"It looks . . . beautiful," I said lamely.

"Well I'm sure you can understand this," Cary said, refusing to give up on me. "It's very roomy and has a lot of storage space. Starting at the bow here, there is a chain locker followed by a double berth. There's a twenty-five gallon fresh water tank, storage under the seats, and behind the seats there are lockers and a bookcase. Here's the folding table hinged on the center board case. The hull is built upside down on a framework made from the bulkheads. No temporary molds means no waste."

"Sold," Kenneth said. "Now, can we please eat?"

Cary looked up from the plans, first at Kenneth and then at me and then he smiled.

"Sure," he said. "I'm starving."

Later, when we were alone on the beach, I pretended to be still upset that he had kept all this a secret.

"I just wanted to surprise you," he protested. "Besides," he added sotto voce, "I couldn't be sure Kenneth was serious. You know how erratic he's been these days. I know he's serious now though. He's put the money up for the plans and given me the green light to start. I'll be building the boat here," he said.

"What about the lobster business?"

"I'm making a deal with Roy Patterson, giving him more responsibility and more of the income. I talked it over with Ma, but she doesn't really understand what I'm trying to do and naturally she's afraid for us. I hope I'm doing the right thing," he added. "I just feel like this is my chance. Once I build one boat and others see it . . ."

"You'll do well, Cary. I'm sure you will."

He nodded with a weak smile.

"I hope so. I know if Dad were alive, he'd be furious about it."

"He never wanted to do anything differently, Cary. It wasn't in him to change, but you're creative and you heard Kenneth say you have a passion for it. If anyone knows about being passionate over something creative, it's Kenneth. In the end you'll make us all proud of you."

"I hope, but for the time being, maybe it would be better if you didn't mention anything about it to Grandma Olivia," he said.

"I don't mention anything about you in front of her and she never asks me anything. It's part of the truce that's fallen between us these days," I said.

He smiled, grateful for that.

"Well, since I'll be here most of the time now, maybe you and I can see more of each other and—"

"I'll stop by as often as I can and bring May, too."

"Kenneth's going to Boston this weekend," Cary said quickly. "He told me it would be all right for me to use his place, if I want."

We stared at each other a moment.

"I can't get away overnight, Cary. She would have the dogs at my heels," I said.

"It doesn't have to be overnight, but we could have dinner here and just for one day maybe, feel like we were . . . you know . . . together."

I thought about it. Somehow, lying to Grandma Olivia didn't seem to be such a bad thing.

"I have an idea. I'll talk to Theresa tomorrow. She'll cover for me," I promised. Cary brightened with hope and we kissed. The wind swept through our hair and the ocean spray sprinkled our faces. It made me feel fresh and alive.

Cary insisted I put my bike in the back of his truck so he could drive me most of the way home. I rode the last mile and a half on my bike. When I arrived, I saw that Judge Childs was visiting with Grandma Olivia. He had been coming over more oft n since Grandpa Samuel had been taken to the home. The two of them usually spent their time sipping sherry in the gazebo. Often, the Judge stayed for dinner.

I hadn't yet paid him the visit he expected. I didn't want to talk about Mommy. It was too painful to think about her. Since I had returned from California, she hadn't phoned or written. It was still difficult to accept the fact that she wanted to be out of my life forever. Sometimes I would walk past the cemetery and see the stone with her name on it. Once, I even stopped to pay my respects to the poor anonymous soul who had been made to take Mommy's coffin and grave. In my secret-put-away heart, I mourned for her the way I mourned for myself, imagining her wishing to be with her own people, whoever and wherever they might be.

Maybe she was, I thought. Maybe being next to the bones of your loved ones wasn't what mattered. Perhaps there was something stronger that bound us after death, some linking of the soul that would someday find me greeting Papa George, my stepdaddy and whoever else I loved and who loved me.

The week after I met Cary at Kenneth's I talked to Theresa in the cafeteria during lunch, planning a way for me to spend most of the following Saturday and Saturday night with Cary at Kenneth's house. With midterms coming up, it was easy to claim we would be studying together. What I wasn't prepared for was Grandma Olivia's reaction to my choice of friends. The way she glared at me when I told my story made me feel she had seen right through the subterfuge, but her irritation was drawn from a more polluted well.

"Patterson? Is that the same Patterson who works for Cary? The Brava?"

"Yes, her father is Roy Patterson."

"That's the best you can do? The best friendship you can form at school? What about the Rudolph's daughter or Mark and Carol Parker's daughter? Isn't Betty Hargate, the accountant's daughter, in your class also?"

"I don't get along as well with those girls and they are nowhere near the student Theresa is, despite her being what you call a Brava. I not ashamed of my friendship with her; I'm proud of it."

"I see I'm not getting you out of this town fast enough," she replied.

"I'm not moving in with the Pattersons, Grandma Olivia. I'm merely preparing study sheets. You want me to be the valedictorian, don't you?"

She raised her eyebrows, considering.

"There's no mother in that house."

"Her father will be home and you know he's a nice man, a hardworking man."

"You intend to eat dinner with them?" she asked, as if I were going to eat with Aborigines.

"I ate there often last year," I said, "before I realized I was so important."

"Don't be impudent. Very well," she said after another thoughtful pause, "Raymond will take you and pick you up promptly at nine P.M." .

"It's Saturday night!" I protested.

"Ten then," she said relenting a bit.

"No one else in my class lives under such strict rules," I complained.

"No one else has your destiny and responsibility," she replied dryly. "Let's not have these silly discussions."

I retreated, feeling I had won as much as I could from her at the moment. When I told Cary, he was ecstatic.

"I'll bring some lobsters and clams for dinner," he said. "We'll have May with us for a while, but I'll take her home in the afternoon."

"That's fine, Cary."

"She wants to know if she can bike out to Kenneth's with you one day. I explained how dangerous it is for her to go on the road by herself. She can't hear cars and trucks."

"I'll come by and get her one day. We'll be all right."

"It'll be a real treat for her," he said. "I haven't been able to do much for her these days and with Ma the way she is . . ."

"It's no problem, Cary. I want to do it," I assured him.

The next day Theresa and I made our final plans at school. The first time I met Theresa I thought she was a very serious girl, pretty but dour to the point of being angry. Since I was new in school, the principal asked her to show me around. We got off to a bad start because she assumed I would look down on her the way other so-called blue bloods did.

I thought she was one of the prettiest girls in the school, with her caramel complexion, black pearl eyes and ebony hair. After she realized I wasn't like the others, she permitted me to get closer to her and we quickly became good friends.

Theresa enjoyed the idea that we were conspiring against my grandmother. She thought of her just as most others did, The Iron Lady, Queen of Snob Hill.

"If she calls for you on the phone, I'll have my brother say we went to the library. Don't worry about my father. He won't ask questions. Since my mother died, he treats me like an adult. Are you going to spend the whole night with Cary?" she asked, her eyes bright with interest.

"No, I have to be back at your house before ten. That's when Grandma Olivia is sending Raymond to pick me up."

"Bummer," she moaned for me. "But, at least you'll have some time alone."

"Theresa Patterson, just hear you," I teased and we laughed. Everyone in the cafeteria gazed at us with jealousy, wondering what delicious secret we shared. Our sealed lips only stirred their curiosity more.

When Saturday came, I was so nervous I was positive Grandma Olivia would become suspicious, but she was preoccupied with a dinner party she was having for Congressman Dunlap and two of his legal aides. The only thing she said that put butterflies in my stomach was that she was sorry I wasn't going to be at the dinner.

"It's important for you to meet important people now," she declared. I thought she would insist I attend the dinner, but she hesitated and added, "but being named class valedictorian is important too. You'll be the first Logan to do so."

The tone of her voice was explicit: Don't fail to do it.

Shaking when I got into the limousine, I took deep breaths and tried to calm down all the way to Theresa's.

As soon as Raymond dropped me off and left, Theresa gave me her bike and I started for the beach. Cary and May were already there, Cary working on the boat. He looked like Adonis, shirtless, his muscles glimmering in the sunlight.

"I was afraid you weren't coming," he said as I walked Theresa's bike over the sandy part of the road. May came running to me. We hugged and I looked at Cary. Neither of us had to say much to each other; it was all in our eyes.

I spent most of the afternoon with May, walking along the beach, searching for shells, telling her about school. She wanted to know more about boys. If any girl needed a big sister, it was May. Aunt Sara wasn't very comfortable explaining things to her. Sex, love and romance embarrassed her. I was the one who had explained what a menstrual cycle was, what changes would happen to her body, what her feelings would be like. Once, we had a long talk about what it meant to fall in love and she told me about a classmate she liked, a boy who had kissed her. Apparently, since I had been away, she had learned much more from her girlfriends at school, for when she looked at Cary and me and the way we spoke, touched and looked at each other, she smiled at us knowingly.

While Cary was bringing May home, I prepared our dinner and set the table. Constantly aware of my curfew, we savored the hours and minutes we had. I waited in front of the beach house, watching the twilight flood the sky with its rosy farewell to the day, flaming the clouds crimson, streaking violet shot through with saffron. Cary returned in the quickest time ever, his truck bouncing hard over the beach ruts.

"Everything's almost ready," I said when he hopped out of his truck and followed me into the house.

"Looks great," he said, but his eyes never left my face. Every time I turned, every time I lifted my gaze from the pots and dishes, I found him staring at me hungrily. My body filled with an ache, a hunger for his lips and his touch. Perhaps it was because we were so far from

259

anyone, alone, in a domestic setting, behaving like married people, whatever the reason, I never felt more desire and passion for him than I did that night. We could barely eat, neither of us saying very much.

Cary leaped out of his seat at the end of the meal to help me clean up. Everything we did seemed designed to keep us under control. It was as if we both understood that the minute we were free of any other distraction, the moment we turned to each other, we would be in danger of consuming each other. Finally, I dried the last dish.

He stood back, gazing at me.

"Melody," he said softly and held out his hand. I took it and he led me out to the guest bedroom. Next to the bed, we kissed and held each other tightly. "I love you," he said.

I took a deep breath, closed my eyes and nodded.

"I love you, too, Cary. Very much."

I kept my eyes closed as his fingers undid the buttons of my blouse. In fact, I stood there, unmoving, waiting as he peeled my blouse down my arms, undid my skirt and drew it below my knees, lifting my leg gently for me to step out of it. Then he kissed my shoulders, my neck and undid my bra, drawing it from me while at the same time, he brought his lips to my nipples and nudged my breasts with his cheeks. My heart pounded hot blood through my body. When his hands lifted from my breasts or my shoulders, I cried out for their return.

Gently, almost in inches, he slipped my panties off. Naked, I stood before him, my eyes locked on his.

"Kenneth couldn't come close to portraying your beauty," he said. "Even if he worked every day for the rest of his life."

I smiled and he undressed himself. Moments later, we were in bed, embracing, moving our arms, our legs, turning ourselves to each other, drawing each other deeper and deeper into each other with every kiss, every touch.

"Are you ready, Cary?" I asked, breathing my last bit

of caution before my thundering heart closed down all avenues of thought and left me longing only for him inside me, making us feel like one.

"Yes," he said with a smile. "Protected."

I felt myself being drawn up higher and higher, dangled above the earth, exquisitely tormented by the danger and the sense of abandon. Our moans mingled until each was indistinguishable from the other. I dug my fingers into his shoulders to hold on and to keep him close. We came at each other like the love-starved people we were; desperate for a loving touch, a longing word.

When it was over, we collapsed in a delightful exhaustion, both gasping for breath, neither able to speak. I took his hand and put it over my heart.

"Feel this pounding," I said, shakily. "It's scary, but wonderful."

"Mine's the same way."

"If we died here together, Grandma Olivia would be very upset," I said and he laughed.

"She'd have everyone involved sworn to secrecy and then she'd have us buried at sea."

"But she wouldn't cancel her dinner party that night," I added.

He laughed and turned to embrace me. We lay there, holding each other, whispering sweet promises, dreaming, constructing our wonderful fantasies, weaving a cocoon of dreams tightly around ourselves. After a while, we stopped and dozed, which almost proved fatal, for when my eyes snapped open, it was nearly nine-thirty.

"Cary!"

I sat up, shaking him to wake him.

"Whaa . . ."

"Hurry, get dressed. Raymond will be at Theresa's before you get me back!"

We both leaped off of the bed and threw on our clothes. We got into the truck and for a few frantic beats it wouldn't start. The engine groaned and groaned.

"Cary!"

"It's okay. Just give me a second," he said. He hopped out and opened the hood, fidgeting.

"Hurry, Cary. She'll make so much trouble for you and your mother if she finds out about us."

He jiggled wires near the battery and tried again, and, thankfully, this time the engine started with a sputter. Then we shot off, bouncing so hard over the beach road, my head nearly hit the roof of the truck cab. Once on the street, he burned rubber until we arrived at Theresa's, just minutes before Raymond and the limousine. I didn't even have a chance to kiss Cary good night. Instead, I jumped out and ran to the house, where Theresa was waiting anxiously.

"You're cutting it kind of close, aren't you?" she remarked with a smile.

"We feel asleep," I whispered.

"No calls, at least."

Moments later, we saw the limousine pull up. I thanked her and rushed out, promising to call her in the morning.

Grandma Olivia's dinner party was still going when I arrived. Her guests were in the parlor talking. I was afraid of what I looked like since I hadn't had time to check my hair or straighten my clothes, but I knew if I didn't stop to say hello, she would be furious. I paused in the doorway.

"Good evening, Grandma," I said.

"Well, did you study hard?"

"Yes, Grandma."

"Good. My granddaughter is the prime valedictorian candidate this year."

Everyone nodded with appreciation.

"Melody, you have already met Congressman Dunlap and his wife."

"Yes, how do you do, Congressman, Mrs. Dunlap," I said, stepping forward. They nodded, smiled and Grandma Olivia looked pleased.

"This is Mr. and Mrs. Steiner and Mr. and Mrs.

262

Becker," she added. I smiled and greeted the other couples. Then I quickly excused myself and hurried up the stairs.

I washed and got into bed, my fatigue now settling into my body firmly. Despite that, I felt wonderful. When I closed my eyes, I saw Cary's loving face before me and imagined his lips on mine again and again. Across the dunes he was most likely in his attic hideaway, thinking about me, gazing out at the same ocean I saw through my window, the water dazzling under the starlight, each whitecap looking like a string of pearls cast back at the shore.

Below me, the voices grew softer until they drifted out of my hearing and I was left with nothing but my own thoughts, whispering promises, counting dreams that took me softly into sleep.

Over the next month, Cary and I were able to meet secretly twice more, each time as wonderful as the time before. His progress with Kenneth's boat continued and it soon began to take shape. Kenneth brought some friends out to see Cary's work and one of them seriously considered hiring him to do a custom sailboat for him as well.

One early spring afternoon after I picked up May and we both peddled out to Kenneth's, I heard a small bark and saw the most beautiful golden retriever puppy poke its head out of the front door of the beach house. May and I ran to pick him up.

"I'm calling him Prometheus," Kenneth announced. "I figure I'll stay with mythological names."

"He's beautiful, Kenneth."

"I thought you'd like him."

May held him and he licked her face, making her laugh.

"She's growing up, too," Kenneth said. "Starting to look like a young lady."

"I know."

"She'll need you around more," Kenneth warned. "Big sister stuff."

263

"She already has," I said. His eyes widened.

"Oh? Well, um, that's great that she has you to confide in. I have a second surprise for you," he declared, obviously eager to change the subject. "I'm putting *Neptune* on display . . . finally. We're going to have a showing at the gallery and a pretty big party afterward."

"Where?"

"I suppose this is the third surprise," he said. My heart began to thump. "Your grandfather's house."

"Judge Child's house? Really? Kenneth that's wonderful!"

"He volunteered our home when he heard about the opening at the gallery and I decided, why not? He couldn't even begin to pay me what he owes me. If I don't take what I can, my brother and sister will anyway," he said.

I didn't like his cynicism and he saw it in my face.

"I don't have to love him to let him do things for me, do I?"

"Yes, you do, Kenneth. You have to love him. He's your father, no matter what," I lectured.

"My father . . . died a long time ago in the aftermath of a confession. This stranger with the same name and resemblance is just some old, rich man," he insisted. "Anyway, I'm not doing it for myself. I'm doing it for *Neptune's Daughter*. I think that has a certain sense of irony, don't you? Sure you do," he said before I could reply. "You're one of the brightest young women I've known, Melody. You understand much more than you pretend to understand."

"But Kenneth—"

"Let it be, Melody," he said. "Just let it be."

He smiled at May cuddling Prometheus. Then he looked toward the boat and Cary.

"We'll all take a maiden voyage in a month and celebrate the birth of something very beautiful. Right?" he asked me.

"Sure, Kenneth," I said. "Maybe you should invite

Holly to the opening," I suggested. I wanted him to have someone at his side.

"I already did," he said.

"And she's coming? That's wonderful. I can't wait to see her again."

"I'm not saying she's coming. She still has to check her chart first and be sure it's safe," he teased, his eyes sparkling with mischief.

We watched May rush out to show Prometheus to Cary and then Kenneth looked at me in the strangest way. I tilted my head because of the way he was staring and the way a fleeting shaft of sorrow crossed his face.

"What's wrong, Kenneth?"

"Just for a second, with that soft smile on your face, your eyes caught in the sunlight, you reminded me of Haille when she was not much older than you. It was as if . . . as if time had gone backwards, as if nothing terrible had happened yet.

"Hold on to these moments, Melody. Hold on to them desperately for as long as you can.

"Too soon," he said, his eyes darkening, "too soon the winds of jealousy come barreling down and sweep it all out to sea.

"I hope," he concluded gazing at Cary and May, "fate isn't teasing you as she did me."

He turned and went back inside, leaving me shivering with anxiety. Kenneth had made it an awesomely fearsome thing to even think beyond tomorrow. I was filled with so many emotions, I thought I would simply explode and fly off in that wind he warned me might come.

Like a reader terrified of turning the page, I stepped away from the house and walked toward Cary to tell him the news.

15
&

The Unveiling

As the date of Kenneth's opening for *Neptune's Daughter* drew closer, the excitement in Provincetown built. National art magazines sent writers and photographers. Reporters from newspapers in New York City, Boston and even as far away as Washington, D.C., and Chicago arrived to do interviews and get pictures. An invitation to the gala affair following the display at the Mariner's Gallery was highly prized. Kenneth told me that since I was now an expert in etiquette and formalities, I would have to help him with the design and wording for the invitations. The gallery owner provided us with a select list of people to invite, claiming these were the people who had invested in art or who carried influence in the community.

Two days before the opening and party, Kenneth called and asked me to accompany him to the judge's house, where we would meet with the caterers.

"I'm not good at these things," he claimed. "I need the feminine viewpoint."

I knew he was just nervous about going to his father's

home. From what I understood, he hadn't been there for years. The Judge was nervous about it, too. That was something Grandma Olivia revealed.

"This has the makings of a wonderful event," she told me, "but we have to be sure there will be no unpleasantness and certainly nothing that would feed the insatiable appetites of the gossipmongers. I know you've spent an inordinate amount of time at Kenneth's house and although I haven't seen it yet, I know and everyone else will know that you were the model for the work.

"I'm depending on you to play a role in mitigating any difficult feelings. In other words," she said with a sharp smirk, "make sure Kenneth behaves himself. See if you can get him to dress properly and do something with that moss on his face he calls a beard and that mop he calls his hair."

"Artists aren't exactly businesspeople, Grandma Olivia. The public understands Kenneth."

"Not this public," she assured me. "Actually," she revealed in a rather rare soft moment, "I'm more worried about the Judge. He hasn't slept a night since he volunteered to host the gala celebration. I told him it was a foolish gesture, but he insisted."

"Everything will work out just fine," I said.

She nodded, studying me.

"You have grown and matured quite a bit since you've been living here. I will tell you that I have heard only good things about you from the school officials, and people admire the way you look after my handicapped granddaughter. I feel validated for my faith in you and your potential. Don't do anything to diminish that faith," she added in her usual threatening tone.

"Thank you, I think," I replied and she almost smiled.

"You have been to visit my sister and have seen Samuel this week?" she asked.

"Yes." I wondered if she also knew Cary had driven me there. If she did, she didn't mention it. "They're both about the same. No improvement. Grandpa Samuel simply sits and stares most of the time, barely acknowledging I'm there."

"There won't be any improvement," she predicted. "That's not a place to go for improvement. It's where you go to wait. God's waiting room," she muttered. "I imagine you'll have me put there someday, too. If I need to be, don't hesitate," she advised. "Hopefully, that won't be for a while, but when my time comes, it comes," she concluded.

For the gala Grandma Olivia suggested I wear the dress Dorothy Livingston had bought me in Beverly Hills. All these months she never mentioned the two expensive outfits hanging in my closet, but I knew she was aware of them.

"There's no point in letting something like that go to waste. If someone was foolish enough to spend that sort of money, well . . . take advantage of it. I'd like to see you in it first, of course," she added.

I nodded and ran upstairs to put it on. She scrutinized me for a few moments and nodded.

"Suitable," she declared, "for such an occasion. You are someone with position in this community now. You should look the part. There will be a number of young men from quality families attending, too. I hope you make acquaintances with some of these people. Of course, I'll see to it that you are introduced properly. What are you going to do with your hair?"

"My hair?"

"I can have my beautician come over and do something special for you, if you'd like."

"No, I think I'll just wear it down. Maybe just trim my bangs. I can do that myself."

"If you insist," she said. "I have a ruby and sapphire necklace that would go with that dress," she added. "It was my mother's."

"Really? Thank you," I said, truly honored that she would entrust me with such a gift, even for just one night.

I told Kenneth about Grandma Olivia's new and

improved persona when he picked me up to go to Judge Childs's. I thought he would laugh and make his quips about the Queen Lady or something, but he was very distracted by his own thoughts and anxiety. I talked mostly to keep from riding in dead silence.

When we turned up the road that led to the Judge's house, Kenneth almost turned the car around.

"This is a mistake," he muttered. "I shouldn't have agreed to it. All we needed was a reception at the gallery."

"Please, Kenneth. You know everyone is looking forward to a big party. We'll make sure it's fun."

"Fun," he said as if that were a dirty word.

The Judge's house came into view. I remembered the first time I had been here, how much more impressed with it I was than with Grandma Olivia's home. The Judge's three-story Adam Colonial had been restored in a Wedgwood blue cladding and had a semicircular entry porch. What made it even more unique was its large octagonal cupola. There was an elaborately decorated frieze above all the front windows.

The driveway brought us to a circle where there was a whirl of activity. An army of groundspeople were everywhere pruning and trimming, cleaning fountains and walkways, washing windows, planting new flowers in the rock gardens. When we entered the circular drive, I could see the huge party tent, in front of which the caterers were discussing their setup with Judge Childs. Beside him was his butler, Morton. Everyone turned to look our way.

Kenneth just sat in the jeep staring at the front entrance of the house.

"It must have been very nice growing up here, Kenneth."

"Yes, it was," he said and stepped out of the jeep.

Morton approached as quickly as he could to greet us.

"Why hello there, Mr. Kenneth. It's good to see you, good to see you," he said reaching for Kenneth's hand before Kenneth lifted it. He shook it vigorously and gazed at me. His face was bright with happiness. "And you too, Miss Melody. You're looking fine. Isn't this going to be a celebration. The Judge was up an hour earlier than usual this morning. Neither of us could sleep just thinking about all the festivities. It's good you're here, Mr. Kenneth. Oh, it's a fine, beautiful day, isn't it?"

He stood there, hoping for some softening in Kenneth's face, some sign that the war between father and son had ended.

"Hello Morton. It's good to see you, too," Kenneth said finally offering him a smile. "You know, Morton here was just as responsible for my upbringing as my mother and father," Kenneth said.

"Oh go on with you, Mr. Kenneth. I didn't do much."

"No, just carted us kids around everywhere, watched over us, played with us. You taught me how to swing a baseball bat, didn't you, Morton? Morton could have been a pro," he told me.

"Oh no, Miss Melody. That's not true. I wasn't that good."

"He was great."

"He's awful excited, the Judge," Morton said slapping his hands together. "You want me to get you two something? Maybe a lemonade or coffee or—"

"No, nothing, Morton. I want to make this quick," Kenneth said. Morton nodded.

"Well, I'll be around if you need something."

"You always were," Kenneth said. "It's good to see you, Morton," Kenneth added, warming slightly. Morton's eyes watered.

"And good to see you. He talks about you all the time, Mr. Kenneth. There isn't a day that goes by."

"Okay," Kenneth said, turning to me. "Let's do this."

I followed and we crossed the lawn toward the caterers and Judge Childs.

"Hello," the Judge said, his eyes on Kenneth. Kenneth barely acknowledged him with a small nod.

"I haven't got much time for this," he said quickly.

"Oh. Well, let's get right to it, then. James will tell us

the menu and how he wants to set up the serving tables. He suggests we have tables inside and outside the tent, but all the food inside. Is that right, James?"

The short, neatly groomed man smiled.

"Yes, Judge Childs. I think that would work. I will have three tables for the entrées: lobster, shrimp, prime roast and duckling, flounder and bass. We will have two long tables for the salads and vegetables and of course, three Viennese desert tables. I suggest we keep the bar outside the tent. It always makes it less complicated when the liquid refreshment is away from the food," he added. "We will, however, have staff bringing glasses of champagne to everyone."

"How's that menu sound?" the Judge asked. Kenneth was staring at the dock, a distracted expression on his face.

"Fine with me," he muttered.

"Now to the decorations," James resumed. "I thought a bouquet of our emperor tulips, jonquils and some daffodils on every table. I would like to suggest a doorway of roses as an entrace to the tent and—"

"This isn't a wedding," Kenneth snapped. He glanced at me for confirmation.

"I think just some flowers on the tables is enough," I said. James nodded with disappointment.

"I didn't know what to do about music," the Judge said. "James here suggested a trio. I thought we could set up a small stage for them over there," he pointed just to the right of the tent. "I'll get one of those portable dance floors and—"

"We don't need people dancing," Kenneth said.

"No? Okay. We'll just have some music. I just thought . . . but if you think that's a bit much."

"The whole thing's a bit much," Kenneth said and walked toward the dock.

Everyone watched him in silence.

"He's just a little nervous about the showing," I explained.

"Of course," the Judge said. "Well then, James can

show us the colors he chose for the tablecloths and napkins."

"They're right in here," he said, gesturing just inside the tent. I followed and looked over his suggestions for interior decorations with crepe paper, balloons and tinsel. I thought it was all spectacular. The Judge was pleased.

"I'll have valet parking, of course. Let's just hope for good weather. Well now, what's left to do?" he questioned, his eyes gazing after Kenneth.

The caterer rattled off a half dozen things, but the Judge had lost interest.

"It might not be a bad idea for you two to talk before all this," I suggested softly. He glanced at me and nodded.

"Yes, I suppose you are right."

He looked tired, old and unsure of himself. Kenneth stood on the dock looking out at the ocean.

"Let me speak with him first," I said. The Judge looked relieved. I hurried over the lawn and joined Kenneth.

"This is stupid," he said. "Half of these people attending think Art's short for Arthur."

I laughed.

"It'll be nice, Kenneth. Let him make a big deal over you. He wants to do it out of pride."

"Out of guilt," he corrected.

"Yes, maybe guilt, too, but at least he cares, feels remorse. My mother shakes off guilt the way you would shake off a fly."

He turned his eyes to me and smiled.

"You feel sorry for him, don't you?"

"Yes," I said.

He shook his head.

"Don't you understand Haille is the way she is because of what he did?"

"No. Look at what she did to me," I replied. "You don't see me turning into my mother."

His smile softened and widened.

272

"Talk to him, Kenneth. Just make a little peace between you. It will be good for you as well as him."

He grimaced skeptically.

"You said *Neptune's Daughter* was your greatest work, the work you're most proud of. Let it be a happy time then, from beginning to end."

"Melody, Melody, what am I going to do with you? Despite everything, you keep pushing the gray skies away, searching for that rainbow."

"Help me find it, Kenneth," I replied, my eyes meeting his gaze firmly. He nodded, sighed, gazing at the water and then turned back toward the house. "Come on," he said.

"Come on?"

"You're his granddaughter. You belong in every family discussion now. No more false pretenses among us. That's my only demand," he said. I trailed beside him as he walked toward the house, his home, a place he hadn't been for years, but a place that held all his childhood memories and the memories of his mother.

We entered and he gave me a tour.

"He's kept it pretty much as I remembered it," Kenneth said. He laughed. "My mother and her antiques. Some of these things are worth a lot of money though."

We went upstairs and he showed me what used to be his room. He stood there for a long time, a sad smile on his face. When we descended again, the Judge was standing in the doorway of his office.

"Well," he said, looking from Kenneth to me. "This looks like it's going to be the event of the year, huh? I haven't seen your piece, Kenneth, but Laurence Baker told me it's wonderful. Anybody make a preliminary offer yet? If not, I'd like to make an offer."

"It's not for sale," Kenneth said.

"What?"

"I'm thinking of donating it to the museum after the showing."

The Judge's mouth dropped open. "Why, that's a

mighty fine idea, Kenneth. Mighty fine," he said when he'd finally recovered.

"Well, if you *were* going to sell it, I'd buy it myself," I said, wishing Kenneth would accept money for his creation.

They both looked at me and then Kenneth laughed. The Judge's face broke into a smile, too.

"I bet she would," he said.

"She would," Kenneth agreed. At least they were agreeing on something.

"I'm glad we're having the party here, Ken. Your mother would be very proud," the Judge said. "Oh, that reminds me," he added quickly. "I found something the other day and thought you'd want to have it." He turned and went into the office. We followed. He handed Kenneth a leather picture frame in which there was a photo of his mother and him when he was no more than five or six years old.

"He had that serious, artistic look even back then, didn't he?" the Judge asked me.

"He sure looks deep in thought," I replied.

"I remember when Louise bought that frame. She considered it a prime find. That design's all hand-engraved or something," he continued as Kenneth continued to stare at the picture of himself and his mother. The Judge found it necessary to keep talking. "I think it was somewhere down in Buzzard's Bay. She would walk into those tiny stores and dig around like some miner looking for gold and come out with the craziest stuff sometimes. When she found that frame, she said she had just the picture to put in it."

"Thanks," Kenneth said.

"Oh, sure, sure. So, how have things been otherwise?" the Judge asked.

"Otherwise?" Kenneth's mouth turned in at the corners.

"I mean . . ." The Judge looked at me.

"Whatever you have to say, she can hear it, too. She is your granddaughter," Kenneth said.

"Yes, she is," the Judge said nodding, "and I must say I'm proud of her."

"Even though it's a deep, dark secret?" Kenneth taunted. The Judge's eyes grew smaller. He blew some air between his lips and lowered himself slowly to the leather settee, gazing down at the floor like a man who had just received some very bad news.

"There's no sense in my apologizing to you, Kenneth. I've done that a hundred times and you won't hear it. Anyway, I don't expect you to forgive me for something I can't forgive myself. But," he said raising his eyes to Kenneth, "none of it has stopped me from loving you, son. I'm proud of you and what you've done. All I hope is that you can come to hate me a little less. That's all," he concluded with a deep sigh.

Kenneth turned away for a moment.

"You betrayed us, you know, all of us."

"Yes, I did," the Judge confessed. "I was a weak man; she was a beautiful and very desirable woman. It's no excuse; it's just an explanation," he followed quickly.

"You've spent most of your life sitting in judgment on people. Who sat in judgment of you?"

"You did, son, and the price I paid was too much. If I could change things, I would."

Kenneth didn't look convinced.

"Really, I would. I would sooner die than take away your happiness. I wanted only the best for you. None of this has had any meaning to me since your mother's death and . . . since all of you children left." He looked at me. "It's sort of a miracle that Melody has come back to us."

Kenneth glanced at me and then he nodded.

"Yes, it is."

"And it just pleases me to all get out that she and you have taken to each other."

"She's a pest," Kenneth teased.

I smiled through my teary eyes.

"Talented, playing that fiddle, too. You're going to play something for us at the party, aren't you, Melody?"

"What? No, I—"

"Of course she is," Kenneth said eying me. "It's part of our deal."

"It is?" I asked worriedly.

"Well good," the Judge said standing again. He seemed to have trouble getting to his feet, swallowing a groan and forcing a smile. "I guess I'll get back out there and see what that dandified fellow's got planned for me. Wants to string pink roses up the driveway next," he said and Kenneth laughed. Then, as if remembering himself, Kenneth stopped and turned toward the doorway. He paused in it, looked down at the picture of himself and his mother, and gazed back at the Judge.

"Thanks for this."

"Sure."

"We gotta go," he said.

"Yes, it looks like I have some unexpected practicing to do," I quipped and Kenneth laughed.

The Judge followed us to the front door.

"I don't have to say good luck. I know everyone's going to be impressed," he declared. Kenneth nodded, and I could tell he wanted to say "Thank you."

When I looked at the Judge, I saw his eyes were full of tears. He bit down on his lip, smiled at me and went back inside.

"I think he's really sorry, Kenneth."

"Maybe," he relented. We got into the jeep and he sat there for a while, watching his father come out of the house, wave to us and walk slowly toward the caterers.

"He was a very handsome man, always distinguished, gentlemanly. He looked just like a judge. When I was a little boy, I thought he had the power to decide life and death. Don't put your faith completely in anyone, Melody. Reserve some skepticism. It's good insurance. Okay," he said smiling at me. "We'll have a good time. If the Queen will grant you leave, you're invited to dinner tonight. Holly will be here any minute."

"She will? Oh great! Of course I can come. Grandma

Olivia wants me to be a good influence on you, get you to look more like—"

"A businessman, I know. I might put on a clean pair of pants and socks," he said and we both laughed.

Holly, I thought. I couldn't wait to see her again.

Holly came laden with gifts for us: charms and crystals, astrological charts, new earrings for me and a bracelet for Kenneth. After dinner she and I took a long walk alone on the beach and talked about my trip to California.

"Naturally, my sister turned everything around, blamed me for sending such a young, impressionable girl to Los Angeles. Philip said it wasn't surprising," she said with a short laugh.

"Oh I hope I didn't make any trouble for you," I said.

"This isn't a new argument. My sister and her husband formed their opinions of me long ago. Anyway, Billy wanted me to be sure to give you his best wishes and love. He was touched by you."

"And I by him. I thought about him and the things he told me many times while I was in Hollywood."

"Your mother didn't have the slightest—"

"She's like someone under a spell, Holly. If I had known as much before, I would never have gone. I sometimes stop at the graveyard and pretend it's her buried there. She might as well be," I added.

She smiled softly and paused to take a deep breath of the fresh ocean air.

"Cleans out my brain," she said. "Well, I see Cary has won over Kenneth, building that boat." She nodded toward the finished hull. "It looks like it's going to be very impressive."

"He's got his whole heart in it," I said, my own heart swelling with pride.

"Not his whole heart. There's some big part of it here," she said, pointing to my chest. I laughed.

"Tell me about Kenneth," she said after a moment.

"He looks like he's in some state of transition, hovering. His chart indicates he's about to change direction."

I told her about the meeting with his father and the quasi cease-fire.

"They're both getting older. It's time for them to settle things," she said, then turned thoughtful. "Does he talk about me much?"

"Oh you're always in his thoughts," I said. "He often says, 'That's something Holly put in your head,' or 'Holly would have a lot to say about that.'"

"Really?" She smiled. "I like it here. I've been thinking about leaving New York."

"And Billy?"

"I'm thinking about giving him the shop. He'd never leave New York."

"Where will you live?" I asked.

"We'll see," she said flashing a smile at me. "I'm about to discover if I can read my own future," she added. "I've got some strong indications." She beamed and looked back at the house.

"I'd better get home," I said, uncertain if I should question her more. "We all have a big day tomorrow and thanks to Kenneth, I have to play my fiddle."

"That's wonderful. Yes, it will be a big day." She took my hand and we ran over the sand dune in our bare feet, laughing, the stars glittering above us, the ocean smooth and gentle and full of promises. It was good to be happy again, to be full of hope.

The next day, people showed up nearly a half hour early to be the first to get into the gallery. Grandma Olivia put on one of her finest dresses, and wore her string of pearls, her diamond bracelets and gold rings. When she appeared in the foyer, she did indeed look like a queen. Judge Childs came by for us, and in his dark blue suit he looked as handsome as I had ever seen him.

"I tried to get Grant and Lillian to come," he said referring to his other children, "but they were both too busy with their own lives. It's a sad thing when families grow apart," he declared, which was something Grandma Olivia seconded heartedly.

"Once you lose the ties that bind, you drift in the wind," she said. She looked at me after most of her deep pronouncements these days, making sure I took note.

Cary, Aunt Sara and May, all dressed up, were waiting outside the gallery when we drove into the adjoining parking lot. Cary looked very handsome in his suit and tie and May, growing like summer corn, was already over five feet one. Even Aunt Sara had put on something bright and cheery and had dabbed on some makeup and lipstick.

"They're just about to open the doors," Cary said as I got out of the Judge's vehicle. "Those people over there are reporters," he added, nodding toward a small crowd gathered on the sidewalk.

"Ken here yet?" the Judge asked.

"No sir. Haven't seen him."

"Be just like him not to show up," Grandma Olivia muttered under her breath. "Well, Sara, how are you?"

"I'm fair to middling, Olivia. It seems like only yesterday," she said, her pale lips trembling.

"Well it's not only yesterday and we've all got to get on with our lives. This is a very happy, wonderful occasion for the Judge. You shouldn't be here if you're not up to it," she said sharply.

Sara forced a smile.

"Oh, I'm fine. And May's very excited about it," she said, nodding at Grandma Olivia's granddaughter, whom she had yet to acknowledge.

"Tell her hello," she ordered and flashed a smile at May who smiled back and signed. Grandma Olivia didn't wait to find out what she said. She stepped forward with the Judge at her side. The gallery doors were opened and the people began to stream in, most greeting Grandma Olivia and the Judge before allowing them to pass through the crowd. Cary, Aunt Sara, May and I followed.

Neptune's Daughter stood in the center of the room,

covered with a sheet. The gallery owner, Laurence Baker, was a tall, lean man wearing a somber expression. The way he moved, gliding across the room, and his soft-spoken manner reminded me of an undertaker. His assistants, a man about twenty-four or -five and a woman who looked to be in her mid-thirties greeted people as well. There was some champagne already poured on long tables and some cold hors d'oeuvres alongside them. People went right for the free refreshments and wandered about the gallery looking at the other works of art while waiting for the unveiling.

"Good afternoon, Judge Childs, good afternoon," Laurence Baker said. "And Mrs. Logan. Thank you all for coming."

"Why wouldn't we come?" she snapped back at him.

"Oh, I just meant . . . it's nice to see you," he said and slipped over to another couple.

The gallery was soon full and Kenneth had not yet arrived. I was beginning to get butterflies in my stomach, thinking he might have decided not to appear. What would we do? How would the Judge handle it, and with the big party all set, the food, the music? I looked at Cary.

"When you saw him last, did he say anything about not coming here?" I asked him.

"He didn't say he wasn't, but he did tell me he wasn't happy about all the fuss."

"You don't think . . . was he drinking today?"

"No. Holly was there with him and they were just spending most of the day walking on the beach and talking. Well," he said with a tight smile, "maybe not just talking."

"You didn't spy on them, did you, Cary Logan?"

"No," he said indignantly. "I could just tell from the way they are acting that things are going well between them."

I was about to apologize when we heard the crowd raise the volume of its murmur and turned to see Kenneth and Holly drive up to the front of the gallery in her tie-dyed car. Kenneth had put on a sports jacket, but he wore an old pair of dungarees and a pair of moccasins without socks. His shirt was opened at the collar.

Holly wore one of her long dresses, sandals and beads that reached her waist. She had crystal earrings and a tiara made of crystals and other minerals.

"Artists," Grandma Olivia muttered.

Despite how Kenneth was dressed, he received an ovation when he entered the gallery. He smiled and nodded and escorted Holly to the foot of *Neptune's Daughter*.

"Well," Laurence Baker said stepping up beside Kenneth, "now that the artist is here, we can unveil his creation. As you all know, Mr. Childs has named his work *Neptune's Daughter*. In your program he describes his own work as a view of Neptune's daughter emerging from the sea, metamorphosing into a beautiful woman. The piece attempts to capture that metamorphosis at a climactic point. Without further ado, let's allow Mr. Childs to unveil *Neptune's Daughter*."

Kenneth stood there a moment, his eyes searching the crowd until they settled on me. He looked impishly happy. Everyone held their breath as Kenneth jerked the cord to reveal *Neptune's Daughter*. The sheet fell away from the statue and the audience released a single gasp, followed by loud applause.

Grandma Olivia's eyes widened as her mouth opened, stretching the skin over her cheekbones. Then she turned to me and we both gazed at each other for a long moment. She knew I had been Kenneth's model, but she didn't expect to see a bare-breasted young woman emerging from the water. She turned back to the statue.

"Well . . . well . . . well," Judge Childs muttered. "I told you this was his best work. What do you think of it, Olivia?"

"I think it's shocking," she declared. "I never expected to see such a realistically portrayed female." She stepped forward and studied the face and then looked at the Judge.

"I know," I heard him say.

"I need some more champagne," Grandma Olivia declared and the Judge escorted her to the table.

"What do you think of it, Aunt Sara?" I asked her.

"It looks like Haille," she whispered. "Just like her."

"Yes, it does."

"Jacob wouldn't have approved," she noted and nodded. "No, that he wouldn't."

"Dad didn't know anything about art," Cary said.

Aunt Sara's face brightened.

"No," she said, "he didn't."

I laughed and signed back and forth with May, who was very excited and loved the statue. We listened to other people complimenting it and complimenting Kenneth, who appeared as uncomfortable with adulation as a man standing in shoes two sizes too small.

Cary and I were about to take May outside for some fresh air when Teddy Jackson, his wife Ann, his daughter, Michelle, and son, Adam, entered the gallery. A cold, electric chill shot through my spine. I hadn't seen the man who was my real father since I had returned, terrified of the moment when I would. Michelle, who disliked me intensely, was actually my half-sister. I couldn't help but search her face and Adam's for any resemblances among us.

Fortunately, the Jacksons were quickly approached by the gallery owner and other members of the crowd.

"Let's go," I urged Cary and we slipped outside.

"It was getting hot in there. Mom's not coming to the party," Cary said. "She wants me to take her home first. I'll bring May and meet you up there later."

"Okay, sure," I replied, still stunned by the sight of Teddy Jackson.

"Are you going with Kenneth and Holly?"

"Yes," I said. "I'm sort of assigned to him to make sure he shows," I added and Cary laughed.

Less than an hour later, the invited guests began to leave the gallery to head up to Judge Childs's home. Kenneth and Holly emerged like two people escaping a long school detention and came laughing and hurrying toward me.

"Let's get something to drink and quick," Kenneth cried. I took my fiddle out of the Judge's car and stepped into the jeep. We took off with Kenneth whooping up a storm. The wind played havoc with my hair, but my complaints went unheeded.

"You got me into this," Kenneth shouted. "Grin and bear it."

We were lucky. It was one of the nicest spring days, the wind warm and gentle, the sky almost turquoise with puffy dabs of clouds. When we arrived the trio was playing, valets were parking cars, balloons were bobbing in the wind. Kenneth and Holly headed straight for the outside bar. People converged around him, shaking his hand, patting him on the back. Holly and I helped ourselves to some of the hors d'oeuvres, and wandered about the grounds.

"What a beautiful place," she remarked. I showed her some of the house as well. When we emerged, the Judge and Grandma Olivia had arrived and were well involved in conversations with the guests. I looked about but didn't see Cary or May anywhere. When I spotted the Jackson family again, I felt myself shrivel inside.

The caterers began serving the full meal. I wanted to wait for Cary, but he still hadn't arrived. I couldn't imagine what was keeping him. Finally, I joined Kenneth and Holly and, despite my nervous stomach, had a little to eat. After we'd finished, Teddy Jackson and his wife came to our table to congratulate Kenneth. He shifted his eyes to me, but I looked away. Behind him, Adam grinned, looking as arrogant, but as handsome as ever. Michelle, as usual, looked like she was bored out of her mind.

My eyes went to the tent entrance, hoping for sight of Cary, but he still hadn't arrived. I was about to go into the house and call him when the Judge stopped by and whispered something to Kenneth. Then they both looked at me.

"It's time I was able to step out of the limelight," Kenneth said gleefully. I groaned. They wanted me to perform. An announcement was made to the crowd as I left to get on the small stage where I had earlier left my fiddle. Most of the people drifted out to hear me play. Kenneth and Holly stood toward the back, both smiling from ear to ear. My eyes fell on Teddy Jackson, who wore a soft smile that made my heart pound so hard, I feared I might faint in front of all these people. Finally, I found the strength to lift the bow and begin.

It was a song about a coal miner's wife who refused to accept the fact that he was dead in a mining accident and sat vigil at the mine entrance for days and nights, refusing to eat or drink anything. And then, one night, the miner emerged and there was a great celebration. Once or twice I thought my voice would break, but I kept my eyes closed and envisioned Papa George teaching me the song. When it ended, I received a wonderful ovation and there were shouts for another song. I played two more tunes and then stepped down. Grandma Olivia looked very pleased at the way some of the younger men were vying for my attention. Still, I didn't see Cary in the crowd, so I excused myself and hurried into the house to call him. He picked up after one ring.

"I'm sorry," he said. "I'm just out the door. Ma was crying so hard and was so sad I just couldn't leave her. She kept thinking about Dad. She finally fell asleep. Did you play yet?"

"Yes."

"Oh, damn."

"But I'll play again and again for you, Cary. Just get here as soon as you can."

"On my way," he promised and I cradled the phone. I stood there thinking about poor Aunt Sara. I was so deep in thought I didn't hear Adam come up behind me until he whispered in my ear and dared to kiss the back of my neck. I nearly jumped out of my shoes.

"Easy," he said as if I were a horse he was trying to gentle. "I saw you go into the house and thought we could have a private conversation. You're really getting prettier and prettier, you know. I was hoping," he continued before I could speak, "that you might have realized how good we could be together. I'm a big deal at my college fraternity already and they're are lots of sorority girls to date, but I can't get you out of my mind, Melody. How about giving us another chance?" he asked stepping toward me.

I backed away, shaking my head.

"Get away from me, Adam. I don't know where you get the nerve," I said. He smiled.

"I like that. I like a girl who doesn't give in easily."

"I'll never give into you. Just stay away."

"Now why don't you just try and give us a chance. We're both a little older and—"

"I told you to stay away from me. Stay away!" I screamed at him when he reached for me again. He stopped his hand in mid-air and grimaced.

"What the hell's the matter with you? Who do you think you are, the princess of Provincetown just because you can play the fiddle and sing? I'm not good enough for you now?"

"No, it's not a matter of who's good enough for whom."

"Then what? What?" he demanded. He looked angry enough to hit me.

"Ask your father," I shouted at him. It came out of my mouth before I could swallow it back. He shook his head with confusion.

"What?"

"Just ask him, ask him why you and I could never be," I cried, the tears pouring over my lids. I turned and ran out of the room, leaving him twisting and turning in a whirlpool of confusion.

At first I felt bad about what I had said, but then I felt good about it, actually relieved. It was as if I had passed the curse along, lifted the weight from my shoulders and placed it on the true sinner's.

16
⁂

Our Last Good-byes

Despite what Kenneth said about losing his enthusiasm for his art, he was busy creating something new only days after the unveiling of *Neptune's Daughter*. The art critics had given it wonderful reviews and he was featured in several magazines and newspapers. *Neptune's Daughter* was delivered to the museum as Kenneth had promised, and later I discovered he had permitted Judge Childs to buy and donate it.

Holly remained after the festivities. I joined them for dinner twice over the following ten days, and once I took May for a bike ride out to the beach and we had lunch with Holly. I saw that Cary was right, she and Kenneth had grown closer. They both seemed very happy.

Cary was working on the detailing of Kenneth's sailboat. The equipment had arrived and he was installing it all himself. A projected maiden voyage was proposed, one that would take the four of us for a day's trip. The boat was in the water now and people from town who had heard about it from Kenneth were coming around to see it. Mr. Longthorpe, a banker, was interested enough in Cary's work to initiate a discussion about his building a boat for him, too. Cary began to design another boat, and we were all very excited for him. I told Grandma Olivia, but she just said it was something only men who .1ad money and time to waste would find interesting. Nothing that involved recreation was important to her. She considered entertainers, sports figures and the like to be frivolous people who had just not grown up. When I talked further with her about it, I understood these were ideas she had inherited from her rather Puritanical father, but ideas she clung to like a holy rod to help her pass through the trials and tribulations that in her mind were the realities this life bestowed upon us. She believed religiously that the Creator put us on this earth just to be tested, just to suffer and endure. That was the closest she came to any religious affiliations, although she entertained the minister and made contributions to the local church. She never ended a lecture or an explanation without referring to the importance of protecting the family, guarding the reputation. That was the only armor we had to ward off "the slings and arrows of outrageous fortune."

I was beginning to think she might not be all wrong. A mutual respect and kind of truce had developed between us, especially as it looked almost certain now that I would be the class valedictorian. She had arranged for me to have an interview with the head mistress of one of the New England prep schools. In her mind I was following her prescription for the perfect life and she was preparing me to walk in her footsteps.

As the school year moved into its final quarter, plans for the annual variety show were being developed and I was approached by the show's director to perform again. I agreed and we began rehearsals soon afterward. The night of the second rehearsal, I came out of the school, expecting to find Raymond waiting as usual. He wasn't there yet, but it wasn't because he was late. My part had ended earlier than I had expected and I had decided to step out and get some fresh air while I waited.

I noticed an automobile across the street and a man sitting behind the steering wheel. For a few moments I stood gazing at the man and the car without fully realizing who it was. When the realization came, I felt as if I had stepped into a pool of ice water. My legs actually turned numb. He rolled his window down and beckoned to me. I didn't move and he beckoned more emphatically. There was no one else around. I hesitated and then crossed the street to the car and Teddy Jackson, my real father, smiled at me and nodded.

"I've been looking for an opportunity to speak to you," he said, "ever since you sent Adam to me. Can we talk for a few minutes?"

I glanced at my watch. Raymond wouldn't be here for at least another fifteen minutes, I thought.

I shrugged.

"Why?"

"We both know you know why," he said, holding his smile. He stopped smiling when I didn't move. "Please."

He leaned over and opened the passenger's door and I went around the car and got in.

"Well," he began, both of us looking forward and not at each other, "I think I rehearsed and replayed this conversation in my mind a thousand times." He turned to me. "How did you finally find out?"

"What difference does it make?" I countered.

"I was under the impression Haille never told anyone. It was a secret she took with her to the grave. Did someone else tell you?"

I looked at him, my eyes burning with the fire in my heart.

"You're afraid someone else in this town may expose you? Is that it?" I shot back at him.

He stared and then he looked through the windshield again.

"I have a family, a wife who doesn't know any of this, a very successful legal practice. I have some reason to be afraid," he admitted. "However, I don't feel good about that. I don't like continuing to be a coward, especially when I see how well you've turned out, how beautiful and talented you are. I'd like to stake claim to you."

"I'm not a piece of property, some acre of land or something to possess," I said. "You don't stake a claim on a daughter."

"I didn't mean for it to sound that way. What I meant was, I'd like to be proud, too. You didn't tell Adam anything, but he was quite upset. He didn't know what to think."

"What did you tell him?"

"I didn't. The coward won out in me again," he said. "I acted just as confused. He's smart though. He didn't buy it and one of these days, he and I are going to have a heart to heart. I guess he won't think it's so wonderful to be a Jackson then," he added a bit mournfully.

"He's spoiled and arrogant," I said. "He needs to be brought down a few pegs, maybe a dozen."

"Yes, he is something of a snob. I will definitely stake claim to that. That's my fault." He paused, gazed at me and then nodded. "I guess I owe you some sort of explanation."

"I don't want anything from you," I said.

"I'd like to tell you some of it. Please."

I said nothing. I just sat there, half wanting to lunge out of the car, and half wanting to lunge at him and demand why he was such a coward all these years. I wanted to pound his chest and pummel his face and scream and scream and scream about the lies, the deceptions, the people who suffered while he built his precious law practice and wonderfully secure family.

"Nearly nineteen years ago, I was a lot less mature than I am now. Not any less than other young men my age," he added, "but I was impulsive and full of myself. My career had begun. I was successful rather quickly, which is not always a good thing; but in my case, I handled it well, invested well, built more and more of a fortune, married a beautiful woman and had my first child.

"Your mother," he continued with a smile, "was the most attractive young woman in this town then, and very

289

seductive. She had a way of directing herself at you that kind of melted your resistance, filled you with fantasies. She was," he said with a laugh, "a terrific flirt."

"I don't want to hear any more about her wild ways," I said. "Every man I've spoken to who has known her talks about her as if she waved a magic wand over them, hypnotized them."

"That's not far from the truth."

"So you don't bear any blame, is that it?" I fired back at him. "It was all her fault. She seduced you and since she seduced you, you felt no obligations?" Tears burned my eyes and my heart thumped like a tiny hammer under my chest.

"No, I'm not going to say that, although I did rationalize it that way for a long, long time," he replied calmly. "I let her blame someone else and cause problems for the Logan family. It was an easy way out for me and I took it."

"Why did she do that?" I asked. "Why didn't she just expose you?"

"I pleaded with her not to, but I think she had other reasons for doing what she did. She didn't do it for me. It had more to do with her relationship with Olivia Logan and the rest of that family. In short, I lucked out and left it that way.

"I don't think you want to know the gritty details," he continued. "Suffice it to say we had a few passionate rendezvous and, well, the rest you know."

"Yes, the rest I know," I said, reaching for the door handle.

"Wait. I didn't just come to see you to tell you all that. I'd like to do something for you," he blurted.

"Oh? Like what?"

"I don't know. Isn't there something you need? Something I can buy you?"

"Buy me a real mother and father," I said. "Buy me a real family with people who love and care about each other."

He shook his head.

"I'm sorry. It wouldn't do anyone any good, least of all the Logans, if I stepped forward and confessed, would it?"

"No. Your confession has to be made to a higher authority." I paused after opening the door and turned back. "There is one thing you can do for me."

"Name it," he said quickly.

"Keep Adam away from me," I said.

"Done. And Melody, I really am sorry," he said.

Just as I stepped out of the car, Raymond appeared with the limousine. I hurried across the street and got in without looking back until we had turned around and were heading back to Grandma Olivia's.

My father was still there, parked, staring ahead at the darkness of his own making.

It took me forever to fall asleep that night. I tossed and turned, my mind fuzzy, full of mists that rolled like the fog. How pathetic my real father had sounded to me. Well all his explanations, his promises and good intentions wouldn't keep the ocean from washing over the deceit. Let it all be swept out to sea where it belongs, I thought. Let me be free of a past that wanted to chain me to despair.

I was exhausted the next day and moved through my classes like a zombie. Theresa kept asking me if I was all right. She thought my mood might have something to do with Cary, because she, herself, had just broken up with her boyfriend. I kept telling her it was nothing like that, but she refused to believe me.

"When you're ready to talk, call me," she said, actually a bit put off.

I had the feeling I was caught in between those webs of confusion that prevented you from doing or saying anything right. It was better to just retreat into a cocoon of silence and wait for it to pass.

When I saw Cary that afternoon, he read my face as quickly as plans for a new yacht.

"More trouble with Grandma Olivia?" he guessed.

"No. We circle each other from a safe distance these days, like two wolves in silent agreement as to each other's territory."

He laughed.

"So?"

I pondered a moment. I had come out with him to Kenneth's dock to keep him company while he completed the finishing touches on the cabin. It was really a magnificent boat and as comfortable inside as he had predicted. He turned from the wiring he was doing on the stove and gazed at me with those green eyes fully focused.

"What is it, Melody? Have you heard from your mother?"

"Hardly," I said with a laugh. "I'd expect to hear from the Queen of England first."

"Then what?" When I wouldn't answer, he turned, putting his tools aside. "If you and I can't trust each other by now with our deepest secrets and feelings, we'll never trust each other," he said and I gazed at him lovingly, appreciatively. I was lucky to have him, to have someone so devoted to me, I thought. Would any of Grandma Olivia's so-called young men of distinguished families have half of Cary's love for me or would they just see me as another part of the puzzle constructed to make them look successful in the eyes of their parents and friends? As if he could read my thoughts, Cary added, "I love you, Melody, and loving you means feeling pain when you feel it, being sad when you're sad and being happy when you're happy."

I nodded. He waited as I took a deep breath.

"Cary, I know who my real father is," I said, "and he lives here in Provincetown."

He stared at me and then slid down against the cabinet to sit on the floor and face me.

"Who?" he asked, holding his breath.

"It's Teddy Jackson," I revealed. For a moment he just sat there stunned, blinking rapidly, his face unchanged.

292

Then, the realizations began to sink in and his mouth opened slightly, his eyes darkening.

"You mean, that skunk, that shark, that ocean scum is your half-brother?" he said. I nodded. "How did you find out?"

"Mommy finally told me before I left Los Angeles," I said.

"And you kept it a secret all this time?"

"I didn't want to believe it or face up to it. I did my best to avoid him and my half-sister Michelle, who, ironically, despises me. I thought I could bury it with the other lies."

"What happened?"

I told him about my meeting my father the night before. He listened, smirked and nodded.

"In character. I'm sorry, but I have to confess something, too," he said. "I have to confess I'm happy."

"Happy? Happy about Teddy Jackson being my real father? Adam and Michelle being my half-brother and half-sister?"

He looked down at the floor.

"There were times . . . because of the things he said, remarks he made, times because of the way he treated you and your mother that I feared . . . suspected . . ." He looked up at me. "I was terrified my father was your father."

"What?" I started to smile and stopped, realizing how horrible it must have been for him to have lived with such an idea.

"I thought that was what he really had confessed to you that day in the hospital when he called you to what he thought was his deathbed."

"But if I knew that, Cary, do you think I would have . . . would have permitted you and me to be lovers?"

"I hoped not, but it was a nightmare of mine."

"Well, I've thought about it too," I said. "We're distant enough cousins so it doesn't matter," I stated firmly.

"You say that now, but Grandma Olivia has your life

plotted like a chart for a sea voyage. Don't you think I know why she wants you to be refined and attend those snob schools?"

"It doesn't matter what she wants. I'm tired of worrying about what other people want or expect of me. You were right when you said we should start thinking about the present and ourselves and not drag up the past anymore," I told him.

He smiled, so warmly and lovingly I wanted to rush into his arms. Once again, he sensed my deepest feelings and rose to come to me. We kissed, a long, sweet but demanding kiss, drawing all the pain and darkness out of each other. He lifted me gently to the sofa and we kissed again and again, our lips moving over each other's faces and necks. His hands were inside my blouse and over my breasts. I turned and moaned and he moved beside me. Somewhere, in the back of my mind, a tiny voice was trying to warn me, begging me to think with my brain and not with my heart, but Cary's lips were gliding ever so gently over my breasts, drawing every tingle out of my body and then sending them back tenfold to travel over my stomach, to my legs. I felt myself drifting, sinking, uncaring. I was tired of being reasonable and logical. I pounced at him, hungry for recklessness.

With not a concern in the world, I put up no resistance and in fact helped him take off my skirt. We made love to each other on that sparkling new sofa, the material soothing beneath my naked back. We were both professing our love for each other so passionately and so blindly that neither of us projected the slightest hesitation. He was in me, holding me, rocking me, driving me as far from the places of sadness in my heart as I could go. I thought of nothing but the taste of his lips and the touch of his fingers. We exploded against each other, melding our souls and bodies for an instant during which I was as much a part of him as he was of me.

We were both surprised by our exhaustion and both had to laugh at our desperation to catch our breaths. For a long moment we just clung to each other, still naked, our hearts pounding. Then he rose slowly and sat up, gazing down at me.

"I—"

I lifted my hand to his lips to stop him.

"No, don't apologize. Don't say anything, Cary. I'm not upset."

He smiled.

"It would have been a lie if I said I was sorry anyway," he admitted and we laughed.

Then we heard the sound of a dog barking excitedly.

"What's that?"

"Sounds like Prometheus. We better get dressed, and fast," he said. We scurried about, pulling on our clothes and heard Holly and Kenneth calling. I brushed back my hair quickly and glanced in the wall mirror, but there wasn't time to do much more. They were shouting now.

"What's going on?" Cary wondered as we climbed up the small stairway to the deck of the boat.

Holly and Kenneth were standing on the dock and in Holly's arms was another chestnut-coated retriever puppy. Prometheus was circling and barking.

"He's going to be company for Prometheus," she declared. "We're calling him Neptune in honor of Kenneth's work."

"Oh, he's so sweet," I said hurrying off the boat. She handed him to me and he covered my face with his licking kisses.

"Everything coming along all right down there?" Kenneth asked Cary, his eyes moving from him to me and then back again. Cary blushed.

"Just fine," he said.

"We're still looking at next Saturday then?"

"No problem I can see," Cary replied firmly.

"Okay, then we should do it on Friday, right Holly?"

"You're not getting away that cheaply Kenneth Childs."

"Getting away with what that cheaply?" I asked.

"If he thinks for one moment we're going to consider that a honeymoon—"

"Honeymoon!" Cary and I exclaimed simultaneously.

They both beamed at us.

"Oh, Holly, congratulations," I cried and we hugged, Neptune squeezed between us. He barked his complaint, which caused Prometheus to join in chorus.

"It's just going to be a small wedding at my father's house," Kenneth said.

"Really?"

"It was Holly's idea to let him marry us. I figured I'd save money so . . ."

"That's wonderful, Kenneth," I said, my face flushed with happiness for them both.

"I had a feeling you'd see it that way," he said. "Well, I guess I'd better get back to work. It looks like this piece is going to be interrupted by something called a honeymoon," he declared.

Cary and I watched the two of them walk back to the house.

"I hope that will be us someday," he said. I took his hand.

"It will," I promised.

He put his arm around me.

Maybe it was changing; maybe the storms had really passed over us at last, I thought.

Two days later Cary drove me up to Grandma Belinda's rest home so I could make my weekly visit with her. Cary liked to visit with Grandpa Samuel. He said he at least got him to talk about fishing. I was anxious to tell Grandma Belinda all the good news. It seemed the only baggage I ever brought with me when I visited her were suitcases full of sadness and tragedy. She was still spending lots of time with Mr. Mandel, but this time I found him first in the lobby, playing checkers with another man. He recognized me and smiled.

"Good, you're here," he said. "She needs company. I've been trying to beat Mr. Braxton here at checkers all week, but I never get the time. She doesn't let me out of her sight," he explained with a twinkle in his eyes.

"Just his excuse for being afraid of losing to me," Mr.

Braxton said. "Blaming that poor old lady. You should be ashamed of yourself, Mandel."

"We'll soon see who's going to be ashamed," Mr. Mandel replied and jumped one of Mr. Braxton's checkers.

Cary laughed.

"She's on the bench in the garden," Mr. Mandel told me.

Cary and I split up in the hallway, he going down to Grandpa Samuel's room first. It was a very bright and warm afternoon. The flowers were in full bloom. Lilacs with their dark purple spikes climbed over the walls and gates. Bees hovered over the honey locusts. The yellow tea roses were especially brilliant and there were petunias everywhere. I knew how much Grandma Belinda liked being outside, how much she enjoyed soaking in the sunshine and drinking in the wonderful rainbow colors all around her.

I saw her on her usual bench, a small smile on her lips, her head back with her eyes closed, basking in the sunlight. Her hands were in her lap and she wore one of her prettier print dresses, with a pearl comb in her hair. I couldn't help but wonder if that was the way I would look when I was her age.

"Hello, Grandma," I said as I approached. Lately, she had begun to remember more and more about me, although she still said very little about my mother and asked no questions.

She didn't reply so I sat beside her and took her hand into mine. The moment I did, a shudder of abject terror passed like an electric current up through my arm and into my heart, which stopped and then started to pound again frantically. Her hand was ice cold.

"Grandma?" I shook her. Her body trembled and stopped, but her eyes remained shut. Her lips parted just a little more. "Grandma Belinda!"

I shook her harder and then I turned and shouted to the nearest attendant for help.

"Hurry!" I screamed. He ran over.

"What's wrong?"

"She won't wake up," I said and he knelt at her side, felt for a pulse, opened her eyes, and then shook his head.

"She's gone," he declared as if she had just gotten up and walked away.

"Gone? She can't be gone. She's smiling. She's pleased and happy."

"I'm sorry," he said shaking his head.

"No. Please. Call the doctor. Call someone!"

"Take it easy. I'll get Mrs. Greene right away," he said. Then he leaned toward me. "She doesn't like us to make too much of a deal of it when this happens," he said in a loud whisper. "It disturbs the others and makes it all that much more difficult around here."

"I don't care what she thinks. Get a doctor!"

He stood up.

"I'll be right back," he promised and hurried away.

"Oh, Grandma Belinda, please don't go. Not yet. We're really just getting to know each other and you're all I have. Please, wait," I begged her, babbling stupidly at her side.

I took her cold hand in mine again and sat there beside her, the tears streaming down my cheeks, rocking my body gently back and forth as I muttered my silent prayers and continued to beg her to stay just a little while longer.

Moments later, Mrs. Greene came hurrying down the garden pathway accompanied by two other attendants and a nurse. The nurse charged ahead and examined Grandma Belinda, making the same pronouncements quickly.

"Get the stretcher from the infirmary," Mrs. Greene ordered the attendants. "Bring it out that side door and take her back in that way. I'll call the mortuary."

"No!" I cried and buried my face in my hands.

"You can come to my office, if you wish," she told me curtly. "I'll have to call Mrs. Logan right away. Don't worry. Arrangements have been made. We do that immediately after we accept a patient."

"How convenient for everyone," I replied as I brushed the tears off my cheeks.

She pursed her lips with annoyance and nodded at the attendants who rushed away.

"Stay with her," she ordered the nurse. Then she pivoted and started to march back to the building.

I turned to Grandma Belinda and brushed back her hair. The nurse smiled at me.

"She died happy, thinking of something nice," she said. "And she loved it so much out here," she added.

"I know," I moaned through my tears.

"This is better than her getting sicker and sicker and lingering in the infirmary," the nurse continued, more for my sake than for Grandma Belinda's.

"I have to tell Cary," I realized aloud and rose.

"I'll stay with her," the nurse promised.

I glanced down at her again. Her lips were turning purple and her smile seemed to fade right before my eyes. I reached down to touch her one more time and then, with my chest feeling as if it had turned to stone, I started away.

Cary was sitting in Grandpa Samuel's room and Grandpa Samuel was still in bed, sitting up. He was in his robe and was unshaven.

"He's not talking much," Cary began, but when his eyes settled on me a moment longer, he knew something terrible had happened. "What is it? You look terrible."

"It's Grandma Belinda, Cary," I wailed. "She's dead. She died in the garden just now, just before I arrived!"

He got up quickly to embrace me as I sobbed. Grandpa Samuel seemed to finally notice us and slowly came out of his daze.

"Laura?" he said. Cary turned to him.

"No, Grandpa. It's Melody. She's just come from Belinda. I'm afraid it's bad news, Grandpa. Belinda's gone."

"Gone?" He looked at me, at my tear-streaked face and bloodshot eyes. "I told her not to do it. I told her it was wrong, but she said it was the best, for everyone's

299

best." He stared down at his hands and shook his head. "She always knew what was best, so what could I say?"

"He's just more confused than ever," Cary explained. "What happens now?"

"They are taking her to the infirmary and then calling Grandma Olivia. The arrangements are already made. They were made five minutes after she was brought here," I added bitterly. "Grandma Olivia thinks of everything, plans, plots, never misses a beat for fear of a moment's embarrassment for her precious family."

Cary nodded.

"Yet," he said, "you appreciate all that at times like this."

I hated to admit he was right, to give her any credit.

"Please, take me home," I said.

"Okay. Grandpa, we've got to go now. I'll be back to see you again."

Grandpa Samuel turned back to us, his face full of seriousness, his eyes small and dark as he nodded with tight lips.

"She decided it was for the best," he said. "But I'm not so sure. Go down in the basement. You decide," he added.

"He's just doing a lot of babbling today," Cary explained. He squeezed Grandpa Samuel's hand softly, patted him on the shoulder and then guided me out.

We didn't stop at Mrs. Greene's office nor did we stop at the checker table to tell Mr. Mandel. I thought it was better for him to find out himself. I still felt like I was in a daze anyway.

"I'm sorry," Cary said as we drove off. "I know how much you wanted to get to know her and to get her to know you."

"It was starting to happen, Cary. Each time I visited, she seemed to remember more."

"I'll go right home and tell Ma," he said after we arrived at Grandma Olivia's. "Take it easy. I'll call you later."

"I'll be all right," I said and kissed him.

I found Grandma Olivia in what was Grandpa Samuel's office talking on the phone. She looked up when I appeared, but continued her conversation with the mortuary.

"Yes," she said, "I want the service short, but I'll stay with the deluxe flower arrangements. No," she added firmly, "you can close the coffin immediately. Thank you."

She cradled the phone.

"Actually, I thought she would live longer than I would. She's younger, and nothing bothered her half as much as it bothers me."

"Maybe you just never saw how much things bothered her. You hardly visited her up there," I attacked.

"Don't use that tone of voice with me. I won't be blamed for trying to protect her and take care of her. One day you'll realize all that, especially when you see how most people look after their sick relatives. The country is full of discarded people," she continued. "At least I made sure she died with some dignity and in some comfort with professionals looking after her day and night."

"She didn't belong there. She belonged at home," I wailed. "She wasn't crazy. She was just confused. Grandpa Samuel doesn't belong there either. You have enough money to keep him taken care of right here in his own home, in his own surroundings."

"To do what? Sit around and dribble down his chin, be carried out and left in a chair on the lawn for everyone to see? None of his so-called cronies would come see him. Most of them are worse off or dead. It would just be another family embarrassment, prolonged; and even if I spent a fortune and got him round the clock assistance, I couldn't change his condition. At least he has good medical care, good dietary care and some companionship where he is.

"Don't be so quick to make judgments about things you know very little about," she advised sharply. "You've come late to this family. You have no real idea about the twists and the turns, the ridges and the valleys

301

that were crossed, the storms I've weathered. Belinda was always difficult and always a problem in one way or another, and Samuel was no prize, but I did the best for everyone," she concluded firmly. "I bear no guilt. Her daughter, that's who bears all the guilt."

She took a deep breath and for a moment looked very pale herself. Then she gathered her resolve and stood up.

"There's much more to do, even though I tried to have everything in order." She paused in the doorway and turned to me. "Were you there when it actually happened?" she asked almost in a soft, concerned tone of voice.

"No. She was already gone by the time I found her in the garden. She . . . was smiling," I said.

Grandma Olivia nodded.

"She probably thought of the Grim Reaper as just another gentleman caller asking her for a date," she said wistfully. "She was a pretty little girl. Everyone always remarked about her perfect features. It won't be long before I'll be taking care of her again. You don't lose your burdens just because you leave this world," she muttered and left the office.

I stood there for a while looking around, thinking, feeling such a smorgasbord of emotions: sadness and grief, confusion and sympathy. I went behind the desk and sat.

Mommy should know, I thought. She should be told her own mother had just died. I stared at the phone. I hadn't attempted to contact her once since my return and she hadn't contacted me, yet I hadn't forgotten the phone number. I sucked in my breath, lifted the receiver and dialed. It rang once and then there was an automated voice.

"I'm sorry, but this number is no longer in service," I was told.

"What?"

I dialed again and again received the same automated message. Where was she? I wondered. She always emphasized how important the telephone was to someone

302

trying to get auditions and parts and assignments. I called information and asked the operator if there was a forwarding number. She told me she had nothing listed.

Frustrated, I thought about calling Mel Jensen, but wondered how I would explain not knowing what had happened to the woman who was supposedly my sister. Nevertheless, I finally called and spoke to his roommate because Mel was at an audition.

"Gina Simon?" he said. "I haven't seen her for a while, months. I don't know where she went. Matter of fact, I think Mel said something about her running out on her lease and the landlord being after her," he added.

"Oh. Well thanks, anyway."

"Do you want me to have Mel call you? Where are you?"

"No, it's all right," I said even more embarrassed. "Just say I wish him luck."

"Sure."

I hung up and sat there a while thinking about Mommy. She hadn't been much interested in her mother all these years that her mother was alive as far as I knew. As sad as it was, I didn't think she would be that upset not finding out when her mother had died.

Maybe Grandma Olivia was right: maybe Grandma Belinda was far better off at the home. At least there, no one pretended to be more than he or she was. They took care of you because they were paid to take care of you, and if they liked you and did something extra, it was honest and simple.

Grandma Belinda's funeral was well attended, but not because so many people remembered her. In fact, some people thought she had died long ago. People came because it was Grandma Olivia's sister and Grandma Olivia still commanded great respect in the community. Government officials attended, as did most of the influential businesspeople and professionals. I saw my father and his wife there, but I avoided looking at him as much as possible and he said nothing to me.

Grandma Olivia did not greet the mourners afterward.

We all went to the cemetery and then the mourners went their separate ways, except for Judge Childs, Kenneth, Holly, Cary, May and Aunt Sara, who returned to the house with us. Grandma Olivia said wakes and feeding large numbers of people only prolong the final good-bye and delayed getting on with life.

Nevertheless, we had something to eat and afterward, we all sat out in the back and talked. Holly took Aunt Sara for a walk with May along the beach. Holly and Aunt Sara got along well these days. She was actually helping Aunt Sara shed her burden of mourning. Grandma Olivia fell asleep in her chair while Cary talked about the boat with Judge Childs and Kenneth.

Finally, Cary and I went down to the dock and watched the approaching twilight with the gulls gliding gracefully over the silvery water.

"I wonder if Holly is right. I wonder if we all return to some spiritual body full of love and then start again," I said.

Cary was silent for a moment and then he turned to me and smiled.

"I started again. I started when you came here," he said. "So maybe it's true: Maybe love is what makes us alive."

I leaned against his shoulder and he put his arm around me, making me feel secure and safe. The sun continued to dip. Clouds drifted toward the horizon as if they were sinking, too. The gulls called out through the shadows.

And I said a soft good-bye to the grandmother I had hardly known, but whose soft eyes filled me with promises to keep.

17
&

An End to the Silence

As Cary had promised, Kenneth's boat was ready for its maiden voyage the following weekend. Of course, Cary took it out on some test runs beforehand and spent the week tuning and perfecting it until he was satisfied. Weatherwise, luck was with us. When Cary came for me early on Saturday morning, it was a nearly perfect day with just a few dabs of clouds over the face of a pale blue sky, and most important, the sea was calm, but with just enough breeze to make for good sailing.

Grandma Olivia said nothing either negative or positive about it at all. She knew where I was going and why, but she ignored my preparations. There was a dramatic change in her demeanor during the week after her sister's death. She was more withdrawn, said less at dinner and spent more time alone in Grandpa Samuel's office reviewing old papers. She dozed a great deal and had fewer visitors.

Judge Childs came around about as frequently as usual, but his visits were shorter and he had dinner with us only once. Toward the end of the week, immediately after he arrived, he and Grandma Olivia went into the office and spent an hour or so behind closed doors going over documents. When he emerged, he looked flustered and tired. He barely spoke to me before he left and after he was gone, Grandma Olivia went directly up to bed, not so much as glancing my way.

She still made daily inquiries as to my progress at school, commented about my appearance, and warned me about not doing anything to ruin the success I had enjoyed and would enjoy, but her words sounded emptier. They were words of duty, automatic words, sentences without passion. Could it be that Grandma Belinda's death really had affected her? I wondered. I was beginning to feel sorry for her, something I thought I would never do.

I didn't mention any of this to Cary, especially the morning of our maiden voyage. He talked excitedly all the way to Kenneth's beach house, giving me little opportunity to get a word in anyway. I had to laugh at his exuberance, but at the same time, I was thrilled by it.

Holly had prepared our cold lobster lunch with salads and Portuguese bread, wine, coffee and carrot cake. She and Kenneth surprised us by buying new matching sailing outfits. It was the first time I had seen her dressed in something reasonably fashionable and I thought she looked fresh and attractive.

"I've got to look the part now, don't I?" Kenneth said, parading about in his captain's hat.

The aura of happiness that settled over all of us was infectious. We fed each other's laughter and joy.

Kenneth and Cary got us underway and we set out to sea, bouncing gently over the waves, the wind stroking our faces, making our hair dance over our foreheads, all of us bathing in the sunlight and the sea spray. The boat was as sleek and as fast as Cary had predicted. It sliced gracefully through the water. Kenneth said it handled with such ease, it could make a novice appear to be a seasoned sailor. He even let me steer to prove it. Cary beamed with pride, strutting over the desk, checking every joint, every mechanical part, just daring something to fail.

After we set the anchor, Cary and Kenneth did some fishing while Holly and I prepared our feast. After we ate I played the fiddle and taught them some of the mountain songs Papa George had taught me. I couldn't recall a time in my life when I felt more contented. All of us sprawled out to rest and actually dozed off a bit before springing back into action and turning the boat toward shore, this time sailing faster, Holly and I shrieking at the waves that splashed over the sides of the boat to soak us. It had been one of the happiest days of my life and I hated to see it come to an end.

Kenneth and Holly had decided to have their wedding the next day at Judge Childs's. It wasn't going to be a very big affair. The Judge would marry them in front of a few friends and there was to be a small dinner party, after which Kenneth and Holly would leave for their week's honeymoon in Montreal. Cary and I had promised to look after the beach house and their puppies, Prometheus and Neptune. Cary said he would take the dogs home with him every night.

We all knew he was going to be busy. Mr. Longthorpe had decided to go ahead and contract with him to build him his yacht. Kenneth offered his home for Cary to use, which meant Cary could utilize the studio and shop. Now there would be reason for him to be at Kenneth's anyway. While he had been working there on Kenneth's boat, the house had become our little paradise, our hideaway from the prying eyes of the world around us. We had only the terns and other birds as witnesses. Now that would continue.

And so as the school year was drawing toward its end, I gradually permitted myself to believe there really was such a thing as a rainbow after the storm. Mommy didn't trouble my thoughts anymore. I accepted that she was gone. I rarely saw my father and never saw or heard from Adam. Michelle avoided me more than I avoided her. It was easy to put it all behind me, to think now of the future, a future that had a place for Cary's and my love.

It was really what I believed as I returned from our day of sailing. Tanned and very contented, I was even eager to share the experience with Grandma Olivia. However, I found the house dark and quiet and discovered Loretta alone in the kitchen. She told me Grandma Olivia had not come down for her dinner.

"It isn't like her to do so, but I brought dinner up to her and she ate in bed," Loretta told me. "That woman isn't right. Something's wrong," she declared, but not with any loving concern. She said it as a matter of fact and went on doing her chores.

All the time I had lived at the house, I always felt uncomfortable going to Grandma Olivia's bedroom while she was in bed. I hesitated to do it now. Although I had developed some level of respect for her, I still wasn't fond of her. I didn't think she was the kind of person who permitted anyone to care for her affectionately anyway. Even the Judge rarely spoke to her tenderly, at least not in front of me. It was as if he thought that if he did, she would either ridicule him or criticize him for it.

Nevertheless, I felt some concern and knocked on her door. There was no response so I knocked harder until I heard, "What is it?"

I opened the door and gazed in at her. She looked like a tiny child in the large bed, her hair loose, her body diminished even more by the oversized pillows.

"I just wondered how you were. Loretta said you didn't come down to dinner and—"

"I'm fine," she said firmly, but then added, "as fine as I can be."

"Is there anything you need?"

She stared at me and then, as if I had asked the silliest question, she uttered a ridiculing groan.

"Need? Yes, I need a new body. I need youth. I need a family with a man as strong as my father was. No," she said, "I don't need anything you can give me." She paused and nearly smiled at me. "You think you've come to where you can start to do things for me?"

"I just meant . . ."

"I'm tired, very tired. The battles wear you down. However, I don't want sympathy and I don't want anyone to feel sorry for me. I'm just stating a fact you will learn yourself one day. You live, you work hard and you die. Don't expect anything more and you won't be disappointed. You can send Loretta up to take my tray. That's what you can do," she said, waving her hand to brush me away.

I started to close the door.

"Just a moment."

"Yes?"

"I don't believe I will be going to the wedding tomorrow. I don't feel up to festivities and parties. It's not much of a wedding anyway."

"Won't the Judge be disappointed?"

This time instead of smiling disdainfully, she laughed mockingly.

"I can't think of anything that means less to me than Nelson Childs's happiness," she said and then, as if her head had suddenly turned to stone, she dropped it quickly to the pillow.

I stared at her. Despite her money and her power, I did feel sorry for her. I had the urge to shout it at her: "I pity you, you and your concern for what's perfectly proper or what's good for the family. Look at what you've become! Look at what you have at the end of your hard, angry life."

The words were teasing my lips, but I swallowed them back and instead I closed the door and went to tell Loretta to pick up her tray. Then I went to bed thinking about Kenneth and Holly's wedding and dreaming of my own, grateful I wouldn't end up like this sad old woman.

Grandma Olivia remained in bed the following morning. She didn't ask for me and I didn't stop by to say good-bye before going to the wedding. Cary, May and

Aunt Sara picked me up and were all surprised to learn that Grandma Olivia wasn't coming.

"Isn't she feeling well?" Aunt Sara asked.

"I don't think so, although I can't imagine the disease or the germ that would have enough nerve to invade her body," I said. Cary laughed, but Aunt Sara looked as if I had blasphemed and had to hide her shock.

The wedding was simple, but very sweet. Judge Childs didn't seem all that surprised at Grandma Olivia's failure to attend. He was too happy about Kenneth's permitting him to perform the ceremony to allow anything to interfere with the joy of the moment. A long table had been set up on the patio. There was champagne and caviar and other assorted hors d'oeuvres first. Then we had a sit-down dinner, catered by the same people who had catered Kenneth's party for *Neptune's Daughter*. That was followed with a beautiful wedding cake.

I met Kenneth's brother and sister and their families, but they were the first to leave. Kenneth and Holly left before any of the other guests because they had to get to Boston to catch an airplane to Montreal.

"Watch Neptune," Holly warned me as I walked with her toward the jeep. "He likes to bury Kenneth's socks in the sand and might just do the same to you and Cary."

We hugged.

"I guess your chart was correct after all," I whispered.

"Yes, yes it was, and if it wasn't, I would have made it right," she declared with a gleeful smile. Then she got into the jeep beside Kenneth. She reached back for me and we joined hands.

"Be careful," she said. "Mercury is not in a harmonious position this month."

"I will," I said and let go of her hand just as Cary stepped beside me. We turned to each other and smiled and thought about the days ahead when we could share the beach house, alone, on a sort of honeymoon of our own.

However, it turned out to be a busy week for both of us. Cary actually began Mr. Longthorpe's boat and I had to start preparing for final exams. Nevertheless, he was there at the end of every school day to pick me up and then to go get May. May had become more friendly with some of her friends and fortunately for Cary and me, wanted to do things with them after school. Aunt Sara let her bring a girlfriend over after school most of the time or allowed her to go to her girlfriend's home so she was occupied.

Usually, I sat on a blanket and studied while Cary worked on the new project. Just before he stopped to take me home, we would go for a walk on the beach or just sit and look at the ocean. Toward the end of the week, it grew unusually hot and on Thursday afternoon, he put down his tools, turned to me and asked if I wanted to go swimming.

"Swimming?"

"Skinny-dipping," he challenged.

Even though we were far from the nearest neighbor and the beach was almost always deserted, the very idea of swimming nude in the daytime frightened me.

"What if someone comes?"

"No one will."

"They might."

"Well, I'm not afraid," he said with that devilish grin and started to take off his shirt. He sat on the sand and pulled off his shoes and socks, looked back at me and then slipped off his pants and underpants. For a moment he just sat there looking at the water. Then he turned back toward me, his eyes so deep, so inviting. "Well?"

My fingers went to my blouse. He rose and walked out to the water to wait. Seconds later, naked, I joined him and he took my hand.

"Ready?"

"No," I said. "It's going to be cold."

"Freezing, but delightful," he promised and we ran into the water, screaming at the tops of our voices, and laughing until the water actually covered us in what felt like icicles. I turned and ran out as fast as I had run in. Cary followed, laughing hysterically at my shrieks. We

311

both collapsed on the warm sand and quickly wrapped our arms around each other.

I was shivering when his lips brushed mine. He rubbed my back vigorously and we kissed again. The sun was warm enough to dry us quickly, but it was the heat of our own passion that drove the chill from our bones. Making love under a daylight sky, out in the open for all the world to see, heightened every tingle, every sensation. The wind was in my hair; there was sand on my face, and my lips were salty from the sea and from his lips. Yet nothing mattered but our great hunger for each other. Before it was over, Neptune came to us and began licking both of us, making us laugh.

"I feel like we're in our own private Eden," Cary said. "Nothing can touch us here. We're blessed, Melody. I'm the luckiest guy in the world."

We pledged our love, wrote our promises in the sand, lay beside each other and gazed up at the blue sky, not thinking about our nakedness.

"I don't know how I will get through each day without you when you go to that snobby prep school," Cary said.

I sat up and braced myself on my elbow, gazing out at the water.

"I'm probably going to hate it," I said. "Maybe I won't go."

"What do you mean? I thought that was settled."

"Grandma Olivia thinks it is, but I'm not sure."

"Really? Well, what will you do?"

I gazed into his face and he smiled.

"Would you just stay here with me?"

"I might," I said and his eyes brightened as if there were tiny candles behind them. Then, they darkened and he shook his head.

"You're the class valedictorian. Everyone will say you've wasted your life."

"I don't live to please everyone, just myself," I said, but he sat up and began to dress. "Cary?"

"Let's not make plans and promises we can't keep, Melody. I'd better get you back to Grandma Olivia's."

I dressed quickly and we left.

"I had a wonderful afternoon with you, Cary," I said after we pulled into Grandma Olivia's driveway. "I've been working on our weekend, too. She thinks I'm sleeping over at Theresa's."

"I know how much you hate to lie," he said.

"If it means being with you, it's not a lie. It's a necessity," I said and he smiled.

"See you tomorrow," he promised and drove away. I watched him go and then I turned and went into the big house, a house that had somehow grown more empty and darker every passing day. Almost as soon as I closed the door behind me, Loretta came hurrying down the hallway to greet me.

"I think you better go up and see about your grandmother," she said.

"Why? What's wrong?"

"She don't answer when I talk to her. I was about to call the doctor."

"Doesn't answer?"

I started up the stairs slowly. Loretta watched me a moment and then walked away as if she had washed her hands of the problem. I knocked gently on the bedroom door, waited and then entered. Grandma Olivia was lying there, her head sunk into her large pillow. She didn't turn to see who it was who had entered. I approached the bed.

"Grandma Olivia?"

I gazed down at her. Her eyes moved toward me, but her mouth was twisted grotesquely in the right corner. Suddenly, her tongue jetted out like a small snake and she made a horrible guttural sound that made me step back.

"What's wrong?"

I lifted the corner of the blanket and looked at her small body. Her right arm was bent against her bosom, the fingers of her hand frozen into a claw. I saw where she had scratched her chest and neck.

313

"I'll call the doctor!" I cried and hurried to the telephone. Afterward, I called Judge Childs, too.

Later, I waited downstairs in the living room while the doctor examined her. He and Judge Childs finally appeared.

"Your grandmother has had a stroke," the doctor declared. "I wanted to send for an ambulance and put her in the hospital, but she insists on remaining here under nurse's care. Nearly shook her head off 'No!' I've sent for someone, a Mrs. Grafton, who will be here shortly. She's a fine special duty nurse, but I think it's only a matter of days before we will just have to get your grandmother to the hospital. Her vitals are stable at the moment," he added and turned to the Judge to see if he wanted to add anything.

"I'll see to everything," he said.

"Will she get better?" I asked.

"At her age a complete recovery is unlikely. She might improve with therapy, but for all that, she is just going to have to be in the hospital. For now, I'd rather she be comfortable and happy."

"Happy?" How could anyone be happy like that? I wondered, and besides, I didn't think she was happy before this had happened.

"Well, comfortable, anyway," the doctor said. "For now, she is asleep. The nurse should be here momentarily," he added and then the Judge escorted him, but returned to me.

"It's no fun being old," he said with a small smile. "However, she's an incredibly strong woman. She might make more of a recovery than the doctor thinks. Anyway, after a few days of this, I'm sure she will be taken to the hospital. At that time I'd like it if you came to stay with me. At least until you're off to school," he concluded.

"Thank you," I said, really not sure what I would do.

"Well," he said glancing up toward her room and then at me, "you going to be all right?"

"Oh yes, I'm fine."

"Call me if you need anything or anything changes," he said and left.

Twenty minutes later, Mrs. Grafton, a woman in her mid-fifties, stout and very professional and businesslike, arrived. I showed her Grandma Olivia's room and she went in to examine her. I had Loretta prepare the bedroom next to Grandma Olivia's for her as well. Then I went to the phone and called Cary to tell him and Aunt Sara what had happened.

"I'll come right over," Cary said.

"No, I'm fine. In fact, I'm tired and I want to go to sleep. I have a math exam tomorrow."

"Okay, we'll check on her tomorrow," he said.

"I'd like to go up to see Grandpa Samuel in a day or so, Cary, to tell him."

"He won't even know you," Cary said, "much less understand what you're saying."

"Still, we should tell him. No one else will."

"Okay. You can't break old habits, can you, Melody?"

"What do you mean?" I asked.

"Even now, you can't stop thinking about other people first," he said and then he laughed. "It's all right. I'm just teasing. I can't imagine Grandma Olivia trapped by a stroke."

"She's human, Cary."

"Could have fooled me," he said.

Afterward, before I fell asleep I thought how terrible it was for a woman to have ruled her family so firmly and authoritatively that they felt no love, sympathy or sorrow for her in her time of greatest need. Surely, no matter how vigorously she claimed it, she couldn't be satisfied with herself and what she had accomplished, even in the name of family.

Grandma Olivia did make some improvement over the next thirty-six hours. The doctor returned and declared that she had regained some of her speech ability.

"It will still be difficult to understand her, but there's been more improvement than I expected," he said.

"She's even gotten more control of her hand. We'll see," he added, not as ready to make dire pronouncements now as he had been before. "The nurse will remain another few days and I'll stop by every day," he promised.

Judge Childs was there most of the day as well. Loretta told me. She said it as if she were complaining he made more work for her. I imagined she thought she would have to do less with Grandma Olivia so incapacitated. When I returned from school the next afternoon, Mrs. Grafton told me my grandmother was asking to see me. I went in immediately. I approached the bed slowly. Mrs. Grafton had her sitting up and had her hair brushed. Her mouth was still twisted and her arm lay awkwardly against her body, but when I drew closer, she fixed her eyes on me and reached out with her left hand to take my hand and pull me closer.

"Naia," she uttered.

"Take it easy, Grandma Olivia," I said softly.

"Naaaa . . . thinssssss chaaaa," she continued. I shook my head. I didn't understand. She tried again and again, but the same confusing sounds emerged. Finally, Mrs. Grafton stepped over and took her hand from me.

"Please try to relax, Mrs. Logan."

Grandma shook her head vigorously.

"She has the spirit," Mrs. Grafton said. "Full of vim and vigor."

Grandma Olivia attempted her sounds again. Mrs. Grafton listened and then she smiled.

"What is she trying to say?" I asked.

"She's said, 'Nothing's changed.' Whatever that means," Mrs. Grafton added.

I nodded and looked at Grandma Olivia.

"I know what it means. It means that even now, she wants to run our lives," I muttered. "I'm sure she's going to get better."

I shook my head in amazement and left.

The next day, Cary found the time to take me to see Grandpa Samuel. Since Grandma Belinda's death, I

316

hadn't been there to visit and neither had Cary. Now, with Grandma Olivia's illness, I felt even more guilty about neither of us going to see him. There was no one to be sure he was being well looked after, no one except us, I thought.

Returning to the rest home was sad for me. I had to remind myself Grandma Belinda was gone. When we entered the lobby, we saw Mr. Mandel sitting alone on a sofa just gazing down at the floor. He looked up and immediately smiled at the sight of us.

"How are you, Mr. Mandel?" I asked.

"Oh, I'm fine, dear. Fine. It's nice to see you again. Very nice." His eyes seemed to go in and out of focus as he tried to understand why we were there. Had Belinda died or not? I could almost hear him wonder.

"We're here to see my grandfather," I explained.

"Oh. Oh yes, yes. What's his name?"

"Samuel Logan," I said.

"Oh yes. I don't think I know him," he said and nodded. Then he gazed down at the floor and grew silent. We said good-bye and went through the lobby to Grandpa Samuel's room, where we found him sitting by the window, staring out, a blanket over his lap.

"Hi, Grandpa," Cary said first. He didn't turn from the window until Cary took his hand. "How are you doing, Grandpa?"

Grandpa Samuel stared at him and then his eyes went to me.

"Yes, Melody's here, too, Grandpa."

He looked at Cary and then at me.

"You got her. Good, good," he said before looking out the window again.

Cary shook his head and shrugged. I stepped forward to take Grandpa Samuel's hand from him.

"Grandpa Samuel, we came to visit you to tell you Grandma Olivia's sick. She has a nurse at the house," I said. "The doctor didn't think she would get much better, but she already has."

He looked at me.

"I told her no, but she said it has to be. Tell your mother I'm sorry," he said. "I told her no."

"It's no use," Cary said. "I told you. We're wasting our time. He doesn't even know where he is anymore. He won't remember us being here afterward, Melody."

"I guess you're right," I said.

Suddenly, Grandpa Samuel turned to us again, this time his eyes more vibrant.

"You go look and you'll see it wasn't me. I didn't sign anything."

"Look where?" I turned to Cary. "Why does he keep saying these things?"

"You know he's confused. It probably doesn't mean anything," Cary reminded me.

"I told her no," Grandpa Samuel repeated. "I told her it was a sin."

We spent another fifteen minutes or so trying to get Grandpa Samuel to understand who we were and why we were there, but he never seemed to grasp the present. He was lost in his memories, drowning in them.

On the way out, I complained to Mrs. Greene about Grandpa being stuck in his room on such a beautiful day.

"For your information," she replied, "he was out all morning and was just recently brought in. Unless you plan on being here twenty-four hours, I would advise you not to criticize," she snapped and walked off.

"I'd rather die in my bed than be brought here," I said. "Grandma Olivia is not wrong in being stubborn about it."

"It's just lucky she can afford to have a nurse around the clock," Cary reminded me. "Otherwise, she would be someplace like this by now."

He took me home and went back to work on the boat. I still had a slew of finals for which to prepare, but as I sat in my room studying, my mind kept wandering back to Grandpa Samuel's eyes and his great fear of being blamed. Why was he so adamant now, at this time in his life? Was it because he thought he was soon to meet his Maker?

318

How had they arranged for my grandmother to be stuffed away at so young an age? I wondered. What sort of diagnosis had the doctors made? What had Grandma Olivia said about her? Curiosity drew me away from my work and I went downstairs and out the back to go around the house to the basement. It was in there that I had found Mommy's pictures and learned about the secrets this family buried in its closets. I thought maybe Grandpa Samuel was right. Maybe I should go back and see what I could find again.

On the north side of the house there was a metal cellar door. I didn't think anyone had been in it since Cary had brought me last year.

I hesitated in the doorway. What did I really expect to find? Did I want to find it? Did I want to read all the horrible things? I paused and thought about the twisted and sick old woman now trapped in her own body upstairs. Perhaps justice had been done. Perhaps it was time to forget.

And yet, I couldn't turn away. Maybe it was morbid curiosity; maybe it was a need to understand. I continued down the stairs and opened the next door, stepping in to pull a cord that turned on a swinging, naked bulb to illuminate the basement. I stood there for a moment, recalling the boxes on the metal shelves where we had found the photographs. I went back to them and began to sift through the cartons, their sides, tops and bottoms, limp from the dampness. There were so many photographs, old school papers, old bills, delivery slips, a trail of purchases and events that were unremarkable, the same sort of trail every family left, I thought.

All the boxes were the same. Grandpa Samuel's declining mind was filled with corridors of distortions, I thought. It was all just part of his garbled imagination now. I started to rise to leave when I saw what looked like a metal box buried under some wooden boards on the other side of the basement. I went to it, lifted off the boards and pulled out the box. It was locked and there were no keys in sight.

Why had this been left buried here and why was it the only thing locked? I brushed it off and took it with me when I left the basement. I didn't go back into the house. I went around to the garage where I knew there were tools and found a screwdriver. It took a while, but I worked one between the lid and the box and gradually, after some effort, got the lock to snap open. Then I lifted the lid and looked inside.

There was a small pile of documents in business envelopes. I took one out, opened it and removed the paper. Then I sat and read.

Of course, I always thought it was just an exaggeration to say 'my heart turned to stone' or 'my blood ran cold.' How could a human heart stop, shudder, crumble and regain itself? How could your body freeze and return to warm?

Yet all of that happened to me and I thought I would never stand, never breathe, never be able to utter a sound. My eyes wanted to sink from the words they read.

However, there was no retreat, no denial, no shaking of the head that would change the reality before me.

I caught my breath and sorted through the remaining papers in the box, reading, growing more and more shocked. Finally, trembling so badly I was sure I would stumble before I stepped outside, I put all the papers back, closed the box, and got to my feet.

No hurricane, no tornado, no earthquake would rock this family as much as what I carried in my hands.

18

At Long Last, Love

I climbed the stairway slowly, each step more ponder-
ous, heavier than the one before. My body was trying
to resist as if I were carrying myself toward fire. I did
feel like someone approaching the doorway to hell
behind which I would surely find the devil herself.
Under my arm, the metal box and its horrible information burned.

The late afternoon sun had fallen behind dark clouds.
Shadows appeared to grow right before my eyes as I
started down the second floor hallway toward Grandma
Olivia's bedroom. My heart thumped with each step. I
felt drugged, dazed, moving through the corridors of a
nightmare. I wasn't even sure I could speak. I thought
that when I opened my mouth, all I would do is hiss.

Just before I reached the bedroom door, it opened and
Mrs. Grafton stepped out. At first she didn't see me in
the shadows. Then I stepped forward into the dim hall
light. My appearance gave her a start and she gasped,
putting her hand to her heart.

"Oh, I didn't see you standing there," she said. She

paused, blinking rapidly as she studied me. "Are you all right?"

"I have to talk to my grandmother," I said in a dreary, dark tone.

"She's going in and out," she said.

"Nevertheless, I have to talk to her," I said. Mrs. Grafton shrugged.

"Suit yourself. I'm going down to get something to eat and then I'll be bringing her dinner."

I nodded and she walked away. I hesitated, my hand frozen in the air between the knob and myself. I was hoping that at any moment this really would prove to be only a nightmare. Perhaps when I touched that doorknob, I would wake with a shudder and find myself in bed.

I didn't.

I turned the knob and entered the bedroom.

Grandma Olivia was propped up somewhat on double pillows. Her hair lay in loose strands around her cheeks. Her mouth, twisted and puffy, was slightly open and her eyes were closed. Crippled, felled by this illness, she would have resembled any one of thousands of elderly people stored in old age infirmaries waiting for the clock to make its final tick. However, her diamond rings and bracelets, her rich satin sheets and her linen nightgown loudly declared that this was still a woman of power and prestige. She could issue orders from beyond the grave.

I stood by the bedside glaring down at her, watching her small bosom rise and fall. Her nose twitched and her lips trembled and parted showing some gray teeth. Her forehead formed folds, as painful ugly thoughts traveled with lightning speed behind her eyes and reverberated in that darkness closed up within her.

I waited and then I put the metal box down on the bed beside her and opened it. Her eyelids fluttered, opened and then closed before opening again. She gazed up at me, her eyes gathering light as she became more and more aware of where she was and who I was. Her mouth opened and she uttered some sound. Surely, I thought, some command.

"I've come to ask you some questions," I said, "and I want you to know right from the start that your illness won't stop me from demanding answers."

Her eyes widened, both with surprise and indignation. She started to protest when I lifted the metal box and held it up high enough for her to see. Her eyes shifted, studied the box and then returned to my face, her face grimacing with new anxiety.

"Yes, Grandma, I found it. Grandpa Samuel talked about it enough to catch my curiosity and I went down to the basement where you had buried all your sins and I found it and what was inside," I said, plucking the first document and holding it for a moment. Then I put the box down and unfolded the document.

She started to shake her head, but I continued.

"I know you are well aware of what is on this and the other papers, but I want you to look at it again. I'm sure you buried everything downstairs so you wouldn't have to look at it again, but now you do."

I thrust the paper out, holding it in front of her. Her eyes moved over it and then she tried to turn away, but I reached out quickly and put my hand on her forehead, easily bringing her head back so she had to look at me and the paper.

"Who did you think you were? Did you think you were God? What gave you the right to do such a thing, to control everyone else's pain and suffering, to determine someone's whole life and the lives of those who loved her and she loved? From where did you get this arrogance of power?"

She began to struggle with speech.

"Fa . . . mmmm . . ."

"How did you get this?" I asked, pulling another document from the box. "How did you get him to do it? It has something to do with all the rest of it, doesn't it? I'm going to find out, Grandma. I'm going to learn every nitty-gritty detail and I'm going to expose all of it," I declared.

Her eyes went as wide as they could and for the first time since I had known her, I saw real fear burning in them. She shook her head vigorously.

"Naaaaa."

"Yes, Grandma, yes. The precious Logan name will be dragged down into the gutter where it belongs. You may have wealth and property, but you're no better than the most common criminal and neither are those who assisted you in this."

"Fammmmmm."

"Oh, you're trying to tell me you did this for the family again, is that it?"

She nodded.

"You were just protecting all the others?" I asked with a cold smile. Once again, she nodded vigorously. My smile evaporated. "That's the biggest lie of all, Grandma Olivia. Whatever you've done, you've done for yourself, to keep your precious high and mighty position in the community, or your precious reputation. Or you did things to get revenge or hurt those who didn't give you the love and respect you thought you deserved. Don't throw the word 'family' at me. Family is just your excuse for evil. I know that now."

She stopped shaking her head and stared. I put the documents back into the metal box.

"I don't know the end of the story, of course, but I will get to the end," I promised.

I closed the box and put it under my arm again.

"As I look at you now, I realize you are only just beginning to get what you deserve, Grandma. I almost pitied you. I almost did what you hate: I almost felt sorry for you, but you don't have to worry about that anymore. I can't find enough forgiveness to sympathize one iota with you. You're home free there, Grandma," I said.

"When I finish this, I'm going to tell the doctor to put you in the infirmary where you belong. You told me not to hesitate when the time came, didn't you? You were so brave then. Well, Aunt Sara, Cary and I will see to it and even Judge Childs will not resist."

I paused.

"I assume he knew about this too, didn't he?" I asked, holding up the box. She stared a moment, closed her eyes and then opened them and shook her head. "He didn't? Why not? You mean there was something he would have denied you after all? Were you afraid of that?"

She nodded and then started to shake her head and reach out for me, but I stepped back.

"There is nothing you could say, nothing, no words, no thoughts, nothing that would justify what you have done and the pain you have caused."

I turned and she cried out in her distorted way, uttering a guttural scream that reverberated through my body. With all her remaining strength, she propped herself up and then cried out again, but I turned my back on her and marched out of the room, the echo of her horrible sound shut away behind me.

As soon as I left her, I went downstairs to the office and called Cary.

"I want you to come and get me, Cary," I said. "I need you to take me someplace."

"When?"

"Right now," I said.

"What's going on? You sound so strange," he said.

"Will you do it?" I replied.

"Sure, but—"

"Thank you. Just be patient with me and I'll explain everything in time, okay? Please," I added.

"Okay, Melody," he said. "I'll come."

After I finished talking to him, I took a deep breath, went to the telephone book, looked up the number and called my father. His wife answered.

"May I please speak with Mr. Jackson?" I said.

"Whom may I say is calling?"

"Melody Logan," I said curtly.

"One moment please."

Seconds later, he was on the phone.

325

"This is Teddy Jackson," he said formally.

"Meet me in your office in a half hour," I said.

"Pardon?"

"Meet me in your office. I have something to show you and something to ask. Actually, a lot to ask."

"I'm not sure I understand," he said weakly.

"You will," I promised. "Be there," I said and hung up, my heart pounding so hard, I had to pause to take a deep breath and calm myself.

I saw Mrs. Grafton walk by with my grandmother's dinner tray. She glanced in at me, but continued toward the stairway.

Grandma Olivia won't have much of an appetite tonight, I thought.

Twenty minutes later, Cary pulled up in front of the house and I ran out to get into his truck.

"What's going on? Something more with Grandma Olivia? Did they take her to the hospital?"

"Not yet," I said. "Take me downtown, Cary."

"To where?"

"My father's office," I said.

"What?"

"Please."

He stared at me a moment.

"What's in that box?"

"I promise I'll explain everything as soon as I can," I said. "Trust me."

"Sure." He shrugged, started the engine again and drove us away.

"Whatever it is, I hope you'll tell me about it soon," he said as headed toward Commercial Street. He glanced at me. "I don't remember you ever acting this strange, Melody."

I took a deep breath but said nothing. He shook his head and drove faster. When we arrived in front of the law offices of Teddy Jackson, we saw the lights were on inside and his car was in its reserved parking space. Cary started to get out of the truck.

"Please wait for me in the truck, Cary," I said.

"Why?"

"This is something I have to do myself first. Please."

"I don't like this, Melody. You're in some kind of trouble. I should know more about it and I should be able to help you."

"I'm not in trouble, Cary. It's not that. Please, be a little more patient," I said.

Reluctantly, he got back into the truck and closed the door.

"Thank you," I said and stepped out.

My father's offices were plush, richly carpeted with real leather waiting room sofas, paneled walls and oil paintings. There was a large legal library and his own office was oversized with a set of back windows giving a full view of the harbor. He was standing by the window with his hands in his pockets gazing out when I entered.

"What's this all about?" he asked, obviously a little annoyed at the way I had ordered his appearance.

"It's about all this," I said, putting the metal box on his large, dark mahogany desk. He stared at it a moment and then walked over.

"What's this?" He opened the box and took out one of the documents. As he read it, his face took on more of a crimson tint. He glanced at me, put the paper down and read another. "She gave you this?"

"No. She had it hidden in the basement," I said.

He nodded, blew some air through his lips and then sat at his desk.

"Who else knows about it?"

"Just me for now," I said. "Cary is waiting outside in the truck, but I haven't told him anything yet. I want to know everything first, every dirty detail."

"I don't know every dirty detail," he replied sharply. I glared down at him and he shifted his eyes guiltily away. "I didn't want to do it, but she blackmailed me," he began and turned back to me.

I sat in front of the desk.

"Go on," I said.

"I didn't think she knew the truth about Haille and

me. I'm still not positive about how she found out. I suspect Haille told her, taunted her with it maybe. I don't know."

He pulled himself up in his chair.

"She came in here that night, calling me to this office almost the same way you did," he added with a small smile, "and she told me what had happened and what she wanted and what I had to do.

"I started to resist and she told me she would not hesitate to expose me, to bring Haille back, to destroy me just when I was getting a wonderful start.

"So I did what she wanted. I took care of all the legal issues," he confessed. "I wasn't happy about it and I couldn't look Jacob and Sara in the face anymore, but in time she had me believing it was for the best."

"Oh, I'm sure you were concerned," I said disdainfully.

"Well, I . . . look, it was her decision," he protested.

"She wasn't the mother; she wasn't the father. It wasn't her decision. You let her play God!" I shouted.

He seemed to shrivel in the chair. His eyes went down.

"What happened to her?" I asked. I didn't want to say anything to Cary before I knew every possible detail and before I knew her final fate.

He looked up.

"Olivia didn't tell you anything?"

"Grandma Olivia had a stroke. I thought everyone in Provincetown knew by now. She can't talk."

"Oh."

"Well?"

"I know only what I was told, Melody. Laura and Robert Royce went sailing. They got caught in a storm and Robert drowned. Olivia told me Karl Hansen picked her up in his fishing trawler and brought Laura directly to her. She was a raving lunatic, suffering from traumatic amnesia. She was naked when he found her at sea and Olivia, well, Olivia thought the worst of that, of course. Anyway, Karl had worked for Samuel and knew who Laura was. Olivia took control after that. She made sure

Karl told no one and then she decided to have Laura secretly institutionalized. I think the whole affair embarrassed her. Legal guardianship was established and Laura was left there where she remains to this day, as far as I know. I never . . ."

"Never cared to find out?"

"It was out of my hands by then," he protested. "I just assumed, as the years went by, that she never . . . that it was for the best."

"Which eased your own conscience," I accused. I stood up. "I expect you will give us any help we need now," I said. He nodded.

"After I had discovered that the man I believed was my father was really my stepfather, I used to dream about the man who was my real father. I used to imagine he was a wonderful person, someone who might not even have known he had me as a daughter, but once he found out, he would come running to me, wanting to love me, to do things for me. I used to dream we would finally have a daughter–father relationship."

"Melody—"

"Now," I quickly continued, "I am grateful that you chose to be a coward. I don't want anyone ever to know that you are my real father," I said. "I couldn't get over the shame."

He stared at me, his face bright red, while I gathered up the papers and put them back into the metal box.

"You're just like her, actually," I said. "No wonder fate brought you together."

"Melody . . ."

I turned and walked away from him, hopefully forever.

Cary read the documents ravenously and then put the papers down and looked at me, his eyes wide, his mouth pulled so tightly in the corners, his lips looked like they would snap.

"I don't understand," he said. He shook his head, refusing to believe in such a betrayal and such deception.

We were sitting in the truck in front of his home. Dark

329

clouds had accompanied the twilight and now there was a steady, hard rain. I told him all that my father had told me.

"All this time we've been thinking Grandpa Samuel was babbling about what had been done to Grandma Belinda," I concluded.

"How could this be? Why?"

Tears spilled over his lids and trickled down his cheeks as if they were tiny watery creatures escaping. He didn't seem to realize it, even as they dripped from his chin.

"Her own grandmother," he said. "My father's mother . . ."

"In her distorted way of thinking, she somehow believed she was protecting the family from disgrace and hardship. There is no way to justify what she did and I condemn her for it as much as you will," I said, "but after living with her and learning who she is and some other things she believes and has done, I understand how this could have happened."

"I don't. I never will."

He closed his eyes and held his head back as if to swallow down some pain.

"My father . . . my father suffered great guilt about Laura."

"I know."

"And Grandma Olivia knew it, too. She must have known it," he said quickly.

"Maybe. Maybe she saw only her own guilt, her own pain, her own fears, Cary."

"She doesn't have an ounce of love in her," he muttered through his teeth. "I hate her more than I have ever hated anyone. I'm glad she had a stroke. I hope she dies tonight," he said.

"Don't become like her, Cary. You only end up so full of hate you can't love."

He stared a moment.

"What do we do? Do I tell Ma now?"

"No. Let's go there first," I said. "Perhaps . . . we can bring her home."

He nodded, smiling.

"Maybe so." He reached for the key in the ignition.

"We'll go in the morning, Cary. It's too late now," I said.

"No. I don't want to think of her being there five minutes more," he said. "We have to go now," he insisted. He looked at the papers. "I know where this is. It's a four, four-and-a-half hour drive."

"But it will be the middle of the night," I reminded him.

"Who cares about that?" he said and started the engine. "I can drop you off, if you want."

"Cary Logan, do you think I would let you do this yourself?"

He shook his head.

"Okay, let's go," I said. "We probably couldn't sleep anyway. Shouldn't you tell your mother something?"

"No, I don't want to utter one more lie, even a white one," he said.

I smiled.

"Okay, but we've got to be prepared for anything, Cary."

"I'm prepared," he said. He started away. "As prepared as I could ever be."

It was a long, hard ride. Cary talked more about Laura than he had ever talked, recalling things they had done together, things she used to say. I sensed these were thoughts he had forbidden himself to have these past few years. He was afraid of what reviving such memories might do to him.

A few times during the journey, he sat there silently, crying, tears streaming down his cheeks as he relived the tragedy and everyone's sorrow.

How could Grandma Olivia attend those services knowing what she knew? I wondered. How could she be so confident she was doing the right thing for the family, so positive that she could bury her feelings, watch her son suffer and not say a word? Instead of a heart in that chest, she surely had a cube of ice, I thought. How horrible her own parents must have been to her to shape her into the woman she had become.

I shouldn't have been surprised. She put her sister away without a single regret and did the same to her husband. Individuals meant nothing in the face of her fanatical faith in the family name. Love was merely a minor inconvenience. Correct behavior, prestige, respect, wealth and power were the five points of her star, and that star was embedded on the face of her soul.

I lay back and closed my eyes and dozed for a while. When I woke, we were near a town. I saw the lights of an all-night restaurant.

"You want some hot coffee or something?" Cary asked.

"Yes, please," I said and we pulled in and ordered coffee and doughnuts.

Cary drank and ate in a deadly silence, his eyes fixed on his anger, brightening with the stream of furious thoughts behind them. I didn't speak. I reached for his hand and smiled at him. He snapped out of his daze and nodded.

"I'm all right," he said. "We'll be all right."

"Yes, we will, Cary. We will," I agreed.

We had another hour's ride before we found the entrance to the institution. It was a tall, gray stone building with a parking lot on its left. It was too dark to see clearly, but we could make out some nice grounds around it. We saw the high fences and then woods.

The outside lights in front of the building were bright. We parked and after Cary shut off the engine, we just sat there, both trying to gather strength.

"Ready?" he asked me finally. I nodded and we got out and walked to the entrance. The door was locked, but there was a buzzer beside it with a little sign that read USE ONLY AFTER TEN P.M. Cary pushed the buzzer and we waited. Because of the reflection of the outside lights on the glass of the doorway, we couldn't see very much of the inside. It looked like a small entryway before a set of double doors. No one came so Cary pushed the buzzer again, holding it longer.

"It's pretty late, Cary."

"Someone's got to be here," he said undaunted.

Finally, the double doors were opened and a redheaded man in a pair of white pants and a light blue shirt stepped out. He looked no more than thirty, thin and slim-waisted, at least six feet tall with freckles over his forehead and cheeks. He peered through the glass before opening the door, scowled and then opened it quickly.

"What'dya want?" he demanded.

"We're here to get someone," Cary said firmly.

"Huh?"

"My sister," Cary said.

"What the hell are you talking about? It's almost three o'clock in the morning," the redheaded man said.

"I don't care what time it is. She's not supposed to be here," Cary said and stepped between the man and the door. The redheaded man recoiled as if he thought Cary would strike him.

"You can't come in here now. Visiting hours begin at ten A.M.," he said.

"We're here and we're coming in. Get whoever is in charge," Cary ordered.

The redheaded man looked from him to me and then stepped toward the double doors. Cary put his hand out to keep the double doors from closing.

"You're going to get into big trouble for this," the redheaded man threatened.

"Good," Cary said. "Now go get a supervisor or someone. Do it!" Cary ordered, so fiercely, the man rushed off. Cary and I followed and entered the lobby. There was a counter with a glass window ahead of us. To the right were sofas and chairs, small tables, magazine racks and a television set. The door directly in front of us most probably led into the institution, I thought.

We waited and finally heard footsteps on the other side

333

of the door. It was opened and a very heavy woman in a nurse's uniform came charging out, her dark brown hair chopped rather crudely at the nape of her neck and ear lobes, her hips rubbing against the stiff material of the uniform, producing a loud swish.

"What's this all about?" she demanded, directing her beady black eyes at Cary. She folded her arms over her heavy bosom like a battering ram and walked within inches of him.

"My sister was illegally brought here," Cary said. "We've come to take her home."

She stared at him a moment, grimaced with confusion and then glanced at the redheaded man.

"Should I call the police?" he asked.

"Not quite yet," she said. Her curiosity was piqued.

"Who are you and who is this sister you are looking for?" she asked.

"I'm Cary Logan. This is Melody Logan. My sister's name is Laura. Show her," Cary said and I produced some of the documents taken from the metal box. She eyed me suspiciously and then took them and began to read. When she was finished, I saw that her face softened a bit.

"You just found out about all this?" she asked.

"Yes, today," Cary said. "Those papers are incorrect. My sister did have parents and not a legal guardian," he said.

"Where are your parents? Why didn't they come here, too, if this is so?"

"My father recently died and my mother . . . my mother is not able to make this journey. In fact, she doesn't know the truth yet," Cary explained.

The nurse handed the documents back to me.

"This is a legal matter," she said. "It has to be handled in a proper way."

"Look—"

"But as for your coming for your sister," she continued, "I'm afraid you're too late."

"What?"

My heart stopped. I stepped forward and took Cary's hand quickly.

"This young lady unfortunately died a short time after she was admitted," she said.

"Died? How?" I asked.

"She drowned. We informed the grandmother about it. She was listed as next of kin."

"How could she drown?"

"It was deliberate, self-induced," the nurse confessed after a moment. "I'm not permitted to discuss the details. There are always legal issues when something like this occurs. It wasn't our fault, however," she added quickly. "I really don't understand who you are and why you're here," she continued.

Cary just stared at her, refusing to believe her.

"I want to see my sister now," he said.

The nurse looked at me to see if she had heard right.

"Don't you understand what I'm saying?" she said.

"Cary, come on," I said.

"No. I want to see her right now. I'm not leaving until I do," he insisted.

"Call the police," the nurse told the redheaded man. He spun around and disappeared inside.

"Cary, it's no use," I urged. He shook his head.

"You're lying," he told the nurse. "She got to you. You were told to say this in case I ever arrived, weren't you?"

"Absolutely not. I don't know anything about you," the nurse said. "And I don't lie about my patients."

Another attendant arrived, an older, bigger man.

"You having some sort of trouble, Mrs. Kleckner?" he asked.

"Yes," she said. "The police have been called, Morris. No one is permitted into the hospital," she said, her eyes fixed on Cary.

"Cary, let's go," I pleaded, but he was as stiff and unmovable as one of Kenneth's statues. It was like trying to uproot a tree.

The larger attendant took his position in the doorway. Mrs. Kleckner turned to me.

"I'm not lying about this. You have to go through proper channels and you will learn I've told you the truth. You're just making things harder for yourselves."

"I'm sorry," I said, "but you have to understand we just learned about all this and it really was done illegally. I'm sure you can imagine the shock. That's why he's so upset. He doesn't mean to make trouble for you. Please understand," I begged.

She considered and then nodded.

"Wait here. I have something that might help you accept what I'm saying," she declared and left us. The attendant was joined by the redheaded man and they both blocked the doorway.

"Cops are on their way," he said gleefully.

"Cary, we're only getting ourselves into deeper trouble," I whispered. He didn't hear me. He glared at the two attendants. Moments later, the nurse reappeared, carrying a small cloth bag.

"These were her personal things. Among them," she said, "is this," she said, lifting a thick notebook out of the bag. "It was her diary. Her doctors encouraged her to keep it, hoping recollections, thoughts would help her revive her identity. Apparently, no one ever came for it. If she wasn't gone," the nurse added in a harder tone, "I wouldn't be giving it to you, now would I?"

I took the bag and the notebook and tugged on Cary's hand.

"Please, Cary. She's right."

He wilted, accepting what he was told.

"Where is she buried?" he asked softly.

"I don't know. You'll have to contact Mr. Crowley tomorrow and ask him for whatever details he has. He's the administrator here. He will be in his office at nine a.m. I'm asking you now to leave these premises. The police are on their way and you will be placed under arrest if you don't go," she threatened.

"Cary—"

"We're too late," he said more to himself than to me.

"I'm sorry," Mrs. Kleckner said, "but I have told you

the truth. I've done more than I have to do and more than Mr. Crowley will approve of, I'm sure."

"Thank you," I said, pulling Cary harder.

He stepped back with me.

"Laura," he said shaking his head. "I'm sorry we were too late."

We reached the truck just as the police car arrived. The officers spoke to Mrs. Kleckner and then questioned us. When I promised we would leave, they let us go.

Cary drove back on the strength of his anger and hate. We hardly said a word to each other. All that mattered to him now was to find out where Laura had been buried. It was mid-morning by the time we drove into Grandma Olivia's driveway. Both of us were physically exhausted, but our emotions gave us the strength to continue.

Loretta came rushing down the hallway when we entered the house.

"Where have you been?" she asked.

"What is it?"

"Your grandmother turned worse last night and was rushed to the hospital," she said.

"She's not going to die," Cary said, shaking his head at me. "She's not getting away that easily."

Loretta's eyes nearly bulged out of her head.

"What?"

"Nothing. We're on our way to the hospital," I told her and we left.

We found Judge Childs in the lobby talking with the doctor when we arrived.

"Melody! Where have you two been?" he asked. "Everyone's been worried sick."

"Never mind where we've been," Cary said. "How is she? Can she talk?"

"I'm afraid not," the doctor said. "She's fallen into a coma."

Cary's shoulders sank. Then he brightened with a thought.

"Do you know about Laura?" he asked the Judge.

"What? What about Laura?"

"He doesn't know, Cary," I said. "She did tell me that."

"What's he talking about, Melody?" the Judge asked.

We went to the hospital cafeteria to get something to eat and I told my grandfather the story. He listened with horror.

"I guess I really never knew her," he said. "To keep all that from me. She was a very determined, private woman who literally needed no one. I'm sorry," he said to Cary. "I'll find out what you want to know. I promise," he said. "You two go home and get some rest. Let me take care of this."

"Thank you, Grandpa," I said and he smiled.

I went home with Cary to help him with Aunt Sara and May, after which we went up to his attic hideaway and fell asleep in each other's arms.

At the moment it seemed to be the safest place in the whole world.

Epilogue

ജ

Grandma Olivia died two days later, having never regained consciousness. Her doctor said it was a blessing because if she would have come out of the coma, she would have been far worse and Olivia Logan was not the sort of woman who could live under institutionalized care.

Cary didn't want to attend the funeral, but a strange thing happened to me. I suddenly saw things from Grandma Olivia's prospective. Why air our dirty laundry in public? Why embarrass the family?

"After all," I explained, "you still want to live and build a life here, Cary."

He listened and then shook his head with a smile.

"You were probably the right choice for Grandma Olivia's throne, Melody. I'll give the devil her credit there, but that's about all," he added firmly. "Okay, I'll put on the proper face. I see I'm going to need you to make sure I do the right things from now on," he kidded.

Kenneth and Holly had returned from their honeymoon and we had all spent a night together going over the recent events.

"She was a cold, hard woman, and so intimidating, most men didn't challenge her, especially the men in her family," Kenneth remarked. "I remember how afraid I was of her when I was younger and used to visit with Haille, Chester and Jacob. When she told us something, we did it and did it fast. I never thought of her as happy though."

"She didn't want anyone else to be happy either," Cary muttered.

None of us spoke. It was better to let the thunder and lightning play itself out and look forward to brighter skies.

The funeral was as large as expected. We decided not to have Grandpa Samuel brought along. He didn't understand what was happening and we all agreed it would be just more confusing and troublesome for him.

I don't know how I got through my final exams, but I did and my grades were as good as I had hoped. I stayed at Aunt Sara's and shut myself up in what had been Laura's room, spending almost two days writing and rewriting my valedictorian speech.

Since Grandma Olivia's hospitalization and death, I had moved in with Cary, Aunt Sara and May again. I hated the thought of being in that grand empty mansion, full of darkness, shadows and family secrets.

The Judge began to go over all the estate documents for us and one day, we all went to his home to listen to what would be. Grandma Olivia had done what she had promised . . . she had left instructions for my taking eventual control of most of the family fortune. In the meantime it was held in a trust supervised by her bankers and brokers and the Judge was appointed executor.

"You will have to decide about the house," he said. "You can put it up for sale or you can move into it."

"Let's put it up for sale," I said quickly. "I don't think it holds enough happy memories for the family."

"I understand," the Judge said.

With such a fortune in our hands, Cary could be confidant that his boat building business would be a reality. He could build on his small beginnings and establish his own company. Kenneth gave him advice and the two of them went searching the area for a good site to put up a factory.

The night before graduation, Cary and I took a walk on the beach. I was too nervous to sleep anyway. So much attention was on me and our family since Grandma Olivia's passing. I was nervous and sure the audience would hang on every word of my valedictorian address.

"Have you given thought to what you want to do, Melody?" Cary asked me. We stopped at the edge of the water and stared out at the moonwalk that led to the edge of the world.

"I'm not going to the prep school, Cary. The kind of life Grandma Olivia was designing for me is not the life I want for myself," I said. "I don't want to strive to get my name in the society columns."

"I know you're very smart and should probably go to college, but—"

"I don't want to go to college just to say I'm in college, Cary. Maybe I'll go next year. But somewhere close. I think I have a clear view of what I want now."

"What's that?" he asked turning to me.

"I want something simpler but more substantial. I want what I never had, Cary. I want a real family, real love."

"Could you have it with me? Now?" he asked timidly. "We could build this new business together and we could build our own house and we—"

I put my fingers on his lips.

"I was wondering when you would have the nerve to ask," I said and he laughed.

We kissed and held each other. The ocean seemed to glitter even more and the stars, the stars were never ever as bright.

The next day was magnificent. Without a cloud in the sky, with the wind warm and gentle, we were able to have an outdoor graduation ceremony. I began my speech with the first lines of a mountain song Papa George had taught me years and years ago.

"I have come a long way from home with just
    a hope and a prayer,
But I got a suitcase full of memories to keep
    me warm on lonely nights."

I turned to my fellow graduates and talked about graduation as a kind of pulling up on the anchor and setting sail—of being captains of our own destiny. We were leaving our parents, our friends and our teachers back on the shore and setting out on a course of our own making. I talked about courage and opportunity and thanked our families and teachers for giving it to us. I ended by singing the first line of *This Land Is Your Land* and an amazing thing happened: the whole audience joined me and sang the whole song.

I was overwhelmed by the applause and the congratulations afterward. People who didn't know me well told me how proud Grandma Olivia would have been. Cary's eyes grew dark and angry, but he kept his rage contained when I gave him a look of reprimand.

Afterward, we had a party at Aunt Sara's. Kenneth, Holly and Judge Childs were there, as well as Roy Patterson and Theresa. Cary made a clam bake and I played the fiddle. Judge Childs said he would take a piece of the graduation cake up to Grandpa Samuel the next day.

Cary and I set a date for our wedding soon afterward. In the meantime, I spent my summer days with May and Aunt Sara while Cary worked on the new boat and began to build the factory on the site he and Kenneth had found.

One morning May came in with the mail and waved something at me, all excited. It was a postcard. It had been sent from Palm Springs, California. There wasn't much written.

Hi,
    I just thought I'd drop you a line to tell you I'm no longer with Richard. I'm with a real agent this time. He's even taken me to Palm Springs for a holiday and he says I have a good chance of making it.
    Wish me luck.

Gina Simon

"Who's Gina Simon?" May signed and then pronounced as best she could.

"Just someone I once knew," I said. "No one, really."

I tossed the card into the garbage can, but later, I went back and retrieved it.

I couldn't help it. I was like someone lost on the desert who had been given a drop of water to cherish. What else could I do?

I went upstairs and put the letter with my other mementos.

And then I looked at Laura's bag of possessions, the only things left from her strange and tragic existence. Neither Cary nor I could get ourselves to do anything about them.

I couldn't just ignore them anymore, however. I reached in and took out the thick notebook which had been her diary. Then I went downstairs and sat behind the house in the big wooden chair that faced the ocean and I began to read.

A long time ago, I lived a fairy tale life, it began. My eyes lifted from the page as I took a deep breath.

Off in the distance a sailboat looked caught in the calm and remained painted against the blue horizon while above it, puffy white clouds waited for the same wind.

All the world was standing still, holding its breath. Even the terns froze on the beach and looked my way.

When the wind began again, it carried a song it wished I would sing for Laura, for Cary, for all of us.

I would sing it, I thought.

Now, finally, I would sing it.

MUSIC IN THE NIGHT

Prologue

&

A long time ago, I lived a fairy tale life. There was always magic around me: magic in the stars, magic in the ocean and magic in the sand. At night when we were only ten years old, Cary and I would lie back on our blankets on the deck of our daddy's lobster boat and gaze up at the heavens, pretending we were falling into outer space, flying past this planet and that, circling moons and reaching out to touch the stars. We permitted our minds to wander and imagine. We said anything we wanted to each other, never ashamed or too embarrassed to reveal our most secret thoughts, our dreams, our intimate questions.

We were twins, but Cary liked to call himself my older brother because, according to Papa, he was born two minutes and twenty-nine seconds before me. He behaved like an older brother from the moment he could crawl and protect me. He cried when I was unhappy and he laughed when he heard me laugh, even if he didn't know why I was laughing. When I asked him about that once, he said the sound of my laughter was music to him and it pleased him so much, he couldn't help but smile and then laugh, too. It was as if we were enchanted children who heard our own songs, melodies that were sung to us by the sea we loved so much.

As far back as I can remember, there was always magic in the water. Cary could wade in and come walking out with the most spectacular seaweed, starfish, clamshells, seashells, and even things he claimed had washed across the ocean from other countries to us. When it came to the ocean, I believed anything he said. Sometimes I thought Cary must have been born with seawater in his veins. No one loved it as much, even when it was nasty and wild.

What discoveries Daddy let us keep, we kept in either Cary's room or mine. We decided everything had some sort of power to it, whether it was the power to grant us a wish or the power to make us healthier or happier just by touching it. We assigned an enchanted quality to each thing we found.

When I was twelve and I wore a necklace made from the tiny seashells we had found, my friends at school were amazed at the way I identified each and every shell, explaining how this one could drive away sadness or that one could make the dark clouds move on. They laughed and shook their heads and said Cary and I were simply foolish and even immature. It was time we grew up and put away childish ideas. There was no magic in these things for them.

But to me there was even magic in a grain of sand. Cary and I once sat beside each other and let the sand fall through our fingers, pretending each grain was a tiny world unto itself. Inside it lived people like us, too tiny to ever be seen, even with a strong microscope.

"Be careful where you step," we told our friends when they were with us on the beach. "You might crush a whole country."

They grimaced with confusion, shook their heads and walked on, leaving us behind, enveloped by our own imaginative pictures, pictures no one else wanted to share. We were inseparable for so long, I guess people thought we had been born attached. Some of my jealous girlfriends once made up a story about me, claiming I had a long scar down

350

the side of my body from my underarm to my waist and Cary had the same scar on his body. It was where we supposedly had been connected at birth.

Sometimes, I thought, maybe it's true, that from the moment we entered this world, our separating had begun, a slow and painful process. It was a separation Cary fought much harder than I did as we grew older.

As a very young girl and even when I first entered my junior high school years, I was comfortable, happy and grateful for Cary's devotion to me. Other brothers and sisters I knew argued and occasionally insulted each other, often in public! Cary never said a really bad thing to me, and if he spoke to me in a manner that suggested he was impatient or annoyed with me, he immediately regretted it afterward.

I knew that other girls fixed their flirtatious gazes at Cary and competed with each other for his attention. It wasn't just a sister's prejudice for me to say Cary was handsome. From the first day he could cast a rope or carry a pail, he accompanied Daddy on the lobster boat and helped in the cranberry bog. He always had a dark tan that brought out the emeralds in his green eyes, and he loved to wear his rich dark hair long, the strands lying softly over the right side of his forehead, just above his eyebrow. It looked so much like silk, girls were jealous and all of them longed to run their fingers through it.

My brother carried himself firmly with the demeanor of a confident little man, even when he was just in grade school. Other boys used to make fun of the way he held up his head and shoulders, striding alongside me with his gaze firmly fixed on where we were headed, his lips tight. Soon, however, they started to envy him, and girls in our classes just naturally thought of him as older, more mature.

Frustrated by their failure to win his attention and interest, however, they eventually found comfort in making fun of us. By the time we were in high school, they were calling Cary "Grandpa." He didn't seem to care or even notice. I was sure it bothered me more than it bothered him, and it wasn't unless someone physically got into his face or insulted me in front of him that Cary reacted, almost always violently. It didn't matter if the other boy was bigger or even if there were more than one. Cary's temper was as quick and as devastating as a hurricane. His eyes became glassy and his lips were stretched so tightly they formed white spots in the corners. Anyone who challenged him directly knew they were in for a fight.

Of course, Cary would get into trouble, no matter how justified his reaction was. It was he who had lost his temper and usually he who dealt the most damage to his opponents. Almost every time he was suspended from school, Daddy gave him a beating and confined him to his room, but nothing Daddy could do and no punishment the school could impose would deter him if he believed my honor was somehow compromised.

With such a devoted and loyal protector watching over me, other boys kept their distance. It wasn't until I entered high school that I realized how untouchable I had become in their eyes. Many girls my age had crushes on boys or had boyfriends, but no boy dared pass me a note in class, and none joined me in the hallways to walk from one class to another, much less walk me home. I walked with some girlfriends or with Cary, and if I walked with girls, Cary usually followed behind us like my guard dog.

When I reached sophomore year, however, I, like most of my girlfriends, wanted a boy who showed serious interest in me. There was a boy named Stephen Daniels, who had lived in Provincetown only a year, who I thought was very handsome. I wanted him to talk to me, to walk with me, and even ask me to go on a date. I thought he wanted to because he was always looking at me, but he never did. All my girlfriends at the time told me he wanted to, but said he wouldn't because of my brother. Stephen was afraid of Cary.

I mentioned it to Cary and he said Stephen Daniels was stupid and would go out with any girl if that girl gave him what he wanted. He said he knew that from listening to him in the boys' locker room. Later, I found out Cary had actually walked up to him and put his face an inch from Stephen's, threatening to break his neck if he should so much as look twice at me. Naturally, I was disappointed, but I couldn't help wondering if Cary had been right.

In the evenings after we had done our homework and helped Mommy with May, our younger sister who had been born deaf and was attending a special school for the handicapped, Cary and I would talk about some of the other kids at school. No matter what girlfriend of mine I mentioned to him, he found fault with her. The only girl he didn't criticize was Theresa Patterson, Roy Patterson's oldest child. Theresa's father, Roy, worked with Daddy on the lobster boat. The Pattersons were Bravas, half African-American, half Portuguese. The other students looked down their noses at them, especially the ones who came from so-called blue-blooded families, families who were able to trace their lineage back to the Pilgrims, families like Grandma Olivia's, Daddy's mother, who ruled over us like a dowager queen.

Cary liked Theresa and enjoyed being friends with her because he liked the way she and her Brava friends defied the other students. When I asked him if he could ever think of Theresa as a girlfriend, he raised his eyebrows as if I had said the silliest thing and replied, "Don't be stupid, Laura. Theresa's like another sister to me."

I suppose she was, but as I grew older and felt Cary's shadow over my shoulder more and more, I began to wish he found some other girl to win his attention. I did my best to recommend this one or that, but nothing I said made him act any differently toward them. If anything, when I mentioned a possible girlfriend for him, that girl suddenly became ugly or stupid in his eyes. I realized it might be better if I just let nature take its course.

Only, nature didn't.

I used to think nature just missed Cary. She walked by one day while he was out on the lobster boat or something. Other boys his age were trying to get dates, hanging out in

353

town, showing off to get a girl's attention, asking girls to do things with them; but Cary . . . Cary spent all his free time with me or his model boats upstairs in his attic workshop, a room just above mine.

Finally, one day at lunch I mentioned my growing concern to Theresa. She rolled her dark eyes and looked at me as if I had just been hatched.

"Don't you hear all the talk behind your back? All the whispering and gossip? There isn't a girl in this school who thinks Cary's normal, Laura; and most of the boys have their doubts about *you*. They don't talk to me about it, but I hear what they say."

"What do you mean? What sort of things are they saying about us?" I asked, trembling in anticipation.

"They're saying you and your brother are like boyfriend and girlfriend, Laura," she replied hesitantly.

My heart skipped a beat and I remember looking around the cafeteria that day and thinking everyone was looking at us, their eyes full of contempt. I shook my head, the deeper realizations taking shape like some dark, ugly beast who had crawled out of a nightmare into my daytime thoughts.

"Look at you," Theresa continued. "You're fifteen now and one of the prettiest girls in this school, but do you have a boyfriend? No. Anyone asking you to the school dances? No. If you go, you go with Cary."

"But—"

"There are no buts, Laura. It's because of Cary," she said. "Because of the way he dotes on you. I'm sorry," she added. "I really thought you knew and didn't care."

"What am I going to do?" I moaned.

She nudged me with her shoulder like she usually did when she was going to say something nasty about one of the other girls in school.

"Get him a girlfriend who'll stir up his hormones and you'll be fine," she said.

I remember she got up to join her Brava friends and I sat there, suddenly feeling very alone and unhappy. Cary came walking into the cafeteria quickly, spotted me, and marched over.

"Sorry I'm late," he said. "Mr. Corkren kept me after class about my homework again. What's going on?" He looked closely at me when I didn't respond. "Did something happen?"

I just shook my head. I wondered how I could tell him and not hurt him.

I put it off and never really tried to make him understand until the year after, when Robert Royce and his family bought the old Sea Marina Hotel and Robert entered school.

For me and Robert, it was love at first sight and that brought with it a special kind of magic Cary couldn't share.

Somehow I had to make him understand and accept. I had to show him how to separate himself from me.

I only hoped it was possible.

1

Young Love

All day my heart had been beating faster than normal, thumping so hard I was sure Cary heard the echo in my chest. When I walked, it was as if my feet didn't touch the ground. I was floating along on a cloud of air, bouncing with a spring in my step. I was positive I had woken this morning with a smile on my face, and sure enough when I looked at myself in my vanity table mirror, I saw my cheeks were flushed with excitement, the excitement of wonderful dreams that continued into my waking moments, dreams that carried me on a magical carpet like some Arabian princess floating through volumes and volumes of enchantment.

Everything around me took on a new and different glow. Colors I had grown used to were brighter, richer, sharper. Every normal sound became part of a grand symphony, whether it was simply the creak in the stairs as I descended to help Mommy with breakfast, or the clink of dishes and pans, the splash of water running in the sink, the opening and closing of the refrigerator and stove, or the tap of Daddy's, May's, and Cary's footsteps in the hallway, and all their voices. Their voices suddenly became a chorus behind the music.

"You look very nice today, dear," Mommy said at breakfast. Daddy glanced at me and nodded. I held my breath because I was wearing just a touch of lipstick, and Daddy hated makeup on a woman. He said it was the devil's touch and an honest woman never tried to fool a man by using paint on her face.

I had chosen my brightest blue dress with the white collar and I wore my gold charm bracelet, the one Mommy and Daddy had recently given me on my sixteenth birthday. They had given Cary an expensive pocket watch on a gold chain that played "Onward Christian Soldiers" when he flipped open its lid.

Cary looked up from his bowl of oatmeal.

"Aren't you afraid you'll swallow some of that lipstick?" he asked, sending a bolt of ominous lightning through my morning of warm sunshine.

I looked at Daddy, but he just snapped the newspaper and glanced at the headlines. Then I threw Cary my most angry look and he went back to his oatmeal.

When we stepped outside to start for school, I stopped in the doorway, felt the sunshine on my face, and closed my eyes. I embraced my books against my breasts, wishing that none of this was a dream.

"What are you doing?" Cary asked sharply. "You want May to be late for school?"

"I'm sorry," I said, skipping forward to join them. He held May's hand firmly in his own. My little sister, locked in her silence, gazed up at me with a twinkle in her eyes, as if she knew it all, as if she had poked her pretty little face into one of my dreams last night and saw my happiness. I took her other hand and we continued down the street. I felt like Alice in Wonderland.

"You're behaving just like all the other dumb girls in our school," Cary muttered, and threw me a look of reprimand. "Making a fool of yourself over some boy."

I only smiled back at him. Today, I thought, today, I am

358

surrounded by protective sylphs, tiny fairy-like creatures who would deflect any arrows of unhappiness away from me.

There were clouds in the sky, but to me it was all blue. Although it was early May, there was a chill in the air, the residue of yesterday's nor'easter. The whitecaps sprouted on the surface of the sea like water lilies, and even this far away from the shore, we could hear the surf roaring in. In the sunlight, the sand was the color of autumn gold. The terns looked like they were tiptoeing over uncovered treasure as they searched for their morning meal.

My hair was pinned back, but some loose strands whipped gently at my forehead and cheeks. May wore a light blue hairband that kept her hair neatly in place.

Cary couldn't care less how his hair looked when he entered school. He would just run his fingers through it and not even go into the boys room like all the other young men to brush and comb in front of mirrors. Instead, he would accompany me to my locker and wait until I had my books before going on to his own. He would stand there even when Robert Royce joined me, and he would glare unhappily, suspiciously, hardly talking, lingering alongside or just behind us like an angry storm cloud. It was the only thing that put darkness in my heart these days.

"Stop daydreaming and watch where you're walking," Cary ordered as a car sped past us.

The invasion of tourists had begun in small ways. The entire Cape was busier now on weekends, but traffic during the week was still at a lazy crawl down Commercial Street. Our route in the morning took us down side streets to May's school. At the gate we each kissed her and signed our good-byes, Cary putting on his best Daddy-like face to warn her to behave herself, as if she ever needed a warning. There was no one sweeter, no one more gentle and fragile and loving than our May. Although Doctor Nolan assured us her deafness had nothing to do with it, May's growth was impeded. She was bright and intelligent, always doing well in school, but she was so tiny for her age, her facial features as diminutive as a doll's, her hands so small they barely covered Cary's or my palms when we held them.

All of us protected and loved her dearly, but sometimes I would catch Daddy gazing at her, unaware that anyone was looking at him, and I would see the most terrible expression of sadness on his face, his eyes glazed with trapped tears, his lower lip trembling just enough to be noticed. Then he would become aware of what he was doing, and he would snap into a firm posture, wiping away any emotion from his face. I never saw Daddy really cry, and the only times I saw him with his head down was when he was praying or after a particularly hard day of fishing.

At her school, May turned back after she had started through the gate and smiled at me impishly as she signed: "Don't kiss Robert too much." She giggled and ran into the building with the other children. I glanced at Cary, but he pretended not to have seen her and started off, his steps so deliberate I thought he would leave footprints in the sidewalk.

It was Friday, and tonight was the school's spring dance. For the first time in my life, I would have a real date for a school party. Robert Royce had asked me. It was to be our first formal date. Up until now, we had just met in places by accident or after we had timidly suggested to each other we might be someplace at the given time.

Robert had enrolled in our school in late February. His parents had purchased the Sea Marina, a hotel with fifty rooms on the northwest end of town. As soon as spring came, they had begun the restoration of the old resort, repairing, painting, planting, and pruning the landscape. Robert was an only child, so there were no other children to help Charles and Jayne Royce. Robert explained that his family had put most of their money into the purchase of the property and had to do most of the work themselves. Because of that, he went home directly after school most days and was very busy on the weekends, especially now that the summer season was fast approaching.

I had hoped Cary would find Robert's devotion to his

360

family and their business admirable. He and Robert really had a lot in common, but from the moment Robert had the courage to step up to me in the hallway and begin a conversation right in front of Cary, Cary's eyes grew small and dark whenever Robert was around me.

Robert always tried to include him in conversation, but Cary's responses were short, sometimes not much more than a grunt or a shrug. I was afraid Robert would be either frightened away or bothered so much by Cary's behavior that he would stop speaking to me and walking with me, but instead he grew bolder and even took a break from working on the hotel and visited me at home one Saturday.

Cary had gone to the dock to work on the lobster boat engine with Daddy and Roy Patterson. I introduced Robert to Mommy and to May, and May fell in love with him faster than I had. Robert was good at picking up signing, too. Before he left that day, he had learned to say "hello," "good-bye," and "I'm very, very hungry."

Later, when Cary returned and Mommy told him and Daddy I had had company, Cary turned white and then bright red when he asked me why I hadn't brought him down to the dock.

"I didn't want to interrupt you," I explained. Actually, I was grateful for the privacy, for not having Cary hovering over us.

He looked hurt and then angry.

"Ashamed of what we do?" he asked.

"Of course not," I protested. "And besides, you've spoken to Robert. You know he's not like that. He doesn't come from a snobby family, Cary. If anyone's family is snobby, it's ours."

Cary grunted, reluctant to admit I was right.

"He probably knew I was down at the dock all day," he muttered.

"What? Why would that matter, Cary?"

"It matters," he said. "Believe me, all these guys take advantage, Laura. You're just too trusting. It's why I have to look out for you," he declared.

"No, you don't, not with Robert, and I am not too trusting, Cary Logan. You don't know everything there is to know about me, and you certainly know nothing about romance," I flared, and stomped up to my room, closing the door behind me.

After my heart stopped pounding and I grew calm, I lay back and thought about my wonderful afternoon with Robert, walking on the beach, holding his hand, just talking. We told each other about ourselves, our favorite foods and colors and books. He was surprised that we didn't have a television set, but he refused to criticize Daddy when he learned it was Daddy's decision.

"Your father's probably right," he said. "You do read more than anyone I know and you're a great student."

He smiled that sort of smile that embeds itself in your mind, prints itself on the surface of your memory, embossed behind your eyelids whenever you close them and think about him. He had azure-blue eyes that turned opaque whenever he spoke deeply or seriously to me, but when he smiled, his eyes brightened as if they had drawn sunshine into them. It was the sort of smile that warmed your heart, infectious, sweeping away any cobwebs of gloom.

Robert was about an inch taller than Cary and just as broad-shouldered. He had longer arms, but was not as muscular. He wore his light brown hair short and always neatly brushed at the sides with just a slight wave in front. Because he was a year older and a senior, we didn't have any classes together, but I knew he was a good student and his teachers liked him because he was polite and inquisitive.

Cary had never been a very good student. He wore school like a pair of pants two sizes too small, reluctant to get in, struggling to be comfortable, relieved when the end-of-the-day bell rang. He hated being shut up and regimented by the clock and the rules. He was truly a fish out of water.

Consequently, Robert Royce's success in school was another thing Cary resented. He hated whenever Robert and I got into discussions about history or a book we'd read for class. To Cary, it was as if we had begun to speak in a different language. On a few occasions, however, Robert did try to talk about his family's problems with the hotel, construction difficulties, the use of tools and paints, things Cary understood and appreciated. Almost as reluctant as someone sitting in a dentist's chair, Cary would settle into conversation, offering his suggestions as dryly and as quickly as he could.

Later, Cary would tell me Robert should stick to quizzes in history and leave the real work to men more qualified. That only brought a smile to my face and a look of confusion to Cary's.

"What?" he demanded. "What is so funny now, Laura? I swear, you walk around with a stupid grin on your face all the time these days. You just don't know how silly you look."

"You simply can't admit you like him, can you, Cary?" I said, and he reddened.

"I don't," he insisted. "There's nothing to admit."

Despite this gloomy prognosis, I hoped and prayed Cary would eventually become friends with Robert, especially after he had asked me to the school dance. Mommy really liked Robert, but Daddy hadn't met him yet and I knew he wouldn't give me permission to go to the dance with him until he had, so the Saturday after he had asked me, I invited him to the house for lunch.

Robert charmed Mommy again by bringing her a box of candy. Cary called it a bribe, but I patiently explained it was only a polite gesture, something people invited to lunch or dinner often do. As usual, he grunted and turned away rather than admit I might be right.

At lunch, Robert sat beside me and across from Cary, who kept his eyes down and refused to talk. We began our meal as usual with a reading from the Bible. I had warned Robert that was something Daddy always did. Daddy paused when he opened the holy book and gazed at Robert.

"Perhaps our guest has a suggestion," he said. Cary started to smile. It was Daddy's little test. He was always lecturing us that young people were slipping into sin faster because they didn't know their Bible.

Robert thought a moment and said, "I like Matthew, Chapter Seven." Daddy raised his eyebrows. He glanced at Cary, who suddenly looked glum.

"You know that one, Cary?" Daddy asked.

Cary was silent and then Daddy handed Robert the Bible. Robert opened it, smiled at me, and glanced at Cary before beginning in a soft, silky voice.

"'Judge not, that ye be not judged. For with what judgment ye judge, ye shall be judged . . .'"

He read on and then looked up. Daddy nodded.

"Good," he said. "Good words to remember."

"Yes sir, they are," Robert said, and Daddy and he began a conversation about the tourist business, the old Sea Marina and how Daddy remembered it. I was afraid Daddy would take off on his and Grandma Olivia's favorite pet peeve—how the tourists were ruining the Cape—but he was civil and said nothing critical.

Cary sulked with his back against the chair, only speaking when he wanted someone to pass him a dish.

Robert confessed that he knew little about the lobster fishing business, and even less about the sea and boats.

"We've been so busy fixing up the place, I haven't had much time for anything else," he explained.

"That's all right. Your parents need you first. Maybe after lunch, you can come down to the dock and see our rig," Daddy said and looked at Cary. But after lunch Cary claimed he had work to do on one of his models and had spent enough time on the boat that week anyway.

I took May's hand and Robert took her other hand the way Cary always did. The three of us followed Daddy down to the dock. I turned and looked back at the house and thought I saw Cary looking out of an upstairs window. For a moment I felt like bursting into tears, but Robert's smile drove that feeling away quickly and we continued on.

Most important, Daddy approved of Robert that day

and so tonight I would be attending the school dance with my very first boyfriend. The school was buzzing like a beehive all day long. Everyone was fidgety in their seat in class and the cafeteria sounded like a hundred more students had enrolled that morning. Only Cary moved like a somber mourner through the halls, his face gray, his eyes dark. He sat silently, eating mechanically in the cafeteria.

"Why don't you ask Millie Stargel to the dance tonight, Cary?" I suggested when Robert and I sat down with him. "I know no one has asked her yet."

Cary stopped chewing and looked at me with such pain in his eyes, I got a huge lump in my throat and couldn't swallow for a moment.

"Millie Stargel?" He laughed. It was a wild, loud, and frightening laugh. "Whose idea was that, *his?"* he said, nodding at Robert.

"No, I just thought—"

"She's a pretty girl," Robert said, "and I bet she'd love to go."

"So why don't you ask her?" Cary retorted.

Robert smiled softly and gazed at me.

"I've already got a date," he said.

"Then why are you looking at other girls?" Cary shot back at him.

"I'm not. I was only saying—"

"See, I warned you," Cary said to me and got up. "These dances are stupid anyway," he said. "Hanging out in the school gym is not my idea of fun. If I go on a date, I'm not going to bring her back to this place."

"Cary," I called as he started away. He just glared back and continued out of the cafeteria.

"He'll be all right," Robert said, and put his hand over mine. "One day he'll meet someone and his heart will pound just like mine did when I first looked at you."

I nodded.

But I didn't have as much confidence in something like that happening to Cary anytime soon.

Not for a moment. And I knew that until Cary was happy, I would have a very hard time being happy myself.

It seemed to me Cary deliberately walked a great deal slower than usual when we left school. He didn't have to be a genius to see how eager I was to get back to the house.

"May will be waiting for us," I complained. "I'm not waiting for you to catch up," I added.

"So go on by yourself," he said, and I hurried away.

May was actually just coming out of her school when I arrived. I signed for her to hurry and we started for home. Cary was so far behind, he was still out of sight of May's school. May asked where he was and I told her he was being a brat. She looked back, confused, but she didn't slow down. She knew why I was hurrying home and she was almost as excited as I was. When we got to our house she asked if she could help me get ready for the dance and I signed back that I would need all the help I could get. May laughed and signed that she thought I was already beautiful, so I wouldn't be needing much help at all.

Despite May's words of encouragement, I wanted to do something special with my hair. I had shown Mommy a picture of a girl in *Seventeen* and told her I wanted to style my hair that way. She said she would help. She was almost as good at it as a regular beautician. So after I showered and washed my hair, I sat at my vanity table and Mommy began to brush out my hair and trim it. May sat on the stool beside me and watched, her eyes full of excitement. She was full of questions.

Why, she wanted to know, did I have to change the way my hair looked?

"This is a special occasion," I told her. "I want to try to look as good as I can."

"Oh, you'll be beautiful, Laura," Mommy said. "You're the prettiest girl in the school."

"Oh Mommy."

"You are. Cary says so."

"He's . . . prejudiced," I said.

"I remember there was a girl named Elaine Whiting when I was in school. She was so pretty everyone thought she would become a movie star. All the boys tried so hard to be the first to ask her to the school dances. I never saw her without every hair being in place and there wasn't a boy whose head didn't spin when she walked by. I bet it's the same for you," Mommy said with a wonderfully happy smile on her face. She was looking at me in the mirror, but her eyes seemed to be focused on her own fantasy. I could tell that neither she nor Daddy had ever heard a nasty whisper about Cary and me. It would just break her heart if she knew what some of the students in the school thought. Ugly rumors could be like infectious diseases, corrupting, rotting, sickening even the most healthy of souls.

"Which boys did you go to dances with, Mommy?" I asked her.

"Oh, no one ever asked me. I was what you would call a wallflower," she said with a smile.

"I'm sure you weren't, Mommy."

"I was frightfully shy, especially around boys. I was glad when my father and Samuel planned my marriage to your father."

"What? Your marriage was arranged?"

"Well, I guess you could call it that, though it really wasn't as bad as it sounds. Our fathers discussed it and I guess Grandpa Samuel told your father and he decided I would do, and he began to take an interest in me.

She paused and laughed at a memory.

"What?"

"I was just remembering the first time your father spoke to me. I was coming home from work at Gray's Pharmacy and he slowed down in his truck and asked if I wanted a ride. I knew who he was. Everyone knew who the Logans were. Anyway, I didn't reply. I kept walking, afraid to even turn my head toward him. He drove ahead and then stopped and waited until I reached him and he leaned out

367

and asked me again. I shook my head without speaking and kept walking."

"Then what happened?" I asked, breath bated.

"He drove off and I thought that was the end of it, but when I turned the corner and started down the street toward my home, there he was. He had parked his truck and was leaning against the door, waiting for me. I tell you I was terrified," she admitted and then glanced at May, who was tilting her head, wondering what Mommy was talking about for so long.

"I almost turned around and went the other way, but I kept walking, and when I reached him, he stood up and said, 'I'm glad you didn't accept my offer out of hand, Sara. Shows you're not a frivolous young lady. Your father and mine have been talking about how we would make a good couple. I'd like permission to come calling on you next Saturday, properly.'

"Well, that just took my breath away," she said. "You see, I had no idea of my father's plan up until then. I didn't even know he and Samuel Logan were friends. Well, once I recovered, your father asked, 'Do I have your permission?' and I nodded. 'Thank you,' he said and drove off, leaving me standing there with the most befuddled look on my face, I'm sure."

"Did he come calling the following Saturday?"

"He did and then we began to go out on dates. Our fathers had discussed our marriage, but Jacob didn't bring me to see Olivia for some time. She wasn't exactly demanding he bring me up to the house." she added.

"Why not?"

"I think Olivia Logan had someone else in mind for your father, someone more . . . wealthy, someone with a social position," she said. "But Grandpa Samuel had gone ahead and discussed it with my father and Jacob took a liking to me, so that was that. No matter," she said with a small wave of her hand. "That's all in the past now. Let's get back to your hair," she said excitedly.

"Did you have a nice wedding, Mommy?" I asked, not

ready to give up the first glimpse I'd gotten into my parents' early life together.

"It was a simple wedding at Olivia and Samuel's home. Judge Childs married us."

"I never heard you talk about your honeymoon, Mommy."

"That's because I didn't have one."

"You didn't?"

"Not really. Your father had to go back to work the next day. We told ourselves we would take a vacation soon, but we didn't. Life," she said with a sigh, "life just takes over. Before I knew it, I was pregnant with you and Cary. Don't look so sad, Laura," she said, gazing at me in the mirror. "I'm not an unhappy woman."

"I know you're not, Mommy, but I just wish you had a chance to travel, to have some fun, to leave Provincetown just once. No one in our family ever leaves here. . . . No one except Uncle Chester and Aunt Haille. Mommy, I never understood why Daddy stopped talking to Uncle Chester and why Uncle Chester and Aunt Haille left Provincetown," I said.

"You know your father doesn't want us talking about them, Laura."

"I know, but—"

"This is such a happy time. Please, dear," she begged. She closed her eyes and then opened them as she often did when she wanted to just forget or skip over something unpleasant. I didn't want to make her uncomfortable, but Uncle Chester and Aunt Haille remained the big mystery in our family, and I just naturally wondered what had complicated their love affair and marriage to make them outcasts in our family.

But Mommy was right: Tonight was not the time to press for answers.

"Okay, Mommy," I said. She looked grateful. I smiled and turned to May, who was signing and demanding to know what all the talk was about. I told her as much as I could. While I was signing, I heard the creak in the

369

floorboards above and realized Cary was in his attic work-shop. I glanced up at the ceiling, thinking about him, thinking about how he would spend one of my most wonderful nights, alone and bitter.

Suddenly, I saw what looked like a pinhole of light in the ceiling. My breath caught and I brought my hand to my chest.

"What's wrong, dear?" Mommy asked.

"What? Nothing," I said. "That looks fine, Mommy. I better lay out my clothes now," I said quickly.

She stepped back and nodded. I glanced up at the ceiling again. The light was gone, as if someone had covered the hole. Why hadn't I ever noticed it before? I wondered. My fingers trembled as I sifted through my closet to find my most beautiful dress, the pink taffeta Mommy had made for me. It was the only formal dress I owned.

It was a good dancing dress, too. All week I had been practicing dancing with it on. May sat on the bed and watched and then, when she got up her nerve, joined and imitated me. We laughed and grew dizzy.

Now I thought about the hole in the ceiling and wondered if Cary had been watching us all that time. Did he feel so left out? Was that why he would do that? How long had the hole been there? The thought of Cary watching me muddled my brain for a moment, and I just stood there, holding the dress.

"Are you happy with the dress, Laura?" Mommy asked. "I know it's not as expensive as some of the dresses other girls will be wearing."

"What? Oh. Yes, Mommy. I just love this dress."

I took it out of the closet and lay it on the bed. Then I took out my shoes.

"Well," Mommy said, "I'd better get downstairs and work on dinner for your father, Cary, and May. Call me when you're all ready," she said. "I can't wait to see you. Oh, and I want you to wear my necklace tonight," she said.

I started to shake my head. Mommy's necklace was her only really expensive piece of jewelry. Even her wedding

370

ring was not that expensive, because Daddy thought it was a waste of money to buy something elaborate when a mere silver band would serve the same purpose.

"I can't, Mommy."

"Sure you can, honey. When do I get a chance to wear it? I want you to wear it for me, okay?"

I nodded hesitantly.

"Come along, May," she signed, "and help me with dinner tonight. Laura has too much to do."

"Oh, I can help, Mommy."

"No you can't, honey. I told you, I never went to a school dance, but I wanted to very much. Tonight," she said with a deep sigh, "you're going for me, too."

"Oh Mommy, thank you," I said. She held out her arms and I hugged her back.

I felt tears prickling under my lids and quickly kissed her cheek and turned away to take a deep breath. After she and May had left, I sat at my vanity table and began to paint my fingernails. I started to daydream, imagining what it was going to be like to be dancing in Robert's arms, floating under the balloons and the lights, feeling him holding me close, occasionally brushing his lips over my hair.

A deep creak in the ceiling pulled me from my reverie and reminded me of the peephole in my ceiling. I gazed up at it and then I got up and went into the bathroom. I was angry, but then I began to feel sorry for Cary. I knew I was shutting him out of a part in my life, a part he could never enter again, yet he had to understand that I was growing up and the things that once amused me, amused us, were no longer enough. *He'll soon realize it,* I convinced myself. *He has to.* In the meantime, I didn't want to do anything else to break his heart.

My thoughts returned to the dance. I was so excited, I had to lie down and rest before I got dressed. I know I dozed for nearly an hour before my eyes snapped open and I sat up, frightened I had slept too long. I was only asleep for twenty minutes, but still I hurried to put on my dress. Then I put on a little more lipstick than ever before and perfected my hair before taking a deep breath and gazing at myself in the mirror.

Was I really pretty, as pretty as Mommy claimed? Robert thought I was and, of course, Cary did, too, but I never felt like the girl Mommy had described. I never thought all the boys were looking my way or that I had even turned a single head. I wasn't ugly, I decided, but I was no raving, movie-actress beauty. I had to keep my feet on the ground and not let my ego swell like so many other girls I knew at school.

Everyone was just finishing dinner when I went downstairs. Mommy slapped her hands together and cried out as soon as I entered the dining room. Daddy sat back, nodding, and May was smiling from ear to ear. Cary wore a strange, dark look.

"You're beautiful, honey. Just beautiful. Isn't she, Jacob?" Mommy said.

"Vanity is a sin, Sara. She looks fine, but there's no reason to blow her so full of steam she explodes," Daddy chastised. However, he wore a very proud expression as well.

"Now you just wait right there," Mommy said, and she hurried out of the dining room.

"How do I look, Cary?" I asked him. I couldn't stand the fact that he wouldn't look my way.

"Fine," he said quickly and dropped his gaze to his plate.

"I might have thought you'd be going to the dance, too," Daddy told him.

"It's stupid," Cary muttered.

"How's that?"

"I'm not interested in any old dance," he snapped. Daddy's eyebrows lifted.

"Well, it's a well-chaperoned affair, isn't it? Teachers are there, right?"

"What's that matter, Dad?" Cary said with a smirk. "Teachers are in school, too, but kids smoke in the bathrooms and do other things."

"What other things?"

"Other things," Cary said, realizing he was digging him-

372

self a hole he might not easily climb out of. He looked to me, but I said nothing. "Dumb things kids do."

"Laura's a good girl," Daddy said, looking at me. "She wouldn't do anything to embarrass this family."

Cary smirked and looked away.

"Of course I won't, Daddy," I said, my eyes fixed on Cary. Mommy returned, her necklace in hand.

"I wanted her to wear this tonight, Jacob," she said, looking to him for his approval. He nodded slightly and she put it on me, fastening it and then running her fingers over the garnets and sparkling diamond. "Doesn't it look nice on her?"

"Be careful with that," Daddy warned.

"I will. Thank you, Mommy."

We heard the doorbell.

"That'll be Robert," I said.

"Oh, she should have a shawl, don't you think, Jacob?"

"Sure. It's getting pretty nippy these nights," Daddy said.

Mommy went to the closet to get hers for me and I went to the door to let Robert in.

He looked terribly handsome in his jacket and tie. He was carrying a small box in his hands.

"It's a corsage," he declared.

"Oh, that's very thoughtful," Mommy said. Robert signed a hello to May, who beamed beside me. Then he opened the box and took out the corsage of red roses, my favorite. They matched the garnets perfectly.

"You'll have to pin it on," I told him. He looked at Mommy helplessly for a moment and then tried, but his fingers were clumsy with his nervousness.

"I'll do it," Mommy said, coming to our rescue. Robert smiled with relief and stepped back to watch her pin it on me.

"There, that's very pretty," Mommy said.

"Thank you, Mommy."

"We should get moving," Robert said. "Don't want to miss the opening dance."

373

"Have a wonderful time," Mommy said. Daddy came up behind her and looked at Robert.

"You look fine, boy," he said. "Now remember," he added with a scowl, "I want her home before midnight."

"Yes, sir," Robert said.

I looked for Cary, but he hadn't come out of the dining room.

"Good night, Cary," I called. There was no response. I flashed a weak smile at Mommy, who nodded, her face full of light, her eyes brighter than ever, and then Robert and I stepped out into the night.

He opened the car door for me and I got in. He hurried around and got behind the wheel.

"Well, I guess I have the prettiest date at the dance tonight," he said and turned to me. "Laura, you look more beautiful than I ever dreamed."

"Thank you, Robert. You're very handsome yourself."

"I guess we'll knock 'em dead then," he predicted and started the engine.

As we backed out, I looked toward the front door, half expecting to see Cary, but he wasn't anywhere to be seen.

2

I Could Have Danced All Night

"Oh, Robert," I said the moment we walked into the school gymnasium and saw how wonderfully the dance committee had decorated, "I wish Cary had come. He wouldn't be so down on the dance if he saw what they've done to this place. It looks like a real ballroom!"

"I don't think that's really what kept him from coming, Laura," Robert said softly. He smiled sympathetically, his eyes soft and gentle. I nodded, knowing he was right.

There was a makeshift stage directly in front of us for the four-piece band. They were already playing, and the floor was crowded with dancers. Above us, ribbons of crepe paper crisscrossed around mounds of multicolored balloons with long tails of tinsel. At the far right, there were long tables with red, green, and blue paper tablecloths set up for the food, and to the left and down the sides of the gymnasium, there were tables with the same color paper tablecloths and chairs. A large poster on the left wall read: WELCOME TO THE ANNUAL SPRING FESTIVAL.

Everyone was dressed up, some of the girls in dresses so formal and expensive-looking, I was sure Mommy would feel what she had made for me was inadequate, even though

I thought my dress was just perfect. However, I was happy now that I had agreed to wear Mommy's necklace. Many of the girls wore earrings, necklaces, bracelets, and rings on most of their fingers. It looked like a contest to see who could be the most overdressed.

"Well," Robert said after we put my shawl on a chair and set my purse aside, "why don't we join the fun?"

He led me onto the dance floor and we began dancing. As we moved across the crowded floor, I felt as if everyone's eyes were on us. When I let my gaze shift from Robert's, I saw some of the girls in my class gathered in a small pack, watching us with twisted smiles on their faces. I felt a tightness in my stomach.

The music was loud and fast. I hoped I didn't look foolish, but Robert seemed pleased. He was a very good dancer and I started to imitate some of his movements with my arms and hips. As long as I concentrated on him, fixed my eyes on his, I felt secure and comfortable. He had such an air of confidence about him. There was enough for me to share.

When there was a pause between songs, we stopped, embraced each other, and laughed. He turned me toward the punch bowl, waving to some of the boys he knew and they waved back, giving Robert the thumbs-up sign to indicate they approved.

"We're going to have fun tonight," he promised, his eyes full of excitement. "We're going to dance until our feet beg for mercy."

"Did I do all right out there?" I asked.

"Are you kidding? If they have a dance contest, we're entering," he said.

"Robert Royce, we are not." Just the thought of such a thing took my breath away.

We drank some punch and ate some chips with cheese dip. Marsha Winslow and the class president, Adam Jackson, joined us. Marsha was in charge of the party. She was a tall, attractive girl who spoke with a slightly nasal tone, as if she were looking down her nose at the rest of the world. She carried a clipboard.

"Excuse me," she said, "but we don't have any record of your paying for your tickets."

"What? Of course you do. I gave the money to Betty Hargate," Robert said.

"Betty has you down, but not Laura," she replied.

"That's ridiculous."

"Are you calling Marsha ridiculous?" Adam asked. "You know, she doesn't get paid for doing all this work that makes it possible for everyone else to enjoy themselves. She's just doing her job."

"I'm not calling her ridiculous. I'm just saying . . . where is Betty? There she is." Robert pointed. "Let's call her over," he suggested.

"Good idea," Adam said, and he waved at Betty, who was standing with Lorraine Rudolph. The two hurried over.

"What's up?" Betty demanded impatiently, her hand on her hip. It was as if she had been asked to wallow with the undesirables.

"Robert Royce claims," Marsha said, rolling her eyes, "that he paid for Laura, too, but that's not indicated on the sheet I have."

"I gave you the money in the cafeteria last Tuesday," Robert insisted. "Remember?"

"Whatever is written on the paper is what I received," Betty said in a singsong, smug voice. "I don't have to steal party ticket money."

"I didn't say you stole it," Robert cried, growing increasingly frustrated.

"I only have one ticket marked off after your name," Marsha repeated. "That means you paid for only one ticket."

"I can't believe this," Robert said.

"Are you sure you just didn't *think* you paid for Laura? Maybe you weren't sure she was going with you last Tuesday," Lorraine quipped, a tight smile on her lips. She shifted her eyes to Adam and back to Robert.

377

"Of course, I'm sure. I paid," Robert maintained.

"All the money checks out," Marsha said.

"That means we don't have more money than tickets issued," Adam added.

"I know what it means," Robert said.

"Do you have the tickets, Robert?" I whispered. He thought a moment and then nodded with a confident smile, pulling them out of the inside of his sports jacket.

"If I didn't pay for them, how did I get them?" he asked Marsha, thrusting the tickets in front of her face.

She gazed at the tickets and then looked at her clipboard again.

"I don't understand," she said.

"Maybe Betty gave him two tickets and he promised to give her the money for the second one later," Adam suggested.

"Yes," Betty said quickly. "That's it."

"No, it's not and you know it," Robert insisted.

"Betty's too responsible to give out tickets and not collect the money for them," I suggested calmly. Everyone paused and gazed at me a moment. "Someone just made a simple mistake."

"Well . . ." Marsha glanced at Adam.

"I don't think Robert would steal a dance ticket, do you?" I followed.

"I hope not," Betty blurted.

"We'll straighten it out later," Marsha said. "Right now, we're all wasting time when we should be having fun."

"Exactly," Adam said, taking her arm. "To the dance floor, Madam Chairman."

The others laughed and then left with them.

"That was a pretty stupid bit of meanness," Robert said, glaring after them.

"Maybe it was just an honest mistake, Robert."

He continued to glare in their direction, just daring one of them to look back at us.

"Somehow, I doubt it," he said. "Those kind don't make honest mistakes."

378

"Let's not let them ruin our night, Robert," I said, touching his hand. He relaxed, smiled at me, and nodded.

"Right. Shall we?" he asked, taking the punch glass from my hand and putting it on one of the tables.

We returned to the dance floor. It didn't take us long to get lost in the music and each other. We soon forgot about the ticket incident and danced until I declared my feet were really begging for mercy. Robert laughed and suggested it was time we had something to eat anyway.

"I guess we've worked up an appetite."

We got in line and filled our plates. Some of the girls in my English class complimented me on my dancing, and girls who had come together without dates gathered around Robert, commenting on his dancing ability too.

Theresa Patterson was there with some of her Brava friends. They kept to themselves, but Theresa gave me a bright, friendly smile when I waved.

As I looked over the endless plates of food I had to give the devils their due: Betty and Marsha had planned a wonderful party. There were steamed clams, of course, and all sorts of chicken dishes, including Southern fried, bowls of tricolor pasta, salads, plates of fruit, loaves of Portuguese bread, rolls, and a table of desserts that would surely be the first to be picked clean.

When we were satisfied we'd taken a bit of everything to sample, Robert and I sat with some of his friends and their dates. Everyone was so excited, they all talked at once. I really was having the time of my life, and when Robert leaned over to give me a small, quick kiss on the cheek, I blushed and told him how much fun I was having.

"I'm so glad," he said. "I was worried when Cary was so negative about the dance. I thought he might—"

"Might what?"

"Talk you out of coming," Robert confessed.

"He could never do that. We may be twins, but I still have a mind of my own, Robert."

"That's good," he said, smiling.

"You should know that by now, and if you don't, you will

379

soon," I promised. Even I was surprised at how seductively it came out. His eyes widened with his smile. I turned away quickly, afraid I would become so crimson, everyone at the table would notice.

After we ate, the music got slower and the lights grew dim. I liked this kind of dancing more because I could rest my head against Robert's shoulder and feel his arms around me. We swayed to the rhythm, neither of us wanting to spoil the moment by talking. Occasionally, I felt his lips on my forehead and hair. My heart pounded so hard, I was sure he could feel it against his chest.

"I'm so glad you came to the dance with me, Laura," he whispered.

"Me too," I said.

"Maybe . . . we can leave a little earlier and just take a ride along the shore. It's a beautiful night," he said.

"I'd like that, Robert."

We moved through the shadows and light. I was dazzled by the glow of the round lanterns, and for a while, it was as if Robert and I were the only ones at the dance. Everyone else just faded away.

That is until I heard Janet Parker's sharp, cold laugh right behind us and turned to see her standing with Adam Jackson, Marsha, Betty, and Lorraine. Brad Laughton and Grant Simpson had joined them as well. Why weren't they dancing? I wondered. Did they come here just to watch and make fun of others? They kept looking our way and laughing.

"What's with them now?" Robert muttered.

"I don't care," I said, but he couldn't stop gazing at them, his eyes filling more and more with fury.

"It's got something to do with us," he said sharply and stopped dancing.

"Robert, forget about them."

"I'd like to know what's so damn funny," he said, taking my hand and crossing the dance floor toward them. They parted, expecting we would walk in between them, but Robert paused.

"Why don't you let us in on your little joke," he said sharply.

"Excuse me?" Adam said with his self-satisfied smirk. "You want to hear a little joke?"

They all laughed.

"What is it with you people?" Robert pursued. I tried to tug his hand, but he was determined to have his say. "Are you trying to ruin our good time? I feel sorry for you if that's all you have to keep you occupied."

"Are you kidding me?" Adam said, surprised that anyone would dare question his actions.

"Well?"

"We just wondered why Laura's brother didn't come to the dance. Couldn't he afford a ticket?" Lorraine asked.

"Robert could have bought him one the same way he bought Laura's," Adam suggested.

"That's not funny," Robert said, stepping toward him. Adam took a step back and held up his hands.

"Hey, take it easy. You wanted to hear a little joke, didn't you?"

"That's not a joke. You're a joke," Robert shot back.

"Whoa, buddy," Brad said. Robert's glare put him back a step, too. They all looked so shallow and cowardly to me, despite their expensive clothing and jewels.

"Come on, Robert," I said. "Let's not waste any more of our time on them."

"The reason we were wondering about your brother," Janet said, "is Grant just came in from having a cigarette and said he saw him loitering in the parking lot."

"What?"

"That's right. He's out there in the cold, dreaming of being in here with his sister," Brad blurted.

Robert's arm shot out so quickly, I didn't realize he had moved until I saw his hand bounce off Brad's chest, sending him back so awkwardly he lost his balance and landed hard on the gym floor. Some of the kids around him started to laugh. He turned red, but after scurrying back to his feet, he kept his distance.

"That was very rude," Betty exclaimed. "Maybe where you come from that happens all the time, but we aren't allowed to do that at our parties." Her eyes widened and she groaned. "Oh no! Mr. Rosner's coming across the floor already. He'll make us cut the party short if there's any wild or stupid stuff and I worked hard to make this a success!" she cried, her mouth twisted and distorted.

"What's going on here?" Mr. Rosner demanded, his hands on his hips. He looked from Brad to Robert and then at the others.

"Just a silly joke, Mr. Rosner," Adam said, smoothly cutting in front of him. "It's nothing. We're all cool."

Mr. Rosner studied everyone and although he wasn't satisfied, nodded.

"I don't want to see any roughhousing," he warned.

"You won't," Adam said. "I guarantee it, sir. As class president, I'll take full responsibility."

"I'm sure you will, Mr. Jackson," Mr. Rosner said. When his eyes fixed on me, he calmed down. "You all look very nice," he said, "and up until now, this has been a very nice affair. I hope you'll continue to make us proud of you."

"Thank you, Mr. Rosner," Lorraine said sweetly. I saw the corner of his mouth twitch as he turned and started away.

"That was close," Adam said, glaring at Robert.

"It wasn't his fault," I said.

"No, that's for sure," Betty said. "Actually, we all feel sorry for him."

"What's that supposed to mean?" Robert demanded.

"Robert, come on," I pleaded, desperate to get Robert away before they could elaborate on their ugly rumors.

"No, what's it supposed to mean?" he pursued.

"Why don't you go out and ask her brother?" Janet quipped and they all started to smile.

"Shall we dance?" Adam asked Marsha, holding out his hand.

"Anything to get away from this incestuous atmosphere,"

she said and they all laughed as they broke up to go their separate ways and leave us standing alone.

"Spoiled, rich—"

"It's all right, Robert. Let's not pay attention to them."

He nodded and then looked at me.

"Do you think Grant was telling the truth? Do you think Cary's hanging around out there?"

"I hope not," I said. "I'm sure he made it up just to hurt us."

Robert forced a smile.

"If you want to go for that ride now," he said finally, "it's fine with me. The air is getting stale in here."

"Yes, I would," I answered him in what I hoped was a cheery tone of voice.

His mood softened.

"Great. I want to be sure to get you home before twelve," he said. "I wouldn't want your father mad at me."

"Most of the time, Daddy's growl is worse than his bite," I said.

"I'm not worried about being bitten; I'm worried about being forbidden," Robert said, slipping his hand into mine, "forbidden to see you."

Our eyes met and I felt a warm glow travel from my stomach to my heart. Was it possible to want to be with anyone more than I wanted to be with Robert? I didn't think so. Surely, this was what love was, and it had happened to me so soon after we had set our eyes on each other, it must be true love. Did that mean it was written in the stars like it had been for Romeo and Juliet? That was fine, as long as we didn't have the same destiny, I thought.

We started out of the gymnasium, gazing back only once to see Betty and Adam looking our way and laughing. It filled me with dread because it was as if they knew something I didn't.

There were some students huddled in the shadows and smoking outside, but I didn't see Cary anywhere. I released the breath I had held in my lungs and walked quickly across the front of the school toward the parking lot. We got into Robert's car and glanced at each other, both of us feeling nervous and excited. Robert took a deep breath and started the car. Then he turned to me.

"You all right with this?" he asked softly.

"Yes, Robert." I slid over to be closer to him and he smiled.

We drove out of the parking lot slowly. I looked back once and thought I saw a shadow scurrying away from a car. In a moment, the shadow disappeared in the darkness and was lost.

"You see something?"

"No," I said, shaking my head and turning back.

We drove quietly for a while, following the road out to the Point.

"I know the artist who lives down that road," I said, when we passed a beach road. "His name's Kenneth Childs. He's Judge Childs's son."

"I've heard of him," Robert said. "In fact, I think we have one of his paintings in the hotel. It was there when we bought the place."

"Most likely. He is one of our most famous artists. He's a nice man, but keeps to himself. Some people call him a hermit."

"I'd still like to meet him. I like his painting in the hotel," Robert said, putting his arm around my shoulders as he slowed the car.

"I took a few exploratory rides down this way recently," he said.

"Oh? And for what reason?" I teased.

"Just to see the countryside," he claimed with an impish little smile.

Moments later he turned down a narrow beach road and then switched off the headlights as he continued a few yards farther. Darkness closed in behind us and on both sides, but before us was the ocean, with the dazzling sea of stars above it and the moonwalk that went to the end of the world.

Many times before, Cary and I had sat in the darkness and looked up at the vastness of space with all the stars twinkling, but it never set my heart pounding as it did this night while I leaned against Robert's shoulder, feeling his breath on my hair and then on my forehead before his lips gently touched my ears, my cheeks, and my eyes. I turned to bring my lips to his and we shared a long, soft kiss.

"Laura," he said, stroking my hair. He put his cheek to mine and whispered in my ear. "When I first saw you in school, I felt as if your face was immediately printed in my mind. That first day, I looked for you everywhere, and if I changed classes and didn't see you, I was sick with disappointment."

"I noticed you, too, but I didn't think you were looking at me in a special way."

"That was because I was too shy to say anything. I thought you would take one good look at my face and know I had fallen head over heels. I was afraid you would laugh at me."

"I never would."

"I know that now," he said, putting the tips of his fingers on my lips. "But I didn't know it until I spoke to you and saw how wonderful you really were. I was walking around in a daydream, even at home. I remember I walked right into the kitchen door and bumped my forehead. My father thought I was taking drugs or something. Then my mother looked at me and said, 'He met a girl. I don't know anything else that would turn a boy his age into a clumsy, absentminded oaf.'"

"She said that?"

"My mother has a great sense of humor," Robert said. "I can't wait for you to meet her."

"Does she meet all your girlfriends?" I asked. He smiled.

"I haven't had many girlfriends, and never one like you," he replied. "Before you, what I felt for other girls was a schoolboy's crush, but when I look at you, Laura, I know it's for real. I hope you feel the same way."

"I do, Robert," I said. "I really do," I added, and we

kissed again. This time he kept kissing me, moving his lips down to my neck. I closed my eyes and let my head rest against his shoulder. His hands moved along my ribs, over my dress, his fingers sliding over the material and then up to my breasts. At first, I instinctively brought my hands up to stop him, but the tingle was so pleasant and warmed me so wonderfully, I let him continue.

Robert sensed my hesitation and then my quick surrender. It made him kiss me faster, harder, longer, his lips rushing over mine before going to my neck, while his hands lifted my breasts, his thumbs riding over the crests of them, caressing my budding nipples.

A soft moan left my lips and I felt Robert gently push me down. He was over me, his fingers finding the zipper behind my dress and carefully moving it down my back. I lifted my arms and he helped me fold the top of my dress to my waist. My eyes were closed as his fingers continued to explore until they unfastened my bra. For a long, delicious moment, my heart pounding, I thought I might die from anticipation and then, when his lips came down upon me, I thought I'd die of pleasure.

The rush of excitement crashed against my better judgment. I knew I should tell him to slow down, but I felt like I was floating, gently undulating on a wave of passion, a wave that was carrying me out too far. "Wait," I heard myself say finally. "We're moving too quickly, Robert. I'm afraid."

He lifted himself from me and I saw him above me, his eyes closed. He took a deep breath and caught hold of the wild passion that was pulling him forward, too.

"You're right, Laura," he said. "I just couldn't stop myself."

"I know a lot of girls wouldn't stop you, Robert. I understand if you're angry with me." .

"No," he said, smiling. "It's just the opposite. I want us to be something special, very special. I want us to move as quickly as we both want to move, and love as we both want to love. I want this to last, Laura. I really do love you."

I nodded.

"I love you, too, Robert." I reached up for him again, but he shook his head and pulled my bra down over my breasts.

"If we don't stop now, I won't be able to, Laura," he confessed. He leaned back against the car door and I sat up and fixed my clothes. He had to help me with my dress zipper.

Then we just sat there in each other's arms, listening to our hearts calm themselves, kissing gently every once in a while, and talking softly about the stars, our love, our dreams. Suddenly, Robert looked at his watch.

"Wow, I didn't realize how long we've been here. We had better get going or you'll be late for your curfew."

He started the engine and put the car into reverse. We heard the tires spin, but the car didn't move.

"What the . . ."

He gunned the engine and the tires squealed, kicking up more sand that slapped at the belly of the car, but still we didn't move. He put the car into drive and tried to move forward, then back, rocking the vehicle, but that didn't work either.

"Oh no," he moaned. He reached over to open the glove compartment to take out a flashlight. Then he got out and shined the light on the rear tires. "I dug a hole in the sand. I didn't realize it was so soft here!"

"Robert, what are we going to do?"

"I'll have to run back until I can find a house with lights on and make a call to a tow truck. I'm sorry. I've ruined everything. There's no way we can explain . . ."

Suddenly, a set of headlights brightened up the sky. Robert brought his hand to his forehead to shade his eyes.

"What the hell . . . Who?"

"Who is it, Robert?" I asked, terrified.

"I can't make him out yet, but . . . I think it's Cary!" he declared after another moment.

I turned to look. I would never mistake that silhouetted form. It was Cary walking along the beach road, his truck headlights on behind him.

"Cary!" I cried as soon as he drew close enough.

"Got yourself in a bit of trouble, I see," Cary said with his hands on his hips, gazing down at the wheels.

"Yes, I didn't realize—"

"That's because you aren't from around here," he said disdainfully. "You think these roads are like the old dirt back roads where you took your other girlfriends, huh?"

"No," Robert protested, but Cary just turned to me.

"This was stupid, Laura," he said to me. "I thought you knew better."

"What are you doing here, Cary? How did you find us?"

"I saw you leave the school dance and thought you were going home. When you kept going toward the Point . . . well, just lucky for you I decided to trail along for a while."

A while? I thought. We'd been here a long time. What was he doing all that time?

He turned to Robert. "I'll back my truck in. I've got a chain on it. We'll hook it to the axle and pull you out. Get in and put the car in neutral," he ordered. Robert got back into the car quickly. "And make sure you don't have any brakes on," Cary warned before returning to his truck.

"I can't believe . . . your brother," Robert mumbled. We turned and watched Cary turn the truck around and then back it up toward us. He approached with the chain and crawled under Robert's car. "Why would he follow us like this?" Robert whispered.

"Lucky for us he did," I replied, choosing not to even think about his question at the moment.

"It's all set," Cary called. "Get ready."

He returned to the truck and slowly drove forward. We felt Robert's car jerk and then lift out of the holes he had dug with the tires. The car bounced along the beach road until we were on more solid ground. Cary stopped and returned to detach his chain.

Robert stepped out.

"Thanks a lot," he said sheepishly.

"I didn't do it for you. I did it for Laura," Cary replied. He stepped over to my side of the car. "You better come home with me, Laura," he said.

388

"I'll take her home," Robert said.

"It looks like it's safer if she drives with me," Cary said, and even in the darkness, I could see Robert turn bright red.

"If I don't come home with Robert, Daddy will wonder why, Cary."

"So?"

"You're not going to tell him about this," I pleaded.

"No, of course not," he said quickly. "Okay, but it's getting late," he warned. He looked at Robert. "And I'm not going to hang around here to bail you out again."

He strutted back to his truck and then drove away. Robert got back into the car and pulled out, driving slowly.

"Why did he follow us, Laura?"

"He was bored, I suppose," I said. It was weak, but it was all I could think to say.

"Was he there all the time, sitting in his truck right behind us? Watching us? Spying on us?"

I started to speak, but just shook my head instead.

"Those idiots back at the dance were right, you know. He was in the parking lot. You've got to help him, Laura. You've got to help him realize you can't be his little sister forever," Robert said.

"I know, Robert. Let's not talk about it right now, please," I begged. Just thinking about Cary's weird obsession with Robert and me brought tears to my eyes and put a lump in my throat.

"Okay," he said, and we were both uncomfortably silent until my house came into view.

"I'm sorry for what happened," Robert said after he parked in our driveway. "Cary was right to bawl me out for it. I just hope it didn't ruin your night."

"No, it didn't. I had a wonderful time, Robert. Really, I did."

"Me too," he said. "I'll call you tomorrow, okay?"

"Let me call you. It'll be easier that way," I said.

"Okay. If that's what you want." He looked worried.

"I'll call. I promise," I said. He smiled and we kissed

389

quickly before I hopped out of his car. "Thanks for a wonderful evening, Robert."

"Good night, Laura."

I closed the door and looked over at Cary's truck. He was already in the house. When I entered, I found Daddy had waited up for me and was sitting in the living room reading. He looked up from his book. I held my breath, wondering whether Cary had decided to say something after all.

"Have a good time?" Daddy asked.

"Yes, Daddy. It was very nice."

"Everybody behaved themselves?"

"Yes, Daddy."

He nodded and then lowered his voice.

"Your brother didn't come home much earlier than you. I think he's got a secret girlfriend. Am I right?" he asked quickly, unable to keep the hope from his voice.

I felt the blood drain from my face as I shook my head. I hated lying to Daddy.

"I don't know, Daddy. He's never mentioned any girl to me," I said.

Daddy stared at me a moment and then shrugged.

"Oh well," he said, "he'll tell us when he wants to. I just hope it's not someone he thinks we'd be ashamed of." Daddy continued to gaze at me with questioning eyes.

I pressed my teeth on my lower lip and shook my head.

"I don't know, Daddy." How I wished it were true that Cary had found a girlfriend, I thought sadly.

"Well," Daddy said, looking at the clock on the mantel, "young Mr. Royce brought you home on time. That's good." He sighed deeply and stretched out his arms. "It is late though, so I guess I'll go to sleep, too," he added and yawned. "Don't forget we're all going to Grandma Olivia and Grandpa Samuel's tomorrow for brunch."

"Okay. Good night, Daddy," I said, happy to get away from his questioning eyes.

I hurried up the stairs. Pausing on the landing, I saw the door to Cary's room was closed and quickly went into my own room, closing the door behind me. I leaned against it and caught my breath. It was only then that I finally felt myself relax with relief.

Unwilling to take off my party dress just yet, I went to my bed and sat there for a while, thinking about the magical night Robert and I had shared. What an evening, I thought, and then my memories of Robert's kisses, Robert's embrace and touch returned, washing over me in a warm reverie. I lay back with a sigh and closed my eyes, thinking about his hands on my breasts, his lips making me tingle. As I thought about him, I moved my hands to where his had been. I started to undress. In moments, I was naked, standing in front of my mirror, gazing dreamily at myself, imagining Robert beside me. Finally, my fatigue hit me and I went to the bathroom to rinse off my makeup. It felt good to crawl under my blanket and snuggle up.

Despite it all, I thought, it was a wonderful night. It really was. I reached over and turned off the small lamp beside my bed and dropped my head to the pillow. The sound of the floor above creaking popped my eyes open and drove away my sweet thoughts. I held my breath and listened. It was Cary, for I heard him open the attic room door, drop the ladder, and descend as quietly as he could.

He had been up there the whole time, maybe peeping through that hole at me, I thought. I felt my body grow hot with embarrassment as my blood rushed toward the surface of my skin. How much had he seen? We had stopped bathing and sharing the bathroom when we were seven or eight, and I began to demand my privacy even more when I began to develop breasts. Cary's curious eyes had made me feel self-conscious. It wasn't long afterward that I stopped walking around in front of him in my underwear. Even then, the way he looked at me and my changing body made me uncomfortable.

I got up and went to my door, opening it slightly to peer out as he returned the ladder. I started to open the door wider and then hesitated. If I confronted him, I'd only bring more embarrassment to myself, I thought. It was late, I told myself; it wasn't the time for this.

I closed the door ever so softly and waited until I heard him go into his room. Then I went back to bed and lay there with my eyes open, trying desperately to drive the troubled thoughts from my mind so I could think only of Robert and our wonderful night together.

But when I turned on my side and closed my eyes, I saw only Cary's angry face after he had emerged from the darkness behind us, his truck headlights casting him in an eerie silhouette. I finally drifted to sleep, only to find that Cary was in my nightmares, along with the distorted faces of my classmates, whispering, leering, laughing, chasing me toward the roaring sea. Everything was so vivid. I woke in a sweat after the first wave washed over me in my dream. My heart was pounding. I sat up quickly and had to hold my hand over my heart and take deep breaths. Finally, I got up and went to the bathroom to splash my face with cold water.

Whenever Cary and I had a nightmare, we would share it the next morning. It was a way we both had to drive the demons out of our hearts, to comfort each other. For the first time, I couldn't tell him about my dream. This time, I had to find a way to drive the demons out myself.

3

Trouble's Brewing

Cary sat sullenly at the breakfast table the next morning. We exchanged few words, but most of the time when he looked at me, I thought I could see the accusations in his eyes. I didn't believe he had any right to make me feel guilty and I refused to act ashamed. If anyone should be ashamed, he should, I thought, following me around at night, peeping through holes in the ceiling.

Mommy was eager to hear about the dance, and I was thankful that at least she could share my happiness. As I spoke, I signed to May, describing the decorations, the food, the music. Of course, I left out the unpleasantness over the ticket and mentioned nothing about Cary pulling Robert's car out of the sand.

"I thought you went to the dance, too, Cary," Daddy said when there was a pause.

"Hardly," Cary said disdainfully.

"Then where were you, boy? It was pretty late when I heard you come in and hurry up those stairs."

"I just met some friends at the Bean Bag," he said quickly.

"How can you hang around a custard stand all night?" Daddy continued.

Cary shot a glance at me to see if I would say anything, and I looked down at my plate.

"We were just hanging out," Cary said. "I didn't realize how late it got."

Daddy shook his head.

"I don't know what you all have to talk about so much that you lose track of time."

"You can pass a lot of time jawin', Jacob," Mommy said, "like when you get together with Pat O'Reilly."

"That's different. We talk about business," Daddy retorted, reddening at the criticism. It was enough to end the topic, for which both Cary and I were grateful.

While we waited to go to brunch at Grandma Olivia's, I took May out to the beach and made some drawings while she sat beside me, asking me questions about my date and about Robert. Drawing was something I did to help relax, just like needlework. I drew pictures of all of us, some from memory, some from things I saw at the moment. Everyone who saw my drawings thought they were very good. I once showed them to Kenneth Childs, who said I might consider taking art classes and developing my talent. I never thought I was good enough to do that, and wasting time trying to be someone I couldn't be was something Daddy convinced me was sinful.

"God grants us enough time to do something worthy with ourselves. Procrastination, chasing foolish dreams, that's what the devil would like us to do," he had said.

I wasn't fixed on anything yet, but I had been thinking lately that I might become a teacher, maybe even a teacher in a school for the handicapped. It made me feel special and filled me with so much pleasure when I was able to teach May something and see her eyes brighten with understanding. I felt as though I had broken through a thick wall, no matter how small the achievement, and I thought I could do this successfully with other handicapped children.

While we were sitting on the beach, drawing and talking, Daddy and Cary went by on their way to the dock.

"We're just going to check on the lobster traps," Daddy explained. Cary stood by, silent, still somewhat sullen. "We

394

won't be long, Laura. You should get yourself and May ready soon."

We always dressed up for brunch at Grandma Olivia's. In fact, we never went there without treating the visit as if it were a special occasion. This was easy for Grandma Olivia, since she was always formally dressed. Even when she was working in her garden, she had her hair pinned properly and wore outfits that most would save for trips into town or visits with company. Grandpa Samuel usually wore a sports jacket and slacks, along with a cravat or a tie. Their home was kept immaculate, everything in its proper place. As children, we were forbidden to wander in the rooms and were terrified of touching anything.

"Okay, Daddy," I said and folded my drawing pad. I signed to May and she folded hers as well. As we headed for the house, I thought this would be the best and maybe only time I would get to call Robert. I was sure he was on pins and needles, worrying about what might have happened after I entered the house last night.

Robert's mother answered.

"Oh hello," she said with enthusiasm, after I had introduced myself. "From the way Robert's been acting this morning, I'd say you and he had a wonderful time last night. I have to say everything to him twice," she added with a little laugh. I heard Robert complaining in the background. "I'd better give him the phone before he throws a fit."

"Hi," he said. "My mother's in one of her hilarious moods today."

"I can't wait to meet her," I said.

"I'll introduce you . . . *as long as you know she'll say anything,*" he added in a voice meant for her ears. He paused and then in a lower voice, asked how things were.

"Everything's fine," I said. "My father was waiting up and I could tell he was relieved that I made it home before curfew. And Cary didn't say anything," I added, knowing he was waiting to hear about that most of all.

"Your father was waiting up? I guess it would have been disastrous if Cary hadn't come to the rescue, but I still can't get over his following us, Laura. Have you talked to him about it?"

"Not yet, Robert. I'm waiting for the right time."

"Don't put it off, Laura," he warned.

"I won't," I said in a little voice. It wasn't something I looked forward to doing.

"I can't wait to see you again," he added in a softer tone.

"Me neither. I'm going to my grandmother's for brunch in a little while. I've got to get ready and then help May get dressed."

"Okay. Thanks for the call," he said in a voice that sent shivers all the way to my toes.

"I couldn't wait," I confessed shyly.

"I'm glad," he said and we both hung up. I hurried upstairs to dress and help May pick out something that wouldn't make Grandma Olivia shake her head disapprovingly.

Grandma Olivia was always uncomfortable around May. We all knew that the signing unnerved her: She said all those hands bending and turning through the air, fingers jabbing, made her stomach jump. She resisted learning any of it and consequently spoke to her youngest grandchild only through an interpreter, usually me or Cary.

Although Mommy seemed to look forward to Grandma Olivia's brunches and dinners, she was always nervous the day of the visit. Mommy reminded me of someone who was preparing for an audition. Pains were taken over how all of us dressed, how well our hair was brushed, our shoes shined, and we were always, even now, reminded about the rules of behavior when at Grandma Olivia's home, including what not to say and what to say. If one of us didn't pass Grandma Olivia's inspection, Daddy usually blamed Mommy, so we did our best to live up to expectations.

We all ended up looking like different people when we were all dressed up, especially May and I, since Grandma Olivia didn't like women to wear their hair loose and down. She said that it made them look like witches, so I had to use bobby pins and combs to wrap my hair neatly, and even May wore a little French twist. Although the old-fashioned hairdos added years to our age, we didn't look overly grown-up, since makeup was strictly forbidden, even for Mommy. She didn't even wear lipstick.

Despite all this, I did look forward to going. Grandma Olivia usually had wonderful things to eat. I especially loved the tiny cakes with frosting and jelly in the center, and even now, even though we were really grown-up, Grandpa Samuel always gave me and Cary, along with May, crisp five-dollar bills when we left.

I had one particular dress that always seemed the most acceptable to Grandma Olivia. It was a navy blue dress with a white collar that buttoned at the base of my throat. Although I had other, equally dowdy dresses, for some reason this one always brought a smile to Grandma Olivia's grim face.

When I stood before the mirror, I reminded myself to keep my shoulders back and my head up, as if I were balancing a book on top. One of Grandma Olivia's pet peeves was the way young people slouched. She claimed posture showed character and embellished good health.

I never told anyone except Cary, but I actually felt sorry for Grandma Olivia. Sure, she had a big, beautiful house filled with extravagant furniture, paintings, and decorations. Her dinners were elaborate and served on expensive china with fine crystal glasses and real silverware.

Yet for all her extravagance, her important acquaintances, and her gala affairs, Grandma Olivia never looked happy to me. If anything, I thought she was trapped by her wealth and position. How sad it must be, I concluded, to go through your life never letting your hair down, never walking barefoot on the beach, never just being lazy or having a potluck dinner; in short, never doing anything spontaneously, but always first having to go through the proper arrangements, as if your whole life had to be lived according to Emily Post.

I knew very little about my grandmother's past. She never volunteered any information and rarely, if ever, told any stories, unless of course, they were to illustrate and support some rule of behavior. Whenever I asked Mommy questions about Grandma Olivia, Mommy would shake her head and say, "Your grandmother had a difficult childhood because of the problems caused by her sister Belinda." What those problems were and how they had made Grandma Olivia's life difficult was left a mystery. Belinda had problems with alcohol when she was younger and eventually ended up in a rest home nearby. Whenever I visited with her, she told me stories and made references to her and Grandma Olivia's youth, but her stories were almost impossible to understand because Aunt Belinda confused the past and the present, mixing up people and places. Sometimes when she saw me, she called me Sara, thinking I was my mother, and once, recently, she called me Haille.

I know Grandma Olivia did not approve of my visiting Aunt Belinda. She treated her sister as if she were poisonous and could infect one of us with her outlandish stories and statements. I rarely brought up her name in front of Grandma Olivia because I knew what sort of reaction I would receive.

With all these no-no's and strict rules to follow, Cary, May, and I practically tiptoed around the big house and grounds, keeping our voices low and keeping ourselves as much out of sight and out of mind as possible.

After we were all dressed, Daddy looked us over as if we were lining up for parade inspection. He straightened Cary's tie and brushed down May's skirt after he spotted a tiny crease.

"I can have her take it off and iron it, Jacob," Mommy offered.

"It's all right," he said. "We'll be late. Let's get started."

The three of us got into the backseat, Cary sitting on one end and me on the other with May between us. He gazed out the window and didn't look at me once during the ride over to Grandma Olivia and Grandpa Samuel's.

"What a pretty spring day," Mommy said as we headed down Route 6. Grandma Olivia's house was midway between Provincetown and North Truro. From the outside, my grandparents' house looked far from cold and impersonal. It was a large two-story, clapboard covered home with a wide-planked whitewashed front door. Over the door was a fan-shaped window of colored glass and, though I'm sure it was meant to be decorative, Cary and I always joked about it looking like a big gloomy frown warning visitors to stay away.

Grandma Olivia was very proud of her home, claiming it was prestigious because of its historic past.

"The original portion of this house was built around 1780," she declared to every new visitor. She usually added, "That was when the prosperous families began to build some of the more fashionable buildings in colonial America. Today," she would continue in that sharp, critical tone of voice of hers, "wealthy people sacrifice classic fashion for ostentation."

The grounds around the house were also beautiful and well taken care of. The carpet-like green lawn was always immaculate, and the flower garden was dazzling with its hydrangeas, pansies, roses, and geraniums. There was even a small duck pond with a dozen or so ducks in it. In front of the house were two large, blooming red maple trees. Between them on the far right was a bench swing with a canopy over it, although I don't think anyone but Cary, May, or I ever used it.

We saw Judge Childs's car parked in the circular driveway when we pulled in. Judge Childs was a frequent guest, especially for Sunday brunch. He was my grandparents' closest old friend. The judge was retired, but Grandma Olivia always stressed the fact that he still had friends in high places and was very influential.

After we got out of the car, Mommy gave us another once-over, straightening May's clothes and again trying to brush out any creases.

Daddy rang the doorbell, and Grandma Olivia's house-keeper, Loretta, answered the door. For as long as I could remember, Loretta had worked for Grandma Olivia and Grandpa Samuel, but she never looked terribly happy about it.

"Everyone is in the sitting room," she declared without much emotion and stepped back to allow us in.

We entered like one of the duck families in the pond, Daddy first, Mommy right behind him, and then the three of us trailing in single file.

There was a short, marble-floored entryway with paintings on both sides, seascapes of the Cape and boats and portraits of sailors. The house was always full of the perfumed aroma of flowers, even in the wintertime.

The sitting room was the first room on the right. It had the look of a showcase in a furniture store window. The oak wood floor was kept so polished, Cary and I used to pretend that we could go ice skating over it. There was a large rug between the pair of beige sofas and under the large dark maple coffee table. Beside both settees were matching maple end tables. On every table, on every shelf, there were expensive-looking crystal pieces, vases and, occasionally, pictures in silver and gold frames of Grandpa Samuel and Grandma Olivia when they were younger, and some pictures of Daddy, Mommy, as well as one group picture of me, Cary, and May taken four years ago. There were no pictures of the ostracized Uncle Chester and Aunt Haille. Bringing up their names in this house was the same as uttering a profanity.

Everything always looked brand new to me. Every piece of metal glittered, as did every piece of glass. The windows were so clean, you couldn't tell if they were open or closed unless you walked right up to them.

Grandma Olivia was in her high-back chair looking like a queen granting an audience when we entered the sitting room. She wore an elegant rose silk dress with a large cameo above her left breast, a piece we knew was an heirloom, handed down from her grandmother on her father's side. Her hair was pulled back in a severe bun with a pearl comb decorated with small diamonds.

Grandpa Samuel sat rather casually compared to Grandma Olivia. He had his legs crossed, a tall glass of whiskey and soda in his hand. He wore a light brown suit and looked

400

his usual dapper self. His face broke into a wide, warm smile as soon as we entered the room.

"Here they are," he declared, "and a pretty handsome and beautiful group of grandchildren, too, hey Nelson?"

Judge Childs nodded. He sat across from Grandpa Samuel on Grandma Olivia's right side. The Judge was a distinguished-looking, elderly man with gray hair shot through with some of his original light brown color. It was neatly trimmed and parted on the right side. He wore a dark blue suit and a bow tie. Despite his age, I thought he was still a rather handsome man. His face was full and his complexion robust, with wrinkles only across his forehead. He had light brown eyes that dazzled with a glow more characteristic of a man half his age.

"Absolutely, Samuel. You and Olivia are very lucky people. Hello, Jacob, Sara," the Judge said.

Mommy nodded and smiled.

"We've got Bloody Marys, if you like," Grandpa said.

"No thank you," Daddy said quickly.

"I know you like Blood Marys, Sara," Grandpa followed, with a twinkle in his eyes. Mommy glanced quickly at Daddy, who was as close to a scowl as could be.

"Oh, I don't think so, just yet, Pa," she replied.

"When are you going to loosen up that collar you have around your wife's neck, Jacob?" Grandpa said, and the Judge smiled.

"That's an inappropriate remark," Grandma Olivia declared. "Especially in front of the children," she added firmly. "Loretta," she snapped, "please take the children into the kitchen and give them some lemonade while we wait for brunch to be served."

"Yes, ma'am," Loretta said.

Grandma Olivia thought it was inappropriate for young people to sit and listen to the older people converse. While we were standing in the doorway beside and behind Mommy and Daddy, she had been looking us over. She nodded at Daddy.

"The children look very nice," she offered Mommy, who beamed immediately. "Now don't go wandering outside and getting messed up," she called after us. "We'll call you to the dining room in a little while. Sit down, Jacob. You're making me nervous standing there like that. Sara."

They moved quickly and Loretta led us away. She gave us the lemonade and then, as we had done many times before, we went out back to the gazebo. Cary stood staring out toward the ocean while I entertained May. Finally, he turned to me, his eyes narrowed as if he were in pain.

"You go down a dirt road like that your first date with a guy. It doesn't look nice. It makes you look like . . . look like . . . an easy target," he said. "I just knew he was going to do that; I just knew it," he claimed and turned back toward the sea.

"First, I'm not an easy target, Cary Logan. I don't do what I don't want to do and we didn't do anything wrong, for your information. Robert is a complete gentleman."

"Ha," he said.

"You don't know him, Cary."

"You'll see," Cary predicted. "Tomorrow they'll be chattering about you in the locker room and Royce will be bragging about how easy you were."

"He will not! And it's dreadful of you to say that he would. You're just . . . just jealous," I accused. His shoulders stiffened and he turned, his face turning pink.

"What's that supposed to mean?"

"You don't have a girlfriend and you don't go out on dates, so—"

"So *what?*"

"So, you're jealous that I do."

"Dates," he said, curling up the right corner of his mouth. "Some dates."

I realized that May had been reading my lips and watching my face. She looked very confused. I tried smiling at her, but she turned and looked at Cary, her eyebrows raising as she gazed at me again. She didn't see us argue often.

"We'll talk about it later," I said.

402

"There's nothing to talk about," Cary retorted.

"Why did you follow us?"

"Why?" He shook his head. "I went to the dance to see what it was like and then, when I saw you two leave early, I just knew I had better keep my eye on you. Lucky for you, I did. I can't believe you have the nerve to question me. If it weren't for me, you wouldn't have made it home in time for curfew."

"You've got to let me—"

"Let you *what,* Laura? Go on. What?"

"Grow up," I said.

He stared, blinking rapidly, and then turned to the ocean again.

"I appreciate your concern, but I need my space, too, Cary."

"Fine," he said through gritted teeth.

He spun around and glared at the house, his anger spilling over like water boiling out of a pot. "I don't know why we have to wait around for them to stop gossiping. I'm hungry. We hardly had anything for breakfast this morning."

"So, go tell Grandma," I challenged.

He pounded up the steps to the door, nearly ripping it off the hinges when he pulled it open. May tugged on my hand and started to sign her questions.

"Cary's hungry," I explained. "He wants to see how much longer before we eat."

She stared after him and then glanced at me, her suspicious eyes small and troubled. I lowered my shoulders in defeat. Why did my most wonderful, new relationship have to bring such sadness? Why couldn't Cary be happy for me? I was near tears and had to turn away from May before she saw my sadness.

Whatever Cary did inside sped things along, because a few moments later, Loretta appeared to say it was time we came in to eat.

It was as wonderful a brunch as ever, with chunks of lobster in Alfredo sauce, shrimp cocktail, delicious home fries, salads filled with almost every vegetable imaginable, and as usual, great desserts, including my favorite, the multilayered, multicolored petit fours.

Afterward, the men went for their walk along the beach, Judge Childs and -Grandpa lighting up their cigars. They took Cary along with Daddy, and Mommy, May, and I were left behind with Grandma Olivia.

Mommy started to tell Grandma about my date and how pretty I looked, when Grandma suddenly rose from her chair.

"I'd like to speak with Laura," she said, interrupting Mommy in midsentence, "if you don't mind, Sara."

"What? Oh. No. Why should I mind?" Mommy stuttered and gazed about the big room helplessly. Grandma Olivia was already to the door of the sitting room.

"Come along, Laura," she commanded. I looked at Mommy, who only shook her head, her eyes wide with surprise. I caught up with Grandma in the hallway, heading toward the back door.

"Why can't Mommy hear what we say, Grandma?" I asked nervously.

"We'll go out to the gazebo," she replied, ignoring my question. "I need some air and a little walk after that meal anyway," she said.

"It was a terrific brunch, Grandma."

"The coleslaw was rather bitter this time," she complained. We left the house, walked down the pathway to the gazebo, and sat on the bench.

"Mommy and May should come out, too," I said. "It's so beautiful, hardly a cloud in the sky."

I gazed down the beach and saw the four men walking, little puffs of smoke from Grandpa's and Judge Childs's mouths caught and dissipated in the breeze. Cary was a few steps behind the adults, his head down.

"We'll send for them in a moment," Grandma Olivia said. "Now that you are obviously becoming a young woman with a woman's . . . interests, I thought it was time we had a little talk, Laura. I don't mean to interfere, but I don't think your mother is prepared for this sort of discussion," she added.

"What kind of a discussion is that, Grandma?"

"A woman-to-woman discussion," she replied, "where one woman has vast experience and wisdom to give to another, younger woman. Although she would have the same good intentions, your mother doesn't have my background, my breeding. She's not as aware of the dangers."

"Dangers?"

I stopped smiling and sat back. I suddenly felt as if my wonderful brunch had all tightened into a small, hard ball at the base of my stomach.

"I don't understand, Grandma. What dangers?"

"You're interested in someone, I understand, and you've actually gone out on a formal date with this person?" she began, her eyes small, but fixed on me with that same intensity that stopped laughter and wiped smiles off faces.

"Oh," I said with some relief. "Yes. He's a very nice young man. His name's—"

"I know his name," she said quickly. "I know of his family and what they do. I know he's been to your home for lunch and you went to the school dance with him last night."

My eyes widened with surprise. I smiled at Grandma Olivia's interest in my social life. She had never asked any questions about it before or cared whether I had gone to a school dance or not. I always thought that sort of thing wasn't significant enough to matter to her.

"I'm sorry I haven't had a chance to tell you about him, Grandma," I told her. Finally, she and I would have a nice grandmother-granddaughter talk, I thought, and imagined she wanted to tell me about her own childhood romances.

"There isn't much that goes on in this town that I don't know and there is nothing that involves my family and the family name that I won't eventually find out about," she declared. "I may not discuss it with you, but I know how well you're doing in school and how much your teachers like you. I know how you are a great help to your mother, and how you've been a respectful, obedient daughter. That's why I think it's so important we have this conversation," she continued.

405

I widened my smile and nodded.

"You're much too young to get deeply involved with any one young man, especially one who comes from a family of some questionable character."

"What?" The little bubble of delight that had started to fill within me suddenly popped.

"Don't interrupt, Laura. Just listen and learn. The Logans, and my family, the Gordons, go back to the Pilgrims, as you know. We have a strong, highly respected lineage. We are looked up to in this community; we are people of worth, status, and that brings with it more responsibility. We have been and remain models of proper behavior, models of respectability. My father taught me years and years ago that the first and most important and valuable thing you own is your reputation.

"You and Cary have been born with a gift. That gift is your family name. You've inherited literally hundreds of years of highly valued reputation. It will open doors for you, gain you respect, and place you high on the ladder of status, but you have a big responsibility, Laura, and that responsibility is to uphold the respectability, the value of our family name.

"Because of that," she continued, "there is a magnifying glass over you and your actions." She flashed a cold smile. "Up until now, you have done nothing even to slightly tarnish our family name, and I'd like to keep it that way. I want you to immediately end this acquaintance. These people are not up to your standard," she concluded. "I intend to discuss it with your father before the day is over as well," she said. She sat back, obviously waiting for my reaction.

For a moment I thought the words would get caught in my throat and my voice wouldn't work. Despite the silvery, soft breeze blowing in from the ocean, I felt as though I had fallen into a furnace. My face was flushed, my heart, although pounding, seemed to have sunken in my chest, the *thump, thump, thump* barely felt through my body. I shook my head.

"I don't know what you've been told, Grandma, but it's

406

all a mistake. Robert Royce is a very, very nice young man, Grandma. He—"

"He comes from a family of innkeepers," she said, practically spitting out the words, as if they were bitter in her mouth. "Do you know what an innkeeper is, Laura? How they started to be? These are people who had nothing, no family name, no reputation. Practically destitute, they open their own homes to strangers, clean up after them, wash their toilets and sinks, serve them food, cater to the wishes of complete and utter strangers, and worst of all, they contribute, are responsible for the pollution and destruction of the Cape.

"Fine homes, beautiful landscapes are all being marred by these . . . these motel and hotel chains. Anyone who can afford the price of a cheap bed can come here and enjoy what we, who built this, who founded it, created and made elegant. You have no business consorting with someone of that ilk, Laura. I absolutely forbid you to continue seeing this . . . this person. He will only bring you down."

"Please, Grandma," I said, choking back my tears, "don't talk like that."

She tightened her lips.

"You must get a hold of yourself, Laura. You must become mature, strong, beat down any foolish little lusts and remember who you are.

"Unfortunately," she said with a deep sigh, "we've already had a terrible time maintaining our family honor because of my sister and your Uncle Chester, but that has been remedied. We don't need something else to disgrace us and weaken our family's reputation."

"Remedied? Your son has left the family. We're not permitted to mention his name in your presence. I don't understand all of it, Grandma. You never talk about him, but don't you ever miss him?"

"He made a choice and one that is unfortunately best for everyone," she said sternly. "I'm not here to discuss the dead. I'm here to discuss you, the living."

"The dead?"

"Laura," she said firmly, "do you understand what I've been trying to tell you?"

"No, Grandma, I don't. I just met Robert. I like him. He's been very nice to me and we had a wonderful time at the school dance. I didn't agree to marry him . . . yet," I said, and her eyebrows rose so fast and so high, I thought they might leave her face.

"You would never marry such a person," she stated, her fear and anxiety deepening the lines in her face.

"I don't judge people by their bank accounts, Grandma," I said. I meant it as a matter of fact, but she pulled her head back as if I had reached across the gazebo and slapped her.

"I don't either, Laura. That's the point I'm trying to make and the point you're missing. Many of these so-called nouveaux riches are resort businesspeople. They have money, but they don't have class or reputation. They never will, no matter how fat their bank accounts become."

"But . . . didn't you ever like anyone who wasn't from an old and respectable family, Grandma? Not even when you were growing up?"

"Of course not," she said. "I wouldn't permit myself to like someone like that."

"That's not something you can permit yourself to do and not to do, Grandma," I said, smiling. "It's something magical. Surely, when you were my age—"

"I was never a foolish young woman, Laura, never like any of these empty-headed girls nowadays. My father wouldn't have tolerated it anyway, especially with my sister being such a disgrace. It would have destroyed him if both his daughters . . ." She paused to pull herself up tight again. "This is all beside the point. We're not here to discuss my past; we're here to discuss your future and the future of the family's reputation," she insisted.

"Can't you remember what it was like to be my age? You couldn't have worried about all this back then."

"Of course I worried about all this." She shook her head. "I knew I should have taken more of a role in your upbringing. Sara . . . Sara is just not equipped and she has too much to do with your crippled sister."

"May is not crippled, Grandma. She has a handicap, but it hasn't stopped her from being a good student and doing most of the things other young girls her age can do. She's very helpful around the house, does her chores, looks after her own things. She's far from a burden to Mommy, Grandma. If you would just let me teach you some sign language, you could talk with her directly and see for yourself how bright and wonderful she is."

"Ridiculous. I have no time for that sort of thing. Besides, you all shield her too much because of this . . . this imperfection. She should be made to expect no favors and she certainly shouldn't be babied. Only then will she have the strength to stand up to her deformity."

"It's not a deformity," I insisted. "And May is smart and strong enough to live a good life with her handicap."

"I didn't bring you out here to waste time on this topic, Laura. I brought you out here to give you the benefit of my years of wisdom and my sense of family responsibility. Unfortunately, I am the one who has to have all the strength in this family. Your grandfather is becoming more and more forgetful. I'm afraid he's falling into his dotage and will end up in a rest home sooner rather than later."

"Grandpa? He looks wonderful."

"You don't live with him," she replied dryly. "Anyway, I hope you have heard some of what I have said and will behave properly, doing the right thing."

"I like Robert Royce, Grandma. I'm not going to hurt him by telling him he's not good enough for the Logans," I said softly, but firmly.

She stared at me a moment and then slowly shook her head.

"I expected more from you, Laura. You leave me no choice but to speak to your father about this."

I felt the tears come to my eyes.

"Daddy likes Robert, too," I said, but I knew how strong my grandmother's influence was on my father. Usually, her words were like Gospel. "Please don't say anything bad about him."

"If I have your word that you will not do anything hasty or foolish with this person," she said. "Too many young people today think nothing of embarrassing their families."

"Of course, I won't."

"Very well. We'll see how things progress. Someday, you will be grateful for what I've said to you today, Laura. You'll look back and laugh at yourself for being so foolish."

She looked confident of that, but inside, I thought, *No, Grandma, I'll never be grateful for your telling me that magic between people is merely empty-headed foolishness. I'll never be grateful for your telling me that people have to be judged by their family lineage instead of the content of their character, that status is more important than anything, even honest feelings. No, Grandma, I won't be grateful; I'll always be full of pity, and not for myself, but for you.*

I said none of this, of course. Instead, I sat silently watching her look toward the beach where the men were making their way back to the house.

"It looks like the great minds have settled the problems of the world and are returning," she said dryly. "Why don't you ask your mother and sister to come out now."

I rose quickly.

"When I was your age, I always thanked my elders for taking the effort and time to talk to me and share with me their wisdom, Laura," she said as I started away. I paused and turned back slowly.

"I know you want only happiness for me, Grandma. I thank you for that," I said.

It didn't please her enough. She gave me the most chilling and piercing look I could remember, a look that sent me hurrying into the house to get Mommy.

4

A Sign from Above

During the days that followed, an uneasy truce developed between Cary and myself. He continually tried to maintain an air of anger and disapproval, once again trying to prove that he knew more than I did about dating. He would talk to me through May, signing and delivering his lectures aloud, even though we both knew she could hear nothing. He claimed May needed to learn what to do and what *not* to do on dates, since I had obviously never been taught the rules. He sounded like Daddy, complaining about young people being too forward, too advanced for their age. At times, when he put on Daddy's face and took on Daddy's voice, I was afraid I would laugh, so I had to turn away to hide my smile. Cary didn't have to imitate Daddy's temper. He had one of his own that was bad enough.

"Now that you're getting older, May," he lectured, shifting his eyes to me, "you have to be careful you don't waste your time on foolish boys or boys who think of girls as trophies and not as people."

"She doesn't have any idea what you're talking about, Cary," I said.

"That's more reason to talk to her now, before it's too

411

late. You're a big influence on her," he growled. "A negative one," he added.

"What's that supposed to mean, Cary?"

"Just what it means. What she sees you do, she'll think is the best thing to do, the right thing to do."

"I haven't done anything in front of her that I shouldn't," I protested.

"Maybe not yet," he muttered.

He was infuriating, but it was better for me to bite my lip and swallow back my words. He simply continued to make his speeches, talking about boys as if they were poisonous. Poor little May was smart enough and sensitive enough to know she shouldn't contradict him, but she looked to me continually to see if I would reinforce or challenge anything Cary said. I said nothing and looked away. Later, when we were alone, she asked me why Cary was so mad at the boys in school. I told her he was just trying to protect her; he was worried about her. She fixed her large hazel eyes on me and waited for me to say more, but I couldn't.

Sadness was like a spider weaving a web around us. Cary's face of gloom cast long shadows in our house. Whenever he entered a room May and I were in, her eyes swung from me to him and back to me in anticipation of some nasty wave that might drown us all in a sea of depression. Cary spent more and more of his time alone, up in his attic workshop. At school, he stayed to himself, even in the cafeteria. Sometimes, he sat with some of the boys from other fishermen families, but his eyes were always on Robert and me, making me feel self-conscious, making me feel guilty for every laugh, every smile, and especially, every touch.

Robert tried to be friendly toward Cary, tried to have conversations with him, but Cary would only respond in monosyllabic grunts, usually hurrying off or simply ignoring him. I told Robert it would just take time. I told him to be patient, that once Cary saw how nice Robert was, he would stop being so protective and concerned.

"I suppose if I had a sister who looked like you, I'd be walking around with a shotgun over my shoulder, too," he

412

told me. It brought a smile to my face and laughter to my lips. Robert had a way of parting the clouds and bringing the sunshine into every desolate moment. I had never known anyone as hopeful or as cheerful. After I met his parents, I decided it was because of them, because they appeared to be so happy and in love themselves.

"A flower blooms best in a happy pot," Aunt Belinda once told me when I visited her at the home. I thought she was referring to Grandma Olivia not being a flower that showed much bloom. I thought she was complaining about her own family life, but I couldn't get her to explain any of the things she said. Most of the time, she would just follow something with a laugh and the words would float from us and dissipate like smoke.

I met Robert's parents one afternoon when school was ended early because of a teachers' conference. I asked Cary if he wanted to come along to see how Robert's parents were fixing up the Sea Marina.

"Why would I want to waste time looking at a run-down tourist hovel?" Cary snapped in response. "And why would you?"

"It's not run-down anymore, Cary, and it's certainly not a hovel."

"Who's picking up May?" he countered.

"I will, if you want," I said.

"If I want? You used to care about your little sister," he remarked coldly.

"You know I care about her, Cary. That's not fair. I said I would pick her up."

"Never mind. You'll probably forget; you'll probably be too distracted by loverboy, and she'll be standing there alone and afraid," he said.

"I'm never that distracted, Cary, but even if I were, May could come home herself easily."

"Sure, and not hear a car when she goes to cross the road."

"She knows how to cross a road."

"I don't think going to see some junk house for tourists is

more important than May's safety," he said. "I'll look after her."

He turned and marched off before I could respond and left me simmering, my hands pressed into tight fists at my sides, my stomach feeling as if it had been twisted and turned inside out. The way some of the other students were looking at me as they passed me in the hallway made me think I had ribbons of steam coming from my ears.

"Are you feeling all right?" Robert asked me when we left school that afternoon. "You haven't said a word."

"I'm fine," I said. "It's just . . . my brother gets me so angry sometimes, I feel like screaming."

"Maybe you should, Laura. Maybe it's time you let him know just how you really feel," Robert said.

"Maybe."

I looked at him, at his face full of concern, and I knew that he was right.

"I'd better wipe the frown out of my face before I meet your parents," I said, "or they'll think you've chosen a witch for a girlfriend."

He laughed and we got into his car and drove to the Sea Marina.

Although the building itself had been neglected, the property on which it lay was prime seaside real estate. Only the front of the hotel had any real lawn. The rear was sandy beach with a pathway that led to a small dock. At one time, the hotel had a sailboat, but it was long gone. All that was left were two rowboats, neither looking very seaworthy, both covered with mildew and both with small leaks. Robert's parents had been concentrating on the building itself, replacing broken shutters, worn, cracked, and broken porch floorboards, painting the walls, repairing the kitchen, putting down new flooring, and replacing the bedding, sitting room furniture, lamps, and electrical fixtures.

"My father's always been pretty handy," Robert told me as we drove up. His father was on a ladder, repairing a loose clapboard.

I knew that the Sea Marina had once been one of the most

414

interesting houses in the area. It had been built as a mansion for a Captain Bellwood, who had developed a successful whaling business when sperm oil was in great demand. As with many great houses, the family lost its fortune and eventually converted the home into a rooming house for tourists. A sign bearing the words THE SEA MARINA was slapped over the entry doors and a new history for the building began. It was never well kept and four or five years ago was finally shut down. Robert explained that the bank had foreclosed on the inn and Robert's parents were able to buy it cheaply enough to have money left over to restore it.

It was a three-story building with twenty-two rooms available for renting. Robert and his parents lived in the downstairs rear of the house. Above the roof was a large cupola with a round dormer. The house had been constructed with a great deal of decorative detail, cresting along the roof line, a widow's walk, paired windows above the front doors, bay windows on the lower floor, and a one-story porch with carved railings and posts. The entire outside of the building had to be stripped and sanded before it was repainted. The cement steps that had cracked and chipped were replaced, as were a half dozen cracked and broken windows. I had ridden my bike past the Sea Marina before and knew how run-down it was before Robert's parents began this prodigious remodeling. It was no wonder he was occupied and working so much of the time.

Mr. Royce saw us drive up and waved. Immediately I saw that Robert had inherited his smile from his father. When we drew closer and he came down the ladder, I also noticed that Robert shared his blue eyes as well. His father was an inch or so taller, with the same lean, muscular frame.

"What are you hooky players up to?" he asked.

"I told you school was out early today, Dad," Robert said. His father winked at me.

"Yeah, he told me, but can I believe him?"

"Yes you can, Mr. Royce," I said quickly and he laughed.

"I see you have a loyal partner there, Robert. You going to introduce us or just stand there looking foolish?"

415

"This is Laura Logan, Dad. Laura, my father, Bob Hope."

"Bob Hope? If I was that good a comedian, do you think I'd be out here sweating over clapboard? Hi, Laura. Well, what do you think so far?" he said, stepping back, his hands on his hips. We all looked up at the Sea Marina.

"It's looking very good, Mr. Royce. It's going to be beautiful."

"Thank you. Robert's had a hand in all this, but you should see what his mother's accomplished inside."

"Come on," Robert said.

"It's nice meeting you, Mr. Royce."

He smiled and gave Robert a look of approval that broadened his shoulders even more.

"Feel free to drop by anytime, Laura. We could always use another hand clutching a paint brush," he said.

"Dad!" Robert protested.

"I'd like to," I said. "It looks like fun."

"Fun? You call this fun?" he joked. "I like this girl, Robert."

"Bye, Dad," Robert said, rolling his eyes and seizing my hand. "Come on, let's meet my mother," he added in a deep, low voice, filling me with trepidation.

We went up the front stairs and inside. Unlike the outside, the inside of the inn looked like it needed weeks and weeks more of work. The floors were still bare, the walls in the sitting room had only been sanded down and prepped for paint, wires hung from ceilings waiting for their fixtures, and doors were still off their hinges, lying against the walls like impatient guests waiting to be checked in.

"Ma!" Robert called from the hallway. We heard what sounded like a collapsing tower of pots and pans and then a curse. "Uh-oh," Robert said. He widened his eyes and held on to my hand as we continued down the hallway toward what had to be the kitchen.

Robert's mother was sitting on the kitchen floor, her face buried in her hands. Pots and pans were scattered around her. She wore a pair of jeans and a flannel shirt knotted at the bottom, the sleeves rolled to her elbows. Her hair, Robert's color, was tied in a ponytail. When she lifted her face from her palms, I saw she had the same soft, perfect features as her son. Even though she was obviously upset at the moment, she had the complexion and youthful glint in her eyes that made her seem ten years younger.

When she focused on us, she smirked, and leaned back on her hands.

"Welcome to the Sea Marina," she said. "Dinner," she continued in a style imitating an English butler, "will be slightly delayed due to catastrophe."

"What happened?" Robert asked.

"Those shelves I put up decided I had put them in the wrong place and rebelled," she explained and pointed to where the brackets had come out of the wall.

"I told you I would do that today," Robert said.

"I didn't think it was going to be a big deal. Obviously, I underestimated the weight of my cookery." She gazed at me and then smiled. "Are you the new cook?"

"What?"

"Ma, you know who this is," Robert said impatiently.

"Oh? Oh," she added and jumped to her feet, brushing off her jeans. "The lobster girl."

"What?"

"Ma!"

"Hi, I'm Jayne Royce," she said, coming forward to shake my hand. "Robert has told me everything about you, so I don't have to ask you a single question."

"Ma."

"Ma, ma. He sounds like a confused sheep. It's ba, ba, Robert. Come on," she said, taking my hand, "let me show you my jewel."

I looked back helplessly as she pulled me along, back through the hallway and into the dining room, so far the only finished room I'd seen. It had a long, dark maple table with very comfortable-looking captain's chairs. There was a silver candelabra and very pretty placemats that looked hand-stitched. There were two teardrop chandeliers that sparkled like ice in the sun, and a large oil painting of a whaling vessel in pursuit was on the far wall. Hanging across the room was another oil painting that I recognized as one of Kenneth Childs's earlier works. It was a beach scene with terns just starting their turn toward the setting sun.

"Well?"

"It's beautiful, Mrs. Royce."

"Please call me Jayne. I call my mother-in-law Mrs. Royce."

I laughed as Robert came up beside us.

"You want to see the dock?" he asked.

"Why would she want to see the dock? It's uglier than a one-eyed bulldog in heat."

"Ma."

"Maybe we should help your mother with those shelves, Robert," I suggested.

"Now here is a girl I could grow to adopt. When you're ready to run away from home, this is the place," she said. "She's very pretty, Robert. You didn't exaggerate."

"Mmm—"

"Don't say it. Wait a minute, Robert," she said, pressing her forefinger into her cheek as she feigned deep thought. "I have it. Why don't you call me Mrs. Royce," she suggested and I laughed. "Come on," she said, taking my hand again, "we'll go back to the kitchen and you can tell me all about life on Cape Cod while I pick up my pots and pans."

I looked at Robert, who shrugged.

"I guess we'll help Mrs. Royce," he said and we all laughed.

It was a wonderful afternoon. I never thought I would enjoy working so much. They wanted me to stay for dinner, but I didn't think it would be right on such short notice. I explained how I usually helped my mother make dinner and should be getting home.

Despite all the restoration work ahead of them, the Royces were happy and confident. The atmosphere of camaraderie, the sense of partnership among them, made me envious.

418

Robert's parents seemed so much younger than mine and so much more relaxed. I felt their love for each other and how concerned they were for each other's happiness. *No wonder Robert has such a warm and hopeful personality,* I thought.

"Well," he said as we drove away, "I warned you my mother was a character."

"I love her, Robert. She's great."

"Yeah, I guess I'm lucky," he said. "And now," he added, looking at me, "I'm even luckier."

Because the school year was approaching its end, studying for exams and preparing our last projects was very important. Although Robert and I didn't share any classes, we thought it might be fun to study together. For that purpose, he came to my house the following Saturday. I had already told my mother and mentioned it to Daddy just before Robert was due to arrive. Daddy and May were playing a game of checkers in the living room at the time. He paused and turned to me.

"Seems you're becoming the talk of the town, you and your boyfriend, Laura," Daddy said.

"No we're not, Daddy." I started to laugh at the idea.

"Grandma Olivia thinks so," he added. "You know how all the news worms its way up to her."

"I know." I grimaced in expectation of what Grandma Olivia had told him.

"Maybe you're getting a little too serious too fast," Daddy suggested.

"I'm not, really, Daddy."

"Everyone's expecting you'll go off to college, Laura. Not many Logans have. Your mother tells me you've shown some interest in becoming a teacher."

"I *will* become a teacher, Daddy."

"Lots of girls make plans and then meet someone and lose their heads, Laura," he warned.

"I'm not lots of girls, Daddy. I'm me," I said.

He nodded, his eyes softening. Daddy never liked chastising me and on more than one occasion, Cary suffered because of that. Poor Cary was always blamed for things we did together, no matter how much I protested and defended him. Daddy believed because Cary was a boy, he should be more responsible.

Once, when we were only ten and we had gone down to the beach at night and gotten ourselves soaked, he took the strap to Cary. I shouted and cried outside the door to Cary's room. Afterward, I went in and put some soothing cream on his welts. He never cried nor complained and when I did, moaning that I should have gotten at least half of the beating, he looked at me and said, "What for, Laura? I can bear it for both of us. I'm happy to take your half."

Because Cary was always so devoted to me, it was hard seeing him upset and angry now. I felt like a rubber band being stretched from both sides, fearful I would soon snap. I wanted Cary to be happy, too; but I wasn't willing to make myself and Robert unhappy in the process. I was hoping Cary would accept Robert soon and we would all be happy together.

Daddy said no more about my relationship with Robert and he didn't oppose our studying together at the house. Cary didn't say anything nasty about Robert coming over, as I thought he might, so I asked him if he wanted to study with us.

"I'm not going to waste my time on that," he replied.

"It's not a waste of time, Cary. I know you're not doing well in some of your classes."

"What of it? I'm not going to college. You are. I'll be working with Dad in our business, where I belong," he snapped.

"You know you want to build boats, Cary. It would be good for you to go to college and take some courses in engineering and design."

"I don't need to sit in some stuffy college classroom full of snobby kids just to learn what I already know," he said.

He did know an awful lot about boats. He had never had

420

reading difficulties when it came to that, and there wasn't a boat, a design, or a concept of which he wasn't aware. Daddy was proud of the way Cary could hold his own in a discussion about our boat or about sailing whenever Daddy's friends were around. Some of them even took to asking Cary for advice.

"If you change your mind—"

"I won't," he declared. "I have things to do at the dock."

Robert had to work until after lunch, but around two-thirty, he drove up. I was waiting for him on the front stoop. Mommy and May had gone into town to do some shopping.

"Hi," he said, getting out quickly, his books and note-books under his arm. We exchanged a quick kiss. "I hated leaving; there's still so much work to do, but my mother practically threw me out. So," he said, "where shall we go?"

"Up to my room," I said. I had been planning on studying there and had my own work set out. "We'll be less distracted. It's too beautiful today and if we stay out here, we won't get a thing done."

It was one of those warm days when the breeze seemed like lips gently brushing my cheeks and the clouds hung lazily under a turquoise sky. The sea conspired with the golden sand to tempt me into daydreams, beckoning with its soft spray and dazzling whitecaps.

"Good idea," he said, his eyes full of more love and devotion than an ocean could hold.

I had never had a boy in my room before. Just the idea of it put butterflies in my stomach. We paused when we entered the foyer.

"Your mother's not home?"

"She took May shopping. My father and Cary are down at the dock."

"Oh." He looked embarrassed, shy about being with me in my empty house.

I took his hand.

"Come on," I said. "We've got a lot to do."

I led him upstairs and into my room. I had made the

room spotless, polishing and cleaning all morning. Twice, Cary had looked in with a dark expression of disapproval on his face.

"This is a nice room," Robert said. He entered and looked at my posters of rock and movie stars. "Who gave you all these?" he asked, indicating the shelves crowded with stuffed animals and ceramic dolls. There was a collection of ceramic and pewter cats on one shelf as well.

"Daddy, Mommy, and Cary, for birthdays, special occasions," I replied. He smiled at the small table with a miniature tea set and a big doll in a chair.

"You don't still play with this, do you?" he teased.

"Sometimes. With May," I added.

He laughed and approached my canopy bed.

"Looks very comfortable."

"You can sit on it," I said and he did, bouncing and smiling.

The bedding, comforter, and pillows all matched the mauve shade of the canopy, and at the center of the two fluffy pillows was a large stuffed cat. He reached out to pet it.

"It looks so real, I had to be sure," he said.

I went to my desk, where I had an open notebook beside a pile of school textbooks.

"I've been going over my history notes."

He got up quickly and looked over my shoulder.

"I got an A in that class," he bragged, "but don't ask me anything now. It went in and then out again."

We both laughed.

"Nice view," he said, walking toward the open window beside my bed.

"We came up here to get away from all that," I reminded him gently.

"Right, right."

"You can have that chair," I said, pointing to the one beside the desk.

"Thank you, Miss Logan," he said with a short bow.

He sat and opened his math book.

"I hate these formulas," he muttered, but didn't lift his eyes from the page.

We both worked silently. Occasionally we would look up, our gazes would meet, and we would smile and look down again quickly.

"Would you like something cold to drink?" I offered, after finishing a section of notes.

"Sure."

"Cranberry juice okay?"

"Fine," he said.

"I'll be right back."

I hurried out and down the stairs, put ice cubes in the glasses, and brought them back up filled with our home-made cranberry juice. Robert was lying on my bed, his hands behind his head, gazing up at the canopy when I returned. I paused, smiling.

"Sorry," he said, sitting up guiltily. "It just looked so inviting."

"No, it's all right." I handed him his juice.

"It's good," he said.

I sat beside him and drank my own.

"Why do they make us take final exams just when it gets so beautiful outside? It's cruel," he said and I laughed.

"It's the end of the school year, Robert. What do you expect?"

"A little more consideration," he kidded.

We gazed at each other. I felt my heart begin to pound as he leaned closer and closer until our lips met.

"I've been wanting to do that for the last hour," he said.

"Me, too."

He took the glass from my hand and put it along with his own on the nightstand. Then he turned to me and we kissed again, this time embracing. I let myself fall back slowly, gently, and he lay down beside me, stroking my hair, kissing my cheeks.

"You're on my mind day and night," he said. "You're the first thing I think about when I wake up and the last before I close my eyes to sleep. On the days we don't see each other I hate the hours until we do."

He kissed me again, this time his hands moving over my shoulders. He brought his lips to my neck, and it was like electricity had exploded from inside my heart, speeding through every vein, to the tips of my toes and back up to my heart again. I took his head in my hands and kissed his hair while he moved his lips down, over my collarbone, unbuttoning the first and second buttons on my blouse, and then kissing the tops of my breasts, unbuttoning another button and another until he could peel away my blouse.

I let him unfasten my bra and lift it away so he could bring his lips to my tingling nipples. *I should stop him,* I thought, but I didn't. He moaned my name and his hands moved over my thighs and lifted my skirt so he could press his palms to my thighs. I put my own hands over them and held his there.

"Laura, Laura," he whispered, "I love you so much."

"I love you, too, Robert."

I let his hands go and they moved to my panties. My heart felt like a clenched fist, pounding at the inside of my chest as if it wanted to get out. When his hands moved over my hipbone and down, I uttered a small cry.

When I was younger and read novels in which girls were seduced or went too far, I swore I would never be like them, no matter how handsome the boy or how much I thought I loved him. How, I wondered, could your body make you do things you didn't want to do? How could any pleasure be so great that you would disregard all your warnings to yourself and surrender? Yet that was what was happening to me. I was moving faster and faster toward the point of no return, that moment when I would be like a swimmer who had gone out too far and was now at the mercy of the waves.

It was like one wave after another, one overwhelming, undulating sensation after another, sweeping me away from the shore of caution.

"Robert," I pleaded, "if we don't stop, we won't stop."

"I can't help wanting you, Laura."

"We're not ready yet, Robert. Let's be ready. Please," I

pleaded, knowing if he refused, if he kissed me one more time or touched me one more time, I would simply fall back and throw caution to the wind.

He held his breath and then pulled back. I lay there, breathless. Robert stepped off the bed and closed his pants. I hadn't even realized he had unzipped them.

Suddenly, I heard a deep, long creak in the ceiling and my heart stopped.

"Wait," I said, pulling him back under the canopy.

"What?" He studied my face. "Do you want me to—"

"No, no, just be quiet for a minute," I ordered.

"What?" He smiled with confusion. "Why?"

There was another creak and then another, then . . . footsteps.

"Cary's upstairs," I said in a low voice.

Robert's eyes widened.

"Huh? Why didn't you tell me?"

"I didn't know he was there."

"I never heard him come in and go upstairs, Laura. And your door's open. We would have seen him go by, wouldn't we? Or," he added with a dreadful pause, "he went by while we were . . . occupied."

"No, he must have been there the whole time, Robert. We would have heard him coming in and up the steps. Those steps creak so loud it sounds like Cary might step right through them sometimes."

Robert shook his head.

"I don't understand. I thought no one was home. You said—"

"I guess he came back when I was outside waiting for you."

"So?" Robert said, shrugging after another moment's thought. "He's been upstairs. What of it? No harm done. We'll just get back to the books." He smiled.

How could I explain? How could I tell him about the peephole in the ceiling, when I couldn't face Cary about it myself? Now I had to, I thought. More than ever, now I had to.

425

"But first," Robert said, "I'd better cool off." He went into the bathroom.

I rose and went to my doorway, listening. Cary was as silent as a ghost now.

"Okay," Robert said, emerging, "let's get back at it."

I looked once more at the attic doorway and then I returned to my desk.

We did study and talked and studied some more. We made plans for the summer months, and Robert talked about his college plans, his desire to become an architect. His drawings were all over the bulletin boards in the art classroom.

"Actually, you and Cary have a lot more in common than Cary wants to admit," I said. "I bet you could design a boat he would like."

"Maybe. I would for the fun of it, if I didn't think he would bite my head off," Robert said.

"He won't. He and I are going to have a real heart-to-heart talk," I promised.

The front door slammed and we heard Mommy and May talking in excited voices.

"It's getting late. I'd better get back. I'll just go down and say hello to your mother. Cary's still upstairs?" he asked.

"Yes," I said, gazing at the ceiling and the hole that, fortunately, Robert had not noticed.

We went downstairs and Robert talked to Mommy and signed to May for a while. He learned some new words with her and then I walked him out to his car.

"See you tomorrow," he said. "I'll get away in the afternoon for that walk on the beach."

"Okay."

He gave me a quick kiss and got into his car. I stood there and watched him disappear, until I heard the front door open and close behind me. Cary stood there, glaring at me. He started down the steps toward the beach and the dock.

"Just a minute, Cary," I said.

"What?"

"We have to talk," I said.

"I have nothing to say. I have to get to the boat."

426

"Well, I have something to say, Cary Logan, and you'd better stop and listen."

He paused and reluctantly turned toward me.

"Talk about what?"

"About the ceiling in my room," I said and walked toward him.

5

☙

Maiden Voyage

Cary turned away and continued toward the dock, walking very slowly. I walked beside him without speaking for a while. It was hard to think of the right words with which to begin.

"You snuck up there, didn't you, Cary? You knew Robert was coming over so you snuck back into the house and up into your attic workshop to spy on us," I said as softly and as calmly as I could.

"You're crazy," he said. "I had something to finish and just went up there. It's not my fault you didn't know I was up there. Anyway," he said, stopping and spinning around on me, "why are you so worried? You do something you're ashamed of?"

"Did I, Cary?"

He stared at me a moment, his eyes blazing.

"Well? Did I?"

"How would I know?" he said, marching over the sand faster now. I ran to catch up with him.

"How would you know? You would look through that peephole, Cary. That's how you would know."

"What?" He stopped again, his hands on his hips. "Peephole?"

"You know what I'm talking about, Cary Logan. If you want, we'll go right back to the house and to my room and I'll point it out to you."

He tried to stare me down again, but this time his eyes shifted guiltily away and his face turned a bright shade of pink.

"Oh," he said, nodding, "I know what you're talking about. There was a knothole in the wood that fell through a while ago."

"A knothole?"

"Yeah," he said. "I just noticed it myself the other day. You think I have nothing better to do than go up there and peep down at you and your boyfriend?"

"I hope you have better things to do," I said, "and if you tell me you didn't do it and you don't do it, I'll believe you," I said.

"I just forgot to fix it, that's all," he said. "I was going to plug it up with some wood glue the other day," he added, looking grateful for being allowed to come up with an explanation. "I just got too involved in what I was doing and forgot."

"Okay," I said.

"I can't believe you would accuse me of such a thing," he continued, now on the offensive.

"Why shouldn't I think it, Cary? You treat me as if I'm some sort of fallen woman now, just because I'm seeing Robert, who, I might add, you have no good reason not to like. He's done nothing to you."

"He and his family are part of the resort business, bringing those tourists up here," Cary said bitterly.

"You know we need the tourists, and that's not you talking anyway. It's Grandma Olivia. Who would buy Daddy's lobsters if there were no tourists, and who would buy our cranberries if people didn't want the products from the Cape? Why do they buy them? It's because we're a famous resort region in America, and it's time everyone accepted that. The only people who don't are those who've inherited so much money, they don't care about anyone else."

"You ought to go work for the chamber of commerce or the tourist bureau," he quipped.

"Maybe I will."

"You would not." He thought a moment. "Would you?"

"I don't intend to, but I wouldn't turn it down out of hand," I said. "It's all beside the point, Cary. You have to judge people for who they are and not for what their parents do or what their grandparents did. Don't be such a Cod-snob," I warned.

He couldn't help but smile because that was a term he and I had invented when we were much younger. He looked away.

"I just don't want anyone taking advantage of you, Laura. You're very trusting and innocent."

"Oh, and you're a man of the world, Cary Logan? Since when?"

"I know what boys are looking for these days," he said sharply.

"Robert's not like that."

"How do you know?"

"I think I would know better than you would, Cary, unless you were eavesdropping on every one of our conversations and spying on every one of our dates," I said. "Are you?"

"No," he said.

"So? Then tell me why you won't at least give Robert a chance. You'll be surprised at how much you two have in common, Cary. You both work for your parents. You may not respect what his parents do as much as you respect what Daddy does, but Robert is devoted to his father's business, just as you're devoted to Daddy's. Nothing's been handed to him on a silver platter, just as nothing's been handed to you. You both work hard for everything you have. You're both stronger and better people than the other boys in our school," I said.

I saw from the twinkle in his eyes that he liked that very much.

"Robert wants to be an architect someday. He's very interested in the work you do with boats, too. Few of your other so-called friends even care. None of them ever come to see your workshop."

"I don't ask them to," he said.

"But why don't you? Because you don't think they're sincere in their interest, that's why. Well, Robert is," I said.

He smirked.

"You've bought this guy, hook, line, and sinker, it seems."

"Cary, can't you have enough faith in me to trust my judgment this one time? You used to respect the things I said and believed," I wailed.

Tears flooded my eyes. When he looked at my face his face softened.

"I'm not saying I don't believe in you, Laura."

He looked at the ocean pensively and then turned back to me.

"Okay, I'll give him a chance," he said. "If that's what you want."

"I do."

"Fine. Now I've got to get down to the dock. I promised I'd help Dad," he said.

"You've got to start studying for exams, Cary," I called as he started away.

He just waved back at me without turning and continued to walk past the pink wild beach grass, strands of his hair lifting in the wind. I stood there watching him for a few moments and then made my way back to the house, feeling I had won some sort of victory, but not sure what it was.

However, the following Monday at school, things were different. Cary was friendly to Robert, so friendly, in fact, that even I was taken by surprise.

"Laura tells me about all the work you and your folks are

431

doing on the Sea Marina. I'd like to check it out one of these days," Cary offered, glancing at me quickly after he had said it.

"Great," Robert said. "I could sure use some advice about the dock. It has to be reinforced, only I'm not sure how to go about it."

"Maybe Wednesday," Cary said, "after school." He turned to me. "We'll pick up May and take her along."

"She'd love that," I said, bursting with so much happiness, I thought I might explode.

"We'll have to tell Ma," Cary said. "Let's not mention it to Dad," he added in a lower voice. I nodded.

Despite my father's need to have a market for his lobsters and his cranberries, he parroted Grandma Olivia's complaints about the tourist industry and the damage it had done and would continue to do to the Cape. I was grateful Cary hadn't brought it up in front of Robert, but I was always on pins and needles when talk turned to tourists and the effects they had on our town. It was a subject Cary and Robert would have to agree not to agree about.

That afternoon, Cary joined Robert and me in the cafeteria for lunch. Robert asked him some questions about boats and Cary talked right through the warning bell. Every once in a while, Robert glanced at me, his eyes wide with surprise. I simply sat there, holding my breath, afraid that if I uttered a word or moved a muscle, I might break the magic spell.

But it didn't break. On the way home from school that day, Cary offered that he might have been wrong about Robert.

"Maybe it's because he's not from around here," he said. "At least he doesn't follow Adam Jackson and that crowd. He asked me to give him some sailing lessons. Maybe this coming weekend," he thought aloud.

I bit down on my lip and nodded. I felt like someone tiptoeing over a floor of fragile glass, afraid that if I stepped down a little too hard, it would all crack, shatter and break around me.

432

"You can come along, too, if you want," he said.

"That sounds like fun, Cary."

"We'll wait and see how the weather is. As for it being fun, that will depend on how good a student he is."

"Robert said he definitely could get away from his work at the hotel?" I asked.

"Well, I promised I'd help him stain the inn's back deck on Thursday. I've got some time," Cary said.

"You would?" I couldn't believe what I was hearing. "I mean, you do? I mean—"

"It's no big deal, Laura. If he holds his own, we'll finish in an hour," Cary said, with more than a hint of challenge in his voice.

On Wednesday, as Cary had promised, we picked up May and went to the Sea Marina. I introduced May to Robert's mother and taught her some sign language to use while Cary and Robert went out back with Robert's father to look at the dock. Whatever Cary recommended pleased and impressed Robert's father, who had only high praise for Cary afterward. We all enjoyed some cold lemonade on the front porch, while Cary and Robert's father continued their talk about the building repairs.

May loved Robert's mother, who gave her an inexpensive watch, still in working order, she had found in a dresser drawer in one of the rooms when they had first taken over the property. It had Roman numerals and a pearl-like casing with a thin, leather strap. May was so excited about it, she walked all the way home with her wrist raised so she could admire it better.

"Daddy's going to ask her about that," Cary warned. "We can't tell May to lie."

To both of us, May was so precious and special, the very thought of having her do something even slightly sinful was upsetting. No one was purer in spirit.

"Let her tell the truth, Cary. We haven't done anything wrong. It's just being a good Christian to help other people. If Daddy says anything, we'll remind him of 1 Corinthians 13, 'And though I bestow all my goods to feed the poor, and though I give my body to be burned, and have not charity, it profiteth me nothing.'"

Cary laughed.

"Serves him right for having us read the Bible every night before dinner," he said.

Daddy did ask about the watch, but he didn't understand May's answer and asked me. I told him the truth. He was quiet for a moment.

"I don't like her taking things from strangers, Laura," he said.

"Mrs. Royce isn't a stranger anymore, Daddy, at least to me," I added. He didn't look happy, but he let it go and May kept the watch.

On Thursday, Cary went home with Robert and helped him stain the rear deck. I didn't go along, but I was so nervous about the two of them together without me around that I couldn't do anything but stare out the window and wait for Cary to come home. True to his word, he wasn't gone much more than an hour. I hurried downstairs to greet him at the door.

"You finished it already?" I asked as he stepped up to our porch.

"What's the big deal?" he said with a shrug. "Painting a hull, now that's a big deal."

"Did Robert think it was as easy as you did?" I asked. I was really asking if they had gotten along.

"He held his own," Cary replied. "I guess I'll spend a few hours teaching him something about sailing on Saturday," he added. "If you want to come along—"

"Oh, Cary," I cried and embraced him. "Thank you." I gave him a quick kiss on the cheek.

He stood there, frozen for a moment. It was almost as if my kiss had burned him. We hadn't kissed each other for some time, both of us self-conscious about it. But I was like springwater gushing. I couldn't help it.

"It's no big deal," Cary said almost angrily. "I'd do it for anyone," he said. "I have to wash up."

He hurried past me and up the stairs.

I knew I should be happy; I should feel very good about it all, but there was a cold chill in the air. It was as if Cary had left his shadow behind and that shadow lingered over me, blocking out the sun.

The next day at school, Robert announced that his parents insisted he take off all of Saturday.

"They said I haven't had a whole day off since we all arrived, and since we're ahead of schedule . . ."

"That's wonderful. Why don't we have a picnic on the beach, Cary?" I suggested.

"All right. Here's the plan. We'll do the sailing lessons late in the morning and then stop to picnic on the beach around Logan's Cove."

"Logan's Cove? Where's that?" Robert asked. Cary and I exchanged smiles.

"It's our secret place," I said. "Cary and I named it Logan's Cove because practically no one else goes there."

"It's about a half mile north of the bog," Cary said. "We don't have to worry about tourists bothering us."

"Oh," Robert said with a twinkle in his eye. "Sounds secluded. I can't wait."

After our Bible reading at dinner that night, Daddy paused before cutting the bread and glanced at me.

"I hear you hope to make your landlubber seaworthy," he said. I looked at Cary for a hint as to what Daddy was really thinking, but Cary's face was a closed book, unreadable.

"We're going to give him a lesson with the *Sunfish*," I said.

"We?" Cary asked with a smile.

"I'm a good sailor, too, Cary Logan. You've said that yourself."

"Yeah, I have, but you don't do it enough to be a good teacher," he explained. Daddy liked that and laughed. Then he grew serious.

"If you take May along, I don't want her in the *Sunfish* while you're teaching him, Cary."

"Of course not, Dad," Cary said.

Even though the *Sunfish* was only big enough to seat two, May was so small, we usually took her with us when Cary and I went sailing. I had already promised her she would be part of our picnic.

"May and I will sit on shore and watch them, Daddy. Don't worry."

He grunted, which was as close to an approval as we would get.

"The weather looks promising," Cary said. Daddy agreed and that was all that was said about it. I was too excited to keep it all bottled up. May sat in my room as I planned the picnic. My hands moved with my thoughts as I paraded back and forth, listing the things we would bring and the food I needed to prepare.

"Maybe I should make shrimp salad. Cary loves my shrimp salad. We could barbecue though, couldn't we? Should we do hamburgers or grill some lobster? We'll need salads and oh, I should make my lemon cake, don't you think? Robert is going to be so surprised when he learns what a good cook I am. What?" I asked May when she started to sign. "Oh, games. Yes, we'll bring something for you and I to do while they're out in the *Sunfish.* No, I'd be too embarrassed to let him see my drawings, May. We'll bring Chinese checkers, okay? And Cary's Frisbee. I'm worried about what I should make. I'll talk to Mommy about it tomorrow. No, let's go talk to her now," I said and reached down for May's little hand. She flew up to her feet and followed behind me as I went downstairs to talk with Mommy.

On Saturday morning as Mommy and I packed the picnic basket, Cary grumbled at us from the breakfast table.

"I don't know why we're not just having sandwiches and cranberry juice like we usually do," he said. "This isn't exactly the Blessing of the Fleet," he added with a laugh. He was referring to an annual event on the Cape when boats were decorated with pennants and priests lead a procession from the church. Everyone dressed up and there was very elaborate food and drink.

436

"Just like a man," Mommy said, "complaining and mocking until he sinks his teeth in and then he quiets down like a church mouse at sermon."

I laughed and Cary turned crimson.

A little over an hour later, Robert arrived. He was dressed in a pair of new sneakers, khaki pants, and a crisp white shirt. His preppy sailor outfit was topped off by a jaunty sailor cap. Cary, who wore a pair of torn shorts, and was barefoot and shirtless, laughed.

"What do you think we're sailing, a yacht?" he joked.

"No, but I thought I'd get into the swing of things," Robert replied, undaunted by Cary's ridicule.

"And you look very nice, Robert," I said. I was wearing a pink sundress over my bathing suit and thought that Robert and I looked like the perfect couple.

"Sailing's work," Cary followed sternly. "You're going to mess up that pretty-boy outfit."

"That's all right," Robert said. "It's not like I have many chances to wear these clothes. Hey, what's all that?" he asked, nodding at the big picnic basket.

"She made a feast," Cary said.

"Gee, Laura, you didn't have to go all out like that . . . but thanks!" Robert said.

"Let's get started. We're missing some good wind," Cary said gruffly, obviously eager to change the subject. May carried our towels and Robert offered to carry the blanket.

The weather was with us: A gentle breeze barely nudged the foamy white clouds along the azure sky. South of us, the sea was already peppered with sailboats.

"Looks like a perfect day for sailing," Robert commented as we trekked over the sand toward our dock.

"Oh, and you know what a perfect day for sailing is?" Cary shot back over his shoulder.

"Me? I know as much about sailing as I do about . . . nuclear physics," Robert replied. "I don't even understand how you get the boat to move."

"The wind gets the boat to move," Cary said. I could tell his mood was already softening and I smiled to myself. Cary

437

was in his glory, talking about the things he loved the most: sailing and boats. "You set the sail at a ninety-degree angle to the longitudinal axis of the boat, keeping the power of the wind on the sail's back surface. That's called running before the wind. In sailing off the wind, the sails are set at a forty-five-degree angle from the axis of the craft. This way, the wind exerts a pulling rather than pushing action, understand?"

"I will when I see it, I guess," Robert said, smiling at me. Cary glanced back.

"This won't work if you don't pay attention and concentrate," he said stiffly.

"I will," Robert promised. "Sorry."

"The wind flows at a great rate of speed along the forward surface of the sail, creating an area of lower pressure ahead of the sail. Understand?"

"Yes. I mean, aye, aye."

Cary shook his head.

"I must be crazy."

"He's paying attention, Cary," I insisted.

"We'll see."

"I just don't understand why the wind doesn't turn the boat over if the sail is at a forty-five-degree angle," Robert said. Cary stopped walking and turned.

"It would if the hull were perfectly flat. Every sailboat has a fixed keel that acts as a flat longitudinal plane to prevent the boat from moving sideways," Cary explained, illustrating with his hands.

"Oh. But if we're moving with a forty-five-degree angle, how do you get the boat to go in the direction you want it to go?" Robert asked. Cary's eyes filled with that glint of pleasure he always had when talking boats. I was glad Robert was asking questions.

"By sailing on the wind, a sailboat makes a course about forty-five degrees away from the wind direction. First you go to the left and then you go to the right, zigzagging. It's called tacking. You should know the terms so you'll know what I mean when I show you and tell you to do something. Coming about means shifting from one tack to the other. We'll do it with the rudder, pointing the bow up into the wind and then away from the wind on the opposite tack, or steering away from the direction of the wind until the sails fill from the other side."

Robert nodded, but I could see he wasn't clear on what Cary was explaining.

"In fore-and-aft rigged vessels—"

"Fore-and-aft?"

"You don't even know what that means?"

"I think I do. Is fore the front?"

"Great."

Robert smiled.

"In fore-and-aft rigged vessels, this maneuver is called jibing, and in square-rigged it's called wearing. If we start to lose control, I'll say we're broaching, understand?"

"Lose control?"

"It can happen," Cary said dryly.

"What happens?"

"We turn over and you fall into the sea and mess up your fancy outfit," Cary said, turned, and walked on. Robert looked at me.

"Don't worry, he won't let our boat turn over," I said. "He hasn't ever."

"That's reassuring," Robert remarked and we followed with May at our side.

May and I set the blanket out on a nice flat spot in Logan's Cove while Robert and Cary launched the *Sunfish*. I had brought along Daddy's binoculars so we could watch them from shore. I knew that once Cary had boarded our boat and set sail, he would be all business. He was really a very good instructor and expert at reading the wind.

They went back and forth, the *Sunfish* bouncing over the waves and looking as if it was running smoothly each time. When I gazed through the glasses, I saw Cary lecturing, pointing, and adjusting, directing Robert to make this turn and that, explaining as they went along. Even so, a few times, they did come close to capsizing when Robert was at the rudder and controlling the sail.

May and I played a few games of Chinese checkers, searched the beach for interesting seashells and waded out along the jetty of slippery rocks, searching for tiny crabs. The terns flew around us and followed us everywhere, especially when we returned to the blanket. They knew about picnics, anticipated crumbs, and eyed us cautiously.

Nearly two and a half hours later, Cary brought the *Sunfish* around and headed for Logan's Cove. They beached where we had set up our blanket. Robert's clothes were soaked, but he looked exhilarated.

"How did he do?" I asked as they made their way up to us.

"Fair to middling," Cary said without much enthusiasm.

"It takes lots of practice," I said. I looked closer at Robert's face. His cheeks and forehead were beginning to look sunburned, but the back of his neck was the reddest, deep crimson. "Oh, Robert, you should have worn some sunblock. You're going to be hurting tomorrow."

"Yeah, I'm going to regret not putting any on. I feel crisp as burnt toast," he said. He gazed at Cary. "How come you're not burnt?"

"I've been out there so long, my skin's used to the sun," he said. "Anyway, I'm starving. Let's eat," he added.

May and I took out the food and as we ate, Robert described his sailing lesson, revealing that Cary had been screaming, "You're broaching!" more than half the time. "I think I finally got the hang of it toward the end, huh, Cary?"

"You're getting there," Cary said. "Actually," he reluctantly offered, "for a landlubber, you didn't do too badly."

"Thanks," Robert said. He was practically beaming. "You're not so bad yourself for an old sea dog."

"Old sea dog, huh?"

"You *are* a bit bowlegged," Robert kidded. I laughed.

"I am not." Cary stood up. "Am I, Laura?"

"Only just a little, Cary," I said hesitantly.

"Is that so? Well, I've got perfect balance on or off land," Cary bragged.

Robert laughed.

"Want to find out, big shot?" Cary challenged. Robert glanced at me.

"Cary, no," I said.

"He's the one who claims to be perfect," Cary said.

"What's your challenge?" Robert asked.

"Ever hear of Indian wrestling?"

"Sure. I'm the Eastern United States champion," Robert bragged.

"Will you two stop? We still have dessert to eat. Sit, Cary," I ordered, pointing to his spot on the blanket.

"We have to earn it first," Cary taunted. "Champ?"

Cary took his stance, his hand out. The object was to pull the opponent so far off balance that he fell. I knew Cary was very good at it, probably from doing balancing acts on boats during heavy seas.

Robert jumped to his feet. May laughed and clapped her hands in anticipation.

"You're going to mess up that sailing costume even more," Cary warned.

"We'll see."

"Will you two stop?" I pleaded. My heart began to pound. Whenever egos came into question, especially masculine egos, there was always trouble.

Robert grabbed Cary's hand, took his stance, and the struggle began. Both were strong. Their forearms bulged and their shoulders strained. Robert surprised me with his balance and I could tell Cary was amazed as well. He had thought he would make short work of Robert. Both nearly toppled the other and then Robert faked a thrust forward and pulled Cary so hard, Cary lost his footing and fell face forward, unable to catch himself before he fell face first into the sand. When he pushed himself up, his cheeks were blistered with sand, as were his chest and legs.

"And still champion of the East Coast, Robert Royce," Robert cried, holding his hands high. May laughed. Cary's eyes met mine and I knew this was not going to end well.

"Let's have a rematch," he demanded.

"You'll have to speak to my manager," Robert said, nodding at me.

"Cary, please, stop. Let's have dessert."

"I don't need dessert. Come on. You were just lucky, Royce," Cary declared. He took his stance and held out his hand. Robert looked at me. I shook my head but he shrugged.

"I can't pass up a challenge," he said. "I have my fans to consider."

"Great." I slammed the basket cover down and sulked as they started their struggle.

It went as before, both nearly toppling the other. Cary was much more intense this time, his determination twisting his mouth and filling his eyes with fire. Once again, Robert made a good feint, only this time when he pulled back, Cary fell forward onto him and the two of them toppled to the sand.

"Tie," I cried, happy it was over, but they didn't let go of each other. The test of strength continued on the ground. Robert laughed and Cary tugged his arm, pushing him back to the sand. In response, Robert clutched Cary's ankle and pulled him to the sand. Then the two of them grappled, turning and twisting, one over the other.

"STOP IT!" I screamed. I stood up. May did, too. "If you two don't stop, I'm leaving."

They grunted, neither relinquishing his hold on the other. The struggle continued. I grabbed May's hand and she looked back over her shoulder as I pulled her away. I marched over the beach and back to our house, leaving the two muscle men grunting and groaning in the sand.

Thanks to their stupid male egos, what could have been a perfectly wonderful afternoon was ruined. Mommy and Daddy had gone to town, so I didn't have to answer any questions. Instead, I went upstairs to my room, May trailing along, wondering what had gone wrong.

"Boys!" I signed angrily. "They can be such idiots. They were getting along so well and now this. I'm tired of it. You're lucky. You still treat boys as if they had cooties."

"Not anymore, Laura. I like a boy in my class," she confessed.

"Don't tell him," I advised. I was feeling so bitter and angry. I seized my latest needlework and sat by the window jabbing the needle in and out of the cloth.

A short time later, I saw Robert and Cary. They weren't walking side by side until they reached the house. Then they stopped and spoke to each other quietly.

"Thanks for ruining the picnic," I hollered out the window. The two looked up.

"We were just fooling around, Laura," Cary claimed. "Why did you run off like that?"

"You weren't fooling around. You're both just two idiots," I declared. "I don't care if I do anything with either of you again."

"Laura," Robert pleaded. "It was just . . ."

I folded my arms and sat back so neither of them could see me. I didn't hear them come into the house and I didn't hear Robert drive off, but I held my curiosity on a tight leash and didn't look out the window. *They're planning something,* I thought, and suddenly heard the two of them singing beneath my window. To the tune of "My Darlin' Clementine," they sang, "We are sorry, we are sorry, we are sorry for what we did. We feel lost and gone forever, oh our darlin' Laura Logan." They repeated it until I stuck my head out and saw the two of them, now with their arms around each other's shoulders, gazing up at me.

I couldn't help but laugh.

"Are we forgiven?" Robert asked.

"You shouldn't be, but you are," I said with a smile.

"Then, can we have our dessert now?" Cary followed. "We worked up another appetite."

"Oh, now the feast makes sense, huh? Come on in," I said, delighted that they had come to a truce.

I signed to May, explaining what was happening now. She shook her head with confusion.

"Being grown-up is going to be harder than I thought," she replied and I laughed.

After dessert, Cary went back to the beach to dock the *Sunfish* and I walked Robert to his car to say good-bye.

"I had a great time. I'm really sorry about our ruining it for you, Laura."

"I'm just happy you and Cary are getting along, Robert. I just hope you two will stay that way."

"We will," he promised. "You're really a good cook," he said. "I enjoyed the picnic."

"Thank you."

He paused and I saw he was thinking of something that was taking a great deal of courage to say, so I helped.

"What is it, Robert?"

"I was just wondering. My parents are going to Boston next Saturday to buy some things for our place. I'm not going," he explained. "How would you like to come over to the hotel and maybe we could make dinner together? We could pretend we were the owners and we had a hotel full of guests and—"

"I don't know," I said, looking back at the house and wondering what I would say to Daddy. Robert looked very disappointed.

"Oh, well, it was just an idea," he said, opening the car door.

"I guess there's nothing wrong with my going to dinner at your house," I said. "I'll tell the truth: You invited me."

"That *is* the truth," he said, encouraged.

"It's not lying if I don't mention that your parents are away."

"No, it's not lying."

"I'll work it out," I promised.

"Great. What should I make?"

"I'll think about it and let you know during the week," I said.

"It'll be like we're married," he said and leaned out to kiss me. "I love you, Laura," he whispered.

"I love you, too," I said and he started the engine, backed out, waved, and drove away over a road dappled with sunlight and shadows.

Perhaps some day we would be married, I daydreamed, and then I thought about Grandma Olivia. She probably wouldn't attend the wedding. She might even excommunicate me from the family as she did her own son, Chester, but like Uncle Chester, that was a chance I was willing to take and a price I was willing to pay for the one I loved.

However, I had no idea just how powerful Grandma Olivia was and how much she could raise the costs.

6
∞

Hopelessly Devoted

*D*espite their wrestling match on the beach, Cary and Robert remained friends, and Cary even went over to the Sea Marina in the middle of the week and helped Robert and his father with some of the refurbishing of the dock. On Thursday, we had a bad storm. The rain fell so hard the drops were bouncing on the streets, pounding the windows and roofs, making the walls of our house beat like the outside of a drum. Daddy couldn't go out on his lobster boat, so he drove us to and from school just to have something to do. It was dark and dreary and unusually cold for this time of year. It didn't begin to clear up until late Friday afternoon.

"At least we know we did a good job on the dock," Robert told me in the cafeteria, "thanks to Cary. The storm didn't have any effect on it at all."

Cary blushed at the compliment. The three of us had been inseparable over the past week. I could see we were becoming the subject of idle chatter, some of the more jealous girls dipping into their dark wells of innuendo and nastiness to bring up new vicious rumors. Someone left a note stuck in the door of my hall locker. It read, *Does Grandpa sit and watch while you and Robert kiss?"*

I ripped it into a dozen pieces, afraid of what Cary would do if he saw it. He didn't mention anything, but I sensed that he was getting ugly notes as well. If anyone bothered Robert, he didn't tell me either. However, on Friday morning, just before lunch, Cary got into a fight with Peter Thomas in the boys' locker room. Whatever Peter said put Cary into a wild rage. He bloodied Peter's nose and gave him a welt on his forehead.

I asked Cary what had happened, but he wouldn't talk about it. He wouldn't say anything in the principal's office, and once again, he was suspended for fighting. The school called Mommy and Daddy, and when they came to pick us up, Mommy cried in front of Cary, which was punishment enough. During the drive home, he sat with his head lowered and listened while Daddy spoke softly, almost like a man pronouncing a death sentence on a convict.

"You're not a boy anymore, Cary. You do a man's work. You've been doing it for some time now. When you're a boy, your parents are judge and jury. They're your government, your court judges, and they pass sentence on your bad deeds. But now, you have to live with yourself and what you do. You have to be responsible for your actions and answer to a higher voice than mine. You hurt all of us and you have to live with that. If they decide to throw you out of school, that will be that."

"It wasn't my fault, Dad," Cary protested.

"Why wasn't it? You beat that boy good."

"He had it coming to him."

"Why?" Daddy pursued. Cary just shook his head.

"He had it coming to him."

"Well, when they make you judge and jury, you can decide that, but for now, you'll sit home instead of being in class where you need to be the most."

Daddy looked to me to see if I could add anything to clear up the mystery. I just shook my head.

"I'm tired," Daddy said as soon as we got home. "I'm going up to bed early tonight."

447

"I'll send up some supper for you, Jacob," Mommy called after him.

The air was so thick with gloom, I thought we'd have to slice our way through the sadness. May, locked up in her world of silence, nevertheless sensed the tension, and sat at Cary's feet, gazing up at him with big, sad eyes from time to time, which only made him feel more miserable. He skipped supper, too, and went up to his attic hideaway.

I heard him moving furniture and when I looked up at my ceiling, I saw he had put something over the hole. Then he was quiet.

I often went up to Cary's workshop to watch him work on his models. It was a small room because of the way the roof slanted, but he had a nice-sized table where he worked on his model ships. The ships he had completed were lined up on half a dozen shelves. He was most proud of his sailing ships, and they held center stage on each of the shelves.

When he'd been silent for over half an hour, I went up to see him. He sat with his back to me and continued to work. ·

"What's that?" I asked.

"A replica of the HMS *Victory,* the flagship of the British admiral Horatio Nelson," he said. "I feel like working on war ships these days."

"Cary, what happened between you and Peter? Please, tell me."

"What's the difference? It's over and done," he said.

"Is it over, Cary?"

He turned and I saw his eyes were bloodshot.

"It won't be over until we're both out of there, Laura," he fired back at me.

"Why?" I pursued. He returned to his model and worked. "Cary, I want to know. Why won't it be over?"

"Because they won't stop," he mumbled. "They enjoy doing it too much."

"Doing what?"

"Belittling me, belittling you, saying disgusting things about us."

"What things?" I asked, anticipating the answer. Little

butterflies of panic fluttered in my stomach when he turned toward me again.

"Things like, 'Do you and Robert take turns? Do you pick a card to see who goes first? Or do you go at it all at once?' You happy now, now that you know?" He looked so strange, and I couldn't tell if it was rage or sadness shining brightly in his eyes.

"No," I said, "but you've got to ignore them, Cary. They're just spiteful and mean."

"I won't ignore them. I'll stuff their garbage words down their garbage mouths," he vowed.

"But you don't win in the end, Cary," I said softly. "You're the one suspended from school."

"It doesn't matter. I get some satisfaction and at least they know they'll have to pay and pay dearly for every remark," he said. Then he fixed his glare on me. "No one's said anything to you? Bothered you?" He got his answer with my silence. "You wouldn't tell me anyway," he said.

"No, because look at what happens," I said. "You want some supper? I'll bring something up."

"I'm not hungry."

I started down the ladder.

"Laura," he called.

"What?"

"Don't let anyone make fun of you when I'm not in school."

"They won't," I said. He went back to his model ship.

Robert called to find out what had happened and express his sympathy. I was afraid that if he knew the whole truth, he, too, would get into fights and then I would be responsible for the two of them doing badly in school.

"You're still coming over tomorrow night, aren't you, Laura?" Robert asked.

"Yes," I said, even though I knew I would regret leaving Cary locked up in his own dark, unhappy world.

"I'll be there by five, okay?"

"Okay."

That night I lay awake for the longest time with my eyes

449

wide open, thinking. What terrible things had we done to cause all the nasty gossip about us? We were twins, born minutes apart. We had been connected in our mother's womb and birth was a great separation from each other as well as from her. When we were younger, we did cling to each other more than most brothers and sisters, even those close in age. I couldn't recall a day or a night when we were apart. I was sure most of our friends believed that when one of them said something to one of us, the other would soon know it. They all sensed that there were no secrets I would keep from Cary or he from me. He just naturally hovered about me, protected me as we grew older. Being twins, it took only a glance or a look for us to communicate a fear or a happy idea.

Perhaps our friends resented this magical connection; perhaps they were jealous and that was why they wanted to hurt us. It was easy for them to turn Cary's devotion to me into something dirty and sick.

And then, a more fearful voice, tiny, hiding in the back of my mind, stepped up to say, "Maybe Cary was so angry because he realized some of what they said was true. . . . He was too devoted to you. Maybe he realized his own problem and maybe his violence was his way of trying to deny it."

I turned over in bed and buried my face in the pillow to shut off that tiny voice and the memories it evoked. Memories of strange looks, lingering touches, intimate words that were meant for lovers, not siblings. I was afraid for Cary, afraid that if I gave this tiny voice even an iota of credence, I would avoid Cary's eyes, find his touch burning, flee from being alone with him. The separation that had begun the day we were born would reach its final stage, and soon Cary, my poor beloved brother, would be alone.

I cried for him, feeling anger and confusion, as well as shame. He was still above me, shut up in his attic workshop. It was very quiet, but I thought I heard him crying. I listened hard, but it was silent again. The wind had died down, yet there was still enough of it to make the walls creak. Outside, the moon played peekaboo with the parting clouds. The surf rose and fell against the dark sand, resembling a giant wet hand reaching out of the ocean, crawling out onto the sand. Night was our respite, the time to put aside the trials and torments of the day, to rest our weary bones and stuff our troubled thoughts into dark corners and then welcome sleep like a long-cherished friend.

I closed my eyes and prayed and waited for the surprise of morning.

The next day, Daddy and Cary went to work right after breakfast and were gone almost all day. They were just coming home when Robert pulled in to pick me up for our date. Both Daddy and Cary knew I was going to Robert's for dinner, but not even Cary knew that Robert's parents had left for Boston and wouldn't be home until late the next day.

With all the trouble circling our lives recently, I was eager to leave our gloomy house. I felt guilty about not telling Daddy and Mommy that Robert's parents wouldn't be there, but I knew if I did, Daddy would scowl and say he didn't think it would be proper.

Instead I waved good-bye to the both of them and got into Robert's car.

"You all right?" he asked.

I forced a small smile, took a deep breath, and nodded.

"Yes, fine," I said.

Robert squeezed my hand gently and then backed out of the driveway. A moment later, we were headed toward the inn and our romantic evening. The Royces had done a lot of work since I'd visited last, and I could tell as we pulled into the driveway that their work was almost complete. Robert gave me the grand tour, taking me from the sitting room to the office and then showing me some of the guest suites. All of them were beautifully decorated, bright and airy, especially the rooms that looked out at the beach and ocean. With its new paint, flooring, wall covering, fixtures, and furniture, the Sea Marina now ranked up there with some of our finest inns.

"We're advertising in the big newspapers and magazines," Robert explained. "Mom and Dad are very hopeful."

"As they should be," I said. "You and your parents did a wonderful job, Robert."

"Thank you."

Being alone in the refurbished, sparkling new inn made us both somewhat nervous. Without realizing it, we were being formal and very polite. Robert opened doors for me and kept his hand on my back as we climbed the stairs. We avoided each other's eyes and talked only about the inn, the grounds, and the upcoming tourist season. It was almost as if we were strangers who had just met.

"I guess we should think about dinner. I bought everything you told me we'd need," he said, and we headed for the kitchen, where we both worked on the preparations. I had him peel potatoes and heat up pots of water for vegetables while I breaded and sautéed flounder fillets.

Robert had already set the dining room table. He had their finest china and silverware laid out, with linen napkins and crystal goblets beside them. There were tall, white candles in the two candelabra in the center of the table. Over the new sound system that had been piped into most rooms downstairs, he played soft romantic music.

"Do your parents know all about this, Robert?" I asked.

"Oh sure," he said. "Mom suggested I use our nicest stuff. Although, I didn't tell them about this," he added and produced a chilled bottle of Portuguese wine. "I thought it would be all right. This *is* a special occasion," he added.

I nodded and went back to our dinner preparations. When everything was ready, I told him to light the candles and sit at the table. I would bring in the meal.

"Let me help," he said, but I insisted and he went into the dining room.

I brought in the food and Robert poured glasses of wine. Shyly we made a toast to the Sea Marina.

"May she have a successful maiden voyage," Robert declared.

We began to eat. Robert raved about everything. We laughed, drank more wine, and pretended first we were the owners and then the guests.

"This is our honeymoon," he suggested. "Where are we from?"

"New York. No, the Midwest. That way we haven't seen the ocean," I followed.

"And now that we have, we're enchanted."

"We don't want to leave. Ever."

He changed his posture, trying to take on the demeanor of an older, stuffy businessman.

"I'm even thinking of looking for work here. Did I tell you, my dear?"

I imitated Grandma Olivia and looked down my nose at him.

"No, you didn't."

"I looked at a small beach house yesterday. Nothing elaborate, but it has a wonderful view. It would be a great place to raise children. They would have the world's biggest sandbox," he said.

"Sandbox? My children won't be permitted to dirty their little hands and feet in any old sandbox."

We laughed and drank more wine.

Suddenly, Robert reached across the table and put his hand over mine, fixing his warm eyes on me and giving me that wonderful winsome smile.

"Have I told you how happy I am, how utterly complete I feel whenever I'm with you, Laura? It's as if the world was created just for you and me. There's no one else and all the beauty is ours alone to behold."

Whether it was the wine or his words that brought an exciting, warm tingle to my stomach, I do not know. All I was certain of was that I felt like I was overflowing with love for Robert, and I never wanted to let go of his hand or this moment. He leaned over to kiss me, a short, soft kiss, so tender and gentle, it was more like the kiss in a dream.

"Laura," he said. "How lucky I am to have found you."

"Me, too," I said, barely above a whisper.

He held on to my hand and then slowly, ever so slowly, he stood up and pulled me with him. Again he kissed me. It was the sort of kiss that grew deeper with each moment, became

453

more demanding and ended only because we were both out of breath. He brought his face to mine and let his lips glide over my cheek and to my ear where he nibbled gently and then whispered, "Shall we go to our room, darling?"

Our room! The thought of it was both thrilling and frightening at the same time. My heart began beating frantically as Robert led me from the dining room to the stairway and to a suite that looked over the beach and the sea.

Entering the room, we were both so nervous we couldn't speak. Standing in front of me, Robert unbuttoned his shirt and took it off, dropping it on the chair. My fingers, as if they had minds of their own, went to my blouse and, though trembling, undid each button. Slowly, I took off my blouse and let it drop beside Robert's shirt on the chair. He smiled and stepped forward to kiss me, his hands moving behind my back to undo my bra.

My heart pounded.

Robert undid his pants and sat on the bed to take off his shoes and socks. I watched him with eyes wide as he removed his pants and folded them over the back of the chair.

The wind made the curtains dance and the ocean outside roared against the beach, but all I really heard was the thumping of my own heart.

I unzipped my skirt, slipped it down my legs and placed it over Robert's pants. Then I took off my sandals and he rose to embrace me. We kissed again, and again it was a long, demanding kiss that took our breath away.

"Laura," he whispered.

I didn't look down, but I felt him move his hands to his waist. I kept my eyes closed as he stepped out of his briefs and then gently lowered my panties. I stepped out of them as if I were stepping gingerly into a warm bath.

For a long moment, we didn't touch, we didn't move. It was as if we had brought each other to the brink, to the cliff from which we could never turn back once we stepped forward.

"You're the most beautiful woman in the world, Laura. I love you so much, my heart aches."

454

Wave after wave of warnings drifted over me, but my body was tingling and the voices of restraint were dying under the rush of desire. I threw all caution aside and made the eventful step forward. Suddenly Robert's hands were on my hips and his lips were pressed to mine, our bodies touching. Everywhere. And yet, we still couldn't get enough of each other. Our legs had to rub against each other, our stomachs, chests. Our hands had to stroke all over until we were clinging to each other like two people holding on for dear life.

Before we knew it, we were in bed, our heads comfortably resting against the fluffy pillows, our bodies entwined under the cool sheets.

"Don't worry," Robert whispered. "I'm prepared."

I closed my eyes and drifted, my head spinning as I waited. Moments later, I felt his lips on my stomach. He worked his way up, between my breasts, over them and then to my mouth as he moved gracefully between my legs.

"Robert," I said weakly, almost too weakly for him to hear.

"This really is our honeymoon," he said before we joined.

I moaned, I cried, I grasped his hair so hard I was sure he was in pain, but he didn't resist or complain. I felt tears streaming down my cheeks and when he felt them, he kissed them away. When it was over, we lay there, still entwined, both of us breathing hard.

Then I gazed down and saw the blood on the bed sheet.

"Oh no, look," I said.

"Don't worry. I'll take care of that." He started to smile.

I pulled away from him, spinning around and pressing my face to the pillow.

"Laura," he said, pressing his palm to my back. "I love you, Laura."

I felt like I had fallen back to earth, like I had been traveling on a cloud, and suddenly, it turned gray and somber and began to rain down on the Sea Marina, releasing me along with the raindrops. My heart was still pounding, but my mind was clearing, the thoughts rushing in like water that had found an opening.

We had done it; I had gone too far; I had lost control. Or had I simply wanted it as much as Robert? Was it a sin to want it? Was all that Daddy taught and preached true, and would he take one look at me and read the sin in my eyes? Would it break his heart?

I thought about Cary, too: about his distrust of all the boys who looked at me or spoke to me. Nothing would convince him that this was good and pure and beautiful. He would say I had simply become someone's little trophy.

"Laura, what's wrong?" Robert asked softly.

"I don't know what came over me. Why . . . how . . ."

"Laura, we didn't do anything wrong. We love each other. Don't start feeling guilty."

"Why shouldn't I feel guilty, Robert?" I snapped and got up to gather my clothes. "This is exactly what everyone would have thought would happen if I came here and spent the evening with you alone. Every accusing eye and word, every sneer—"

"But we didn't do anything wrong. We love each other, want each other."

"I drank too much wine," I said, flailing about for an excuse.

"You don't mean that, Laura. You don't mean the only reason you made love to me like you did was because you got drunk." Robert lay there, looking at me with such pain in his eyes.

"I don't know what I mean," I wailed. "I just feel like we went too far, that we ruined something true and pure."

"That's foolish."

"It's not foolish to me, Robert!" I cried.

"Okay, okay," he said, holding up his hands. "I'm sorry. I didn't mean you were foolish, but you know in your heart, this was what you wanted, too."

"That's just it. Maybe I did, but maybe I was wrong to want it."

"You weren't wrong," he insisted.

"That's something boys usually say," I shot back.

"Not this boy. I say what's true and good for us. I don't

find myself in bed with every girl I meet and I don't fall in love with every girl I meet, but I fell in love with you."

I put on my sandals and looked at him.

"I'd better go home," I said.

"Laura—"

"Please, Robert. I just want to go home."

"You're punishing yourself unfairly," he said, rising. He started to dress.

"I'll go down and clean up while you dress," I said. "You better do something about the bed sheet, too."

"It's all right. I can do it later."

I left anyway and hurried down the stairs. I was already clearing the table when he caught up with me. He seized my wrist.

"I said I'd do that, Laura. Stop this. Stop punishing yourself."

I tried to swallow, but couldn't. I just stood there, nodding softly. He embraced me and held me, stroking my hair.

"Laura, Laura, Laura," he sang. "If I thought I made you unhappy . . ."

"I'm all right," I said, straightening. "Just take me home. I'll feel better after I get some sleep."

"That's right. Things always look better in the morning, don't they?"

"Not always," I said prophetically. I looked back at the dining room table. Our dinner had been so beautiful, so dream-like. Then why was I so confused, so twisted with mixed feelings?

All the way home, Robert cajoled, pleaded, begged me not to think poorly of him or myself. He repeated his love for me and swore he would go to the ends of the earth to follow me if he had to. He said he would rather walk on fire than hurt me in any way ever.

I tried to talk, but all my words got jumbled and stuck in my throat. All I did was look out the window at the dark ocean and the crashing waves. I didn't understand my own feelings. How could I explain them to him?

457

"Give me some time," I told him when we arrived at my house.

Sadly, he nodded.

"I was hoping this would be a special night . . ."

"It was," I said. I kissed him quickly on the cheek and ran to the front door. I didn't turn back to wave. I went inside and up to my room before anyone could see my face. Then I went to the bathroom and threw cold water on my cheeks.

"Laura? Is that you, honey?" I heard Mommy call from my doorway.

"Yes, Mommy."

"Everything all right?"

"Yes, Mommy. I just had to go to the bathroom," I said. "I'm fine."

"Okay. Would you like some hot chocolate?"

"No, Mommy. I ate and drank enough."

"Oh. Is Mrs. Royce a good cook?"

I swallowed and closed my eyes. Robert had told me she was a good cook.

"Yes, Mommy," I said. I felt like I had stuck pins in my own throat. No one believed in me more than Mommy and no one would refuse more to believe I had lied or been deceitful.

"That's nice, dear. You can tell me all about it tomorrow, if you want. Good night, Laura."

"Good night, Mommy."

I heard her go to her room. Then I took a deep breath and got ready for bed. I tossed and turned all night, seeing myself in a rowboat that was being flung from one wave to another, the sky black and full of cold rain. Out of the storm clouds Daddy's face appeared, raging. A long finger of accusation pointed at me from the heavens.

"You have sinned," he bellowed. It was a chant caught in the wind. "You have sinned."

I woke up in a cold sweat.

"I haven't sinned. I haven't. I love Robert and he loves me. That's not a sin. That's—"

I pressed my hand to my mouth, embarrassed to find

myself talking aloud. Slowly, I lowered my head to the pillow and stared into the darkness until my eyelids grew so heavy again, I couldn't keep them open.

Sunlight burst into my room like a bird crashing madly into the window. My eyes snapped open and I sat up quickly. I had perspired so much during the night, my nightgown was cold and wet. I pulled it off my body quickly and went in to take a warm shower, turning my face into the water and letting it pound on my closed eyes and cheeks.

No one but Cary seemed to notice how quiet I was at breakfast. Daddy was excited about a new location he had discovered for lobster fishing and talk of the day's work dominated the conversation. Every once in a while, Cary glanced at me and I could see from the way he studied me that he sensed something was wrong. Every time his questioning gaze met mine I glanced away quickly. I was eager for everyone to finish eating so I could escape to the kitchen to help Mommy clean up.

Cary poked his head through the kitchen doorway just as Mommy and I were finishing.

"I'm going over to the bog," he said, "if you and May want to come along."

"Go ahead, dear," Mommy said. "We're almost done."

"I—"

"I know it's not as exciting as it used to be," Cary snapped. "Forget it."

"No!" I cried. He looked back, surprised.

"I'd like to go, too. I'll get May."

We joined him outside and the three of us, just as we used to, walked over the beach to our cranberry bog. It was all in blossom and looked like a pale pink ocean.

"Daddy says it will be a fair crop this year, but no record breaker," Cary remarked. He leaned over and inspected some of the blossoms.

We didn't harvest until the fall and even with everyone helping it was still quite a process. It was Cary's job to run one of the harvesting machines. He had been doing it since he was ten.

"Looks healthy," he remarked. He gave May a blossom. Then he sat and put a twig in his mouth as he gazed out at the ocean. "So how was your dinner? Are you a member of their family yet?"

"No, Cary. And you don't have to be so sarcastic. We had a nice dinner," I added quickly.

"Um." He glanced at me. "Everything all right?"

"Yes," I said.

"You don't look all that happy this morning."

"I've been thinking about a lot of things," I said.

"Oh?"

"Things I have to work out for myself," I added. He grimaced.

"Used to be a time when you and I trusted each other with our problems, Laura."

"It's not that I don't trust you, Cary. Sometimes girls have to deal with girl issues, issues boys just won't be able to understand."

"Sure," he said, his mouth twisted with skepticism.

"I'm telling you the truth, Cary Logan. You don't have to sneer at everything I say."

"You mean you're not going to discuss this with your precious boyfriend?"

"Cary!"

"What?"

"Nothing," I said, shaking my head, my tears escaping from the corners of my eyes.

"What is it, Laura?" he asked with a face full of concern.

"Boys are just . . . boys!" I cried and got up. I tried running down the sandhill, but sand has a way of giving and I know I looked clumsy and foolish, nearly losing my balance as I hurried back to the house.

All that day I found myself bursting into tears for no apparent reason or warning. I tried to hide my face and spent most of my time alone in my room under the guise of studying for finals. The truth was my eyes just floated over the pages of my notes, my mind not grasping any of the

460

lessons. Robert called, but I kept our conversation short and I heard the unhappiness in his voice when I ended the call.

I returned to my room and my mind once again returned to the night before.

Why? I demanded of my annoying conscience, why should I feel any guilt? I love Robert and I believe he loves me. What we did all people who are in love do.

But other people wait until the proper time, until they are blessed and until they swear their love and loyalty before God in a church, my conscience, in Daddy's voice, replied.

No. I shook my head. Love is what's holy, not words pronounced by a priest. Love, pure and simple.

Is it love? Can you be so sure, so positive? Will you be in love like this next year? Will Robert?

Yes, yes, yes, I shouted in my thoughts.

Suddenly there was a gentle knock on my door. I quickly wiped away my tears with the back of my hand.

"Who is it?"

Cary opened the door and leaned in.

"Laura, if I did anything or said anything to hurt your feelings today, I'm sorry," he said. "I just wanted you to know that before you went to sleep."

"You didn't," I said. "But thanks."

"Good. Night, Laura."

"Good night, Cary."

He closed the door and walked softly away.

During the following week, Robert would leave a letter in my locker at the end of every day. Each letter declared his love for me more than the letter he had previously written.

I want to apologize to you, Laura, but I tell myself what we did was not wrong and neither you nor I should feel guilty about it. I love you and only you and making love is only another way of saying it. There's no one to forgive, he added.

I tied his letters up and kept them hidden in my desk at home, reading and rereading them so much, I thought the words were starting to fade. I wanted to believe every word he wrote and everything he said to me. I wanted that more

461

than anything and I fought hard to silence the voice of conscience that berated me and threatened me with the punishments of damnation.

Every night that week at dinner, Daddy seemed to pick the readings from the Bible as if he knew what was going on in my mind. One night Isaiah, Chapter 1: "Ah sinful nation, a people laden with iniquity, a seed of evildoers, children that are corrupters . . ."

I looked down at my lap and when I looked up, I felt the heat in my face and Cary's penetrating gaze, his face still full of questions and concern.

The next night it was my turn and Daddy asked me to read from Romans, 8. I began, but my voice cracked when I read, ". . . for to be carnally minded is death; but to be spiritually minded is life and peace . . ."

My throat closed and I had to stop, pretending to be choking on something I had nibbled before we sat at the table. I drank some water and Cary scooped up the Bible and completed the reading for me. Daddy looked at me with troubled eyes.

"Are you all right, Laura?" Mommy asked.

"Yes, Mommy."

"Maybe you're working too hard on your schoolwork," she said. "You should take a day off and maybe go sailing or enjoy the beach."

"I'll see, Mommy," I said. "I'll be fine."

Robert's letters kept coming, his pleading growing more frantic as I continued to remain aloof in school. He was absent on Thursday and, since Cary was already eating with friends, I sat with Theresa Patterson in the cafeteria.

"You look lost without Robert," she said. "Where is he?"

"He's . . . I don't know. I guess he wasn't feeling well this morning."

Theresa's dark eyes searched my face and then she moved a little closer.

"There are a lot of girls who are jealous of you, Laura. Most of them would steal him away if they could. Can they?" she asked with a small smile on her lips.

"I don't own him, Theresa. No one owns anybody else," I replied.

She shook her head.

"That's not the right answer, Laura. You should be a tiger when it comes to holding on to your man. See Maggie Williams there. She'd jump you and tear out your hair you so much as batted your eyelashes at Artrus. Everything all right with you and Robert?" she finally asked.

"Yes," I said.

"I know that boy dotes on you, Laura. That's why the other girls were making all that hissing about you and him and Cary. They're jealous. Good," she said. "I like to see them eat their hearts out," she added, glaring at the girls across the room, the ones who would never be seen sitting beside a Brava.

She turned back to me.

"You make that boy happy, Laura, he'll make you happy. Know what I mean?" she said, winking.

I shook my head.

"If you're a good lover, your lover is good to you," she said and laughed. "Never mind. I don't want to pry. But I warn you," she sang, "you turn your back on him once, and Robert Royce is going to be snatched away."

Was she right? I wondered. Was Robert losing patience with me? Would he turn away? And would I regret it, forever?

If only these answers were as easy as the answers that came to me on my final exams, I thought, life would be so simple.

7

A Woman's Heart

Once, when I was much younger, I looked up and saw Mommy staring at me while we were both sitting on the porch and doing needlework.

"What's wrong, Mommy?" I asked because she had the strangest, soft smile on her face. She looked like a little girl, amazed at some wonder of nature.

"Oh, nothing, dear," she said. "I was just thinking how much you remind me of Belinda sometimes."

Then, as if she realized she had said something blasphemous, she bit down on her lower lip and shook her head vigorously.

"Don't ever tell anyone I said that, especially your Grandma Olivia, Laura. I shouldn't have said that. You don't really look like Belinda. Not at all," she emphasized and went back to her needlework.

Although I never mentioned it to anyone, not even Cary, I never forgot Mommy had said it, and whenever I had any opportunity to look at a picture of Aunt Belinda, I searched her face for similarities.

Then, one day, on a whim, I asked Cary to take me to the rest home. He refused at first. For us it was as off limits as a

464

local bar. It was pretty much understood that Aunt Belinda was an embarrassment to our family and she was so mentally confused, it would be a waste of time to speak to her. If I asked about her, Daddy would say, "It's not your affair. Forget about her." Nevertheless, probably because of the remark Mommy had let slip from her lips and the curiosity it had stirred in me, I wanted to meet Aunt Belinda.

Finally, Cary agreed to drive me there one day, but he refused to follow me inside.

"I'll wait out here for you," he said. "Don't be more than a half hour."

That was my first visit. It was our secret for a long time. He drove me there one other time, but that was months ago. Neither of us spoke much about Aunt Belinda. Cary didn't ask any questions about my visits. It was as if he thought it was so forbidden a subject, even to show curiosity was a sin. He would rather act as if it never happened.

Occasionally, because it had been done so many times before in conversation, he would make a remark like, "That's something only crazy Aunt Belinda would do or say." She was truly a skeleton dangling in our family closet.

The day of my conversation with Theresa in the cafeteria, I asked Cary to drive me to the rest home.

"What? Why? You haven't been there for months," he said.

"I know. I feel sorry for her, Cary, but I want to talk to her about other things."

"What other things?"

"Things," I said. "If you won't do it, I'll have to ask Robert," I said. That was enough to cause him to make a decision quickly.

"I'll do it, but I won't go in with you."

"I know. I'd rather that you didn't anyway," I said.

He looked at me with a face full of curiosity, but he just shook his head.

"You've been acting really strange these past few days,

Laura. Sometimes keeping a secret buried so long can make it fester like a sore," he warned.

"I'll be all right, Cary. Just do me this favor. Please."

It was almost impossible for Cary to refuse me anything if I asked him strongly enough.

"As soon as we get May home, we'll go up, but it can't be for long, Laura. You know we can't let Daddy know."

"I know. I think that's wrong. She's really a very lonely, sweet old lady and no threat to anyone," I said.

He didn't reply. We picked up May from school and walked home quickly. Then he and I got into the truck and drove to the rest home.

We rode for nearly a half hour before Cary turned up a side road heavy with pine, wild apple, and scrub oak. It seemed fitting that our aunt who was kept a secret and whose past was to be forgotten had been put in such an isolated place.

The rest home had a pretty setting. The ocean was directly behind it and the grounds in front of the building consisted of a long, rolling lawn with benches, a rock garden, and some fountains.

The Wedgwood-blue home was a three-story building with a front porch the width of the building. Behind the building there was an elaborate garden, more benches and fountains, and a gazebo twice the size of Grandma Olivia's. There were some full red maple trees, more scrub oak and pine, and the pathways were lined with trimmed bushes. I had spent my second visit with Aunt Belinda out among the gardens.

After he shut off the engine, Cary turned to me.

"Remember. Not more than thirty minutes," he ordered, tapping his watch. "We want to get back before Daddy gets home and starts asking questions."

"Okay, okay."

I got out and walked the flagstone walkway to the short row of steps. I glanced back at Cary, who stared at me with a face the picture of worry. He looked about as if he were afraid to be caught here, as if he were the driver for a gang of bank robbers.

I entered the building. The lobby had light blue curtains, a blonde oak slat wood floor with dark blue oval area rugs. There were large paintings of country scenes and ocean scenes, some with fishermen, some simply with sailboats. The cushioned chairs and settees were all done in a light blue floral pattern. There were small wooden tables, book and magazine racks, and several rocking chairs were lined up in front of the large, brick fireplace.

There were only a few residents seated, a pair of elderly gentlemen playing checkers, with the rest just reading or talking softly. I didn't see Aunt Belinda.

The receptionist turned from a nurse and hurried toward me.

"Yes?"

"I'd like to see my aunt, Belinda Gordon. I've been here before," I said. "My name's Laura Logan."

"Oh, yes." She turned to the nurse. "Do you know where Belinda Gordon is at the moment, Jenny?"

"She's in her room. I brought her there about ten minutes ago."

"Is she all right?" I asked quickly.

"She was tired. She spent almost the whole day outside," the nurse said. "Come on. I'll take you to see her," she offered with a smile.

I followed her down the corridor through another door to Aunt Belinda's room.

She was sitting in her chair, her eyes closed. The moment after we appeared in her doorway, her eyes snapped open and she blinked rapidly.

"There's someone here to see you, Belinda," the nurse said. I stepped into the room.

"Hello, Aunt Belinda. It's Laura. Jacob and Sara's daughter," I added when her face registered no recognition.

She smiled.

"Oh, yes. Laura."

467

I pulled the chair near the window closer to her and sat. "How are you feeling?"

Aunt Belinda was no taller than Grandma Olivia. If anything, she was an inch or so shorter. They both had small features, but I thought Aunt Belinda was prettier. She had sapphire-blue eyes, which even here were brighter, happier. Her smile was softer. There was a childlike innocence to her, despite the tales of promiscuity and the notoriety of her youth.

"I'm a little tired today. How is your family?" she asked.

"Everyone's fine, Aunt Belinda."

"You're Jacob's daughter?"

"Yes," I said, smiling. Just as before, she had trouble remembering the details.

"Jacob has how many children?"

"Three, Aunt Belinda. I have a twin brother, Cary, and a younger sister, May, remember? Don't you remember me coming to see you before?"

"Oh, yes," she said. She stared a moment and then leaned forward. "Have you seen Haille, then?" she asked in a whisper, her eyes on the doorway.

"No, Aunt Belinda. I have never met Haille."

"Oh. Well . . . isn't it a nice day?" she said, gazing out the window.

"I came to see you, Aunt Belinda, because last time you were telling me about the first time you fell in love, really in love. Remember?"

"Oh? Oh, yes," she said with a smile. "I remember." Her face grew darker. "It was a forbidden love, a love to be kept in the shadows, full of whispers and stolen kisses. When we saw each other in public, we couldn't show our feelings. Then I lost him," she added sadly. "I lost him forever and ever."

"But how did you know it was love, Aunt Belinda?"

"Oh, it was love all right. Why? Did Olivia say something again? She's always telling on me, running to Daddy and whining that Belinda did this and Belinda did that. Well, she's not so lily-pure."

She pouted.

"No, Grandma Olivia didn't say anything, Aunt Belinda. I just wanted to hear about love. Somehow, for some reason, I think you know more about it than anyone else in my family," I added, more to myself than to her, but she perked up.

"I do." She leaned forward and took my hand. "I've been in love many times."

"Many times? But I thought there was only one great love of your life. That's what you told me the last time," I said, not hiding my disappointment.

"There was, but I lost him and then forever after I was always looking for him," she explained.

"Always looking for him? I don't understand, Aunt Belinda. Where did you look?"

She laughed.

"Wouldn't you like to know?" Her eyes grew small, suspicious. "Did Olivia send you here to find out?"

"Oh no, Aunt Belinda. She has no idea I'm here."

She stared, skeptical, and then nodded softly.

"Every time I fall in love with someone, Olivia falls in love with him, too. She always says she was first, that he liked her first and I stole him away by being promiscuous. Well, no one likes her because she's a cold fish. She won't even hold hands in public! You can run back and tell her I said that, if you want."

"I won't tell her anything you say to me, Aunt Belinda," I assured her.

"If you love someone," she continued, "you're not afraid to touch him or have him touch you. Olivia says that's ridiculous. She says it's not necessary to touch all the time and she hates kissing. Oh, she'll deny that; she'll say she kisses in private, but she doesn't. I know. Young men have told me. She turns away all the time." She laughed and then leaned forward again. "You know what I heard Samuel told someone? He told them she won't make love with the lights on and never with the covers off. Like she has something someone is dying to see."

She paused and looked at me closely again.

"What did you say your name was, dear?"

"I'm Laura, Aunt Belinda. Sara and Jacob's daughter Laura. How can you be in love so many times, Aunt Belinda? Isn't love something special?"

"It always was, every time," she replied. She pulled in the corners of her mouth and nodded. "You just make sure they respect you and treat you like a lady. Don't let him know you love him right away. Let him twist and torment himself and then," she said with a wide smile, "when you finally say yes, he will think you have given him the world.

"I was in love once," she added wistfully. "A long time ago, a sweet boy, handsome. He thought the sun rose and set on my moods. 'When you're sad,' he said, 'you bring the rain clouds. But when you smile, the sun is bright and strong.'

"Wasn't that sweet? It's poetry. He wrote poetry. Olivia found the poems and tore them up. She said if I complained, she would show them to Daddy and he would see what I was up to.

"I wasn't up to anything. I just . . . wanted someone to love me and I wanted to love him."

She paused, took a deep breath, and then looked at me again.

"You remind me of someone," she said and blinked rapidly for a moment. Her expression changed. It was as if she had just set eyes on me. "Do you know my sister Olivia Logan? Her maiden name was Gordon, same as mine," she said with a light, thin laugh.

"I'm your niece, Aunt Belinda. I'm Jacob's daughter, Grandma Olivia's Jacob."

"Yes," she said. She smiled. "How pretty you are. Are you a schoolgirl?"

"Yes, I'm in high school."

"And you have a boyfriend, or do you have many boyfriends?"

"Just one," I said.

She looked out the window.

"I'm waiting for him. I sit here by the window every day and I wait. He promised he would return, you know. And he would bring me flowers and candy. They don't want me to have any candy," she whispered, gazing at the door. "But he hides it in the flowers."

She brought her hand to her mouth and giggled like a little girl.

Then, she suddenly started to hum.

"Aunt Belinda?"

She continued to hum and stare out the window.

"I'm going, Aunt Belinda," I said, rising. She paused and looked at me.

"You tell Olivia I'm not sorry. She's the one who should be sorry. If it weren't for her, he'd still be my boyfriend. We would be out there," she said, gazing at the garden, "walking hand in hand and he would be telling me sweet things."

She returned to her humming and staring.

I leaned over and kissed her on the cheek, but she didn't seem to feel it. I paused in the doorway and gazed back at her. She looked so small and alone, left only with her memories and haunted by her regrets and losses.

That would never be me, I pledged. No one will keep me from my love.

"Well?" Cary said after I got into the truck and we started away. "Did you get what you wanted from her?"

"Yes," I said.

"What was that?"

"An answer to a question."

"What question?" he asked, glancing at me. "Laura?"

"Something only a woman would understand," I said.

"Oh brother. That stuff again."

"Yes, Cary, that stuff again," I said and pressed my forehead against the window as we bounced over the road and onto the main highway. Cary accelerated, blowing air out of his tight lips and shaking his head.

"It's all because of him," he muttered.

"What?"

"Nothing," he growled and tightened his shoulders as he turned himself away and drove faster.

When we got home, I thanked him and hurried toward the house, Cary right behind me.

"Robert called," Mommy said as we entered. Cary looked at me and then ran up the stairs, pounding the steps so hard, the entire staircase shook.

"Thank you, Mommy. I'll be right in to help with dinner," I said and went to the phone.

"Where were you today?" I asked as soon as Robert said hello.

"I had such a headache this morning, Mom thought I was coming down with the flu or something. She said I had a little fever and gave me some aspirin and told me to take the day off. Normally, I'd have to be chained to the bed, but things haven't been too normal. Did you miss me?"

"Of course. I wouldn't have asked if I hadn't."

"How are you doing? You looked so distracted after school yesterday. I hardly had a chance to say a word and I don't think you heard anything I said anyway."

"It's all right, Robert. I've just had so much on my mind with finals and stuff."

"Stuff means me, right?"

"Yes."

"I still love you, Laura. You can refuse to answer my letters, grunt after everything I say in school, but I won't stop loving you."

"I know. I don't want you to," I said.

"Really?"

"Of course. How do you feel now?"

"I'm getting better fast," he said. "I'll be in school tomorrow. Laura, can't we see each other soon?"

"Yes."

"This weekend?" he asked hopefully.

"Yes, Robert. I would like that."

"Great," he said with relief. "I'll—we'll plan tomorrow, okay?"

"Okay, Robert. I've got to go help Mommy with dinner."

"I'll be at your locker tomorrow morning, probably before you," he said with a laugh. "I love you, Laura."

As soon as I cradled the receiver, Daddy entered. He took one look at me and then tilted his head with curiosity.

"What's going on, Laura?"

"Nothing, Daddy. I'm just going to help Mommy with dinner. Did you have a good day?"

"Fair to middling. Where's Cary?"

"Upstairs."

"In the attic again, I suppose. That boy should have been born a bat so he could live in a belfry," Daddy muttered and went to wash up for dinner.

After dinner Mommy insisted I go up and study and not waste time helping her with the cleanup.

"Besides," she said, signing to May, "May's big enough to help out by herself now."

Up in my room, I began to worry that I had lost my ability to concentrate and would do poorer than I expected on my finals. If I continued to do as well as I had, I would be my class's valedictorian next year. I knew how important that was to Mommy and especially to Grandma Olivia.

I hadn't been at my desk long before I heard the phone ring. I listened, wondering if Robert was calling again. No one called me to the phone, so I went back to my notes. Then I heard Daddy's heavy steps on the stairway. I looked up because I sensed he had stopped at my door. He knocked.

"Yes?"

He opened it and stood there, his hands on his hips.

Daddy always seemed to feel out of place in my room. My things were too dainty, too sparkling for him to touch. Even though he gave money to Mommy and approved of the gifts, the stuffed animals, the dolls, and ceramics, he looked uncomfortable around them. When I was just a little girl, not much older than May, Daddy rarely came into my room. He always said his good-night from the doorway. Once or twice he came to my bedside when I had a fever and when I had the measles.

473

"Laura, where did you go today?" he demanded.

"You mean after school?" I replied.

"You know what I mean, Laura," he said, his voice dripping with disappointment. I never lied to Daddy face-to-face and I wasn't about to now.

"I went to see Aunt Belinda," I admitted.

"Who took you there, Cary or Robert Royce?"

"Daddy—"

"Who took you there, Laura?"

"I took her," Cary confessed from his attic doorway.

Daddy spun around and glared up at him.

"You know I told you distinctly never to go there, Cary."

I never knew Daddy had strictly forbidden him. It made me feel worse for asking him to do it.

"He didn't go in, Daddy. I went in to see her myself. Cary waited in the truck and he didn't want to take me. I made him."

"You can't make a young man Cary's age do anything he doesn't want to do," Daddy said.

"She didn't make me," Cary said.

"You turn those truck keys over to me, Cary. I don't want you using it until I say again, hear?"

"Okay," Cary said. "Here." He tossed them down and Daddy caught them in his right hand, which only turned up the fury in his eyes another notch. Then he looked at me.

"I thought we were clear on this matter, Laura. I thought you understood I didn't want you going up there, that it disturbed your grandmother."

"But why, Daddy? I don't understand how it disturbs anyone for me to go see a lonely old lady."

"It's family business," he said.

"So? I'm part of the family. Why can't I visit her?"

"Belinda is the black sheep of the family. It's a matter of reputation, family honor," he said.

"Why is she the black sheep?"

"I don't have to go into details, Laura. She was not a good girl, a decent girl. She gave Grandma Olivia's father and mother a lot of grief and that behavior continued long after

474

they were gone, only then it fell on Grandma Olivia's shoulders. She's done right by her and that's that. It's embarrassing to me to have to learn my children disobeyed me. It says in the Bible, honor thy father and thy mother, Laura. It's a sin not to. Remember that," he warned.

"But—"

"There are no buts. I absolutely forbid you to go up there again, understand? Do you?" Daddy demanded.

The tears that came to my eyes blurred my vision. Daddy looked out of focus, but his anger was so great, his face so red, I couldn't look away.

"Yes, Daddy."

"I hope this is the end of it and I never get another phone call from your grandmother about it. She's very upset."

I shook my head.

"It also says 'For if ye forgive men their trespasses, your heavenly Father will also forgive you . . .'"

"Don't quote Scripture to me, Laura. I know Scripture and I know you should obey your father," Daddy said, his face so crimson now I thought his blood pressure must be sky-high.

"Okay, Daddy."

"Let it be," he said.

I nodded and looked down. I heard Cary slam his attic door shut. It sounded like a gunshot in the house. Daddy turned and descended the stairs, each of his steps sounding like a judge's gavel, pronouncing harder and harder sentences on all of us.

It was difficult to get back to my studying. It took all the concentration I could muster, but I was finally able to run through a few chapters and go over some quizzes before I got too tired to focus any longer. After I crawled into bed and put out the lights, I heard Cary come down the ladder. I got up quickly and went to the doorway. He was just turning to go to his room.

"Cary . . ."

"What?" he snapped.

"I'm sorry about what happened with Daddy."

"I told you it would. I don't know why you had to go up there, why it was so important right now," he said. "Girl stuff," he added and started toward his room.

"Cary!" I called, but he continued walking away from me. He closed the door hard.

I never felt more like crawling under my blanket and disappearing.

I apologized again to Cary in the morning when we walked to school.

"Forget about it, Laura," he said. "You know Dad. He'll calm down and it will be all right again."

"I just don't understand it, Cary. If you met Aunt Belinda once, you would see what a sweet little old lady she is. She can't be a threat to anyone and I'm sure she doesn't even remember half the things she was accused of doing."

"It's not our business," Cary said.

"But why isn't it, Cary? We're members of this family. Why can't we ask questions and express our opinions, too? We're old enough now," I insisted.

"It's the way it is," he replied. Then he stopped walking and spun on me. "Somehow all this is because of you and Robert, isn't it? It has to do with your great love affair, right?"

I blushed before I could utter a reply.

"You don't have to answer. I know the answer," he said, walking ahead. We had just dropped off May when he quickened his steps and kept in front of me the rest of the way to school. As soon as Cary saw Robert waiting at my locker, he glared at me and then hurried away to join his own friends.

"Something wrong?" Robert asked immediately. He looked after Cary, who was plowing through other students, knocking shoulders, and clearing a path.

"I'll tell you about it later," I said and organized my books and notebooks for another day of school.

Cary remained distant, barely looking at me in classes or in the hallways. He sat with his friends in the cafeteria and I

476

sat with Robert. It was then that I told him about Cary and me getting into trouble for visiting my forbidden aunt.

"How weird," Robert said. "No one will tell you exactly why she's off limits?"

"No one thinks we're old enough yet," I muttered.

"I've got relatives I haven't seen, but it's only because they're wrapped up in their own lives. My mother calls them the funeral family." He laughed at my look of puzzlement.

"Funeral family?"

"We see them only at the funerals of other family members. She says as far as she knows, these people have only black clothing."

He laughed and I smiled.

"That's better," he said. "That's more like my Laura. Do you want to go to the movies this weekend? I can splurge. My father paid me back wages. I can take you to dinner, too. I can even afford the Captain's Table!"

"I'll see," I said and then quickly added, "what my father says. I want to go."

"Good," Robert said, slipping his hand under the table to take hold of mine. He squeezed it gently. "Good."

I wanted to wait until a little more time passed before I asked Daddy's permission to go to dinner and a movie with Robert. Fortunately, over the next few days, Daddy's mood improved because he was enjoying a good lobster catch and there was talk that the prices for the cranberries would go up in time for our harvest this year. One night after dinner and after I helped Mommy clean up, I stopped in the living room and asked him if it would be all right for Robert to take me to a movie.

"And dinner first," I added.

"Dinner?" Daddy's eyebrows rose. "The tourist season hasn't even started yet really, and he's got money to waste?"

I smiled.

"He doesn't think it's a waste to take me to dinner, Daddy," I said.

Daddy shook his head.

"When I was your age, going to a restaurant was something I did only with my parents."

"It's different now, Daddy."

"Aye, that it is, and not all for the better."

"It's just a date, Daddy. I'm old enough to go on dates," I said softly, giving him my best smile.

"Ask your mother about it," he said finally. This was the same as him saying it was all right. Of course, I knew Mommy would approve.

I told Robert the next day at school, which made him very happy. We were both back to our old selves, holding hands, laughing, enjoying our time together. I felt a whole new energy, and I was eager now to face my exams and end the year on a high note.

When Cary, Robert, and I left the building at the end of the day, however, we were surprised to see Grandma Olivia's Rolls-Royce in front of the school and Raymond waiting beside it. He waved as soon as he spotted us.

"What's going on?" I wondered aloud.

"Your grandmother would like to see you, Miss Laura," Raymond said.

"See me?"

"She asked me to bring you up to the house right after school."

I looked at Cary, whose gaze dropped to his feet.

"I'll see about May," he said and started off.

"Something wrong?" Robert asked me.

"I don't know. I'll call you tonight," I promised and got into the luxurious automobile. I hadn't ridden in it all that much and never before alone. I felt self-conscious about driving off in a chauffeured Rolls with other students looking after me.

When we arrived, I went right inside and found Grandma Olivia alone in the living room, seated in her favorite chair, her thin-framed glasses on her pearl chain resting against her bosom. She had been reading the society pages in the Boston newspaper and set it aside.

"Hello, Grandma. You wanted to see me?"

"You can sit over there, Laura," she said, nodding at the sofa across from her. I sat and waited as she pulled her shoulders up.

"Is this about my visiting Aunt Belinda?" I asked quickly.

"No, not directly," she said, pursing her lips for a long moment. "You and I, you'll recall, had what I thought was a very important conversation. I was hoping you had listened to what I said and would behave accordingly. That you would be a source of family pride and accomplishment and continue to be a good daughter, a good granddaughter. But you have chosen, it seems, to fly in the face of all my words of wisdom and be defiant."

"It's about Robert," I said, nodding. "I told you, Grandma, that he is a very nice young man and I—"

"Nice young men don't invite impressionable young women to their homes when their parents are away and seduce them," she spat.

For a moment I could swear my heart actually stopped. I know I felt faint.

"What?"

"Don't deny it. I can see it's true in your face and denying it only makes it worse."

"Who—I don't understand." Did she have spies everywhere? Was every living soul in this town on her payroll?

"There's nothing to understand. What you've done and what you seem bent on continuing to do is disgraceful. I want it put to an end tonight. I will not say a word of this to your father and your mother if you obey, but if you don't—"

I shook my head and stood.

"Sit down, I'm not finished with this conversation, Laura."

"I won't listen. I don't want to hear another word, Grandma. You don't understand and you have no right to run my life like this."

"Of course I do," she replied, as if I had spoken the silliest words. "I'm responsible for the health and welfare of this family."

479

"Why?"

"Why?" She laughed. "Why? I'll tell you why," she said, fixing her eyes on me and narrowing them into slits, "because the men in it are not capable of it. They've never been capable of it, and the other women haven't the stamina or the backbone.

"Now, back to what I was saying. You are apparently seeing so much of this boy and being so openly intimate with him, you have people talking. Some of my closest friends have come to me and—"

"You have people spying on me, Grandma? Am I being followed?"

"Of course not, but they have eyes. They have ears and they know how important the family reputation is to me," she said.

"They're just gossips who have nothing else to do with their lives," I cried. "I'm no princess, Grandma, and you're not a queen. We're not royalty because we can trace our family lineage back to the first settlers here. We're just like everyone else. We put our shoes on one at a time," I said, the tears streaming so freely down my cheeks, they dripped off my chin.

"Have you no self-respect?" she hissed. "Don't you care at all about what you do to my family name?"

"Your family name?"

"Our family name. I explained how important that is, how reputation—"

I straightened my shoulders to match hers.

"I'm not doing anything I'm ashamed of, Grandma Olivia. I have a personal life and I'm old enough to make my own decisions about it."

"That's idiotic talk. Age has nothing to do with it. There are people twice your age who are twice as foolish and some of them are in this family," she said.

"How do you know you're always right about everything, Grandma?"

"It's my unfortunate destiny to be right about everything," she said calmly, resting her hands on the arms of the

480

chair, "because with that comes the awesome responsibility of looking after the family."

"You don't have to look after me," I said.

"Apparently, I do, even more than I first thought. I'm warning you, Laura. Don't defy me. I'll go to your father tonight and reveal what you have already done. Just think what such a revelation will do to your parents."

I shook my head, unable to speak.

"Now, quietly end the relationship, do well in your schoolwork, and continue to be a helpful, loving daughter. In time you will see my wisdom. After your next year, I'll see that you are admitted to the best of the Ivy League schools and you'll be admitted to the most prestigious sorority there. You'll meet a young man who is deserving of your name and your life will be wonderful."

"As wonderful as yours has been, Grandma?" I threw back at her. She stiffened. "With a sister locked away in a rest home and deserted by her family, and with a son who's been disowned. No, thank you," I said.

"Laura! Stop being impudent! You will do as I say or I will carry out my threat," she snapped back at me.

I felt myself wilt. Mommy and Daddy would be devastated to hear about my evening with Robert. All their trust in me would be gone.

"Now go home. Raymond's waiting for you outside. Study for your tests and put an end to this stupidity immediately. I will not have another member of my family be defiant and go astray. I didn't take action early enough with my sister and my younger son, but I am determined to do so with you," she vowed.

It was as if she spoke from the heavens. Her words rained down on me and landed like a heavy weight upon my shoulders.

There was no more to say to her. I turned and walked away, moving like someone in a trance. I didn't even remember the ride home. When I got into the house, I ran up the stairs and into my room before anyone could see me or ask any questions. I threw myself on my bed and started to cry. I cried until my chest ached and then I turned and sat up and wiped my tear-streaked face.

I got up and opened the desk drawer where I kept Robert's wonderful letters. I stared at them and started to think about him when something caught my attention. I lifted the pack and studied it for a moment. The letters were out of place and they had been bound again, but sloppily. My heart sank.

Cary, I thought, must have found them and read them and told Grandma Olivia what was inside them.

8

A Heart Betrayed

I had been the lead in several of our school plays, but I didn't think I was a good enough actor to keep Mommy and Daddy from seeing how sad I was that night. I was pale and tired-looking, no matter how I tried to smile or how I tried to make my voice sound happy.

Cary didn't ask me any questions about my visit to Grandma Olivia's house, and he hadn't even told Mommy that Raymond was waiting for me at the end of the school day. Mommy just assumed I had something to do after school and had walked home myself. Neither she nor Daddy heard or saw Raymond drive me up to the house in the Rolls-Royce.

May was the one who signed the questions, wondering where I had gone after school, what I had done, and why I looked so sad. I signed back quickly, just telling her I was busy with schoolwork. Daddy didn't notice and Mommy was too preoccupied with serving dinner, proud of the new recipe for meat loaf she had found in an old Provincetown newspaper. Cary kept his head bowed, his eyes on his plate throughout most of the meal. It was Daddy's turn to read the Bible and while he did, I kept my gaze locked on Cary.

He couldn't look at me and whenever he accidentally did, he shifted his eyes guiltily away. He was the first to leave the table, claiming he had better get upstairs and do some studying. Daddy was happy to hear that and didn't question his quick retreat. While I helped Mommy with the dishes, she talked enough for both of us, planning things for the summer, including a trip to Boston. Finally, she noticed me standing quietly beside her and reminded me that I should go up and study, too.

I was grateful for the escape, but once again it was hard, if not impossible, for me to focus on my schoolwork. My eyes drifted constantly from the pages of my books and papers and my attention settled on the drawer where I'd hidden Robert's letters as my thoughts wrapped themselves around images of his face and the sound of his voice.

Just before her bedtime, May came in to spend some time with me. I took a break and did some needlepoint with her while she talked about her friends at school and asked me questions about high school life. Finally, she got tired and went to sleep. I did, too.

Moments after I had turned off my lights and crawled under my blanket, I heard a gentle knock on my door. It was so light, I first thought it was just some pipes rattling in the walls. I listened again, heard it, and rose. When I opened the door, I found Cary standing there in his robe and slippers.

"What?" I said quickly.

"I tried, but I couldn't fall asleep without talking to you," he said.

"I'm not surprised," I replied curtly. I stepped away from the door and returned to my bed. I sat on it, my legs folded under me.

Cary entered and quietly closed the door. He stood there gazing down at the floor for a long moment. I turned on the lamp on my nightstand. The brightness made him squint.

"What is it, Cary?" I finally asked.

"I was just wondering what happened up at Grandma Olivia's," he said.

"Somehow, Cary, I think you already know," I said and looked quickly from him to my toes. I always thought I had ugly toes. They were too big, but Robert said they were perfect. He claimed everything about me was perfect. *How blind love can make someone,* I vaguely thought. *I'm far from perfect.*

"What do you mean, I already know?" Cary replied. He gazed at me and I stared back, undaunted.

"Someone told her I had been at the Sea Marina at night, alone with Robert."

"So? Anybody could have told her that, Laura. Anyone could have seen you go there. Maybe you told one of your friends at school. Maybe you bragged about it to Theresa Patterson," he added quickly. "Maybe—"

"Maybe you told her, Cary," I said firmly.

"I would never—"

"Cary, for as long as we have been alive, you couldn't lie to me easily. You're not doing a good job of it now either," I said. "I don't know whether to just cry or scream my loudest at you."

He stared.

"I might have said something to her," he admitted. "She's . . . well, you don't know what it's like to be interrogated by her. She called me to her house a few days ago and—"

"Why didn't you tell me, Cary?" He was silent. "Were you ashamed? Was that it? Ashamed that you betrayed me?"

"Yes," he admitted.

"Why? What happened?" I asked. "Cary, you might as well tell me everything and stop playing these silly games with me. You *might* have said something? You would know if you said something, Cary."

"Okay, I'll tell you what happened. She started with her questions about my taking you up to see Aunt Belinda. She was very angry about that and she bawled me out for not knowing better. She wanted to know what was so important about us seeing Belinda. I told her I didn't see her; it was

485

just you and she got . . . I don't know . . . very mean-looking. She was really scary, Laura. I've never seen her like that. She told me to sit down and she stood up. She's only up to here," he said, holding his hand to about his chest, "but suddenly, she looked gigantic to me. She hovered over me and demanded to know why you went to see Belinda. What did you discuss? What did Belinda tell you? As fast as I told her I didn't know, she asked another question, firing them at me so fast, my head began to spin. I thought I was in one of those police stations you see in the movies. You know, interrogation rooms with the bright light in the person's face?"

"So then you told her about my letters, didn't you, Cary?" I asked directly.

His eyes shifted to my desk drawer and then back to me.

"I don't know what you—"

"Cary, you can't lie to me," I reminded coldly. "I know those letters were read. I had them folded and tied together a certain way. May wouldn't read them and Mommy and Daddy wouldn't read them. Who does that leave?"

"Well, I was worried about you. I knew you kept his letters in that drawer. I came in here to talk to you one day just as you were putting them away. When you started acting weird, I knew it had something to do with Robert Royce. So I came in here and just read a few."

"You read my personal letters," I said, shaking my head. It was one thing to suspect it and another to hear the confession from his lips.

"I care about you. I don't care about any personal letters," he claimed. Then he paused and softened his face. "Were they true, Laura? I mean, what he says happened between you and him in his place?"

I shook my head and looked away.

"I should have known you would read them," I muttered.

"The stuff in those letters, that was the girl stuff you went to talk to Belinda about, wasn't it?" he asked.

"No," I said. "It was far more than that."

"We never talked about those kinds of things, Laura. We

never really talked about sex, but I always thought that you would be different from the other girls in our school, that you would never—"

"I'm not like the other girls. I am different, Cary," I insisted, my voice cracking with emotion.

"That's what I think, too," he said, quickly nodding. "I think it's all his fault," he said firmly, twisting my words.

"It's not all his fault!" I cried, pounding my thighs with my small fists. The sight made Cary wince. I lowered my voice. "It's nobody's fault. I never did anything I didn't want to do. I happen to . . . I happen to love Robert, Cary, and he loves me, too. Now you've gone and made things very hard for us. You had no right to do that."

"I just did what I thought was right for you, Laura. I only wanted to protect you. I—"

"You had no right," I insisted, furiously shaking my head at him. "What did you tell her exactly? I want to know all of it, every ugly detail."

"I didn't tell her anything exactly. I told her how funny you had been acting and how suddenly you wanted to go see Aunt Belinda, that you said she knew about girl stuff.

"As soon as I said that, Grandma Olivia pounced. 'Girl stuff?' she demanded. 'Laura is still seeing that boy, then? How serious has it gotten?' she demanded. I tried to make it seem like nothing. Honest, I did, but she kept at me, asking if I knew if you had ever been alone with him. She's the one who suggested the inn, now that I think about it. Yes. That's what she said. 'Has she gone to that inn?' From the way she was asking me, I thought she knew and was just checking to see if I would be truthful. I told her you had been with Robert at his place for dinner. She asked if I knew if his parents were there. I said I didn't know, but I guess you're right: I'm not a good liar, because she asked me again in a sharper voice. I said I thought maybe his parents were gone and then she was the one who told me what you had done. It was as if she had read the letters herself, Laura. I swear," he added with his hand up as if he were about to take the witness stand in a courtroom.

"And you didn't deny any of it? You let her believe it," I concluded.

"She took one look at my face and said I didn't have to say another word. My eyes said it all. She's spooky. You know how she is. She's—"

"She's a very unhappy old woman, Cary. That's what she is, and now she's succeeded in making me unhappy, too," I said. "And you helped her. Are you satisfied?"

"No, of course not. But Laura, he shouldn't have . . ." Cary looked away. "If he loved you like you said, he would respect you more and that never would have happened."

"I don't want to talk about it anymore, Cary. I'm afraid that anything I say to you might get back to Grandma Olivia anyway," I added.

It was as if I had slapped him hard across the face. His head actually jerked to the side and his eyes filled with such pain, I couldn't look at him.

"I'm sorry, Laura, but I just did what I did because . . . because I love you," he blurted and turned quickly to rush out of the room.

I remained sitting there for a long, long moment, staring at the closed door and hearing Cary's words echo in my ears. How could I ever explain all this to Robert? Who could ever understand the madness of my family?

I tried to sleep, but fretted in and out of nightmares, waking with small cries, burying my face in the pillow and then falling asleep again, only to wake before the morning and then finally fall into a fitful sleep once again. I was in such a deep sleep when morning did come, I didn't hear anyone moving about the house. It was May who finally woke me, shaking my arm.

My eyelids fluttered and I looked at her without understanding why she was there. Then I gazed at the clock and flew out of bed. She followed me around my room, signing her questions. Was I sick? Was Cary sick? He wouldn't say a word to anyone, she claimed. I was fine, I told her. I just overslept.

Mommy was at me the moment I appeared.

"Aren't you feeling well, Laura? You didn't look so well last night, now that I think about it."

"I'm fine, Mommy. Just a little tired," I said. "I'm sorry I overslept."

"Your brother's acting strangely, too," she complained. "Just like when the two of you were May's age and younger. If one of you had a stomachache, the other did, too. Remember when you both got the chicken pox, not more than a day apart?"

"Yes, Mommy."

"Maybe it was something in that new recipe," she mused.

"No, Mommy. If there was something wrong with the food, you and Daddy and May would be sick."

"Yes, that's true."

"We're just a little tired," I said. It wasn't a lie. I was sure Cary hadn't slept much better than I had.

I drank some juice, had some toast and jam, and scooped up my things to join May and Cary, who were waiting at the door. Daddy had already left for work. Cary's eyes were full of remorse and sorrow, but I chose not to look at him. I didn't say a word as we started out for school. May was full of curiosity and signed questions all the way. After we dropped her off, Cary turned to me.

"I'm sorry, Laura," he said. "I didn't mean to get you in any trouble."

"Let's not talk about it, Cary. I'm still trying to come up with a way to explain things to Robert."

He nodded and walked a little ahead of me all the way to school. When we arrived, he quickly went to his locker and left me to talk to Robert alone. Robert took one look at me and the sweet, happy grin disappeared from his face.

"What's wrong? You look like you lost your best friend," he half-kidded.

"I think I did," I said.

The first warning bell rang before I could say anything, and I knew I didn't have enough time to explain it all.

"I'll tell you at lunch," I promised. "There isn't time now."

Robert nodded, his face darkly serious and full of worry. Between every class he tried to catch up with me so he could find out what was wrong.

"Are you all right?" he asked. "You look really tired, Laura."

"I *am* really tired," I admitted.

"Your brother's doing a good job of avoiding me today. I caught him looking at me and when I looked back, he turned away. He's back to muttering or grunting whenever I try to speak to him. What's going on?"

"We'll talk at lunch," I said, and I, too, hurried away.

However, when lunch hour finally arrived and I approached the cafeteria and heard the happy chatter of the students, all full of excitement about the approaching end of the school year and summer vacation, I stopped a few feet from the door. My feet felt frozen to the floor.

"What's the matter with you?" Theresa Patterson asked as she came up beside me. "You look like you've seen a ghost."

I turned to her. A tear escaped from my eye and I shook my head instead of speaking.

"Laura?"

I ran back down the corridor and out a side door, bursting into the afternoon sunshine and letting the tears come more freely now that I was alone. I walked to an old oak tree and plopped down in the shade, hugging my knees, gently rocking back and forth. My shoulders shook as I sobbed.

"Laura," I heard minutes later. Robert was rushing over the lawn toward me. "What happened? Why didn't you come into the cafeteria? I waited and waited until Theresa told me she saw you run outside."

He knelt beside me. I wiped my tears away and tried to smile.

"I'm all right," I said. "I just wasn't in the mood for all those eyes and all those inquisitive faces today."

490

"Why? Tell me everything," he demanded as he sat on the grass beside me.

"Oh Robert . . ." I started and then sucked in my breath. "Cary read the letters you wrote to me. He went into my room when I wasn't there and he read them," I wailed.

"Uh-oh," Robert moaned. "No wonder he's been treating me like someone with a contagious disease today. I'm sorry, Laura. I shouldn't have put any of that in writing. Has he been nasty to you or—"

"No, it's not just Cary," I said. I paused and looked around at the slow-moving traffic, the soft cotton clouds lazily crossing the horizon, and the songbirds flitting from tree to tree. The world looked so calm and beautiful that it made the knots in my stomach and the chill in my heart seem worse.

I told Robert about my great aunt Belinda and how my grandmother Olivia had questioned Cary at length about my visiting Belinda at the rest home.

Then I described how Grandma Olivia's interrogation had turned to my personal life and specifically my relationship with him. Before I could go on, Robert sputtered out, "You mean, Cary told her what I wrote in my letters?"

"Not exactly," I said, "but it had the same result."

Robert shook his head, amazed.

"What happened after that?"

"That was why she had the driver here for me yesterday, Robert," I said.

"Oh. You mean, she called you to her home to question you about you and me?"

"Yes."

He blew a low whistle through his closed lips.

"I'm sorry, Laura. I guess I really messed things up but I couldn't help myself. I had to tell you how I felt and you wouldn't talk to me. . . ."

"Don't blame yourself, Robert. Cary knows he was wrong," I said, grinding the tears out of my eyes and catching my breath. "It's just that Grandma Olivia is the head of our family and she could make things hard for everyone."

"What does she want? Should I go to see her? Maybe—"

"Oh no, Robert. Never. Don't even talk about it," I said and he saw the terror in my eyes. He nodded.

"Well, what should I do?"

"There's nothing to do at the moment," I said. "Except . . ."

"Except what, Laura?"

"Except stay away from each other for a while. At least until things calm down," I added quickly. He stared at me a moment and then shook his head.

"What's a while?"

"A while," I said, shrugging. "We've got our finals to think about anyway."

"You think I care about my finals now?"

"You have to, Robert. You want to go to college. If you did poorly because of me, I would feel ten times worse."

He plucked a blade of grass and put it between his teeth.

"I'm keeping you from eating lunch," I said, trying to joke. "You must be hungry. You're eating grass."

He stopped chewing and smiled. Then he shook his head slowly.

"I don't think you understand how much I love you, Laura. It's easy to say we should keep away from each other for a while, but it's nearly impossible for me to do. I'm going to camp out near your house and hope for a glimpse of you every night."

"Robert—"

"Seeing you in school will be like torture. What am I supposed to do, stay away from you here, too?"

My lips started to tremble, my chin quivering.

"I'm sorry," he said. "I'm doing it again. I'm thinking only of myself and putting you in a difficult position." He stood. "All right, I'll try to cool it, as they say. For a while," he added. "But Laura Logan, you mark my words. You will be my wife someday. You will be the woman I live with

492

forever and ever, and no powerful grandmother, no over-protective brother, no one can stop it from happening."

I nodded, pressing my lips together and swallowing the lump in my throat. Robert smiled one last time before he turned and walked back into the school, his shoulders slumped, his heart as dark and as broken as my own.

Each succeeding day without Robert, without his smiles, without hearing his voice, receiving his phone calls, was a day of gloom. The sun might as well have kept its face behind a wall of storm clouds, as far as I was concerned. I did my chores, I studied and helped May with her work, but I know when I moved about, I resembled a zombie, a robot without a heart or soul. When I had time to be alone, I walked off and sat on the beach and watched the waves comb the sand, gently rolling over each other, beckoning. Sometimes I went down to the edge of the tide and walked barefoot through the foam. The terns followed me, circling, calling, gazing with curiosity at my sad, forlorn figure alone on a vast sea of sand.

Often I caught Cary watching me from afar, afraid to speak or to approach, distant, a sad figure himself, looking just as lost. He was struggling within himself to find a way to make me happy, to apologize, to win my forgiveness. I kept telling myself that I had to forgive him, that Grandma Olivia had forced him to talk, but that small voice inside me wondered if Cary hadn't told Grandma Olivia so that he could have me all to himself.

Mommy continued to ask questions about my health and even Daddy began to scrutinize me more closely. I blamed it on my studying.

The following weekend we all went to Grandpa Samuel's birthday celebration. It was an elegant party, a clam bake with two bars set up, one at each end of the grounds. There was a large blue and white tent under which tables were set up with linen tablecloths. Grandma Olivia despised the use of plastic plates and forks, so everything was served on real china and with real silverware. A small army of waiters and waitresses, servers and kitchen helpers was hired to help that evening. There were over a hundred and fifty guests, all wealthy businessmen, politicians, their families, and, of course, the best families from the Cape. People attended from as far away as Boston and Hartford, Connecticut.

A string quartet was set up in the gazebo and played all afternoon, culminating with everyone singing "Happy Birthday" to Grandpa Samuel. It was really one of Grandma Olivia's best parties, but I was still in no mood to be happy about anything. Late in the day, she pulled me aside.

"Apparently," she said, "you are following my advice. That's good, Laura. That's good for everyone," she added.

Before I could utter a reply, she called to one of her guests and went off arm in arm, leaving me feeling a little more empty inside. When I turned, I saw Cary was staring at me. I walked away and started toward the dock.

"What did she say?" I heard Cary ask and turned to see he had followed me.

"She said she was happy to see I had followed her advice and that it was good for everyone," I told him.

He shook his head.

"I'm sorry, Laura," he said for the hundredth time.

I folded my arms and looked at the sea.

"She has no right to run our lives," he continued. "I can see you're going to get sick from unhappiness," he added in an angry tone.

"I won't get sick," I said defiantly.

"You're as pale as driftwood," he remarked. "Look," he said, stepping closer, "there's nothing wrong with my being friends with Robert, is there?"

"What do you mean?" I asked.

"Nothing, except I was teaching him how to sail, wasn't I? So, I'll just invite him over to go sailing tomorrow and you and he can—"

"Can what, Cary?" I asked, my heart starting to beat with the possibilities.

"Go sailing yourselves."

"You would do this for me?"

494

"Yeah, I would," he said, looking away.

"You'll get into trouble with Grandma Olivia, Cary."

"I'm not afraid of that," he said boldly.

Just then the wind picked up and whipped the strands of my hair around my face. Someone shouted and we looked back to see a flower display topple.

"Uh-oh, some poor slob is about to be bawled out for not setting that up properly," Cary said and laughed. "Grandma Olivia might take away his breathing rights."

I couldn't help but laugh, too.

"That's more like it, Laura. Remember when I told you that your smile lights up the day?" he said shyly, breaking off in embarrassment. "Don't worry, I'll call him later. And this time, she won't get anything out of me either," he promised.

And suddenly, the sun did peek out from behind a cloud and the warm rays washed over me, making me feel reborn.

That night I dared a phone call to Robert. Cary had already called and invited him.

"I was going to call you," he said. "Cary's invitation was such a surprise, I didn't know what to make of it. What's going on? Why the change of heart? One day he comes at me like he's my biggest enemy and the next . . ."

"He's so sorry for what he's done, he's trying to make it up to me, to both of us," I said.

"Actually, I don't care what his reasons are. I'm going to spend the day with you. That's all that matters, Laura. You don't know how sick at heart I've been these past days," he moaned.

"I do know, because I've been the same way," I said.

"My mother's been asking questions constantly about you. She thinks I did something to drive you away and she wants me to know that if I did, I'm really stupid. She'll let up on me now that she knows I'm going to see you tomorrow," he said with a laugh.

It was as if the blood had returned to my body, my heart began beating once again. I caught myself smiling crazily, and I knew I was walking around with a glow around my face.

I was the first up in the morning, and started to make breakfast for everyone. Mommy was so happy at my display of energy, she talked a blue streak as she helped me set the table. Even Daddy looked more relaxed, amused. The only dark thing he said was we should keep an eye on the weather. He said the sky had the look it usually took on right before we get hit with a nor'easter.

To me the sky looked beautiful. Even the clouds gathering on the horizon were welcome to my eyes. The wind was up, but Cary thought it was perfect for sailing. He spent part of the morning with Daddy at the cranberry bog while I prepared our lunches for the picnic on the beach.

"I'm glad you're taking some time off, Laura," Mommy remarked. "You've been working too hard. There's no sense in getting sick before you take your finals and end the school year now, is there?"

"No, Mommy."

"We're very, very proud of you, Laura. Everyone in the family is proud of you. Why, just the other day at the party, your grandmother came over to me especially to remark about how delighted she was to hear about your accomplishments at school. She wanted me to be sure to tell you that, and that she had a special surprise for you."

"And what's that, I wonder?" I asked, keeping my eyes on the sandwiches I was wrapping.

"Well, we're not supposed to tell you yet, but Daddy said she told him she's established a fund in the bank to take care of your entire college needs. That's a lot of money, Laura. It's nice to know your grandparents care that much about you," Mommy added.

"Money's not the only way to show you care for someone, Mommy," I said.

"Oh, no, but it sure helps," she said with a light laugh. "Just think how that takes the worry out of your father's brow," she continued. "You know how he's been about the ups and downs in the business. He's not one to harp on bad times, but we've had our share," Mommy assured me. "Your daddy's very happy that Grandma Olivia thinks so much of you, too."

I swallowed away the tightness in my throat.

"I'm glad, Mommy," I said and hurried to pack the food in the basket.

I had wanted this to be an extra-special day. I had put my hair up, then down, then up again and tried on nearly everything in my closet trying to find the perfect outfit. I finally chose a pair of heather-gray shorts and a white tank top, a pair of sneakers with no socks, and just for a happy touch, I wrapped my navy silk scarf around my ponytail. I felt as light as air and floated up and down the stairs all morning until it was time to go.

Robert arrived just after Cary had returned from the bog. We all met outside. May had the smaller basket cradled in her arms.

"Well, thanks a lot for inviting me," Robert told Cary. "It looks like a perfect day for this, huh?"

Cary studied the weather a moment and nodded cautiously.

"As long as we come in before late afternoon. The wind's picking up a bit and it will be a good ride," he said. "But you're an expert now," he added with a note of challenge.

"Well, I haven't forgotten what I learned, if that's what you mean."

"Laura knows enough to be a judge of that," Cary said.

"Well, let's get going then," I said, impatient and worried that too many words would stir up old wounds.

"I'll carry that," Robert said, taking the bigger basket from me.

We walked down the beach, Robert and I glancing longingly at each other as Cary led the way.

"You want to test me?" Robert asked Cary when we reached the sailboat. "Go ahead, ask me anything," he challenged.

"The only real test is the test the ocean gives," Cary replied coolly.

Robert laughed nervously, his eyes flitting from me to the boat and then to Cary.

"Laura, why don't you take May to Logan's Cove while Captain Robert and I bring the sailboat over," Cary suggested.

"Okay. Be careful," I said to Robert and took May's hand. We had the blanket out and were sitting and organizing our picnic lunch when the sailboat appeared around the bend. Robert was doing all the work. The boat bounced hard on the waves and then straightened and turned toward us, the sea spray shooting up around it as it headed toward the shore.

"It's wonderful!" Robert cried. "Invigorating. Much more exciting than it was the last time, Laura."

"I can see that. How did he do, Cary?"

Cary busied himself with beaching the sailboat and then turned.

"Fine," he said. He gazed at the sky. The small dots of clouds had grown fatter and toward the south we could see longer strands of white. "But I think you two should go out right after lunch and if it gets too rough, head right back," he said.

"Boy, just that little bit worked up my appetite," Robert followed.

I was too excited to be hungry. Cary didn't eat very much either. He sat pensive, staring out at the ocean. Robert talked about the Sea Marina, how successful their first few weekends had been, and how they were close to being fully booked for July. Cary made little comment. I never saw him so deep in thought. He looked nervous, too, stealing glances at me and then quickly gazing back at the sea or down the beach. Finally, he stood.

"I think May and I will go looking for seashells while you two do some sailing," he said. "Keep your eyes on the sky, Laura," he added and signed to May, who rose quickly to take his hand. The two of them started down the beach.

"Well," Robert said with a sigh, "we're finally alone for the first time in a century. At least that's the way it feels to me," he said. "Ready for your maiden voyage with Captain Blood?" he asked, shooting to his feet and reaching for my hand. "M'lady?"

I laughed and let him pull me up. Then I took off my sneakers and threw them into the sailboat. I gazed down the beach at Cary and May, who were already some distance away. Cary looked like he was watching us and then turned back to help May hunt for interesting shells. Robert helped me into the sailboat and pushed off, jumping in quickly and taking hold of the rope.

"Let's sail all the way to China," he yelled into the wind.

The sea spray felt good on my arms and my face. More gracefully than I had anticipated, Robert took us out and filled the sail with wind.

"Not bad, huh? I guess the sea is in my blood after all, thanks to you," he said.

I sat with my back against him and screamed at the bouncing we endured until we got farther and farther out and the water calmed.

"The last time I went out with Cary, I saw another cove," Robert said. "It looked very private, too," he added. "Why don't we find it and call it Laura's Cove," he whispered.

He kissed my hair and my forehead and I turned and reached up to meet his lips with mine. The sailboat twisted and we both screamed.

"I better keep my mind on the business at hand," Robert said.

"Just let out a little line, Robert, and she won't spill us into the sea."

"Aye, aye, Captain."

We sailed on, the wind whipping the sail, the bow cutting into the waves. We were going at a good clip and as we made the turn around another bend of shore the wind died a bit and the ride became slower, smoother. Robert grew more confident.

"This isn't as hard as everyone makes it out to be," he declared.

"Don't get too arrogant, Robert," I warned. "It takes a

while to become as good a sailor as Cary. Cary says the sea doesn't easily forgive mistakes, either."

"I know, but I do have a flair for it, don't I, Laura?" he asked, fishing for a compliment. "Well? Don't I?"

"Yes, yes." I laughed. We kissed again and sailed on. Finally, I felt relaxed and happy.

Perhaps all of our lives will be like this now, I thought. We'll round another bend and find sunshine and happiness. With the wind in my hair and Robert's arms around me as our sailboat sliced through the water, it was easy to believe in fairy tales. Cary and I had grown up with faith in the magic of the ocean. Who could blame me for wanting Robert to share it as well?

Who would ever blame me as much as I would soon blame myself?

9
Swept Away

*F*or a long time, I had no memory of that fateful afternoon. My mind locked it in a dark closet and threw away the key. As hard as it is to believe, I even forgot Robert's name.

I was lying comfortably in his arms as he turned the sailboat toward the shore. The cove was small, with just a patch of beach, really, but he had discovered it and claimed it as our special place. When we drew closer, I sat up. The wind had grown a bit stronger and the clouds flowing in from the south now looked a bit darker and thicker. I should have said, "Let's go back, Robert," right then and there, but I didn't. I, too, was hungry for love and I, too, was titillated by the prospect of our own private little world.

Robert leaped out of the sailboat and guided it onto the shore. Then he reached for my hand and I stepped out. He found a piece of driftwood nearby and planted it in the sand. Then he tied his handkerchief around it so it flapped in the wind like a flag.

"I claim this beach for Laura Logan and hereby name it Laura's Cove," he said, standing proud and strong like some historic explorer.

I laughed and clapped my hands. He took a sweeping bow

and I laughed again. Everything made me laugh that after-noon. All of it, the air, the freedom, the renewal of love and promises had made me giddy. I was drunk on dreams.

"We have to christen our piece of paradise," he declared and stepped up to me.

He embraced me and kissed me full on the lips. The wind whipped my hair and the sea spray felt cool and refreshing on my arms and neck.

"I missed you," he said. "Oh, how I missed you. I kissed you a thousand times in my mind, Laura. I held you every chance I could get."

He kissed me softly on the tip of my nose and then my chin before we joined our lips again. After that, he reached into the sailboat and pulled out the blanket. He spread it out and we embraced and lowered ourselves onto the sand. I lay back against his chest.

"We can't stay long, Robert," I remember saying. "Cary and May—"

"I know," Robert replied and stroked my hair, running his palm over my cheek as if he were blind and committing every feature of my face to his memory forever and ever. I wanted him. Oh, how much I wanted him.

He sensed my desire and began to kiss me on my neck. His hands moved to my waist and he gently pushed up my tank top. In moments we were both nearly undressed, embracing, clinging to each other as if the whole world had become water and we were floating on the surface.

"I will not let anyone take you from me," he whispered, "even for a short time."

His words filled my heart and drove away all the doubts about our love, about myself, about what and who we were. *Yes,* I heard myself begin somewhere deep down inside my very soul, *yes, yes, yes.*

Our kisses were long and hard and hungry, the kisses of two loving people who had been locked away from that love for too long. I don't even remember how we became totally naked, but we were, and without hesitation, almost without skipping a beat, we were making love, throwing all caution to the wind that whirled around us.

It began with a maddening rush and then slowed to an undulating rhythm that took me up and down, to heights and ecstasy and moments of quiet when I could catch my breath; but soon the hunger for another taste of ecstasy overpowered me and I tightened my embrace around him, holding him, refusing to permit it to end.

I remember hearing his small laugh of delight and seeing his face, his eyes full of so much love and pleasure. I told myself what we were doing couldn't be anything but good and beautiful. He smothered me in kisses; he chanted my name; he quieted my small cries and held me as tightly as I held him. We rode on each other's passion until we were exhausted.

He slid off me and lay beside me, his face against the blanket, but his eyes on me. I turned and looked into his eyes, into his beautiful smile of contentment.

"I love you, Laura," he said.

"I love you, too, Robert."

He put his arm over my shoulder, lay his palm against my naked back and closed the distance between us. We lay there, quietly, our eyelids fluttering, suddenly feeling heavy. We both decided to just rest for a little while, and then, like some magic spell, sleep washed over us and we both drifted.

I was the first to wake up. The wind had picked up considerably, spitting sand and water over us. I turned quickly and when I looked up, I saw only low, dark clouds whirling toward us. Seconds later, I felt the raindrops, but the worst and most terrifying sight was the sailboat drifting away. In our haste, we hadn't beached it securely. It was a good ten to fifteen feet from the shore already.

"Robert!" I screamed.

He opened his eyes and sat up quickly.

"Oh, no. The boat."

"We have to get it before it gets washed out too far!" I cried. He leaped to his feet and dove into the water, swimming as hard as he could to the boat. The waves were already at least two feet high. He struggled and reached the side of the sailboat, heaving himself up and over. The sail was flapping hard, the small mast swinging from right to left. Robert struggled to get a good hold on the line, but when he tightened the sail against the wind, the small boat began to turn over and he didn't let go fast enough. It looked like it jumped out of the water, spilling him into the ocean as it capsized.

"ROBERT!"

I was a good swimmer, but not strong enough to battle those waves for very long. It took a monster effort, nearly exhausting me, but I managed to reach the boat quickly. I grabbed hold of the boat and called to Robert again. He surfaced on the other side of the boat, looking dazed. It wasn't until he swam toward me that I saw why. When he had tumbled into the sea with the boat following after him, some part of it had struck him on the head. A thin, but steady stream of blood trickled from under his hair, down his temple, and over his cheek.

"Robert, you're hurt!" I cried. He nodded, but he still looked confused.

We bobbed with the boat as the waves grew higher, stronger. The wind was intensifying, too, and the rain had become stingingly sharp and cold. I looked back at the shore. All our clothing, the blanket, everything was being washed by the tide and slowly sucked into the sea. The shock of it all happening so quickly panicked me. I struggled with the boat in a vain and fruitless attempt to right it. Robert was just bobbing, holding on to the side, either unsure of how to right the boat or so confused he hadn't even thought to try.

"Climb over the hull, Robert, and start to pull the boat upright. Climb!" I cried. "Robert, do it now. We're being swept out farther and farther with every roll of the waves."

Finally, he seemed to understand. He pulled himself up and reached for the side of the boat, using his weight to turn it upright. He didn't weigh enough and wasn't strong enough, so I joined him as quickly as I could and both of us pulled desperately as the wind whipped against our backs like a cold, wet rope and the rain became a torrential downpour, blinding us.

More desperate, frantic, realizing the danger fully, we gave it all our might and the boat began to turn over. Robert was too excited by our small success and jerked wildly at the hull.

"Just let it turn, Robert," I screamed, but he continued leaping up and down, pulling and grunting, defeating his own efforts.

Finally, the mast came up, the wet sail came out of the water. We were doing fine. We would get it upright, I thought. We'll be all right. Then, another heavy, fierce gust of wind lashed at us and I lost my grip, sliding back into the sea. The boat began to turn over again and Robert lunged with all his strength to prevent it from happening. I saw him fly over with the boat and disappear on the other side. We were at least another twenty feet from shore by now. The rain was falling so hard, I could barely make out the tiny patch of beach.

"Robert!" I called when I didn't see him. "Robert, where are you? Robert!"

He didn't respond and he didn't swim back to me. I kept my grip on the hull and fought my way around the boat. At first I didn't see him, and then I saw his head, just under the surface, his hand floating toward the mast. I moved as quickly as I could, taking hold of the mast and then his hand, pulling with all my might until his head appeared. His eyes were glassy, dazed. There was a wider, faster stream of blood now on his temple and cheek. I thought he mouthed my name and smiled, but it was hard to see clearly with the salt water burning my eyes and the rain pounding my face.

I held on to him. He seemed incapable of moving on his own. His right arm never came out of the water and his head slowly lowered to his shoulder as his eyes closed.

"ROBERT!"

I tried pulling him closer, but I was losing my grip on the

mast. The water had made it slippery and difficult to hold. If I didn't let go of Robert's hand soon, I might lose my grip completely and get washed out to sea with him, I thought. My shoulders ached, my neck muscles screamed, and my hand felt as if it were being torn off my wrist.

"Oh, Robert, wake up. Help us. Robert!"

He bobbed with the waves that took us up and down. When I turned and looked back, I saw we were out of sight of the shore. The ocean was sweeping us away.

I remember thinking about Cary, expecting him to appear any moment in another boat, flying over the waves, coming to our rescue. He would be angry, but very, very worried. He would scoop us both out of the sea and wrap us in warm blankets and get us home.

"Please hurry, Cary," I moaned. "Please."

I held on to the mast and on to Robert's hand, but the weight of his body was pulling on my wrist and arm. His fingers lost their grip on mine and he started to slip away.

"Robert. Oh, Robert, wake up!" I pleaded. I thought about shaking his arm, but I was afraid the motion might cause me to lose the tenuous grip I still held on the mast.

The ocean water hit my face while I was calling to him and I swallowed too much. I gagged, coughed, choked, and felt myself losing my grip on Robert and I struggled to hold on to him. I couldn't let him go.

New England weather, I thought, famous for its quick changes. I should have known. I should have known better. It's my fault, my fault.

The ocean was relentless. It would not be denied its sacrifice. I made a desperate last effort to hold on to Robert and the mast and then I felt his fingers slide down over my palm. His body lifted in the waves as if he were rising up to say his last good-bye, and then he went under.

I yelled his name as hard and as long as I could. I started to let go of the mast to search for him, but my own desperation to survive wouldn't permit my fingers to loosen their grip. I know I screamed and shouted his name until my voice gave out, my throat ached, and then I closed my eyes and turned to put my other hand around the mast. I pulled myself closer to it and laid my cheek against the cold metal. The boat continued to bob, to rise and fall in the wind and the rain.

A deep and thick darkness fell over me. Even when I opened my eyes, I saw nothing. The last thing I thought was silly in light of what was happening and what had happened. I moaned and cried, "I lost that beautiful silk scarf Mommy gave me. I'm sorry, Mommy," I cried.

My body shook as much with my own sobs as it did from the cold water and the freezing rain. I lay there with my head resting against the mast and felt the hull on my left side. It was reassuring. I remember thinking, I'll just sleep a moment and then, the storm will stop.

The magic will return.

The sun will warm us.

We'll laugh again and make promises to each other again. Won't we?

We? I couldn't remember his name. I could see his face, see his smile, even hear his voice, but who was he?

And then, the worst terror of all struck me.

Who am I?

I have put together what happened next, working over time on the events, the vague memories, the words I had heard as if it were all part of some grand thousand-piece puzzle. Some of it was told to me later on, but I always had to measure what I remembered against what I was told.

The storm continued to build that afternoon, preventing any real search for us. The wind and the waves carried the overturned sailboat farther out to sea. A fisherman by the name of Karl Hansen was fighting his way back to shore. He had worked for Grandpa Samuel and Grandma Olivia for years, but was pretty much retired now, only venturing out now and again with his own net. He saw the overturned sailboat and drew close enough to spot me clinging desperately to the mast. He began to shout. I remember first thinking the wind had found a voice. I thought it was part of the magic and just listened with a small smile on my face, my eyes closed as he called and called. Then I felt something hit my shoulder and I opened my eyes to see a man tossing a net my way as his boat bobbed in the rough seas.

"Take hold. Wrap it around you," he ordered, yelling through his cupped hands. "Take hold!"

He threw the net again and again. Each time, I looked at it but didn't move. I couldn't let go of the mast. My hands had locked around it, and no matter how hard I tried, I couldn't will my hands to reach out for the net he threw.

Finally, Mr. Hansen brought his boat closer until he was able to leap into the sea. He had a thick rope tied to his waist and when he reached me, he quickly untied himself and wound the rope around me.

"You've got to let go," he said. "Don't worry. I'll get you on my boat."

He was a short, stout man with a full gray beard and gray hair. I should have recognized him, but I didn't. He recognized me.

"Laura Logan?" he cried. "Mrs. Logan's granddaughter. Sweet Mary and Joseph. Let go of the mast when I tell you, girl."

I remember I screamed and screamed and tried to resist his effort to pull me away from the mast, then finally he got me free and swam back to his boat, towing me along behind him.

The wind was furious; the rain unrelenting. The struggle was getting to be too much for him. His own boat was in danger. I'm sure he questioned whether he could continue the effort, but continue he did. Finally, we reached the boat and Mr. Hansen was able to lift me up quickly and swing me on board.

I was naked and freezing, my teeth chattering so hard, I thought they would shatter against each other. The waves were tossing Mr. Hansen's boat mercilessly. He had to get back to controlling the roll. He found a blanket and threw it over me first and then he attended to the boat. We went farther out until he found enough calm water to give him a

508

chance to tend to me. He returned and helped me into the cabin, where he set me on a small cushioned bench.

"What happened to you, girl? How did you get caught out here? Was your brother with you?"

Brother? I thought. I have a brother?

I didn't respond. I lay there, going in and out of consciousness. I don't remember how long it took for us to reach shore, but he made a tactical navigation decision and brought us to Grandpa Samuel and Grandma Olivia's dock. The wind had let up some and the rain had slowed.

The next thing I knew, Mr. Hansen was running for help. He returned to get me up and out of the boat, and then literally carried me into the house. A small, angry woman greeted us and directed him to bring me to a guest room downstairs, where he set me gently on the bed. The elderly lady stood behind him, waiting. I didn't know who she was then. All I saw was her face of rage as she glared down at me. It all seemed to be happening to someone else. It was as if I were watching a movie.

"Where did you find her?" I heard her ask.

"She was clinging to an overturned sailboat about a mile and a half off Dead Man's Cove," he replied. "Those things are too small for weather only half as bad as this."

"You found her by herself, then?"

"Yes, ma'am. I hope her brother wasn't out there with her," he said. "No one could survive that," he added.

"It wasn't her brother," she said. "She was naked when you found her?"

"Yes, ma'am."

"Disgusting," she muttered.

I was still so cold I couldn't move my arms or legs. I lay curled up in a ball, breathing heavily, my body shuddering. She drew closer.

"What were you doing out there, girl?" she demanded, glaring at me with cold eyes of steel.

I couldn't talk; I couldn't even shake my head.

"Something sinful, just as I predicted," she concluded, nodding.

"I'll get a search party up after this dies down," Karl Hansen said.

The old woman spun around.

"You'll do nothing of the kind, Karl," she snapped at him. "You won't mention a word of this."

"But . . . surely, there was someone else on that boat, Mrs. Logan."

"I know there was someone else. I'm sure he was naked, too," she added disdainfully. "It's not something I want anyone else to know," she said, nodding at me. "The both of them were caught in some sinful act."

"What sinful act?" I wanted to say, but I couldn't.

She turned back to him. I saw the look of surprise and confusion on his face, but I didn't understand why. I didn't know where I was and I had forgotten how I had gotten there. All I knew was I was very cold and no one seemed to be paying much attention to that.

"You never found her, Karl," she told him. "I need your word on that."

"Pardon, Mrs. Logan?"

"You never found her," she said firmly. "Leave it all to me now."

"But Mrs. Logan—"

"You will be handsomely rewarded for your loyalty to me, Karl. I know your wife is sick and you have been having a hard time making ends meet. You won't have to worry at all about her doctor bills anymore or anything else for that matter. As long as I can rely on your word," she added.

He gazed at me and then at the small, angry woman he called Mrs. Logan.

"Well. I suppose there's nothing more to do about this, really. You'll see to her and whoever else was out there. Well, God rest his poor soul," Karl Hansen said. "I'm sure he didn't survive. There's nothing we could do anyway except locate the body and there's no rush to do that."

"Exactly. Now remember, Karl, you never found her. You

510

just made your own way toward shore and got washed up here. It was hard enough for you."

"Yes, it was, ma'am. That it was. There's no lying about that."

"Precisely," she said. "Raymond will see that you get home and I will have something for you in the morning. I'll also see that Ruth gets the personal nursing care she requires."

"Well, thank you, Mrs. Logan. That's very kind."

"As long as we understand each other, Karl," she added, her small eyes very cold and threatening. He nodded quickly.

"Oh, absolutely, Mrs. Logan. Absolutely."

"Good," she said and turned back to me. "Good."

She escorted him out and then returned a few minutes later. She simply stood there, gazing down at me.

"How could you do this?" she demanded. "How could you deliberately lie and deceive me and do this?"

My teeth chattered and I moaned.

"Don't you have even the slightest concern for this family? Do you know what kind of a disgrace this could bring? Why, they might even put this in the newspapers. People from outside of Provincetown, friends, acquaintances from everywhere could learn of it. Well? Don't you have anything to say?"

"I'm cold," I finally said.

"Cold? That's the least of your problems. Fortunately, Mr. Hansen won't tell anyone a thing, but . . . don't you hear a word of what I'm saying to you?" she snapped. "You're staring at me as if I were speaking Greek. And wipe that silly smile off your face," she ordered. "I won't have it."

"I'm sorry," I said. "I'm not smiling. I'm just cold. My hair is soaked," I said. I started to rub the blanket up and down my arms and legs.

"I'm sure you are sorry now. Although it does us no good to have you say it," she said and wagged her head. "How did this happen?"

"What?" I asked.

"What? Are you an idiot? This!" she exclaimed, thrusting her hands toward me. "You've lived here long enough to know when to come in from a storm and when to be cautious. What were you doing out there? Were you so wrapped up in your lust that you ignored the weather? Well?"

"Out where?"

"In the ocean, you fool. What is wrong with you?"

Then I remember giggling. I couldn't help it. She was a funny little old lady to me. Her hair was held tightly back with pearl combs and she wore a flower print dress with a rope of pearls around her neck. When she got excited, the blood under her skin rose up her neck like mercury in a thermometer, and she seemed to bounce on her feet after every sentence.

"You think this is funny?" she asked, astounded.

I shook my head.

"What happened to him?" she asked.

"To who?" I responded.

She stopped being angry for a moment and stared intently at me.

"Don't you remember anything?"

I shook my head.

"You know where you are, don't you?"

Again, I shook my head.

She stared and then tilted her head a little as she thought.

"What's my name?" she suddenly asked.

"That man called you Mrs. Logan," I said. "Isn't that your name?"

"My God." She covered her mouth and stared at me. Then she lowered her hand slowly. "What's your name?"

I thought, but no name came to mind.

"I don't know."

She stepped back as if I had some contagious disease and stared at me again.

"Madness on top of disgrace. It's happening again. First, to my sister, and now to you, and I'm supposed to bear the burden, face the community, hold on to my prestige and position, and keep this family name as respected as it once was, as it should be?"

She paused and then raised her small fist toward the ceiling as if she were threatening God.

"This will not happen," she declared. Then she turned back to me. "Don't you move from that bed," she ordered.

I didn't think I could move. I had just barely managed to straighten my legs.

Minutes later, she returned with an armful of big, fluffy towels and then went into the bathroom. I heard her run water in the tub. She was moving quickly, and she looked like a goblin to me and I couldn't help smiling again. It made her angry when she emerged from the bathroom and saw the smile on my face.

"Get up," she ordered. "I'll handle this myself. Go on, get up!"

I swung my legs out slowly, the muscles in my thighs screaming, and when I pushed to sit up, I felt my shoulder stinging. The blanket fell away. I looked at my arm. Blood vessels had burst all along it, so that there were black and blue marks from the inside of my wrist, up over my elbow, right to my shoulder. Even she gasped.

"Everything hurts," I complained.

"And rightly so," she said, regaining her regal, stern demeanor. "Stand up and walk into the bathroom. Go on. I don't have the strength to lift you," she added, her hands on her hips. I realized she had put on a light blue housecoat over her dress. I tried to stand, but my legs wobbled.

"I can't," I moaned.

"You can and you will. Stand!" she ordered. She reached forward and seized the top of my hair, tugging me hard.

I screamed. The breath nearly left me, but I rose. I reached out to brace myself on her shoulder. She stepped back and at least gave me her hand.

"I can't carry you. Walk," she commanded.

Each step was excruciating. My back, my legs, even my feet ached. I made my way toward the sound of the running water, reaching out to steady myself against the doorjamb, and then I entered the bathroom. She moved ahead and shut off the water.

"Get into the tub and soak yourself. Go on. Do what I say and do it now," she ordered again.

I don't know how I did it, but I reached the tub and lifted my leg to step into the water. It was so hot, however, I howled and pulled my foot out quickly, losing my balance. I fell back and sat hard on the floor.

"You're disgusting," she cried.

"It's too hot," I moaned.

"It has to be hot, you fool. Now get up and get into the water. Go on. Do it." She hovered over me. "If you don't, you'll surely get pneumonia."

I got to my knees and crawled to the tub. Then I took a deep breath and rose to put my foot in again. It took the breath out of me and I grew so dizzy, I thought I would faint. She put her hands on my hips and held me steady, permitting me to rest against her for a moment.

"All right, now lower yourself into the water. Just do it quickly," she commanded.

I took a deep breath and did so, crying out as I settled into the steamy liquid. My body began to itch and then tingle. I kept taking deep breaths. Finally, I grew more comfortable and then it did suddenly make me feel better. I closed my eyes.

Suddenly I felt something being poured over my head.

"You have to wash out the salt," she said. She scooped water onto my hair, scrubbed it, and then forced me to lower myself until I was under the water so I could rinse my hair. She kept me down so long, I thought she wanted to drown me in the tub. I came up gasping.

"Just lie there and soak," she said and left the bathroom.

I'm sure I fell asleep for a few minutes. Then I sensed her nearby again. She had returned and stood above me, looking down at me with an expression of utter disgust.

"Well?" she demanded. "Do you know who you are now?"

I thought and thought. Then I shook my head.

"I don't know," I wailed. "Who am I?"

"You're a fool and I don't suffer fools in this family anymore," she declared. She sighed deeply. "Who am I?"

I tried to remember. I had even forgotten what that man had called her before.

"I don't remember what that man called you," I moaned.

"What, has your brain turned to cranberry jelly?" she asked.

"Cranberries? I remember cranberries."

"Well, I'm glad about that. What else do you remember? Do you have any family, friends?"

I thought and just found a blank, dark place in my mind with no faces, no words, no voices. I shook my head.

"I don't know," I said.

She stared.

"Maybe you don't. Maybe . . . this is a blessing in disguise. Yes," she said, her face lighting up and her eyes widening, "it is."

She left again and for what seemed like quite a long time. When she returned this time, she had a white terry cloth robe in her hands.

"Get out. Dry yourself off and put this on," she said. "Someone will be here for you soon."

"Someone?"

Good, I thought. There was someone. Surely, I would remember everything soon. I crawled up and out of the tub with great effort. My body was beyond exhaustion, the muscles working on their own memory and not my commands. It seemed to take me forever to dry myself. She grew impatient.

"For God's sake," she said and seized one of the towels. She began to rub me vigorously. I felt as if she would peel away my skin. My every movement was still filled with pain and I ached everywhere.

"There," she said. "Now put on the robe and return to that bed," she instructed.

I did what she said. The moment my head hit the pillow

515

and I closed my eyes, I fell asleep. I woke when I heard voices near and above me. My eyelids refused to stay open at first and then, with stubborn effort, I did get them to do so.

Coming into focus was a tall woman in a starched white uniform. She stood next to the small elderly lady. The woman in white scrutinized me a moment and then made a small, tight smile.

"Hello. My name is Clara. What's your name?" she asked and took my wrist into her fingers to feel for my pulse.

"My name's . . . My name's . . . I can't remember!" I cried.

The woman looked at the elderly woman and then back at me.

"Do you know whose home you are in?"

I shook my head.

"How old are you?"

"I don't know."

"How did you get here?" she followed quickly.

"I don't remember. Where am I?"

"Are you home?"

"Am I?"

"See?" the elderly lady said.

"Yes. It's classic, I think," the woman in white said. "Her pulse is strong."

"It's not her pulse I'm worried about," the small elderly lady said.

Clara nodded.

"You understand what I want and how I want it done," the elderly lady said.

"Precisely. You have made the appropriate phone calls, I imagine?"

"Of course," the elderly lady said. "It's all arranged. I'm relying on your discretion. You will be rewarded," she added.

Clara smiled. "You won't be disappointed."

"Good."

Clara turned back to me.

"I'm going to help you now," she said, "but I need you to help yourself, too. Okay?"

"Yes," I said.

"Good. I want you to get up and walk with me. We're going to get into a car outside. I'm going to take you to a nice place, okay?"

"Okay," I said. I raised myself up on my elbows and Clara reached under my left arm and helped me get out of bed. When I stood up, I felt terribly stiff and said so.

"That's all right," Clara said. "You won't be stiff too much longer. I'll help you," she said. She smiled. She had a nice, friendly smile, a much nicer smile than the elderly lady could ever have, I thought. I was glad to be leaving.

The elderly lady followed behind us as we continued out of the room, down a long corridor to the front doors of the house. I remember thinking it was a big house and there were things about it that looked familiar, but I didn't remember coming here. The elderly lady walked ahead of us and opened the door.

It was still lightly drizzling out, and the cold air hit me like a slap in the face. I shuddered and Clara wrapped her arm around my shoulders.

"There, there, now," she said. "We'll be warm soon."

She guided me out and to the dark car that was waiting. I didn't see the driver. Clara opened the door for me and I was guided carefully into the rear of the car. Then Clara stepped back.

"You want to say anything to her?" Clara asked the elderly lady.

"No. Tell them I'll be there tomorrow to make the arrangements and give them a check," she said.

"Very good, Mrs. Logan."

I snapped my head around. Mrs. Logan? I remembered that name, but who was she? She glared at me, her eyes beady, icy, her mouth pinched tight. I was glad when the door was closed and she was out of sight.

Clara got in from the other side and sat beside me.

"All right now?" she asked. I nodded. "You'll be fine," she said. "Soon, you'll be fine."

I smiled back at her. She nodded at the driver and the car began to move away from the big house and into the rain, into the darkness that lay ahead.

I stared for a moment and then spun around and looked back, but the lights of the house were already gone and the darkness had closed in behind me. It was as if I had walked through a door and the door had been shut tight. I wanted to go back; I wanted to open the door again, but I couldn't find my way.

"Where are we going?" I asked Clara.

"Someplace else," she replied. "Is that okay?"

I thought for a moment.

"Yes," I said. "It's okay."

I wasn't sure why, but vaguely I realized that yes, yes, it was better to be someplace else.

10

&

My Name Is . . .

I fell asleep again in the car and didn't wake until the car hit a bump and jarred me from my trancelike slumber. It was very dark outside because an overcast sky kept the moon and the stars hidden. When I gazed out the window, I saw only my own reflected face in the glass, the face of someone so lost and confused, her eyes were filled with question marks and her lips frozen in a vain struggle to find some word, some thought to voice.

I turned and looked at the woman in the nurse's uniform dozing beside me. Her eyelids fluttered as the automobile jerked and turned, but they didn't open. I gazed at the back of the driver's head and I wondered who these people were and where I was going. Should I know? Had I been told?

I struggled with the questions, but it was as if I had fallen into an echo chamber because all I could hear were the questions coming back at me. The answers were like schools of fish swimming in the opposite direction, far, far out of reach and uninterested in turning back. I could only watch them disappear, their scales glimmering for a moment and then gone, perhaps forever.

My body was sore, yet I couldn't remember why that was either. It hurt to straighten out my arms and legs and the back of my neck felt as if someone with powerful fingers had grabbed it and squeezed for hours. My eyes ached even when I kept them closed. I groaned and twisted to make myself more comfortable and the woman beside me woke with a quick jerk of her shoulders. She looked about, seemingly confused herself for a moment, and then turned to me and smiled.

"How are you, dear?" she asked. The driver turned a little but didn't look back at us.

"I'm sore," I said. "Why am I so sore?"

"Don't you remember anything about what happened to you, why you are in pain?"

I thought and thought, but it was like opening a book and finding it had only blank pages. I turned one after another and saw nothing written on any of them.

I shook my head, my lips trembling, my tears feeling more like smoldering ashes under my eyelids.

"Don't worry," she said. "It will all come back to you someday."

"It would be better for her if it don't," the driver muttered.

"We'll be needing none of your comments," she snapped at the back of his head. "You're here to drive and nothing else," she added sternly. He cringed as if her words were actually slaps and then he grunted and drove on silently.

Suddenly, there were lights ahead cloaked in what looked like banks of fog. As we drew closer, I strained to make out the shape of what appeared to be an entryway to an estate. It was a very tall iron gate with a wide, red brick column on each side. The light came from a large ball lamp atop each column. The driver slowed to a stop at the gate.

"One moment, dear," the nurse said, patting me softly on the knee. She got out of the car.

The fog twirled about us like smoke. I leaned forward to watch her poke numbers on a pad built into the side of the column on the right. The iron bars groaned loudly as the nurse returned to the car.

"Where are we?" I asked.

"Just relax, dear," she said in reply.

When the gate was completely opened, we drove through and began a climb up a winding hill, climbing up out of the sea of fog.

After the second turn, a five-story, gray brick and wood structure loomed above us, rising out of the darkness like the bow of a great ship. As we drew closer, it looked like a medieval castle because there was a large cupola at the center of the roof. On both ends there were dormers with windows that caught the reflection of the light below cast by tall pole lamps illuminating the parking lot. Most of the windows in the building were dark, but there were some dimly lit rooms on the first floor.

When we turned into a parking space, I saw there was a cement stairway up to the front entrance. It was really too dark to see much of the grounds, but I could make out some large weeping willow trees to the right. They looked like giants with their heads bowed.

"What is this place?" I asked. The sight of it had stirred no memory, recent or otherwise.

"It's sort of a hospital," the nurse replied with a small, but quick smile. The driver snorted. She glared at him a moment and then turned back to me. "You'll be well looked after here," she said.

"Is this where I live?" I asked.

"For now," she said.

She got out and came around the car to open my door and help me out. The driver remained behind, slouching down and lowering his chin to his chest. The nurse knocked on the window and he lowered it.

"I'm not going to be that long," she told him, but he didn't act as if he heard her or cared. She turned back to me. "Come along, dear."

She led me toward the stairs. There was an iron railing on the right. I held on to it as we climbed the steps because I felt a little dizzy. When we reached the front entrance, she pressed the buzzer and then looked at me and flashed another snapshot of a smile.

The doors looked heavy and thick. They were tall and wide and had no windows. I leaned back and looked up at the roof. I thought I saw a bat fly from one end to the other. It was so quiet and the air was very moist and enveloping. I could practically see the droplets of moisture dancing like small fairies around us. Off to the right, a streak of lightning sliced through the blackness, and then instantly disappeared. My stomach felt as if it were filled with broken glass. I felt so lost, so detached, floating in space, longing for the pull of gravity to bring me back to earth, back home, back to my name.

We waited and waited. Finally, the door opened and a tall, lean man with hair that looked like it couldn't decide whether to be red or blond stood before us. He, too, wore a white uniform. He looked very sleepy, his eyelids drooping. He seemed to be in his twenties and had freckles all over his cheeks and forehead, even on his lips.

"Weren't you expecting us, Billy?" the nurse asked him gruffly.

"What? Yeah. Sorry, Clara," he said. "I fell asleep waiting," he added dryly.

"Well now that we're here, we'd like to come in," she said sharply. He stepped back quickly and we entered.

Nothing looked familiar inside either. It was a large room with gray-and-blue cotton–covered sofas and chairs. There were about a half dozen light maple wood tables. Only three of the small lamps in the large room were turned on, but I could see that there wasn't much on the walls, just some paintings of ocean scenes with sailboats and fishing boats and a few paintings just of colors in rectangular shapes. The floor was a dark wood with oval area rugs here and there. At the far end, there was a large fireplace made of fieldstone.

The freckle-faced man she called Billy looked at me for the first time, his gaze sweeping up from my feet to my face as if he were measuring me for something to wear. His eyes widened with a little more interest and alertness when I gave him a friendly smile.

"This is her?" he asked, his voice filled with surprise.

"Of course it is. Who did you think it was, the new Miss America?" Clara quipped. He smirked.

"She looks pretty good. I just thought . . . Mrs. Miller said we should just show her to her room and get her to bed," he concluded once he saw the expression of impatience on Clara's face.

"So let's do it," she said. "I don't have all night to dillydally with you."

He turned and started toward the stairway, pausing at the bottom step.

"She's going to be on the second floor. She can take care of her own basic needs, right? She looks like she can," he added, gazing back at me.

"Why don't you leave the diagnosis and treatment to the doctors and just take us to her quarters. It's late and I'm tired, too, Billy," Clara replied with more fatigue in her voice than anger this time.

"I'm just asking," he whined and started up the stairs. The nurse guided me up. We turned at the landing and went down a long hallway. The lights above were very bright, creating a glare off the gray tile floor. Occasionally, the clean white walls were smudged. Here and there I saw what looked like squiggly lines made with dark crayons. Suddenly, I heard someone wailing. Moments later I saw a woman and a man in white hurry through the corridor.

"That's Sara Richards having another whopper of a nightmare, I bet," the young man said. "The last time that happened, she scratched her face so badly they had to cut her nails back to her knuckles. She's headed for upstairs, for sure," he predicted.

"Thanks for the cheerful news," Clara said.

What was upstairs? I wondered.

Billy paused at a doorway and reached for a set of keys hanging on his belt. He rifled through them, chose one, and opened the door. He switched on the light and we entered.

523

The first thing I noticed were the bars on the windows. How odd, I thought, for a hospital. Other than that, the room looked very pleasant. There were pretty blue and white curtains around the windows and a pretty blue flowered wallpaper on the walls. The bed was twin size and looked comfortable. It had a light blue comforter and two plush pillows with a thick, dark mahogany headboard. Beside it were two matching nightstands, on the right one of which was a lamp shaped like a ship lantern in brass. Across from the bed was a small dresser and to the right of that was a desk and a chair. There was a cushioned, blue-and-white patterned chair between the two windows. On the wall across from the bed was a painting of a garden with lawn furniture. The word Impressionist came to mind, shooting out of some dark closet, followed by the face of someone I should be able to remember. Was it a teacher? A friend? Family? It was gone too quickly for me to come to any conclusion.

"Isn't this nice?" Clara said.

"Yeah, you know the facilities here are quite good when you consider," Billy said before I could respond.

"Consider what?" Clara asked. He shrugged.

"That most of them don't know where the hell they are anyway," he said.

"You've got a great attitude, Billy. Mr. Sensitivity himself."

He laughed.

"I just call it like it is," he said.

"Spare me," Clara told him and he laughed again.

Clara crossed the room and opened the closet. There was what looked like a hospital worker's powder blue uniform dangling on a hanger and a pair of white terry cloth slippers beneath it. Other than that, the closet was empty.

"All right," she said to Billy, "I'll settle her in."

"What about the paperwork?" he asked.

"I'll be down in a little while to take care of it. Just have it ready for me."

"Aye, aye, Captain," he said with a mock salute. He gazed

at me and then nodded at her. "Good," he said as if I had done something difficult by merely walking in and up the stairs. He turned to me again before leaving. "What's her name?"

She hesitated a moment as if she had forgotten and then said, "Lauren."

Lauren? I thought. That didn't sound right.

"No, that's not my name," I said.

Her eyes widened and her eyebrows curled up.

"Oh? You remember your name?"

I thought and then shook my head.

"So how do you know it's not Lauren?" she asked.

I stared at her and then at him. He was wearing a wide, silly grin.

"I . . . just . . . know," I faltered.

"Until you remember your name, that's your name," she replied dryly. "Now, Lauren," she said, pronouncing it emphatically so I would not contradict her again, "come over here and get into this." She took the shirt and pants off their hangers and handed them to me. "You should get settled in and get some sleep. Tomorrow is a big day for you."

"Yeah, the first day is always the hardest," Billy commented.

Clara turned to Billy, shooting him an angry look. He flashed another smile at me and then left quickly.

I got into the shirt and pants while she turned down my bed. The sheets smelled freshly starched and the blanket felt brand new.

"Comfortable?" she asked me as she tucked me in and arranged my pillow under my head.

"Yes, but I still ache all over. Why can't I remember what happened to me? Was I in some sort of accident? A car accident? Did I fall?"

"Tomorrow, the doctor will see you and then we'll see what can be done to help make you more comfortable," she said instead of answering my question. "In the morning, another nurse, the head nurse, Mrs. Kleckner, will show you around and take you to breakfast. You're going to be fine," she added.

"How long will I be here?" I asked.

She stared at me a moment.

"I don't think you'll be here as long as your grandmother thinks," she said.

"My grandmother?" I thought about the small elderly lady back at the house. "That woman was my grandmother? Why was she so angry and mean to me?"

"Never mind now," she said quickly, as if she had already told me too much. "There's plenty of time to work on your return."

"Return? From where?"

She thought a moment.

"From . . . oblivion, I guess," she said. She paused and looked at me, a small smile on her lips. "Can't you remember anything about yourself? How old you are? Any member of your family? Anything?"

I closed my eyes, tried to remember and then shook my head.

"Everything is so muddled. I hear voices and see quick flashing pictures, but it's like my mind is full of bubbles that keep bursting when I try to seize one," I replied.

She laughed.

"You'll be fine," she said and patted me on the hand. "Get some sleep."

"Will I see you again?" I asked quickly as she turned and started for the door.

"No. I don't work here. I work for a doctor who has patients here," she replied from the doorway.

"My doctor?" I asked.

"No, not exactly," she said. "Don't worry about all those details. Just do what they tell you to do and you'll get better sooner than you think," she said. "For now, what you need the most is some rest."

"I know I want to go home," I said, "but I just can't remember where that is."

She smiled warmly.

"You will. Someday," she said. Then she looked sad. "Good-bye, Lauren." She switched off the lights, and as she closed the door behind her, I heard the distinctive click of a lock.

Trying to forget that I had just been locked into my room, I lay there in the darkness, listening. Through the walls I could hear someone crying softly. Above me there were footsteps moving rapidly and then a deep, long silence that was soon filled with the sounds of creaking walls and floors, the slam of a door and more footsteps.

Why was I here? Why did Clara call that old lady my grandmother? She didn't act like a grandmother, I thought. Why wouldn't Clara tell me more? Who told her to call me Lauren? Maybe that was my name.

I closed my eyes. All these questions and thoughts were giving me a headache. A myriad of faces flashed against the insides of my eyelids, some smiling, some laughing, a young man looking serious and then someone began to whisper. I struggled to hear what he was saying, but his voice drifted back until there was only silence and blackness.

I was so tired. Clara was right. I needed rest. Maybe in the morning, I would remember who I was. All my questions would be answered and this would all be over.

For now, that was my only prayer.

I woke when the door to my room was thrust open with such force and abruptness, it sent waves through the air. A much older nurse than Clara stepped in carrying a package under her arm. Her hair was the dirty gray color of old silver coins and the strands cut just below her earlobes looked thin and harsh as wire. Her forehead had rows of deep wrinkles that exploded at her temples to produce spidery webs extending to her cheeks. Her cheeks were a bit puffy, making her small, wide nose look like it was sinking into her face and would soon be swallowed up by those cheeks. She had a thin, uneven mouth, the right corner of her lower lip dipping just enough to reveal some teeth. The roundness in her face fit her chunky, short body, yet she had long arms with wide hands and thick fingers.

She paused, breathing in and lifting her hefty bosom as she contemplated me for a moment. I thought she looked like a pigeon with her chest out as she strutted to the bed. She placed the package at my feet.

Her appearance had startled me so that my heart thumped. As soon as I regained my senses, I sat up and gazed about in confusion, trying to remember how and when I had been brought here. The soreness in my body had gone deeply into my muscles. My arms felt heavier and just the thought of standing was exhausting.

"Good, you're awake," this new nurse said.

She went to the windows and when she turned her back to me, I saw she had a rather prominent birthmark at the base of her skull. Small hairs grew along its perimeter so that it looked like a large black bug had landed there. She opened the curtains wider to let in more sunlight. I could see clear blue sky.

She spun on me, her hands on her hips.

"I'm Mrs. Kleckner," she said. "I'm the head nurse here. Your bathroom has all that you need in it. You'll find a toothbrush, toothpaste, a new hairbrush, soap, and shampoo in the cabinet. Can you get up and give yourself a shower this morning or do I have to take you to the special bathroom for the disabled?"

"I think I can do it myself," I said.

She approached the bed.

"Hold out your hands," she ordered. "Go on."

I did what she asked and she watched them tremble and then turned them over and watched them again.

"Touch the tip of your nose," she commanded. "Do it," she said when I didn't move quickly enough.

After I had done that, she took my pulse, looked at my eyes and then stepped back.

"Do you remember why you were brought here? Do you remember how you were brought here?" she asked before I could answer the first question.

528

"I came in a car. There was another nurse named Clara. She said I had been with my grandmother." I looked up. "The nurse kept calling me Lauren, but I don't think my name is Lauren," I said.

"Really? Then what's your name?"

I thought a moment, but I couldn't think of anything that sounded right.

"I know it's not Lauren," I said.

"That's nice. You know it's not Lauren. You know it's not Susan, too. And you know it's not Joyce and you know it's not Matilda, I bet," she rattled with a smirk. "You probably know you're not fifty or sixty or seventy names, but do you know how old you are?"

"How old? I can't remember," I said. "Why can't I remember my own age and my own name?"

My lips started to tremble.

She nodded as if confirming what she thought to be true.

"A shower is the way we begin the day. There are clothes for you in this package," she said, indicating what she had brought in with her. "Underthings, socks, a pair of shoes, a skirt, and a blouse. Other things are being brought for you today. First, I'll show you the cafeteria and you'll have breakfast. After that, you'll meet Doctor Southerby and have your first session. I understand you have some trauma on your arms and legs," she said and drew closer again.

She lifted the blanket away from me.

"Lower those pants," she ordered.

I started to do so and once again, I didn't move quickly enough to satisfy her. She finished lowering them herself and inspected the bruises on my thighs and my calves as well as my hips and ribs.

"You did take a beating," she remarked.

She lifted the shirt over my head so roughly, I cried out.

"My arms, my shoulders!"

She held my arm up and inspected the black and blue marks. When she released it, I studied my hands and my forearms, too. My fingers looked scabby where the skin had been peeled away. What could I have done to myself?

529

"What happened to me?" I moaned, near tears.

"You'll live," she said dryly, lifting the right corner of her mouth so that it put a bulge into her cheek. "This will all go away in time."

"But I don't understand. How did this happen to me?" I asked her.

She didn't smirk exactly. She pressed her lips together, puffed her cheeks out a bit more, and made her eyes small.

"It's your responsibility to tell us," she said. "When you do, you'll be on your way to recovery."

"What's wrong with me?" I asked in a shrill voice. "Why can't I remember anything about myself? No one wants to tell me anything. Please!"

"The doctor will tell you all about that. My job is to get you ready and see after your basic needs first," she said calmly, clearly unmoved by my emotional outburst. Then she fixed her eyes on me. "I'll warn you now," she continued, stepping back and folding her thick arms under her heavy bosom. Her elbows looked dry, the skin scaly like a fish. "This is not a five-star hotel. I don't want to hear complaints about the food or the service or the size of your room. I don't want to hear how we don't have enough to do to entertain you. I'm a nurse, not some camp counselor for wealthy, spoiled children."

"Am I a wealthy, spoiled child?" I fired back. I thought she almost smiled.

"That's something you'll have to learn for yourself. The plan is for you to make your own discoveries about yourself, with our help, of course. That's how you get better. My telling you everything I know about you doesn't help you."

"I don't understand. Where am I?" I asked.

"Where are you? You're in a mental clinic, my dear," she said.

"A mental clinic?"

"One of the best in the state, if not *the* best, and very exclusive, too. Now, take your shower. I'll be back in twenty minutes and I expect to see you dressed and ready for breakfast. There's no reason why you can't do it all for yourself. I have a few patients on this floor who really do need my assistance and I must get to them now."

My lips started to tremble. I thought my whole body would soon start to shudder uncontrollably. She saw something was about to happen and stepped closer.

"Get hold of yourself," she ordered. She put her hands on my upper arms and shook me. "I don't permit any of my patients to sit in their rooms and feel sorry for themselves. The quicker you get better, the quicker you get out of here," she said, "and make room for someone else who really needs us. Shower," she concluded, pivoted on her soft shoes, and marched out of the room, closing the door behind her.

I took a deep breath.

Remember, I chanted. *Try, try to remember. Please. If you remember, you can go home.*

I squeezed my eyes closed and searched my brain, but it was as if my shouts for help were locked in a small part of my mind, shut up and smothered. I looked down at my hands and my feet, seeking some mark, something that would stir a memory. Nothing happened.

I sighed with frustration, rose, took off the shirt and pants, and went into the bathroom. There was a mirror over the small sink. I stared at my face, bringing my fingers to my lips, my nose, even touching my eyes. I was like a blind person trying to identify someone through my fingers, but what I felt, what I found rang no bells. I leaned in to look very closely at my reflection. I was looking at the face of a complete stranger. It was as if I had been dropped into someone else's body.

"Who are you?" I asked the image in the mirror and waited.

Suddenly, I heard a roaring in my ears. A memory flashed, the memory of holding a seashell to my ear and listening.

The ocean is in there, someone was saying. I sensed I was just a little girl.

Look inside. Do you see it?

I closed my eyes. There were smiling faces and there was laughter and there was the ocean in the seashell. Everyone who looked at me smiled.

"Who am I?" I screamed at them, but they just continued to smile. "WHO AM I?"

I directed my screaming at the image in the mirror and the image just screamed back. I don't know how long that went on before Mrs. Kleckner returned. She spun me around with those strong hands of hers and then she slapped me sharply across the face and I stopped.

"What are you doing? You frightened some of my other patients."

"I don't remember my name," I wailed. "I don't know who that is in the mirror. I'm afraid. I feel like I'm dangling in space. It's terrifying!" I cried.

"Don't be ridiculous. You're safe here. You're not dangling. Now, didn't I tell you to take a shower and get dressed? You'll see the doctor this morning and your therapy will begin. Now, get into the shower," she said and reached over to turn it on. "Go on, get in and stop this nonsense now. No one is going to pamper you. You have to cure yourself and help yourself."

She glared at me.

"It will go better for you if you cooperate," she said, not cloaking her threats.

I ground the tears away and stepped into the shower, adjusting the water so it wasn't as scalding hot as she had it. She waited a moment and then left me alone.

Despite the shower, I felt deeply exhausted after drying off. It took great effort to dress, get on my socks and shoes. Where did this clothing come from? I wondered. Was it mine? Everything did fit well.

The door opened again and Mrs. Kleckner stood there inspecting me.

"Good," she said. "Come along. I'll show you the eating facilities now and tomorrow morning, you'll get yourself up and to breakfast on your own, understand? Do you understand?" she repeated when I didn't answer quickly enough.

"Yes," I said.

"This way." She turned and I joined her. We walked down the corridor toward the stairway. A tall, dark-haired girl was there ahead of us. She didn't glance our way, but instead bounced happily down the steps, waving her hands as if she were sweeping cobwebs away from her head.

Mrs. Kleckner sighed deeply and shook her head, but she said nothing. We started down the stairs. The dark-haired girl was already down and away. I was moving too slowly to satisfy Mrs. Kleckner, so when we reached the bottom of the stairs, she seized my hand and jerked me along.

"It's time to wake up," she declared and forced me to stride step for step alongside her until we reached a large doorway, from which I could hear dishes and silverware clinking and voices in a low but continuous murmur, punctuated by some laughter. When we turned into the doorway and entered the cafeteria, everyone stopped talking and looked at us.

There were a little more than a dozen people, all looking relatively my age, whatever that exact age was. The dark-haired girl who had been sweeping the air around her as she descended the steps broke into a long, shrill laugh. She was at the counter getting her food from a sweet-looking elderly lady in a white uniform.

"Quiet," Mrs. Kleckner cried. The dark-haired girl stopped with such abruptness, I couldn't help but be impressed with Mrs. Kleckner's authority. All eyes were on us now. There was a boy close by who didn't look much more than ten or eleven, gazing at me with a small smile on his lips. Sitting at his table was a tall, very thin girl with hair the color of ripe apricots. She had big dark eyes and a mouth with soft, perfect lips. Her cheekbones were clearly visible under her tissue-like skin, which was pale and thin enough to pass for transparent. I saw how thin her arms were, too. Despite her fragile appearance, she sat straight and firm and looked at me with a soft, friendly air.

Across from her, his eyes down, was a handsome young man with hair as dark and shiny as black pearl. He wore it

533

brushed neatly on the sides and long down the back of his neck. For a moment I thought of someone else. A name almost appeared, but when this boy flashed a quick, timid look at me, I forgot the face in my memory and smiled back at him.

"We have a new resident," Mrs. Kleckner said.

"Hooray for her," a chubby boy with blond hair cried. The two boys at his table laughed, but then stopped as if they could turn it on and off like a television set, their faces moving from comedy to tragedy in a split second.

"That's enough of that, Carlton," Mrs. Kleckner chastised. He laughed silently, his cheeks jiggling, and then he suddenly looked as if he were going to cry. I glanced at Mrs. Kleckner, who didn't seem to notice or care.

"Her name," she continued, "is Laura."

I turned and looked at her, seeing a small smile on her face. All along she knew I had been right. The other nurse had mistakenly called me Lauren and not Laura, but I had been unable to remember. However, even though I sensed Laura was my real name, I couldn't connect it with anything else, especially a surname.

"I want you all to make her feel at home here," Mrs. Kleckner added.

"Home sweet home," someone in the back muttered.

The dark-haired girl by the counter suddenly spun around and then spun around again as if she were dancing a ballet. One of the attendants nearby moved quickly to her side and seized her hand. He spoke to her quietly and she gazed at the floor.

When I looked to the right, I noticed a female attendant hand-feeding a boy who looked at least twelve or thirteen. She encouraged him to feed himself, but he merely stared ahead, opening his mouth and chewing mechanically as she scooped the food into it and then wiped his lips.

"Go to the counter and get what you want," Mrs. Kleckner said. "There's juice, cereals, and eggs, if you like. Mrs. Anderson is our cook. She can make some special

534

things for you if your requests are reasonable and she has enough notice. You can sit anywhere you like," she added.

I crossed the cafeteria, feeling all eyes upon me. The dark-haired girl had been moved along and sat with the attendant at her side. She sipped on a glass of orange juice and stared ahead.

"Hello, Laura," Mrs. Anderson said. She had a wonderfully happy smile, her eyes bright and cheery. "Would you like some scrambled eggs this morning?"

"Yes," I said. "Thank you."

I suddenly realized that I was very hungry. I chose grapefruit juice and plucked a roll from the basket. Mrs. Anderson scooped the eggs onto a plate and put a piece of melon beside them.

"Enjoy your first breakfast with us," she said.

"Thank you."

I took the plate, put it on my tray, and turned. Many of the other residents were still staring at me, but a number had gone back to their own breakfasts and conversations. Some looked absolutely terrified that I would stop at their tables as I made my way through the room.

"Sit here. You'll be safe," a pretty red-haired girl said. There was another, shorter and younger-looking girl with her. The younger girl wore a jeans skirt and a frilly white blouse. Her blond hair was tied in two long, thick pigtails.

"Thank you," I said and took the empty seat at their table.

"My name's Megan Paxton," the red-haired girl said. She had a button nose and a small mouth. Her eyes darted about as if she expected trouble.

"I'm Laura," I said, confident of that little bit of information.

"Laura what?" the younger girl asked. She looked like a doll because of her tiny features.

"I can't remember my full name," I said. "I can't remember anything," I admitted, as if that were a crime and this was a jail instead of a clinic.

535

"Around here, that's an advantage," Megan said. "You're lucky," she said dryly. "I can't forget anything. When did you arrive?"

"Some time last night. I think," I said. "It all still seems fuzzy in my head." I drank my juice.

Megan darted her eyes about again. I began to look in the directions she was surveying to see if there was something I should notice, too.

"Is something wrong?" I asked.

"I'm just waiting to see if he's still here. They claim," she said, widening her eyes and hoisting her eyebrows, "that they fired him yesterday."

"Who?"

"Garson Taylor, one of the attendants. He tried to rape me," Megan said.

"Really?"

"Of course, really," she snapped. "What do you think, I'm making it up? Well, *do* you?" she drove at me, her face full of fire, her eyes wide.

"No, I'm . . . I'm sorry. I was just surprised by what you said."

"Well don't be surprised. Be alert. All the men here have one thing on their minds and you don't have to take two guesses to figure out what it is either," she said. "When they look at you, they're looking through your clothes."

"That's terrible."

"Tell me about it." She considered me a moment. "Maybe you were raped," she said. "And it was so traumatic, it caused you to forget everything. That's very common." She nodded, firmly convinced in her diagnosis.

I stopped eating and gazed at her. I started to shake my head.

"Why are you shaking your head? You said you don't remember anything. I bet that's it. Right, Lulu?" she asked the young girl. The small girl nodded.

"Yes, Megan," she said obediently. Megan looked satisfied.

"Her name isn't really Lulu. I named her that," Megan explained with a smile. "That's because she's a real lulu. Right, Lulu?"

The small girl laughed.

"My daddy's coming to see me today," she said.

"Oh, will you stop? She's been saying that for two years. Her father doesn't even write her letters," Megan said. "You would think she'd understand, face reality by now."

"Yes, he does."

"Okay, Lulu. Believe what you want. Fathers are the biggest liars of all anyway," Megan said. "Can you remember your father?" she asked me.

"No," I said.

"He's the one who raped you then," Megan threw back at me.

I nearly choked on my eggs.

"I never said I was raped."

"Of course you didn't, but it's a very logical reason why you can't remember." She leaned over to whisper. "Be very careful after you've gone to bed. They all have keys to our doors," she said, leaning back, "that is how Garson Taylor got into my room. Fortunately, I was able to shout loudly enough to bring others. He claimed he wasn't even in my room. Can you imagine?"

She looked about nervously again and then turned back to me, her haunted eyes wide and full of alarm.

"If he's still here we're all in danger, especially a new girl like you. Watch the doctors, too," she added.

"The doctors? Why?"

"They like to touch you here all the time," she said, touching her small breasts, "and pretend it's necessary."

She stared at me and then bit down on her lower lip so hard, I thought she would draw blood.

"You'll be all right," she said. "We'll all be all right. Someday. Right, Lulu?"

"What? Yes. My daddy's coming today," she told me. "He's going to take me home."

"I'm happy for you," I said.

"Oh, spunks," Megan said. "Let's go to the rec room. We can listen to some music and talk."

"We can just leave and go there?" I asked.

"We can do anything we want," she declared. "We're paying the rent. At least you know this much about yourself, Laura: You're rich."

"I am?"

"Of course you are, stupid. It costs about forty thousand dollars a year to stay here."

I sat back, amazed.

"I didn't realize," I said. "I—"

"Just don't let any of them take advantage of you. You don't have to put up with any of it." She gazed at the door. "If he's still working here, I'm going to raise holy hell," she said. Then she gazed at my plate. "Finish your breakfast. We've got things to talk about," she ordered. "I've got to make you aware of all the dangers!"

11

Return to the Land of the Living

I didn't get the chance to spend time with Megan after breakfast because as soon as I was finished and rose from the table, Mrs. Kleckner approached me to tell me Doctor Southerby was waiting for me.

Megan seized my wrist as I turned to follow Mrs. Kleckner out of the cafeteria.

"He's the worst," she whispered, "because he's young and unmarried. Watch yourself."

I nodded as if to thank her for her warning and she relaxed her grip on me so I could walk after Mrs. Kleckner. We went to the right and down the corridor to an office on the left. A pleasant-looking dark-haired woman of no more than forty looked up from her desk and smiled as we entered. She wore a dark green dress and had pretty pearl earrings that matched a pearl necklace on a gold chain. She looked as perfectly put together as a mannequin in a showcase window. Not a strand of her hair was out of place, but she had a warmth to her smile that made me feel welcome.

"Mrs. Broadhaven, this is our new patient," Mrs. Kleckner declared.

"Yes. Doctor Southerby is waiting to see you, Laura," she said to me and rose from her desk.

Despite Megan's warning, I was eager to meet the doctor, eager to find out what was wrong with me and finally be cured.

"When you're finished here, maybe Mrs. Broadhaven will show you around the clinic," Mrs. Kleckner said, nodding at Doctor Southerby's secretary. Mrs. Kleckner's tone made it clear it wasn't a request as much as it was an order.

"I'll be very happy to," Mrs. Broadhaven said, apparently not bothered by the sharpness in Mrs. Kleckner's voice. She went to the door to the inner office, smiling at me as she turned and waited.

I took a deep breath and followed her. Hopefully, the answers to all my questions and the light to wash away the darkness lay behind that office door.

"This is our new patient, Doctor Southerby," she announced as soon as she stepped in.

Even though Megan had warned me, I was rather surprised at how young the doctor looked. He rose immediately from behind his dark cherry wood desk, a desk so large it looked like it was wrapped around him. Everything on it was neatly organized with folders in a neat pile and an open pad before him. On the wall behind him hung his framed diplomas and awards. There were two large windows behind his desk that looked out at the grounds. I saw the weeping willow trees I had seen silhouetted in the dark the night before. Everything looked green and plush today.

"Good morning," Doctor Southerby said. "Please. Come right in." His voice was deeper than I would have expected and he had a Southern accent. His light brown hair was trimmed short at the sides, but with a small pompadour at the front.

"Please," he said quickly, nodding at the chair in front of his desk, "make yourself comfortable. Thank you, Mrs. Broadhaven," he told his secretary.

She gave me a smile of reassurance and left, closing the

540

door softly behind her. Doctor Southerby turned back to me.

He had turquoise eyes that radiated a warmth and friendliness that immediately put me at ease. His smile brightened them even more.

Not a very tall man, perhaps only five feet ten, he nevertheless projected a strong, firm demeanor with his shoulders back, his handshake assertive, definite. He had a firm, straight mouth and a taut jawline. In his dark gray suit, light blue shirt and matching tie with a jeweled tie clip, he appeared very distinguished and confident despite his youthful look.

He returned to his chair behind the desk.

"Did you get some rest last night?" he asked. "I always find it hard to sleep well in a new place, myself."

"I was so exhausted I didn't have time to think about it," I said and he laughed.

"Most likely, most likely," he said. "Well, let me introduce myself properly." He leaned back in his chair and pressed the tips of his fingers together. "I am Doctor Henry Southerby and I will be in charge of your case."

He spoke calmly, relaxed, while I felt like butterflies with their wings on fire were circling madly in my stomach. I could barely sit still.

"What is my case? Why am I here? What happened to me? Why can't I remember the simplest things about myself?" I blurted out all at once. "I couldn't even remember my real name! I still can't remember my surname."

The high notes of hysteria in my voice didn't seem to faze him. He simply nodded, gently.

"I can understand your anxiety," he said, "and I want to put you at ease as quickly as I can. That way, you'll recover faster. It would be best," he continued, "if you remember things on your own. My simply filling up the empty spaces won't be enough. For one, you might reject the information again and then we could be worse off than we are now."

"Reject the information? I don't understand," I said, shaking my head. The calmer he was, the more anxious I felt. "Why did I reject such important information about myself, my name, my family, where I live? It's terrifying. Am I crazy? Is that why I'm here? What's wrong with me?" I pursued, my voice so shrill it hurt my own ears.

"I assure you that what's wrong with you at the moment won't last. And once you are cured, there's very little chance this will happen again," he replied in a mellow voice. It didn't satisfy me, however.

"What will not happen? What do I have, a disease? What?" I asked. He couldn't talk fast enough for me.

"From what I understand about your situation, I feel safe in a preliminary diagnosis of psychogenic amnesia," he said, although he looked uncomfortable about committing himself so quickly.

"I know what amnesia is," I said, shaking my head, "but that other word—"

"Psychogenic simply means your amnesia probably isn't due to any organic mental disorder. There's no physical reason for you to be unable to remember things. You didn't suffer any injury to your brain; physical injury, that is. There are no drugs or alcohol involved. You're not an epileptic, and," he said with a smile, "you're not pretending to be forgetful."

"What happened then? What's caused this?"

"What's happened is you have experienced a very traumatic event, an event of such emotional and psychological magnitude that your brain has shut down its memory chambers to prevent you from suffering," he said softly, leaning over the desk toward me. "It's really a self-defense mechanism the mind employs and is not uncommon in situations such as yours.

"This trauma arose from an event that overwhelmed your coping mechanism. Another term for this today is dissociative amnesia, the inability to recall important personal information."

"What was it?" I asked, my heart pounding. "What was the traumatic event?"

542

"It's important you remember that on your own, Laura," he said.

"Laura, but Laura what? What's my full name?" I demanded. "Tell me."

He nodded.

"Your full name is Laura Logan," he said. Then he stared at me for a moment. "What does that do for you, hearing your full name? Do you remember any more about yourself? Close your eyes and repeat your name. Go on," he urged.

I did so and then I shook my head.

"I don't remember anything," I wailed. "I can't," I cried more desperately.

"You will," he promised me. "I'll take you back gradually until it all rushes into your consciousness again. If you're just patient and—"

I shook my head.

"I can't stand it!" I cried. "I look in the mirror and feel like I'm looking at someone else. It's horrible. I'm walking around on pins and needles. My head keeps echoing with questions, over and over and—"

"Easy, Laura. Don't upset yourself," he said, but the tears were already flowing down my cheeks, burning as they traversed my face and dripped off my chin. I shook my head violently, shook it so hard, it revived the ache in my neck.

"No, no, no. I want to be cured *now!* I want to remember *now!* Tell me everything. Tell me why I'm like this!" I screamed at him.

He stood up.

"Easy, Laura. Please. You're just upsetting yourself and making it all that much more difficult for us to help you here."

"I don't want to be here. I want to be . . . where do I want to be? I don't even know that!" I shouted. I gazed down at my arms, the black and blue marks still vivid. "Look at me. What happened? Tell me everything! Please, tell me," I begged and then I rose and looked about the office, looked

543

for an avenue of escape. I felt like running and running until I couldn't run anymore.

He was around his desk instantly and at my side.

"Laura, relax now. Sit calmly. Come on," he said, putting his hand on my arm gently but firmly.

Megan's terrified face flashed before me.

"He's the worst," she whispered.

Who were these people who knew more about me than I knew about myself but kept it secret? What was going on?

"NO!" I screamed again. I pushed him away and then I heard a terrible ringing in my head. I pressed my palms to my ears. Someone was shouting *Laura*. There was water everywhere, water rushing over me until I couldn't hear my name anymore.

"NOOOOO!" I cried and then, all went black.

I woke on a gurney in a treatment room someplace in the building. The walls and the ceiling were stark white. Mrs. Kleckner was at my side and Doctor Southerby was on a telephone, talking softly to someone when I opened my eyes.

"She's regaining consciousness, Doctor," Mrs. Kleckner declared. I started to sit up, but she put her hand on my shoulder. "Just relax for a while," she commanded. "Doctor?"

He cradled the receiver and approached.

"How are you feeling now, Laura?"

"My head hurts," I said with a grimace. The pain felt like a metal band being tightened from one temple to the other.

"We'll give you something for that," he said.

"What happened?"

"You got too excited." He smiled. "You know how a circuit breaker works?"

I thought. Yes, I did know, but I had no idea why.

"Yes."

"Well, the mind works the same way. When it gets overloaded, it shuts down. Now you see why I've got to get you to relax first before I can help you?" he asked. "I want you to learn to trust me, Laura. Only then can I help you, and I want to help you," he said firmly. He held my hand and gazed down at me, his eyes washing over my face and then fixing on mine. "Do you believe me?"

I nodded, but not with enough confidence to please him. He smiled nevertheless.

"In time you will and then you'll cure yourself, Laura. This unfortunate situation won't be long. I promise," he said. "Really." He patted my hand.

I wanted to believe him. He was saying the things I wanted to hear.

"Sit up now and take this pill," he said, indicating the pill Mrs. Kleckner was waiting to give me. She placed it in my mouth and gave me some water. I drank and swallowed.

"For now," Doctor Southerby continued, "I'd like you to return to your room, get some more rest, and then we'll talk again."

"I want to talk now," I insisted.

"I know you do, but I don't want to chance any recurrences of what just happened. You're very fragile right now, Laura, more fragile than you can imagine. You need to rest up a bit so you can go about your recovery with full strength. Trust me about this. I promise," he said, "you won't be here a minute more than you have to be." He nodded at Mrs. Kleckner.

"Try to stand up now, Laura," she said.

I sat up and my head began to spin so rapidly, I actually lost my breath for a moment and thought I was going to black out again.

"Easy, easy," Doctor Southerby said. "You better wheel her over," he told Mrs. Kleckner. Moments later they both eased me into a wheelchair. I lay my head back and felt myself being moved out of the treatment room. I kept my eyes closed all the way back to my room.

Once there, Mrs. Kleckner helped me into bed.

"Just rest," she said. "I'll be back to check on you in a little while."

"I want to go back to Doctor Southerby's office and get my treatment," I moaned. "I want this to be over."

"You will go back," she said sternly, "but you heard the doctor. He wants you to be rested, stronger, otherwise he's just wasting his time and his time is very important. He doesn't only work here with the privileged. He works at another clinic, too."

"The privileged?"

What was privileged about being here, about being disturbed and sick? I wanted to ask. I tried to open my eyes, but whatever they gave me made my eyelids feel so heavy. In moments, I was asleep.

I woke when I felt my whole body shaking. Megan Paxton was at my bedside, tugging on my hand. She looked at the door and then back at me.

"What happened?" I muttered. My eyes felt like cobwebs had been built over them. My eyelids remained glued shut.

"They gave you something," she whispered. "You've got to be careful. One of them can come in here and rape you while you're asleep," she said. "They did that to me. Stay awake," she warned. "Or sleep with one eye open."

"I'm so tired," I muttered. She shook me again.

"Stay awake," she ordered.

"What are you doing in here?" I heard and forced my lids open enough to see Mrs. Kleckner in the doorway. "Come out of there immediately, Megan," she commanded, her hands on her hips.

"I'm just seeing how she is. What's the big deal?"

"You know you're not supposed to go into anyone else's room without permission from me. Now come out and let her rest, Megan. Now!" she insisted.

"Stay awake," she whispered to me as she left.

My eyes shut closed again and when I woke the next time, Megan's presence in my room seemed more like a dream. I felt groggy, but I wanted to get up and move about, so I lifted myself from the bed and went into the bathroom. I washed my face in water as cold as I could get it and that helped some. When I came out of the bathroom, I found Mrs. Kleckner waiting.

"I see you got yourself up. That's good. How do you feel?" she asked.

"Weak, but I don't want to sleep anymore," I added quickly, afraid she had another pill waiting.

"Very well. As long as you feel up to it, I'll show you about the facility myself then," she said.

"When do I see Doctor Southerby again?"

"Tomorrow," she said. "He had to leave the clinic for other appointments. If you're strong enough, you can go to the recreation room and meet some of the other patients. It's good for you to interact with other people. Doctor Southerby left strict orders about that. He doesn't want you hibernating in this room."

"I don't want to hibernate. I'd like to get some fresh air, too," I said.

"I'll see that one of the attendants takes you out before dinner," she told me.

"Dinner? What about lunch?" I asked. She laughed, a short laugh that sounded more like a cough.

"You slept through lunch. There's tea and crackers or cookies in the recreation room, if you like, and soft drinks in the refrigerator. Come along," she said and I started after her, my steps not as steady as I would have liked. She noticed and held my arm in the corridor.

"Once you move around, get your circulation going, you'll get stronger," she said.

"What did you give me? What was in that pill?"

"It was just a light sedative. Doctor Southerby has prescribed it for you to take at night so you get a good rest."

"I don't like taking pills," I said. She paused and looked at me.

"You remember not liking them or you just decided?" she asked.

"I . . . just don't like them," I said.

"Well, we all have to do things we don't like to do once in

547

a while. You're no different just because you can't remember who you are," she commented and led me to the recreation room.

There were only seven patients there, two boys who looked about twelve or thirteen playing a game of chess and the rest of the patients sitting and reading or just staring out the windows at the walkways and gardens behind the building. Megan, Lulu, the very thin girl, and the good-looking young man I had seen in the cafeteria were sitting on two sofas facing each other with a table between them. There were magazines and books on the table. Lulu was writing feverishly in a long, yellow pad and didn't look up as the others did when I entered.

On the right I saw a small stove, a refrigerator, a sink, and some cabinets.

"There's hot water for tea there," Mrs. Kleckner indicated, "and some cookies, if you like. Tea bags are in the cabinet and milk and soft drinks are in the refrigerator."

"Thank you," I said.

She brought me farther into the room.

"This is Mark and Arthur," she said, referring to the two boys playing chess. "You two remember Laura, don't you?" she asked. They looked up at me and then back at their chessboard with hardly a smile of greeting. It was as if nothing more than a breeze had blown by them.

"You already know Megan Paxton and Edith Sanders," she said, referring to Lulu. "This is Mary Beth Lewis and Lawrence Taylor," she added.

Mary Beth gave me a warm smile of welcome. Lawrence glanced at me quickly and then looked down.

"I'll leave Laura with you so you can all get to know each other better," she told them with a mechanical smile. "If you need anything, ask Miss Cranshaw," she told me and nodded at the attendant sitting in the corner and reading a magazine.

Miss Cranshaw gazed our way for a moment and then folded the magazine and sat back to watch us. I thought it was because of the look Mrs. Kleckner had given her. She didn't look much younger than Mrs. Kleckner. In fact, she could easily be older, I thought.

Mrs. Kleckner left us.

"Sit here," Mary Beth said, moving over on the sofa to make a place for me. Lawrence looked up, but quickly shifted his eyes from mine.

"Have you remembered your full name yet?" Mary Beth asked.

"It's Laura Logan," I said.

"How come you didn't know your own name?" Lulu asked, perking up.

"She's got amnesia, stupid," Megan said. "Why do you think she's here? For the food? Or for the stimulating company?"

"Oh," Lulu said, turning to me meekly. "I'm sorry. Does it hurt?"

"Not the way you think. It is painful not to be able to remember anything though," I said. Lawrence gazed at me and smiled softly before looking out the window.

"Do you know why you have amnesia?" Mary Beth asked.

"If she knew why, she wouldn't be here," Megan answered for me.

"She's right. I don't know," I said. "All I know is it's because of something terrible that happened to me."

"If that was the case, most everyone in this place would have amnesia," Megan quipped.

"What can you remember about yourself?" Lawrence asked and then pressed his lips together as if the words had escaped before he could stop them. He had thick eyebrows and dark eyes that flashed with interest before shifting away.

"Not very much, really. Actually," I said, looking at all of them, "nothing."

"Nothing?" Mary Beth cried. She started to smile.

"I didn't really remember my full name. Doctor Southerby told me," I said.

Mary Beth stopped smiling. She formed a big O with her lips. It looked like she had blown a bubble.

"He wouldn't tell me what had happened to me either. He wants me to remember on my own."

"It's classic," Megan said as if she were a doctor herself. "Once I heard her story, I knew she had suffered some terrible experience, and as a result, her mind's gone completely bonkers. Remember that girl they moved to the Tower," she continued, "the one who tried to cut her wrists with the broken plate? Every day she couldn't remember what she had done or said the day before. It was as if her mind erased itself every morning and started over. Remember? What was her name?" she asked Lawrence. "You tried to talk to her all the time."

He turned beet red.

"I didn't try to talk to her all the time," he said, flashing a look at me.

"Fine. You didn't. It was all in my imagination. What was her name?" Megan demanded.

"Lydia," he said quickly. "Lydia Becker."

"Right. Lydia Becker. Every day we each had to introduce ourselves to her again. It was as if she had just arrived. Remember, Mary Beth?"

"Yes."

Megan laughed.

"I started giving her a different name for myself each time just to see if it mattered. It didn't."

"What did you mean when you said they moved her to the Tower?" I asked.

"She's still here, but on the top floor. We call it the Tower because Megan thinks once you are taken up there, you are shut away for the rest of your life, like in a tower," Mary Beth explained and shrugged.

"You are! No one who's been brought up there ever comes back to this floor, do they?" Megan fired at her. She glared angrily for a moment and then turned to me. "You can just imagine what goes on. She could be raped and not even remember it the next day. If they ever want to take me up there, I want you all to promise to kill me."

Lulu laughed.

"I mean it," Megan said. "I'd rather be dead." She glared at Lawrence, who immediately looked down.

"Why are you here?" I asked Mary Beth.

Megan laughed loud and hard.

"Are you kidding? Why is she here? Look at her. She thinks she's fat."

"I am overweight for my size," Mary Beth said.

I started to smile, but saw the look on Lawrence's face that told me not to.

"She eats and then throws it all up," Megan said. "One of these days, they'll tie her to her bed and shove a tube down her throat."

"Oh, I'm sorry," I said, not knowing what else to say. I had the feeling words were like footsteps on thin ice here.

"Go on, ask Lawrence why he is here," Megan taunted. I looked at him. He held my gaze for a brief time and then blushed and looked down at his hands. They looked long and graceful. He had them folded and was twirling his thumbs. "Can you guess why he's here?" Megan continued.

"I have no idea," I said. "He looks very healthy."

His eyes lifted to mine and I thought he smiled, but then I realized he had the sort of face that could easily be deceiving. Was it a smile or a look of pain? As if to answer, he moved his lips slightly, lifted them almost imperceptibly in the corners, brightened his eyes and fixed them for a second on me, but almost as soon as he realized I felt his interest, he shifted away. Was he merely overly shy? That wouldn't be enough to keep someone here, would it? I wondered.

"Well, Lawrence, tell her what's wrong with you," Megan challenged. "Go on. Don't leave her hanging and guessing."

He shook his head.

"Oh, go on, tell her," Megan taunted. "It's a sign of improvement when you can talk about your own problem," Megan explained.

He glanced at me again and then looked away. I thought his eyes were starting to look a bit teary.

"Lawrence hasn't made much improvement yet. Young

551

Mr. Taylor," she continued, "has what the doctors describe as a panic disorder. Don't you, Lawrence?"

"Can't you leave him alone?" Mary Beth said.

"What am I doing to him? Lawrence, can't you speak up for yourself?"

"I—"

"Yes, Lawrence? Hold it, everyone," Megan said, raising her hands. She turned and looked toward the two boys playing chess. "Quiet down over there. Lawrence Taylor the third is about to say something. Go on, Lawrence," she said.

He looked at me and then rose quickly, his face flushed.

"Where are you going?" Megan cried.

"Will you leave him alone," Mary Beth said.

Lawrence glanced at me and then hurried out of the recreation room.

Megan laughed.

"Lawrence," she said, "is unable to perform today. Everyone gets his money back."

"That wasn't very nice," I told her.

She smirked.

"As Mrs. Kleckner says, if we baby each other, none of us will get better."

"And what's wrong with you then?" I demanded, still feeling sorry for Lawrence.

"Me? I'm . . . unable to have significant relationships. I don't trust anyone. Can I trust you?" she asked, her eyes growing watery. "Can I trust you?" she asked Mary Beth. "What about you, Lulu?"

"I'm writing to my father," Lulu said with a smile, "telling him about our new friend."

"Oh great. Another letter to the dead. I have to go to the bathroom," Megan said, rising. "Will everyone please excuse me?"

She folded her arms over her breasts and walked out.

"Megan is not a very happy person," Mary Beth said. "So she's not satisfied until everyone around her is unhappy, too."

"I can see that," I said. My stomach rumbled. "I think I'll have some tea. Would you like some?"

"No," Mary Beth said quickly. "I never eat between meals."

"Tea isn't really eating," I said.

"I've got to go to my room and get something," she said with a voice of panic. "I'll see you at dinner." She rose and left quickly as I got up to go to the stove and pour hot water into a cup with a tea bag. I took one of the cookies and looked at Lulu. She was so sweet, so dainty. How could her parents let her be here and not with them? I wondered. When I returned to the sofa, she looked up from her notepad.

"How do you spell acquaintance?" she asked me and I told her. "I'm describing you as a new acquaintance," she explained and wrote on. "Is that all right?"

"Of course," I said.

"I like making new friends and my daddy likes to hear about them. He told me to write him a letter every day. Sometimes, I write two a day. And I have piles and piles of letters from him," she said. Then she paused, put the notepad down and looked at me. "I think I'll have a cookie, too."

When she got up, I leaned over and looked at her pad. I went from surprise to shock and confusion.

There wasn't a word written on it, just lines scrawled in every direction.

At Mrs. Kleckner's directive, Miss Cranshaw took me out to the gardens and walkways to get some fresh air.

"We like you to stay on the pathways," she said. "You can sit on the benches, even on the grass or under a tree, as long as you remain in this area," she added, gesturing at the boundaries.

The grounds were beautiful, with beds of flowers, bird-baths, some stone and marble statuary, and tall, thick oak and maple trees. The hedges, the grass, and the gardens were all well maintained. A groundsperson was weeding in one of the gardens as we walked through. None of the other patients at the clinic were outside, as far as I could see.

"I'd like to just sit here for a while," I said, moving to a wooden bench halfway down the long, center path. The sight of the soft clouds, the scent of the grass and the flowers, and the touch of the breeze on my face was deliciously familiar. I liked being outdoors; I liked nature. What else did I like? It was strange, discovering such basic and simple things about yourself.

"You have about an hour before dinner," Miss Cranshaw said. "I have to look after a few patients and then I'll come get you when it's time to come in," she said.

I thanked her and sat back, watching two songbirds flit from the birdbath to a statue of a cherub. They paraded on the small angel's shoulder and then gazed at me before lifting off to fly toward the oak trees.

It's so quiet, so beautiful and fresh here, I thought. It was a perfect place for recuperation. The only problem was I didn't know from what I was recuperating and now a part of me was afraid to know, afraid to go back. If it was something so terrifying that it would cause me to forget the most basic things about myself, it must be horrendous, I thought, too horrendous for the doctors or nurses to want to tell me.

A movement near one of the sprawling oak trees caught my eye and I turned to see Lawrence Taylor emerge from the shadows and step onto a path. He walked slowly with his head down. When he drew closer, he looked up and saw me and he stopped quickly.

"Hi," I said. "It's so pretty out, I wonder why there aren't more people outside."

For a second he looked like he might run off. Then he took a deep breath and replied.

"No one comes out here this time of the day. It's too close to dinner," he said. "Everyone usually follows a strict routine here," he added. He looked to his right and then glanced at me as if he had to steal each and every look.

"How come you're outside then?"

"I like being alone now," he said. "Out here."

"Why do you like being alone?"

He shrugged.

"I always have," he said. "Well, not always. I used to be afraid to be alone," he confessed. "That's why they think I'm improving."

"Do you have any brothers or sisters?" I asked.

"No." He smiled and looked away.

"What's so funny?" I asked. He didn't reply. "Well?"

"I was going to ask you if you did and then I remembered you don't remember anything," he said.

"That's funny?"

He looked down. I was angry at first and then, I suddenly laughed. He looked up, a puzzled expression on his face.

"Maybe it is funny," I said. "I do feel ridiculous." He held his gaze on me for the longest time yet and then he drew closer.

"Doctor Thomas told me sometimes it's better to laugh than cry," he said. "If you have more of a sense of humor about yourself, you don't take things as seriously and you don't worry as much," he explained. "I try to follow his advice, but I still don't laugh all that much."

"Sounds like good advice though," I said. "How long have you been here?"

"Two years," he replied. "It seems like forever."

"Two years! You didn't go home and come back?" He shook his head. "Why can't you go home? You seem fine to me," I said. I wanted to add, "unless shyness is now considered an illness."

"I have these spells. I get chest pain, dizziness, and I start to shake uncontrollably."

"Why?"

"It's what Megan told you. I have a panic disorder," he admitted. "I have very low self-esteem, but as I told you, I'm getting better," he added quickly, as if he were afraid I would be frightened away. "At least now I can take walks by myself. It used to be, I never left the building. However," he continued, "every time I think about leaving the clinic, I break out in a cold sweat and feel faint."

"You want to leave though, don't you?"

"Yes. I'm trying. I really am now. I wasn't trying so much in the beginning. I didn't care as much."

"Did you always have this . . . panic disorder?"

"No," he said.

The whole time he spoke to me, he kept squeezing his right hand with his left and nibbling on his cheek.

"Why don't you sit here for a while," I suggested. "Relax. Tell me what it's like here. I've only been here one night," I explained.

He looked at the space beside me on the bench as if it were a high hurdle he could never reach.

"I don't bite," I said. "Or, at least I don't think I do. I don't remember biting people, but maybe I did," I added, tilting my head and pretending to think about it. "Since I can't remember, I can't swear I didn't. I might even be a killer." He smiled. "See, I have a sense of humor," I told him.

He widened his smile and then, with a sudden, abrupt, and definite move, like someone charging into a fire, he sat beside me.

"You really can't remember anything? Nothing?" he asked. When he spoke, he avoided looking directly at me for more than a fleeting second.

When he did look at me, I could see the sensitivity in his dark eyes. His pupils looked like two shiny black pearls. They made me think of another face, but I saw only the eyes in my memory, and then, when I saw the mouth, the eyes faded.

"I have these flashes, pictures, sounds, but as soon as I try to understand them, to trace them back to something, they disappear," I complained.

"What's an example? What do you see, hear?" he asked with interest.

"Water, the beach, boats, but little boats, toy boats."

"You mean like model boats?"

556

"Yes, yes, model boats, but it makes me shiver, even now, even in the sunlight, to think about boats," I said and hugged myself. My teeth actually chattered.

Very tentatively, inches at a time, he reached out to touch my hand.

"You are cold," he said, impressed.

I nodded and he wrapped his hand around mine.

"That feels good," I said, smiling. He smiled and held on to my hand. The longer he held on to it, the more confident he became.

"Well, what do we have going on here?" we heard, and Lawrence let go as if my hand had shocked him.

We turned to see Megan coming toward us. She marched stiffly with her hands clenched at her sides and her arms unbending.

"Hi, Megan," I said.

"I wondered where you were when I came back. Lulu said you had asked to go outside. Isn't this cozy?" she added, looking from Lawrence to me and back to Lawrence. "You don't know each other five minutes and you rendezvous in the garden and I find you holding hands."

Lawrence moved away from me quickly.

"We just bumped into each other out here," I said. "I didn't know Lawrence was outside."

"Really?" she said, her eyes narrow with suspicion. "How'd he get you to let him hold your hand?"

"He didn't get me to let him, Megan. I told him I was cold and he was just trying to warm me up," I said.

"Sure. That's how it starts," she said. "I'm surprised at you, Lawrence Taylor. You haven't touched another person here since I've known you. You must be someone special," she said to me.

Lawrence's face was crimson, but his lips were white with fear. He shook his head.

"I just—"

"The male in you has woken," Megan declared like a doctor diagnosing a terminal illness. "I'll warn the girls and the female attendants and the rest of the world. Everyone

557

should know to be on guard. Lawrence Taylor's lusts have been miraculously resurrected. His hormones are raging. Beware!"

"No . . . I—"

"Oh, stop it," she snapped and then looked around. When she turned back to us, her expression was completely different. "I have a private, secret place I'll show you later," she told me, "if you're good. However, I hope you're not like Lydia and forget everything every day. I really don't like wasting my time on people."

"I don't think that's my problem, forgetting things I learn," I said.

"You don't know what your problem is. *That's* your problem," she replied. "Look at him," she continued, nodding at Lawrence. "Pathetic."

I turned and saw he was trembling and that sweat had broken out on his brow.

"Lawrence," I said, reaching out to touch him.

"I'm okay. I'm okay. I think it's time to go in for dinner." He stood up. "I didn't mean anything. I just . . ."

"It's all right, Lawrence. Really," I said. "Please stay with us."

He looked at Megan.

"Yeah, Lawrence. We're hungry for your wonderful company," she said.

"I'll see you inside." He glanced at me and turned away. "I've got to do something before dinner," he added and walked toward the building.

"I wonder what that could be, Lawrence," Megan called after him. "What could you do alone in your room? I hope it's not what I think it is. I hope it's not what other boys your age do with themselves."

Her words and laughter made him walk faster.

"Why do you pick on him like that?" I demanded. "He was doing so well."

She looked at me as if I spoke another language.

"I don't pick on him. I don't pick on anybody." She paused, making her eyes smaller. "Are you siding with them already? You just got here and you're siding with them?" she accused.

"With whom?"

"With whom?" she mimicked. "You'd better be careful," she warned. "You just better be careful. First they win your trust and then . . . then . . ." Her lips trembled and her chin quivered. She had her hands clenched into fists and her arms extended and against her sides again. She looked like a soldier frozen in place.

"Megan? Are you all right?"

Her eyelids fluttered. Then she looked at me and relaxed.

"Of course I'm all right. I have to be all right. I have to be sharp, aware. I'm . . . going back inside. I've got to get Lulu. She doesn't know enough to get herself to dinner. She keeps waiting for her daddy. Her daddy. Daddies," she spit, as if it were a profanity. "She should be happy he never comes around."

She turned and walked after Lawrence.

Why did she hate daddies?

12

Shadows of My Mind

*E*veryone seemed more subdued at dinner. Their voices were low and there was very little laughter. Those who were unable to feed themselves were seated together and served by the attendants. The rest of us moved through the cafeteria line. There were two choices for an entre: turkey or halibut. Everything smelled and looked good. Mrs. Anderson supervised with pride. If I closed my eyes and listened, I couldn't tell I was in a clinic.

"Does this cafeteria remind you of your school?" Lawrence whispered from behind me.

"It's familiar," I said, "but I can't recall anything specific."

"I went to a private school," he said. "I always did. The food was pretty good there, too, and it didn't have many more students than there are patients here," he added, but he sounded like it wasn't a happy experience.

"Some of us back here are hungry," Megan said to prompt us to stop talking, take our food, and move down the line.

I hurried along, noticing how Mary Beth skipped taking

bread or dessert and then pushed her food apart, as if to let anything touch would contaminate everything.

This time Megan, Mary Beth, Lulu, Lawrence, and I all sat at the same table. No one else seemed to want to join us.

"What are you waiting for?" Megan asked me. "Eat before it gets cold."

I hadn't realized I was sitting there, not touching any silverware, while everyone else, even Mary Beth, had begun.

"I don't know," I said, sensing a blank that wanted to be filled in desperately, "but you're right. I feel like I am waiting for something before we eat, something that should happen first . . ."

"My daddy used to tell us all about his day at work at dinner," Lulu said. "And then he would tell us stories about when he and my mother were young."

"He was probably never there for dinner. Didn't your parents get divorced when you were a baby?" Megan reminded her.

"I still remember," Lulu said and glanced at me to see if I believed her. I smiled at her and she smiled back.

"Maybe you said a prayer first," Lawrence suggested. "At my private school, the headmaster led us in saying Grace before every dinner."

"Yes," I said. "Maybe . . ." I nodded. "I think that's it," I added excitedly.

"Okay. I'll say it. Everyone wait. Hold your fork, Lulu." Megan stared ahead and raised her arms slowly toward the ceiling. "Grace," she declared, clapping her hands. Then she dug into her potatoes, laughing.

"Yes," I said, nodding. "Yes, that's it. You're right, Lawrence. I can remember that. I think I can remember . . . the Bible. We read from the Bible," I continued. Lawrence smiled, his eyes happy for me as he nodded softly.

"This is good," he said. "If everything comes back to you this fast, you can leave before you know it."

"Goody, goody for her," Megan said. She started to eat again and then paused to consider me. "Do you really remember something?"

561

"Just vaguely, someone reading . . . it's like I'm remembering myself reading." I shook my head. "It doesn't make any sense. I hear a different voice, but I see a face so similar to my own, it's like . . . I'm looking at myself."

"That doesn't sound like anything," Megan said after a moment of thought.

"Sure it does," Lawrence said, suddenly assertive. Megan widened her eyes and he turned back to me. "You better have something to eat," he suggested softly. "You'd be surprised at how much strength all this mental work takes."

"Yes," I said and started. Even that tiny bit of memory returning filled me with encouragement and stimulated my appetite. I really am going to get better, I thought.

Halfway through the meal, I glanced at Mary Beth and saw she was eating, but after every bite, she wiped her mouth with her napkin and put the napkin on her lap. I caught sight of it after she took another mouthful of fish and saw that the napkin was filled with the food she had spit back into it. Actually, she was barely eating anything.

The attendant named Billy, who had greeted Clara and me at the door when I first arrived, had been standing on the side with another attendant watching our table. Suddenly, he rushed over and pounced.

"Mary Beth, you're spitting out your food," he accused, his hands on his hips. He nodded at her plate.

"No, I'm not!"

"Let me see your napkin," he demanded. "Come on. We've got strict orders from Doctor Thomas about you."

"I'm eating!" she cried, on the verge of tears.

"Leave her alone," Megan said. He turned to her.

"Mind your own business, Megan. There's plenty to mind there," he said. He turned back to Mary Beth.

Mary Beth's panic had flushed her neck and face. She looked like she was trembling in her seat. I felt sorry for her. Her eyes were darting about, searching for some avenue of escape.

"You're scaring the hell out of her!" Megan cried. Billy ignored her and continued to hover over Mary Beth.

"The doctor said if we see you spitting out your food, we've got to tell him and then they'll put you upstairs and force-feed you," Billy reminded her.

"The Tower!" Megan declared. "Don't even think of trying it," she told Billy. She even poked him in the rear with her fork. He spun on her again.

"Look," he said, "if you interfere with our work with other patients, you'll end up there, too. And don't you ever poke me with anything. That's an exhibition of violence," he chastised with a smile that revealed his row of glitteringly white teeth. "And you know what *that* means," he threatened.

While he glared with fury at Megan, I reached under the table, took Mary Beth's full napkin off her lap and dropped mine in its place. She glanced at me gratefully. Billy turned back to her.

"Well? Hand up that napkin. Come on," he said, gesturing with both hands.

She reached into her lap and gave it to him slowly. He seized it. The disappointment registered on his face when he opened it and nothing fell out. Megan roared and then clapped.

"Billy Screwball screws up again!" she cried, clapping her hands over her head. Conversations throughout the cafeteria stopped and everyone looked our way.

"Cut that out," he told her.

Megan continued to clap, which caused one of the boys I had seen playing chess earlier to start clapping, too. His friend followed and then the whole table joined in. Soon, everyone in the cafeteria who could clap was clapping.

Billy's face took on a look of rage and he threw the napkin back at Mary Beth. Then he marched back to his position in the cafeteria, shouting at the patients to quiet down. Megan finally stopped clapping and soon everyone followed. One boy, however, kept breaking out into applause and laughter for no reason every once in a while during the remainder of the meal.

"Thanks," Mary Beth whispered to me.

"That was pretty smart," Megan told me. "You saved her butt with quick thinking."

Lawrence smiled at me, too, his gaze steadier now and full of pride and admiration.

"You better eat something, Mary Beth, or I'll feel responsible and guilty if you get sick," I told her.

She took a forkful of fish and put it in her mouth, chewing demonstrably and turning toward Billy as she did so. He looked away with disgust.

"Billy's such a dork," Megan said. She glared back at him until he turned his back to her and kept his eye on the other patients. "He doesn't scare me with his threats. He knows if he so much as put a finger on me . . ."

She turned back to me and stopped talking and eating.

"What's wrong with you?" she asked.

"That girl," I said, nodding to a girl who sat across the cafeteria from us, "what is she doing?"

Megan looked.

"Oh, that's Tamatha Stuart. She's mute. She won't talk, so she does that sign language to communicate. It's so stupid. She's not deaf. I don't know why they pamper her. She should have been given shock treatment. I—what?" she asked me when she saw the expression on my face get more emphatic.

"I know what she's saying with her hands. I understand it!" I said, even surprised myself.

"Really?"

"That's awesome," Lawrence said. "Someone you know must be deaf," he added.

I looked at him. It was as if a thick, heavy door had been opened just an inch or so, and there was light streaming through. I thought I saw a face peeking out at me through the darkness. But who was it?

My eyes began to blink rapidly, uncontrollably. I wanted to see who was behind that door. I felt as if I were struggling to tug that door open just a little bit more, pulling, pulling. . . . I couldn't stand the effort.

"Laura?" he said. "Are you all right?"

"You're upsetting her," Megan said.

"What am I doing? I'm not doing anything," he moaned. "Laura?" he said, turning back to me.

Suddenly, it just came over me. I heard a cry, the cry that had been haunting me ever since I arrived, someone was desperately crying out for my help.

I spun around in my seat and looked behind me and to the sides.

"What is it?" Lawrence asked. "Laura?"

"Someone . . . is crying . . ."

The noise in the cafeteria became the roar of the sea. There was water everywhere. The wind itself was calling my name: *Laura! Laura!*

My heart started to pound. I felt the whole room turn. It was as if I were in a boat and not a chair, and the boat was being tossed violently. I grasped the table.

"No!" I cried. I closed my eyes and felt myself swaying.

"What's the matter with her?" I heard Lulu say.

Lawrence reached over and touched my hand tentatively.

"Are you all right?" he asked. "Laura?" His voice merged with the voice in my mind, especially when he repeated, "Laura?"

I felt nauseated. I started to shake my head and then my whole body began to tremble. I was holding the table so firmly that the dishes began to clank. A glass fell over.

Megan shouted to Lawrence because I was tipping over backward. He seized my chair, but I started to slide off it. My body felt as if it had turned to liquid, all my bones melted. I was pouring toward the floor. Lawrence held me, but I slipped from his grip and fell down, down, down, waving my arms about me. Billy and a female attendant came rushing over to us.

"What's wrong with her? Does she have epilepsy or something?" someone asked. It sounded like Megan.

My tongue was swelling and I couldn't get any air. I felt myself drooling and then I started to scream, or at least I thought I did. Then, all went black.

When I woke this time, I was back in my room. A man in

a white lab coat was taking my pulse and one of the night nurses was beside him.

"She's stabilizing," he said. "Laura? How are you doing?"

I blinked rapidly.

His voice echoed.

"Laura, how are you?"

"Laura . . . Laura . . ."

"NO!" I screamed, or at least I thought I did. My whole body began to tremble terribly. It was as if the bed were coming apart beneath me. "I'm sinking!"

"Hold her!" the man said. "Easy . . ."

There was a pinprick in my arm and then, after a few moments, a wave of darkness washed over me. My body sank deeper and deeper into the bed. I felt like I was going underwater. I tried desperately to stay conscious, but wave after wave of blackness was rushing in, pushing me farther and farther down. The sound of my name drifted off, and then, I was asleep.

When I woke again, there was sunlight streaming through the curtains. I heard the sound of water being run in a sink and then a nurse emerged from the bathroom with a washcloth and a pan. She put the cloth on my face as I blinked and blinked, trying to focus in on something that made sense to me.

"So you're finally awake. Good," she said, twisting her mouth. "You gave everybody a bad time again, I heard."

She lifted the cloth from my forehead and gazed down at me. I opened my mouth, but my voice wouldn't work.

"So, let's hear about it. How are you now? Do you have any pain? Any nausea? Well?" she demanded when I was silent. I shook my head. "Are you hungry?"

I thought about it. I was a little hungry, but when I went to say yes, nothing happened.

"Well?" she asked. "Can't you talk this morning?"

Talk? I thought. Could I ever talk? I tried to speak and only a deep guttural sound emerged. The nurse looked surprised.

"What is it?" she asked.

I lifted my hands and as naturally as people speak, I began to sign.

"What the . . ." She stepped back and watched as I spoke through my hands.

"Yes, I am hungry," I told her, "but where am I?" I asked. She shook her head.

"This is a surprising turn of events," she said, looking quite impressed. "The doctor will be here in an hour. If you want to eat any breakfast, you should get up now," she said.

I signed okay and rose from the bed. I felt groggy, but strong enough to stand.

"Some more clothes were brought here for you last night," she told me. "They're all brand-new apparently. Everything still has a tag on it. Some of it is in the closet and some is in the dresser. Choose what you want to wear, get dressed, and come out to breakfast," she said. "Well?"

I signed okay.

"So you can't talk now, is that it? Fine. I could use a little more quiet around here," she said. "I'll see you in the cafeteria. Get dressed," she ordered and left the room before I could ask her where the cafeteria was.

Confusion resembled a great cloud of smoke circling me. I moved slowly, unsure of myself, making discoveries about the room and the bathroom as if I had never been here before. How long had I been here? And where was here?

I paused in the bathroom and looked at myself in the mirror. The face I saw seemed to change right before my eyes, and for a moment, I thought I was looking at a boy. It only lasted a second or two, but it made my heart pound and took my breath away.

After I dressed, I poked my head out of the room and looked up and down the corridor. The floors gleamed under the rays of sunshine that came through the windows. Suddenly, the door across from me opened and a girl about my age stepped out. She looked sickeningly thin.

"How are you?" she asked softly. "We were all worried sick about you last night."

567

"I don't know," I said with my hands. She started to smile and stopped.

"Why are you doing that?" she asked.

"Doing what?" I signed. She seemed to understand.

"Why are you doing that stuff with your hands, sign language?" she asked. "Has something happened to your voice? Can't you talk?"

I shook my head. She just stared at me, her face so thin her eyes looked like they were floating in their sockets. I could even see the bones in her jaw and cheeks through her thin skin. A thought brought a strange, soft smile to her thin lips.

"You look like you don't remember me," she said and then asked, "Do you?" I shook my head again. "I'm Mary Beth."

"Who am I?" I asked her, pointing to myself and then raising my hands and shaking my head to make her understand my question.

"You don't know who you are?" After I shook my head emphatically, she said, "You're Laura Logan. I don't know anything else about you because you didn't remember anything to tell us when you first came here," she said. "This is terrible," she added, gazing down the hall and looking for someone, as if I were hurt and bleeding.

I rubbed my stomach and indicated my mouth.

"You're hungry?"

I nodded and she relaxed.

"Just come with me," she said. "Come on," she urged, reaching out for my hand. I took her hand and we went down the hallway together to the cafeteria.

"How's she doing?" a dark-haired girl at the table Mary Beth had brought me to asked as soon as we appeared. The handsome boy beside her looked up with interest, as did the young girl on her other side.

"She can't talk. She's using sign language and she's forgotten everything, Megan. I don't mean about herself either. Now she doesn't know who we are, where she is, everything!" Mary Beth wailed.

568

"Oh no," Megan said, gazing back at the attendants who were standing and talking to each other. "They'll put her in the Tower right next to Lydia Becker, for sure. Look, Laura, I'm Megan, Megan Paxton. This is Lawrence and this is Lulu. You're at the clinic. You go up there and get what you want to eat and come back. Act as if you remember everything, okay?"

I looked at Lawrence, whose look of concern impressed me. Then I nodded.

"If you tell them you forgot everything about this place, they'll want to give you some other treatment, something like electric shock maybe. That could mean you'll be going to the Tower!"

I signed question after question, but no one understood. I wanted to know how long I had been here. Why was I here? Where had I come from? And what was this Tower?

"You sure you can't talk today?" Megan asked with a grimace. I shook my head. "Great. You're in deep water, I'm afraid," she said. "It's hard enough around here to protect yourself when you can talk."

"I'll take her to the cafeteria line," Mary Beth offered.

"That's like the blind leading the blind," Megan quipped. "If you help her pick out her food, she'll starve."

"Don't worry. I'll make sure she gets what she wants to eat," Mary Beth insisted.

"I can take her," Lawrence said, rising.

"Me too," Lulu said.

Why was everyone so concerned about me?

"Remember. If you make it look like she's helpless, they'll notice and that will be it," Megan warned. "Sit down, Lulu."

"Just follow me," Lawrence said softly. "I'll do all the talking and you just nod, okay?"

"All of a sudden he can help someone. Before this, he couldn't tie his own shoelaces if someone was watching," Megan remarked with a twisted smile.

Lawrence ignored her and directed me to follow.

"I can understand a little sign language," he said. "And I

can learn the rest fast. Don't worry. I'll protect you," he promised.

After I got my food and returned to the table, I did feel less tentative and insecure. I listened to their conversations and ate. Every once in a while, Lawrence turned to me and asked me how I would say or ask for something through signing. I showed him and he committed it quickly to memory.

Someone else, someone in my past, learned sign language that quickly, I remembered. I could see myself teaching him. Who was he? Everything I did raised another question about who I was and where I belonged, and every question felt like a needle in my side demanding attention.

"You shouldn't be encouraging her," Megan warned. "She won't snap out of it as fast."

"She'll be fine," Lawrence said, smiling at me.

"Listen to him, Doctor Lawrence Taylor. Hang a shingle over your room door," Megan said. She looked at the doorway and then leaned in toward me. "Here comes Mrs. Kleckner. You better not act too stupid," she advised.

"How are we doing now?" Mrs. Kleckner asked after she approached our table.

"Fine and dandy, Mrs. Kleckner. We're an absolutely happy little group of idiots and screwballs," Megan remarked with a fat smile.

"You're not really very funny, Megan. I'm hoping you'll realize that soon. For your own sake, as well as everyone else's," she added.

"Oh, I'll try, Mrs. Kleckner," Megan promised with a false smile on her lips.

Mrs. Kleckner turned to me.

"I understand you've lost your voice."

I looked at Megan and Lawrence and then at her before I nodded.

"Very well," Mrs. Kleckner continued, "you have your session with Doctor Southerby now. Come along, Laura," she said.

570

I looked at the others. Their eyes were wide with concern.

"Good luck with *your doctor*," Megan said as I stood up. "I hope things go better for you *this* time," she added, telling me I had met him before. I smiled, signed my thanks, and left with Mrs. Kleckner.

Doctor Southerby wasn't in his office when I was brought there. Mrs. Kleckner had me take a seat in front of the big desk and then left. I sat quietly waiting, gazing at everything and wondering how it could be that I had been here before. None of it looked even vaguely familiar. A side door opened and Doctor Southerby entered. He smiled softly and went to his desk.

"So," he began as soon as he sat, "you've had a little setback, I understand. Lost your voice?"

I didn't know what else to do, so I nodded.

"You can use sign language," he said. "I know it well."

I felt like I was in a foreign country and had finally found another person who spoke my language. The questions flowed out of me so quickly, my hands could barely keep up. Doctor Southerby's eyes followed and his smile widened and widened.

"Whoa," he cried. "Let's take it one at a time. You're in a clinic for people who have mental and psychological problems. It's a clinic mainly for young people. It was established by a foundation funded by wealthy people and has become one of the more prestigious and successful institutions of its kind in the northeast, if I may say so," he added proudly. "I'm one of the chief therapists here and your case has been assigned to me.

"As we were discussing yesterday, you suffered a serious traumatic experience and it has affected your memory. You have a form of general amnesia, but it is the sort of amnesia that won't last long. I feel confident of that."

"Yes," he said after I signed my question, "when you first arrived here, you could speak, but you couldn't recall anything about yourself."

I signed, "Why can't I speak now?"

"I don't know yet," he said, looking very thoughtful. "I'm just learning about your background myself and the information I need is slow in coming, unfortunately," he said with a grimace. "However, since you know sign language so well, it is something that is obviously in your background. Someone close to you is deaf. Does that jog your memory a bit?"

I thought.

"Yes," I told him, "but I can't remember much about her right now."

"You will. Suddenly, you will see someone else doing it and you'll realize who it is," he promised. "Until then, since you are unable to speak . . ."—he reached into a drawer and came up with a notebook—"I would like you to write down everything you remember; everything you think and anything that occurs to you about yourself, or people here, anything," he said, handing me the notebook.

I took it gingerly.

"I know you have a lot of anxiety. Do you experience flashbacks, hear voices you don't recognize?"

I nodded.

"You're eating well, apparently. That's good. Do you have any numbing, any part of your body that feels detached?"

I shook my head.

"Good. Just so you'll know what to expect from me . . . I'm going to try to get you, slowly, of course, to relieve the trauma you have suffered. We have to undo any unnecessary shame and guilt. It's all right for you to get angry and eventually to grieve, Laura. When you're able to do so, you will return fully to yourself. I might employ hypnosis. We'll see, okay?" he said, his voice soft, comforting.

I nodded.

"That's good. Okay, Laura," he said, "let's do something now. Let's both relax and you tell me whatever comes to your mind . . . words, pictures, anything. Go on," he said, "close your eyes and just let your mind wander."

I did so. Pictures flashed, but each for only a split second. I saw sand and water, faces that I couldn't attach to names, small boats, and cranberries in a bog. I described each thing to him.

"That's good, Laura. That's progress. In a short time, all these apparently unconnected images will start linking up for you and you'll start to find meaning. You're on your way home. I promise," he said.

"The best thing for you to do here is relax. Enjoy our facilities, write in your notebook, and rest. You're going to cure yourself," he said. He sounded so confident and sincere, I felt better.

He talked about other patients with similar problems and how they overcame them to return to active, healthy lives. He assured me that whatever was wrong with me would end and I would never return to the clinic once I left.

"Try to say something to me before you leave today, Laura," he concluded. He got up and walked over to me, taking my hand into his and looking so intensely into my eyes, I couldn't look away. "Go on, say your name. Try," he urged.

I opened my mouth and moved my lips.

"That's it," he coaxed. "Go ahead."

My tongue lifted and fell. I felt the muscles in my neck and throat strain.

"Lawwwww." I started to gag, tears burned under my eyelids, and I felt my cheeks turn red and hot.

"Okay," he said, patting my hand. "Okay. It will come back."

He patted my hand and returned to his chair.

"I have to do some research on you, Laura. I have calls out to gather the information I need. You and I will meet again tomorrow," he said, "and in a week's time at the most, you'll see some dramatic changes. Okay?"

I nodded and smiled. I decided he was a very nice young doctor, someone I could probably trust, only at the moment I had nothing to trust him with except my immediate feelings. He took me out to his secretary.

"Mrs. Broadhaven didn't get to show you some of our facilities yesterday, Laura. She wants to do that now, okay?"

573

I nodded and the pretty woman rose and led me out.

"We have a very nice arts and crafts studio here," she explained. "It's just down the hall from the lounge."

I gazed through the door at some patients watching television, playing chess, and reading. In the rear, a young man was playing Ping-Pong with an attendant.

"Here's the studio," she said, pausing at another door farther down the corridor. I looked in and saw Megan wearing a frock and dabbing roughly at a soft clay figure she was forming. Lulu and Mary Beth were painting with watercolors at a table in the corner. A tall woman with beautiful red hair and a milky white complexion approached us.

"This is Laura," Mrs. Broadhaven said. "I'm showing her around, but she might come right back here," she added, seeing the interest on my face. "Laura, this is Miss Dungan, our art therapist."

"Hi, Laura," she said, offering her hand. "You can choose any format to work with: clay, oils, watercolors, wood. We can make ceramics, too."

I sensed something familiar. I know an artist, I thought, but I couldn't remember his name. Miss Dungan saw how hard I was staring at Megan's sculpture.

"Do you want to try that today?" she asked.

"It might help you remember things," Mrs. Broadhaven suggested.

I nodded.

"I'll bring her right back," Mrs. Broadhaven told Miss Dungan.

She then showed me the library, where I saw Lawrence sitting at the table, poring over a book. He had a small pile of other books beside it. As soon as he saw us, he blushed.

"We're very proud of our library facilities here, Laura," Mrs. Broadhaven said. "It's as good as many small college libraries. Isn't it, Lawrence?" she asked him.

"What? Oh . . . yes," he said. He looked frightened, I thought, and I wondered why. His eyes shifted quickly and I saw that his hand was shaking.

"Well, Laura. What would you like to do? Go back to the

574

studio?" Mrs. Broadhaven asked. Either she didn't see what I noticed about Lawrence or she chose to ignore it.

I nodded, looked back once more at Lawrence, who now had his hands over his eyes, and then we left to return to the art studio. Miss Dungan set me up with a smock and then placed me at a table with a mound of clay. After showing me how to use some of the tools, she went to attend to other patients. Megan, who had been working intently on her piece, paused and came over to sit beside me. She looked at my formless mound and then at me.

"They're hoping you'll do something revealing. You know, something they can analyze. They like to get into your head, dissect you like a frog." She laughed. "I know what Doctor Thomas expects me to say every time I do a piece. He sits back and nods and nods and then asks me what do I think I've made. Without hesitating, I say, 'A phallic symbol.' You know," she added when I didn't respond, "a penis." She laughed. "I don't. I try to make something else, but just because everything I make has some vaguely similar shape . . ."

She paused and shook her head at me.

"How long are you going to be dumb? I talk to myself enough as it is. Can't you talk to me and pretend to be dumb with the others? Forget it," she added quickly. "Do your own thing. Everyone else does."

She looked away and when she turned back, the crazy look in her eyes startled me.

"Today's visitors' day, you know. They'll be around to see their precious children working and playing in therapy. My mother probably won't come. You *know* my father won't. No, you don't know that, but I'm telling you he won't. Maybe my mother will come," she added. She looked at me. "I wonder if anyone will come for you," she said.

And suddenly, that became the most intriguing idea of all.

Visitors came throughout the remainder of the day. Some spent the time with their children in the lobby or rec room, but most went outside and walked in the gardens. I saw that Lawrence's mother and father came to visit him. They were an elegant-looking couple. His father was tall, easily six feet two or three, with graying hair. When he turned my way, I saw he had a strong, handsome face, his features chiseled much like Lawrence's. His mother was an attractive woman who wore her light brown hair in a stylish bob. She wore a pretty flowered dress and shiny black heels. From where I watched, it looked like Lawrence's parents were doing all the talking. Occasionally, Lawrence nodded and then he turned and saw me staring at him and his parents through the window of the art studio. He looked embarrassed, but smiled nevertheless and then moved his hands to wave hello. I waved back and smiled. Both his parents looked my way and Lawrence quickly turned and continued to walk. His mother's gaze lingered on me a moment before she joined him and his father.

After that, I caught a glimpse of Mary Beth walking with her mother. Mary Beth had her head down and her mother was talking so quickly it looked like she was giving a lecturing. Her mother was a very pretty woman, tall and thin with shoulder-length blond hair that curled slightly around her face. She looked like a model or an actress. They disappeared around the corner, Mary Beth never raising her head and her mother never stopping her lecture.

Megan, Lulu, and I remained in the studio working throughout the afternoon. No one came to see Lulu, and Megan let me know that her own mother had sent word she couldn't be here today.

"It's not hard to figure out why she hates seeing me," Megan muttered, sitting at my side again as I worked on my sculpture. "She blames me for what my father did to me. Can you imagine that? She gets a divorce and she blames me for her life now? I know it's true. You don't have to look at me like that. The doctor agrees with me. Oh, he won't come right out and say it, but he's met my mother and he agrees.

"So what? So let her blame me. Who needs her?" she said.

"What did your father do to you?" I signed.

"What?" she said, as if suddenly realizing she had been talking to me. "What are you saying? I can't understand all those stupid hand movements. I don't know why you suddenly can't talk. I thought finally, finally I would have someone with some brains to talk to and then you go and lose your voice and start doing this. What are you saying?"

"She's asking you about your father," Miss Dungan said as she passed us with an armful of colored paper.

"My father?" She turned to me. "Why are you so interested all of a sudden? You think I'm making things up? Is that it?"

I shook my head vigorously.

"Just mind your own business," she snapped and returned to her clay figure. Suddenly, she began pounding it madly.

Miss Dungan came rushing over.

"Megan, what are you doing! Please honey, stop that," she said calmly. Megan continued to batter the clay until it lost all shape. Then she sat down hard in her chair and started to laugh.

"Sorry," she said, "I guess there's nothing to analyze this week."

She laughed again and then began to cry; but strangely, although there were tears flowing from her eyes, her face remained still, her lips unmoving.

"You better take a little rest, honey," Miss Dungan said and put her arm around Megan's shoulders. "Come on," she urged. Megan stood and let herself be led out of the studio.

I returned to my own sculpture for a while and then gazed out the window and saw that Lawrence's parents had gone. He was alone, sitting on a bench, staring in at me.

When Miss Dungan returned, I asked her if I could go outside now.

"I suppose so, sure," she said. "We'll leave your piece just as it is and you can return to it tomorrow, okay?"

I nodded and left the studio. Lawrence looked up and smiled warmly as I came down the pathway.

"Hi," he said. "How's your artwork coming along?"

I shook my head.

"I wouldn't exactly call it a work of art," I signed. He seemed to understand and nodded. I liked the fact that he didn't try to convince me otherwise and fill my head with false ideas about being talented.

"You want to take a walk? If we go down the path there, we can get a view of the ocean."

I turned and gazed in the direction he indicated.

"It's still pretty nice out," he continued. "My parents had to leave early. They had a social function to attend. They usually do."

I turned back to him, hearing his note of displeasure.

"They're not crazy about coming here in the first place. It's an embarrassment. I'm the only member of my family to end up in a loony bin. Oh, I didn't mean it that way," he said quickly. "I mean, I don't think of you as loony. I'm loony, Megan's a real loon, but you're not."

"Something's wrong with me," I signed. I pointed to my head and shook it.

"Whatever's wrong with you will be easily cured. You won't be here anywhere near as long as I've been, I'm sure. Want to walk?"

I was reluctant, but I finally agreed and we started down the path.

"My father's a stockbroker," he said. "Very successful one, too. He's got some high-profile clients, big portfolios. I don't know exactly how rich we are, but I know we're really rich. My mother usually buys whatever she wants. You should see her closet. It's as big as some people's bedrooms. She even has a vanity table in there."

I smiled.

"I'm not exaggerating," he said. "When I was a little boy, I hid out in that closet. She always yelled at me for it. She's got clothes hanging in there with the tags still on them. I don't think she even remembers half the things she buys.

578

"And you should see her jewelry. She's got enough to stock a small store. What about your mother? Have you tried remembering her? Did you live in a big house?"

I thought and shook my head.

"No? That's strange. I bet your mother is probably the first person you're going to remember. Well, there it is," he said, stopping. I looked up.

Through the tall maple trees, I could see the ocean, its blue sheen glimmering in the late afternoon sunlight.

I stepped back.

"What?" he said.

I shook my head.

"You're afraid of the ocean?" He thought a moment. "It has something to do with what happened to you then. I was reading about your problem. I looked it up in our library. That's what I was doing when you came in with Mrs. Broadhaven. The only way you're going to get well is for you to confront what happened," he said. "That's Doctor Southerby's job, to get you to do that."

He looked at the sea and then at me.

"You want to try to get closer? Maybe it will revive your memory and—"

I shook my head emphatically.

"Okay," he said. "We'll go back, huh?"

I nodded, but chanced another glimpse of the water. Images began to parade through my mind: faces, lobster traps, boats, the beach, a cranberry bog, someone singing, and then someone calling my name, whispering at first, and then calling me louder, louder. It seemed like . . . I was calling myself.

I felt my throat tighten with the effort to pronounce someone else's name.

Lawrence's eyes widened as I brought my hands to my neck and shook my head.

"Is something wrong? Are you all right? Laura?"

Impulsively, I threw myself into his arms and buried my face against his shoulder as I sobbed, cried for reasons I

579

couldn't explain. All I wanted to do was cry and keep crying until my well of tears went dry.

At first, Lawrence just stood there with his arms at his sides, not knowing what to do. Then he embraced me slowly and held me closely, kissed my hair, my temples, stroked my back and kept repeating my name.

"Laura . . . Laura . . ."

Finally, my sobbing ended and I pulled back slowly. He looked happy, but very concerned.

"Are you all right now?"

I nodded and he wiped the tears from my cheeks with his handkerchief.

"I better get you back before they come looking for us," he said.

He turned me around and reached for my hand. We started along the path again. This time, I didn't look back at the ocean, not even for a second. I was happy when it disappeared behind us, but I knew that soon, very soon, I would have to return, perhaps by myself, and stare at the water until the truth and my memory broke free of the chains I had thrown around it.

Only then would I get those chains off myself.

13

§

Close Call

I had three sessions with Doctor Southerby the following week. He was happy to see I was following his advice and filling my journal with thoughts and feelings. He spent the first ten minutes reading them and then asking me questions about the things I had written, never insisting I try to answer if I showed any reluctance. I performed my sign language so spontaneously and gracefully, he joked about my having once been deaf. Then he grew serious and returned to the idea that I talked to someone who was deaf on a daily basis.

"That seems logical, doesn't it, Laura?" he asked.

I nodded, even though I felt I'd rather not answer. He had a way of holding his kind eyes on me firmly, but not with intimidation. I felt so captured by that gaze, a gaze filled with sincerity and compassion, that I could barely turn away. His eyes were mesmerizing. In fact, during our third session, he decided he would try hypnosis. I had no idea if he learned anything. One moment, I was staring ahead and the next, I was blinking and wondering how long I had been in his office. Did he get me to speak under hypnosis? If he did, he didn't mention it afterward.

"It's very good that you feel less and less anxious, Laura, especially about being here," he explained after I had agreed to be hypnotized. "Trust is essential if we are to make any progress with your problems."

I smiled and nodded. I did trust him more and more, and I even looked forward to our sessions. Some of the others, especially Megan, thought that was strange.

"It's like enjoying someone putting his fingers through your skull and feeling around in your brain," she said after she had asked me a little about our sessions and saw I was happy talking and listening to Doctor Southerby.

When she heard I had permitted him to hypnotize me, she went bonkers.

"Are you really crazy? When you're out of it like that, you have no idea what he's doing to you. Maybe he took your clothes off," she suggested. I started to laugh and her face crumbled not with anger, but with sadness.

I tried to sign an explanation, tried to tell her how good Doctor Southerby was and how he would never do something like that, but the tears were filling her eyes quickly.

"I thought you were different. I thought you believed me and understood. Everyone else laughs at me."

I shook my head.

"I'm not laughing at you," I signed.

However, the tears were already streaming down her cheeks. She had her hands clenched into tiny fists and for a moment, I was afraid she might hit me.

"You mark my words," she flared. "You'll be sorry you didn't listen to me someday. You will," she concluded, her voice strong and hateful, as if she were pronouncing my death. Then she marched away, her body straight, her arms extended and stiffly swinging like a toy soldier's. Lately, she was doing more and more of that, leaving us all and going off by herself, closing her door in her room or wandering about outside, avoiding people.

My own periods of depression, my feelings of nervousness, had diminished, but not the inner voices and the flashbacks. Doctor Southerby made me think as much as I could about those I had described in my journal. He probed my mind, his suggestions and questions resembling a scalpel in the hands of a skilled and graceful surgeon, knowing just when to push forward, when to pull back. If something became too sensitive, my lips would begin to tremble. In fact, my whole body would start to shake and my heart would pound so hard and fast, I had trouble breathing.

He would stop, touch my shoulder, ask me to close my eyes and take deeper breaths. Then, he would change the subject, and soon, I would relax again. During our fourth session, he had Miss Dungan bring in the needlework I had completed and we talked about the picture, why I was attracted to it and what I thought about when I looked at it.

Most of my free time was spent in the arts and crafts studio now. During my second visit there, I went from sculpture to needlework. That day, I saw another patient sewing quietly in the corner and I walked over and watched her for a while. My fingers felt as if I were doing the work along with her. Miss Dungan noticed my interest and suggested I try it. In minutes I was doing it comfortably.

"From the way you're at that," Miss Dungan said as she nodded gently, "I would safely say you've done it many times before. I guess your fingers don't have amnesia," she said, smiling.

She let me choose my own picture and I had selected one of a little girl playing on the beach. As I filled in her legs, her dress, and her face, the little girl became clearer and clearer in my mind, flashes of her smile, her eyes, and even the sound of her voice popping in and out of my memory. It was someone I knew and loved very much. But who? Her name was on the tip of my tongue and her voice tingled inside my head. All I had to do was think harder.

Yet, every time I started to open one of the secret doors holding the truths about my past, I found it locked up tight. Something in me knew that as soon as I remembered one thing clearly, it would all come tumbling out of the remaining dark places in my mind and with it, one terrible, terrible memory. Sometimes, the effort literally took my breath away and I had to stop, close my eyes, and wait for the trembling and the pain in my heart to pass.

"This is not unusual," Doctor Southerby told me when he saw how distressed I was after he read about this in my journal. "There's a tug-of-war going on inside you, Laura, and one day soon, the side of you that wants you to return to the world will win and it will be over. I promise," he said.

He really made me feel good; he gave me hope.

I discussed most of this with Lawrence, who was there waiting for me after every one of my sessions. He pretended he had just happened to be in the corridor on his way to the library or the rec room. I knew he was pretending, but I didn't mind. I enjoyed teaching him more sign language and then using what I taught him to explain and discuss things with him.

"Maybe the whole world should use sign language, Laura," he told me one afternoon. "When you have to draw a visual idea of your thoughts, you think about it more and don't say as many stupid or cruel things to the people you supposedly love and care for," he said.

I guessed from the way he lowered his eyes and then looked away so I couldn't see the hurt on his face that he was really talking about his parents. Only his mother had visited him this last time and when I asked about it, he said his father had to go off on a business trip.

"It's harder to lie to people through sign language," he continued. "It's a greater commitment because it involves more of yourself. Afterward, it's more difficult to tell people, 'I didn't say that,' or 'That's not what I meant.'"

He turned to me and sighed deeply, smiling through his fog of depression.

"Maybe you're lucky not having anyone visit you," he said. "That way no one close to you can lie to you."

I started to shake my head.

"We've always lied to each other in my family," he continued bitterly. "My mother always says it's better to tell little white lies and avoid unpleasantness. The thing of it is, everyone knows everyone else is not telling the truth, but we

584

all make believe we don't. It's like . . . like we tiptoe over thin ice and it will just take a little nudge of the truth to crack the world under us and drop us into oblivion.

"All I had to do this last time is say, 'I know you're lying, Mom. Dad's not away on any trip. He just wouldn't come this time.' He can't stand coming here. Every time he comes, he wears this sour face, gazes around disgustedly. I know what he's thinking. He's thinking, What's he doing here? What's a son of his doing here?

"I don't want to be here either," Lawrence protested. "I don't. I . . . I don't like being thought of this way. I lost all my friends on the outside. How am I ever going to go back out there? What am I supposed to say when people ask me where I've been and what I've been doing all this time? Most of them know anyway and will just treat me like some sort of leper."

He dropped his head and didn't raise it until I reached out to touch his cheek. Then he smiled again.

"Now that you're here, I guess I don't mind it as much," he said. "At least you listen to me and I'm not afraid to talk to you."

"That's because I don't talk; I just sign, so you can get your words in faster," I signed and he laughed. Then he stopped abruptly.

"I don't laugh with anyone else," he told me. "Really, not even with my parents. Especially not with my parents," he added. "You're a special person, Laura. I know you are. That's why I made myself concentrate and learn as much as I could about sign language. If that's the way you're going to communicate for the rest of your life, I'll be here to understand and talk to you for the rest of mine," he pledged.

The softness in his eyes reminded me of someone else's eyes. Even the sound of his voice was more than vaguely familiar. If I closed my eyes and listened to him talk, I almost . . . almost fell back through the darkness toward the light.

I told Doctor Southerby about Lawrence, about our little

talks, when he asked me if I had made any friends. I asked him about Megan and Mary Beth and Lulu. He didn't go into detail, but just said they all had serious problems, too. He assured me that everyone would get better in time, if they truly made the effort.

"You've got to want to help yourself. That's the key," he lectured. I knew he meant it as much for me as anyone else in the clinic.

I told Lawrence that and he nodded.

"I admit I don't want to help myself as much as I should yet," he said. "Not yet. But," he added quickly, "the day you walk out of here, I'll work hard at following you."

Is that a promise? I inquired.

He nodded, and I was so happy for him that I leaned forward on the bench and gave him a quick kiss on the cheek. His eyes nearly exploded. He raised his hands slowly and touched the place where my lips touched him, as if to confirm they had indeed been there.

From that day forward, Lawrence looked at me differently. His eyes would linger on my face longer. He wasn't afraid to be caught staring at me, and if I did catch him, he simply smiled. Most important, he stopped shaking whenever he was with me. I saw he was growing stronger in small ways, eating better, participating more in the recreational activities, talking more to the others.

One visitors' day, he appeared abruptly in the art studio. Megan, Lulu, and I were the only ones there. Once again, Megan's mother hadn't appeared and Lulu's mother had written to say she had an important legal obligation. Megan told her it probably had to do with her finding another lover.

"She'd rather be with him than with you here in the nuthouse," Megan said.

I wished she hadn't said such a thing. Whenever Lulu had trouble with her family, she acted even younger, behaving like a baby, crying and sulking until she had to be taken to her room.

The moment I saw Lawrence in the doorway, I knew

something dramatic and serious had happened. His face was flushed, but he stood firm, his eyes full of excitement. He hurried across the studio to me. I looked up from my needlepoint, a small, quizzical smile on my face.

"I did it," he bragged and strutted to the window. He looked out at the gardens, at the other patients and their families and then turned back to me. "I burst the bubble today. I risked falling through the ice."

He turned. I held my smile.

"She came without him again. This time it was supposedly because of some major company problem. It's Sunday!" he cried, raising his voice and his arms. "How can there be a major company problem? I told her she was lying for him and she couldn't deny it!"

The commotion caught Megan's attention. She left her mound of clay and approached, her tools still in hand.

"What's going on?" she demanded.

Lawrence turned and looked at her and then at me.

"Nothing," he said quickly.

She stared at him and then at me and then looked at him again.

"Ooooooh, I see," she said, "secrets. You two have secrets now," she said, smirking. Then her face filled with fury, her eyes blazing madly, her lips thinning. "So, keep your stupid secrets. See if I care. See if anyone cares."

"That's right," Lawrence said suddenly, surprising me by not backing down as usual. "We do have secrets. So mind your own business, okay?"

Megan's mouth dropped and she turned to look at me. I tried smiling at her, but she narrowed her eyes and shook her head. There was no retreat in her. A strange smile twisted her lips.

"You two have done it, haven't you?" she asked, stepping toward him.

"What?" He shifted his eyes to me and then to her, stepping back as she stepped forward.

"You've done it, haven't you, Lawrence?" she asked

disdainfully, her smile sharper. "You and Miss Laura Perfect have joined at the waist."

"What? No," Lawrence said, shaking his head more vigorously.

"Sure you have," she pounced. "Where did you do it? In your room? In hers? In the grass? Where?" Megan screamed.

"What's going on over there?" Miss Dungan said, looking up from across the room. She had been helping another patient with his fingerpainting so intensely, she hadn't noticed what was happening in my corner of the room. She hadn't even seen Lawrence enter the studio.

He looked her way anxiously, his eyes full of panic.

"Well, go ahead, Lawrence. Tell Miss Dungan what's going on. Tell her where you two did it," Megan challenged.

Lawrence grew more terrified. He seemed unable to move. It was as if his feet had been nailed to the floor.

I started to sign to him, but he was beginning to tremble harder, faster. Megan laughed. Miss Dungan rose and started toward us. Lawrence looked at me helplessly.

"I'll tell her myself then," Megan said. "I'll tell her what you two have been doing. I'll tell everyone," she taunted and started to turn toward Miss Dungan.

Lawrence rushed at Megan. I raised my arms and managed a guttural noise, but it was too late. He grabbed Megan around the neck. Miss Dungan screamed as he pulled Megan back. Her face turned crimson and she stuck her carving tool into Lawrence's wrist, but he didn't relinquish his grip until Miss Dungan grabbed his arm and I rose to push him away from Megan. Then he charged out of the art studio.

"He's bleeding," I signed at Miss Dungan.

"I know. Megan, are you all right?"

She was leaning against the table, gasping for breath, coughing and rubbing her neck.

"Yes, I'm all right," she managed. Then she blinked hard, as if she were trying to get something out of her eyes before turning back to Miss Dungan. "You saw it," she said. "He tried to rape me."

"What?"

I shook my head when Miss Dungan looked to me.

"He tried to rape me. All of a sudden, he was at me and if I didn't fight him off—" She looked at me. "He raped you, too, didn't he? Tell her! He came into your room one night," she continued, her eyes widening with the elaboration, "and put his hand over your mouth and—"

I shook my head more vigorously.

"No, no," I signed.

Megan stopped, the tears rolling down her cheeks. She took a deep, painful breath.

"Why don't you people believe me?" she asked tearfully.

"Maybe you should go to the infirmary, Megan," Miss Dungan said softly. She stepped up to her and put her arm around Megan's waist. "Come along. Let Mrs. Cohen check you over."

"I'm all right," Megan insisted, pulling away abruptly. "I fought him off. He didn't do anything. But he could have," she added quickly. She fixed her wild, angry eyes on me. "You weren't much help," she told me. Then she spun around and returned to her clay, as if nothing had happened.

Miss Dungan and I watched her for a moment. She was humming and working more vigorously on her clay.

"I have to see about Lawrence," Miss Dungan said. "Are you all right?"

"Fine," I signed, "but I'm worried about Lawrence."

"I'll see about him," she said and went to her intercom.

Lawrence frightened himself more than anyone else. The attendants found him down by the ocean, sitting on a rock. He had walked through the water, soaking his shoes, socks, and pants, and was hugging his knees, his head down, when they located him. He was shaking so badly from his panic and the chill of the ocean water, he had to be taken to the infirmary. Later, I found out his hands were clenched into fists so tightly, he nearly stopped the blood circulation to his fingers and he dug his fingernails into his skin until his palms bled. He had to be put on tranquilizers. They called his parents, but neither his mother nor his father visited. I was worried so much about him, I didn't think much about myself for days and my session with Doctor Southerby didn't go as well as usual.

A week later, Lawrence was released from the infirmary. In the meantime, Megan had behaved as if nothing at all had happened. She hadn't told a soul about the incident and had never brought it up with me. She often abruptly went from being as mute as me to talking incessantly about everything and everyone, mainly at the dinner table. Lulu and Mary Beth inquired after Lawrence and were simply told he wasn't feeling well. In this place, everyone accepted that as enough and didn't follow up with more persistent inquiries.

As if she felt she had to direct her slings and arrows at someone new, Megan zeroed in on different patients in the cafeteria and complained about the way they ate, talked, or moped about. She seemed to know everyone else's problems and always laid the blame on his or her father. She was so cruel to Lulu at times when it came to Lulu's father, I had to intervene, pulling Lulu's attention away and teaching her sign language.

"Why don't you just stop this already," Megan fired at me. "You were talking when you came here. It's just an act, an act to get them all to feel sorry for you. Oh," she said suddenly, her eyes shifting away from me, "look who's better."

Everyone turned to see Lawrence enter the cafeteria. He looked like his old self; unfortunately, that meant that once again he was unsure, timid, eyes downcast. He avoided looking our way and walked directly to the food line, stepping back when another patient went to reach for a second dessert. He didn't come to our table after he had gotten his food either. Instead, he sat at the first table available, one at which two younger boys ate, neither showing any interest in him, nor anyone else for that matter.

"Why doesn't Lawrence sit with us?" Mary Beth asked.

"He's probably too ashamed of himself," Megan said. "He peed in his pants," she whispered to Lulu. "Just like you do sometimes. Did you know that Lulu here has to wear diapers every once in a while?"

"Stop it!" I shouted emphatically with my hands as I stood up.

"What's the matter with you, Laura Perfect?" Megan teased. "You never wore diapers?"

I marched away from the table and joined Lawrence. He looked up with surprise as I sat beside him. I smiled and asked him how he was.

"I'm okay," he said softly, dropping his eyes. "I'm sorry if I embarrassed you."

I forced him to look at me and told him I wasn't embarrassed. Megan was the one who should have been embarrassed. Now she was pretending it never happened.

He shot a quick look her way. She was glaring at us.

"You don't have to worry about her," I continued. "She doesn't want anyone to talk about it. It's almost as if *she* suddenly came down with a case of amnesia."

He looked a little relieved, but I noticed how peaked and tired he was. Later, I learned that was probably an effect of the medication he had been given. It took the better part of another full day before he regained some of his newfound courage and outgoingness. He joined us in the rec room after lunch the next day and watched me play a game of checkers with Mary Beth.

Megan was in one of her mute moods again that day. She had barely uttered a word, and when Lawrence sat down beside me, she looked away and then started singing under her breath. After a while, we all turned to her. She was staring out the window and we heard, "Twinkle, twinkle, little star, how I wonder what you are. Up above the world so high, like a diamond in the sky . . . ."

591

She turned when she realized we were all staring at her.

"My daddy . . . used to come into my room and sing that to me and tell me to look up at the ceiling and the stars would appear. So, I looked while he . . ."

Tears rolled out of her eyes.

"I hate secrets," she said, staring at Lawrence. "I hate having to keep secrets!"

She got up and walked out quickly.

"What's with her?" Mary Beth said.

I shook my head and looked at Lawrence, who gazed after her and then back at me, his face full of sadness and pity. I smiled at him. He didn't hate her for what she had done to him. He truly felt sorry for her.

Megan didn't appear for the rest of that afternoon. At dinner, we all got our food and sat, but she didn't come into the cafeteria. Billy, the attendant, approached our table suspiciously.

"Where's Queen Megan?" he demanded. "She knows what it means if you don't show up for dinner," he said pointedly, directing himself at Mary Beth, who quickly looked down at her lap.

"She said she would be right along," Lawrence told him firmly. Billy raised his eyebrows.

"What are you, her lawyer?"

Lawrence turned crimson. Billy laughed and returned to his position, but he kept looking at our table and at the door.

"I'm going to go get her," I signed to Lawrence and rose as inconspicuously as I could. I left the cafeteria and hurried up the corridor to the residential wing.

Megan's door was closed. I knocked and waited and then knocked again. We weren't able to lock our doors from the inside, so I knew I could enter her room, but she wasn't exactly the type of person who would forgive you for barging in. But I wanted to warn her about Billy and what he would do if she didn't show up soon, so I opened the door slightly and peeked in.

At first I thought she was gone. She wasn't sitting in a

chair or lying on the bed, but I heard what sounded like water running in the sink so I entered the room and knocked again on the door to get her attention. She didn't appear. I walked slowly to the bathroom and gazed in.

There she was, sitting on the closed toilet cover, her arms over the edge of the sink. I stepped forward and looked. Her wrists were under a sinkful of ruby red water, so dark it looked like she had cut off her hands. She gazed up at me, her eyes wet with tears, her cheeks streaked, and she smiled.

"Hi, Daddy," she said. And then she began to sing, "Twinkle, twinkle, little star . . ."

I felt my throat close and then open, as the shock of what I saw hit me. I ran to the door, gasping for breath as I tried to summon up my long-lost voice.

"He . . . hel . . . help!" I screamed, finding my voice. "HELP, HELP! HELP!"

Two male attendants and Mrs. Kleckner came running down the hall.

"What is it? Why are you shouting?"

"Megan!" I cried and pointed. "She's trying to kill herself!"

They sped past me and I fell back against the wall, sliding down slowly until I was crouched along the baseboard. The commotion drew some of the staff from the cafeteria and Lawrence and Mary Beth came out, too. Lawrence saw me sitting on the corridor floor and came hurrying over.

"What happened?" he asked.

"Megan tried to commit suicide," I said gravely. He looked down the hall at the staff gathering around her room and then looked back down at me.

"You've got your voice back," he said.

I nodded. Sometimes miracles happened at the strangest times.

Thankfully, I had found Megan in time. She needed only a day in the infirmary. However, they took her upstairs afterward, instead of permitting her to return to her room and to us. We all felt just terrible for her.

593

"She's probably heavily sedated," Lawrence said at dinner that night.

"When she comes out of it and realizes she's in the Tower, she'll get even more depressed," Mary Beth said. "You know how she is about the Tower," she reminded Lawrence and Lulu. They nodded.

"Maybe she won't be up there long," Lulu said hopefully. Despite the way Megan had often treated her, Lulu really liked and needed Megan.

"You know, when someone goes up there, they usually don't come down," Mary Beth reminded her. Lulu started to cry and rock in her chair.

I reached over and took her hand in mine.

"Maybe it will be different for Megan," I said, stroking her hand. "She's pretty tough and knows how to take care of herself around here, right?"

Lulu smiled and nodded.

"Why give her false hope?" Mary Beth insisted.

"What do you mean?" I asked. "They can't keep her up there forever."

"If they can't make any progress with you upstairs, sometimes they move you someplace else," Lawrence said. "Someplace where they handle only serious cases, not a rich person's country club clinic like this."

"Oh."

"I'm glad you found your voice," he said, smiling. "It's really nice to hear you talk again."

"Yes," Mary Beth said and I noticed she looked a lot healthier—like she had gained a couple of pounds since I had first arrived. Lawrence told me she had made significant progress in that she finally admitted she wasn't overweight. The end of her ordeal was in sight.

I felt bad for Megan. Despite her bouts of nastiness, I missed her. I told Lawrence how I felt when we went for a walk together after my work in art therapy. Lulu trailed along with us. She seemed to be the most lost without Megan, who in her strange fashion had defended and looked after Lulu as much as she ridiculed her.

"Poor Lulu. Maybe we shouldn't call her that anymore, Lawrence."

He laughed.

"I think it's gotten so she wouldn't answer if someone called her Edith," he said.

"I'm going to start doing that. She's never going to get better if we don't help her face reality, too."

"You're right," Lawrence said. "Here you are worrying about everyone else's problems but your own."

"You once told me helping others helps you, too."

"Yes," he said, smiling, "I did, but that was more of an excuse to get you to let me be involved with you more."

"You didn't need an excuse for that, Lawrence," I said and his smile widened.

We sat on our favorite stone bench, the one that had become a symbol of the boundary for me, because beyond it was the hill that led to the view of the ocean, a view that put ice into my veins.

Lulu walked around us, occupying herself with wildflowers.

"I'm looking for a four-leaf clover," she said. "My daddy told me it brings good luck. If I find one, I'll give it to him when he comes to visit."

"Why doesn't her father ever visit her?" I asked.

Lawrence turned to me, a strange look on his face.

"I thought you knew," he said. I shook my head.

"I know her parents got a divorce. At least that's what Megan said."

"Yes, but not long after that, her father was killed in a car accident. Lulu won't believe it. She never went to the funeral."

"Megan never said—"

"Megan can be cruel, but not *that* cruel; at least to Lulu," Lawrence said. "Maybe . . . maybe she didn't want it to be true. She seems to hate all men, especially all fathers, but I think she really wants to love one, to have a real father. We all know what her father did to her. He put her here. Just like my father put me here," he added angrily.

"Who put me here?" I wondered aloud. "You know so much about everyone else, Lawrence. What do you know about me?"

"Nothing more than what you've told me, which isn't much," he said, smiling. "Everyone's asked about you, but it's like you're the top secret patient. A nurse brought you here one night and that's it."

"Yes," I said, "that's it."

I stood up.

"Going back?"

"No," I said firmly. "Going ahead." I started toward the crest of the hill and then paused.

Lawrence came up beside me and took my hand.

"I'm going to confront my demons, Lawrence." Determined, I took another step forward. "I'm going to do it."

"I'll go with you, Laura. Let me help you."

I took a deep breath and nodded. Then I took another step and another, until we were going down the hill. Lulu remained at the crest, watching us. We walked slowly until we rounded the turn in the path and the ocean came into view. It was as if someone had knocked the wind out of me and I closed my eyes as I struggled to take slow, deep breaths. Lawrence squeezed my hand.

"I'm right here," he whispered.

I opened my eyes and we walked ahead. The waves became more vivid, the spray splashing off the rocks, the breeze harder, faster. Seagulls screamed through the sky and swooped down to feed. The scents of seaweed and salt air made my head swim. The ocean's roar grew louder, stronger.

I paused and closed my eyes again. The darkness lifted like a curtain and I saw a young man, tan and strong, standing shirtless on the deck of a boat. He had eyes like mine and his nose and mouth were also similarly shaped. He was waving, beckoning. . . . I looked down. There was a small hand clasped in my own, a girl no taller than Lulu, smiling.

"Laura . . ."

Was that Lawrence or the boy on the boat calling me? I released my grip on the little girl's hand and she started to sign.

"She's deaf!" I cried.

"Who?" Lawrence asked.

I opened my eyes. We were close enough to the rocks and the sea so that the spray reached our faces. I turned to him, my heart thumping.

"I have a little sister who's deaf," I said, "and I have a brother who is . . ."

"What?"

"My twin," I declared and turned away to run back up the hill. I dug into the ground with my feet so hard my legs ached, but I charged up, terrified by the rush of memory. Lawrence called to me, but I didn't turn back. Instead, I kept running, passing Lulu, who looked surprised and confused, and then down the walkway and back toward the clinic.

I burst through the door and charged madly down the corridor, nearly knocking over the janitor who had just finished scrubbing the tile floor.

"Sorry," I cried as I ran toward Doctor Southerby's office. Mrs. Kleckner was just coming out of the staff quarters. She shouted and stepped in my path, holding her arms out so that she could stop me.

"What's wrong? Why are you running through the building, knocking into people? You know that's not allowed," she chastised.

"I've got to see Doctor Southerby right away," I said, gasping for breath.

"You just don't burst in on Doctor Southerby, young lady. There are other patients here. You wait for your appointment," she said.

"No, I have to see him. You don't understand. I have a little sister who's deaf. That's why . . . I know how to sign, and I have a brother—"

"That's wonderful," she said. "Congratulations. Now just turn around and get yourself cleaned up for dinner. You

597

look like a wild woman. You'll frighten the other patients half to death."

"But, I have to see him now!"

"If you don't listen to me, I'll have to have you confined to your room or worse," she threatened. "I don't condone wild behavior here, no matter what's supposedly wrong with the patient. Those who can't follow the rules are placed elsewhere. This is not a high-security clinic for the mentally disturbed," she added.

I stepped away from her.

"No, this isn't, although I know you would like it to be," I said defiantly. "Well, we shouldn't be treated like criminals just because we have mental problems. We're people who have had difficulties in their lives, serious difficulties."

"I know," she said dryly, "overindulgences. Having too much can become a problem. Where do you put everything? How do you handle all the special privileges? Very serious difficulties," she said with a sardonic smile.

"Why are you working here?" I asked, shaking my head. "You don't care about the patients. You have no respect for us. You should be working in a prison hospital. That's really where you belong," I fumed.

"Really? How come all you blue bloods know what's good for everyone else but yourselves? Spare me the career guidance and behave yourself."

I straightened up as if a rod had been inserted in my spine and fixed my eyes on hers.

"I want to make an appointment with Doctor Southerby," I insisted. "I can do that at least, can't I?"

"I'll make the arrangements for you," she said. "Go on, get ready for dinner. You look a mess."

I hesitated a moment, debating. She looked like she was made of stone and if I tried to move her, I would only anger her and delay my visit with Doctor Southerby.

"I have to see him as soon as possible," I said and then turned and walked back toward my room. Lawrence and Lulu had come in and were looking for me.

"Are you all right?" Lawrence asked when he caught up with me outside my room.

"Yes, I just had a real memory and I wanted to share it with Doctor Southerby, but Mrs. Kleckner stopped me and told me to clean up for dinner. She said she would make my appointment for me."

"That's good," Lawrence said. "I'm happy for you, Laura. This might be the beginning of the end of your time here," he said.

"Maybe," I said and went into my room. I was too frustrated and furious to appreciate my progress at the moment.

However, when I looked at myself in the mirror, I saw that Mrs. Kleckner was right about one thing: I did look wild. My hair looked like I had run my fingers through it for hours, my face was flushed, and my eyes were bright with excitement. I decided to shower and change for dinner.

I was just putting on my shoes and going in to brush out my hair when Mrs. Kleckner appeared in my doorway.

"I've made you your appointment," she said. "Tomorrow at ten."

"Thank you," I said.

"Go to room one-oh-one in the morning," she added and started to leave.

"One-oh-one? But that's not Doctor Southerby's office," I cried. "Why do I have to go there?"

She turned back to me slowly.

"Your case has been transferred to Doctor Scanlon," she said, not without some pleasure.

"But I don't want to be transferred. I want to talk to Doctor Southerby," I said. My heart was racing. Why would I be transferred now?

She sighed and rolled her eyes toward the ceiling.

"I want, I want, I want. Don't you people have any other words in your vocabulary? It's not important what you want; what you *need* is decided by the people in charge here," she said. "Your transfer to Dr. Scanlon has been decided and that's that," she added, her words hammering into my brain.

"I won't talk to anyone else but Doctor Southerby," I insisted just as firmly. I faced her with all the defiance I could muster.

She stared at me a moment and then stepped toward me, a cold smile on her face.

"If you refuse your therapy, you'll have to be transferred upstairs, and if we can't help you upstairs, you'll be transferred to a different sort of institution, one that suits your needs better," she said. "Believe me, that's what will happen." She started to turn away.

"But Doctor Southerby is helping me," I moaned. How could I fight such raw power over me?

"Doctor Scanlon is just as good. In fact, he's Doctor Southerby's superior. You should be grateful you've been given the opportunity, that he has made time for you, but being grateful for things is not in the character of most of the patients here. Why should you be any different?" she added. "Don't be late for dinner," she warned.

She left me staring after her, wondering what I had done to deserve to be transferred to Dr. Scanlon. After all, getting my memory back wasn't something to be punished for. Was it?

14
&

Out of the Shadows

My mind wandered all through dinner that night. I kept drifting back to the memory of walking with my little sister on the beach toward the boat where my twin brother was waving, beckoning. The images burst like flashbulbs in the backdrop of my empty and dark mind: a tiny smile, a lobster trap being pulled up from the bottom of the sea, castles in the sand, starry nights on the beach, and the deep voice of a man I knew must be my father reading, reciting. It sounded like a chant, and then the woman I knew must be my mother singing a lullaby. My early memories mingled with later ones in a hodgepodge of faces, voices, and sights. I felt like I had fallen into a giant crossword puzzle. I was just another letter searching for the others that joined me to an entire word: family. The letters spun around and around in my head until they spelled out a name.

"May," I suddenly said.

"What's that?" Lawrence asked. Everyone stopped talking and looked at me.

I turned to him.

"Her name is May."

"Whose name?" Lulu asked.

601

"My little sister. Her name is May," I said more enthusiastically. "I just can't think of my brother's—"

"Easy," Lawrence said, reaching to touch my hand. "Don't try to remember too much at once."

I looked at his concerned face and nodded.

"It must be exciting for you, though," Mary Beth said, "regaining your past, your identity. Pretty soon, it will all come back to you."

"Yes." I nodded. "Yes, it will. Doctor Southerby was right."

I finished my dinner quickly because I had let most of it get cold while I sat there thinking. After dinner we usually went to the rec room to watch television, read, or play board games. This evening I didn't feel like doing any of those things. I was too excited by the closeness of my memories. I just wanted to sit in a corner by myself and struggle with images and words until I put together more of the puzzle.

Mary Beth, feeling sorry for Lulu, spent more time with her, playing the games with her that Megan used to play.

Lawrence sat across from me reading *A Tale of Two Cities*. He read a lot, and when he talked about some of the books he read, I remembered having read them, too.

"You must have been a good student," he remarked, "to have remembered all the characters."

Now I wondered. Was I a good student? Where did I go to school? Who were my friends? What did I want to become? Not having the answers to the simplest of questions had become more than an irritation. I sat there feeling as if an explosion might happen any time in my mind and send me rushing back to my past. I guess I looked like a hen about to lay an egg, because Lawrence suddenly looked up from his book and laughed.

"I wish you could see the expression on your face, Laura. You look so poised, so tense sitting forward like that. You look like you might jump up and yell 'Eureka!'"

"It's the way I feel. The images keep floating by, circling, circling, drawing closer. I can hear my mother's voice, my father's, too, and I'm beginning to see their faces. It's like a continually growing light is bringing them out of the darkness. Does that make any sense?"

"Yes," he said. "Actually, it makes a lot of sense, Laura. You're one of the really lucky ones here. You're going to get better," he said, "and very soon," he added, not without a little sadness in his voice.

"So will you."

"Yes, I will," he said. "I'd like to meet you again on the outside and do something . . . normal, like take you to a movie or go dancing. Something."

"Me, too," I said, smiling, "but who knows where I live? Maybe it's hundreds, thousands of miles from where you live."

"Distance wouldn't matter to me." He looked at me intently, his eyes burning bright.

Noticing the way he gazed at me made me wonder if I had had a boyfriend before my accident. I knew Lawrence would be disappointed, but that wasn't what kept me from remembering. I realized it had to be something else. But what? Why did my heart start to pound just at the idea?

Suddenly Mary Beth got up and came over to us. One of the younger girls had been talking to her and what she said made her look unhappy.

"Denise says she overheard Billy and another attendant talking about Megan. She says they said Megan's mother is having her transferred to a real nuthouse. From the way they described it, it doesn't sound nice. They called her a straitjacket case." She looked back. "Lulu's very upset. She heard most of it. Now she's just sitting there sucking her thumb. I don't know what to do. I don't want her to end up in the Tower, too."

"Poor kid," Lawrence said. "And poor Megan."

"When does she stop being a victim?" I asked aloud.

Lawrence fixed his eyes on me thoughtfully for a moment.

"When she wants to," he said.

"You think she wants to be like she is?" Mary Beth asked him angrily.

"I've been doing a lot of reading lately about some of this. Megan feels responsible for what happened to her. She blames herself and she looks for sympathy. It's all she knows how to do at the moment," he said. "The doctors have got to make her see what happened to her was not her fault."

"Maybe you're talking about yourself," Mary Beth snapped, her eyes furious.

He gazed up at her.

"Maybe," he admitted and then looked at me. "Maybe I'm talking about all of us."

I shuddered and looked around at all the other patients. Someone from the outside sticking their head in the doorway to gaze at us might not easily understand how troubled most of us were. For the moment, everyone looked as normal as anyone on the outside—playing cards, games, watching television and laughing, talking, and reading.

It struck me how difficult it was to know about someone simply by looking at them. Maybe it took years and years before anyone really knew anyone. Lawrence was growing more and more attached to me, but what if all that I remembered would devastate him? What if I were exactly like the people he despised? Would my true self, my identity, come rushing back over me and wipe away any identity I had established with him? He and I were truly strangers, a pair of lost souls who happened to meet for a while and soon had to return to our bodies, and those bodies might not be so attracted to each other afterward, I thought.

"I feel like going outside," I said and stood up.

Mary Beth and Lawrence looked at each other and then smiled.

"What? Why are you two looking at me like that?"

"You can't go outside now," Mary Beth said. "The doors are locked, and if you tried to open them, the alarms would go off."

"We *are* prisoners here," I moaned. "All I want to do is walk in the garden, look up at the stars, feel the night air.

604

What's so terrible about that? Why won't they let us out at night?"

"It's dark," Mary Beth said. "They can't keep watch over you as easily."

I flopped back into my chair, sullen, my arms wrapped around me.

"I could get you outside," Lawrence whispered.

Mary Beth widened her eyes.

"No, Lawrence. You'll get into big trouble."

"How?" I asked.

"The cafeteria staff is gone by now. They go in and out through a side entrance off the kitchen. It's not locked and there's no alarm on it."

"How do you know that?" I asked.

He hesitated and then leaned toward me.

"I did it once. I thought I was going to run away, but the moment I stepped out the door, I froze," he confessed.

We were silent a moment.

"I'm going back to Lulu," Mary Beth said. The conversation was obviously frightening her. Lawrence watched her return to the table before he continued.

"I know how she feels. When darkness falls and the doors are locked, the outside of the building feels and looks like the outside world. It's as if the boundaries of this place shrink. She's not ready to return, so she's even afraid of the thought of going out at night," he explained.

"You know a lot about everyone, Lawrence. You could study and become a doctor yourself," I said. I really meant it. He blushed at the compliment.

"It's just that I spend a lot of time in the library. Most of the people here don't know what's available." He leaned toward me again. "There's even a book by the head doctor, Doctor Scanlon," he said. *Causes of Family Dysfunction.* After I read it, I thought he was using my family as his resource material for the book."

I knew he was waiting for me to comment, but I couldn't stop this feeling of restlessness. It felt like a hive of bees was buzzing inside me. I had to see the stars, feel the night air.

"Will you take me to the kitchen?" I asked finally.

"Really?"

"I want to go outside and look up at the stars. I think it might help me. There's something about the stars. . . . Something that's teasing my memory," I explained. "It would mean a lot to me."

He grew serious.

"All right," he said after a moment's thought, "we'll do it." He gazed at the attendants. "You go out first so we don't look suspicious. Go to the bathroom, wait a minute, and then come out. I'll be down the hall and if it's all clear to the cafeteria, I'll wave you on. Are you sure you want to do this? They could send you or me or both of us upstairs and you know what that could mean," he added.

"I don't want to get you into trouble, Lawrence. Maybe you should just tell me where it is instead of showing me."

"No," he insisted. "I want to do this for you. Go ahead. Go to the bathroom and give me a minute."

I still hesitated. He nodded toward the door, urging me on. I looked at the attendants and then rose as quietly as I could. Nevertheless, one of the attendants gazed at me as I approached the door. I smiled at her and mouthed the word "bathroom." She smiled back at me and I left the room. I waited just as Lawrence had told me and then I stepped out of the bathroom. The hallway was empty, but up toward the cafeteria, Lawrence appeared, stepping out of a doorway. He gestured for me to hurry.

I practically ran to him and we went through the doorway and then into the cafeteria. All the lights were out now, but there was enough of a glow from the lights outside to silhouette all the tables and chairs so we didn't bump into anything and make any noise. Lawrence moved quickly to the kitchen doors, then held up his hand for me to stop and be still as he listened. He slowly opened the doors.

There was a small light on over the stove. From what we could see, there was no one around.

"This way," he whispered. We walked through the kitchen to the pantry and then to a small hallway. "That's it," he said, nodding at a metal door at the end of the hallway.

"Thank you," I said. I approached the door slowly and then looked back at him.

"They're going to start looking for you soon, Laura. When they don't find you in the bathroom, there's going to be trouble."

"If they ask, tell them I went to my room for something," I said. "I won't be long."

"I'd like to come with you," he said, but he seemed incapable of taking another step forward. "It's just that . . ."

"It's all right. You've done enough, Lawrence. Go back before you're missed, too. I'll be fine," I said.

I reached for the door. When I opened it, I hesitated, afraid there might be an alarm he didn't know about, but nothing happened except the cool night air came rushing in at me.

"If you don't come right back—"

"I will. I promise," I said.

I could see that he was shaking. He wanted to pierce that invisible border so much. I stepped out and closed the door behind me quickly to end his suffering as much as to give myself the courage. For a moment, I simply stood there, listening to the sounds of the night. Then I walked away from the building so I could get away from all the lights.

It was a night filled with stars, clear and sharp so that the constellations were easy to locate. My eyes traced the length of the Big Dipper. The mere sight of the luminous dots sparkling above me took my breath away. I had to sit. I didn't even notice the coolness anymore. Words, pictures, and thoughts were rushing at me like shooting stars themselves, approaching and then veering away just when I was about to understand something or see something clearly.

I closed my eyes and sat back, my arms stretched out, my hands open, palms up, waiting to be touched, to accept my identity and everything that would follow. I thought I felt another hand in mine and I could hear a voice, a young man's voice, whispering, his lips so close I could almost feel them brushing against my ear.

I moaned. His face began to rise out of the black pit of forgetfulness, first his eyes and then his lips and then—

"What the hell do you think you're doing?" I heard and opened my eyes to see Billy standing there, smoking a cigarette. He had a wry smile on his face. "Huh?"

"Nothing," I said.

"How did you get out here?" he asked sharply.

"I just wanted to see the stars," I said. I started to stand and he stepped toward me, flicked his cigarette, and continued to move until he was between me and the building.

"Tell me how you got out," he demanded.

"I just found a door that wasn't locked and walked out," I said. He was close enough so that I could see his eyes narrow suspiciously.

"Just found a door, huh? Are you sure you didn't come out here to meet someone? Huh? Someone named Arnie by any chance?"

"What? Who?" I said, shaking my head.

"Arnie's had his eye on you."

"I'm not meeting anyone. I don't even know who Arnie is," I insisted and tried to go around him, but he stepped quickly into my path.

"I know how you young girls can get, locked up like this, away from your boyfriends," he continued, drawing closer. I retreated a few steps. "Arnie's a joke. I know how to treat my girls." The right corner of his mouth rose into an impish, lusty smile.

He reached out and put his hands on my waist.

"Let me show you," he said, pulling me toward him and bringing his lips toward my mouth. I turned away just in time and started to struggle as his hands moved over my ribs toward my breasts.

"Let me go!"

"Come on. There's nothing really wrong with you," he said, trying to get me to turn my mouth to his. "You're the prettiest girl here. I've been watching you ever since you arrived here, and I know you've been looking at me, too. Come on," he urged, cupping my breast with one hand while the other lifted my skirt.

I squirmed and struggled.

"If you don't cooperate, I'll turn you in," he threatened. "I'll get you and whoever helped you into big trouble. You'll end up in a straitjacket like Megan. Stop fighting," he insisted. "Stop it!"

I was afraid so I stopped squirming and his hand moved up my leg, over my panties, his fingers tracing the trim along the edge and then he lifted them away. I sobbed as he ran his fingers over me.

"You're sweet," he said, putting the tip of his tongue in my ear.

"Please," I pleaded.

"I'm not going to hurt you. You'll like this," he said, moving me back to the bench. I could sense he was undoing his trousers with his left hand as his right continued to move over my breast and then moved to undo the buttons of my blouse, slipping in to struggle with my bra.

"You're beautiful, so beautiful," he muttered.

I started to cry and to pull away again.

"Laura, don't make me angry," he said, stopping my resistance.

Suddenly, both of his hands were under my skirt. He pulled my panties down as he nudged me onto the bench. I was afraid to scream. I thought I would faint and then . . . someone whispered my name. Although the voice wasn't loud, it was close.

"Laura!" Billy froze, still holding his hands on my thighs. "Laura, you better come back inside."

"Who the hell's that? Lawrence?"

"Let me go," I said, pulling free and stepping away from him. I pulled up my panties quickly.

"LAURA!"

"Get out of my way," I told Billy. He thought a moment, looked toward the building, and then let me pass.

"You tell anyone about me and I'll tell about you," Billy cried as I ran toward the kitchen doorway. Lawrence was standing there with the door open. I ran toward him.

"What's wrong?" He looked at me aghast, jumping back as I pushed him out of the way and slammed the door.

"Let's get back to the rec room," I said. I didn't want him knowing about Billy and doing anything rash. It would only get him in trouble, I thought. It struck me that even in her madness, Megan might not have been so wrong about some of the men in this place.

Lawrence caught up with me outside the cafeteria and seized my hand, turning me back to him.

"What happened out there?" he demanded. "You look like you've seen a ghost. You're so pale and——"

"I almost . . . remembered someone," I said. "Someone special."

"Special?"

"Someone very special," I added.

He understood. His eyes flinched with pain and he released my hand.

"Oh. Well that's good," he said. Then he smiled. "That's good, only . . . I wish that someone were me."

I woke the next morning feeling as if my bed had been a boat adrift on the sea as I tried to sleep. That was how much I had tossed and turned. I was exhausted, drained. It was as if all the memories that had drifted away had come back during the night and added weight to my head. They lay in waiting now, bunched in a knot, anticipating my unraveling them and returning them to their rightful places.

I strained to sit up, my head spinning for a moment. I grew so dizzy, I lost my breath. When something like this had happened earlier, Doctor Southerby described it as an anxiety attack. He advised me to try to relax, take deep breaths, and concentrate on something pleasant.

Even after I had done what he had advised, my head still felt like it might just snap off my neck. I wobbled when I walked and a number of times, stopped to press my hand to

610

the wall to steady myself. My stomach was hollow, empty, but I had no appetite. When I gazed at myself in the mirror, I saw how drained I looked, how pale my face was and how my eyes were empty, without thoughts behind them, orbs of glass that merely reflected whatever was in front of me.

My hands shook when I went to wash my face. Had I caught Lawrence's panic attacks? I had a ten o'clock appointment with Dr. Scanlon today. I realized I was afraid, afraid of having to meet and confide in a new doctor, especially after it took me so long to trust Doctor Southerby.

Somehow, I managed to get myself to breakfast, although I couldn't remember walking there. I must have looked like someone floating in a dream, sleepwalking her way through the clinic. Everyone was there already and starting to wonder about me.

"You don't look so good," Lawrence said.

I blinked and realized I was standing in the middle of the cafeteria. He was just heading back to the table with his tray.

"I don't feel so good this morning."

"Why don't you sit at the table and I'll go get you what you want," he offered.

"Thanks, but I'm not that hungry. I'll be all right," I said and went to the line.

I barely picked at my breakfast. Lawrence grew more and more concerned about me.

"Maybe you should go see the nurse," he said.

"No, I'll be all right. It will pass," I assured him, even though I wasn't so sure myself.

He wanted to stay with me and be sure I was okay, but he had his therapy session right after breakfast and had to leave. He did escort me to the rec room lounge before he went off to talk to his therapist.

As the hour of my first meeting with my new doctor drew closer, my heart began to thump and my dizziness became so intense, I had to sit with my eyes closed and wait for the spells to pass. Finally, I felt someone nudge my arm and looked up at Mrs. Kleckner. She was squinting, her forehead creased in thick folds. Her complexion was as gray as her hair, the tiny veins at the crests of her bony cheeks more vivid and more like crimson spiderwebs than ever.

"It's nearly ten o'clock. You're going to miss your appointment," she said.

"I don't feel so good," I groaned.

She stared down at me.

"Do you have any pain?" she asked.

"Not pain exactly. I have these dizzy spells and feel nauseated every once in a while." I put my hand on my stomach.

She lifted my wrist and took my pulse. Then she felt my forehead. The palm of her hand was clammy, cold, and rough.

"You're fine," she said.

"But I'm sick. I feel very sick," I insisted.

"It's all part of your condition. That's why you have to see the doctor," she concluded abruptly. "Get up. I'll escort you to his office. Come on. He's a busy man. You should count yourself one of the luckier ones to have Doctor Scanlon look into your case. Frankly, I think there are a number of far more serious patients for him to consider, but I'm not the one who gets to make that decision. Unfortunately."

She held out her hand. Reluctantly, I took it. I was afraid I might topple over if I didn't. After I stood, she put her hand behind my back and gave me a firm push, keeping the pressure against my back until I started walking out of the room. I felt a little stronger as we continued down the hall. My eyes went longingly to Doctor Southerby's closed office door as we passed it.

"Keep going," she said. "Come along. The clock is ticking. Even the wealthy can't bribe Father Time," she muttered.

We stopped at room 101 and she opened the door for me.

"Laura Logan," she announced as I entered.

A small woman in her late fifties looked up from her desk.

Her light brown hair was streaked with gray and she had gelatinous dull brown eyes hidden behind a pair of thick-rimmed glasses with rather large lenses. Her thin nose had a bump at the bridge that seemed to have been made specifically for her glasses. She stretched her uneven lips a bit in a weak effort to smile and turned to find a folder on the desk.

"One moment, please," she said, rose, and walked to the inner office door. She wasn't much more than five feet tall, wide in the hips with thick calves barely visible beneath the hem of her lavender knit dress. She knocked, entered, and closed the door behind her. A moment later she reappeared.

"The doctor will see you now," she told me.

"Behave yourself," Mrs. Kleckner advised and released her grip on my elbow.

I glanced at her disgruntled face and then walked into the office, past the receptionist, who stood like a statue, her back straight, her shoulders against the door. It was as though she were afraid I might touch and contaminate her. She stepped out and closed the door as soon as I had entered. I looked back and then turned to Doctor Scanlon.

Now that I was in his office confronting him, I recalled seeing him in the building a number of times, but I had never thought of him as a doctor, much less the head doctor. I thought he was always in a great hurry and imagined him to be some sort of salesman. He never looked at anyone in particular or smiled, nor had I ever seen him in a conversation with a patient, as I had other therapists, especially Doctor Southerby.

Doctor Scanlon wasn't much taller than his receptionist. He had hair the color of weak tea. The strands were so thin his scalp was visible and I could see that his head was covered with spots that looked like enlarged freckles.

At the moment, Dr. Scanlon had his back to me and was gazing out his window. His office faced the rear of the building and the pathway that led down toward the ocean. It was where I had sat on the bench the night before, when Billy had accosted me.

He turned and looked at me, his hazel eyes wide with

interest, but an interest that gave me the feeling I was under a microscope.

"Take a seat please," he ordered, nodding to the chair in front of his desk. "I like my patients to face me during their initial consultation. Later, you can lie on the couch if you like. Patients," he continued, pronouncing the word as if it designated an alien species, "can sometimes free associate easier when they're lying down. Did you sit or lie on the couch with Doctor Southerby?" he asked quickly after I sat.

"I sat," I replied.

He nodded and then gazed down at the folder his receptionist had brought in before I had entered. Still standing, he turned the pages, reading as if I weren't even there. Then he nodded and closed the folder. He dropped himself into his oversized chair, folded his hands on his desk, and leaned toward me.

"I'm Doctor Scanlon and I'm going to try to help you," he began.

"Why can't I stay with Doctor Southerby?" I demanded in response.

He didn't answer immediately. First, he closed his eyes, and held them that way for a moment, as if my question had given him great pain, and then opened them.

"Doctor Southerby works at another clinic as well as here. Actually, he has more responsibility at the other clinic. His patients at the other clinic now need more of his time and he had to cut back on his responsibilities at this clinic," Doctor Scanlon explained with obvious reluctance.

"We are a bit short of professional help these days," he continued. "Normally, I don't take as direct a role in the treatment of our patients. I'm here to consult and assist and confirm a diagnosis and treatment, but he left a gap and a gap must be filled," he added, giving me what I thought must have been his best efforts at a smile. I didn't think I liked being referred to as a gap.

"So," he went on, leaning back in his chair now, "after you were brought here, you were diagnosed with psychogenic amnesia and Doctor Southerby was helping you return to

614

your past, helping you find your identity. I see from his notes that he was happy with your progress."

"I remembered more yesterday," I said quickly. I wanted to get this session over with as soon as I could. I felt very uncomfortable. It was clear to me that Doctor Scanlon didn't have Doctor Southerby's sincerity. He saw me less as a person and more as a patient, another statistic. In my way of thinking, the patients were lucky he usually didn't take a direct role in their treatment.

"Oh? And you had some sort of a reaction to that, I see. I have a report here," he continued, opening the folder again, "that you exhibited some acting out yesterday."

"Pardon me? Acting out?"

"You were running wild in the corridors, nearly knocked over a custodian, screamed hysterically, made demands, and nearly had to be restrained."

"I was excited. I wanted to see Doctor Southerby," I said. "I didn't mean to be loud, and I don't think I needed to be restrained."

"Umm-hmm," he groaned, without looking at me. He continued to stare at the papers before him. How quickly Mrs. Kleckner had written me up, I thought.

"I wasn't hysterical. I was excited about my memories," I added firmly.

He did smile, but it wasn't warm.

"You're here because you're having trouble evaluating and controlling your own behavior, Laura. It's best we give consideration to the way the professional staff evaluates your behavior, don't you think? Now, what was it that got you so excited?" he asked, but looked down at the folder again.

"I remembered my little sister's name and I remembered I had a twin brother," I blurted, impatient with the pace of things. If he kept reading something after everything I said, I would be here all day, I thought. And besides, why hadn't he prepared for me better?

"Really?" He fixed his eyes on me. "What else did you recall?"

"Visions of faces, memories of voices I know belong to my parents. I think we have something to do with lobster fishing and we have a boat and we live near the ocean and my little sister is deaf," I said, trying to contain my exuberance so it wouldn't be misinterpreted. However, as I told him these things, they began to reappear in my mind. My heart began to pound again and I closed my eyes.

"Why do you think you had forgotten them and yourself?" he asked.

"I don't know."

He sat back, again lifting the corners of his lips into that arrogant smirk.

"Well, I can see from Doctor Southerby's notes that you have at least come to the understanding it might have something to do with an event that disturbed you greatly. What we call psychological trauma. Is that still true?"

"Yes," I admitted, my lips trembling again.

He leaned forward, once again fixing me under his microscopic gaze.

"You look very tired. You didn't sleep well last night?"

"No," I said. "I kept waking, hearing voices, hearing someone call, someone who sounded like me. And then I felt very cold. It was as if I . . ."

"What?"

"I was soaking wet," I said, realizing just at the moment exactly what it was I had felt. "Yes, that's what it was: something to do with water . . . the ocean."

His eyes widened.

"I see. I don't like this," he suddenly added. "Take a deep breath and try to stop yourself from thinking about these things for the moment."

"What? What do you mean? Stop? Why should I stop?" I fired my questions like bullets that seemed to just bounce off his coldly analytical face.

"I don't like what's happening to you physically. It's classic. You're rushing back too quickly, I'm afraid. You're in danger of crashing into your trauma and that could cause irrevocable damage, psychological damage. There are a number of similar cases in my ward for severely disabled patients. Some have become comatose and live off intravenous feeding, and some have to be led around like lobotomized people, mere shadows of themselves, never smiling, never laughing, blind and deaf, the walking dead. You don't want that to happen to you, do you?"

"No," I said, terrified. "Could something like that really happen to me?"

"Of course it could. I wouldn't tell you otherwise. I read here that you've already lost your ability to speak once. I'm telling you not to frighten you as much as get you to be more cooperative. I like a patient who wants to cooperate with his or her own treatment. It makes it easier for all of us, especially the patient."

He widened that short, tight smile.

"The brain is the most complex part of our bodies. There are layers and layers of conscious and unconscious thoughts. Your memories are like buried treasure right now," he continued, "and the pathways to them have been shut down. If we reach too quickly or too clumsily for them, they could fall deeper and deeper into the abyss. We must be very, very careful how we go forward."

He paused and flipped through the folder again, shaking his head with disapproval.

"I see that Doctor Southerby failed to prescribe any medication for you. From the way you've described your nights, I think it would be wiser at this stage if we did. I want to be very careful with you, Laura. You're very tender, very sensitive, raw at this moment, and we have medication that can cushion you, protect you."

"I don't like taking medications."

"No one likes taking them, except those who become addicted to them, of course," he added. He wrote something on a pad.

"Won't I ever see Doctor Southerby again?" I asked mournfully.

"Hopefully, you will be cured and gone by that time," he said. "I'm sure you'd like that better, wouldn't you? You do

617

want to go home, home to that little sister who needs you, and your twin brother and your parents, who I am sure miss you."

"Well, where are they then?" I asked. "Why don't they come to see me?"

My question startled him.

"In your case, it is not advisable just yet. Too much too soon, as I said, could cause you to have a breakdown and do what I just described: drive your past even farther away."

"Why?"

He hesitated.

"I'm not sure it's wise to tell you that just yet."

"I have to know. Why?" I insisted.

"Very well. It's because what happened to you is something you blame yourself for. You are the way you are because of guilt," he explained.

"So then, whatever happened was my fault? What did I do that was so terrible?"

"Maybe nothing," he said, "or maybe something that contributed to a tragedy," he continued. "You have to proceed in steps. First, gradually return to yourself and then deal with the guilt. Okay?"

"No. It's not okay. Why doesn't my family come to see me?" I exclaimed.

"There are frequent reports," he said.

"Reports? I would never be satisfied with only reports. Did I do something that hurt them? Is that why I suffer this guilt?"

"You know it's better if you make your own discoveries," he said rather dryly.

I thought for a moment. Could it be that my parents weren't any better than Lawrence's or Megan's?

"No, I don't want to wait anymore. I want to know everything, and now," I said.

"Miss Logan—"

"And I want to see Doctor Southerby. I have to see him. I have to tell him what's happened. He can help me. I know

618

he can help me. Please." I started to cry, my sobs growing stronger, longer with every passing second.

"Miss Logan, get hold of yourself."

"WHY . . . DON'T MY PARENTS . . . COME TO SEE ME?" I screamed.

He pushed a button on his desk and then he rose. The office door opened and Mrs. Kleckner and a male attendant came rushing in. The look in the attendant's eyes frightened me.

"We're acting out again," Doctor Scanlon announced, as though he and I were conspirators. "I think it would be better for now if she went upstairs."

"Upstairs?" I said, looking at them. "NO!"

I leaped up and stepped away from them, shaking my head.

"Easy," the attendant said, moving slowly toward me. "My name is Arnie. Don't worry, I'll take good care of you."

"I'm not going to the Tower!"

"Whoever gave that floor that ridiculous name?" Doctor Scanlon asked Mrs. Kleckner.

"One of our patients, I'm sure, Doctor." She turned to me. "Now, don't make this any harder on yourself than it has to be. You have to do what the doctor says. Come along," she said.

I shook my head.

"Please, I'll be good. I swear I'll be good. I'll go back to my room. I won't complain. I won't ask for Doctor Southerby anymore. Leave me alone. Please," I pleaded.

"Now, now, don't be afraid," Doctor Scanlon said. "We're here to help you, Laura. We won't let anything bad happen to you. You know, you have a grandmother, too, and she would be even more upset than your parents if we did anything to harm you," he added with a cold smile.

"My grandmother?"

Flashes of an older woman standing outside a car, looking in at me, shaking her head with disgust, returned. She had

619

sent me here and I couldn't recall any expression of love in her angry face. What had I done to displease my whole family?

"NO!" I cried. "Stay away from me. Leave me alone." I held my hands out.

Arnie came around behind me and swiftly brought my arms down to my sides. I had little strength to fight him and soon he held me tightly in his grasp. Doctor Scanlon rushed around the desk and Mrs. Kleckner pulled up the sleeve on my blouse. I struggled and squirmed, but Arnie was too strong. Doctor Scanlon poked me with a syringe.

"You're going to be fine. Everything will be all right," he murmured. "Take it easy. Relax. That's it."

"My head," I moaned, "feels so heavy. It's felt so heavy all morning."

"That's right. Close your eyes. Get a wheelchair," he ordered.

Moments later, I felt myself being lowered into a wheelchair and then a strap was pulled tightly around my waist. Arnie's strong hand kept my shoulders back when I tried to sit forward.

"Just take it easy," Mrs. Kleckner said.

"Put her in three-oh-seven," Doctor Scanlon said.

As they began to wheel me away, I had barely enough strength to utter one last request.

"I want . . . Doctor Southerby. He can help me. I want to see him."

"I want, I want, I want," Mrs. Kleckner chanted behind me. "That's all you patients ever say."

Arnie laughed. I heard an elevator door open and opened my eyes as they wheeled me in. The door closed. Mrs. Kleckner smiled down at me.

"I knew this one belonged upstairs," she said.

And then, all went black.

15
☙

I Remember You

When I opened my eyes again, I thought I was still asleep, still dreaming. I felt like I was floating, hovering just above my bed, looking down at the empty shell of my body. My surroundings were white and sterile, more like an examination room. The walls were bare and the small windows had their dark gray curtains drawn closed so tightly they looked sewn together. The door of the room was slightly ajar and through the crack between it and the jamb came the only light, a dull, yellowish glow.

My bed smelled strongly of starch. The sheet was stiff and tucked tightly around me. Because my pillow was so soft, my head was barely raised. When I turned to look around the room, I saw there was a table with a long top drawer and a counter of some imitation wood beside the bed. On it was an ivory-white bedpan and a metal bowl with a washcloth draped over the edge.

When I tried to sit up, I was shocked to discover I was strapped down, thick belts of leather across the top of my body, just under my breasts, my arms tucked against my sides, and another belt across my legs. I could barely move.

621

It put a hot ball of panic in my stomach that rolled from side to side.

"Help me!" I cried. "Someone, please."

I waited, but heard nothing, no footsteps, no voices, nothing. I cried out again, waited, and cried out once more. The silence was maddening. Wasn't there anyone else here? My struggle against the straps was futile, even painful. I sighed deeply and gave up, closing my eyes and whimpering softly.

I must have fallen asleep again, because when I opened my eyes, I heard water running in the sink. There was someone in my bathroom.

"Who's there?" I called.

Moments later a tall, thin woman with rust-color hair stepped out. I could see her shoulder bones outlined against her white uniform. She had long arms with jutting wrist bones and very long hands, hands that looked strong and capable. When she circled the bed and came around on my right, I could see her face more clearly.

She looked half asleep herself, her eyelids drooping so that there were barely two slits revealing small hazel pupils. She had a long thin nose and a very wide mouth above a cleft chin. She reminded me of Mary Beth and I wondered if she were suffering from anorexia, too. If so, why wasn't she a patient instead of an employee?

She didn't seem impressed with the fact that I was awake. She moved about the room as if she had been taking care of me for weeks and weeks. It made me wonder just how long I had been here. Without greeting me, in fact barely looking at me, she placed the basin of water on the table and pulled back the sheet to undo the straps.

"You have to sit up. I'm going to wash you down a bit," she mumbled. Her voice was so deep it sounded almost manly. This close to me, I could see tiny black hairs curled at the side of her chin. "And then I'll give you something to eat," she said.

As she spoke, she avoided looking directly at me.

"What happened to me?" I asked. "Why was I strapped into bed?"

She paused and finally glanced at me.

"I don't know," she said and continued undoing the straps. "Can you sit up by yourself?" she asked.

"Where am I? Who are you?"

"My name is Clare. You're in room three-oh-seven," she said. "Can you sit up please."

I thought hard and vaguely recalled the events that led to my being brought upstairs.

"I need to see Doctor Southerby," I said. "Can you tell him Laura Logan needs to see him as soon as possible? It's very important."

"I'm just a nurse's aide," she said. "I don't tell anyone anything."

She began to wash my right hand and my arm with as much interest as she would have in washing a dirty dish.

"I can do that myself," I said, anger rushing in to replace fear. "Why was I strapped down in bed? Why can't I get up and walk around? Can't I just take a shower or a bath?"

She kept washing and rinsing as if I hadn't said a word. My anger began to simmer my blood into a rolling boil.

"Can't you tell me anything?" I demanded as forcefully as I could.

She paused.

"I have some meat loaf, mashed potatoes, peas and carrots, some bread, apple juice, and strawberry Jell-O."

"What?"

"That's your supper," she said. "That's all I can tell you. That's all I know."

She started on my other hand and arm. I pulled it back abruptly.

"I said I can wash myself."

She held the cloth a moment and then shrugged.

"Here. Do it. I'll get your food," she said and dropped the cloth in my hand before turning and walking out of the room. I put the cloth on my face and took a deep breath.

I have to get out of here, I thought. I have to find Doctor Southerby and get out of here. I put my legs over the bed and stood. My whole body swayed like the pendulum in a grandfather's clock. Nevertheless, I turned to the closet, hoping to find my clothes. At the moment, I was wearing a loose hospital gown and was barefoot. The tile floor felt like ice beneath my feet. Taking a deep breath, I stepped away from the bed and walked to the closet. However, when I opened the door, I looked in at empty hangers. There were no clothes, no shoes, nothing but a layer of fine dust.

"What are you doing out of bed? Get back in, quick, or I'll get fired," the tall woman cried. She had my tray of food in her hands and moved across the room to the table quickly. As I turned, she took hold of my arm to help me back. The room spun around me.

"Why am I so dizzy? What did they give me? My legs feel like rubber."

"I don't know anything about medicines. Just get into the bed."

"Why don't you know anything if you work here? Where's the doctor? I need to talk to someone who knows something," I moaned.

She practically lifted me onto the bed, tucking the blanket around me. My head fell back against the pillow.

"I'll crank the bed up for you," she said and pushed a button that raised my head and upper torso until I was nearly in a seated position. Then she moved the tray table so the food was in front of me. "Can you feed yourself, or do you want me to feed you?"

"I can eat by myself," I said. "I can do everything for myself if you people will just let me."

"Good. I got two other patients on this floor and neither can do much for themselves. They can't even wipe their own noses most of the time and they're not much older than you."

She started away from the bed and then stopped and returned to fasten the straps over my legs.

"Please, can't you leave them undone?" I asked.

"You might fall out and then I'll get fired," she said.

"Why do you work here if they'll fire you for anything that happens?" I asked.

She finally smiled.

"It's a good job. They pay me more than I can make most anywhere else, and there's just me and my mother now. She's too old to do anything for herself and she doesn't get much social security."

"How long have I been here? You can tell me that at least," I said.

She shrugged.

"Not more than a day, because I would have seen you before," she said.

We heard the sound of footsteps in the hall.

"Uh-oh," she said, her face whitening with fear. "That's Doctor Scanlon making his rounds along with Mrs. Roundchild. She cracks the whip here."

A woman of about forty with hair the color of pencil lead turned into the doorway, a step ahead of Doctor Scanlon. She had gray eyes and a narrow face with a strong, full mouth and a nose so straight it could be used as a ruler. She wore a dark blue cardigan sweater with pearl buttons over her uniform. I thought she had a nicely shaped figure and a rich complexion. However, all that was feminine and soft about her body was negated by the firmness in her lips and the piercing chill in her eyes.

"What are you doing?" she asked Clare.

"I was just on my way to three-oh-four. I got her settled with her dinner and—"

"Well then, get on with it. See to the others. They can't complain for themselves, you know." Her words were sharply pronounced with an English accent.

"Yes, Mrs. Roundchild."

"Wait. Why is that closet door open?" she demanded, nodding at it.

"Closet door? Oh." Clare looked at me, her eyes frantic. She reminded me of some small creature looking for a way to escape.

"I was trying to find my clothes," I said. "I want to go back downstairs, Doctor Scanlon," I explained, turning my attention to him.

"You will," he said. "Soon."

Mrs. Roundchild spun on Clare.

"You let her get off the bed and open the closet?"

"When I went to get her food, she did it herself," Clare said.

"You undid the straps and left the room?" Mrs. Roundchild practically lunged at Clare.

"She wanted to wash herself, so I thought to save time, I would go get her food and—"

"That's a demerit, Miss Carson. It will go on your record. You know all about our liabilities here and you've been told what to do and what not to do. It clearly states on the door that this patient does not have off-bed privileges at the moment."

"I know, but—"

"There are no buts when it comes to regulations. You've been here long enough to know that."

"It's not her fault," I said. "I insisted I wash myself."

Mrs. Roundchild considered me.

"It's admirable that you want to take the blame, but it's not honest now, is it?"

"Yes it is," I said.

"Are you a liar?"

"What? No, I just . . . it *was* my fault. I told her I would wash myself."

"She knows she's supposed to be in charge, not you. Why are you still standing here, Clare?" She swung around to look at the meek woman paused in the doorway.

"I'm sorry," Clare whined and hurried out.

Doctor Scanlon approached the bed with Mrs. Roundchild right beside him.

"That's good, you're eating," he said, nodding at my food. I hadn't touched a morsel.

"I'm not hungry," I said. "Doctor Scanlon, why can't I go back downstairs? Why am I being kept here?"

"You have to remain under strict observation for a while, Laura. Here, you can get more personal treatment," he added and glanced at Mrs. Roundchild.

"I don't need more personal treatment. I was doing fine until you wanted to start giving me some drug," I complained.

"First, it's not just some drug, Laura. I'm giving you something that's designed to keep you from being too anxious and having a bad reaction to your returning memories," he explained calmly. "Second, I really don't think you're in a position to know what's best for you."

He glanced at Mrs. Roundchild, who looked like she disapproved of his taking the time to defend his decision.

"I want my clothes," I moaned. "And I don't want to be strapped into bed like this."

"The medications I'm giving you can have some side effects, Laura. They can disorient you sometimes. This is just to protect you."

"I feel like a prisoner," I cried, the tears gathering under my lids and making my eyes watery and my vision hazy.

"You're not a prisoner. You're a patient, and we're here to help you get better. Mrs. Roundchild is one of the two specially trained head nurses who run this floor. I have the greatest confidence in her. She will see to all your needs."

"What's happening to me?"

"I feel you are on the verge of a complete recouping of the past with a minimum of selective amnesia. My sense of this is you could at any time remember the trauma and when that happens," he continued, "it will be like being hit by a freight train. Believe me. I've seen situations similar to yours many, many times."

His words frightened me. I settled back, my tension and resistance melting away. I saw that pleased him. He looked at Mrs. Roundchild and she stepped forward, reaching down to bring up a button attached to a plastic wire.

"If you need any assistance, you press this and someone will come in due time, but don't think they will fall out of the ceiling. We're understaffed here and people are always busy. Have patience," she warned, "and we'll do our best to see to it that you are comfortable and safe."

"Can't I at least have my arms free? I'd like to get a drink of water for myself or scratch myself when I itch," I said.

"I think that will be okay as long as you promise not to undo the strap around your legs. That will guarantee you won't fall out of the bed," Doctor Scanlon said. "What do you think, Mrs. Roundchild?"

"I'd like to keep the top strap around her waist as well. At least until she's stronger," she added.

"Fine. All right, Laura?"

I nodded. What else could I do?

"If you undo them," Mrs. Roundchild threatened, "we'll have to restrain your arms again."

Doctor Scanlon took my pulse and then checked a chart dangling from the end of the bed. While he did so, Mrs. Roundchild tightened the straps securely.

"Let's remain with this current pharmaceutical protocol," he told Mrs. Roundchild.

"Very good, Doctor," she said. She looked as though she were going to salute as well.

He turned back to me.

"I'm going to let you rest now, but Mrs. Roundchild will keep a close eye on your condition. If there are any dramatic changes, she'll inform me immediately and I'll be here as soon as I can," he promised.

"Does Doctor Southerby at least know what's happened to me?" I asked softly. He didn't like the question and hardened his mouth, turning his eyes to granite as well.

"Doctor Southerby knows you are now under my direct care. He has no concerns," he replied sharply. "Just so you'll know," he added after a moment, "Doctor Southerby interned under me. He thinks of me as his mentor. Do you know what that means, mentor?"

"Yes," I said. "You were his teacher."

"More than that. Doctor Scanlon was his idol," Mrs. Roundchild corrected. "And rightly so," she finished. Doctor Scanlon smiled at her and the two of them left my room.

I gazed down at my food, my appetite still gone. Nevertheless, I nibbled on some of the cold meat loaf, drank some juice, and lay back. A little over an hour later, Clare returned for the tray.

"I'm sorry I got you into trouble," I said.

"I got myself into trouble," she replied, took the tray and left without a word.

Fifteen minutes later, I had to use the bedpan. I pushed the buzzer for it to be taken away, but no one appeared for more than a half hour. Finally, Mrs. Roundchild came with Clare right behind her.

"Empty that," she told her, nodding at the bedpan. Then she handed me a cup with two pills in it, and gave me a glass of water. "Your medication," she said firmly.

"Will it make me tired? I'm still so weak and tired from before," I complained.

"Your medication," she repeated, holding it out. "Doctor Scanlon wouldn't prescribe it if it wasn't necessary, Laura. I'm sorry to have to be so firm with you, but it's an awesome responsibility to care for people who can't care for themselves."

I plucked the pills out of the cup and put them in my mouth while she hovered over me, watching me swallow the water and the pills. She nodded.

"Good," she said. Clare returned the bedpan to the table and they left me.

Never did I feel more alone. Strapped down, in a barren room with no one to talk to, nothing to look at, not even anything to read, I did truly feel more like a criminal than a patient. It was as if I were being punished, not helped. I listened hard, but the sounds that I heard from the corridor were few and meaningless. There were no voices and little movement. If they were so understaffed, why wasn't there more going on?

I had to close my eyes. The pills are working, I thought. They're making my eyelids heavy again. In moments I was asleep, and soon after, I was dreaming. Wonderful, familiar faces began to reappear, rising out of the darkness. My mother was smiling at me and my father was looking at me with love in his eyes. A little hand reached for me. It was May and she was afraid. My brother stepped up beside her. His name seemed to be closer, my tongue struggling to form it.

"Come home, Laura," he said. "Please, come home."

"Laura," my mother called. "Laura, come home."

"We need you back here, Laura," my father said.

May was signing and crying.

I struggled, twisted, and pulled against the straps in my sleep so violently, that I woke myself in the middle of the night. My skin burned where I had chaffed my waist and my legs. I groaned and cried out. The door to my room was nearly closed completely, so that most of the dim light from the corridor was gone. I was alone in the dark.

I closed my eyes again, drifting off. This time I immediately felt a wave of cold ocean water wash over me. I gasped. There was a hand reaching up and the top of a head emerging from the water. I struggled to get a grip on that hand and then . . . I really felt something in my hand and my eyes snapped open.

"Shh," I heard, and turned to see Lawrence kneeling by the bed.

"Lawrence? What are you doing here?"

"Don't talk too loud," he said. "I snuck up to see you. We heard what happened to you and I tried to get information all day, but no one knew or would say a thing. Mary Beth and Lulu send their love."

"How did you get up here?"

I sat up until the strap cut into my waist.

"There's another stairway that's used to bring up supplies mainly. It's right near here. I didn't know what room you were in, of course. I checked two others before finding you. The chart on your door says that they don't want you to be disturbed. Has something terrible happened to you, Laura? Have you remembered something horrible? Is that why they brought you up here?"

I told him what had happened with Doctor Scanlon and what he wanted done with me and why.

"I don't see why that meant you had to be brought up here," Lawrence commented.

"Neither do I. I want to go back downstairs, be with people, move about on my own."

"Did you tell him that?"

"Yes, but he keeps saying they're doing this to protect me, to ensure that I don't hurt myself."

"I don't know why they can't protect you downstairs just as well," Lawrence said. I nodded.

"Anyway, at least I know where you are now. I'll come up to see you as much as I can, but it will have to be at night. If I get caught, they'll lock me up someplace, too, or ship me away like Megan."

"I can't believe you got up here. You know everything about this clinic," I said. He was barely visible in the dim light from the hallway, but I saw him smile.

"I've been here long enough to know every corner of the place," he said. "Are you going to be all right?"

"I'm scared, Lawrence," I said, holding on to his hand. "I don't want to be here, but I'm frightened of putting up too much of a fight. What if Doctor Scanlon's right? He's the head doctor, isn't he? They said even Doctor Southerby learned from him."

"I don't know, but I don't want you to be frightened, Laura," Lawrence said softly. He rose and brought himself closer to me. I knew what courage it took for him to come up to see me, how much of his own problem he had to have overcome.

"Thank you for coming up here, Lawrence. I want you to know that it means a lot to me that you snuck up to see me."

"I couldn't sleep, thinking about you and worrying about you," he said.

We heard footsteps in the hallway.

"Someone's coming," I whispered and watched frantically as he crawled underneath my bed.

Moments later, the door opened and Mrs. Roundchild

stood silhouetted in the hallway light. She stared in at me. I closed my eyes and waited, praying she wouldn't come in. She stood there for the longest time and then she left, closing the door behind her. Neither Lawrence nor I spoke or moved until we heard her footsteps die away. Finally he got to his feet.

"That was close," I said. "You'd better go."

"All right."

I started to sob. I didn't want him to go. I felt more secure, more at ease with him holding my hand. He leaned toward me again and I touched his face. His lips drew closer and closer until they met mine. It wasn't so much of a kiss as it was a brush of lips and a sigh.

"I wish I could stay here with you all night," he whispered. "I wish I could put my arms around you and hold you and protect you from your own fearful thoughts. When I'm with you like this, I don't think about myself and I don't get panicked, Laura. I need to be with you as much for myself as for you," he admitted. "We're good for each other, Laura."

"I don't think I'm good for much right now, Lawrence. I'm no better than an invalid. I can't even get off the bed to go to the bathroom."

"You'll get better and I'll get better. You'll see," he promised.

"You've been so nice to me, Lawrence. I'm glad we got to know each other," I said.

"I hope we can get to love each other," he followed quickly. I think the darkness made him brave. It brought a smile to my face.

He held his face close to mine for another moment and then he kissed me again, only this time, he held his lips to mine longer and made it into a real kiss.

I moaned softly, desperate for a loving touch, for affection.

He kissed me again, moving his lips over my cheeks and back to my lips. Then he kissed my forehead and held me.

"Robert," I said softly, my cheek against his chest.

"What did you say?" He pulled back. I opened my eyes.

"What's wrong?" I asked quietly.

"I thought you called me by another name just now. I thought you said Robert."

Neither of us moved a muscle.

I searched my thoughts and waited, but it was as if a dark cloud had suddenly appeared, shutting away the light and enveloping me in darkness once again.

"I don't know," I said, frustrated. "I don't understand." I started to cry. "You see, Doctor Scanlon is right. I am disturbed, too confused to be on my own."

"Don't, Laura. Please." He kissed away a tear.

We heard the sound of a cart being wheeled in the hallway and we waited until it passed my room.

"You'd better go," I whispered.

"I'll be back tomorrow night," he promised. He kissed me again. "Good night, Laura."

"Good night," I said. He held my hand until he started away and had to let go. I watched him walk to the door and peer out. Then he was gone.

Moments afterward, alone in the dark and quiet room with only my thoughts for companionship, I had to wonder. Had I dreamed Lawrence's visit or had he really been here?

In the morning, I realized I must have cried most of the night in my sleep because my pillow was soaked with my tears. I knew my dreams were full of sadness, but I couldn't remember the details of a single one. It was as if everything had been written in the sand and as soon as I woke, the ocean came up and washed out each and every word, carrying them back to the depths of the sea. There was nothing to do but start all over.

A different nurse's aide brought me my breakfast. She was just as closemouthed as Clare and seemed even more afraid of doing anything wrong. All I learned about her was her first name, Della. She was a heavy black girl with very pretty

633

ebony eyes. She wore her hair very short, which made her look even chubbier than she was, I thought. She emptied the bedpan, gave me fresh water, and helped me wash.

"When can I take a bath or a shower? These sponge baths aren't enough."

"I don't know," she said. "You have to ask the nurse."

Just like Clare, Della avoided looking at me most of the time she was in my room. It made me feel as though I were ugly, a hideous creature that no one could bare to look at.

Doctor Scanlon finally appeared late in the afternoon. He gazed at my chart and then pulled a chair up beside the bed.

"I see that you had a restful twenty-four hours. That's good," he commented.

"Restful? I woke with a soaked pillow and my arms and legs are chaffed from all the tossing and turning I did against these straps. Please take them off. Please," I begged.

He considered.

"All right. I'll trust you to watch yourself." He scribbled something on his pad. "Now, tell me about your memories. How are we doing on that score?"

I described my visions, the ones I could remember. He seemed to tiptoe gently about the descriptions I gave him of the ocean, the waves, the hand coming up.

"Your memory is returning, Laura. We're handling this right. I'm more convinced than ever. Continue to cooperate, take your medication, and let your mind feel at ease enough to permit the past to seep back into your consciousness slowly. It won't be long before you walk out of here," he promised.

"However, with the trauma threatening to make itself heard dramatically and completely, I'd like to increase your medication a bit. Just to play it safe," he added and made another note. "Okay?"

"Okay," I said and he gave me the phoniest smile he had given me yet.

"To reward you for your cooperation, I'm leaving instructions for you to be taken on a short walk through the halls so you get some exercise. How's that?"

634

"I'd like that," I said. At this point, I thought, I'd like anything that resembled or suggested a normal life.

"We'll do it before it's time for your next dosage of medicine so you can be a little more alert."

He rose.

"We're in control of your problems rather than permitting them to be in control of you, and as long as we keep it that way, we're on the right track," he concluded.

Clare returned at the start of the late afternoon shift and announced that she had been instructed to take me for a short walk. For that purpose, I was given a light blue cotton robe and a pair of cotton slippers. She undid my restraints and helped me put on the robe and slippers.

"Maybe this will help your appetite, too," she commented, noticing how much food I had left over from lunch. Then she bit her lip as if she had said something blasphemous.

"I hope so," I said. "It's not because the food is terrible. I'm just not hungry," I added quickly, imagining the same people prepared the food for the Tower floor.

She helped me to my feet. I was shaky at first, but as I took one step and then another, my blood began to circulate and I felt stronger. We left the room and paused in the corridor.

It was very different up on this floor. The hallway was just as immaculate, but there were no paintings, no chairs, and the windows were covered with heavy drapes that blocked out all signs of the sun. I noticed also that there were very few rooms at the far end of the hall. Instead, there was a glass double door through which I saw Mrs. Roundchild talking with another nurse. To my right was a sharp turn in the corridor.

"What's around that way?" I asked.

"At the very end of this corridor is the Zombie Ward," Clare said.

"Zombie Ward?"

"The patients in there don't talk except to scream or cry. Many of them just sit or stand for hours staring at nothing, shaking their arms or their heads madly. They've got to be fed and washed all the time. There are young people in there who took too many drugs and burned out their brains," she added.

"How horrible."

"You're lucky compared to them," she said.

We walked in that direction. After a while, Clare lessened her hold on me and I took stronger steps. When we made the turn, I looked down the hallway and saw there were glass doors there, too. I could make out some patients sitting in chairs and a couple of young women standing.

"I'm not supposed to take you that far," Clare said, nodding toward the glass doors. I kept walking in that direction anyway. "You got to turn back now, Laura," she said.

Suddenly, from a room on our right, we heard a loud crash, the sound of a bedpan slamming to the floor and then a shrill scream.

"Oh no, it's that Sara Richards again. Just wait here," she ordered, and went into the room. I continued to walk toward the doors.

As I drew closer, I thought I saw a familiar face. It intrigued me and I sped up until I was only a few feet from the doorway and could look through the windows. There, standing with her wrists all wrapped in bandages and staring at the doorway, was Megan. Her mouth was open, drool seeping out and down the sides. Her eyes were wide but vacant.

"Megan?" I whispered.

Clare came up beside me quickly and grabbed my elbow.

"You can't be down here. Come on, let's go back, Laura."

"But that's a friend of mine from downstairs, Megan Paxton. I thought she was being moved to some other hospital. What happened to her? She looks terrible."

"I don't know, but if she's in there, it wasn't good. Please, let's get back before Mrs. Roundchild catches us and gives me double demerits. When you reach ten, they fire you. Come on, Laura," she urged and turned me.

I looked back as we walked.

Megan seemed to recognize me. She lifted her arms and held them up and then, I thought she screamed. I couldn't hear anything. Maybe she wasn't making any sounds, but she was trying to scream. A nurse moved to her quickly and directed her into a room and she was gone.

"Megan," I murmured.

"You have to get back into your bed now," Clare said as we rounded the turn and headed toward my room.

Mrs. Roundchild was gazing our way suspiciously.

"Poor Megan," I said.

And then I wondered, could that happen to me? Would I end up on the Zombie Ward, too? Maybe no one gets better here. Maybe they all just end up locked away in the Zombie Ward. Or worse.

"Time for your medicine," Mrs. Roundchild said, bursting into the room moments after Clare had helped me into bed. She thrust the cup of pills at me.

"I don't need them. I want to try to sleep tonight without them," I said.

"You have to take your medication. Besides, you told Doctor Scanlon you would. Why are you being obstinate now?"

"I'm afraid," I said. "Too many drugs might burn out my mind."

"That's ridiculous. Who told you such a thing?" She turned to Clare, who was hurrying to clean up the bathroom and leave.

"No one told me," I said. "I'm just afraid."

"I'll stand here all night if necessary until you take your medication. And if you don't, we'll have an I.V. hooked to your arm and we'll feed them to you intravenously," she warned.

"But they make me so groggy. I'm already exhausted just from that little walk," I moaned.

She held out the pills, her expression unchanging and unsympathetic.

637

"Are you going to take these pills voluntarily?" she finally asked.

Reluctantly, I took them from her. She watched me wash them down, her hands on her hips, her eyes beady.

"Strap her in," she said.

"But Doctor Scanlon said I don't need to be strapped in. He promised," I cried.

"As head nurse I have to make decisions on the spur of the moment if necessary. You just said the walking made you tired. I don't think you'll be safe tonight without being strapped in," she said.

"Look at my legs, how red they are," I said.

"That's nothing compared to what could happen if you fall on your face. Strap her in," she commanded.

Clare moved quickly to obey her.

"I want to see Doctor Scanlon," I demanded.

"He'll be here tomorrow at his usual hour."

"I want to see him now!"

"Don't raise your voice to me, young lady. Your grandmother might be paying for your treatments and making big donations, but you're still a guest of this clinic. We don't take just anyone—no matter who they are," she said and marched out of my room.

Clare gave me a look of sympathy and then quickly followed after her.

"I want to see the doctor!" I shouted at the nearly closed door.

No one returned or responded.

Soon, the pills began to take effect again. My eyes drooped and I felt weaker. It was futile to struggle against them. Sleep and remember, I thought. Sleep and remember who you are and then you will be free.

Vaguely, I thought about something Mrs. Roundchild had said . . . something about my grandmother. What did all that mean? That was my last conscious thought.

I knew the dosage Mrs. Roundchild had given me was considerably greater, as Doctor Scanlon had promised, because I didn't wake during the night. Lawrence had been

638

in my room, too. I knew because when I woke, I found a tissue in my hand with the words *"I love you. Guess who—"* scribbled on it. It made me smile, but also put fear in my heart because I was afraid someone would find it. I quickly crumbled the tissue into a ball and put it in my bedpan. No one would want to look at it now, I thought.

Doctor Scanlon didn't come to see me the entire day. I kept asking about him, but as usual, neither nurse's aide knew anything and Mrs. Roundchild simply said, "He'll be here when he'll be here."

The only thing I could count on regularly was my medication. They had me taking it twice now, once in the morning, once at night. The night dosage affected me just the way it had the night before. Soon after I took it, I was asleep, but this time, my dream woke me, or at least I thought I woke.

Once again, I saw a hand come out of the ocean and then a head began to rise to the surface. When I saw his eyes, I started to scream. He was sinking again and I was struggling to reach him. I heard his voice. I heard him say, "Help me, Laura. Help me. I want to be with you always. Help me. Come to me."

I felt his lips on my face and reached out to embrace him and cradled his head against my breast where he could fall asleep safely. Just before morning, I woke with a start. I wasn't imagining it now. I did feel something against my breast and turned to see Lawrence, his head resting on me, his body curled up beside me.

"Lawrence," I cried. His eyes fluttered. "When did you come? I don't remember."

"I was here, Laura. I've been here for hours and hours."

"They're giving me more medicine, Lawrence. It makes me so tired. I'm afraid not to take it, I'm afraid of what might happen to me. Lawrence," I said, seizing his hand, "Megan, Megan wasn't transferred to another hospital. She's here. She's in what they call the Zombie Ward. I saw her. She looks terrible."

"Zombie Ward? I know about that place. She's really that bad?"

"I almost didn't recognize her. She looked so wild she frightened me. Oh, Lawrence," I moaned, "what if that happens to me? What if the medicine and my dreams drive me mad? Don't let them put me in that place."

He shook his head sharply.

"Never. I'll never let them lock you away in there."

"If only I remembered everything they would let me go," I said with a small sob.

"I think it's happening, Laura. I heard you cry out in your sleep for someone, someone you were losing. That must be your traumatic experience, the event that caused your illness," he said.

"You did? Who was it? Did I say a name?"

He hesitated.

"I'm afraid to tell you. After what you just told me, I'm afraid of doing something wrong," he said.

"You've got to tell me. I can't stand this emptiness, this darkness. Please. Whom did I cry for?"

"It was the same name I heard you say before."

I thought a moment.

"I can't remember what I said before, Lawrence. The medicine that they're giving me has already turned my mind into a glob of mush. Whose name did I call out?" I repeated more firmly. "You must tell me, Lawrence. I don't want to end up like Megan. Please."

"Someone named Robert," he replied.

The sound of his name took my breath away. I stared at Lawrence.

"I think it was someone you cared for very much," he said sadly.

"Yes. Yes," I said, seeing the darkness begin to retreat and the light begin to slip in from behind the cloud of my memory. "He was. He is."

And I knew that today, today I would remember everything. I was filled with mixed emotions, anxious, terrified, and yet hopeful it would mean the end of my ordeal. Finally I would be free.

16

❧

Reunited

"*I* hate to leave you," Lawrence said.

Through the slight opening in my window curtain, we could see the dawn beginning. The light that cleared away the darkness gave me hope that something similar would happen to the darkness in me as well.

"You have to go, Lawrence. I'll be all right now," I said, smiling. "I will. Somehow," I said, my eyes shifting as I gazed ahead, "I know I will."

"I wish they wouldn't give you so much medicine. It doesn't seem right," he worried aloud. He leaned over and kissed me softly on my forehead and then smiled. "I'll see you later," he promised, squeezing my hand and walking toward the door. He paused to check the hallway and in moments, he was gone.

"Robert," I whispered in the silence that followed. It was as if my lips were trying on the word to see if it fit. "Robert."

I closed my eyes and a series of pictures rolled maddeningly by. I concentrated, slowing them down until I saw my family clearly, heard their voices clearly, the sounds of their laughter, their chatter at dinner, Daddy reading from the

Bible, and then—Cary. His name emerged in a bubble rising out of the confusion, and with his name came a litany of his words: his compliments and his complaints, his warnings and his hopes.

A small sailboat bobbed on the surface of a pond. I understood it to be one of Cary's models. I had memories of him working hard on them, hunched over his table with his soldering gun and his glues, his fingers turning and fitting the miniature parts into their tiny places. I realized I was remembering his workroom. With each memory, each vivid picture, my home was returning. I saw my own room, my stuffed animals, my beautiful, beautiful bed. I saw Mommy in the kitchen making a delicious clam chowder. I saw Daddy sitting in his favorite chair reading the newspaper and mumbling over some event. May was at his feet putting a puzzle together, waiting for me to help her with her homework. They were all waiting for me to come home, to come back.

I saw myself running up to the front door and tugging on the door knob when it didn't turn. The door wouldn't open. Why was it locked? I pounded and called.

"MOMMY! DADDY! CARY!"

No one came to the door. I turned and looked around desperately, but instead of seeing my front yard, I saw the sailboat, only now it began to grow larger. The pond became the ocean. Someone was in the boat, steering it toward shore. He was calling to me, beckoning. The boat drew closer and closer until I saw him vividly, my Robert.

"Laura," he was calling. "Come back. Laura . . ."

Now I was running down the beach toward the boat, but the more I ran, the farther away it became. I ran harder and began to call to him. I seemed to run over the same sand repeatedly, never making any progress as he continued to call and to beckon.

"What's wrong with you?" I heard someone ask and instantly all my memories evaporated. Mrs. Roundchild stood by the side of my bed with my medication in hand, gazing down at me. "Why are you crying?"

"I . . . can remember lots of things now. I remember my family and my home," I said. "And I remember Robert and a boat and—"

"That's good. Here," she said, "take your medicine. Clare's bringing your breakfast."

"Maybe I shouldn't take any more medicine now," I said. "Now that I'm really remembering things, maybe it's better I have a clear mind."

"Why is it everyone wants to be a doctor here?" she asked, almost with a smile. "I'm sorry, but you have to spend a little time in medical school first."

"I'm not trying to be a doctor, but it just feels right that I shouldn't take anything."

"Really? Well, up until now, has Doctor Scanlon been wrong? Haven't you begun to remember things and do it in a fashion where you don't hurt yourself or get mentally incapacitated? Isn't that true?"

"Yes," I said. "I suppose."

"You suppose? Well, I know. I've been a head nurse on this floor for nearly five years now and I've seen many, many different kinds of illness, a number of cases similar to your own. I've seen Doctor Scanlon treat them successfully, too. So, I don't have to suppose," she said.

Tears filled my eyes once more.

"I just want to go home," I said.

"You will if you do what you're told." She paused for a moment, her expression softening. "I don't mean to be cruel to you, Laura, but I must be firm. I have an awesome job here. I am responsible for a number of people who are not able to be responsible for themselves. Many of these people have and will continue to hurt themselves if I don't follow doctor's orders in regards to them. There is a lot to do and little time to do it. Everyone needs specialized, personal treatment. It makes it hard to waste time, do you understand?"

643

"Yes," I said in a small voice.

"Good. Then take your medicine. Doctor Scanlon will be here to evaluate you and your progress and we'll see what he wants to do after that."

With trembling fingers, I plucked the pills out of the cup and put them in my mouth. She handed me the glass of water and I swallowed them down.

"Very good," she said. "Your breakfast is on its way."

She left the room and moments later, Clare arrived with my tray. She raised my bed and moved the table over me.

"I'm getting better," I told her. "I'm remembering things quickly now. I'll be able to go home."

"That's nice. I'd like to have less to do," she said. She paused. "But whenever someone leaves the floor or gets moved to the Zombie Ward, there's always someone else to take their place. I heard they have a waiting list as long as my arm," she added.

"Can you find out about a patient for me? Can you find out about Megan Paxton?"

"They don't like me asking about patients. If anyone working here is caught talking about the patients, they could be fired instantly," she said. "I gotta get breakfast to the others," she added before I could plead with her any more. She quickly left the room.

I sighed with disappointment and frustration and began to pick at my breakfast. I ate what I could, then closed my eyes, and dozed off. When I woke, my bed had been lowered and my tray taken away. I stared at the white ceiling.

Robert's face began to form on the white background. It looked like he was emerging from a cloud. I saw his soft eyes and gentle smile. Strands of his light brown hair fell over his forehead. He was laughing and then suddenly, the white background began to whirl around him. His head started to spin along with it and the white ceiling turned into water. His arm emerged, his hand reaching out for me.

"Laura . . ."

I screamed.

Maybe I fainted. Maybe I fell back to sleep. I don't know,

but when I woke this time, Doctor Scanlon was seated beside the bed. He had just taken my pulse and was making some notes on his pad. He looked very calm, so calm that I couldn't imagine he heard me scream.

Suddenly, I noticed there were two younger men in doctor's hospital coats standing at the foot of the bed looking at me. Both carried clipboards. One had dark brown hair and wore glasses; the other had longer, light brown hair and light blue eyes. He was taller and wider.

"Hello, Laura," Doctor Scanlon said. "This is Doctor Fernhoff and Doctor Bloom. They're both interns, studying with me. From time to time, they'll each look in on you, too. So," he continued, "Mrs. Roundchild tells me you've remembered a lot more about your family and your home. Is that so?"

I nodded.

"Good. Now, let's talk a bit about those memories. Were they all pleasant?"

I shook my head.

"I see. What was unpleasant?" he asked.

I gazed at the two interns. Doctor Fernhoff, the man with the glasses, was staring at me so intently, I felt self-conscious.

"I . . . remember . . . there was someone," I said, "someone I cared for and something happened to him."

"Yes," Doctor Scanlon said. He glanced at the two interns. Neither cracked an encouraging smile nor changed expression. "Go on. What happened to him?"

"I think . . . it has to do with the ocean. He was in a sailboat."

"Yes, go on, go on," he urged, as if he were playing a tug-of-war with my mind.

"I don't know. I . . . think he might have fallen out of the boat."

I gazed at Doctor Bloom. Something in his softer face told me I wasn't far off.

"What else do you think, Laura? You must tell me what you remember and what you believe happened."

"He and I were in the boat," I said, "and I think we were caught in a storm. Is he all right?"

"Who?" Doctor Scanlon pursued. "Who is this person in the boat with you?"

"Robert," I said and it all tumbled out. "Robert Royce, a boy from my school."

Doctor Scanlon sat back, a look of satisfaction on his face.

"That's good, Laura," he said, nodding. "You've come a long way."

"But is he all right?"

"Is he?" Doctor Scanlon fired back at me.

"I don't know. I can't remember," I cried frantically. "He's not all right. He can't be all right. Please, say I'm wrong. Tell me!" I begged.

"You must not think of it as your fault," he said.

"Why would it be my fault? Was it my fault? What did I do?" I demanded.

"That's enough for now," he declared with finality. He gathered up his charts and stood.

"No, it's not enough. How can it be enough? You've hardly been here five minutes."

"The length of time I'm here isn't what's important. It's what happens *during* the time I'm here," he said, as if I were one of his interns, too.

"I can't remember everything, but I remember a lot. Can't you help me remember it all, finally?"

"I think it's best we take it one step at a time, Laura. Tomorrow is another day," he declared with a regal air. His two interns made quick notes on their clipboards as he turned to them.

"I want to go home," I moaned. "I remember my mother, my father, my little sister, and my brother. Why don't they come to see me now?"

"Perhaps they will very soon," he said. "Classic case," he said, nodding at me. The two interns widened their eyes and pressed their lips simultaneously. "As you know," he lectured to them, "dissociative amnesia most commonly presents a retrospectively reported gap or series of gaps in recall for aspects of the individual's life history. As illustrated here, these gaps are usually related to traumatic or extremely stressful events."

"It's a common battle-fatigue syndrome," Doctor Fernhoff said.

"Precisely. However, today, we're seeing it more and more with early childhood abuse. I'd like you both to keep a close observation on this case. She's on the verge of crashing through her trauma and the immediate aftermath is most instructive."

They nodded and stared at me. I felt like an amoeba under a microscope. The way their eyes fixed on my face made me cringe.

"I want to go home," I moaned.

"We have to deal with the patient's perception of the event," Doctor Scanlon continued. "It's critical we deal with her sense of guilt as soon as she recalls nearly one hundred percent, for it is precisely that sense of guilt that put her into dissociative amnesia. Again, classic symptoms for classic cases, i.e., mothers who survive accidents when their children don't, husbands or wives who survive, et cetera.

"I'm giving her a series of EEGs. As you know," he continued in his teacher's voice, "regions of the brain that are involved in memory function also affect the stress response. Traumatic stress results in changes in these brain regions; alterations in these brain regions in turn may mediate symptoms of posttraumatic stress disorder.

"Unfortunately," he continued, looking at me, "Doctor Southerby neglected to give her an EEG on admittance, so we lost a potential comparison there, but . . ." He smiled at them. "We'll make the best of it."

He gestured at the door and they turned.

"Please let me go home," I cried. Why wouldn't they answer me?

"Our next patient is a more classic case of child abuse,"

he rattled on as they walked away. "We have a twelve-year-old Caucasian male . . ."

I watched them leave the room and then I dropped my head to the pillow because it suddenly felt like it had turned to stone.

As Doctor Scanlon had explained, later that day I was taken for tests. Electrodes were placed on my head and machines read my brain waves. Doctor Scanlon's interns supervised and studied the results, although no one told me what they were. I was simply brought back to my room and put to bed. When I complained, Mrs. Roundchild permitted me to sit in a chair for a while, as long as I didn't walk around or try to leave the room.

I sat there all day, thinking about my memories, feeling the details fill in, the colors and shapes growing richer and richer with each passing minute. It was as if my recollections, which began as simple line drawings, were now being painted by a wonderful artist. Not only did pictures and words return, but aromas, scents, and tastes did as well. More than ever, I wanted my mother. I cried for her all day, but no one listened. Every time Mrs. Roundchild or one of the interns appeared, they offered me promises, punctuating every hope with "Soon."

Soon was not soon enough, I thought. Only right now was soon enough. Because I became more vocal in my demands, Mrs. Roundchild had me returned to bed and strapped in again. She called Doctor Scanlon and then came back to my room to inform me that he wanted me to take my medication earlier than usual tonight. She said he claimed I was about to make a dramatic breakthrough. Once again, they held up the promise that this would all be over . . . soon.

I took the pills after dinner and immediately fell asleep. In moments I was drifting on the sea. I was in the sailboat and Robert was smiling with pride at his ability to guide us over the waves. We were heading for a cove. It was coming back to me with the promise of love and all that lay just around the bend.

* * *

In my dreams I saw Robert and this girl who appeared to be me pull the sailboat onto the shore quickly and, laughing and teasing each other, go up the beach. I saw her fall to the sand and then I saw him fall first to his knees, and then to all fours above her. He gazed down at her, his eyes full of love, and he reached out to touch her hair, her cheek, to let her hold his fingers to her lips so she could kiss the tips of them. The girl moaned and the boy leaned over to kiss her softly on the lips, moving his mouth up her face, over her cheeks to her closed eyes.

For a while, he touched her only with his lips. He held himself above her, moving to her forehead, her hair, and then back to her lips before moving to her neck and then, ever so gently, lifting up her shirt.

In the distance the clouds began to gather. Neither the boy nor the girl noticed the change in the wind, the hectic and nervous cries of the birds, or the lift of the water as the tide rushed in faster, higher. They were completely entranced with each other, mesmerized, lost in the whisper of their own voices pledging endless love, promising.

I saw them undress, peel their clothes away quickly, but not roughly. Naked beneath the sky, they held each other first gently, and then desperately, wanting their lovemaking to be bigger, greater, more intense than it had ever been before. And it was.

Exhausted, they collapsed against each other, held each other tight. With this exquisite exhaustion came contentment. They closed their eyes and remained entwined, soon falling asleep. I tried to cry out a warning, but they couldn't hear me.

The sky darkened. The wind grew stronger. The water rose and fell with a slam against the rocks, and the small sailboat was washed away from shore. By the time they finally woke, the boat was out to sea.

Suddenly, I was no longer a third party, an observer. I was on the beach, shouting. Robert was swimming desperately for the boat. I saw it all and rushed forward to help him. That was when the darkness fell again, slamming my memory closed, ripping the sounds away, leaving me in a terrifying silence.

"Robert," I called. I started to swing my arms about madly until I felt someone holding me and opened my eyes to see Lawrence at my side.

"Laura, Laura," he cried.

I reached up for him and he embraced me.

"Were you having another bad dream?" he asked. "Maybe the medicine is causing your nightmares."

"I don't know," I sobbed. "I've got to get out of here, Lawrence. They don't really want to help me. They just keep giving me drugs that make me sleep and keep me weak. I want to go home, Lawrence. I know who my parents are and I know where I live. I remember almost everything! I've got to go home right away."

"You want to leave the clinic now? Tonight?" he asked.

"Yes, desperately. They're turning me into some sort of guinea pig, using me for a study. They want to prolong my treatment for as long as they can. I know they do. I want to go home. Help me, please," I begged.

He thought a moment. I pressed my fingers around his hand firmly.

"Okay, Laura," he said. "I'll help you, if that's what you really want to do."

"Thank you, Lawrence. Thank you."

I undid the strap around my waist and ripped the blanket away. Lawrence undid the strap around my legs and I started to get out of bed.

"Wait," he said. "Let me think first."

"There's no time to think. Get me out of here, Lawrence. Please."

"You need clothes, Laura. You can't go outside like that," he said. "I know. When we get downstairs, we'll go to your old room and get something for you to wear and then we'll go to the door off the kitchen, the one I showed you," he said.

"Yes, yes. But we've got to hurry."

"We've got to be careful," he corrected. "If we're caught,

650

they're sure to take more drastic measures with both of us." He went to the door and peered out. "It looks clear," he said.

I swung my feet over the side of the bed and stood. For a moment I swayed and nearly fell, but I steadied myself quickly. He came to me to take my arm, and we both went to the door. He looked again.

"When we go out, we go around the corner and take the first door on the left, Laura. We'll go down the stairway and stop at the bottom floor so I can check the corridor again. I've done this enough times already to be an expert. Don't worry," he added.

I nodded, eager.

Lawrence took my hand and led me from the room to the doorway. We slipped away quickly and started down the steps. My head was spinning, but I didn't let on how dizzy I was until I slipped on the landing and he had to catch and hold me.

"You're so weak, Laura. How can you leave the clinic?"

"I can do it, Lawrence. Once I'm away and out in fresh air, I'll be fine."

He held me for another indecisive moment, and then he guided me down the next flight of steps, until we were at the bottom floor and he was checking the hallway. After a few moments, he nodded and we scurried out and down the hallway to the residential area. Minutes later, we were in my old bedroom. We didn't put on the lights for fear of attracting attention. I went to the closet and found a pair of jeans and a sweatshirt, but there were no shoes or sneakers. I had to wear my slippers.

Lawrence remained at the doorway with his back to me as I dressed.

I paused by the small table and looked at the journal I had been keeping for Doctor Southerby. No one had bothered giving it to Doctor Scanlon. I was tempted to take it with me, but hesitated. I didn't want any reminders of this place, if I could help it, I thought. I wanted to leave this place behind me for good.

"I'm ready," I announced.

Lawrence looked at me and shook his head. He didn't move.

"What?" I asked.

"I can't let you do this by yourself, Laura. I'm going to go with you."

"You're going to leave the clinic, too?"

"Yes," he said. I could almost feel him trembling in the dark. Lawrence had told me that he hadn't been off the grounds for years.

"You don't have to do that, Lawrence."

"I want to," he said.

He watched the corridor and indicated I should be still. Seconds later, we heard talking and through the crack in the doorway saw Billy and Arnie walk down the corridor. They paused near my door. Billy whispered something to Arnie and they broke out into laughter as they continued down the hallway, disappearing around the corner.

"Now," Lawrence said, and we shot out and hurried down the hallway to the cafeteria. Just before we reached the kitchen, the doors opened and a janitor stepped out pushing a pail on rollers. He didn't look right or left or he would have seen us with our backs against the wall, watching him go through the cafeteria and out into the hall. We waited.

I looked at Lawrence. He seemed suddenly frozen against the wall.

"Shouldn't we go now?" I asked him. He nodded, but he didn't move.

"Maybe you should go back, Laura. I don't know if this is the right thing to do. No," he concluded. "It isn't. I shouldn't have done this. Please, let's go back," he said. He was trembling badly, and even in the subdued light, I saw how white his complexion had turned.

"No, I can't go back. I have to leave," I said. I started away and entered the kitchen myself. Moments later, Lawrence was behind me.

"How will you get home?" he asked when we confronted the metal door.

"I don't know."

"You don't even know which way to go. Laura, this is wrong," he said, seizing my arm to hold me back. "Laura . . ."

His voice seemed to die away after he pronounced my name, the word falling lower and lower as if everything he was saying were being said from the top of a deep well and I was on the very bottom. I felt like I was shrinking.

"Laura . . . don't go. Laura . . . come back."

"Yes, Robert," I said. "I'm coming back."

"What? Laura, it's me. Lawrence."

I went to the door.

"Laura! Wait!"

I pushed the door open and stepped out into the night, and then, I heard him calling again.

"Laura, come back! Come back!"

"Yes," I said. "I'm coming, Robert. I'll be there soon."

I turned and started around the building. Above me, the sky was thick with clouds. There were no stars, no promises for tomorrow.

I stumbled, but ignored the pain. I could hear his voice in the wind. Sometimes it was loud and sometimes it sounded far, far away.

"Laura, wait. Where are you going? You can't get to the highway that way. Laura."

Lawrence grabbed me at the elbow and spun me around.

"Laura, what are you doing? You lost your slipper back there," he said and gave it to me. I stared at it a moment and then at him.

"I'm not going back," I said. "Tell my grandmother I'm not going to give him up."

"What? You're not making any sense, Laura. Aren't you cold?" he asked, embracing himself. He looked around us. The weeping willow trees shook in the wind. "That wind is wild tonight. There's a storm brewing."

"Of course there's a storm brewing," I said, "but that won't stop us. You can tell her I said that."

I slipped my foot into the slipper and continued down the path, past the benches and the gardens.

"Tell whom? Laura, you're not making any sense. Laura!" he shouted.

Someone inside the building heard him. A light went on and then another. I heard doors opening and voices calling out into the night. It drove me on faster. I was running down the hill now, slipping and sliding, losing the slippers again, but not slowing down. Something inside me told me not to slow down for an instant or it would be too late.

And besides, he was calling louder and more desperately each time.

"I'm coming, Robert. I'm coming, my darling Robert," I cried into the darkness.

Ahead of me, the ocean thundered as the waves slammed against the rocks and the sea spray flew into the night. My eyes had grown accustomed to the darkness, but shapes were still only silhouettes. Some of the rocks had been stroked so long by the water, they gleamed like jewels in the night.

I fell and scraped my arm on a rock. It stung, but I didn't pay any attention to the pain. Instead, I got back to my feet as quickly as I could and listened. His voice was gone. The ocean was drowning him out.

"Robert!" I screamed.

"Laura! Where are you?" The voice seemed to come from behind me, but then I heard it again, this time from directly in front of me. "Laura. I'm here. Laura!"

"Yes, yes, Robert. I'm here."

I moved more carefully over the smaller rocks, until I reached the water and the tide slapped at my legs. Concentrating hard, I could see the boat rising and falling. The small mast was broken and lay over the side, the sail soaked. I started into the water.

"Robert!" I called. "Robert!"

The boat lifted again, only this time it came down on its

654

side and then turned completely over, and after it had, I saw him, bobbing in the water, his arm up.

"Laura . . ."

"Robert, I'm coming. Wait."

He disappeared for a moment. I charged ahead, the water now up to my waist.

"Laura!" I heard someone scream behind me, but I didn't turn back. That was Grandmother Olivia's trick to get me to give him up. Don't look back, I thought, or you'll be like Lot's wife and turn into a pillar of salt.

I started to swim toward the boat. His head reappeared and then that arm slowly emerged from the dark water, just as it had many times before in my dreams. I tried to shout to him as I swam, but it was difficult because the water slammed into my face and I swallowed some, gagging for a moment. The waves lifted and threw me back, but I continued, swimming as furiously as I could now. I wasn't far from the boat.

His head lifted slowly and his eyes—even in the darkness without a moon and stars—his eyes were luminous and full of love.

"Robert, my darling," I called to him and swam and swam and swam. When I looked up, the boat wasn't any closer. Was it just the strong tide keeping me back?

My arms ached. My clothing weighed me down. I treaded water and stripped off my jeans and then my shirt. The tide carried off its bounty quickly and I turned back to my swimming, putting all my strength into every stroke. I felt myself lift and fall with the water and when I looked out again, there was the boat, but not any closer.

"Robert, I can't lose you. I won't lose you. Don't let them take you from me. Please."

Miraculously, he appeared only inches away, his head emerging from the sea, his arms out toward me. I stretched until our hands joined.

"Robert—"

"Laura," he said. "My Laura."

I felt him draw me closer to him until his arms were

around me. The water didn't matter anymore. I didn't feel how cold it was or how rough it was. In his arms I felt safe and warm. We kissed.

"I waited for you," he said. "I knew you would come back to me, so I waited for you."

"I'm so glad, Robert. I'm so happy."

I turned toward the shore. Someone was waving madly. He was up to his waist and waving.

"Let's go back," I said, "together."

"No, Laura. We can't go back," Robert said. "Come . . ."

He gestured with his head toward the overturned sailboat.

"Oh," I said. I smiled, understanding.

We swam together for a few moments and then I reached forward to touch the boat. Robert did, too. We turned to each other and we brought out lips together and kissed as the darkness swept in over us.

But I was happy, as happy as I had once been.

I was with my love.

Forever.

Epilogue

❧

*T*he black Rolls-Royce climbed the hill to the clinic slowly, rising over the crest of the knoll. The automobile came to a stop in front of the main entrance as the sun was covered by a long, dark cloud. The driver got out and quickly opened the door for Olivia Logan. He reached in to take her at the elbow, but she shook him off.

"I'm all right, Raymond," she snapped. She paused after emerging and looked at the building as if it were alive and the windows now glittering like mirrors were the dozens of eyes greeting her.

"Just wait right here," she ordered and made her way to the steps.

Raymond watched her obediently for a few moments before getting back into the Rolls. He reached for his newspaper and lowered the back of the seat.

Before Olivia Logan reached the entrance, the door opened and Doctor Scanlon, with Mrs. Kleckner on one side and Mrs. Roundchild on the other, stepped forward to greet her. She paused and looked at them, her eyes full of contempt and accusation. The three seemed to wilt; Herbert Scanlon, the most. It was as if his clothes were growing on his body. His shirt collar widened and he pressed the knot of his tie between his right thumb and forefinger before reaching out to take Olivia's hand.

"Where is she?" Olivia asked.

"We have her in the infirmary. I'm sorry," Doctor Scanlon began. "I—"

Olivia put up her black-gloved hand, palm forward.

"Save your explanations for later," she said. "Take me to her."

The three separated, Mrs. Roundchild stepping back so Olivia could enter the building.

There wasn't anyone in the lobby. The patients were all at lunch. Olivia paused, struck by the silence, and then continued as Herbert Scanlon directed her to another doorway and the corridor beyond. The two nurses trailed behind, neither looking at the other, neither saying a word.

"The patients are all in the dining room," Doctor Scanlon said.

"Except one," Olivia remarked.

He glanced back at his nurses and continued walking. When they reached the end of the corridor, they turned right at a door labeled INFIRMARY. Dr. Scanlon opened it and stepped back for Olivia to enter. The nurse, wearing a nametag, Suzanne Cohen, rose so quickly from her desk chair it looked like she had been sitting on springs. She looked at Doctor Scanlon, her face gray with concern.

"This is Mrs. Logan," he said. "She's here to see Laura."

"Oh yes," the infirmary nurse said. "I'm so sorry," she added.

Olivia closed her eyes and shook her head.

"I'm not interested in hearing apologies," she replied. Sue Cohen glanced at Doctor Scanlon and saw from the expression on his face that she should move quickly.

"This way," she said, and led them through the small lobby to a rear door and down a short hall, on either side of which were examination rooms, radiology, a laboratory, and at the very end, a room that fortunately was used rarely. It had no label on the door, but everyone who worked there knew it to be their morgue.

She opened the door and stepped back.

Olivia approached slowly and gazed in at the steel gurney covered with a sheet, on which lay the body of her granddaughter. The room had no particular odor. It seemed aseptic, devoid of any character, or light.

Olivia approached the gurney. Doctor Scanlon moved quickly to get beside her.

"Let me see her," Olivia demanded.

He lowered the sheet to her neck and Olivia gazed for a long moment.

Now, now that she was here and they were around her, she would make demands.

"How did this happen?"

Doctor Scanlon was prepared.

"Another patient with whom she had developed something of a relationship snuck up to our special floor and helped her escape down a stairway used by the employees. He knew of the one door we don't keep alarmed and showed her the way out of the building. He claimed she wanted to go home."

Olivia turned with interest.

"Home? Then how did she end up in the ocean?"

"You have to understand," Doctor Scanlon said, "that this other patient is a seriously disturbed young man himself. It's taken an enormous effort to get him to be lucid enough to give us any sensible details. This entire event has put him into a regression that—"

"I'm not here to discuss him," Olivia said sharply.

Doctor Scanlon nodded.

"Apparently, from what I've been able to garner, she heard voices."

"Voices? What voices?"

"Mainly the voice of her young man, the one who drowned. Lawrence—that's this other patient's name—said she kept calling for Robert. He said as soon as he showed her the way out, she turned toward the sea and ran. He tried to stop her, but she was determined."

"She went down to the ocean and deliberately drowned herself?" Olivia asked incredulously.

"That's not uncommon, suicidal tendencies in cases such as hers, Mrs. Logan."

"Then why wasn't she guarded, day and night?" Olivia snapped at him.

"I . . . well, she was on our most secure floor."

"Secure floor? And yet this other patient was able to get to her and take her away?"

"No one expected . . ." He looked to Mrs. Roundchild, who stepped forward.

"She was strapped in, medicated. We had just looked in on her. He must have been hiding in the doorway, watching," she explained.

"Send them away," Olivia commanded with a wave of her hand.

Doctor Scanlon nodded at the nurses and they all backed out of the room. As soon as they had, Olivia turned on him.

"You know I could sue this clinic and you for every penny you are worth. Word of this sort of negligence would destroy you," she said, her eyes small, but full of fire.

Doctor Scanlon could barely swallow. He nodded.

Olivia held her hateful glare on him like a spotlight, hot and intense. Finally, she turned back to Laura.

"It's your good fortune, however, that I don't want word of this to leave these premises."

"What? But in any death, there's an inquest, reports . . ."

"It's your problem," she said. "I don't want this in any newspaper. We're going to give her a proper burial and that will be all. This could devastate my family," she added and turned, "and I won't permit it."

"I understand. I'll do the best I can."

"No, you'll do what I ask, not the best you can." She looked at Laura again. "We see the results of the best you can do. I want more than that."

He nodded, sweat trickling down his brow.

"Do you want any of her things, anything you sent?"

"Not at the moment, no," Olivia said. "I hesitate to ask, because I have some doubts about your competence now, but was she making any progress?"

"Oh, yes. I think in time I could have effected a complete recovery," he bragged.

"What did she recall before . . . before this?" Olivia asked.

"Her family, her parents, her brother and sister, and most of the tragic event," he replied.

"She said nothing about me?"

"Not a word during my sessions and from what I see of Southerby's results, not a word with him either," Doctor Scanlon said.

"What about him?"

"That's taken care of," he said quickly.

"Good. I want it all taken care of, Herbert." She turned again and fixed her piercing eyes on him, turning his spine to ice. "I mean it."

"I understand. Is there anything special you want at the gravesite?"

"No," she said. "Leave me for a moment," she ordered.

"Yes, of course. I'm sorry, Mrs. Logan. Truly."

She said nothing and he left.

For a long while, she stared at Laura's face. Then she took a short, deep breath and looked up at the ceiling.

"I'm sorry about you," she said. "I know you won't ever understand now, but what I did, I did for my family. Family is all that really matters, family name, family loyalty. It's who we are when we come into this world and who we are

661

when we leave it, and we must cling tenaciously to it all the time in between, Laura."

She gazed at her granddaughter and thought how beautiful she looked, even in death.

"Somehow I knew that after you lost your precious Robert, you would never have a really happy moment, Laura. Maybe . . . maybe you weren't so mad, as sick as the doctors think. Maybe you heard him calling.

"In a strange way," she whispered, "I envy you, my dear."

She reached out and touched Laura's cold face. Then she turned and left the room.

Doctor Scanlon escorted her to the front entrance.

"My lawyer will be in contact with you to be sure all is done as I instruct," she said.

"Yes, I understand," Doctor Scanlon said with a small nod.

"I want you to do something else for me."

"Of course," Doctor Scanlon said without hesitation, without hearing it first.

"I want you to tell that young man, that other patient something."

"Yes?"

"I want you to tell him I don't blame him for anything. Tell him I thank him for being her friend. Will you do that?"

"I will. It will help him, Mrs. Logan. It's very kind of you."

"I'm not doing it for him. I'm doing it for Laura and," she said, looking at the Rolls-Royce, "for myself."

She started down the steps. Raymond got out quickly and opened the door. Doctor Scanlon wiped his face with his handkerchief as he watched her get into her automobile. When the door closed, he backed up and closed the clinic's front door.

Raymond got in and started the car. It moved slowly toward the driveway.

The sun escaped from under another cloud and shot its rays downward over the car, over the grounds, over the ocean, where the waves were now gentle, the whitecaps glimmering. Two terns lifted into the warm air and flew side by side, sweeping down together toward the sea, and then rose toward the sun as if it were a promise kept between them.

In moments, they were gone.